VANCOUVER

The Gem of Canada
Is Aglow with Four Romances

GAIL SATTLER

BARBOUR
PUBLISHING

Gone Camping ©1999 by Barbour Publishing, Inc.
At Arm's Length ©1999 by Barbour Publishing, Inc.
On the Road Again ©2000 by Barbour Publishing, Inc.
My Name Is Mike ©2000 by Barbour Publishing, Inc.

Cover image © GettyOne

ISBN 1-58660-963-7

Published by Barbour Publishing, Inc., P.O. Box 719, Uhrichsville, Ohio 44683, www.barbourbooks.com.

 Member of the
Evangelical Christian
Publishers Association

Printed in the United States of America.
5 4 3 2 1

VANCOUVER

GAIL SATTLER lives in Vancouver, B.C., where you don't have to shovel rain, with her husband, three sons, two dogs, six lizards, and countless fish, many of whom have names. She writes inspirational romance because she loves happily-ever-afters and believes God has a place in those happy endings. Gail was voted as the #1 Favorite Heartsong Author in 1999, 2000, and 2001 and has now been retired to the Heartsong Authors Hall of Fame. She has many books out with Barbour Publishing, in novels, novellas, and works of non-fiction. Gail invites readers to visit her website at http://www.gailsattler.com.

Gone Camping

Chapter 1

Roberta ignored the pounding at the front door as she blew her nose.

Molly's muffled voice accompanied more pounding. "Robbie, Robbie! I know you're home. Please, let me in!"

Roberta glanced at the clock and wondered why Molly wasn't at work. Despite her red-rimmed eyes and blotchy face, Roberta opened the door. Immediately, Molly threw her arms around her.

"Oh, Robbie!" she moaned, "I just heard what happened! You didn't answer your phone, so I came over as fast as I could."

Just when she thought she had herself under control, Roberta started to sob again. "Today I discovered for myself that the rumors were true." Tears streamed down her cheeks. She made no effort to wipe them.

Molly hugged her tighter. "How did you find out?"

After a few more stifled sobs, Roberta managed to continue. "I went to work early to surprise Mike, but I was the one who got the surprise. Mike and Suzie were in the corner of the stockroom. . .and they were. . ." Roberta gulped, trying to sniffle back more tears while fighting for the right words. "I didn't even say anything. I turned and ran. Like a fool I hid in the washroom and bawled my eyes out. Mike stormed in, and the whole office heard his rampage. Then this was waiting for me on my desk." She thrust the crumpled piece of company letterhead at her friend.

Molly stared at it, mouthing the words as she read.

Dear Miss Garland,

 This letter is to inform you that effective immediately, your services are no longer required.

 Enclosed is your final check. Your vacation pay, other monies owed to you, and letter of recommendation for your years of service will be forwarded by post.

 Good luck in future endeavors.

Regards,
Michael Flannigan, Sr.
President

Molly slowly handed her back the letter. "So. The wedding's off, and his dad fired you. . ."

All Roberta could do was nod as the tears threatened to break through again. As a Christian, she valued trust above all else in a relationship. Not only did Mike obviously not feel the same, but he had betrayed her in the worst way.

"When I arrived to pick you up for lunch and Suzie said you no longer worked there, I thought it was a joke, except no one was smiling. Then I asked what Mike thought about it, and she just laughed." Molly clasped her hands in front of her. "Oh, Robbie, I don't know what to say. But if it makes you feel better, the receptionist told me Mike didn't deserve you anyway."

"Thanks," Roberta sniffled. Not that it helped.

"You don't have to put up with that treatment, you know." Molly crossed her arms. "They can't fire you. You can take them to court."

Roberta shook her head. "What for? To get my job back? I loved my job, but how could I ever face those people again? And how could I work beside Mike or his father?" Roberta sniffed again, lowering her voice. "Or Suzie. I'll get another job. On my way out, Michael Senior said he would give me a considerable severance package. Life goes on."

"I know!" Molly raised one finger in the air and broke out into a wide smile. "You need to get away from all this. A change of scenery. You need a vacation!"

Roberta wiped her eyes with her sleeve. "I'm unemployed. I can't afford a vacation. While I don't think I'll go looking for another job tomorrow, I doubt I'm going to be taking a wild vacation."

"No, not a wild vacation. After work tomorrow I'm going camping with Gwen and her twin brother for a week. Do you want to come? Their tent-trailer has three double beds in it, but I'm sure Garrett won't want to spend the night under the same roof as us girls anyway. It'll be fun."

Roberta shook her head. "No, I'm not going to tag along with you and your friends."

"Don't be silly. You're my friend, so naturally you're their friend too. You remember them, don't you?"

Roberta remained silent as she thought for a minute. Certainly she would have remembered friends of Molly's that were twins. "Sorry, I don't think so."

"We were planning on meeting Garrett at the campground."

"Why in the world would you want him along? Is there something going on between you two that I don't know about? Does your friend mind her brother coming?"

Molly shook her head. "No, nothing like that. It was Gwen's suggestion. Maybe he has some time off work or something. He's really good-looking and very nice, but not my type."

Roberta backed up a step. "I don't want to tag along. I think I'll just stay at home, thanks."

Molly snorted. "Not a chance, Robbie. In fact, I insist. Not only that, you can help us. If you took the camper tonight, then we'd be assured of a great spot for our week's vacation. No reservations, first come, first served. So you can be the first one there!"

Roberta almost visualized the gears whirring in Molly's head. She held her hands up, palms facing Molly, in an attempt to ward her off. "You can't make me do that. You know I've never been camping in my life. Besides, if I went tonight, that would mean I would be out there all alone. No way!"

Molly made a calculated laughing sound. "You won't be alone. Garrett will be there."

Shaking her head furiously, Roberta didn't drop her raised hands. "Oh, no. I'm not spending the night in the middle of nowhere with a strange man keeping watch over me. You've conned me too many times for me to get sucked in like that. Not this time. No way. I'm staying home."

"He's not strange. I've known him for years."

Roberta noticed Molly's lack of reference to everything else she mentioned. "No."

Molly shrugged her shoulders. "How about if I spent the night with you?"

Roberta dropped her hands to her side. "What?"

"The campground at Rolly Lake is only a couple of hours' drive from downtown Vancouver. Not in rush hour, of course. If I leave work early and beat the traffic, then I could be there in time for a late supper if you pick up the groceries. How about it?"

"No."

"We can have a wienie roast, just you and me."

"Really? Uh, I don't know. . ."

"Hurry up." Molly checked her watch. "I have to be back at work in a few minutes."

"But I don't think—"

"We'll have a great time. . ."

"But I—"

"Going, going. . ."

Roberta raised her hands, then slapped them to her sides. "Oh, all right! I'll go!"

"Great!" Molly shouted and clapped her hands. "I'll tell you everything you need to know." She reached into her purse and handed Roberta her key ring. "Here. Drive me to work."

"What? Why?"

"So you can go get the camper. My car has a hitch. Yours doesn't, does it?"

Roberta laughed for the first time that day. "Of course not."

"Let's go. I'll tell you how to set it up on the way there. It's important to do everything in the right order. Maybe you should write down some instructions while I drive."

"How are you going to get home?"

"With Gwen. We can only have two cars parked on the spot, so the only two cars we can use are mine and hers."

That answered that. Kind of. While Molly drove back to her office, Roberta tried desperately to write down Molly's rush of instructions, a near impossibility in the moving vehicle.

"Sleeping bags are already in it. Bring your own pillow. See you about sundown. Bye!"

Roberta smiled hesitantly. As Molly raced out the car door and disappeared into the entrance of the office tower, Roberta couldn't help but feel she was making a big mistake.

～

Roberta experimented with the brakes, testing the added weight of the full trailer behind her before she had to come to a stop in real traffic. She sucked in a deep breath and willed her hands to stop shaking. She could do this.

All the way down the highway, despite strict adherence to the posted speed limit, she couldn't help but notice the long lineup of cars behind her. Every time another irritated driver whizzed past, she tightened her already iron grip on the steering wheel. When at last she arrived at the park entrance gate, she heaved a sigh of relief.

Slowly, she bumped down the gravel road to the designated camping area, where she used her best judgment to pick one of the many large sites still available. A sign instructed campers to pick a spot, and a park ranger would register it later.

One day she would get Molly back for this.

Stopping the car and trailer a little beyond the entrance to the site, Roberta mentally prepared to back in. With no one to help direct her, she desperately tried to remember Molly's rapid-fire list of instructions during the twenty-minute drive back to work. All Roberta could remember were cautions to steer the opposite way when backing up. As well, Molly's friend's mother had warned her about something called "jackknifing." She'd heard the term mentioned in reference to big highway trucks, but never knew what it meant.

On the bright side, no one was around to laugh if she backed in wrong. However, at some point, someone would come by, and she was blocking the one-way gravel road.

Roberta craned her neck to examine the wide opening one last time, sucked in a deep breath, and shifted into reverse. After considerable manipulation, she managed to back up most of the way into the spot, but the trailer was crooked and too close to the picnic table. At least she hadn't hit it.

Her second and third attempts were worse.

Roberta dropped her forehead to the steering wheel with a bump while she mentally kicked herself for letting Molly convince her to do this. She had arrived at the house when Gwen and Garrett's mother was already late for an appointment. All the woman had time to do was throw her a massive set of keys, tell her how to release the pin lock, and quickly help her hook the trailer to the back of Molly's car. Then she had driven off, leaving Roberta standing in the driveway.

Roberta pressed her forehead into the steering wheel and drew in a deep breath. After one more attempt, if the trailer was still crooked, she would give up and leave it where it was, even if it was on top of the fire pit.

"Hi there," a pleasant baritone voice resounded from beside the door. "Need some help, Miss?"

Roberta rolled her head on the steering wheel and raised her eyes to see a tall man standing outside the open window, smiling at her. She raised her head to see him better. His green baseball cap bore the emblem of the Parks and Recreation Division. Together with a pair of large dark sunglasses, the overall effect shielded most of his face. Below the sunglasses, he had the nicest smile she had ever seen. A khaki-colored shirt bearing a crest with the same emblem as the hat accompanied baggy black shorts, which showed off strong hairy legs. Beat-up hiking boots with wool work socks sticking above the rim completed the picture of a rugged park ranger.

"At the risk of looking like a helpless female, I've never pulled a trailer before, much less backed one in. I appear to be doing something wrong."

The ranger grinned, showing off some rather attractive dimples and a flashing white row of straight teeth. Sunlight glinted off the frames of the dark sunglasses, emphasizing the deep tone of his skin. For a split second, Roberta considered him very attractive and wished she could see his eyes. But then, her better judgment took over. After the way Mike treated her, it would be a long time before she would even look at a man again.

"You've never driven with a trailer before? I could never tell." His smile widened.

Roberta scowled back.

He rested one hand on the mirror. "If you want, I could back it in for you."

Roberta narrowed her eyes while she considered his suggestion. Molly had told her any of the park rangers would be able to help if Garrett was unavailable. However, even if Garrett were available, she would never know it. She had no idea what Garrett looked like, or what time he was due to arrive. She wasn't sure what to do.

She tilted her head to study him further. This man was a park ranger, not a petty hoodlum about to steal Molly's car. She was obviously doing a poor job of trying to back the trailer in place. The offer of help from a ranger was too good to pass up.

She met his eyes and forced a smile. "Yes, please." As she stepped out of the car, she couldn't help but notice how tall the ranger was as he passed her on his way in.

The ranger bumped his knees against the steering wheel before reaching down to adjust the seat so he could position his legs comfortably. Roberta hadn't considered Molly's car that small, but when the ranger straightened, the top of his hat scraped the ceiling.

He shifted the car into gear and inched forward until the car and trailer were aligned properly. He then backed in smoothly, positioning the trailer perfectly with the first effort.

He stepped out and tipped his hat. "Will that be all, Miss?" he asked, smiling at her again.

Roberta dared not ask him to help unhitch it. Besides, she had her notes. "Thank you very much. I appreciate your help, but I think I can manage on my own from here."

"Very well," he replied. Holding the brim of his cap, he straightened it on his head. "See you after you're settled so we can get you registered." He smiled again and left.

Roberta checked her notes.

Her list said to block the tent-trailer, then support it and unhook it. She stared at the trailer, still attached to Molly's car. That had sounded so simple while Molly barked out instructions. A few pieces of wood had surrounded the tires in the Gwen's mother's driveway, so she did the same.

Roberta stood back to admire the start of her project. Molly had mentioned something about legs under the trailer, so Roberta lowered herself gently in the gravel to her hands and knees and pulled down four spring-loaded contraptions, one tucked in each corner, and adjusted them until they touched the ground.

According to the list, the next step was to unhitch it, so she started turning the crank to raise the hooking thingie above the hitch. Nothing moved. She cranked and cranked until she started to sweat and stopped. Roberta swiped a sheen of moisture off her brow, needing to take a breather. When she stood back, she noticed a clip on top of the locking mechanism. Roberta narrowed her eyes and scowled at it. What a stupid place to put a safety latch.

She fought with it until her fingers were sore, and finally it released. After flexing her numb fingers, she started cranking again. Finally, using considerable effort, she had barely worked it high enough to drive Molly's car forward when she heard the same baritone voice behind her.

"Hi, how's it going, Miss?" the ranger said cheerfully.

Roberta felt far from cheerful. She was sweaty, her fingers were sore, and her shoulders ached from all that cranking. And while she was thinking of cranking, she felt cranky.

"Fine," she replied curtly. Standing straight, she realized she should try to be pleasant. Even though she was getting nowhere fast, if the ranger was back, then he probably thought she should have finished setting up by now, and she still didn't even have the car pulled away. She couldn't read the expression behind the ranger's dark glasses, but she thought he was frowning.

"I think you should have a piece of wood under there, or you're going to find it will sink in the gravel."

Roberta sagged. After all the work and sweat, she didn't want to consider that she would have to do all that work, all over again. She squeezed her eyes shut. In the back of her mind, she recalled seeing a piece of wood under the pin in the driveway.

"Oh," was her only reply.

The ranger studied her, making her feel even dumber. "Want me to do it for you? I see you've already been working hard at it." It might have been her imagination, but Roberta thought he was struggling to keep a straight face.

At work, she only ever lifted a few books and light boxes. For someone so badly out of shape, cranking the trailer up was hard work. She was sorry it showed.

The thought of her ex-job froze her where she stood. Thanks to Mike, the ex-love of her life, she was now unemployed. She could still barely believe Mike's father defended his conduct by firing her.

The more she thought about it, the more she realized she should have figured it out. Instances started to pop into her mind, making her realize that everyone, including Mike's father, knew what was going on and hid it from her. Naively, she had ignored every hint of any indiscretion. She'd listened to every one of Mike's many excuses, refusing to believe Mike was anything less than loyal and happily in love with her. For awhile, he'd even started to attend church with her.

Roberta turned back at the ranger, who had been watching her the entire time she'd been staring off into space. What she really wanted was to be left alone. If she treated him politely and answered him, maybe he would go away.

"That would be nice, thank you very much. I guess I'm more out of shape than I thought." She forced herself to smile graciously.

With no apparent effort, the ranger turned the crank, easily lifting the shaft off the ground, slid in the piece of wood, then cranked it up high enough to clear the ball and drive forward.

Roberta noticed the ease with which he turned it. She hopped in the car, drove forward a few yards, parked it, and returned just as the ranger cranked the trailer back down to the right spot.

"You know, my family has this same kind of tent-trailer, and it gets hard to turn the crank at exactly the same spot. How about that?" He smiled again at her.

Roberta gritted her teeth. The last thing she felt like doing was making conversation with a strange man while she was alone in the middle of nowhere. She did not smile back. "Thank you very much. I think I can handle it myself from here."

He nodded, tipped his hat again, and strode out of the campsite. Roberta assumed he would continue making his rounds.

Checking her notes, the next step was to crank the roof of the tent up. She dragged her hand over her face at the thought of more cranking.

She tried every key on the key chain, and finally the last one fit in the lock for the storage compartment. Finding another crank, she inserted the key into the slot at the back of the trailer and went back to work.

After turning forever, the roof finally reached the top. Her back ached, so she stretched her arms above her head to try to release the kinks, then resigned herself to the next step. According to the list, she had to pull out the beds and insert the support bars.

Roberta emptied bazillions of poles from the storage compartment, then sorted them into piles. With her head bent and hands on her hips, she tried to figure out what in the world they would be for. Unable to do so, she skimmed the list with her finger, hoping a name for their uses would help her match them up. About halfway down the paper, while standing in the midst of the poles in neat piles about her feet, she heard that same voice again.

"Hi. Making any progress?"

Her finger still on the paper, she raised her head. The ranger again stood a few feet away, his long legs slightly spread and planted firmly. Resting his hands on his hips, he held a clipboard loosely in the crook of one arm. He wore an annoyingly smug smile on his face, but his lips were pressed together tightly, like he was trying not to laugh.

She said nothing as she glared at him, waiting for him to say something.

"You've never done this before, have you?"

Roberta blushed. If only there had been more time for Molly to give her better instructions. If only Molly's friend's mother hadn't been in such a rush to get going. If only she had told Molly to forget this dumb idea and stayed home. "No, I haven't. It's not mine."

"Ah," he mused, tapping the end of his pen against his cheek, the other hand still resting on one hip, holding the clipboard. "Like I said earlier, my family has one just like this. Want me to help you set it up? There's hardly anyone here, so I think I can spare the time."

"I appreciate your concern, but I really can do this myself. If you really want to help, how about if you tell me which poles go where, and I can do the rest."

His chin lowered almost imperceptibly as his smile faded. Finally he was getting the hint. "Of course." The clipboard remained in the crook of one arm, and he used the pen to point to the various piles as he spoke. "The ones with the flat ends support the pullouts, and the ones with the small round ends go inside to hold up the tent on top of the beds. Those are for the awning, and those look like they're for a tent, which you don't appear to have with you. Are you sure you want to do this by yourself?"

"Yes, thank you very much." Try as she might, she couldn't keep the sharp edge out of her voice. Mike had always insisted on doing everything for her, expecting her to be grateful, when all he did was make her feel useless, then guilty for not appreciating him. She refused to let this ranger treat her the same.

He nodded and left again, this time not tipping his hat.

Roberta heaved and pulled the large pull-out sections for the beds, struggling with every inch until she got them into position. Then she wiggled and manipulated the support poles until she could be sure that everything was secure.

For a moment she stood still to admire her work, then pulled the list out of her pocket. She eyed the poles the ranger had said held up the sides of the tent by the beds. However, the list said that the next step was to insert the door.

Roberta froze while she stared at the gaping, doorless opening in the side of the tent-trailer. Slowly, she ran her hand along the empty frame, then dragged her palm down her face.

After some searching, she located the door under a pile of sleeping bags on the bed inside the trailer. Delicately, she gave it an experimental push to discover it was heavier than it looked. The top of the frame showed a series of slots, and the bottom of the frame had a few clips to hold it in place. Now, all she had to do was get it there.

She picked it up, tipping it awkwardly to try to fit it into place. The harder she tried to fit it in, the heavier it became. Then, just as she thought she had it, it slipped. Roberta jerked her knee upward to prevent it from crashing to the floor, which smashed it into her kneecap. She gritted her teeth to prevent herself from screaming.

"Are you all right?"

That voice again. Mr. Ranger was back.

Roberta looked up, bringing herself face-to-face with a large pair of dark sunglasses and a big, bright smile.

"I'll live, thank you. Nothing's damaged." Except her pride. Her temper was working overtime, though.

"Want me to do that for you?"

Without a word, she grumpily handed him the heavy door and stepped out of the trailer opening. Of course he showed no indication of it being heavy. He effortlessly slotted it into the holes, gave it a little push, and fitted it neatly into the bottom of the frame. Fastening it to the bottom half of the door, he never lost that insipid smile. Roberta glared back.

"Done." He wiped his hands on the back of his shorts. His smile faded quickly as he saw her grumpy face. "Feel free to call me if you need any more help." And he left again.

Roberta stomped outside to the picnic table where she had left the list. It was gone.

Since the campsite was almost completely surrounded by trees, Roberta assumed it had to have blown off the table. The bright white of the paper would contrast with the darkness of the ground cover, making it easy to find. Walking a bit farther into the trees, she paused to inhale a deep breath of fresh air.

Somewhere in the forest, squirrels chattered and birds chirped. The wind rustled the leaves, and in the distance, Roberta could hear children laughing, playing at some far-off campsite. A slight breeze carried the pleasant scent of a campfire and burnt hamburgers. Roberta smiled.

Despite the trouble she'd had so far in setting up, Roberta considered the possibility that maybe Molly was right. Getting away from the city into the peaceful surroundings of the campground could go a long way toward helping her sort things out.

On her quest to find the missing list, Roberta glanced upward, searching for a glimpse of the nearby squirrel who chattered brightly from the high branches. As she walked, her sandal caught in a branch on the ground.

With one foot caught helplessly while the rest of her weight still continued forward, Roberta couldn't maintain her balance. She flailed her arms, but it didn't help. The trees flashed by as the ground came closer and closer.

Roberta landed with a thud. As she bounced on the ground, her foot slid out of the sandal, causing her to skid along the rough terrain. In the process, her already sore knee struck a jagged rock. Her arm scraped against a branch, leaving a painful stinging welt.

Arms and legs splayed, Roberta lay facedown in the rocks and sticks. Instead of moving, she began to consider the possibility that despite the serene setting, maybe, just maybe, this camping business wasn't such a good idea after all.

Sprawled inelegantly on the ground, she briefly considered standing up, except that surely something else would go wrong. On the other hand, if she continued to lie in the dirt long enough, maybe she would wake up and find this had all been a bad dream. She let her mind wander. Maybe she could get comfortable down here among the rocks and branches. She could have a nap if some rabid chipmunk didn't come along and bite her.

Footsteps. Running. No, anything but that.

"Miss! Miss! Are you all right!?"

Not Mr. Ranger again! Roberta pushed herself up on her hands and knees, barely managing to prevent her left knee from buckling as she put her weight on it. When she rubbed the scratch on her arm, her fingers came away sticky when she moved her hand away.

Watching blood slowly seep out of her new wound, Roberta wondered what else could go wrong. She turned to the ranger, unable to keep the bite out of her voice as she spoke. "Look, I just tripped. Nothing serious. Thank you for your concern, but I really want to be alone, okay?"

"I was concerned when you didn't get up."

"I'm fine!" she snapped. "Now why don't you just go away!" She narrowed her eyes and glared at him, trying her best to get him to take a hint.

Instead of leaving, Mr. Ranger stood still. His lower lip quivered, like he was trying to stifle a smile, making Roberta wish she could see what he was looking at behind his dark glasses.

His smile dropped, and he cleared his throat. "You're bleeding. Do you have a first aid kit?"

"Probably, but it's nothing I can't handle."

"Okay, fine," he mumbled. Again, he turned and left.

She gritted her teeth. The last thing she needed was for Mr. Ranger to laugh at her. Contrary to Molly's promises, her camping adventure was turning out to be more trouble than it was worth. She reached up to push her hair back off her forehead when her fingers poked a hard object. Roberta wrapped her fingers around a long, slender object and pulled. Along with a stick, she also pulled out a number of strands of her hair.

With a growl, Roberta broke the stick into small pieces and threw them on the ground. She slid her foot back into her sandal, then stomped the stick into smaller pieces, trying to get some revenge against the great outdoors.

"How did I let Molly convince me to do this?" she shouted at the little squirrel, who for some reason turned and ran away.

Roberta limped back to the camper. If it wasn't for Mike, she would be sitting at her desk, calmly working away in an air-conditioned office. The thought of her job made her even angrier at the unfairness of it all. She had been fired because her fiancé was fooling around on her, yet there was nothing she could do about it.

Roberta flopped herself on the bed. Her knee ached and her arm stung, but she was too angry to care. She was determined to get the stupid camper up without the instructions or she would die trying.

She stomped outside and studied the poles on the ground. When she figured out which pile Mr. Ranger said supported the tent above the pull-out beds, Roberta lugged those poles into the camper. She threw them on one of the beds, and they clanged loudly as they bounced together.

Roberta didn't care. One pole at a time, she pushed and wiggled and pushed some more until every pole was slotted into place and the tent-trailer was in the shape it was supposed to be.

For the next step, Roberta crawled under the middle bed. Supporting it with her back, she hooked the support section into the slot. Still pushing up with her back beneath it, she pulled down the collapsible leg, positioned it properly, and crawled out.

Finally done, Roberta stood in the center of the trailer and heaved a sigh of relief.

Now she had a table. Success.

With that success, she closed her eyes and smiled, thinking of how a cup of steamy coffee would hit the spot, despite the heat of the summer afternoon.

When she opened her eyes, her smile disappeared. In order to make coffee, she needed to use the propane-powered elements, but she had not hooked up the propane tank connection. The bed and support bars were now pulled out over the propane tank. Instead of relaxing, she now had to crawl under the overhang to hook up the propane.

Roberta squeezed her eyes shut. Just when she thought she had everything done, something else had gone wrong.

Cringing with every movement, Roberta hunched beneath the overhang and crawled underneath the bed, trying to ignore the gravel digging into her already sore knees as she screwed the hose onto the tank. Not wanting to take chances with the connection, she thought it best to exchange the screwdriver for a wrench, except she didn't know where to find one. She'd discovered Molly's friend's tenttrailer held many cubbyholes and compartments, and wished she had a map to locate them all.

Roberta gritted her teeth with every painful contact of the gravel on her knees as she backed out from her cramped work space. Unfortunately, she misjudged the distance she'd crawled forward, because in crawling backward, she straightened up too soon and hit her head on the overhang.

At the same time as she bit her lip to prevent herself from saying something she shouldn't say out loud, Roberta heard a sound from a few feet behind her. Holding her head, she backed out the rest of the way and turned to come face-to-face with good old Mr. Ranger again. It was apparent that he sincerely tried to suppress the urge to laugh, but he didn't do it very well.

"What do you want now?" she barked at him, still holding her head.

Mr. Ranger's mouth straightened. "Let's get you registered. Have you got that propane properly connected? I see you don't have a wrench there. It may not be tight enough."

Roberta squeezed her eyes shut and stiffened from head to toe. The events of the day roared through her mind. Her disastrous morning at work. Molly railroading her into this idiotic camping trip. The nerve-wracking drive. The trouble setting up. Then, every time she turned around, there was Mr. Ranger, always showing up whenever she did something stupid or clumsy. Now, here he was again, telling her something she already knew. Of course she needed a wrench. She wasn't brain-dead.

She knew the Bible spoke of patience, but not a single verse came to mind. "I know I need a wrench!" She waved her hands in the air as she hollered at him. "I just have to find out where it is! I was going to do that when you barged in on me again. Don't you have something better to do? Some wild animals to document or something?"

Mr. Ranger frowned and stepped backward. "Sor—ry!" he mumbled sarcastically. "I'll sign you in and be out of your way." He flipped to the right page and held up his pen, ready to write. He cleared his throat. "Name and number of people in your party."

Roberta glared at him. "Roberta Garland. The whole group won't be here until tomorrow."

He looked up with the frown still on his face. "You mean you're here alone for the night?"

"No. One friend will be here tonight, and two more tomorrow. I don't know how long everyone will be staying." She glared at him, wishing she could see his eyes beneath those dark glasses.

They stared at each other in silence.

After about a minute, Mr. Ranger let out a sigh. "Look, I've got a wrench in the truck. I see you're limping. I can get some ice for that knee, and I can check that propane hose for you, if you want."

Roberta scowled at him, but he only scowled back at her, looking like he was starting to lose his patience with her too.

Visions of Mike flashed through her mind—how he always did everything for her, and instead of acting gracious, he lorded it over her, only making her feel stupid and incompetent.

"I don't want your help. I don't want anyone's help!" Roberta screamed. "Coming out here like this wasn't my idea. I don't even care if I blow myself up anymore! Leave me alone!" Tears burned the back of her eyes.

Mr. Ranger stared at her. As his mouth gaped open, Roberta realized she was taking all her hurt and anger and frustration out on this helpful stranger.

Her lower lip wouldn't stop quivering. Unable to stop it from happening, the tears that threatened earlier burst to the surface. "I'm sorry. I'm having a bad day. Please just go away," she sobbed. Without waiting for a response, Roberta turned. She ran into the camper, slammed the door, and threw herself on one of the beds, leaving poor Mr. Ranger standing by himself, pen still poised in midair.

She knew he could hear her crying through the canvas walls, but she didn't care. When she lifted her head to wipe her eyes, she peeked through the screened window to see him still standing in the middle of the campsite, looking around as if wondering what he should do. When he finally turned around and left, Roberta lowered her head and cried herself out.

When her tears were exhausted, Roberta wiped her face on her sleeve. She felt like an idiot for bursting into tears in front of poor Mr. Ranger. Not only had she looked like a hysterical female, she never should have screamed at him like that.

Feeling utterly useless and totally dejected, she sat at the small table. She plunked her elbows on the table, rested her chin in her hands, and stared out the screen window into the thick forest of trees while she absently twirled a lock of her hair in her fingers.

Suddenly, her hand froze. Then, slowly, Roberta placed a hand on each ear. One dangly earring was still in place, but the other ear held nothing.

Roberta groaned. Not only were they her favorite earrings, they were a gift from Molly, who would be there shortly.

First Roberta made a thorough search of Molly's car but found nothing.

Then, remembering her struggle with the door, she searched the floor of the camper, but still found nothing.

She sank to sit cross-legged on the cold floor. The movement caused her knee to ache, reminding Roberta of her earlier fall, which made her wonder if she'd lost the earring as she bounced along the ground.

Roberta pushed herself to her feet. She limped outside, carefully watching the gravel with every footstep. When she reached the right area, she sat in the gravel and began to pick through the gravel, leaves, and other debris, trying to ignore her revulsion at what unknown dirt and germs she was touching.

As she diligently searched, she heard footsteps behind her.

"Hi. I just thought I'd check and make sure you were okay."

Mr. Ranger. Again.

Not wanting him to see her red, puffy eyes or her shiny nose, Roberta kept her head down and continued to pick diligently through the small rocks. "I'm fine, thank you," she sniffed, knowing she looked anything but. She wished from the depths of her soul that he would leave.

He didn't. "What's the matter? Lose something?"

Roberta was ready to give up, except she didn't want to stand up and let him see her face. "Yes, I lost an earring." She tried to think of some way to tell him to leave her alone, but he got the next word in.

"Want me to help you look?" Without waiting for an answer, he squatted until he was hunkered down beside her. "What does it look like?" he asked cheerfully.

Roberta sighed. The sooner she located the missing earring, the sooner he would go away. "Just like this one." She sighed again, tipping her head and lifting her hair so he could see it.

"Okay, let's look for it." He picked through the ground cover, so she resumed her search as well.

"When is your friend coming?" he asked politely as he meticulously picked through the dirt.

Roberta kept her head down but raised her eyes to study him. As before, she couldn't see his face behind the brim of his hat and large, dark sunglasses.

He appeared to be serious in his search, but Roberta couldn't help but wonder why he kept coming back. Since she was alone, she wondered if perhaps he was preying on her, taking advantage of the fact that she was alone and helpless. Such a situation would be prime if he wanted to pick her up.

The possibility made her wonder if this was how Mike had picked up other women when he claimed he was madly in love with her, as she now realized that Suzie wasn't Mike's only other conquest. The thought made her start to simmer again.

"Soon!" she snapped. She began to throw the sticks and rocks farther than necessary as her most recent memory of Mike, in the corner of the storage room with Suzie, their lips locked together, flashed through her mind.

Not fully recovered from her last bout of crying, she struggled against the telltale constriction in the back of her throat. She dared not speak, for fear of losing control again. She bit her bottom lip and held her breath to try to maintain some semblance of dignity. It didn't help. Another river of tears rushed down her cheek, but this time she managed to keep silent.

"Found it!" Mr. Ranger raised his head and reached toward her, the earring lying in his palm.

As she met his gaze through his dark sunglasses, his bright smile faded. Her hand shook as she accepted the earring from him. Of course, just her luck, a tear dripped off her chin and landed on his wrist. He flinched, and she froze.

"Hey, are you all right?" he asked, his voice soft and gentle. "Will your boyfriend be here soon?"

Roberta squeezed her eyes shut, but she couldn't stop her tears. She had no boyfriend, and she planned never to have a boyfriend again. It wasn't worth the heartache.

"Why can't you go away and leave me alone?" she sobbed as she ran back into the camper, gasping for breath.

By the time she had once again cried herself out, Mr. Ranger was gone.

Chapter 2

Ranger Lamont sat at the table at the park office, resting his feet on an empty chair. Up until today, this job had been a lot of fun, but today he experienced his first troublesome camper.

That lady in site 27 was a nutcase.

Originally, he had only been trying to help a first-time camper. Normally, he wouldn't have interfered, but she was obviously alone and totally inept. It was almost as if she had never even seen anyone set up a tent-trailer before, let alone done it herself. She looked like she really needed some assistance setting up the camper, despite insisting she could do it alone.

He wondered if she was perhaps trying to surprise her boyfriend, whom she claimed was coming later. Most likely after he finished work, he would join her for supper, which was not uncommon. The campground was only an hour and a half's drive out of the Vancouver city limits, about two hours from downtown, and slightly more than half an hour for those living in the suburbs.

Knowing how the poor woman was struggling, he hoped her significant other would appreciate her efforts. For her, it appeared to be a monumental undertaking.

Every time he came back to check her progress, things became worse instead of better. When he saw her lying on the ground not moving, he had almost been ready to call an ambulance.

Then when she started screaming at him, he was ready to call the funny farm. At about the point she ran into the trailer sobbing something about having a bad day, he decided to keep his distance.

He was more than willing to help a lady in distress, but at that point, this lady was more distressed than he wanted to handle. Although, he hated to do that, because he had the impression she could use a friend. Despite being a bit unstable, she seemed like a nice person.

He checked the time once more and decided to make the registration rounds again.

He shook his head. He sure hoped her boyfriend arrived soon.

❧

Roberta sipped her coffee as she organized the inside of the camper. She hoped Molly would arrive soon, because that meant she could stay inside while Molly paid the money, and she wouldn't have to face Mr. Ranger again.

In preparation, Roberta rolled out the sleeping bags on the beds. For tonight, it would be only the two of them. Molly said she would get up early and go directly to work from the campsite, which would leave Roberta alone all day. But now that the camper was set up, Roberta found she actually was looking forward to a day in the great outdoors with no distractions, and especially with no men.

As she familiarized herself with the camper's layout, she found where everything was stowed. She removed her pillow and the duffel bag with her clothes and toiletries from Molly's car and placed them on one of the beds, then hauled the cooler out of the trunk and placed it beside the picnic table.

Molly had told Roberta not to worry about food beyond tonight's supper and tomorrow's breakfast. She wasn't supposed to be concerned with any other details beyond getting a good spot and setting up. Her mission accomplished, Roberta was now ready to cast her troubles away and relax.

One of the things she discovered while digging through the storage compartments was a hammock. She had never been in one before, and from what she saw on television, they appeared comfortable. Plenty of trees graced this campsite, giving her many choices of where to tie it. Therefore, Roberta looked forward to curling up with a good book.

She tied the hammock securely to a couple of large trees, then tugged on it as hard as she could to be sure it would support her weight. She pushed on one of the wooden crosspieces and stood back. The hammock swayed and spun one complete revolution, making her wonder how she could climb on it without falling off. She knew people actually slept in these things, but she had no idea how they climbed in.

Carefully and hesitantly, with her book tucked under her chin, Roberta grasped the hammock. With a hand on each side and one knee braced up, all she had to do was lift the other leg, hoist herself up onto her hands and knees, and then she could sink into the center and flip over onto her back. Once her other leg was off the ground she could balance her way in. No problem.

Doing as she pictured the steps in her mind, Roberta raised her left leg, which put most of her weight being supported by her right hand. Roberta stiffened as she realized she was leaning too much weight on one side, because the hammock was starting to pitch. She tried to redistribute her weight, but that only made the hammock swing the other way as she balanced precariously. Her fingers clenched as hard as she could onto the sides, both hands clinging to the top portion as she braced herself on one knee, the other leg hanging over the edge as the hammock continued to lean. The ground moved precariously.

To her horror, the hammock continued in a rolling motion, the whole thing happening in slow motion like some outtake in a B-grade movie. Roberta hung on for dear life.

The hammock picked up speed as it continued to turn in its rolling motion. Her foot lifted off the ground when the hammock pitched, flipping completely over. The book slipped out from under her chin and shot into the bushes at the same time as she landed on the ground under the hammock with a thud, flat on her back.

With the wind knocked out of her, Roberta gulped for air. It didn't hurt too bad, but she was unable to move as she struggled to breathe, staring up at the bottom of the hammock.

Gravel crunched, increasing in volume, as the running footsteps came closer. "Miss! Are you hurt!? Can you speak!?"

Roberta looked up. Way up. She considered the odd perspective her position granted her. First she stared at Mr. Ranger's battered and worn hiking boots, then up the length of a pair of long, hairy legs. A tight pair of lips accompanied by large, dark sunglasses and a green hat peered down at her.

He hunkered down beside her. Reaching one hand out, he waited for her to respond and offer her hand to him so he could pull her up.

Not a chance. Embarrassment flooded her as she lay on the ground, flat on her back, looking up at him. She ignored the pinch of gravel digging into her back, and the new scrapes on her bare legs. "I think I lost my book."

Mr. Ranger smiled down at her. "Ah. I thought I saw something fly up and land in the bushes as you went tumbling over. Do you need some help getting into your hammock?"

Roberta squeezed her eyes shut as she continued to lie, unmoving, on the ground. She didn't want to know that he had seen her newest misadventure. This whole day could have been a nightmare, except the pain in her knee and the gravel digging into her back confirmed that she was indeed wide awake.

He reached out again, and this time Roberta tried not to blush as Mr. Ranger helped her to her feet.

"I guess there must be a trick to this."

"You know, I've got a hammock exactly like this. Did you buy it at Hank's Outdoor Store on the corner of Third and Main?"

"No."

He shrugged his shoulders, smiling. At her answering frown, he turned his head toward the bushes. "Well, then, let's find your book, and I'll show you how to get in."

Roberta couldn't believe his arrogance. First he had a camper just like Molly's friend, and now he had a hammock exactly like this. Mike always did the same thing, always trying to impress her, but this time she refused to fall for it. Just because he was the park ranger didn't mean he was an expert at everything. She would have eventually figured things out for herself. She didn't need or want his help.

Without speaking, she immediately began to search for her book so Mr. Know-it-all Ranger wouldn't find it first. Out of the corner of her eye, she saw it sticking out of a small bush, allowing her to grab it before he could. "I've got it!" she called out to him.

As she watched from a distance, Mr. Ranger straightened and sauntered to the hammock. He inspected the knots, probably not trusting that she was capable of tying them properly. Once satisfied, he offered her his hand and smiled again from below the dark sunglasses. She wished she could see his whole face.

"Want me to help you get in?"

Roberta backed up.

"I guess not." He frowned. "Then watch me, and I'll demonstrate." He backed up to the hammock until he was almost in a sitting position, then leaned to one side as he sat down. When his back was down, he lifted his legs in. Linking his fingers behind his head and crossing his booted ankles, he appeared quite comfy as the hammock swayed slightly.

"See?" He smiled again.

Roberta glanced up and down his tall frame at the way his lithe body fit into the hammock. He looked tall even lying down, and she guessed his height to be close to six-foot-two. Even though half his face was hidden, he seemed very good looking. She wondered if he came on like this to all the lone women that came camping.

Roberta grunted in response.

Still wearing an infuriating smile on his face, Mr. Ranger continued to watch her. "This is how you get out." She watched him get out in the same manner as he got in, only in reverse.

"Demonstration complete. Have fun." He turned and left, tipping his hat on his way out of the campsite.

Watching him turn down the road and walk away, Roberta sighed. She didn't know what he'd come for that time, unless he had meant to ask her to pay. In that case, he had obviously forgotten when he saw her fall off the hammock. She shuddered to think that he would be back again.

Once he was far enough away, and not likely to come back, Roberta tried once more to enter the hammock, feeling more confident of her ability when he wasn't watching. Doing exactly as Mr. Ranger showed her, she settled in without incident, and sure enough, the hammock was indeed comfy.

As she started to read, Roberta decided that maybe camping wasn't such a bad idea after all. When Molly arrived, which hopefully would be soon, they could start supper. Roberta had brought what she thought was a typical camping meal of hot dogs and everything that went with them, and she could hardly wait.

The more she read, the more she relaxed, and the more she enjoyed the calming sway of the hammock. Appreciating the lull and the soothing rocking motion, after a couple of chapters, her eyes drifted shut.

❦

The phone rang in the park office.

"Parks and Recreation, Ranger Lamont speaking."

"Garrett? Is that you?" A burst of static blurred the line.

Garrett raised his voice, trying to be heard over all the noise. "Molly? I can't hear you very well. Where are you calling from?"

Molly's voice screamed over the background noise. "I'm calling from the hospital. Mom had another asthma attack. She's going to be fine, but can you go find Robbie? It looks like I won't be there tonight. I have to stay with Mom."

"Your friend never showed up."

Molly gasped. "What do you mean Robbie never showed up? Garrett, she's never pulled a trailer before, and she's got my car and your family's tent-trailer. If she's had an accident or something, I'll never forgive myself! It took awhile, but I had to really convince her because she's never been camping before. Are you sure she isn't there?"

Garrett's mind raced, trying to fill in the holes obscured by the static, until Molly's words sank in. When he had talked to Gwen, he heard only the name Rob, not Robbie. He naturally assumed it was a guy they were talking about. "Your friend is a she?"

Garrett closed his eyes. Robbie. Roberta Garland. The nutty woman in site 27. The hammock that looked just like his. The trailer with the crank that got stuck in the same place. He had thought the car looked familiar. It was Molly's car.

"Garrett, haven't you met Robbie before?" Molly shouted over the noise. She paused. "But then, she didn't remember ever meeting you either. Maybe you two really haven't met."

Garrett said nothing. No wonder the woman was such a basket case. Gwen had told him earlier that Rob's fiancée had been caught making out with someone else in the storage room. They had an ugly fight in front of all the staff, and after that, Rob had promptly been fired. It hadn't dawned on him that Rob could be female. Garrett closed his eyes, remembering his own words, asking her when her boyfriend was coming. Under the circumstances, it was no wonder she had broken down and cried again.

Garrett knew how persistent Molly could be when she got herself stuck on something. It appeared Molly had been hard at work again, this time convincing her poor dejected friend to go camping to get away from it all. No wonder Robbie was so incompetent. Not only was it not her tent-trailer, she had never even been camping before. Under those circumstances, she hadn't done too badly.

He sighed as he remembered the sight of Robbie sailing over the hammock as it flipped over with her on it. He thought she had seriously hurt herself that time, but instead she had made a joke about losing her book. She had even been friendly for a few seconds.

The phone line crackled again.

"Garrett? Are you still there? Hello?"

"Yes, Molly, I'm still here. Just thinking, that's all. Yes, your friend Robbie is here. She's set up and everything is fine. Let's just say she hasn't been too receptive to my assistance." He frowned as he recalled her expression as she screamed at him to leave her alone, then ran sobbing into the camper. "About now she's all settled into my hammock reading a book. Maybe I'd better go introduce myself."

The volume of the static increased. Garrett was ready to end the conversation, but Molly's raised voice again broke through. "You're going to have to do more than that. I can't come tonight like I promised. I was going to ask if you'd stay with her for the night and keep an eye on her. She's had a pretty rough time of things."

Garrett's frown deepened. "You're kidding, right?"

"No, Garrett, I'm very serious. You're going to have to look after her for me."

Garrett gritted his teeth. Molly didn't know what she was asking. Twice already her friend had screamed at him to leave her alone. More important, he had no intention of spending the night in the same campsite with a woman, unchaperoned. "I'll talk to her and see what she says. That's all I'm going to promise, Molly."

"That's fine with me. I have to go. There's someone else waiting for the phone. See you tomorrow after supper when I come with Gwen. What site is she in?"

"Site 27. At least she picked a good spot."

"Great. See you tomorrow, and tell Robbie I'm sorry."

"Sure. Bye, Molly."

Garrett hung up the phone, his ear ringing from both the loud static and Molly's shouting. For a few seconds, he squeezed his eyes shut. He imagined himself walking up to Robbie, a stranger, to announce that she was in his hammock, in his camper, and if that wasn't enough, he was going to spend the night in the campsite with her. Based on her reactions to his presence so far, and knowing now why she was reacting to him the way she had been, he couldn't even guess her reaction to Molly's request.

Garrett picked up his hat and sunglasses and put them back on as he walked out the door toward site 27, deep in thought.

❦

Roberta lay in the bottom of a small boat, rocking as the waves sloshed against the side, the lull of the splashing soothing her. Clouds drifted through the bright blue sky. Birds sang overhead.

Suddenly everything darkened. A voice drifted from a cave, and she could feel an evil presence. It called her name. Frightened, she cowered as she continued to lie in the bottom of the boat. A dark claw reached toward her neck, ready to strangle her. A voice again called her name. The ugly clawed hand touched her.

Roberta jolted to a sitting position and screamed. With the book still in her hand, she flung her arms out. Upon impact with something hard, the book flew out of her hand. She grabbed onto taut pieces of cloth at her sides, and gasped for breath while she became aware of her surroundings.

As the world swayed back and forth, Roberta slowly remembered that she was at a campsite, and she'd been reading a library book in a hammock, of all things.

To give a name to her nightmare, Mr. Ranger stood beside her, except he looked different. He wasn't wearing his hat, and the sunglasses she'd never seen him without were askew on his face. Both hands covered the lower half of his face, and blood dripped out from between his fingers.

Realizing what had happened, everything fell into place.

She had hurt him.

She covered her mouth with her hands. "Mr. Ranger! I'm so sorry! Are you all right? Let me get something for you!"

Roberta tried to get out of the hammock quickly, but fell out on her hands and knees, banging her sore knee for the third time and this time taking off a few layers of skin. She tried to ignore the sting as she ran into the camper for a towel, hobbling as fast as she could.

Grateful she had already discovered where the towels were stored, she pulled one out and quickly limped back to Mr. Ranger. She offered him the towel at the same time as she bent down to press her knee, wishing she had brought a second towel for herself, because she was bleeding too. "I'm so sorry! I didn't mean to hit you! I feel so awful!"

Mr. Ranger removed the sunglasses and pressed the towel against his face. "Don't worry about it. I'm sorry for startling you, Robbie. I should have thought before I woke you." He repositioned the towel. His deep baritone voice came out muffled as he spoke through the towel. "How's your knee? You should get some ice on it."

Roberta looked up at him from her crouched position as she continued to press her hand to her wounded knee. This time she could only see the top half of his face. The hat and glasses were gone, but the towel obscured his face from his nose down.

Above the towel, Mr. Ranger had beautiful dark brown eyes, long lashes, and gorgeous, thick, straight dark hair, although it was quite messy from having his hat knocked off.

She studied the top half of his face, trying to imagine what both halves would look like together.

❧

Garrett looked down at Molly's friend as she hunched over clutching her knee. He had sure seen stars when she hit him in the nose with that book. With all the accidents he witnessed today, he should have known better than to get too close.

"What did you call me?" he asked slowly, still speaking through the towel.

Her face turned red. "I called you Mr. Ranger. For some reason I've been thinking of you as Mr. Ranger in my head every time you've come by. Why did you call me Robbie? Only my friends call me Robbie. How did you know that?"

Garrett shuffled the towel to hold it to his nose with his left hand as Robbie narrowed her eyes to glare daggers at him. He examined his right hand and wiped it on his shorts, just in case, before extending it to her for a handshake.

"Molly just called me. Allow me to introduce myself. I'm Garrett, Gwen's brother. We're going to be camping together."

She stared at him with her mouth open. She did not reach out and shake his extended hand. Instead, all the color drained from her face as she buried her face in her palms.

"Oh, no!" she moaned as she bowed her head.

Chapter 3

Garrett held the towel away from his face and dabbed at his sore nose with the back of his hand to make sure the bleeding had stopped. In addition to the dull throb on his cheekbone where the frame of his sunglasses had smashed into his face on impact with the book, his eyes still watered from the blow to his nose. If he hadn't been wearing the sunglasses, she would have taken his eye out with the corner of that thing. He had never considered a book to be a lethal weapon before. He'd heard the pen was mightier than the sword, but this was ridiculous.

Garrett looked down at Robbie, who still refused to look at him. She remained hunched over, her face hidden by her hands. With her track record today, Garrett could see why she didn't want to face him, and he felt bad for her, but it couldn't be avoided. They were more or less forced into each other's company.

He cleared his throat and picked up his hat. "Molly phoned to say her mother had an asthma attack. She has to stay with her mother tonight, so she asked me to check up on you. I hope you don't mind."

Robbie uncovered her face and looked up at him with big, round green eyes. She didn't say a word.

He ran his fingers through his hair, scrunched his hat in his hand, then stared at the crinkles he'd made in the canvas. "She also told me what happened. I'm very sorry. I didn't mean to upset you earlier."

When she still didn't say anything, Garrett looked at her again. She remained hunkered down near the ground, looking up at him with sad doe eyes. Garrett forced himself to smile. This did not look like the start of a fun evening.

He tried to think of something to say, but nothing came to mind. All he could do was stare down at her. The one time she smiled at him, it struck him how pretty she was. She was pretty even now, almost cowering, her face pale, in that half-kneeling squat. Delicately featured, she had deep sea green eyes and a long, flowing, wavy mane of beautiful hair so light brown it was almost blond.

Earlier, he remembered restraining himself from reaching out and touching her hair to remove the stick that lodged in it after she'd fallen, but he was stopped by her foul expression. At least now he understood why she was in such a state of emotional upheaval.

❦

Roberta continued to stare up at Mr. Ranger, better known as Garrett. Molly hadn't mentioned Gwen's brother was a park ranger, but at least now it made more sense why he would be joining them on the camping outing. He worked here.

Without the hat and dark glasses, she could see both halves of his face together for the first time. His dark brown hair, so dark it was almost black, suited his strong features. Cut short at the sides and longer on top and at the back, the style emphasized his Roman nose, which didn't make him in any way unattractive but instead added to his appeal. The dark tone of his skin matched his deep chocolate brown eyes. They were set off by strong, heavy eyebrows that accented the masculine appeal in his face.

If she had to typecast a ranger, Garrett would definitely be a match. Everything about him shouted "the great outdoors." Tall, muscular build. . .he even looked great in shorts, and she hadn't seen many men who had such nice legs. She'd gotten a good view of those legs from the ground up.

A large red blotch marred his right cheek, probably where she had hit him with her book. By tomorrow it would most likely be a big ugly bruise. She tried not to cringe at the knowledge that it was her fault.

All day long she'd made a complete fool of herself in front of him, in addition to treating him so badly. Even if she had never liked the know-it-all type, that didn't give her the right to be rude. Most important, since he was Molly's friend, she was obligated to be nice to him.

He wiggled the arms of his sunglasses, gently slid them back onto his face, and replaced his hat. He smiled, but Roberta didn't smile back. "Let's go sit down somewhere more comfortable." He reached out his hand toward her after wiping it again on his shorts.

She stood on her own. Out of rebellion, Roberta refused to touch his hand. She agreed to this camping vacation to be left alone, not to have one of the park rangers watch her, even if it was at Molly's request. She knew Molly was only concerned, but Roberta was an adult and didn't need or want a baby-sitter.

She opened her mouth to protest, but the words died in her throat. The reason for Molly's concern, Mike's betrayal, brought back the image of Mike and Suzie together, and Mike's ugly words as she left the office. She walked to the lawn chairs in silence. She refused to break down and cry in front of Garrett again. The poor man had seen enough tears. From this moment on, Roberta decided to be strong.

⁕

Garrett ignored being shunned. He watched Robbie limp over to one of the lawn chairs, where she sat all prim and proper, folding her hands in her lap and saying nothing. He tried to think of a good conversation-starter to take her mind off her troubles. "How do you like my hammock? I see you had a little nap in it."

"Yes," she replied quietly. "It's very nice." She lowered her head and stared at her hands.

There was a long pause.

"You did a good job setting up the tent-trailer, especially for someone who's never been camping before. It even looks level."

"Thank you," she replied equally as quiet. "But you did all the hard parts."

Another long silence.

"You picked a real good campsite. This is one of the largest and most private, with all the trees surrounding it. It will be nice and quiet tonight. Most of the campers who come Thursday just park their units to reserve the spot and leave. It will be full tomorrow night."

"Yes," she nodded, her voice still soft. "That's what Molly said."

More silence.

Garrett resisted dragging his hand over his face. He'd had enough trying to make conversation. He had things to do. He wasn't here on vacation.

"I've got to get back to work now. I'll stop by and peek in on you from time to time. The rangers usually have dinner in about an hour and a half. Since Molly isn't coming, would you care to join us?"

"No, I think I'll stay here. Thanks anyway." She stared down at her lap and picked at a thread.

"By yourself? You don't have to be alone, you know. You're more than welcome to come join the guys." The other rangers might even be jealous if he brought along a pretty woman to supper break, even if she didn't talk much. Knowing the rest of them, if she remained quiet, they'd all start to show off, trying to impress her. The last laugh would be on them.

"I'll be fine, thank you."

This was one depressed lady. For as much as he tried to think of something to cheer her up, not a thing came to mind. Perhaps bringing her into the ranger camp to sit among all the guys wasn't such a great idea, but he did have to agree with Molly—Robbie shouldn't be left alone. He just didn't know what to do about it.

He watched as she sat in the chair, her dainty hands folded in her lap, staring down at them. She was even starting to make him feel depressed. He started to nervously brush a fleck of dirt off his shorts before he stopped himself.

"Look," he said as he stood, "if you don't want to join the rangers for dinner, that's fine. I can come here. I know it's awkward when you don't know anyone. I'm off around midnight tonight. Maybe we can talk then. I have to go, but I'll see you later, okay, Robbie?"

Roberta finally looked up at him. "Okay."

Garrett waited for her to continue, but she didn't. Rather than make the silence any worse, he stood, adjusted his sunglasses on his face, and touched the brim of his hat. "Enjoy the peace and quiet. See you at supper time." He turned and strode off, back to the ranger camp.

It didn't matter that she was no longer in front of him. He could still see her face in the back of his mind. He knew those big, sad eyes would haunt him until the end of time.

Garrett walked along the camp road to check for unregistered arrivals, but his mind was not on his work.

Usually he didn't go for the helpless femme fatale type, but he couldn't stop thinking of Robbie. He couldn't equate her downcast spirit as they sat together with the feisty woman he'd seen attempting to be a first-time successful camper all by herself. When she screamed at him, she'd displayed a burst of temper and independence any five year old would have been proud of.

It was probably just as well that she was out camping rather than at home brooding. When he had something to think about, the serene atmosphere of the great outdoors always served to remind him of God's presence all around, which told him God was ultimately in control, no matter what disaster befell him. For tonight, though, he did have a problem knowing Molly wouldn't be there to spend the night.

Although this particular campground was generally family oriented, he didn't feel comfortable with a woman camping alone. He hadn't exactly been thrilled to hear Gwen and Molly planned a camping trip by themselves, so he jumped at the chance when Gwen invited him to join them. He had planned to bow out once Molly's friend Rob arrived, but now it turned out there would be three women, which wasn't much better. Molly was a bad enough camper, but Robbie's camping skills defied description.

Therefore, until Molly and Gwen arrived, it was up to him to keep an eye on Robbie, not that he knew what to do or say. Only time would tell.

Roberta stared at the empty fire pit. Molly wasn't coming. It was bad enough she let Molly convince her to try this stupid camping idea, but now, except for Mr. Ranger Garrett, she was all alone. She didn't know what to think or what to do.

Not that she cared to admit it, but she was nervous all by herself out in the middle of nowhere. She didn't know what kind of pressure Molly had put on Garrett, but if it was anything similar to the way Molly pressured her into going camping, Garrett would be visiting again. Since Roberta was all alone in unfamiliar surroundings, she was grateful for the presence of someone she knew, even if it was second hand. At the same time, she really wanted to be left alone and didn't want him to come back.

Roberta's stomach grumbled. Because of the scene at work and then Molly's arrival at her house, she had skipped lunch. Now that all the action was over, she was starving.

Not moving from the chair, she stared blankly at the cooler, which contained the supper she'd brought for herself and Molly. Even though he'd offered, she doubted Garrett would abandon his good supper and the company of his ranger friends to join her for scorched hot dogs. Besides, she'd been so rude to him that she didn't expect him to return except to fulfill his obligation to Molly.

She turned her attention to the empty fire pit. The fire wasn't going to start itself. Since Molly wasn't coming, and she knew Garrett wasn't likely to return, the only way to have a campfire was to make one herself.

Roberta remembered passing a stockpile of firewood by the entrance to the campground. She slipped her camera into her pocket in case she saw the little squirrel again and walked in the direction of the camp entrance.

At the opening to the pullout, she stopped to read a sign about campfire safety, which stated, among other things, that a campfire was not to be left unattended.

She studied the haphazard pile of firewood.

Almost everyone she knew, except her parents, had gas fireplaces and never burned real logs. When she was growing up her parents never allowed her to start a real fire in the fireplace, unless it was at Christmas time. Then it was the manufactured kind they bought at the grocery store that burned in pretty colors, and all she did was light the wrapper to get a fire started.

Trying to ignore the scrape of the rough bark against her tender skin, Roberta selected a few dry logs. In an effort to calculate how long each piece would take to burn, Roberta juggled the logs in her arms in an attempt to compare them to the pressed Yule logs. The real thing seemed lighter, but weight gave her no indication of how long it would burn.

Since she didn't know the answer, Roberta decided it best to have too much wood on hand at the campsite, rather than too little. Besides, since she didn't have anything better to do, she had plenty of time to accumulate mass quantities of firewood.

She studied the large stack of logs. Her biggest challenge would be to carry the wood by hand, since she didn't want to get pieces of bark and mud in Molly's clean car.

After the third trip, Roberta lost the bounce to her step. Trudging back and forth in the heat of a summer day, carrying dirty hunks of heavy wood, was not turning out to be her idea of a dream vacation. As she stared at her meager pile of firewood beside her fire pit, she wondered how much more she would need to last the night. During the daytime the temperature was hot, but the evenings cooled quickly, probably more so out here in the wilderness than in the city.

She swiped her arm across her forehead and fanned herself by waving the front of her T-shirt. Even though she had been selective, the logs seemed to get heavier with every trip. Not having the energy anymore to do it properly, Roberta wiggled her foot to dislodge a rock stuck between her toes while she counted the logs in her stash. While it probably didn't take much wood to cook one little wiener, she was more concerned about evening, when she would need enough wood to stay warm.

Therefore, Roberta wiped her hands on her shorts and headed down the gravel road one last time.

Bent at the waist, while picking through the pile for the lightest pieces of a decent size, she heard that all-too-familiar deep baritone voice behind her.

"Hi, Robbie. Want me to carry some for you?"

Roberta cringed. She straightened and turned around to look up into a huge pair of dark sunglasses. Even though for this moment she couldn't see his eyes, at least now she knew what they looked like.

Garrett stood tall, smiling down at her, his feet slightly apart and his arms crossed over his broad chest. The man was huge.

Roberta gulped, then lowered her head as she searched for more nice pieces of wood.

He didn't miss a beat. "I see you're getting a nice little pile of firewood back at the campsite. Between the two of us, one more trip ought to do it."

Roberta squeezed her eyes shut. He'd gone looking for her. She wasn't that helpless, or hopeless, that she couldn't do this by herself.

She glared at him in silence. With Garrett wearing his sunglasses, she couldn't see his eyes. Giving him a dirty look didn't do any good when he wasn't paying attention. Therefore, she ignored him right back and continued to pick through the woodpile. Once she selected a good armload, she turned to see him standing beside her, waiting patiently, his arms full with approximately triple the amount of wood she could hold.

She opened her mouth to protest, but self-preservation stopped her. With what he now carried, she would now have enough to last the whole night, plus part of tomorrow, maybe even 'til Molly and her friend arrived.

"Let's go," she mumbled.

They walked quietly for a few minutes, which was a welcome change. Although his voice was pleasant, Garrett talked far too much for Roberta's liking. Unfortunately, as usual, he was the first to break the silence.

"Don't you just love to sit by a crackling fire in the dark?"

"Uh, sure."

He looked down at her as they walked side by side. "Have you ever made a campfire before?"

Roberta kept her gaze decidedly forward. "No."

"Do you know anything about building a fire?"

"No."

He faced forward again as he continued to talk. "Would you like me to show you? I've got a few free minutes. I can chop up some kindling for you. Since you've got my camper I know where the ax is."

Roberta nearly fell over her own feet as she walked. She hadn't thought about needing to chop the wood she was diligently piling up where the fire would eventually be. Now that she was thinking about it, she did need his assistance. She hadn't exaggerated when she said she knew absolutely nothing about building a campfire.

She tried to sneak a sideways glance at him as they walked together. She felt bad that he felt obligated to be with her because of Molly badgering him, especially when she knew personally that once Molly got her mind stuck on something, nothing could change it. Yet, as much as he got on her nerves, she at least owed him some courtesy for all his help, regardless of his reasons. "Yes, thank you. I'd appreciate that."

He turned to her, smiling his response. A strange quiver unsettled her stomach, but she convinced herself it was only because she was over-hungry. Mike had been nice to her too, at least in the beginning of their relationship. He'd been so nice, in her inexperience she'd quickly fallen in love with him. It was only now she could look back and see that instead of wanting to help her, Mike had only wanted a helpless female on his arm to feed his enormous ego.

Roberta promised herself she would never put herself in that position ever again.

Instead of returning Garrett's smile, she faced forward and trudged into the campsite.

Garrett opened a compartment on the outside of the trailer and pulled out a rather large ax. Then, to her shock, he started unbuttoning his shirt.

Roberta stepped backward. "What are you doing?" she gulped.

"I thought you wanted me to chop some kindling for you?" Garrett slung his shirt over the back of one of the lawn chairs, walked to the pile, selected the largest log, and stood it up on end. Holding the ax across the front of him, one hand on the end of the handle and the other about two thirds of the way up, he shuffled his feet to stand with his legs planted firmly apart.

Roberta gulped and stared. He hadn't been pushy on purpose. One look at him told her he loved what he did as a ranger. He stood before her as the personification of Mr. Great Outdoors. Broad-shouldered and bare-chested, with muscles tensed and ready, he steadied the ax in his large hands as he contemplated the log in front of him.

While Garrett stared at the log, Roberta stared at Garrett. Rugged and powerful, he was gorgeous. The hat and dark glasses shielding his face added a touch of mystery to his appearance.

"Stand back," he commanded as he raised his head in her direction to be sure she was a safe distance away.

He heaved the ax high in the air behind his head and swung it down solidly, cleanly splitting a thin piece of wood from the log. Repeating the procedure a number of times, he soon reduced the heavy log to a mere pile of kindling.

Resting the ax on its head, he wiped one arm across his brow, then wiped his hands on his shorts. "I'll split one log more for you, and then I'll be on my way."

All Roberta could do was nod.

He pulled off his hat, ran his hands through his hair, then placed the hat back on his head as he picked through the pile for another log to split. He didn't keep looking back at her—in fact, he paid her no attention whatsoever. He was only there to do a job, which he was doing quite efficiently.

Once he'd picked another suitable log to split, Garrett positioned himself as before. Holding the ax across the front of him, he assessed the log. He turned his head, and as best Roberta could tell, he was probably watching her from behind the dark sunglasses. "Just checking where you are. Don't move while I'm doing this. You're supposed to stand to the side of someone who is chopping wood. If the head of the ax flies off you could get hurt."

"Okay," she mumbled.

He touched the tip of the ax to the log, then inhaled deeply. He moved slightly and started to raise the ax, but as he did so the log fell over. He sighed, rested the head of the ax on the ground, and with his free hand, he reached toward the fallen log.

Roberta watched him, mesmerized. When he righted the log, she let her hand drop down. The motion caused her to brush a hard shape in her pocket. Slowly, she wrapped her hand around the object—her camera.

Roberta smiled. She hadn't seen the squirrel, but watching Garrett chop wood turned out to be far more interesting than any four-legged creature.

She couldn't help herself. She raised the camera and quickly snapped a picture. As she waited for the sound of the auto-advance to finish, Garrett managed to steady the log to stand on end. She again positioned the camera, intending to attempt to snap the picture at the exact second the ax landed to actually split the wood.

He positioned the ax. Garrett tensed at the same time as he raised his head to look up at her. "I'm ready. Don't. . ." As he caught sight of her, his voice trailed off. His smile instantly degenerated into a miserable scowl. "What are you doing?" he barked.

Roberta lowered the camera. "I'm going to take your picture. Smile." She deliberately failed to mention she had already taken one. Raising the camera to her face again, she took a step back. "Go ahead and chop the wood. I have an idea."

If looks could kill, Robbie would have been six feet under. "Put that thing away."

Once again, she lowered the camera. Even without seeing his eyes, his tight frown and pinched lips told her he wasn't pleased.

He stiffened and let go of the center of the ax handle, holding just the end of it with one hand while the head rested on the ground. "I said put that thing away," he said from between clenched teeth.

She held the camera behind her back.

"Away. Put it away."

Roberta turned the camera off and tucked it back into her pocket. "Why don't you like having your picture taken?"

He clenched his teeth. "I just don't. Okay?" he said in a straight, even pitch. Despite the fact that she obviously didn't know him very well, any fool could see he wasn't kidding. She didn't understand, because up until now, he had been so mild mannered. Roberta thought it best not to push her luck. She took her camera out of her pocket and laid it on the picnic table, where he could plainly see it, while he glowered at her, watching her every step.

Obediently, she stood in an acceptable location while Garrett silently split the other log. Roberta watched in admiration but said nothing as he repeatedly swung the heavy ax, making perfect, even pieces every time.

When he was done, he remained uncharacteristically silent for possibly the first time. Purposely leaving the camera on the picnic table, Roberta ran into the camper.

Garrett inhaled a deep breath and watched her disappear, still feeling irritable, and hating himself for it. He knew he shouldn't have been so harsh with her, after all, she couldn't have known. The poor woman had enough problems without having to deal with his hang-ups. All he wanted to do was keep an eye on her, although he didn't know why. She was certainly less than receptive to his presence. He didn't usually fall for her type, but something he couldn't name would have kept him watching her, even if Molly hadn't asked. He rested his hands on his hips and waited, staring toward the camper, wondering what was taking her so long. His gaze drifted to the camera, still lying on the picnic table. His gut clenched at the thought of it.

When she finally reappeared, she handed him a clean towel. He lifted his hat and sunglasses with one hand and wiped his face, then rubbed the sweat off his chest and shoulders. Instead of giving it back, he tossed the towel over the back of the lawn chair.

"Thanks," he mumbled as he picked up his shirt. More quickly than he'd ever done before, he buttoned it, tucked it into the waistband of his shorts, and left before he said something he'd regret.

Roberta's stomach grumbled, making her grateful he left when he did. Before starting the fire to cook her hot dog, she lifted the ax to put it away. As she did so, she turned to the pile of logs, then shifted the weight of the ax in her hands to get a feel for it.

Garrett had made the whole thing look so easy.

Digging through the pile, she found a log that would balance nicely on one end. Following Garrett's example, she wiggled it into the ground to steady it fully, picked up the ax, and touched the blade to the center of the log. She was ready.

The ax was heavier than it looked. She tried lifting it high, but it was too heavy to heave over and behind her head like Garrett had. As carefully as she could, she lifted it as high as she could without the fear of falling backwards, then swung it down, aiming for the center of the log.

The blade barely caught the edge. Instead of splitting a piece off, the ax lodged in to a depth of a few inches and stuck. Roberta pulled and heaved and twisted, but couldn't get it out. Out of frustration, she pushed the log over, with the ax still firmly wedged into the wood. Using one foot to steady the log, she wiggled the ax until it came out. She dropped it on the ground, then stopped to catch her breath.

Perhaps the woodcutting was best left up to Garrett.

After she tucked the ax back into the bin and pushed the log back into the pile, Roberta set to work building a fire. Since she started the Yule log burning by first lighting the paper, Roberta used some newspaper she found stashed beneath the ax to start the real logs, and very soon she had a good fire roaring. Rather than use a stick to roast her wiener, she used a long metal pole she found inside the camper, and soon her hot dog was nicely roasted.

She helped herself to everything she'd brought to share with Molly, and sat in a lawnchair beside the fire. Before she began to eat, Roberta stared at the plate in her lap. It had been a long time since she had stopped to be thankful for God's blessings, yet today, surrounded by the beauty of God's creation, she felt compelled to offer a prayer of thanks, as she sat in the wilderness, alone.

Despite the bad things that had happened to her, she could be thankful. Molly was with her mother, who was fine after her asthma attack. Even though Roberta had lost her job, she received a severance package to see her through financially until she found something else. This time she didn't want to work in downtown Vancouver, but she knew she could find a good paying jobs in the suburbs, closer to home.

She couldn't see the city from where she was now, but she knew that somewhere in Vancouver, Mike and Suzie were having a great time now that she was gone.

Mike. Her teeth clenched. It wasn't God's fault Mike was an unfaithful jerk. She really should have known what kind of guy he was. At first, Mike said he "kind of" believed in God, and he even had attended church a few times with her. Soon he convinced her to start missing services, until she hadn't been going for months. She wondered if Mike had ever been a believer. She now suspected he had gone to church with her in the beginning only to win her trust.

She had never felt like such a fool. Thinking of Mike as she now knew him to be, she realized he was no loss. Now that the shock was over, she was thankful she found out in time, before the wedding. The real loss was her job.

And so what? She could always find another job, maybe even a better one. Her best friend, Molly, had come to her rescue, providing a break from routine to give her time and opportunity to get her head together. Even though she was more alone than she'd originally planned, God had provided Garrett to help if she should need it. That he got on her nerves didn't make him any less available. Perhaps he was to also be a lesson in patience.

Roberta bowed her head and thanked God for taking care of all her needs. Just as she raised her head and lifted the hot dog to her mouth, a familiar voice echoed behind her.

"Nice fire. Looks like you're going to make a decent camper yet. I see you found the roasting poles. Am I invited?"

Roberta turned around to see Garrett's lithe form striding to the fire pit, all traces of his anger from their last encounter forgotten. She had been enjoying the silence until now.

"Help yourself. Everything I brought is in the cooler." She doubted what she brought for Molly would be enough for a big man like him, but what she had, he was welcome to share.

She heard him digging through the cooler, pausing every once in awhile to open a few lids.

"Hey, potato salad, great! And carrots, already cut up and everything. This looks like grape juice. You're sure I can help myself?"

"That's what I said."

Roberta heard him without really paying attention to what he was saying as he complimented her on the food she brought, comparing it to an allegedly miserable campfire meal at the ranger camp. He stepped into the camper to get himself a plate and utensils, yakking constantly the entire time. She hoped he would at least be quiet while he was eating.

Plate full, he sauntered to the campfire, dragging a lawn chair with him. He smiled as he accepted the pole with his hot dog. She ate her dinner, nodding politely as he kept up enough conversation for both of them, until finished roasting his supper.

Conversation abruptly stopped. Just in case he was choking on his dinner, Roberta turned her head to check on him. Garrett sat in the lawn chair, his head bowed. She stared as he didn't move or speak for a few seconds. He nodded once, still silent, then raised his head. Even though she couldn't see his eyes through the sunglasses, she knew he was staring back at her.

"Yes?" he asked, then opened his mouth and took a massive bite out of his hot dog.

Chapter 4

Roberta concentrated intently on the fire, poking the glowing embers with a long stick she had found earlier.

He prayed over his meal. Without any prompting.

She didn't know anything about him, nor did she know what Molly had told him about her, or if Molly had told him about Mike.

After Mike made all the right moves to earn her trust, Roberta wasn't so sure Garrett wouldn't do the same. Pretending to be a committed Christian had done wonders for Mike. She wouldn't fall for the same thing again.

"I like this brand of potato salad. I buy this kind too."

Roberta made a mental note to ask Molly more about him, just to satisfy her curiosity. Until then, for safety's sake, she planned to keep her distance.

"Did you bring any marshmallows? If not, I can bring a bag from our stash at ranger headquarters." His sly little grin told her there was more to the story, but she didn't ask for more details.

She shook her head.

Garrett checked his watch. "It's time for me to get back. I'll check in on you when I make the rounds. Catch you later, and thanks for supper, Robbie. I always love a home-cooked meal."

Roberta stared at the cooler. The only thing about their meal of flame-blackened hot dogs and store-bought potato salad that could be considered "home-cooked" was that she had sliced the carrots by hand. "You're welcome."

She remained seated in the lawn chair as Garrett left the campsite. Instead of walking to wherever he was going, he drove away in a small pickup truck emblazoned with the Parks and Recreation logo on the door.

At home she would have simply put the plates in the dishwasher. Out in the middle of nowhere, first Roberta had to pump some water out of the tank in the camper, heat it in a pot, then wash everything using plastic tubs on the small counter. She poured the water down the sink, but it didn't occur to her until she heard water splashing on the ground beneath the trailer that there was no plumbing system. She was merely dumping the water on the ground under the tent-trailer, which she thought rather disgusting. When the dripping sound finally stopped, Roberta froze, wondering where the water would go and hoping that she had not created a dirty river that would run through the campsite, where she would be walking.

Next time, instead of using the sink, she would have to carry the water outside and dump it in the bushes, to be safe.

Now that she was done, Roberta walked outside. She'd never taken so long to wash two plates and a handful of cutlery in her life. By the time she settled into the hammock with her book, the daylight had diminished considerably. As well, it was slightly darker being tucked inside the hammock. After reading only a few pages, Roberta laid the book down on her stomach and rubbed her sore eyes.

She looked up into the ever-darkening sky. It was never really dark in the suburbs of Vancouver. But here, with no electricity available for miles, and without the glow of the city lights, she suspected the dark of night would be very dark.

Slowly, Roberta maneuvered herself out of the hammock. While on her mission of discovery she had unearthed an old lantern. The time to light it would be now, before it got too dark to make out the instructions.

The instructions were worn but not impossible to read. Although she turned all the knobs and things to the right place, she wasn't positive she did everything exactly right. Therefore, as a precaution, she carried the camper's fire extinguisher outside.

Before attempting to light the lantern, she walked to the entrance of the campsite and looked both ways down the road. Naturally, since this was the one time she was actually hoping to see Garrett, she didn't.

In the few minutes it took to check down the road, the sky darkened even more, telling her she couldn't wait forever. Earlier, she recalled yelling at Garrett that she didn't care if she blew herself up. This was her chance to prove it.

With the lighter in one hand, the flashlight in the other, and the fire extinguisher at her feet, Roberta read the instructions one last time. She pumped the lantern till her best guess thought it was right, flicked the lighter on, and stuck the flame inside the little hole with the arrow pointing to it.

A poof sounded as it caught. A small flame burned on the outside casing where she had dribbled some fuel, but no explosion ensued. She watched as the thing sputtered and hissed and flickered ominously. Hoping for the best but expecting the worst, Roberta lifted the fire extinguisher, pulled the pin, and aimed.

"Let me guess. You've never worked a lantern before."

The sudden deep timbre of Garrett's voice nearly made her pull the trigger. She lowered the fire extinguisher to her side and glared at him. "What gave me away? My shaking knees or the fire extinguisher? Would I be correct to assume that since it hasn't blown up yet, I'm probably safe?"

Garrett laughed so hard he had to wipe tears from his eyes, which made Roberta notice he wasn't wearing the sunglasses. Of course, it was dark so he didn't need them, but by now she was beginning to wonder if he slept with them on. He had also changed out of his shorts and now wore uniform pants. The stripes on the side emphasized the length of his legs.

He laughed as he spoke. "Sorry for laughing. The fire extinguisher was actually a good idea, especially with your track record today." He paused and wiped his eyes again. "More people should do that. I've seen a couple of those things catch fire. Congratulations. You've got more sense than some of the jokers that come through here."

Roberta wasn't sure if she should take that as a compliment or not.

He continued to laugh. "In fact, I could tell you stories about what people have set on fire out here."

She wasn't amused. She didn't want to hear about it, but she knew that by the end of her camping vacation, she probably would anyway.

During the course of his laughter, the flame on the outside of the lantern burned itself out. "Here. Let me set that for you." He pumped the unit up a bit more to brighten it and adjusted one of the knobs. The annoying hissing faded to an acceptable level. "There. How's that?"

While bright enough to cast some questionable shadows among the trees, the light wavered, making it little better than a glorified stationary flashlight. "Is that as bright as it gets?"

"It's not exactly a quartz-halogen spotlight. This is a campsite, not an art studio. Most people only sit around the campfire and roast marshmallows and stuff. If you sit close enough, you may be able to read your book if the print size is okay. But if you pick up that book again, I'm afraid I'm going to have to keep my distance."

"Really? Promise?"

Garrett almost looked hurt, but then he smiled, probably thinking she was joking. "No," he replied.

It was just as well for the moment. She needed a favor. "I have to make a trip to the outhouse. Can you stand here and watch the fire for me? The sign said not to leave a fire unattended. Since you're one of the park authorities, I figure you'd be a good one to ask."

"I'd be honored," he said solemnly. Garrett removed his hat and held it over his heart and bowed.

"Very funny," Roberta grumbled. "I'll be right back." She made a hasty retreat to the ladies' outhouse, which was a few sites down the road. Away from the fire, the air possessed a chill, convincing her to change into her jeans when she got back to the camper.

On her way out of the facilities, a man stood at the side, nearly scaring the life out of her.

"Hi there," he said. His gaze drifted from her head to her feet, then he smiled.

She would have stepped back into the outhouse, except she didn't want to appear frightened. Roberta looked around, hoping he was talking to someone else, but they were alone. Suddenly she regretted not bringing her flashlight, not for the light, but for a weapon. "Are you talking to me?" she asked, checking around one more time.

"Yes. I've been watching you. Are you alone?"

The hairs on the back of her neck rose in alarm. "Me? Alone? Of course not."

He stepped closer. "Don't be frightened. I'll keep you company."

Her heart stopped, then picked up in double-time. If this man only wanted someone to talk to, he could have approached her during the daylight in the wide open spaces, not in the bush at dusk when there was no one else around.

Throwing dignity to the wind in favor of personal safety, Roberta stepped sideways, heading for the path to the open gravel road. She forced herself to speak louder than usual, trying her best to keep the tremor out of her voice as she backed up. "I'm not interested in any company. Come any closer, and I'll scream!" Not giving him a chance to respond, she ran back to her campsite, where Garrett stood beside the campfire, his arms crossed over his chest.

"You took an awful long time. I was getting ready to come and get you." He paused as he glanced down at her. "Are you all right? You seem a little out of breath."

Roberta opened her mouth, but then snapped it shut. If she told him about the stranger who'd approached her, he would never leave her alone. She shook her head, then stared at the entranceway to the campsite to make sure she hadn't been followed. "I'm fine, thank you," she gulped.

Garrett frowned. "I'm off duty after we close the park gate at eleven. After everything is settled I'll be back after midnight to check up on you, if you're still up then."

Roberta tried very hard not to check her watch to see how much longer that would be. Like a fool, she had run straight back to her own campsite for the strange man to plainly see where she was staying. If he didn't already know which site was hers, he knew now.

For the first time today, she didn't want Garrett to leave. But since he had to, she thought of her options. Either she could lock herself in the car until Garrett came back, or, if that was unreasonable, she could simply leave. Other people had set up their campers and then left to go back to the city, to return on Friday after work. Likewise, it would take her less than an hour to get back home, where she would be safe.

But she wasn't going to let some stranger manipulate her. All her life, she'd allowed people to lead her and manipulate her for their own gain. Roberta steeled her nerve. That was about to stop. The stranger was probably harmless. Besides, if he became a real threat, any scream in the relative silence of the campground would carry for miles. Someone would immediately come to her assistance.

She smiled at Garrett. "Sure. I'd like that very much. See you then."

Roberta expected him to nod and leave, but he didn't. He narrowed his eyes and held eye contact. After a few very long seconds, he turned his head to the road, then back to her. She suspected she had taken too long to reply, or been a little too eager for his return, because he continued to study her strangely.

Instead of leaving, he once again turned his head toward the entrance to the campsite. "I'll be right back," he said curtly. Before she could reply, he walked to the road, hopped into the park truck, and drove away.

Roberta sat in the lawnchair beside the fire. Unable to read, and in an effort to calm her shattered nerves, she instead concentrated on the noises of the night. Frogs croaked and crickets chirped in the distance. She couldn't hear any birds or squirrels like during the day, but every once in awhile she heard what was probably a coyote far in the background.

Most of all, the stars were phenomenal. Double, or even triple, the number of stars were visible, twinkling in the black night sky. The night was beautiful and peaceful.

And cold.

Roberta shivered, even though she changed into her jeans. She rubbed her arms, then chided herself. She didn't have to be cold, she had a jacket in the camper. The second she slipped it on, she felt better. She smiled and started to return to the fire, but before she left the safety of the tent-trailer, she peeked outside to make sure the site was still vacant.

Seeing no one, she returned to the lawnchair, telling herself not to be so paranoid. Molly had been right. Sitting beneath God's heavens was a great way to unwind.

Roberta leaned her head back to enjoy the stars, until she heard footsteps approaching. Despite the speech she gave to herself to calm her jitters, she squealed, jumped out of the chair, and turned to face the intruder, wishing she had the flashlight in her hand.

"Hi there. Miss me?"

Her breath released in a whoosh. "Garrett." Not that she actually missed him, but she was actually happy to see him. "Have a seat. After all, they're your lawn chairs."

Instead of joining her at the fire, Garrett walked to the camper and threw in a duffel bag that had been slung over his shoulder.

"What was that?"

"Just my stuff."

"Stuff?" Roberta narrowed her eyes. "What kind of stuff?"

"Just my toothbrush and sleeping bag and stuff."

"Why?"

"I don't feel comfortable about a woman spending the night all alone out here. Besides, Molly asked me to keep an eye on you."

The meaning behind his actions suddenly dawned on her. "You're not serious," she demanded more than she asked. "You're not staying here tonight."

"Yes, I am. It's my family's camper. You can get the registration out of the drawer. My name is on it."

Roberta tapped her foot and crossed her arms. "That's beside the point."

Garrett raised one arm in the direction of the entrance to the campsite.

"I know something frightened you earlier, even though you won't admit it."

She couldn't deny it, so instead she gave him her best menacing look.

His frown deepened. "I knew it. Remember, Molly told me to look after you. You don't want to cross Molly, do you?"

She opened her mouth to tell him she didn't care what Molly thought, but he interrupted her.

"This is no big deal. When I'm not working here, I live with my mother and my sister. I can respect your privacy if you can respect mine."

"No." She didn't care what his living arrangements were, nor did she care about mutual friends. She wasn't sharing accommodations with a man.

"It's a camper—a combination living room, kitchen, and everything else rolled into one. You get one side, I get the other. It's okay."

"No way."

"Fine. Then I'll sleep in my pup tent, but I'm staying in this campsite tonight."

Her mouth opened, then snapped shut. Up until that strange man approached her near the outhouse, she had been nervous but perfectly willing to spend the night alone. Now she wasn't so sure. If Garrett, an official park ranger, and a big one at that, stayed in the campsite, she would be safe. Her only alternative was to go home, but that would be admitting defeat.

"All right, but you'd better not snore or walk in your sleep or anything bizarre."

He placed one hand over his heart and lifted up the other arm elbow height in the form of a pledge. "Not me. Scout's honor."

Roberta crossed her arms and tilted her head. "Have you ever been a scout?"

He grinned. "No. But I'm the park ranger. Does that count?"

"Maybe," she grumbled. If he had said anything about being a born-again Christian as evidence of his virtue, like Mike had, she would have screamed and left.

"Good." He dropped his hands to his sides, threw a few more logs on the fire, and sat in the lawn chair beside her. Not knowing what else to do, Roberta leaned forward to warm her hands.

"I thought you were working until after midnight."

"I booked off. Someone's covering for me. They know where I am if they need me."

"Oh."

The fire snapped and crackled as it burned. Sparks flew upward into the night, flickering as small particles of light until they darkened and floated to the ground as ash. The lantern, hissing slightly on the table, illuminated only the immediate area. In the blackness, the night seemed more still and peaceful than the most deserted city street.

Garrett's voice seemed unnaturally loud in the pristine night. "Want to talk?"

She knew the golden silence couldn't last. "About what?"

Bent over in the chair with his palms raised to the fire and elbows on his knees, he shrugged his shoulders. "Oh, anything. The weather. Cars. Your love life."

Her love life.

Frogs croaked somewhere in the background. Probably momma frogs and baby frogs. She'd never have baby frogs. "I don't have a love life. Not anymore."

"I heard."

Roberta sighed. "I don't know what Molly told you."

Thankfully, he continued to stare into the fire. She couldn't have faced anyone right then. "Molly told Gwen who told me that you caught your fiancé cheating on you, and then you got fired. That's all I know."

"Something like that." Roberta snorted. The more she thought about it, the stupider she felt. She should have seen it coming, yet she hadn't. "You don't want details, do you?"

"Only if you want to tell me. I'm a pretty good listener."

She didn't know why, but she told him. She hadn't even told Molly, her best friend, all her deepest inner thoughts.

Her concentration didn't leave the fire as the whole story poured out. She told him how Mike was the boss's son, about how after years of working there how flattered she'd been when he started paying attention to her. She'd been so excited when Mike started to attend church with her, doing and saying all the right things, claiming to share her beliefs and faith in God. How when Mike talked of family, children, and then marriage she'd been thrilled. She didn't want to be a society wife, but when the time came for Mike to take over his father's company, as his wife, she would uphold the social position and do her duty. She was happy, and she would have done anything for him.

But soon after their engagement became official, Mike started missing church. At first she went alone, but soon he convinced her to start skipping services until she hadn't been to church for months. All the while, Mike kept pressing her to sleep with him. She refused.

Then she started picking up on little rumors. With her head in the clouds, she ignored them, which led to this morning, when she caught him making out with Suzie. She even told Garrett of her humiliation when they argued in the women's washroom, screaming for everyone in the office to hear. Following that, she was fired. Now here she was, staring blankly into a fire in the middle of nowhere, pouring her heart out to a stranger.

Yet, even when everything was said, her eyes remained dry. Talking about it, rather than brooding, put the situation into a new perspective. If she were as in love with Mike as she thought she was, she should have been more upset and unwilling to talk about it, much less to someone she didn't know.

She tried to figure out when the relationship started to deteriorate, and now realized it had been a long time ago. She had been so caught up in the flurry of their engagement and pending wedding plans, including meeting everyone Mike thought she should know, she hadn't thought about the declining state of their relationship.

Roberta couldn't believe how she had allowed Mike to sweep her off her feet. From that moment on, she refused to let another man do that to her again.

She continued to stare into the fire, warming her hands. Her backside was getting cold, but she ignored the discomfort as she continued to think. Despite the trauma and hardship of losing her job, the end of her relationship with Mike wasn't such a bad thing after all.

Without warning, Robbie yawned. Her cheeks heated up, and she immediately covered her big mouth with her hands. "I'm so sorry, I didn't mean to be rude. I guess I've had a rough day. I should turn in. You can stay up if you want."

Garrett shook his head. "Us rangers have to be up and on duty by sunrise. I think I'm going to hit the sack too."

They stood at the same time. As Roberta faced forward, she stared straight into the middle of his chest. She tilted her head up to make eye contact to wish him good night, but before she could, the words caught in her throat.

"Oh, Garrett, your face!"

"My face?"

Before she thought about what she was doing, she rested her fingertips on his cheek.

"You've got a huge bruise. This is my fault. I'm so sorry."

He covered her hand with one of his, pressing her fingers to his cheek. "Don't worry about it. It doesn't hurt."

His cheek was warm in contrast with the cool night air. Roberta made no attempt to pull away. It seemed only natural when Garrett rested his hands on her shoulders and massaged the back of her neck with his thumbs. "You feeling better?"

Strangely, she did. Not lowering her hand, she smiled. "Yes. Thank you."

Slowly, Garrett's arms moved from her shoulders to her back, and she felt him pulling her against him. At first she stiffened, but when he did nothing except simply hold her, she relaxed and leaned into his warm chest. Even when she responded, and he could have taken her acquiescence as encouragement, he only rubbed one thumb in little circles on her back.

Roberta's throat clogged. No one had ever held her like this. Her parents had nicely patted her on the head when she needed comforting, Mike only held her when he had more than a friendly hug in mind. Except for this morning with Molly, she never touched her female friends.

She didn't know Garrett at all, but his comforting hug was exactly what she needed. She leaned into him even more and sighed.

Without warning, she felt herself suddenly standing alone in the cool night air.

"I think I should set up my tent so you can turn in. Now I know why you had those poles earlier. I've got the tent here, and I couldn't remember what I did with the poles. Now I know."

Roberta held back a shiver as she sank into the lawn chair. She raised her hands up to the fire, but it didn't help.

Garrett pulled the poles in question from the compartment in the camper, and soon his pup tent was set up. He disappeared into the camper, and within minutes, he came out wearing a T-shirt and sweatpants instead of his ranger uniform.

Roberta rose and mumbled a "good night" as she stepped into the camper. Instead of putting on her pajamas, she also changed into an old T-shirt and sweatpants to sleep in. Because it was so cool, she left her socks on and slipped into the sleeping bag.

First she made sure the flashlight was within arm's reach, and then she unzipped the window to watch Garrett quench the fire. He poked it a few times with a stick, then turned off the lantern. Suddenly, everything became completely pitch black except for the twinkle of the stars above.

So he could see where he was going, Roberta shone the flashlight through the screened window, but he pulled a solid heavy-duty flashlight with the Parks and Recreation logo out of his pocket and turned it on. The beam was at least triple the strength of hers. "Thanks for the thought, but I came prepared." He grinned and disappeared into his tent.

Feeling like an idiot, Roberta quickly zipped the window shut.

She listened in the dark to the sound of the zipper on Garrett's sleeping bag, and the glow of his flashlight went black.

"Good night, Robbie," he called. "Sleep tight."

Bugs chirped, and in the distance, something howled ominously. Easy for him to say. "Good night, Garrett."

Roberta closed her eyes and laid back, and soon the sleeping bag which surrounded her like a cocoon became warm inside. She wanted to fall asleep, but the sounds of the night kept her from relaxing. She opened her eyes, but what she saw wasn't much different from when she had her eyes closed, it was so totally dark.

She forced her eyes to close, but suddenly she heard the sound of crunching in the gravel outside. Her heart pounded. She swallowed hard to make her voice work.

"Garrett!" she said in the loudest whisper she could force out. "Are you sleeping? Do you hear something?"

❧

Garrett was already awake. In fact, he hadn't been sleeping. He'd been lying there, thinking about Robbie's sad story. She needed a friend, and since Molly wasn't there, it was up to him to be that friend. He'd promised to listen, so he had. Even when she wasn't talking, he listened anyway.

He could only imagine how bad Robbie had been hurt. In any relationship, Garrett valued trust and faithfulness above all else. He'd had a few relationships over the years, but never anything serious enough to be badly hurt when the relationship ended, regardless of the reason.

When Robbie finished talking about her ex-fiancé's betrayal, he didn't know what to say. He did the only thing he could think of, and that was to hold her. Except, his plan to just comfort her backfired. When she nestled into him, instead of the calming gesture he had intended, touching her made his pulse heat up and his brain freeze. It scared him.

At twenty-six years old, he'd recently begun to wonder if he'd ever find a special woman who could ignite that spark, especially since his job entailed either spending most of his time alone or being with other park rangers who were also all men. He'd spent many hours in prayer, turning it over to God. If the woman who was to be his soul mate was out there, God would allow her to cross his path, or he would remain single.

Because Robbie was a city girl and not the least bit interested in wildlife biology, he knew she wasn't that woman. But in a strange sort of way, he looked forward to spending the next day with her, in between his ranger duties.

But for now, he had something else to deal with.

He'd heard something too.

Something, or rather someone, was prowling in the campsite. From the sound of the footsteps, he could tell this was definitely not an animal, at least not the four-legged kind. If one of the other rangers needed something, they would have called him on his radio first, not entered the campsite when all was dark. To his knowledge, the camp had never experienced any trouble with intruders, but there was always a first time.

He tried to make his voice sound sleepy and unconcerned, when deep down he was furious. He had wondered earlier if someone had bothered her when she asked him to watch the fire. Now he suspected he knew the answer.

"Go back to sleep, Darling," he said loudly enough for anyone to hear a male voice plainly. Hopefully, the intruder would fail to notice the tent in the darkness and would think his voice came from inside the camper. "It's probably just a raccoon."

The gravel crunched, getting softer, then fading to nothing.

He lowered his voice. "It's gone. Go back to sleep, Robbie."

If Roberta had been the least little bit sleepy before, she wasn't sleepy now. She couldn't imagine why Garrett would have called her "darling," unless he was half asleep and in his dreams he was thinking of his girlfriend. Just because she didn't like him didn't mean no one else could. All she knew was that whoever "darling" was, the poor woman would have a hard time competing for airtime.

Girlfriend aside, Roberta had thought that whatever was outside sounded bigger than a raccoon. However, Garrett was the park ranger, so if he thought the noise sounded like a raccoon, it must have been a raccoon. But thoughts of wild animals were the least of her concerns. Now that she was fully awake, she had to go to the outhouse. Tomorrow night, and every night while she was out camping, she would remember to limit her liquid intake.

⁂

Garrett lay on his back, staring blankly at the peak of the tent above him. He had to alert the other rangers to the possibility of a prowler. He had his walkie-talkie, but in the small space of the campsite in the silence of the night, Roberta would hear every word he said and know something was wrong.

"Garrett? Are you sleeping?"

"No, I'm not sleeping." The opposite of sleeping, he was plotting how he could sneak off. "What's on your mind?" Hopefully she wasn't scared, even though this time she had a reason to be.

"Garrett, I have to make a trip to the outhouse."

Garrett broke out into a smile, then forced himself to become serious as he unzipped the tent door. He flicked on his flashlight and slipped his feet into his untied hiking boots. When the camper door opened and Robbie stuck her head out, Garrett stretched his arms over his head and lowered his voice, trying to look bored. "Let's go." Not taking the time to tie the laces, he shone the flashlight on the camper's single stair for Robbie. As she closed the door behind her, he patted his walkie-talkie in his back pocket.

They walked in silence to the outhouses, where he waited for her on the path. When she was inside, he told Tyler about the possibility of a prowler trespassing in site 27 and to be on the lookout for someone checking out the campsites while people were asleep, and especially in the campsites where people had left their tents or trailers for the night to reserve the spot and gone back into the city. He almost wished it was his turn for night duty.

"Who are you talking to?"

Garrett tried not to flinch at the sound of Robbie's voice. Someone must have finally oiled the hinge, because he hadn't heard her come out of the outhouse. "I was just checking up on the other rangers, that's all." He held out the walkie-talkie for her to see and turned it off. "Let's get back to sleep, shall we?"

They walked back to the camper in silence. Garrett shone the light for her as she stepped back into the camper. He listened as she zipped up her sleeping bag, then crawled into his tent.

"Good night, Garrett, and thank you," she called softly.

"Good night, Robbie, and you're welcome."

Garrett almost had to bite his tongue. He'd almost called her "darling."

Chapter 5

Daylight came early in the wilderness. Roberta awoke to the smell of coffee and the sound of faint stirrings outside. She opened her eyes, orienting herself to the small sleeping compartment of Garrett's camper. The early light gave the unit a strange glow, giving everything inside a yellowish hue. As soon as she opened the camper door, she smelled food. Good food. Bacon and eggs. Garrett stood beside the picnic table, using a small green camper's cookstove.

Trying to be discreet, she quietly slipped out of the camper and up the entrance to the campsite for a trip to the outhouse. She almost thought she made it undetected, but his head turned, and he smiled and nodded as she left.

Upon her return, two plates of bacon and eggs and toast and two cups of steaming coffee sat on the picnic table.

"Good morning, Robbie. Did you sleep well? I did."

"How did you cook this out here? Are we going to eat all this for breakfast? What time is it?"

He turned off the flame and raised his head to the sunrise, the brilliant colors already starting to fade. "5:17 A.M."

Roberta looked up. Wisps of pink and purple clouds were losing their colors to bright white against the blue of the early morning sky as she watched. Birds twittered and squirrels chattered. "How could you tell that?"

"I checked my watch."

She would have said something nasty if her stomach hadn't growled. "Where did you get that thing?" She swooshed her hand in the air over the stove. "And all this food?"

"Ranger camp. I've got connections. I make breakfast like this every day."

"If I ate breakfast like this every day I'd weigh six hundred pounds. I brought cereal for breakfast. There's milk in the cooler that's got to be used up."

"I suppose we could eat that too. Unless it's some kind of healthy granola stuff. I won't eat that."

She had always assumed that anyone who made a career out of being in touch with nature would lead a healthy lifestyle, including plenty of exercise as well as a nutritionally balanced diet. Somehow, she couldn't see a breakfast of high-fat, high-cholesterol bacon and eggs with thickly buttered toast fitting into that plan.

"It's sugar-sweetened processed kid's cereal, loaded with food coloring and preservatives. Multicolored sugar bombs. The kind my mother would never allow me to have when I was a kid. You're welcome to help yourself if you want."

He grinned ear to ear and rubbed his stomach, which she couldn't help but notice was extremely flat. "Yummy."

A plastic tablecloth covered the picnic table. Despite the questionable nutritional value, not to mention the megacaloric content of the food, she could hardly wait to dig in. This time, she knew what to expect as he sat down. Just as he started to close his eyes, she stopped him. "It's okay, Garrett, you can pray out loud."

His eyes widened as his head rose. He stared blankly at her, then smiled again. Something inside her stomach flipped, but she was sure it was only the growlies.

He bowed his head and folded his hands on the table. "Thank You, dear Lord, for all You've given us, including this food, this wonderful day, and that we can share it with our friends. Amen."

At Roberta's mumbled "Amen," he dug in. Not only did he consume a huge plate of his own breakfast, but he also helped himself to a large bowl of cereal. He even drank every last drop of the milk.

He turned his wrist to read his watch as he chewed his last mouthful. "Sorry to be rude. I'm on duty, and I'm late."

While she stared at his empty plate and her still half-full one, Garrett disappeared into the camper. In what seemed like seconds, he reappeared in his uniform, including the pants with the stripe down the side, the hat, and the dark sunglasses to complete the picture. He'd also done up the laces on his hiking boots. From the dark shadow on his jaw, she suspected he would be shaving at the ranger camp, where they probably had electricity.

"I've got beach duty after lunch. Want to go for a swim?"

"Swim?"

"There's a beach down that path over there. It takes about fifteen minutes to walk. You can swim, can't you?"

"Of course I can swim!"

"Good. See you after lunch." Tipping his hat, he smiled beneath the sunglasses and walked away with his duffel bag slung over his shoulder and his rolled-up pup tent under his arm. Roberta couldn't help but notice that he'd again forgotten the poles to go with it.

She smiled until she realized she had been railroaded again. Yesterday Molly had wangled her into going on this camping vacation, and now Mr. Ranger Garrett had conned her into a swimming expedition. Plus, he left her to do all the dirty dishes.

Since it was so early, despite all the time it took to heat the water on the propane elements, wash, then dry and repack all the dishes in their plastic boxes, she had plenty of time before lunch and Garrett's expected return. Unless he made the rounds as often as he did yesterday.

Short of hiding, she considered what she could do and where she could go that he wouldn't find her. Very few people were in the campground, and those who were, she suspected were mostly still asleep. The only place she'd seen so far besides her own campsite was the wood stockpile at the entrance. She had seen a sign directing campers to a nature trail, so she decided to check it out.

Preparing for the heat of the day, she changed into her shorts and sandals. After brushing her teeth, she picked up her camera and the rest of the bag of bread that Garrett brought, and she was on her way. If she had three hours to kill, she might as well feed the squirrels or any other wildlife that came along.

After constantly stabbing her toes on twigs and mulch as she walked, Roberta settled down on a log and spent most of her time trying to take pictures of a very elusive squirrel who must have felt the same way as Garrett about having its picture taken. For awhile, every time she clicked the camera or moved slightly, the squirrel ran away, but after a few tries, he seemed to get used to her and finally ate in front of her. She wondered how one tiny squirrel could eat so much at once, and why he sometimes hid while he was eating it. However, she still managed to get a few good shots of the squirrel with a tiny piece of bread tucked neatly between its cute little front paws.

The little critter must have sent out some kind of secret squirrel radar code, because just as she was about to leave, a whole flock of squirrels descended from the trees. Before she knew it, the whole loaf was gone, except for two pieces she remembered at the last minute to save for her own lunch. She wondered if other campers gave the squirrels the good pieces and left the crusts for themselves. Once they saw no more food forthcoming, the squirrels deserted her. Roberta braved the path again, constantly stopping to empty pieces of the great outdoors from her sandals. Next time she would wear sneakers.

With no sign of Garrett when she arrived at the campsite, she made herself a sandwich and enjoyed her lunch in peace.

"There you are. I've been looking for you. Where were you?"

"I went for a walk to feed the squirrels."

Sunlight glinted off Garrett's sunglasses as he crossed his arms over his chest and tilted his shoulders slightly back. He would have presented an intimidating stance, if she hadn't remembered how tender his embrace could be. "I didn't know where you were. You were gone a long time."

"So?"

His frown deepened. "I was worried."

She shrugged her shoulders. "I wanted to be alone and check out Mother Nature. You've been very nice to keep an eye on me, but you don't have to check up on me every minute of every day."

Garrett lifted his hat, swiped his hair back, then replaced his hat. "Maybe I have been overdoing it a bit. I apologize."

All the harsh words she nearly let loose were forgotten at the sight of his smile. For such an annoying man, he really had a kind smile.

"I'm sorry too. I didn't mean to be rude. You've been very kind, and I do appreciate it. I guess I haven't been myself lately."

"I can understand that. Still want to go to the beach?"

She opened her mouth to protest, but the words didn't come out. It wasn't as if she had anything better to do. She nodded. "Sure. It'll only take me a minute to change."

They walked to the beach in silence at first, but soon Garrett started explaining things he probably thought might interest her along their way, pointing things out in the strangest places. Roberta said very little, content to listen. Some of the things he said were interesting.

❧

Garrett couldn't help himself. Towering above her as they walked side by side, he tried to be a gentleman and not gawk at Robbie in her bathing suit. Most women would have draped their towels over their shoulders as they walked, but Robbie wasn't most women. She wrapped the towel around her waist like a skirt, and instead of her dainty little sandals, she wore a tiny pair of pristine white sneakers and little white ankle socks with baby pink pompoms on the back. He felt like Grizzly Adams clomping along beside her in his favorite hiking boots.

Instead of staring, all he could do was look around and talk about points of interest along the way. He also talked about things that weren't very interesting. Anything. Plants. Animals. Birds. He wasn't usually such a motormouth, but he had to do something, anything rather than stare.

He turned his head as he pointed and explained about a particular species of squirrel that chattered at them in the treetops. He made the mistake of glancing at her when she asked a question. Garrett squeezed his eyes shut for a second and pointedly kept his focus straight ahead.

The near-deserted beach stretched out before them. Garrett assured her that tomorrow would be another story. In a few hours, people would start arriving as they got off work for the weekend.

"Enjoy it while you can." He sat on the grass and leaned back, resting his weight on his palms, his arms stretched out straight behind him, his ankles crossed.

"Aren't you coming in?"

"Nope. I'm on duty." For a second, he almost hoped the expression on her face was one of disappointment, but she simply shrugged her shoulders, untied the towel from her waist, then laid it out on the ground. She ran into the water, then at the right depth, lifted her arms over her head and dove in the rest of the way.

Robbie shot up out of the water, glistening in the sunlight as a spray of water splashed around her. She arched her back, tipped her head backward, and used both hands to swipe her wet hair from her face, then stretched her hands to the sky, radiating total freedom.

He forced himself to blink and added up the hours until he was off duty.

She smiled and waved and dove back in. Garrett forced himself to start breathing again. The next time she came up, she started walking toward the shore, so he stood and walked to the water's edge to meet her. "This is wonderful!" she called from the waist-deep water.

Rather than stand there staring like an idiot, Garrett turned his head and noticed a movement in the designated picnic section. He raised his hands to his mouth to call out to her. "There's someone with a dog in the restricted area. I've got to go kick them off. I'll be right back."

≈

Roberta waved as he walked away, then turned around to dive into the cool water once again. She'd never been swimming alone, but with Garrett on the shore, she didn't feel alone, until he left. She swam back and forth a few times, then stood still to catch her breath.

As she stood, she heard a child splashing nearby and turned to watch. A little boy about four years old played happily on a float toy in water that was almost shoulder height on herself. Worried, she glanced around the near vicinity, searching for a parent. She knew many children took swimming lessons, but no matter how well he swam, he shouldn't be unsupervised, especially in water that would be over his head.

The child tried to stand on the float toy, lost his balance, and fell off. The float toy bounced away atop the surface of the water. The little boy screamed and flailed his arms and started to go under.

Roberta hurried to him and grabbed onto his little arm, pulling him out of the water. The child still kicked wildly and thrashed about.

"It's okay! I've got you!" she tried to call over his yelling. "Calm down! You're fine now!" Frantically, Roberta tried to get a grip on his other arm, but couldn't. The child continued to flail about and scream.

Since the boy wouldn't settle down and no one was on shore to come and help, Roberta carried the boy into more shallow water and left the stupid toy to float away.

When she was finally at a point where the boy's feet could touch the bottom, a man approached. He grabbed the child roughly from her arms. Ignoring her, the man swore at the little boy as he gave him a resounding smack, making the child scream even louder.

She was about to rebuke the man for allowing the child to go into the deep water unsupervised when he turned, belched in her face, and made a crude comment. The stench of liquor almost made Roberta gag as he stepped closer. He shuffled the child to one arm and reached forward. Quickly, Roberta stepped back, but when she did, her toe hit a rock. For a split second she stopped moving, and in that split second, the man grabbed her wrist.

Her throat tightened. "What are you doing? Let me go!" She glanced down to see a rather ugly tattoo on his wrist, then looked up into his face.

The man sneered at her and said nothing. Roberta sucked in a deep breath to start screaming, when Garrett, fully dressed, appeared in the water beside the man.

His lips were drawn into a tight line, and his cheeks were absolutely rigid. At the sight of Garrett, the child screamed louder. From Garrett's expression, Roberta wondered if he was going to hit the disgusting man.

"Let her go," Garrett demanded, enunciating every word clearly and slowly. As Garrett stepped even closer, the man dropped her hand.

Instead of leaving it at that, Garrett crossed his arms, squared his shoulders, and clenched his fists tight. "Now apologize to the lady. And you had better thank her for saving the child."

Instead of apologizing, the man yelled a string of obscenities in Garrett's face.

"That does it. Out of the water and get off the beach." Garrett straightened to his full height, towering over the rude man by at least three or four inches. The wet shirt clung to his muscular body, emphasizing his height and the width of his powerful shoulders. Roberta sure wouldn't have dared cross him.

The man continued to swear and stomped out of the water, carrying the still-screaming child. Garrett followed him to the water's edge and stood defiantly on the shoreline, watching the man pick up his belongings and pull the child roughly by the hand down the path to the campsites.

Garrett walked to an untidy pile at the water's edge containing his boots and socks and his walkie-talkie. He spoke into it briefly, touched his soaking wet shorts and the clip on his belt where the unit usually rested, then held the walkie-talkie in his hand instead.

Roberta ran to retrieve her towel and handed it to Garrett. He wiped his arms, but nothing else, and gave it back. "Let's go sit down at the picnic table and put our shoes and socks back on."

By the time they reached the table, her feet were dry. They sat side by side as Roberta pulled on her socks and sneakers, then waited for Garrett to lace his hiking boots. He neatly folded the tops of his wool socks over the rims of the boots, picked up his walkie-talkie, and they walked to the path leading back to the campsites in silence.

His shorts had stopped dripping, but were still soaking wet and hung on him like wet rags. Compared to the pristine ranger of this morning, his bedraggled appearance almost sent her into a burst of giggles.

"I've got to get some dry clothes, then get back on duty. If it's any consolation, I logged this and I'll be filing an official report. Any minor infraction and his group will be asked to leave."

"Thank you, Garrett." She didn't know what else to say.

He raised his hand and rested his fingers on her cheek. His head lowered, making Roberta think he was going to kiss her. Her heart pounded. Then, instead of what she expected, his eyebrows knotted above the sunglasses and he remained motionless. "Are you sure you're all right?"

Roberta leaned into his hand, finding strange comfort in the roughness of his fingers against her cheek. She shuffled her feet to bring herself slightly closer to him, until she could sense the cool dampness radiating from him. Part of her wanted him to kiss her. Oddly shaken by the thought, she quickly rationalized it away. This latest incident must have upset her more than she realized. "You've asked me that more times in the last twenty-four hours than I can count."

He let out a sad little laugh. "Do these kind of disasters happen often to you?"

"Never."

He shook his head as he gently ran his thumb along her temple. "I feel like this was my fault. If I had been there, watching, it wouldn't have happened."

His presence on shore would probably have prevented the man from touching her, but that didn't make anything Garrett's fault. She was about to reassure him when his walkie-talkie beeped. His hand dropped, and she immediately missed his touch.

"Excuse me." He flipped the switch and raised the unit to his cheek. "Lamont."

Being so close, Roberta could still hear the caller's voice. "We followed him like you said, and we've got him. Site 45. Left the fire at a full burn while he was gone, and there's open liquor everywhere. Soon as you get here, we can evict him."

"I'm on my way," Garrett replied. He reached down to the clip on his belt, but instead of clipping his walkie-talkie to it, he pulled his hand away when his fingers brushed the dampness. He held the unit at his side. "I've gotta go. I'll be back when I can."

With that, he turned and left.

Chapter 6

Roberta had no idea if it was normal for someone to be kicked out of a campground, but she didn't think so. She couldn't tell if the victory made her proud or angry with Garrett. On the other hand, knowing the man had been kicked out and his weekend ruined gave her a tremendous amount of satisfaction. A stab of guilt then got the better of her. As a Christian, she was supposed to forgive him. She'd have to work on that.

Before the arrival of Molly and her friend at suppertime, Roberta planned to rehearse a list of questions to find out what Molly could have said to cause Garrett to stick to her like glue.

Until then, Roberta settled slowly and gently into the hammock with her book under her chin. At first she smiled, knowing Garrett wouldn't come near her as long as she had the book in her hand, but then she kicked herself for thinking such a thing. Over the breakfast table, before he put his sunglasses on, she saw the slight discoloration of the bruise on Garrett's cheek. Regardless of how she felt about him, she still felt guilty, and hoped no one, especially the other rangers, had seen it. She wanted to make it up to him, but didn't know how.

After lunch, Roberta prepared to enjoy the rest of the afternoon reading, but in the peace and quiet and the warmth of the summer day, she couldn't keep her eyes open. She hadn't realized she'd fallen asleep until the sound of footsteps in the gravel jolted her awake.

She opened her eyes to see Molly walking toward the tent-trailer.

Slipping more gently out of the hammock this time, Roberta ran to greet Molly.

"I'm so glad to see you! How's your mom?"

Molly sighed, then shrugged her shoulders. "She had a rough night, but she's okay now. She really scared me this time. How about you? Did Garrett make it by a few times?"

"Define 'few,'" Roberta mumbled under her breath, then smiled at her friend.

"Come on, we're going to unload the boat first."

She followed Molly back up to the entranceway. A large canoe was strapped to the top of Molly's friend's car. Behind it was a small utility trailer, filled with boxes, oars, and camping paraphernalia.

"Robbie, have you met Gwen before?"

Gwen waved from behind the wheel. Considering they were twins, Gwen didn't look that much like Garrett. While they shared the family resemblance,

Gwen's features were much finer. While not delicate, Gwen was beautiful, if not drop-dead gorgeous. And thin. And probably tall too. Her smile could have lit a banquet hall. Robbie smiled politely as Molly introduced them.

They turned onto a dirt road labeled "restricted use only," but Gwen assured her they had Garrett's permission to be there. The smooth, pristine lake stretched out before them, and a small dock jutted over the water. Roberta stood back as Molly and Gwen heaved the canoe off the top of the car.

Gwen tied the canoe securely to the dock, and they returned to their campsite. Gwen backed the car with the trailer into the right place the first time, and they unpacked it quickly. While Gwen went into the tent-trailer to make coffee, Molly sat with Robbie at the picnic table.

Molly plunked her elbows on the table, rested her chin in her palms, and grinned. "What do you think of Garrett? He kind of keeps to himself, so this job in the middle of nowhere is perfect for him."

Roberta opened her mouth to ask if there were two rangers here named Garrett, but Molly spoke again before she had a chance.

"Look, there's a big rock on the table, with a piece of paper under it." Molly threw the rock into the bush and picked up the note. "It's from Garrett. Look at his handwriting, it gets worse every time I see it. No wonder he likes this job. No paperwork." She briefly held the paper in front of Roberta's face, as if that would give her time to analyze it, then snatched it back when Roberta held out her hand. "It says, 'I came to check up on you, but you were armed so I didn't wake you.'" Molly shook the paper, then looked at Roberta. "What does this mean?"

Roberta blushed. She grabbed the paper out of Molly's hand, crumpled it up, and threw it into the fire pit. "Nothing," she mumbled. "Absolutely nothing."

Gwen appeared, setting three mugs of hot coffee on the table. "I don't know about you guys, but I'm starved. Fresh air always makes me hungry. I'm going to start supper." While Gwen assembled everything to make a fire, she glanced at the neatly stacked pile of wood. "I see you have a good stock pile here. Did you manage okay by yourself, Robbie?"

"Oh, yes, Garrett helped me carry the firewood, then chopped up all this kindling for me."

Molly and Gwen looked at each other.

"I'm glad Garrett helped you." Gwen cleared her throat, then spoke in a more normal tone. "You did a good job setting up the tent-trailer too. Did it take you long?"

"Probably. I must have taken longer than usual, but Garrett helped with the hard parts."

Gwen hesitated for an almost indiscernible moment. "I see you got Garrett's hammock up. Comfortable, isn't it? You were sleeping when we got here, weren't you?"

"Yes, I was out like a light. Although I'm embarrassed to admit that the first time I tried it I fell out. Garrett showed me the right way to get in and out without hurting myself."

Gwen stopped playing with the wood and turned her head. It almost looked like she was going to say something, but instead she turned back to lighting the fire.

The three of them barbecued a good supper over the fire. The dishes were nearly done when Roberta heard familiar heavy footsteps approaching in the gravel.

"Good evening, ladies."

Gwen and Molly gaily chorused together, "Hi, Garrett!"

Roberta grunted.

"Enjoy your supper?"

"Naturally. I cooked it," Gwen replied. "Have you eaten?"

"Yup."

"Good," she continued. "Because we didn't save you any."

Everyone laughed except Roberta.

"The place is full, as I expected. The naturalist phoned in sick, so I'm going to have to do the programs this weekend. I won't have much, if any, free time. In fact, I have to get moving right now to go set up."

Knowing he started at dawn, Roberta wondered if he was normally expected to work such long hours. She remembered reading some literature about information programs and slide shows to be presented throughout the weekend at varying times every day. Some of them had sounded very interesting, and judging from her one-sided conversation with Garrett on the path to and from the beach, he possessed a good knowledge about the flora and fauna of the area.

Gwen laughed out loud. "Maybe we'll go sit in the back and heckle you."

Garrett frowned. "Better not."

"Okay, we'll sit in the front."

Garrett said nothing, but his frown deepened. Gwen smiled widely and pushed him on the arm. He stood solid as a rock. "Try and stop us."

Molly joined her teasing. "I'm starting to think of a million questions already."

Garrett remained silent.

Gwen continued. "Lighten up. Don't you want a cheering section?"

"No."

"How about a fan club? Doesn't that sound like fun?"

All he did was give his sister a dirty look.

Finally, Roberta couldn't stand it. In a way she felt sorry for him. He didn't deserve to be embarrassed by his sister in front of the campers. His position of authority demanded that he be respected as a park ranger, not harassed during a presentation. "I think we can find something else to do, don't you?"

Gwen sighed loudly. "Oh, all right. I'll behave, but under protest."

"Thank you," Garrett grumbled, and he turned around and left.

Gwen grumbled the entire time while the three of them washed the dishes, but her smile gave her away. "I'd been looking forward to pestering him, but I'm not going to do it alone. Maybe as Robbie gets to know him better, she'll see Garrett needs a little convincing to come out of his shell."

Molly giggled. "Forget it. He's a lost cause."

Roberta listened as she stacked the dishes in their respective plastic boxes. At first she'd wondered if she'd met the wrong Ranger Garrett, but now that she knew she hadn't, she really didn't understand what Molly and Gwen were talking about.

"Are you coming?"

Roberta nearly dropped the plastic tub of cutlery. "Are we going somewhere?"

"Yes. To Garrett's presentation. We only promised to behave. We didn't promise not to go. Come on."

She really had wanted to learn a little about the animals and natural phenomena of the area, but not at Garrett's expense. "I don't think so."

"Come on," Molly said, waving her hand to try to convince Roberta to join them. "It's going to start soon. The flyer said tonight they have a slide show about the local parks. It's going to be interesting. We were planning on going even if Garrett wasn't going to be the one doing it."

"All right. Why do I let you do this to me?"

Molly laughed. "Because I know what's best."

"Not likely."

Upon their arrival at the small amphitheater, Gwen sat center front, Molly sat beside Gwen, and Roberta sat beside Molly. Garrett kept glancing at them nervously but said nothing, which Roberta thought was unusual, but a welcome change. Since it was already dusk, he wasn't wearing the sunglasses, which emphasized how handsome he was in his uniform. Yet, his appearance was slightly marred by the slight discoloration on his cheek. Roberta suspected Gwen wouldn't lose a chance to tease him about it, once she noticed.

For awhile Roberta watched as Garrett smiled and chatted with the campers surrounding him. She also noticed most of them were female.

More and more people arrived, until the small amphitheater was almost full. Garrett started his presentation with a short speech while he showed a map of the local provincial parks. He then started a slide show, where he gave an explanation about each picture shown.

Next, he elaborated on the presentation and invited questions. When all queries were answered, he thanked everyone for coming and encouraged all present to take advantage of the features and activities provided by the Parks and Recreation Department. As he sent everyone on their way, Roberta thought Garrett would have made a good teacher.

She was anxious to leave him alone, but Gwen and Molly wanted to stay. Having seen enough of him in the last day and a half to last a lifetime, Roberta returned to the campsite alone, grateful she had brought her flashlight. She remembered the hard way how very, very dark it got at night with no streetlights.

After piling everything up to start another fire, she fetched the lantern. She was in the midst of searching the camper for the matches, when she heard the footsteps crunching in the gravel of their campsite.

Her hand froze on the drawer. Molly and Gwen's chattering and laughter would be heard long before she heard their footsteps. She knew Garrett would be there long after them, since he would need to pack the projector and other paraphernalia and return them to ranger headquarters after the last of his audience left.

She doubted it would be another park ranger.

Already on her hands and knees from picking through the cupboard, she flicked off her flashlight and stayed low, slowly lifting her head to peek through the corner of the window.

It wasn't Garrett, nor was the man a ranger. All the valuables were locked in the cars, so if it was a would-be thief, he would get nothing. Roberta gritted her teeth, hoping the man wouldn't check to see if the camper was locked, because it wasn't.

The man remained in the center of the campsite. "Hey, little darling," he called out, "where are you?"

Roberta's stomach churned. It was the same man who approached her last night at the outhouse. But he hadn't called her "darling" then. The only one who had called her that was Garrett, in his dreams.

Her mind raced. It wasn't a raccoon last night, it was him! He had come in to the campsite in the middle of the night, expecting her to be alone.

Roberta covered her mouth with her hand to prevent herself from screaming. The flashlight in her hand could be used as a weapon as a last resort, but she doubted she'd be very effective against a man that size, or any man, for that matter. At only five-foot-four, she wasn't much threat to anything or anybody. Even the four-year-old child had gotten the better of her. She suddenly regretted not taking the self-defense course advertised in the newspaper last fall.

After what seemed an eternity, his steps retreated and disappeared.

She knelt to peek out the window to be sure he was gone. Her heart pounded and her hands shook as she slowly opened the door and poked her head out, an inch at a time. Searching the area slowly, she exited the camper when she was sure he was truly gone.

Panic started to overtake her. She wanted to bolt and go home, but she'd already given Molly her car keys, so that wasn't an option. Above all, she couldn't stay in the campsite alone.

Flashlight in hand, she fled the campsite and ran to where she hoped everyone else would still be.

❧

After all the campers left the amphitheater, Garrett packed everything up. He closed the lid on the last box as Gwen and Molly chatted with another ranger.

Out of the corner of his eye, Garrett saw Robbie running toward him at a breakneck pace. Her wide eyes showed fear, and her abrupt halt as she skidded on the cement beside him bespoke frenzy. His breath caught as she grabbed his arm and started shaking it.

She gulped for breath so badly he barely made her words out. "A man. . .outhouse. . .raccoon. . .looking for. . .hid in. . .went away. . ."

"Calm down, Robbie." He tried to speak slowly and softly, but his heart hammered in his chest. "Take a deep breath and tell me, slowly, what's wrong."

She squeezed her eyes shut, then opened them wide. Garrett rested his hands on her shoulders and waited. From the way she couldn't catch her breath, he suspected she had run the entire way from the campsite to the amphitheater.

Molly came running. "Robbie! What's wrong? Are you hurt?"

Roberta swallowed hard as her gasping subsided. Garrett could hear the tension in her voice as she spoke. "That man from last night. He came into the campsite looking for me. He called me 'darling' just like you did. It wasn't a raccoon, you idiot!" she screamed. She thumped his hands off her shoulders and settled her fists on her hips. "I was all alone hiding in the camper, terrified! I couldn't stay there so I ran here."

Garrett opened his mouth to speak, but she started up again. She grabbed one of his arms and shook it again and continued to shout at a slightly lower volume level, but her voice was still raised and tight and rapid. "Even I could tell it wasn't a raccoon. How could you be so stupid! Can't you tell the difference? Even I could tell it was footsteps! Why did I let you convince me it was a raccoon?"

Totally ignoring their audience, Garrett trapped her hands between his forearm, which she held like a steel trap, and his hand. He lowered his voice to speak slowly and evenly. "Listen to me. I knew it wasn't a raccoon. I can certainly tell the difference between an animal and a human. I didn't want you to be frightened. I made sure to speak loudly so he would know you weren't alone and he wouldn't bother you again. Do you understand?"

He paused long enough for his words to sink in. Robbie nodded.

"When we went to the outhouse I radioed the rangers and told them to be on the lookout for a prowler, but they couldn't find him. You have to trust me, Robbie. I did what I thought was best so he wouldn't think you were all by yourself. Just don't go off by yourself again until we find out who he is."

"Okay." She nodded again, and he allowed her to pull her hands away. "I won't go anywhere by myself."

Molly stood to the side, gawking. "Come on," she said, "let's all go back. No one will bother us if the three of us stick together."

Garrett didn't like the three of them camping alone, but there was nothing he could do about it. "With one man short, I'm going to have to stay at the ranger camp for the weekend."

Gwen stepped in. "Don't worry about us, Bro, we'll be fine. Safety in numbers."

Roberta stared at the ground.

Molly touched her shoulder. "Let's go back now. I can hear some popcorn calling me. Come on, Gwen."

Gwen nodded and said a quick good-bye to the ranger she was talking with.

Garrett had turned his back to lift the boxes when he heard Gwen's voice behind him.

"Darling? Last night? What exactly was going on last night?"

"None of your business," he grumbled, balancing the boxes so he could carry them all in one trip. He steadied the pile and walked to the truck, ignoring his sister.

He shuffled the boxes in the truck bed, watching the three women walk down the dark road, three flashlight beams zig-zagging across the road as they made their way.

He didn't know what to do. As much as Robbie felt singled out by the prowler, in all likelihood, the prowler would act the same with any lone woman. The thought didn't ease his mind.

He knew he should be out walking around the campsite, keeping an eye out for trouble, but his heart told him to stay in site 27 with his sister, Molly, and Robbie, even though it wasn't likely they'd be bothered.

Being Friday night, if anyone was going to get drunk and disorderly, tonight would be the night. Already the rangers had kicked out one undesirable group before the rush traditionally started. Not only did the group have a car full of beer and half-empty liquor bottles littered all over the site, he'd also detected the smoke from a hastily butted joint. That group was trouble looking for a place to happen, and it wasn't going to happen at his campground. As good as it felt to evict them for leaving a campfire unattended, Garrett would have derived more satisfaction from punching the guy's lights out for harassing Robbie, but as a peace officer and park representative, he couldn't. He needed to work this out with God, but for now, the picture in his mind of the man holding Robbie's wrist made him see red.

Garrett shoved the last box roughly to the front of the truck bed. He had to get started making his rounds, checking up on the campsites, although he'd never felt less like it. If he was being honest with himself, he would admit the real reason he wanted to join the three ladies was to talk to Robbie, even though she'd made it quite plain that she didn't want to talk to him.

He was a glutton for punishment. As soon as most of the campers turned in for the night and he could make arrangements, he knew where he was going.

Chapter 7

Gwen and Molly burst into peals of laughter at another of their jokes. Roberta just smiled. With fresh, though slightly burnt, popcorn and a large pitcher of icy Kool-Aid, they sat around the campfire, huddled in their jackets, telling jokes and behaving as she thought typical campers would behave. She only half listened as Gwen started in on another joke, with Molly butting in and trying to guess the punch line.

She'd called him stupid. She'd taken all her frustrations out on poor Garrett. He hadn't deserved that. He hadn't said a thing, he'd taken it all in stride. Neither had he brought up about her hitting him in the face with her book. Even if no one else noticed the bruise, she knew it was there. Fortunately neither Molly nor Gwen had said anything yet, at least not that she knew of.

Gwen and Molly roared with laughter again, so much that neither of them heard the sound of the Parks Department truck or the crunching of footsteps in the gravel. Roberta did.

"Hi! Did anyone save me some?"

Gwen and Molly jumped, spilling their popcorn, then laughed even louder. Roberta stared at the ground.

Molly stuck her tongue out. "Make your own. You and your ranger buddies spend more time sitting around goofing off than doing any real work anyhow. I know what you really do all day. Nothing."

Garrett grinned. "Think what you want. It's hard work handing out maps and pointing out the signs that lead to the nature trails all day. And beach duty, with all those bikinis. It's a tough job, but someone's gotta do it." He smiled so wide his dimples appeared and his teeth shone in the flickering glow of the campfire.

Gwen threw a handful of popcorn at him. He never lost his grin.

"Gotta go. Catch you next round." Garrett started to walk to the truck, but Roberta didn't want the earlier incident hanging over her head. She ran after him.

"Garrett! Wait!"

He stopped with one hand resting on the truck's door handle. "Yes, Robbie?"

She stood beside him, but she couldn't face him. She stared at the ground, knowing by now he'd seen a lot of the top of her head.

"I'm sorry about earlier. I know you did what you thought was best, and you were right. I apologize."

"It's okay, Robbie, I know you were upset."

She cringed. That's all he'd seen of her was upset, and she didn't like it.

Normally a friendly, happy-go-lucky person, no one she knew would equate the Roberta Garland of the last few days with the Roberta Garland they already knew. On the other hand, nothing had ever gone wrong in her life before. She coasted happily along from day to day without any hindrances or stumbling blocks in her path. If this was the way she behaved when troubles happened, then maybe she didn't know herself either.

"Is that it? I've got to get back to work, Robbie."

She raised her head and blinked dumbly up at him. "Uh, yes," she mumbled, nodding as she spoke. She almost turned around, but his smile stopped her. One day the woman he called "darling" for real would be a very lucky woman. But instead of daydreaming about Garrett's future, she had some serious thinking to do about her own.

"See you next round, then." He gripped the brim of his hat, tipped his head slightly forward, and drove away slowly, looking for whatever it was that rangers looked for.

With that burden lifted, she returned to the campfire, but she continued to think about Garrett, much to her dismay. Not only had she questioned his intelligence and his judgment, she'd done it in front of his sister and Molly, and also within earshot of several other campers. Garrett was the local authority, the camp police, so to speak. Judging from the way he talked about the other rangers, he seemed to rank above them. Yet, he'd forgiven her in a flash. If the situation had been reversed, she doubted she would have done the same.

Molly and Gwen bantered jokes back and forth, and Roberta only listened with one ear while she thought about Garrett. After one particular loud burst of laughter, Gwen suggested they pack up for the night. Roberta readily agreed. She knew the hard way that morning came early in the middle of nowhere.

She poured water on the fire while Molly and Gwen poked around in the embers. The wood hissed as the water touched it, and all three of them stood clear of the steam.

Obviously not wanting to go to bed, Molly grumbled. "When I'm camping, why do I wake up earlier than my alarm clock?"

Gwen nodded. "I know. Happens to me too."

Roberta nodded as well. "Yes, we were up early this morning too."

Molly and Gwen exchanged glances. "We?" they asked in unison.

Roberta blinked and looked at them. "Yes, Garrett and I were up at dawn. He had to go to work." She was about to complain how he left her all alone to do the dishes, but stopped. Molly's and Gwen's sticks remained planted in the ashes as they stared at her like she'd grown another head. "Why are you looking at me like that? We weren't the only ones up at that hour."

"Garrett spent the night with you? Here?" Gwen asked, lifting the stick out of the ashes.

Roberta gulped. "In his tent." She'd done nothing wrong. "He said Molly asked him to keep an eye on me. When some weirdo scared me, I guess he took it upon himself to be my guardian angel or something. To tell the truth, I was glad he did, because someone came into the campsite in the middle of the night, but Garrett scared him off."

They said nothing, but continued to stare, eyes wide and completely motion-less. Roberta glanced back and forth between the two of them, then averted her gaze to study what was left of the fire. "Ever since I got here, every time I turn around, Garrett seems to show up again."

Gwen's and Molly's eyes opened wider.

Roberta held the bucket tighter. "What? Why are you two staring at me like that?"

"You're talking about Garrett, right? My brother, the ranger guy who was just here?"

"Of course I know who Garrett is, Gwen! I've certainly seen enough of him over the last couple of days."

"Wow." Gwen turned her head toward the entrance to the campsite, the last place they had seen Garrett, then back to Roberta. "He's usually pretty shy and tends to keep to himself."

"Could have fooled me," Roberta mumbled. "I wish he would leave me alone." She hadn't asked for him to check up on her constantly. But in the end, she was glad he did.

Molly yawned. "Forget him. Let's get ready for bed. One last trip to the out-house, and we can change."

After their trip, they locked themselves in the camper. Molly started to giggle. "I feel like a teenager having a slumber party. What we need now is a big pizza, loaded with everything so we can get indigestion and then sit and talk all night."

"No, thanks," Roberta moaned.

"Oh, Robbie, you're such a party pooper!"

"Molly, we're going to be sleeping together in this little thing for a week and a half. If we're going to be doing whatever it is that campers do, why in the world would we stay up all night and talk if we're going to be together night and day? Don't you think we'll get a little sick of each other?"

"No way! We're party animals!"

Roberta snorted. "Good night." She pulled the top of the sleeping bag up to her chin. "Party without me."

Before Roberta fell asleep, she heard either Molly or Gwen snoring. So much for their party.

They all managed to sleep well past sunrise. They enjoyed Roberta's cereal for breakfast, and after taking a remarkably long time to wash three bowls and three spoons, they were ready for some action.

Following much discussion, they decided to observe Garrett at the amphithe-ater. The morning's schedule promised a nature talk about the animals native to the area. Much of his speech Roberta had already heard on the path to the beach, but she sat and listened politely.

Even still, he managed to pique her interest. In addition to an entertaining and informative presentation, Garrett displayed pictures of the animals. He described and drew their footprints, and then encouraged all the campers to try to find some animal tracks and figure out what kind of animal made them. He named a few good places to check out and opened the floor for questions. Caught up in the excitement of the crowd, when the presentation was over, Roberta felt confident enough to enter the trails and go hunting for tracks.

Gwen wanted to stay and talk to Garrett when everything was done, because although they lived in the same house when he wasn't staying at the ranger camp, she hadn't seen much of him lately. Molly didn't want to listen to Garrett and Gwen's private conversation, so Roberta took the opportunity to drag Molly onto the nearest nature trail to begin their adventure of discovery.

They were considerably farther down the path before Molly finally developed a little enthusiasm. Bending over and scanning the ground, both of them searched for evidence of animal habitation.

Try as they might, Roberta and Molly couldn't find anything. Molly gave up first and picked a fallen tree to sit on. "Haven't you given up yet?" she called, not trying at all to keep the boredom out of her voice.

"No. I was feeding the squirrels around here yesterday. They had to leave some footprints, don't you think?"

"You mean I've been hanging around here when all you've been doing is searching for lousy squirrel footprints? You've got to be kidding!" Molly stood, ready to return to the campsite.

"Molly!" Roberta scolded good-naturedly. "Sit down. I know they were here, so there have to be some footprints. I'm going to turn into a nature lover, you wait and see."

"Hmph. I won't hold my breath."

"Quit being so. . ." Roberta's breath caught. "Look! I found something! Right here! Footprints!" Roberta tried her hardest not to jump up and down at her success.

Molly wasn't as enthusiastic. Slowly, she shuffled her way to the tracks that held Roberta's rapt attention. She rubbed her chin as she examined the neat set of tracks. "Those are too big for a squirrel."

"Garrett said there are lots of rodents and the like out here. But this is one of the tracks he drew. Think. What kind of animals did he mention?"

Molly tilted her head as she thought. "Chipmunk? No, that would be the same size as the squirrel. Coyote? No, this is a rodent, too small for a coyote."

Roberta tapped her foot and put a finger up to her chin as well, to help her think. "What else did he draw? Raccoon? No, that was narrow. Hold on, I think I remember, it's a. . ."

They looked at each in horror.

"Skunk!" they hollered in unison. They screeched and ran down the trail back to the campsite as fast as their legs would carry them.

⊰⊱

Garrett leaned his head back and laughed. He could picture the scene Gwen had just described, imagining their mother struggling to handle the situation. Just when his laughter subsided enough to speak, Molly broke into the clearing in a breakneck run, full speed, arms waving, screaming his name, with Robbie close behind.

His stomach clenched. Both of them looked like they had seen a dead body. Ignoring Gwen in midsentence, he jumped to his feet and bolted off to meet them. "What's wrong? What happened?"

Molly's chest heaved as she gasped for air, holding one hand up to her throat. "Garrett! In the bush! On the trail! It's. . .it's. . ."

Garrett hoped she wasn't going to be sick. After all the things that happened around Robbie, it could be anything.

Robbie managed to blurt it out first. "Skunk!" she wheezed. With her arm outstretched, she pointed to the entrance of the trail as she puffed. "Over there. . . by the tree. . ."

Garrett's breath came out in a rush. He hadn't even realized he'd been holding it in. "That's it? You saw a skunk?" He bent his head and pinched the bridge of his nose with his thumb and forefinger. "A skunk?" he asked again, in complete disbelief. "You almost gave me heart failure over a little skunk?" He shook his head, still holding the bridge of his nose. One of these days. . .

Robbie regained enough breath to stop gasping for air as she spoke. "We didn't actually see it, but we found its footprints, just like you drew." She continued to point to the path, staring with her eyes wide, as if she expected the wild killer creature to appear and maim and destroy them all.

Garrett covered his face with his hands and groaned, trying to contain himself. "You mean you didn't even see it?" He hated campers like this. It could have been days ago the skunk was there if all they saw was tracks.

Robbie's arm dropped to her side. "It was there! I know it! A skunk! It could have attacked us!"

Garrett lifted his face out of his hands. Robbie's eyes still held the wild fear of a frightened doe. He tried to speak slowly, evenly, and calmly. "Skunks do not attack people. Skunks are timid animals. If a skunk sees a human, it runs one way and the person runs the other way. They're more afraid of you than you are of them. The only thing they do is spray, and they only spray when threatened. Did you threaten the poor little animal that wasn't even there?"

Robbie's and Molly's faces reddened. "Oh," Robbie mouthed. She and Molly turned and looked at each other like bad children who had been caught with their fingers in the cookie jar. "Then maybe your next nature talk should include what to do if you see a skunk." She made a sad, pathetic little laugh, then backed up.

Garrett didn't laugh. He didn't say anything. He pressed his lips together tightly to avoid saying something he would regret. At least Molly should have known better. Molly had been camping before.

The corners of Robbie's lips curved up for a split second in a quick grin, probably meant to disarm him, then dropped. "Maybe I'd better go back to the campsite now. Anyone coming with me? Molly?"

Molly took one look at him, glanced back at Robbie, then nodded. "Yes, I think I forgot to turn off the television," she said in a timid little voice, not like Molly at all. "We had better go right now."

Garrett glared at them, standing frozen to the spot, his hands planted firmly on his hips as they hustled down the path leading to the campsites.

"What was that all about?"

He turned to see Gwen scowling back at him in a pose identical to his own.

"What do you want?" he barked.

"Who bit you?" she snapped back. "Why in the world did you get so mad at them? They're inexperienced!" She waved one hand in the air, then planted it back on her hip. "They were genuinely afraid of getting attacked by a wild animal!"

They stared at each other in silence as her words sunk in. The air whooshed out of Garrett's lungs. Gwen was right, he shouldn't have been so angry. He knew Robbie didn't know the least little bit about wild animals, and Molly wasn't much better. Yes, they had overreacted, but so had he. Never again did he want to experience the soul-wrenching terror that something seriously wrong had really happened to Robbie this time.

Getting blasted by his sister completely defused his anger. He shrugged his shoulders. "To tell the truth, I don't know," he said lamely.

"What do you mean, you don't know?" Gwen tapped her foot.

Garrett crossed his arms over his chest. "Give me a break. You're acting like Mom when we were little kids. I don't owe you an explanation!"

"Yes, you do. Molly is my friend, and Robbie is our guest."

"Robbie has been nothing but a pain since she got here." He tried not to shout but failed. He waved one arm in the air in the direction they'd last walked. "Every time I turn around, she's either doing something wrong, hurting herself, or she's got some creep or weirdo after her. Now she thinks she's about to be attacked by some poor defenseless animal that wasn't even in the vicinity! Women!"

Without waiting for a response, Garrett turned and stomped off, leaving Gwen standing alone in the middle of the empty amphitheater with her mouth hanging open.

※

Roberta stuck the knife deep into the peanut butter jar, diligently helping Molly prepare lunch as they both worked in complete silence. She'd made a fool of herself in front of him. Again.

They'd made a big deal out of nothing, but really, they hadn't known any better. What if a wild skunk had appeared out of the bush? What if they had frightened it, and it had attacked them? What if. . .

"Peanut butter sandwiches, my favorite." Gwen's voice broke her train of thought. It was just as well.

Conversation was slow to get started, and they all carefully avoided any subject matter relating to wild animals or Garrett, but soon Molly and Gwen were laughing and joking once more, while Roberta listened and smiled politely.

"So," Gwen mumbled around a mouthful of sticky peanut butter, then noisily gulped her drink to wash it down, "what are we going to do on this lovely sunny afternoon?"

Molly looked up at the sky, then glanced between Roberta and Gwen. "I know! Let's go for a swim. The beach here is really nice, Robbie. Lots of nice soft sand."

"Hmph," Roberta grumbled. "I'm not interested. I've already seen the beach."

"You have? You told me you'd never been here before."

"Yesterday. Garrett took me to the beach."

Gwen's head shot up. "Garrett? He was working yesterday."

"I know. He said he had beach duty, so he took me to the beach. It's very nice. Clean and well cared for." She smiled as Gwen and Molly stared blankly at her. "They're really strict about no dogs allowed. When I was swimming, he kicked someone with a dog off the beach." She neglected to tell them how he ran into the water fully dressed to save her.

Molly shrugged her shoulders.

Roberta felt the heat rising into her cheeks. "A little boy fell off his float toy yesterday. I pulled him up out of the water, but his father was, well, he wasn't very nice to me. Garrett, well, he helped me again."

"What did Garrett do?"

Roberta's finger drew little circles in the layer of ash that had blown onto the picnic table. She'd never forget her shock at seeing Garrett appear in the water fully dressed, the expression on his face when he ordered the boy's father to let her go, or her impression that Garrett was going to deck the guy.

"He got them kicked out."

"Kicked out?" Gwen asked, her eyes almost bugging out of her head.

"Wow. . ." Molly's voice trailed off.

"Well," Gwen said, "if Garrett kicked the guy out yesterday, he won't be there to bother you again."

"I guess."

"Well, want to go again, then? It's a nice hot sunny day," Molly said.

Molly and Gwen cleaned up and then they scurried into the camper to change. The beach was crowded.

"It wasn't like this yesterday." Roberta turned her head to scan the entire beach, milling with people. They'd be hard-pressed to find a spot to lay all three towels side by side and still have a little privacy. "Yesterday there couldn't have been more than a half dozen people here. Plus one dog, who wasn't here long."

After finding a spot to spread out their towels, they raced to the shoreline to wet their toes. Gwen and Molly shivered and backed up. "Oooh! It's so cold!" they complained.

"Last one in's a rotten egg!" shouted Roberta as she sprinted in until she could no longer run, and then she dove. Rising out of the waist-deep water, she swooshed her wet hair off her face as she stood and turned to the shore. "Cowards!" she yelled.

Her mouth stayed open long after no sound came out. Standing alongside Molly and Gwen was Garrett. She wondered what he was doing there, and if he had been watching her. When he saw he had her attention, he waved.

"Hi! I'm on beach duty again," he called out, as if he had heard her thoughts.

Roberta frowned, not moving from her safe position waist-deep in the water. "Just run in!" she called out to Gwen and Molly. "You're only torturing yourselves by inching in."

Garrett smiled and waved, leaving Gwen and Molly alone on the shore as he sauntered slowly down the beach and into the picnic area.

Despite her instructions, Molly and Gwen continued to inch their way in, cringing every time they got a little deeper. Finally Roberta couldn't stand it. She ran and flopped down on her stomach in front of them, spraying them with a cascade of water, causing them to throw up their hands and screech.

"No fair!" shouted Gwen. "You're already wet!"

Gwen splashed her in the face, then Roberta splashed back, getting Molly in the face. The three of them laughed and splashed each other like little kids, squealing and splashing, until they heard a voice.

"Excuse me, ladies."

They all froze. Garrett stood on the shore, his arms folded across his chest, looking every inch the authoritative Mr. Ranger. "I have to ask you ladies to stop splashing. You're disturbing others in the water."

Red-faced, they slunk down and swam off quietly without splashing a drop. Meeting at the rope that signaled the end of the designated swimming area, they continued their playful cavorting where no one else was near. Treading water, they splashed and laughed in private, swimming underwater and playing on the rope and buoys until they'd had enough.

Upon reaching the shore, they coated each other liberally with sunscreen, stretched out on their towels until they were warmed up, then headed back to the campsite.

Even though he was gone, all the way down the path, Roberta kept picturing Garrett as he stood on the shore in his uniform. Tall and powerful and handsome, in a rugged sort of way, even though he wore shorts, which should have looked silly on a man. He instantly had the respect of everyone on the beach, herself included.

She couldn't get his image out of her mind.

Chapter 8

Following a delicious supper of barbecued chicken and slightly burnt potatoes, Roberta, Molly, and Gwen tried to decide what to do until nightfall. Taking a vote with two for and one against, they decided to attend Garrett's evening presentation at the amphitheater.

Grumbling all the way, Roberta tagged along, deliberately trying to slow them down, hoping if they arrived late, there wouldn't be any empty seats and they would be forced to turn back. Or, if they were late enough, it would be too awkward to enter once Garrett started and they would leave.

They arrived with plenty of time. Gwen and Molly headed center front, again.

Roberta watched from her seat as Molly and Gwen chatted with Garrett while he prepared his materials and the slide projector. As darkness fell, he pointed to the empty seats beside Roberta, ordering Gwen and Molly to sit down, and he called the audience's attention to begin his topic of the night, which was hiking.

Despite her bad attitude, Roberta found him fascinating, and she immensely enjoyed his presentation. Sparked with a touch of humor, he illustrated good and bad examples of a typical hiker, complete with volunteers from the audience, followed by an in-depth description of the local trails and suggested difficulty levels.

Every once in awhile their eyes met, and every time, Roberta's heartbeat quickened. At the conclusion of his presentation, a group of young women surrounded Garrett, vying for his attention. Rather than compete, Roberta, Molly, and Gwen returned to their campsite. Molly and Gwen complained about the women, but Roberta didn't care.

Gwen used the last of the kindling to build the campfire for the night. Not long after that, she threw in the last log, as well. This time, Molly and Roberta used Gwen's car, which still had the little utility trailer hooked on the back, to haul a huge pile of wood back from the stockpile.

Molly wiped her hands on the back of her jeans. "So, who gets the honors of chopping it up? Garrett cut it for you before, didn't he?"

Roberta nodded. "Yes. He made it look so easy. I learned otherwise, the hard way."

Gwen grinned. "I know. It takes practice, and I'm probably better at it than you are, but Garrett slices through it effortlessly. Maybe next time he makes his rounds, we can sucker him into cutting us some more. I know he won't have time tomorrow, because Sunday is a busy day for him. That's when most campers leave, and all the sites have to be tidied up for the next batch. By tomorrow lunchtime, this place will be almost empty. We'll have the whole place almost to ourselves."

"Really?"

"Yes," Gwen replied. "The beach too. Usually all that's left by Sunday afternoon are a few families with little kids."

"Sounds like you know the routine. I guess you do a lot of camping."

"Yes, we do. We've camped since we were little kids. Everyone loved it, but especially Garrett. It was no surprise when he got this job until he finishes university."

It hadn't occurred to her that Garrett would be anything but a park ranger. "What's he taking?"

"Wildlife biology."

"I don't know why I asked."

Gwen swirled the last of her coffee in the bottom of her cup, then drank it down. "Our family used to do a lot of camping. When we got a little older, I especially loved camping with Garrett. Because he's so big, and so, you know, staid and upright and all that, Mom and Dad trusted us off by ourselves. I got to hang around with all his friends, and they were always extra nice to me, with Garrett around."

"What's it like, having a twin brother?" Roberta didn't have any brothers or sisters, but she did have a stepsister. While they got along fine, they had never been close. She missed the camaraderie she saw between her friends and their siblings, which she had never experienced firsthand. The easy interaction between Gwen and Garrett showed her all the more what she had missed.

Gwen poked a marshmallow onto a stick and held it over the fire. "Different than a regular brother or sister, I'm told. We used to tell each other everything. I used to think all brothers and sisters were like us, but I found out later it isn't so. We've always been really close, friends and family at the same time. If it's possible, my brother is my best friend. Sometimes I don't say a word, and he looks at me and says 'I know' and I know he knows. You know?"

Roberta smiled. "I see," she said. At least she thought she did.

The marshmallow caught fire. Molly shrieked, Gwen blew it out, blew on it some more to cool it, then popped it into her mouth.

"Yeah. I always keep an eye out for the vultures who want to get their hooks on him. Sometimes it bugs him, but only a woman knows what another woman is after. He usually appreciates it a few weeks later."

Roberta wasn't sure she wanted to hear this. She tried to figure out a way to change the topic, but nothing came to mind before Gwen started up again.

"At least out here in the middle of nowhere, he can keep to himself. He seems to like it that way."

Although Gwen had expressed that aspect of Garrett's personality before, Roberta couldn't equate the loner Gwen described with the same Mr. Ranger who wouldn't leave her alone.

Gwen absently stabbed another marshmallow onto her stick. "Funny thing, I haven't seen him for a long time, he's been out here all summer, and I thought we'd have lots to talk about—but I think for the first time, he's holding something back."

She didn't know if she was supposed to say anything, because she really didn't know either of them, so Roberta chose to keep silent.

"We've always shared everything, but today when I started to tease him about that mark on his cheek, and I asked him who hit him, he got real quiet. It was weird. I didn't know what to do."

Roberta gulped. "I did it," she mumbled, bowing her head.

"You did that? You hit my brother?"

Roberta's voice hushed to a whisper. "It was an accident. It's a long story."

"Now I know why he was so evasive about it."

Fortunately, the sound of approaching footsteps crunching in the gravel interrupted them.

"It's about time," Gwen called out without turning her head. "Wanna chop us some more wood? You know, help us poor defenseless campers."

"You've got to be kidding. Whatever happened to, 'Hi, good to see you'?"

"Hi. Good to see you. The ax is over there."

Garrett sat in the empty chair in front of the fire. "You have to feed me first."

After talking about him when he wasn't there, Roberta found it difficult to face him. Without uttering a word, she walked to Molly's car, selected something for him to eat out of the cooler in the trunk, and returned to the fireside. Very carefully, she jabbed two wieners onto a stick and held them to the fire to cook. Studying them intently so they didn't burn, she almost didn't notice the lack of conversation around her until the silence dragged. When she turned her head, Garrett was staring at her, and Molly and Gwen were staring at Garrett.

"You're cooking them for me? You don't have to do that."

Roberta mumbled her reply, not really intending anyone to hear. She didn't want to be pressed for the answer, but she could feel Gwen and Molly staring at her.

She raised her eyes without moving her head to see Garrett turn to glare at them, and when they took the hint to mind their own business, Garrett turned back to her. "I'm sorry, Robbie, I didn't hear you."

She rotated the stick to cook the other sides of the wieners. "I said, you've done so much for me, I wanted to do something for you."

It must have been a trick of the glowing firelight, but Roberta almost thought his cheeks darkened.

"I think they're done now. Here."

She tucked the wieners into the buns she'd already prepared. Garrett accepted the hot dogs in reverent silence, not breaking eye contact. He closed his eyes for a few seconds, opened them, then still maintaining eye contact, took a big bite.

Molly's voice broke the silence. "First thing in the morning, we're going to take the canoe out. Nothing beats the early morning stillness of the lake. Then in the afternoon, we'll go swimming again."

"You ladies do know they're forecasting rain for the afternoon, don't you?"

Roberta's spirits lifted, then fell. "I guess that means swimming's off. What in the world do you do out here in the middle of nowhere in the rain without electricity?"

Gwen merely shrugged her shoulders, undaunted. "Who cares about a little rain? We're going swimming, so we're going to be wet anyway. As long as there's no lightning, it's still fun. Not only that, we'll have the entire beach to ourselves."

Roberta tried to picture it but couldn't. "I never thought of it that way."

"Gwen. I don't think—"

"Oh, Garrett. Lighten up!"

He stood. "Suit yourselves. Now I'd better chop that wood for you and get back to work."

❧

Birds twittered in the treetops, and muted pink and mauve clouds colored the early morning sky. Squirrels chattered in the distance, and the scent of someone's campfire brought with it the delicious smell of sizzling bacon, a vivid comparison to their own breakfast of soggy cereal in warm milk.

Roberta stood in the water up to her ankles, her pants rolled up to her knees, shivering. The lake had been much warmer yesterday.

She managed to grab the second oar before it floated out of reach. It wasn't her fault they hadn't been fastened down properly. "Got it!" she called out, then covered her mouth with one hand. Sounds carried for miles out here in the perfect stillness. The smell of someone's breakfast meant there had to be at least a few people up at this ridiculous hour, but she doubted there were many. In fact, it was probably the rangers, not campers, who were having such an early breakfast.

Quickly, she returned to the shore and tried to pull her socks over her cold, wet feet while she tried to remember who had this bright idea.

"Hop in, Robbie, and I'll push off for you."

Roberta pulled her sweater tighter around her body. "If you don't mind, I think I'd rather watch. You two can have the first ride." After accidentally dumping the oars out so easily, she wasn't entirely sure the canoe was safe for people.

"It's not difficult."

"You two go ahead first."

"You can sit on the bottom in the middle."

She wasn't convinced the thing would safely hold three people, so Roberta shook her head.

"Suit yourself. See you in about half an hour."

"Take your time."

Roberta waved as Molly and Gwen paddled off to the center of the lake. Unlike the ocean with its never-ending waves, the surface of the inland lake was perfectly still and shone like glass, reflecting the trees along the shore and the awakening blue of the sky above. The only disturbance to the water was the ripples caused by the oars breaking the surface, striking the water at the same time, lifting out of the water in unison. Behind them, a small wake in the shape of a narrow triangle rippled the water as the canoe sped in a silent line off into the distance.

Just before Roberta could no longer make out their individual shapes in the distance, they lifted their oars out of the water at the same time, flipped them to the other side in unison, and continued on their journey. Of course she'd seen people in canoes before, but after being involved in pushing it through the sand and into the water, she couldn't figure out how they managed to steer the thing in a straight line.

"Hi, Robbie. I expected to see you paddling off into the sunrise."

She didn't turn; she didn't have to. It was enough to feel his presence as she stood surrounded by the beauty of God's creation. "Good morning, Garrett." If he'd expected her to be in the canoe with the others, she wondered why he came. She continued to take in the beauty of the scenery around her, long after the canoe disappeared around the bend. She'd never been outside early enough to witness the latter part of a summer sunrise, or any part of the sunrise, for that matter. Maybe it was something she would have to do more often, although in the big city of Vancouver, the sunrise never looked like this.

The quiet serenity of the moment calmed her soul like nothing else. Only a few wisps of pink clouds remained as the sky brightened. The crystal blue morning sky reflected in the perfect stillness of the lake, briefly disturbed by a duck taking off.

Out of nowhere, she heard music. For a split second she thought she'd been caught up in the Rapture, but then realized it was a guitar strumming softly behind her. When Garrett started humming quietly along with it, her breath caught at the timbre of his deep, soothing voice.

"That's beautiful. Do you do this often?"

"Every Sunday. Care to join me?"

She did, without hesitation. Garrett sat on a small blanket, his legs crossed, the guitar in his lap. The brilliant early sunlight glinted off the corner of his sunglasses, but the brilliance of the glare didn't compare with his megawatt smile as she sat across the blanket from him.

Garrett sang softly, and Roberta hummed along with him, not remembering all the words. It was a song she'd sung a few times in church, but it had been a long time since she'd been, and she didn't really remember it. At that moment, she knew that had to change.

She knew the next song well, as well as the next few, so she joined him. For the last song, he picked a slow, worshipful song. Roberta closed her eyes as the words poured from her heart. She'd often heard people quote the Bible verse that where two or three were gathered together in Jesus' name, God was there in their midst. She'd agreed on the surface but never experienced it before. This time she knew. God was there, with her and Garrett as they sat together on the blanket beside the still lake at the crack of dawn.

Garrett played the song once more, humming the melody, while mixed thoughts and words cascaded through her head. The words to the song mixed with her words of prayer as she talked to God, really talked, for the first time in a long time. It took her awhile to realize that Garrett had stopped playing. For a brief minute, he held the guitar in silence, then laid it on the ground beside him. "Would you like to join me in prayer?"

"Yes," she whispered, nodding at the same time.

She could see herself in the reflection of his sunglasses. So much was she concentrating on trying to see his eyes through the dark lenses that she didn't realize he was reaching for her hands until he touched her. With both of his hands holding both of hers, he smiled gently, and they bowed their heads.

Roberta couldn't speak. But Garrett prayed enough for both of them. He praised God for the beauty around them, for each other's company, and for the salvation so freely given not only to the two of them, but to everyone who believed. Before Roberta realized he'd changed topics, she listened to him pray for her—for the healing of her heart and soul, and for God's guidance to direct her to the perfect soul mate as her life's partner. Garrett even prayed for Mike, for forgiveness and guidance. At first she thought she'd choke, but she surprised herself by realizing that she had forgiven Mike. She agreed in prayer for everything Garrett asked God on Mike's behalf. She felt cleansed and released and free.

Silent tears streamed down her cheeks as they sat without speaking, hands held, sitting cross-legged, across from each other on the blanket, heads bowed.

She didn't know how he knew the right moment, but at his mumbled "Amen," they raised their heads and he released her hands. She scrambled to stand, but didn't back away from him. They stood toe to toe, and it was all Roberta could do to tilt her head back and gaze up to his face. Before she thought about what she was doing, she rested her hands on his waist and her forehead to the center of his chest.

"Thank you for including me in your private worship time today." She paused to take a deep breath. "You don't know how much I needed that."

Although she certainly didn't expect a major speech from him, she didn't expect him to be totally silent. Without saying a word, he slowly and gently wrapped his arms around her and held her tight. Nestled against his huge frame, she basked in the security and protection he offered, until he augmented the warmth of the embrace by tucking her head beneath his chin. Roberta snuggled into him, slid her arms from his waist to around his back, and hugged him tight.

He was big and warm, and solid, and she'd never felt so cherished and loved in her whole life.

Loved? She pushed herself away. This was Garrett. Mr. Ranger. Molly's friend's brother who got stuck helping a pathetically distraught tagalong when he surely must have had dozens of better things to do.

"Aren't you supposed to be working today?"

The strange loss she felt when she pulled away from him was mirrored in Garrett's face for a few seconds, until he turned to pick up his guitar. "Yes, but I always take a little time off at sunrise Sunday morning to do this. The other guys respect that. They know I'll be back soon."

All she could do was nod.

"I'd better be off." He didn't leave but stood in front of her, holding the guitar in one hand.

Roberta nodded again, unable to stop staring as she processed what he said. The other rangers knew what he did and where he was going. He did this every Sunday, going through the trouble to make special arrangements, adjusting his work schedule. Sometimes she barely had the courage to tell her co-workers she went to an organized church service on Sunday morning, when there was nothing else to do. She suddenly felt ashamed. This, too, would change. Roberta made up her mind. God caught her in her weakest moment and lifted her up when she'd pushed Him aside. She quickly counted the opportunities and blessings she didn't deserve. From now on, every Sunday, she would go to church to freely worship.

Garrett raised his free hand and brushed his fingertips along her cheek, then dropped his hand to his side. "See you later, Robbie."

He turned and left without a backward glance.

❧

The sky turned overcast, as predicted. The forecast said "unsettled," but Garrett estimated rain within an hour.

He was supposed to be working, but all he could think of was the ladies in site 27. He knew that once Molly made up her mind to do something, it was as good as done, and sometimes his sister was no better. If Molly said they were going swimming, then the weather was secondary. However, he doubted Robbie knew what it was really like to swim in the rain.

During his short walk to their campsite, the sky continued to darken. Upon his arrival the site seemed deserted, but as he walked toward the tent-trailer, he heard Molly's voice easily through the canvas walls.

"I guess we don't have to worry about sunburn. Or towels. Or a blanket."

Garrett knocked on the door. "Hey, in there! You're not really going swimming, are you?"

He waited for the door to open, but instead, he again heard Molly's voice, loud and clear. "Who wants to know? You a cop?"

Garrett chuckled, then cleared his throat. He deepened his voice and spoke in the authoritative voice he used for troublesome campers. "Yeah. Park ranger. Official business. Open up in the name of the law."

He heard Molly giggle. "Come i—innnn," she called sweetly.

Garrett smiled, liking the sound of Molly's invitation. The second he opened the door, three pillows whapped him, sending him backward a step until he gained his bearings.

Before he could raise his arms to protect himself, another onslaught caught him.

"No fair!" he called out, lifting his hands and bowing his head to protect himself. "Resisting an officer! You're all under arrest!"

After a few more hits each, they stopped. He raised his head to peek over his arms to see if it was safe. "What do you ladies think you're doing? Don't you think you're a little old to be having pillow fights?"

"Old!?"

"Oh, no. . ." He saw it coming in time to cover his head again. "Truce!" he called out from beneath his arms, hoping they could hear him begging for mercy over their giggling. "I surrender!"

When he thought he was safe, he looked up. They were already changed into their bathing suits.

"I think my question's been answered. You're kidding, right?"

Gwen tapped her bare foot on the camper floor. "Does it look like we're kidding?"

He didn't bother to reply. On the remote chance of the weather changing, he had traded for beach duty for the afternoon. But the weather hadn't cooperated, and it felt like the rain would start any minute.

So often, campers did foolish things on their vacations, justifying themselves by saying they only had a few days' vacation and they were determined to do everything they planned, no matter what. With Molly and Gwen, he hadn't been surprised, but he didn't expect Robbie to go along with them.

All three ladies stood, staring at him, their arms crossed over their chests. He accepted the fact that he was outnumbered.

Garrett shrugged his shoulders. "Suit yourselves. Just don't say I didn't warn you." Before they could respond, he turned and left.

The rain set in while he made the rounds at the boating area. His patrol complete, he ran to the truck and drove to the beach, donning his bright yellow slicker before walking out into the pouring rain. As he expected, the beach was deserted, except for Molly, Roberta, and Gwen, splashing about in the lake. He stood on the shore, his arms crossed, not caring about the scowl he knew was on his face. Grinning like idiots, they waved at him. He raised one hand with a single wave back and recrossed his arms. They ignored his disdain and dove beneath the surface, all three of them in different directions. Witnessing enough, he headed back to the truck and back to the office. They'd be sorry. Maybe not now, but they'd be sorry.

A rainy day provided a good opportunity to catch up on his paperwork. With a cup of coffee beside him at the desk, he drafted up the duty roster and scheduling for the following few weeks, made a few phone calls, ordered some supplies, and began to read all the reports that had piled up on his desk in the hot weather.

One report in particular caught his interest. It was a follow-up to his warning to the other rangers about the prowler who'd frightened Robbie.

Garrett sat back in the chair to study the other ranger's comments. The next night, Dean discovered a man trespassing in another campsite and issued a warning. The man had suspiciously checked out the next morning, and thankfully nothing had been found missing. Although it was impossible to be positive it was the same man without a confession, the timing and pattern were the same, and no more instances had been reported.

Garrett smiled as he signed the bottom of the page. Robbie would be happy to hear the situation was dealt with. Not that he wanted her to wander around alone at night in the campground, but he felt better about it.

He continued to read and initial more reports, then stopped when he picked up his own report concerning the eviction of the rowdy group containing the man who bothered Robbie in the water.

Garrett laid the paper on the desk and stared off into space. Despite the fact that she wasn't his type, he couldn't stop thinking about her. He probably should have been feeling sorry for her, but he didn't. True, she was devastated about her fiancé cheating on her. Who wouldn't be? The thing he personally valued the most in a relationship was trust, and he couldn't imagine a worse way to break that trust. His heart made a strange flip-flop in his chest as he remembered the series of events upon her arrival, how distraught she was. But instead of dwelling on it, she was dealing with it, and unlike so many people he'd seen facing a major upheaval in their lives, she was moving forward.

She was obviously a believer, and from what she'd told him, her ex-fiancé wasn't. From the little he knew, Mike wasn't the right person to be her life's partner. Already, she had figured out she was better off without him, and he was strangely satisfied with her decision.

They'd prayed for her to find that perfect partner God had in mind for her, but even though he'd prayed for it, he didn't like the idea that she would now go back to the dating scene. He wondered if Robbie would mind him checking up on her periodically through Molly. He almost laughed out loud. Robbie had made it more than obvious she wanted nothing to do with him, but if that were the case, he didn't understand why he had felt such a closeness when they worshipped and prayed together.

Garrett continued to stare into space. Just as he prayed for Robbie to find the man God wanted for her, he often prayed for God to show him to his own special someone. This morning he hadn't. He no longer wanted to pray for it.

He let his gaze drift out the window, and he noticed the day had brightened. The rain had stopped.

He filed the last report away and checked his watch. If anyone was going to be stupid enough to use flammable liquids to try to light their campfires for supper, this was the time. Garrett gulped the last sip of his coffee, preparing himself to make the rounds to prevent anyone from blowing themself up for the sake of a roasted wiener.

But he knew where he was going first.

No noise emanated from the tent-trailer as he approached it, making him wonder if they were still at the beach. He was about to turn around when he heard Molly's voice from within, whining.

"What I wouldn't give for my blow-dryer right now."

"Oh, Molly," Gwen whined back, "where's your sense of adventure?"

"I don't have a sense of adventure anymore."

Garrett smiled. He wasn't going to say "I told you so," but he could think it. He knocked. "It's me," he spoke into the door. "Can I come in?"

"Only if you have a battery-operated blow-dryer."

He opened the door anyway. Pale, with her teeth chattering, Robbie sat at the table, huddled with her sleeping bag around her, over her jacket and long pants. Gwen stood beside the propane burner wrapped in her jacket trying to warm her hands on the flame beneath the old aluminum coffee percolator as she waited for it to bubble, a towel wrapped snugly around her still wet hair. Her stiff posture and the jerky movements of her hands betrayed how uncomfortable she was. Molly sat awkwardly on one of the bunks, completely tucked inside her sleeping bag, only her head peeking out.

"Did you have a nice swim?" Garrett asked, fighting the urge to smile.

He couldn't help himself. He pressed his lips together tightly as they all glared at him. He knew this would happen. He and Gwen had done this before, when they were in their teens. Against their parents' advice, they'd gone for a swim in the lake when it was raining, and then they had run all the way down the path in their bathing suits in the pouring rain to get back to the camper. For the rest of his life, he'd never forget that particular camping trip, and how cold they'd been that day. He hadn't stopped shivering until the next morning.

He had tried to tell them. They wouldn't listen. Roberta visibly shuddered, and all three of them looked up at him like frozen, drowned little rats.

He felt his lower lip tremble, and he could no longer keep the corners of his mouth from tipping up. "Goodness, Gwen, you don't have as good a memory as I gave you credit for!" Unable to hold back any longer, Garrett burst out laughing. Three cold, wet bathing suits hit him in the face.

Chapter 9

Roberta nearly dropped her supper plate when Garrett stepped into the site. He wasn't wearing his uniform. All she recognized of his attire was the battered hiking boots. A light jacket blew open in the slight breeze, showing a sweatshirt with some kind of wild animal picture, accompanied by very worn jeans that fit him perfectly. The casual clothes made him appear even larger, if that were possible.

She nearly tripped over her own feet when she recognized the duffel bag he carried. Although she knew it was coming, she'd managed to push it to the back of her mind. She could no longer bury her head in the sand. He was off work now and here to join them on their camping vacation.

He casually tossed his belongings into the tent-trailer, except for a cylindrical bag that Roberta recognized, which he leaned against the picnic table, then sat to join them, helping himself to a cup of coffee.

Molly craned her neck at the bag on the ground. "What's that?"

"My tent."

"Tent?" Molly stared at it like it was radioactive. "What do you mean, tent?"

"Tent. Portable sleeping accommodation."

"What's it for?"

"I'm going to sleep in it, Molly."

Roberta gulped. "No, Garrett. Please, don't feel you have to sleep outside again."

"I won't be outside. I'll be inside my tent. I'm not sleeping in there with you ladies." He jerked his thumb over his shoulder, and all three of them turned their heads, as if they'd never seen the tent-trailer before.

She wondered if he would have slept inside the camper if she hadn't been there. She opened her mouth to speak, but Garrett cut her off.

"I know what you're thinking, Robbie. I would have slept in the tent anyway, even if you weren't here, so don't worry, okay?"

She clamped her mouth shut. Even though the sun came out and the ground was surprisingly dry, she still thought it would be cold and lumpy, but she was learning the hard way what it was like to try to change his mind, once it was made up.

"Hey, Bro, since you're here, if you want some food, you can have whatever's left over."

Garrett grinned as he walked back to the picnic table.

"Hey! What's this?"

At the sound of Garrett's suddenly sharp voice, Roberta nearly choked on her mouthful of barbecued pork chops.

All three heads turned. Garrett held in his hand a battered mug containing a few wildflowers she'd picked earlier.

"I couldn't find anything else to use," Roberta mumbled, hoping she hadn't desecrated his favorite coffee mug by mistake.

"I didn't mean the mug. I meant these." He plucked the flowers out of the water and held them up for everyone to see.

"It was a flower arrangement."

"I beg your pardon?"

"You know, a flower arrangement. A centerpiece in keeping with the great outdoors."

"Where did you get these?" He held the flowers out towards her.

"I picked them from over there." Roberta pointed to the edge of the clearing, where a number of pretty wildflowers were growing.

"It's against the municipal bylaws to pick wildflowers."

Roberta cringed. "Oops. I didn't know."

Garrett dragged his palm down his face, then stared at her. "There's a sign right at the entrance to the park, next to the notice about the firewood. If every camper who came here picked just one flower, there would be no flowers left. The plants wouldn't come back the next year, and they'd be destroyed forever. I'm supposed to either report you or issue you a warning."

Roberta stared at him, not caring that her mouth was hanging open. She didn't doubt that he would do it.

Molly's voice drifted from behind her. "You're off duty. You're out of uniform."

He didn't comment, but his stare told Roberta how seriously he took her infraction. However, even though it didn't seem like a big deal to pick a couple of small flowers, she could see his point. Like so many things in life that started small, if not checked properly, they would soon escalate. Like what happened in her Christian walk.

It had started with omitting saying grace when she went out because Mike said he felt awkward praying in public. That developed into missing church every once in awhile, then more and more often. It had been such a gradual process that now, except for her recent talks with God since she'd come camping, she didn't remember the last time she'd prayed or even read her Bible. It started with one small thing, and if she had continued much longer, she wondered if there would have been anything left of her Christian lifestyle, just like the little wildflowers that could disappear forever, one small flower at a time.

"I'm sorry. I'll never do it again."

"It's okay. You didn't know." She watched as Garrett turned back to Gwen, completely unaware of the thoughts racing through her head. "Are you sure I can eat the rest of this potato salad? And the last pork chop?"

Fortunately, the incident was quickly forgotten as Garrett consumed the rest of the food. By the time Roberta and Molly finished the dishes, the sun had completely set. Gwen had a cheerful fire going, and Garrett had set up a few tarps near the camper in case it rained again. He also had his small pup tent set up in the flat grassy area next to the tent-trailer. He sat beside the fire, spearing a marshmallow onto a stick. Roberta purposely sat in the end chair of the row of four, which were placed neatly to the opposite side of the drifting plume of smoke. Gwen sat on the far end, and Molly sat between Roberta and Garrett.

"Oops, forgot my cup," Molly mumbled, and rose to disappear into the camper.

Grabbing the bag, Garrett smiled and shuffled one seat over to sit beside Roberta. He slowly waved the raw marshmallow on the end of the stick in front of her nose. "I'm an expert marshmallow roaster. Wanna share?"

"Uh, I don't think so," she mumbled.

He held the marshmallow close to the glowing embers and turned to smile at her. "You don't know what you're missing." His shining smile made her breath catch. Roberta turned to study the fire.

Garrett didn't take the hint. He leaned closer and whispered in her ear. "You'll make Gwen jealous. She's wanted to know my secret method for years."

Roberta turned to stare, but all he did was grin at her. Over his shoulder, she could see Gwen and Molly staring at the two of them. Her face warmed, but not from the heat of the fire.

As soon as he noticed her looking over his shoulder, Garrett's grin dropped. He pulled the half-roasted marshmallow out of the fire and turned to his sister. "Don't you two have something better to do?"

Gwen and Molly shook their heads and rested their chins in their palms, leaning forward. "No, not really."

He sighed loudly, then continued to roast the marshmallow in silence while Molly and Gwen chattered away. If Roberta didn't know any better, she'd think Garrett was coming on to her.

While Molly and Gwen chattered away, she supposed good manners dictated that she should talk to Garrett, since she would have to speak over him to join in their conversation. Instead, she watched Garrett, which was a mistake, because he caught her looking. Without a word, he blew on the marshmallow to cool it and held the stick in front of her, offering it to her.

"I'm sorry. I don't really like marshmallows."

He smiled that killer smile she was beginning to know and love. "They're different roasted. Consider it changed, refined by fire, the impurities burned away, refined like silver, tested like gold, the end result being perfect and pure, just like Zechariah 13:9."

After a line like that, she couldn't help but accept the transformed marshmallow. The rich, creamy roasted texture melted in her mouth. It was delicious.

"Want to roast one yourself?"

"I don't think so. I've never roasted a marshmallow before, and I'd likely incinerate it."

He stabbed a new one onto the stick. "Here. I'll show you." He placed the stick in her hands, then covered both hands with one of his. With his other hand, he gently guided the stick to point the marshmallow to the side of the flames, near the glowing embers at the bottom of the fire. "Now we patiently wait."

Roberta waited, although not too patiently. She didn't know when it started, but Garrett's thumb trailed up and down her wrist, massaging gently, lulling her into a calm relaxation as they waited for the marshmallow to slowly brown.

"So, what do you think of camping?" his low voice murmured almost in her ear.

She turned her head to discover her face only inches from his. She froze, mesmerized. Their eyes locked, and she couldn't have looked away to save her life. In the flickering orange glowing light, his eyes shone with sincerity and seemed to gaze into her soul. "I like it," she mumbled.

"Good," he murmured.

She wasn't sure they were really talking about camping, so she didn't say anything more.

Slowly, he pulled her hands up but didn't break eye contact. "If you don't watch it, your marshmallow is going to burn."

Blinking rapidly, Roberta tried to regain her bearings. She stared at the golden brown marshmallow, steaming on the end of her stick. Gingerly, she touched it, then pinched it cautiously, pulled it off, and popped it into her mouth. It melted in her mouth just like the first one, except this time she ate it slowly, savoring it, as if it were an expensive truffle from the downtown specialty chocolate store on Robson Street.

Garrett held eye contact the entire time.

This time, some of the molten marshmallow had dribbled onto her finger, so she stuck her forefinger into her mouth to suck it off. His gaze dropped to her mouth, and he watched. In a split second, she yanked her finger out of her mouth and wiped it on her jeans.

Fortunately, neither Molly nor Gwen seemed to notice anything strange. She turned back to Garrett, but he simply smiled at her and stabbed another marshmallow onto his stick and started yakking away about some of their family's camping experiences. Roberta shook her head.

Garrett continued to talk. At first she was content to listen, but soon she began to answer his questions, and then gradually contributed more and more to the conversation until she found herself enjoying talking with him.

Before she knew it, it was after midnight. She knew sunrise came early, so they quickly packed things up and doused the fire.

She mumbled a quick good night to Garrett and followed Gwen and Molly into the tent-trailer.

But she couldn't sleep. Before long, someone started snoring, which didn't help. She couldn't stop thinking about the exchange by the campfire. They were just roasting marshmallows, but she'd almost felt like he was going to kiss her.

Earlier in the evening, the sky had clouded over again, obliterating their view of the stars, making the night even darker. As she lay in her sleeping bag, it was so dark she couldn't tell if her eyes were open or not. She tried to count sheep to lull herself to sleep, when a shuffling noise came from outside. Her eyes shot open as she listened.

Then something fell off the picnic table.

She knew Garrett's tent lay only a few feet from the window of her side of the camper. Roberta unzipped the window.

"Garrett!" she whispered loudly through the screen. "Garrett! Did you hear that?"

A light came on inside his tent, and his head appeared in the opening.

He briefly shone the flashlight in the direction of the picnic table, then turned it off. "Go back to sleep. It was just a raccoon."

Roberta froze. She'd heard that line from him before. "That's what you said last time," she called out in a loud whisper. Whoever was snoring paused, snorted, then started up again.

The light in Garrett's pup tent went on again. He unzipped his sleeping bag, then she heard the shuffle of clothing. He crawled out of the pup tent with the flashlight at his side, pointing to the ground, and stood beside her at the screened window. "Robbie, believe me," he whispered into the opening. "It's a raccoon."

A scraping sound drifted from beneath the picnic table.

"Garrett. . ." Roberta couldn't keep the waver out of her voice. "Do something!"

He chuckled softly, then aimed the flashlight beam toward the noise. "Look."

From beneath the picnic table, animal eyes glowed from the reflection of the light. He aimed the beam directly at it. A raccoon huddled in the corner, eating bits of cereal that had spilled at breakfast time.

Roberta gasped. She'd never seen a live raccoon before, only on television. Aside from the fact that it was much bigger than she expected, the black mask around its eyes and the way it huddled under the table made it look like a cuddly little bandit. "It's so cute!" She looked toward the door, then started to wiggle out of her sleeping bag, when Garrett's open palm pressed on the screen.

"Robbie!" he called in a harsh whisper. "What are you doing? Where do you think you're going?"

"Uh, to see it. . . ," she stammered, then glanced back and forth between his hand pressing against the screen and the path to the camper door.

"Don't let their adorable expressions deceive you. Raccoons are vicious. I hope you don't think you're going to walk up to it and pat it. When a raccoon feels threatened, it will attack. It's not a cute little puppy dog. It's a wild animal, very used to fighting for survival. Never forget that."

"Oh."

They watched it finish the rest of the cereal and waddle off in search of more treats left by other sloppy campers. Garrett's palm still lay pressed against the screen. Roberta was amazed at the size of his hand. Very lightly, she touched her fingertips to his, then trailed her hand down 'til the heel of her palm rested against his. His fingers extended a couple of inches beyond her own. She stared at their hands, touching, with the screen between. "Sorry to wake you for nothing. I've never seen a raccoon before."

Garrett's voice came out hoarse and croaky. "Then it wasn't for nothing." He dropped his hand, then backed up a step. "Good night, Robbie."

At sunrise, armed with a handful of quarters, Roberta tiptoed past Gwen and Molly, who was still snoring, exited the camper, crept past Garrett's quiet tent, and headed to the amenities building to have a shower.

Upon her return nothing had changed, except the sunrise had brightened. The sun shone gaily in the blue sky above, promising another gorgeous day for camping. Rather than chance disturbing anyone, Roberta eyed the silent hammock. Did she dare?

She dared. She tiptoed into the camper, snagged her book, and returned to the hammock. Very carefully, she settled in it like Garrett had shown her and lifted the book.

Approaching footsteps crunched in the gravel. "Hi. You're up early."

Not having read a word, she rested the book on her stomach. "Good morning, Garrett."

He stood beside the hammock and peered down at her. His duffel bag lay slung over one shoulder, and his wet hair evidenced that he, too, had snuck off for a shower. He also held a steaming mug in one hand. "So, did you dream about patting raccoons? Or feeding them, perchance?"

"No." During what little sleep she did manage to get, she dreamed about him. Roberta inhaled deeply. Coffee. He had coffee. She wanted one, but she suspected he had been to the ranger camp to get it.

"I'm sorry, I didn't know you were up, or I would have brought you one too. But I'll share."

She narrowed her eyes to stare at the steaming cup. After a gentle sip, he held the mug forward a few inches. It seemed a little too intimate to be sharing a morning coffee, so Roberta shook her head and raised her book. "That's okay, but thanks, anyway."

"Do you know what their plans are for today?" He jerked his head toward the camper.

She lowered the book back to her stomach. "No, but since the day looks promising, we'll probably go to the beach."

"Sounds like a good idea."

He didn't say anything, so she raised the book again.

"How long do you think they'll sleep? The day's a-wastin'."

The book dropped back to her stomach. "I have no idea," she replied. "We were up at dawn yesterday. It's only 6:30 now." She acknowledged Garrett's nod. When he didn't comment further, Roberta lifted the book.

"Gwen usually gets up early camping," he said, glancing back at the camper, "but I don't know about Molly. What do you think?"

The book dropped. "Molly sleeps like a log. I have no idea." When he didn't comment further, she picked it up again.

"I don't know how you could sleep with all that snoring in there."

Roberta squeezed her eyes shut, thumped the book back down to her stomach, then stared up at him. He smiled down at her. She hadn't slept well, but it hadn't been Molly's fault, it was his. "It didn't bother me," she said and lifted the book.

"Yes, the fresh air does that to a person. I always sleep better out here. Do you find that?"

She stared at the book, not seeing the print.

"Oh, are you trying to read? That's a good book. Watch out for Stanleigh. He's got something up his sleeve."

Roberta squeezed her eyes shut, but kept the open book up in front of her. "Garrett!"

Garrett chuckled softly as he walked away, speaking over his shoulder. "Enjoy your book, then, but you might be able to read it better if you turned it right side up."

She slammed it shut, groaned out loud, took aim, and threw it at him.

"Heads up!" he shouted as he projected its trajectory. Using his duffel bag like a baseball bat, he swung and deflected the book, sending it flying into the bush. He laughed out loud, making no effort to retrieve it.

Gwen stepped out of the camper. "What's going on out here? What time is it?"

Garrett stopped laughing but grinned ear to ear. "Better get that coffee going. I won't mention any names, but someone's crabby in the morning." He snickered and crawled into his pup tent.

Chapter 10

Garrett, wake up. You've been sleeping all day."

"Leave me alone, Gwen," he mumbled, and covered his face with his forearm.

Instead of leaving him alone, her finger poked him in the ribs through the fabric of the hammock.

"You win," he grumbled without opening his eyes. "I'm awake."

"I can't believe you fell asleep like that. It's almost supper time. I tried to wake you before we went swimming, but all you did was grunt, so we went without you."

Garrett stared blankly at the trees above him, but he still couldn't make his eyes focus. The morning had been a complete disaster. Having four people in such a small accommodation required careful placement of all utensils and personal goods. It took until lunchtime to take the tarps down and get organized before they could choose their afternoon activity, which ended up being another trip to the beach.

He'd been looking forward to going, but after a big, delicious lunch, the long hours of working from sunrise to midnight all week had caught up with him. He'd only intended to have a short nap, but apparently, it had been longer.

Garrett still couldn't make himself move. In the background, he heard Robbie telling Gwen to leave him alone.

The sweet sound of her voice brought Garrett to complete wakefulness. It wasn't like him to sleep all afternoon, but in addition to his long hours all week, instead of sleeping he'd tossed and turned most of the night thinking of Robbie.

Compared to the state she was in when she first arrived, he could barely believe she was the same person. Yet, over the space of a few short days, he'd personally witnessed her change. He realized now she'd had it in her all along.

He continued to listen to her voice in the background, simply enjoying the sound. If he had to be honest with himself, he had to admit that he wanted to spend more time with her, even if she wasn't quite so receptive of him. The musical sound of her laugh made him smile even though he hadn't heard the joke, in addition to doing strange things to his heart.

He couldn't believe how he'd flirted with her last night, if one could do such a thing beside a campfire. If it hadn't been for his sister and Molly in the near vicinity, he would have kissed Robbie. As it was, he'd nearly kissed her anyway.

When she called out to him as the raccoon scrounged through the campsite for food, the connection he felt when she touched his hand rocked him to his core.

"If you expect to eat, you'd better be prepared to work for it after sleeping all day."

"No problem." He rolled out of the hammock and helped himself to a barbecued feast, ignoring Gwen as she nattered away at him over her opinion of him sleeping all afternoon.

He pretended to gripe when they told him to wash the dishes, not admitting he welcomed the chance to have something to do with his hands. He also wanted to watch Robbie from a distance. Strangely silent, Gwen dried the dishes, but left everything on the table for him to put away. He didn't mind.

Molly and Roberta made a fire, and all three women huddled around it while he tidied everything up. He suggested they go for a hike to enjoy the evening, but they complained about being too tired. On the other hand, after sleeping all afternoon, Garrett was wide awake and raring to go.

It didn't take much convincing for him to haul another load of wood, nor did he protest when they cajoled him into cutting it all into smaller pieces, even though he knew it would burn faster that way.

He still had lots of energy. They complained he was making them more tired just watching him.

What he really wanted to do was go for a long hike up the mountain, but the sunset had already begun. He knew the dangers of venturing outside the designated camping area after dark. He had no intention of merely walking around the campground because he did that often enough when he was working.

When they all went to bed early, Garrett once again tidied up the campsite, fixed up his tent, then watched the fire for awhile.

He couldn't believe it. He usually enjoyed spending time alone, but this evening he was bored.

Garrett stacked up the lawn chairs beneath the awning, doused the fire, and extinguished the lantern. He crawled into his tent and somehow managed to drift off to sleep.

Roberta only half listened to Gwen and Molly's endless chatter the entire walk to the beach. Garrett walked alongside them, not saying a word, much to her disappointment.

Even though the day was already hot, the beach was nearly deserted, just like Gwen predicted.

As before, Molly and Gwen inched in, making faces as the cool water tortured them with every slow step. Roberta ran in, with Garrett running at her side. He splashed in slightly ahead of her, diving in a split second before she did. Roberta rose out of the water and, as always, tilted her head back and swooshed her wet hair back off her face. When she opened her eyes, Garrett stood before her, his hair also slicked back, his body glistening in the sunlight. Tan lines on his muscular arms drew her attention to his physique in general. Although she'd already seen him without a shirt, she had to force herself not to gawk.

Roberta turned her head. This was Garrett. Mr. Ranger. Molly's friend's brother. Someone she'd never see again after her camping vacation was over.

She didn't want to think about never seeing him again, yet she had to. Yesterday when they went swimming without him she'd had the feeling that something, or rather someone, was missing. She didn't want to miss him, but she did. Throughout the afternoon, she kept expecting him to show up. She was disappointed when he didn't.

But today he was with her, promising to be fun.

Together, they watched Molly and Gwen, who were in only up to their hips. They gasped and flinched with every little step as they walked into deeper water.

Garrett met her gaze, grinned, and winked, making her aware that the ever-present dark sunglasses were missing. Roberta caught her breath and nodded back.

They dove in again, surfacing in front of Molly and Gwen. Garrett slapped the surface of the water with both hands, then laughed when they screamed. Roberta froze. She liked the sound of his laughter. Instead of joining in the splashing, she chose to watch as he splashed them again.

Molly shrieked. "No! No! Stop! Garrett, we're going to get kicked out! You'll get fired!"

"I'm not on duty, and no one here knows I'm supposed to know better." With that, he slapped the surface again, showering all four of them. "Besides, it's a weekday. We're almost the only ones in the water, so who cares?"

Gwen splashed him back, which Roberta thought rather pointless, since he'd already been completely immersed twice, as had she. He couldn't possibly get any wetter.

Without warning, Garrett ducked under the surface, flipped Gwen up by her legs, then swam away, surfacing where she couldn't get him. When Gwen and Molly approached Roberta, suspecting her of some degree of involvement, Roberta sank beneath the surface and joined Garrett a distance away, begging him to save her. This time, it was a relief to only be kidding.

❧

As their vacation went on, Roberta relaxed more and more. She found that the more time she spent with Garrett, the more she enjoyed his company. In the mornings, the four of them discussed and voted on the chosen feature activity of the day, and they stayed together the entire time. Evenings they spent talking and joking around the campfire, enjoying the sunset and continuing the playful banter until bedtime.

On Wednesday they awoke to an overcast sky. The odd raindrop had already begun to fall, so they scrambled to resurrect the tarps, then stood beneath them, dry if not warm, and watched it rain. For awhile they played a board game Gwen found in one of the cupboards. Roberta even laughed when Garrett pretended to have difficulty choosing whether he wanted to be her partner or sit close beside her.

Because of the rain, they couldn't barbecue, and since it was Roberta's turn to cook, she did the best she could on the two propane burners inside the tent-trailer. She had thought the close quarters all day, marooned in the small unit or in the lawn chairs beneath the tarp, would drive them all crazy, but they'd had a good time in spite of the weather.

She had to laugh when Garrett started the usual evening campfire huddled under an umbrella at the edge of the tarp. Amazed that no smoke drifted under the tarp, they sat close to the fire, welcoming the heat after a damp, chilly day. After spending the entire day in the confines of the campsite, except for the occasional trip to the outhouse, they called it an early night. Roberta couldn't believe she'd enjoyed the day so much.

The sound of the rain on the camper roof lulled all four of them to sleep.

"If I were at ranger camp, I'd be eating bacon and eggs."

Roberta noticed Garrett consumed every bit of cereal in his bowl and every drop of milk, despite his dissatisfaction.

Gwen crossed her arms and glowered at him. "If you want bacon and eggs, then you can cook breakfast. Don't expect me to go through all that work in the morning. I'm on vacation."

Molly's eyes opened wide. "Bacon and eggs. . .wow. . . Someone has to go grocery shopping this afternoon. If we buy bacon and eggs, you can cook, we'll all eat it, and then you can clean up the mess."

Garrett smiled. "I can handle that."

Molly enthusiastically created a shopping list filled equally with things they needed and things she wanted. It took them all morning to agree on what they would eat every day as they made up the shopping list, and then they argued about who was going to go do the shopping. In the end, Roberta insisted she would go later that afternoon, since she hadn't paid for a thing so far, and she had been there almost a week.

Roberta and Molly were elected to do the lunch dishes. Another ranger making the rounds stayed to talk to Garrett on the road, leaving the women alone at the picnic table as they worked. Molly tilted her head toward Garrett, then leaned toward Roberta. Roberta leaned closer to hear Molly's whispered words. "So, what's going on between you and Garrett?"

Roberta flinched. She didn't know the answer herself. "Nothing," she mumbled.

"Could have fooled me," Molly whispered, glancing at Garrett as he laughed at something the other ranger said.

Roberta carefully studied the scratches on the plastic plate as she dried it. "Nothing's going on," Roberta mumbled again.

"Don't think I haven't noticed the way he's been hanging around you."

Roberta had noticed herself, but she had lost the ability to decide if that was good or bad. "He's just being friendly, I'm sure."

Molly snorted in a very unfeminine manner. "Just watch out. He's, like, really religious, you know."

Roberta paused, then wiped the plate with more force than necessary. In her opinion, the degree of Garrett's faith and conviction spoke volumes about his character and strengthened her opinion of him. But most of all, she wondered why Molly thought his faith would be a concern. Molly knew she was a believer, even though she'd allowed Mike to draw her away from the church temporarily. She dearly wished Molly would make a decision to follow Jesus, but Molly remained passive, and it hurt. Knowing from experience that Garrett held nothing of his faith back in his everyday lifestyle, Roberta wondered if Garrett's good example could make a difference to Molly.

"We've had a few good discussions, and I find his commitment refreshing."

"Oh." Molly mouthed the word more than actually said it.

Garrett jogged down the entranceway to stop beside them, thankfully halting their conversation. "A few of the guys are having a flag-football game, and they're short a few players. Are you ladies interested?" He paused as he looked down at Robbie, not needing to say how much shorter she was than everyone else. "If you want to be the cheering section, Robbie, we'll understand."

Roberta tightened her lips. A challenge had been issued. "I've got back pockets. I'll play."

"Are you sure about this?"

"If they need me to even up the sides, sure I'm sure." She'd played flag-football before. Once. When she was in grade seven. It was fun, as best she could remember.

Crossing the field on their way to the designated meeting place, a football flew toward them. Garrett jumped and caught it in one fluid motion and threw it back in a long, even pass. Roberta wondered if perhaps she had been a little premature in her enthusiasm to join the game. Tennis was more her speed, especially when she considered the size of Garrett's ranger friends.

"Garrett's on my team!"

"You can have him! I want the redhead!"

Molly blushed and giggled but didn't miss a step. "I'm on his team."

Gwen and Molly exchanged winks. Roberta shuddered and opened her mouth to protest, but they beat her to the draw. Just her luck, they did need her to play to make the teams evenly numbered.

The tallest one of the bunch approached her and winked very obviously. "If you're on my team I won't care if we lose."

Roberta blushed. Before she could open her mouth to respond, Garrett stood beside her. His fingertips brushed her shoulder, and he stood so close she wondered if she could have slipped a piece of paper between them. "She's on my team," he stated bluntly. The man met Garrett's stare and backed away. Roberta wasn't quite sure what just happened, but she wasn't in a position to protest.

Everyone stuffed colored pieces of plastic, which suspiciously resembled pieces of a tarp, in their back pockets. They agreed on boundaries and started to play. She wondered about Garrett's decision to play football still wearing his sunglasses, but she decided not to question his judgment.

Shorter and slower than everyone else, even Molly, Roberta still did her best. Her strength was catching, so unfortunately she became the recipient fairly often. She quickly became winded being chased all the time, so she didn't understand why they kept throwing her the ball, because she never got very far.

During a much-needed break, they pumped some water from the well and splashed water on their faces, while a few of the men simply held their heads under the running water.

Refreshed, Roberta continued with renewed vigor. Despite her hesitations, she found herself enjoying the game and having a good time.

Roberta heard someone yell at her to receive a pass once again. Running to catch it, she saw Gwen approaching at full speed out of the corner of her eye, meaning to intercept, with Garrett quickly catching up, since he was on her team.

In a hurry to catch it before Gwen, when Roberta jumped, she misjudged her distance. Her fingertips brushed the football in the air, and she started to fumble the ball. Desperately trying to catch it before it fell out of her hands completely, she forgot about Gwen. Just as she thought she had it, still in the middle of her jump, Gwen crashed into her with a thud. Before she hit the ground, she heard Garrett mumble something, Gwen and Garrett grunted in unison, and the three of them fell to the ground together.

Instead of hitting the ground, she heard as well as felt the rush of air as she landed on top of Garrett. Gwen bounced off to the side, rolling in the grass melodramatically until she came to a stop on her stomach, arms and legs splayed. Having overdone the theatrics so badly, no one gave her any sympathy but laughed instead.

Although Roberta's landing was softer than Gwen's, Roberta wished she would have landed on the grass, because now she had to get off Garrett with her dignity intact.

She scrambled to her feet. "Oops, sorry," she mumbled, as she backed up a step. Something crunched under her foot, twisting her ankle. Still feeling shaky from her recent mishap, she couldn't regain her balance soon enough. Rather than make it worse, she simply let herself fall, landing with a thump in a sitting position with her legs sprawled out.

She sat inelegantly beside Gwen, who was lying face down on the ground, and Garrett, who was lying face up, as everyone else came running to check for casualties.

Before she checked in the grass to see what she'd tripped on, she noticed Garrett wasn't wearing his sunglasses.

Roberta felt sick.

She didn't want to look, but she had to.

Beside her foot lay the remains of Garrett's sunglasses. Before he got to them first, Roberta grabbed them. One arm stuck out at a horrible angle. She wiggled it just a little, and it snapped off completely. With one piece in each hand, she whipped them behind her back.

Garrett rose to his feet and stared at her. He didn't say a word.

Roberta gulped, tried to smile, and failed miserably. "You don't want to see them. It will be less painful this way."

He didn't comment.

Roberta scrambled to her feet, still holding the pieces behind her back. "I'm going to go into town now to pick up the groceries. If you come with me, I'll buy you a new pair. I'm really sorry."

After a charged silence, Garrett sighed. "No, I probably shouldn't have been wearing them. It's not your fault. Don't worry about it."

"I mean it, Garrett. Please? For me?"

She gave him her best puppy-dog look as he hovered above her. She could see the indecision on his face, but finally his features softened, and he nodded. "Okay. I don't have a spare pair, so I guess I don't have much choice."

"If we're going to be back in time for supper, we had better leave now. Molly, can I borrow your keys?"

Before Molly could respond, Garrett stuck his hand in his pocket and pulled out his own keys. "If you don't mind, I've been inside Molly's compact car. I'll drive."

He walked away before anyone could protest.

Chapter 11

A beat-up four-wheel drive vehicle of some kind inched into the campsite. Roberta almost told the driver he was in the wrong place when her breath caught. The driver was Garrett.

He leaned out the window. "Hop in."

The immaculate interior contrasted radically with the exterior, which had apparently seen more than a few mountain adventures.

"Like it?" He grinned.

As Roberta ran her hand along the plush seat, her attention drifted to a large dent on the hood of the vehicle. "This thing looks like you drove it over a cliff."

Garrett's smile faded. "It's been rolled a couple of times when I was off-roading, but I'm a safe driver. I never take unnecessary chances."

Roberta hadn't meant to question his driving ability. She rested one hand on his forearm, then almost forgot what she was going to say at the odd squishy feel of the hair under her palm. She yanked her hand back, and he stared down at his arm, as if she'd left some foreign substance on his skin.

"That's not what I meant," she stammered. "I trust you. It's just. . ." She shook her head. "Never mind. We'd better get going. I'm sure you're going into serious withdrawal without your sunglasses."

Saying it out loud made her realize she did trust him, not merely that he wouldn't do something foolish and get them killed on the road, but really trusted him. For anything.

Upon their arrival at the mall, Roberta led him to her favorite department store and straight to the sunglasses. Within seconds, she spotted the perfect pair, almost identical to the ones she broke.

"Here, try these."

He put them on without looking in the mirror, wiggled them, then nodded. "Yeah, they feel fine."

"Aren't you even going to look at yourself?"

He shrugged his shoulders, removed them from his face, and read the tag. "What for? They fit right, they're a good quality name brand, and they offer a good level of UV protection."

"Don't you want to know what you look like in them?"

He slipped them back on and scrunched up his cheeks as if feeling them on his face, which raised the glasses up along the bridge of his nose, then let them drop. "No."

Roberta couldn't believe her eyes. She found it difficult to believe he could be so handsome in sunglasses he hadn't even bothered to see on his face.

He took them off and started to walk toward the cashier when Roberta stopped him.

"Hold on a sec," she said. "Let me see those."

He handed them to her without thinking. Roberta turned and proceeded to the cashier.

"Robbie? Where are you going?"

"I broke your other ones, so I'm paying."

"You don't have to do that." He held out his hand to take them back, but she didn't cooperate.

"I broke them, I replace them."

Since she was unemployed, Roberta cringed at the price. But knowing Garrett worked outside all day, every day, he needed to have good quality sunglasses. She suspected the ones she broke were equally as costly.

While waiting for him to unlock the car door, she removed the price tag. He opened the door and held it for her, but instead of settling in, she handed him the new sunglasses. "You'd better take them now, before I sit on them or something."

After thanking her politely, he slid them on, nodded, and walked around to the driver's side.

"Do you mind if we make a quick stop at my place? Since we're already half-way there, I'd like to check my plants and take in my mail. I live in Coquitlam, not far from Lougheed Mall."

"Just tell me where to go."

She directed him to her small rented duplex.

It felt strange to be back. Although nothing had changed, she remembered the state she'd been in when she left. Even though it had been only a week, she felt like she'd done a year's worth of maturing in the short space of time. She stood in the middle of the living room, staring, feeling oddly out of place.

❧

Garrett followed Robbie inside, closing the door behind him. He left his brand-new sunglasses on the coffee table as he checked the place out. The furniture, while sparse, was well-chosen, comfortable, and well-matched. "Nice place." He honestly liked it. It suited her. Clean, neat, practical. "You live alone, right?"

"Yes, I do. Is it that obvious?"

"You have one couch, one painting, and everything you have matches everything else."

She smiled in reply, warming his insides.

He followed her into the kitchen, where she flooded some plants that were sitting in the sink. "I left on such short notice I didn't ask anyone to house-sit, so I left my plants like this and hoped for the best. Looks like they're going to live."

While she fussed with her plants, a rainbow reflection caught Garrett's attention. He expected to see a prism or crystal ornament hanging by the window, but the window was bare. He followed the path of the light with his eyes to discover the source was on the table. His stomach clenched when he saw it was an engagement ring.

He whistled between his teeth when he held it up and turned it to catch the light. "What a rock," he mumbled. Even though he'd never priced engagement rings, any fool could see this one cost a small fortune. He would never be able to afford a ring like this as a park ranger, perhaps not even after he graduated and found a better paying job.

Robbie sighed and shrugged her shoulders. "Yes, it's very expensive. I didn't pick it out, but I did have it appraised for insurance purposes. That ring is worth more than my car. After I found out the value, I was afraid to wear it."

After a comment like that, Garrett didn't feel right holding another man's ring, whether she was wearing it or not. He laid it quickly on the table and turned away, but then Roberta picked it up. She tossed it in the air, caught it, then threw it carelessly onto the counter. Garrett cringed when it landed, tinkling as it slid until it hit the tile wall and stopped.

He'd almost expected her to get all teary-eyed again, but instead, she stared blankly out the window. "For all the money spent on that gorgeous ring, it's worth nothing to me. All it represents is a hollow promise that's been broken into a million worthless pieces. To be given a ring a fraction of that value with a sincere commitment of love and trust and loyalty would be worth far more than all the gold and diamonds in the world."

Garrett couldn't have said it better, so he said nothing.

Robbie ran her fingers through her hair, stared at her open palm, then grimaced. "I'd feel awkward saying this to anyone else except you, but I think you've already seen me at my worst. I need a real shower, not the quarter-a-minute kind. Would you mind if I basked in the luxury of my own shower while we're here? I think I have some magazines or something if you want to read. I promise to hurry."

"Your couch looks softer than those wooden picnic benches. Don't rush on my account."

To prove his point, Garrett sauntered into the living room, lazed back on the couch, and linked his fingers behind his head. "Wake me when you're done." He winked as she appeared in the doorway between the kitchen and the living room.

⋘⋙

Roberta quickly laid her clean clothes on her bed, then locked herself in the bathroom. She'd always considered the shower to be a place of quiet contemplation, and she'd never appreciated it more than today.

Despite the heartache of a week ago, and though it had been a rough ride, she thanked God for the final result. God was faithful through it all, even though she hadn't been. She'd pushed God aside and ignored Him when she thought she was pursuing her own happiness. God knew better. God knew Mike and what would have been in store for her had she stuck with him. It had been a tremendous slap in the face, but she now appreciated seeing Mike's true colors before it was too late.

When she'd felt all but deserted, God put Garrett in her path. He'd taught her a lot about herself, and for that she'd always be grateful. She'd have to do something special for him before their holiday ended, because she'd likely never see him again. The realization made her strangely sad.

Having the burden of Mike's betrayal lifted almost made her sing the last song she'd sung with Garrett at the lakeside, a song of reverence and respect for God's enduring love. However, her singing, especially in the shower, was far from professional caliber. God wouldn't mind, but she thought Garrett might. In fact, if she started singing unaccompanied, knowing the way Garrett so readily appeared to help her when he thought she needed it, he would probably think she was in pain and break down the bathroom door and embarrass them both. She'd embarrassed herself in front of him enough in the past week to last a lifetime.

She had just turned off the water when she heard the doorbell. She scrambled out of the shower to grab her towel and hurry through the adjoining door to her bedroom when she heard the creak of the front door opening. Instantly she relaxed, grateful not to have to hurry. Whoever it was, Garrett could either tell them to make themselves comfortable, or if it was a salesman, send him away.

Her hand froze on the towel bar when she heard an angry voice.

"Where's Robbie?"

Mike. She sucked in a deep breath and yanked the towel down.

Garrett answered, pointedly polite. "My name's Garrett. You must be Mike."

"Yeah, Garrett," he sneered, spitting out Garrett's name. "What are you doing here? Where's Robbie?"

Garrett used the same overly pleasant tone as when he was handling a difficult camper. "She's busy, and I'm waiting for her. Can I help you with something?"

Roberta didn't bother with her dripping hair. She frantically tried to dry herself as quickly as possible, scurrying to her bed to collect her clothes.

"I need to talk to her. I want to make a deal."

She didn't like the sound of Mike's voice, an irritated tone she'd heard only once, when he was very, very angry. She'd never been so grateful for Garrett's presence, although she didn't want Garrett any more involved in her personal problems than he already was.

Garrett replied, pleasant again, but firm. "I don't think she wants to talk to you."

"That's too bad. I'm going to talk to her, whether she wants to hear it or not."

"Well, Mike, I beg to differ. I think you should go. By the way, Friend, have you been drinking? Or anything else that we don't want to talk about?"

"Look, Pal, that's none of your business. Where has Robbie been for the past week? With you?"

Garrett's voice lost its pleasant edge. "I don't think that's any of your business."

The conversation continued to heat up. Roberta wanted Mike gone, and she wanted him gone now. She tried to slip on her underthings.

"I'm her fiancé. I make it my business."

Roberta stood on one leg, trying to force one damp foot through the leg opening of her shorts, and nearly fell on the floor at Mike's words. As usual, he made it his business when he wanted something. The selfish creep. She bounced on the bed, then shoved both feet in while sitting and stood to fumble with the zipper.

Garrett's voice dropped to a low, even pitch. "You're not her fiancé anymore."

Mike made a choked laughing sound, not that it sounded like he thought Garrett's reply was funny. "Well, well. Surprise, surprise. How long has this been going on? Are you the reason she's been holding back on me? Hmm, Garrett?"

Roberta's hand froze, and she managed to yank the zipper up with a jerk, nearly catching her fingers. Couldn't Mike understand that she wouldn't sleep with him, or with Garrett either, because she had morals, something Mike obviously knew nothing about.

"That's enough. Let me show you to the door."

"I'm not leaving without my ring!" Mike shouted.

"You're leaving. Now."

She couldn't believe the angry sound of Garrett's voice, and she couldn't believe Mike wasn't long gone. Robbie pulled her T-shirt over her head, soaking the neck opening with her dripping hair, then nearly choked herself as it got stuck.

"If she's ready to play by my rules, then I'll think about giving her back her job."

"Why, you. . . She'd never. . ."

Roberta nearly lost her lunch. She tried to ram her hand through the sleeve opening and missed. She didn't need or want her job back, and she wanted Mike out of her house and out of her life forever. She didn't know how she could ever have thought she loved Mike, and even less how she could have considered marrying him.

She needed to put a stop to the ugly scene in the living room. Fully dressed at last, she started for the bedroom door just as she heard the sickening thud of a fist finding its mark. She couldn't tell who hit whom. Although Mike deserved it, she couldn't see Garrett throwing the first punch.

Just as she ran down the hall in bare feet, she heard cursing as Mike hit the sidewalk, a rustling of her bushes, hopefully the rosebush, followed by the slam of her front door.

"What's going on in here?" she called frantically as she skidded to a halt. Garrett stood, his back to her, leaning with his palms pressed at shoulder height against the door.

"Garrett! Say something!"

"You had a visitor."

She waited.

Slowly, he turned to face her with a slightly crooked smile. "He's gone now." One eye was already starting to swell shut.

Roberta covered her mouth with her hands. "Oh, Garrett!" she gasped.

He winced at the same time as he grinned.

"Oh, Garrett, I'm so sorry! Does it hurt?"

"Am I expected to be brave or truthful?"

Roberta cringed. Turning toward the kitchen, she called over her shoulder as she started to run, "Let me get you some ice. Sit down."

Instead of sitting, he followed her into the kitchen. She guided him to one of the chairs before she dumped some ice into a plastic bag, then covered it with a clean dish towel and gently pressed it to his eye.

When he flinched at the contact, Roberta nearly cried. She twined the fingers of her other hand through the hair at the back of his head to steady him, and maintained the pressure with the compress.

He raised his hand to push it away, but she shook her head.

"It's not that bad, really," he complained.

"Quit trying to be valiant. I know Mike works out at the gym." Garrett flinched again when she moved the compress as the ice melted and shifted. "Don't move," she whispered hoarsely.

Obeying her command, he stiffened, not moving a muscle, until she removed the cloth to reshape it.

"Am I all better?"

"Hush," she choked out, still trying to assimilate what she'd heard. Mike had let her know in no uncertain terms what he thought when she turned down his advances, but he had never resorted to violence or threats in the past. After his performance today, she didn't think it wise to take the chance. Date rape really happened, and she had no intention of becoming another statistic.

She raised the compress to reapply it, but before she could, Garrett grasped her wrist.

"It's okay, Robbie, I don't think any more ice would make a difference. What's done is done."

"I'm so sorry. This is all my fault."

He gave her such a sad smile she had to bite her bottom lip to stop it from quivering. "I should have seen it coming. Now forget about it. We'd better go get those groceries, or else we'll have to face the wrath of two very hungry campers when we're late with their supper."

All she could do was nod.

On their way out the door, Garrett picked up his sunglasses off the table and very gingerly placed them on his face.

Roberta couldn't help but stare. The large sunglasses managed to hide most of the swelling, but she could see some discoloration already starting below the lower part of the frame.

For the first time since they were alone together, Garrett remained silent. Overcome with guilt about everything that had happened to him because of her, she found herself doing what Garrett had done up until now. Chattering. Endlessly. She talked about her neighborhood as they drove away, her family, her perception of her camping experience. It warmed her heart when he smiled at her admission of how out of her league she was when she first arrived and how much she'd learned. She asked him questions about his studies, his future career plans, and about what in the world a wildlife biologist would do, especially in the winter when there weren't any campers to harass.

He outright laughed at that, doing strange things to her insides.

Garrett never removed the sunglasses the entire time they shopped. Quickly filling their list, Roberta insisted on paying as Garrett packed. Knowing they wouldn't have time to cook a decent meal by the time they returned, Roberta bought a bucket of chicken, and they headed back to the campground.

Garrett couldn't believe Molly and Gwen's reactions as they pulled into the campsite. He'd expected them to be anxious for supper, but they'd nearly pounced on poor Robbie, complaining bitterly about starvation, until they saw the bucket of chicken in her hands.

Except for the food, they hadn't been missed. While eating, Molly and Gwen described their day of searching the campground for the group of rangers they'd played football with. Disappointed at not being able to find them, Molly and Gwen gave up and went to the beach, where they had been pleasantly surprised to find the same group of rangers, off duty. They'd had a wonderful time.

Garrett remained in the background as the women ate, listening to them chattering away. Fortunately, no one paid attention to him. On the drive back, when Robbie wasn't looking, he'd snuck a peek at his eye in the rearview mirror, and it looked worse than it felt, if that was possible. Almost swollen shut, every time he blinked, the mere contact of his upper and lower eyelids against each other created such pressure that he saw stars all over again. He'd developed a pounding ache all through the left side of his face, and even though it left him with no depth perception, he kept his left eye shut. With the sunglasses on, hopefully no one would notice.

Not wanting to cause a scene or embarrass Robbie, he slunk into the hammock once he finished his supper, where no one would pay any attention to him.

He made no effort to help them build their campfire or light the lantern as sunset approached. He linked his fingers behind his head and crossed his ankles in the hammock, pretending to be asleep. He'd never had a black eye before, and he wondered how long it would throb like this, making him also wonder if he'd be able to sleep tonight. The day changed into nightfall, and still he stayed in the hammock, silent. With darkness came the chill of the night air, but he didn't want to leave the haven of his hammock. He'd have to take off his sunglasses sooner or later, and although he knew it was unrealistic, he thought if he waited long enough, maybe they wouldn't notice.

Knowing they wouldn't ignore him forever, he was still caught off guard when Gwen called him. "Wake up, Garrett, or you won't be able to sleep tonight."

He didn't answer, hoping she'd leave him alone, and that no one would notice the hammock trembling because he was shivering. He mentally kicked himself for not changing into long pants when he had the chance.

"Garrett!" Gwen called, this time from above him. He looked up at her and grinned, hoping that she couldn't see his face in the dark shadow of the hammock. "Are you sick or something? You didn't eat any marshmallows. I didn't know there were so many in one bag."

"Oh, I must have fallen asleep," he mumbled.

"Are you still wearing those things after dark? Are you nuts? Let me see them. These are the new ones Robbie got you, right?" Before he realized what she was doing, Gwen reached down and pulled the sunglasses off his face. He couldn't protest without causing a scene, so he painted a grin on his face, hoping she wouldn't look at him. He'd managed to hide his face all evening, first with the sunglasses and then under cover of darkness. If his face remained enough in the shadow of the hammock, their secret would be safe for awhile longer.

"Aren't you cold? I've got a jacket on and I'm by the fire. Are you avoiding us for some reason?"

He was. But he wouldn't admit it, especially to his sister.

"If you don't get out of there, I'm going to dump you."

He didn't need this attention. "You'd better not."

Without warning, she grabbed one side of the hammock and lifted it up. Caught off guard, his arms shot out to the sides in a reflex action. He grabbed the edges of the hammock to keep from falling out. Gwen let it go, causing the hammock to rock back and forth violently. His head pounded from the sudden movement, and it felt like something stabbed him in the eye. Completely forgetting himself, he sat up with a jolt. "Knock it off, Gwen!"

She never replied. Her eyes opened wider than he'd ever seen. She gasped and leaned closer to him. "What happened to you?"

Three pairs of eyes stared at his face. Robbie visibly paled. Her mouth opened, but no sound came out. He bared his teeth in what was probably the phoniest smile of his life, the mere movement making his face hurt. Mustering his dignity, he rose from the hammock and seated himself at the empty lawn chair by the fire.

"Would you believe me if I said I had an accident with a big tree?"

No one spoke. Gwen shook her head.

"I had a disagreement with Smokey the Bear?"

Robbie broke the silence. "It's my fault," she squeaked out in a tiny little voice. Garrett cringed as she continued.

"Garrett and Mike had a bit of an altercation."

Molly gasped. "Mike? When did you see Mike?"

"He kind of showed up when we stopped by my house."

Molly's eyes opened wider, if it was possible. "You had a fight? A fistfight? You?"

Garrett couldn't help himself. He smiled, despite the pain the movement caused in his face. "It wasn't exactly a fistfight, Molly." Although, after the shock of Mike plowing him in the face, he'd been very angry. Instead of striking back, he'd picked Mike up by the scruff of his neck. Exhibiting great restraint, he'd thrown Mike, arms and legs flailing, outside into the bushes before slamming the door. He didn't know how he hadn't hit Mike back, but after the fact, he was grateful for the grace God gave him not to lower himself to Mike's level.

Molly walked to him, leaning forward to get a better look at his face. "Well, I hope you flattened the little creep!"

"Molly!!!" Robbie gasped as she ran to his side.

Garrett grinned. "We'll just say I escorted him out the front door against his will."

He raised his hands to the fire, leaning forward to warm himself, signaling his wish to change the subject. As always, Gwen knew he had no intention of discussing it, and she led the conversation into tall tales and bad jokes.

Midnight came quickly. Garrett crawled into his pup tent and the women retired into the camper for the night.

Chapter 12

Any other day, the fussing would have amused Garrett. He might even have appreciated being spoiled. Not today. The swelling had subsided enough to not be painful, but he knew the bruise was still ugly. Worse than the women hovering, he knew the other rangers would tease him. He didn't want to explain how it happened, but he could only wear the sunglasses until sunset.

"Would you like another cookie? Or more coffee?"

If he had any more coffee he'd burst his bladder. "No, thanks, Robbie. But I know what I would like. Why don't we all do something away from the campsite? I have to go back to work this afternoon, so this is my last chance at any time off. By midafternoon, the weekend campers will begin to arrive, and I'll be due back on duty."

Molly groaned. "Don't you want to relax? You walk around all the time."

"It's different when I have a routine to follow. Who wants to check out the waterfall?"

Robbie perked up. "Waterfall?"

"Yeah." Garrett pointed north to the trail leading up the mountain. Robbie's head turned to follow the direction of his finger. "At an average pace, it takes about an hour to reach it. If anyone here can handle it."

Gwen and Molly shot him a dirty look. He knew they didn't like to walk in the wilderness. Even if they did, it wasn't them he wanted to walk with. Garrett smirked beneath his sunglasses.

"I'd rather play football," Molly grumbled.

Garrett gritted his teeth, then smiled at Robbie. "I'll bet you could take some great pictures."

"Pictures?" Robbie turned her head to the direction of the camper, where her camera sat in the middle of the table. Up 'til now he'd managed to stay clear of her with that thing, but some things were worth the sacrifice.

He could almost see the gears whirring inside her head. "Okay!" she chirped. "I just have to change. I'll be right back!" She ran inside the camper, and all the curtains pulled shut.

"Garrett, I have to make a trip to the little girl's room. Care to come for a walk with me?" Judging from Gwen's stone face and less-than-discreet glances to the road, he didn't think he was going to like what she intended to say. But all that coffee, graciously delivered, had taken its toll.

Gwen remained silent until they were well out of earshot of the campsite. He didn't know why. If this one was like any other of their normal conversations, no one would be able to follow it, anyway.

"Don't think I don't know what's happening, Garrett."

He hated these conversations. Garrett sighed loudly. "Why don't you tell me all about it?"

"This is different. Tell me what's going on."

Garrett nearly stumbled. No matter how much time they'd ever spent apart, he'd never had to explain himself to his sister. Never. "I don't know if I can."

"You're falling in love with Robbie, aren't you?"

He walked slowly in step with Gwen. "Does it show?"

"It does to me." They stopped in front of the path to the outhouses, but Gwen remained on the main road with him.

Garrett shoved his hands into his pockets and stared at the ground. He'd never been at a loss for words with his sister before and found it difficult to explain what was happening in his head. He thought about it for a minute, then faced her. "She's different than anyone I've ever met. I know she's not really my type, but there's something about her that makes me feel complete, like the last piece of a puzzle fitting into place."

Gwen nodded. "I was afraid of that."

"Oh? How so?"

Gwen laid her hand on his shoulder, and he didn't think this was a good sign. "Has it occurred to you that she might not feel the same way?"

"Don't be ridiculous, Gwen. All I need to do is talk to her."

"I don't think so this time, Bro."

"I've prayed about it. God's answered me. I know it."

Gwen shook her head. "All I can say is, don't get your hopes up. Sometimes these things can be one-sided. You know I'll pray for you, but I don't want you to be disappointed."

He shook his head, but he didn't say anything. All he had to do was talk to Robbie.

They returned to the campsite in silence, where Robbie waited for him dressed in a stark white T-shirt, a pair of cream-colored sweatpants, and her white sneakers, which weren't as white as they used to be. He tried to smile as she fiddled with the camera slung around her neck.

"Oops. Let me get an extra film from the camper. I'll be right back."

While Robbie disappeared inside, Gwen joined Molly.

Garrett could see Molly looking around, trying to be discreet, which was a first for Molly. After his conversation with his sister, he strained to hear what they were saying.

Molly leaned to Gwen. "He's got it bad, doesn't he?" she said in a loud whisper he couldn't help but overhear.

Gwen nodded. "Yup."

"She doesn't, does she?"

"Nope."

"This could be interesting."

"Yup."

That was okay. Garrett knew that this time, his sister was wrong.

※

Roberta walked beside Garrett as they wandered along the mulch pathway of the nature trail. For the first time, Garrett didn't fill every minute yakking about the squirrels, birds, trees, bushes, clouds, weather, or anything else that crossed his mind. At first she enjoyed the peace and quiet, listening to the soft crunching of their footsteps on the path, the birds chirping, and the chattering of the odd squirrel without an explanation on the species or genus or a description of their habitat. But after awhile, she couldn't stand it any longer.

She opened her mouth to ask if something was wrong, but as she did, she heard water trickling and splashing in the distance. "Listen! We're close to the waterfall! I can hear it!"

"Yes," Garrett replied softly. The low timbre of his beautiful baritone voice almost made her lose her step. "A few more minutes, and we'll be able to see it."

The volume of the moving water increased as they continued, until finally she could see it.

The water cascaded over the edge of a small cliff, bouncing and splashing on smooth, shiny black rocks below. The entire scene glittered in the sunlight, creating a small shimmering rainbow to the right above the stream. The brightness of the water contrasted magnificently with the dark bushes surrounding it, creating a natural frame, showing off the elegant beauty of the flowing water as nothing else could.

She lifted her camera.

Garrett stood back quickly.

After snapping a few pictures, she lowered it and let it hang freely about her neck. She watched his head lower almost imperceptively, as if analyzing the status of the camera. Roberta sucked her lower lip, wondering if she should ask. Encouraged by his silence, she did. "Can I take your picture by the waterfall?"

He stiffened, and his lips tightened. She couldn't tell where he was looking behind the sunglasses. "I won't smile."

She tried to bite back a nervous laugh. "I didn't expect you to, although your smile must do your dentist proud. Besides, with that hat and your sunglasses constantly covering your face, a smile would seem out of character. All you need to complete the image is a big cigar and a submachine gun."

His mouth opened as if he was going to say something, but then he stopped and smiled. In a flash, Roberta raised the camera to one eye and clicked without taking the time to focus, hoping for the best, then lowered it just as quickly. "Why do you hate having your picture taken?"

The smile faded, making her sorry she had asked. She waited, unsure if he would tell her the reason or tell her to mind her own business. He stared off into the waterfall and rammed his hands in his pockets. She joined him at his side.

"You know Gwen and I are twins?"

"Yes."

"When we were little, my dad lost his job. To make some money, my mom took us to audition for magazine ads and the like, having cute little twins to pose. One agency signed a contract with us." He stared into the water, bent to pick up a rock, and threw it in. "Awhile after we started, I finally saw some of the pictures. I'll never forget how awful they were or how it felt to look like that."

"Oh, come on. I'll bet you were a cute kid."

"I wasn't. At a certain age, Gwen and I looked almost exactly alike. Instead of cutesy twin pictures, the photographers tried an experiment, and it worked, at least from a commercial standpoint. For one particular ad sequence, they made her up and posed her as the cute little girl she was, and dressed and made me up to be the identical doofus little boy. The ads were a success, so they kept on with the same theme. I was completely humiliated, yet I knew it was important to my parents, although at the time I didn't know why, so I did my best and stuck with it, but I wouldn't wish that on any kid."

He cleared his throat and picked up another a rock. "My mother honestly thought people laughed because they thought we were cute, but the truth was that the contrast between the perfect little girl and the pitiful little boy made me feel pathetic."

Roberta didn't know what to say, but the sight of a grown man fighting unpleasant childhood memories tore at her heartstrings. "I'm sure no one meant it personally."

"I was just a kid, and I took it very personally. I still can't get over my hatred of cameras. As if you couldn't tell." He turned his head, and she thought he was looking at her, but she couldn't tell for sure. "I make myself scarce when the camera comes out at family functions too."

Roberta wished she could say something to ease things, but her mind was blank, so she said a silent prayer for peace of mind for him. They watched the waterfall, standing side by side.

Garrett finally broke the silence. "Do you have any plans for when you get home?"

Roberta wasn't sure what he meant. "Not really, except for trying to find another job, but I don't think I'll have any problems. I've got a steady work history and a good letter of recommendation. I guess today is the end of any time off for the rest of the summer for you. Then you're going back to university in the fall, right?"

"Yes." He stuck his hands back in his pockets. "Do you think Mike will bother you again? If you need any help keeping him away. . ." His voice trailed off, becoming drowned out by the steady drone of the waterfall.

"I don't think he'll be a problem. You already showed him he was less than welcome."

Conversation lagged. Garrett inched closer, then grasped both her hands in his. "Can I ask you a personal question, Robbie?"

She wasn't sure she wanted to hear his question, but she couldn't imagine things getting much more personal than anything she hadn't already told him or his confession of why he hated cameras. She doubted his parents knew how he felt. Although she suspected there were few, if any, secrets between him and Gwen, she didn't think even Gwen knew this. So Roberta nodded.

"Why did you say you'd marry him? Were you in love with him, I mean, really in love?"

So she was wrong. Things could get much more personal. Roberta wondered if she could avoid the question, but he held her hands just firmly enough that she couldn't pull away without looking churlish after he'd bared his soul to her. As she answered, she could see her own reflection in his sunglasses looking back at her. "At the time, I thought I was, but now, looking back, it was more familiarity. We were always together, every day all day at work over the space of years, then dating in the evenings. I guess the engagement seemed a natural progression. We obviously don't share the same faith or even moral standards. In the end, I don't know what we shared. So I guess I really didn't love him, in the happily-ever-after sense." She gulped. "Why do you ask?"

"Because I think I'm falling in love, Robbie." One of his hands rose. He tenderly brushed his knuckles against her cheek, then ran his fingertips gently along her jaw, stopping under her chin. "With you."

Her voice came out in a squeak. "But you barely know me." She barely knew herself. This past week had been a lesson in life like she'd never experienced.

"I know that. It doesn't make sense, but it's true. Please tell me I'm not the only one who feels this way."

In a moment like this, Roberta couldn't handle staring back at her own reflection. As if he knew what she was going to do, he released her hands. She twined the fingers of one hand with his, just to keep touching him, and with her other hand, she plucked off his sunglasses. The swelling of his black eye made her wince in sympathy. Her heart tightened, knowing it was her fault.

The bright sunlight caused him to blink a number of times until his pupils shrank to small black dots, emphasizing more of the dark chocolate brown of his eyes. Roberta stared into his eyes, thinking back over the past week, about how different he'd turned out to be than her first impression, yet in many ways, no different at all. Nothing less than a gentleman the entire time, he'd listened to her with the right mixture of sympathy and distraction as she poured out the story of her failure at the most important relationship in a person's life, and her poor judgment regarding Mike's character. His steadying influence held her together when she needed it, and through his spiritual guidance she had managed to grow in spite of it. She couldn't help but feel the bond that had developed between them. But love?

She had thought she loved Mike, and that was the biggest disaster of her life. But Garrett was nothing like Mike. Mike used his power and influence as his father's son to intimidate people to do his bidding, where Garrett was a natural leader. His inner strength and quiet confidence left no question of his authority. Over the years of working with Mike, she'd grown used to him because she'd had to, as her supervisor and the future owner of the company. Familiarity had bred more than contempt. She'd allowed it to happen out of weakness. She saw that now.

Nothing going through her mind and heart felt the same when she thought about Garrett. At first she'd tried to get rid of him, but within a few days, she had missed him when he wasn't nearby. When he wasn't talking for the sake of talking, which she now suspected he did to distract her from her troubles, she enjoyed his company more than anyone else's. It was a foregone conclusion she found him attractive. Plus, when they prayed and worshipped together, she had felt a bond like no other.

Above all, he had been totally open and honest with her, as she had been when they barely knew each other. She could do no different now.

"No," she whispered, barely managing to speak above the volume of the rushing water, "I don't know what's happening, but you're not the only one who feels something."

Whatever he said, and she suspected it was her name, was lost as his mouth descended on hers. The sunglasses nearly fell out of her limp fingers as the touch of his tender lips seared into her memory.

For such a large man, his embrace was tender and his touch gentle as he lifted his mouth, angled his head a little more, then kissed her again. Roberta lifted herself as high as she could on her toes, leaning into him, crossing her wrists behind his neck, his sunglasses dangling from her fingers.

He made a sound that rumbled deep through his chest and kissed her again and again. Her knees nearly turned to jelly when his hands inched upward, along her sides, over her shoulders, until he cupped her face with both hands, and gave her one more slow, lingering kiss, ending with his lips suspended over hers and barely touching, while at the same time his thumbs gently rubbed her nape.

Slowly, she sank to rest her heels on the ground, burying her face in the center of his chest, and slipped her hands around his waist. He held her firmly but gently, like she was the most precious thing in the world. His chin rested on the top of her head.

"I'm sorry. I have to be back on duty in an hour. We have to go back."

She backed up and offered him his sunglasses. Instead of simply taking them from her, he lifted them out of her hand with one hand, then slipped the fingers of his other hand between hers. After he slid the sunglasses back on his face, he led the way back, still holding hands.

The simple gesture demonstrated his sincerity like none other, both comforting and casual, yet understatedly possessive. In a word, cherished.

They walked hand in hand, in silence. There was no denying something had developed between them, but she couldn't define it. If this was love, then it was a quiet comfort, riding side by side with an excitement deep inside, unlike anything she'd ever felt before. She tried to ask God for an answer, but she kept getting too distracted by the warmth of Garrett's hand as he walked beside her.

Or was this what it was like to be, as the classic phrase said, "caught on the rebound"? She'd often heard the phrase but never understood it. Now, here she was, walking through the forest holding hands with a man she had only just met, when a week ago she wore another man's engagement ring. She'd just kissed him too. Not just a friendly peck kind of kiss, but the kind that made a woman's insides melt.

A week. The thought echoed through her brain. What was she doing? Had she lost her mind?

The path widened to the opening onto the road through the campground. A week. They talked of love, and she'd known him a week. And on vacation, yet not even a normal lifestyle setting. What was she doing?

She pulled her hand out of his.

"Robbie? What's wrong?"

Garrett's confusion nearly broke her heart. "I have to go to the bathroom," she stammered, and ran for the amenities building, leaving him standing on the gravel road, alone.

Chapter 13

Dressed in his uniform and ready to go back on duty, Garrett waited at the entrance to the campsite. It didn't take a rocket scientist to see something was wrong, and he didn't want to leave without talking to her. Ephesians 4:26 reverberated in his head. He couldn't let the sun go down on her anger, not that he thought she was exactly angry, but he couldn't let this go unattended. Time was too short.

He nearly laughed. Time? He'd known Robbie a week, but in that short week, his head and heart had been turned upside down. From the moment Robbie did a flip over his hammock, his heart had done a flip over her. But, he wasn't foolish enough to believe in love at first sight. Rather than diminish his initial attraction, the additional time spent with her beyond that only magnified it.

His heart skipped a beat, then restarted with a thud as Robbie entered the campsite.

"Robbie? Are you all right? Can we talk about it?"

Her face paled, and she shook her head. He opened his mouth to speak, but nothing came out.

"I can't talk now; I have to think. I'm sorry, Garrett."

He didn't like the sound of that, but she'd given him no choice. He would wait.

Roberta busied herself at the campsite, trying to fill her mind with meaningless activity, and failed. The sight of Garrett back in his uniform did strange things to her insides. He was Mr. Ranger again. Tall, dark, handsome, dedicated to his job, committed to his faith in God. If his past performance was any indication, anything he committed himself to, he would pursue with equal unfailing devotion.

Beyond the shadow of a doubt, he meant what he said about falling in love with her. Now that she was away from him, she knew she was in the process of falling in love with him too. However, she didn't know if she could be equal to his expectations. According to Gwen, many women had wanted to be in her position. The fact that she was scared her to death.

Before she drove herself into a frenzy, Gwen and Molly returned for supper. Busy discussing the rangers they'd met once again, neither Molly nor Gwen noticed how jumpy she was as they prepared their dinner. Molly blabbered on about the ranger who had teased her about her flaming red hair, and from the sound of things, they had exchanged phone numbers, with Garrett's recommendations.

To keep herself occupied, Roberta volunteered to take care of all the dishes after supper, while Molly and Gwen set up tarps, since the sky had clouded over. Diligently, she scrubbed every dish and glass meticulously until everything sparkled, which was difficult to do with plastic.

Seconds after Molly and Gwen excused themselves for a trip to the outhouse, Garrett showed up on his ranger rounds.

"Hi, Robbie." He stood beside her, waiting for her to respond. Not looking up, she rewashed one of the pots, trying to scrub out a black spot that looked like it had been there for years.

"Will you tell me what's wrong? Have I done something. . . ?"

Roberta shook her head. "You haven't done anything wrong, Garrett. Please understand."

Noting the absence of retreating footsteps, she turned to see him not only still there, but with the dish towel in hand, drying the clean plates she had neatly stacked on the drainboard. His hand froze midwipe when he noticed her staring at him. "What? I do my share of the housework, even in the great outdoors."

She nearly dropped the pot. "Aren't you supposed to be on duty, like, being Mr. Ranger?" she squeaked out.

"Please, don't hide from me, Robbie."

She buried her hands in the soapy dishwater. "I'm not hiding," she mumbled. "Things are happening too fast for me."

Garrett finished drying the last plate, then stacked it neatly with the others.

While helpless to protest with her wet, sudsy hands, Garrett touched his fingertips to her cheek, then trailed them lightly to her ear as he brushed back a stray strand of hair. "Okay. You know where to find me."

Just as he'd done on the first day she met him, he straightened, touched the brim of his hat, and walked out of the site.

❧

Roberta stared into her bowl of soggy cereal, pushing all the matching colors into groups and patterns. Molly and Gwen watched her but fortunately didn't comment. Rather than go searching for the rangers with them, Roberta grabbed a half bag of stale bread and left for the nature trail. She'd seen more than her share of rangers.

With less enthusiasm than the last time she tried this, she sat in the same spot as a short week ago, absently feeding and taking pictures of nature's little creatures, thinking of the resident nature expert.

Being in close quarters, she actually had come to know him fairly well. She knew what activities he liked and didn't like, she knew about his family, his job, his interests. He was devout, honest and sincere, truthful to a fault, and tremendously loyal. Over and over, she listed his good and bad qualities in her mind, but she still had to be realistic. She'd only known him a week. A short week.

She didn't believe in love at first sight. However, she'd known Mike for years, so that was no indication of knowing a person's character either. She needed more help than her own experience could offer. She didn't know many verses by memory, but Proverbs 3:5–6 came to mind.

"Trust in the LORD with all your heart, and lean not on your own understanding; in all your ways acknowledge him, and he will make your paths straight."

Roberta fell to her knees, alone in the quiet forest, and prayed.

Dear Lord God. I'm so sorry I've pushed You aside. Now here I am, asking for help. I know I made a bad choice with Mike, but now I see that You showed me before it was too late, and I thank You for that. But what about Garrett? Am I falling in love with him? Is he the one You've meant for me? Please show me what to do. I'll trust in You from now on, because You are God, the Master and Creator of all.

Roberta scrambled to her feet, her mind clear. She had let her bad experience with Mike distort her budding relationship with Garrett. She didn't have to marry the man right away—she didn't have to marry the man at all, but she could get to know him better. If things progressed, God would direct her to know if the relationship was good and right. He'd shown her what a creep Mike was. He could also show her what a swell guy Garrett was.

Roberta threw the bread on the ground, scooped up her camera, and ran down the path, all the way to the camper. Garrett would show up sooner or later. He always did.

While she waited, she made idle conversation with Gwen and Molly, constantly checking over her shoulder, forcing herself not to jump to her feet every time someone walked by or a vehicle slowly drove down the road. Garrett did not appear to be making the rounds.

Supper was a tasteless affair of the last of their food and leftovers thrown together. Just before sunset, someone walked down the entranceway into the campsite, but even though she recognized the ranger uniform, it wasn't Garrett. Her heart sank. It was Molly's ranger friend.

Roberta grabbed her flashlight and headed down the road. If he wasn't going to come to her, she would go to him. She walked through the campground, sticking to the main road, turning her flashlight on as night started to fall. He was nowhere to be found. After more than a week of use, the white beam started to turn yellow. Roberta smacked the flashlight a few times, but it continued to dim, then went out.

She stood in the middle of the road. She could either go back to the campsite, knowing he wouldn't show up, or go to the ranger headquarters, where he was doing whatever it was that rangers did. With the other rangers. If he was there.

Glancing both ways, Roberta started to hear little noises in the bush. Holding back a shudder, she walked quickly back to the campsite. She didn't want an audience when she talked to him. Besides, in the morning, being Sunday, she knew where she could find him.

❧

At sunrise, Roberta awoke.

Molly snored away as Roberta tiptoed out of the tent-trailer, using as much stealth as she could. Not wanting to arrive breathless, she walked down the road, onto the nature path, then chose the fork to the lake.

As she approached the clearing at the shoreline, she heard his guitar and his voice as he sang quiet songs of praise. When she could see his face, she noted he wasn't wearing his sunglasses, and his eyes were closed. Rather than intrude, she stood back in the bush and watched, thinking of what to say now that she was here.

His eyes opened as he changed songs, but Roberta remained frozen. Today his songs were different. While still reverent, it took her awhile to realize the connection. He was singing songs of trust, expressing his confidence that God was in control, and giving God complete reign in his life. Then he stopped and laid the guitar on the blanket beside him. Instead of closing his eyes, he slumped and buried his face in his hands to pray. Although he mumbled, she could still make out a few words, including her name and something about letting her go.

Roberta couldn't watch. She could no longer intrude on his private moment with God. She forced herself to walk away slowly and quietly, then once she figured she was out of earshot, she ran the rest of the way to the camper. She quickly slipped back into her sleeping bag and lay there, her eyes open, staring at the top of the tent, until Gwen awoke.

Garrett did not show up for breakfast.

When all the dishes were done and put away, they started packing up the camper and taking it down, ready to go home.

Roberta couldn't remember feeling more depressed. For every stage that was taken down, she remembered Garrett's part in helping her set it up and, at the same time, the fool she had made of herself in front of him. Yet he had kept coming back. Now when she wanted him, he didn't. Her eyes burned as she took down Garrett's hammock.

Finally hooked up and ready to go, Roberta surveyed the campsite. This had been the best vacation of her life. She had a wonderful time, she had found herself—and true love. And lost it.

They drove to the dock, and Roberta helped heave the canoe atop Gwen's car. Just looking to the side where Garrett sat every Sunday morning caused her throat to tighten, nearly choking her.

Back at the site, they made one last check for forgotten articles, then drove away. As they cleared the park entrance, Roberta saw Garrett standing almost hidden by the trees, his arms crossed over his chest, watching. He didn't smile. He didn't wave. He'd broken her heart—or had she broken his?

She reminded herself that the past week was just a vacation. Some time to get away from the troubles of life, and that vacation and all that went with it was now over. It was time to go home and get things back to normal.

Molly chattered constantly the entire trip home. Dutifully, Roberta thanked her for providing a much-needed escape and the chance to get her head together. As soon as she dumped her clothes on her bed, Roberta hopped in her own car to dash off and buy a few days' worth of groceries before the store closed. While she was there, she dropped her film off at the one-hour photo department so it would be ready when she was done.

When she picked up her pictures, a large envelope was attached.

A giddy teenaged girl explained that she had won a free enlargement. Since Roberta hadn't answered the page, the clerk had picked one of the photos to enlarge and told her if she wanted a different one, she could return it at no charge in exchange for a photo of her own choice.

Roberta wanted to go home, not hang around waiting for a picture. Being her camping pictures, she doubted she would need a 16 x 20 portrait of a squirrel.

With her groceries sorted and put away, all that remained was the envelope of pictures on the table. First, she opened the large envelope to see her free enlargement.

Roberta sucked in a deep breath as she pulled out a large photo of Garrett standing tall and erect, bare-chested, muscles flexed and ready, holding the large ax, poised to cut her firewood on the first day with him. Her brain froze as she stared at the photograph, bringing back with astounding clarity every event from when he backed the trailer into the campsite for her to the last sight of him as she left with Molly.

He had won her love without trying, by only being himself. Honestly. Naturally. She had rejected him out of her own fear and self-doubts. By the time she admitted to herself what had happened, it was too late. She couldn't blame him for letting her go. She'd behaved abysmally.

Instead of looking at the rest of the pictures, she lowered her head to the table and cried.

❦

Roberta woke up in her soft, warm bed at dawn. As much as she tried to sleep in, her internal body clock had not yet reset itself. Tossing and turning, she gave up, showered, and dressed.

She started to make herself a large pot of coffee, when a flash beside the stove caught her eye. On the corner of the counter, Mike's engagement ring lay where she had tossed it the day Garrett had been there. Just looking at the expensive trinket turned her stomach.

She opened the lid to the garbage can, ready to toss it where it belonged when the phone rang.

"I want my ring back," Mike demanded without any salutation or polite chitchat.

"You broke off the engagement, therefore the ring is legally mine. Everyone in the office heard the whole thing, so try and take me to court over it."

"It's worth a lot of money. If you give me the ring, you can have your job back."

Roberta held the phone in front of her and stared at it, unable to believe what he said. According to what she heard with her own ears a few short days ago,

Mike wanted more than just the ring before she got her job back. She hung up without replying.

The sparkle of the ring in the sunlight stopped her once more from tossing it in the garbage can. Holding it up into the sunbeam, she let the beauty of it catch the light. The ring was gorgeous, and she knew what it was worth. It would be a horrible waste to throw it out. She let the lid drop shut and dropped the ring into the bottom of her purse instead.

The second she touched the coffee can, the phone rang again. This time it was Molly, loaded with questions. "How are you, are you still upset, has Mike called, has Garrett called? Just checking to make sure you're okay." On and on.

After assuring Molly that she was feeling just peachy, she hung up. Everything she did made her think of Garrett. Seeing the ring made her think not of Mike, but of Garrett holding it in the light. Mike's phone call reminded her what slime Mike was, in comparison to Garrett's upstanding morals and unselfish ways. Even her dirty clothes reminded her of camping, which made her think of Garrett all the more.

She spent the day cleaning up and doing her washing.

The next day, she did the ironing and went out looking for a job.

The next day, she did the same.

All day, every day, she could think of only one thing. One person. Garrett. What was he doing? Where was he? What was he thinking? Was he wearing the sunglasses she had bought him? Was he thinking about her?

She depressed herself terribly.

Enough was enough. Roberta decided she had pined over Garrett too long, and it wasn't going to get any better. She drove to the mall, marched into the jewelry store, and asked for the manager, where she presented him with Mike's ring and the appraisal certificate.

She had no regrets selling it. The jeweler gave her a fair price on the ring, nowhere near what it was worth, but a decent price on a used ring. Now it could be a bargain for some couple somewhere who were truly in love.

After she made all her purchases, she still had plenty of money left over. Smiling, she patted her purse and headed home. She packed some suitable clothes, then left a message on Molly's answering machine not to worry. The second she hung up the phone, Roberta put her plants back in the kitchen sink and took off.

The hour-long drive to the campsite was the longest hour of her life. When she arrived, she managed to pick a nice, small, private campsite. Emptying all the paraphernalia onto the ground, she was ready to begin, but quickly became overwhelmed. In her excitement, she hadn't realized the volume involved. The kind elderly man who owned Hank's Outdoor Store had had his staff load up the car for her. Now that she saw the gear strewn about her feet on the ground, she couldn't believe the volume of goods necessary for a short camping trip. A lot of it she was familiar with from Garrett's family's camping accessories, but beyond that, she had no idea what to do with most of this junk.

She had absolutely no idea how to set up her brand-new tent.

But she knew who she could ask.

She glanced upward at the position of the sun in the sky, then checked her watch. Garrett would have already started the afternoon presentation. Leaving everything as it lay on the ground, she headed for the amphitheater. Rather than disturb anyone by walking in late, she sneaked into a seat on the end near the back, where she sat and watched Garrett.

While he smiled at the crowd and presented his information in an entertaining manner, he lacked his usual enthusiasm.

In the back of her mind's eye, she pictured him sitting alone and dejected, praying beside the lake. The loss of his cheerful disposition was her fault. Again.

At the close of his presentation, he followed his usual routine, asking if anyone had questions or comments, and politely if not enthusiastically answered every one of them. Finally, no more hands were raised.

"Is there anyone else?" he asked, scanning the crowded amphitheater for any stragglers.

Roberta raised her hand.

Garrett pointed to her. "Over there."

She stood and faced him across the little amphitheater full of people. She saw him flinch momentarily as he recognized her, and then he stiffened his posture.

"Yes?" he asked.

Roberta gulped and clasped her hands in front of her churning stomach. "This has nothing to do with your topic, but I do have a question, Mr. Ranger. You see, I'm not a very good camper, and I don't seem to be good at putting things together. I've got this tent and stuff, and I think I'm going to need your help."

They stared at each other as a hush grew in the crowd.

He had no comment.

She swallowed hard. "I miss you, Garrett. And I'm sorry."

Garrett's face paled and his voice trembled when he replied. "Don't do this," he said, barely loud enough for her to hear.

Roberta blinked hard. Her voice started to crack, and she didn't care. "I'm sorry," she repeated. "I do love you, Garrett."

"Robbie," he choked out. He clenched his hands into fists and rammed them into his pockets.

Tears welled up in her eyes, and she forced herself to keep them open. She knew everyone was staring, but she could only see Garrett, and he was fast becoming blurry.

All heads and eyes turned on Garrett as he stood at the front, constrained and ramrod-straight. She squeezed her eyes shut. She'd made a spectacle of him, and herself too. This was not the way she had meant for this to happen. She'd botched everything from the first moment she saw him, and now she had embarrassed him in front of all these people.

Roberta turned to leave, rejected by his silence and lack of response. She clenched her teeth, determined not to run until she was out of sight of Garrett and the crowd.

Garrett called out, his voice choked. "Robbie, wait!"

He ran up the center aisle and through an empty section, jumping over some of the seats in his haste.

Very gently he touched her shoulder with his fingertips. "Robbie, nothing's changed. I still love you, you know."

She knew he meant it. It was herself she wasn't sure of.

"I love you too, and I've handled this badly, but I need more time. Can we take this slowly? Can we, you know, date and stuff?"

Garrett bent his head, then brushed a lock of hair off her face. "Yes, I'd like that. But be warned. I intend to try my best to convince you to marry me."

She smiled and bit her quivering lower lip. "I think I'd like that."

"Robbie. . ." His voice trailed off, like he didn't know what to say. He tipped her chin up with his fingertips, and the corners of his mouth curled up slightly. "Do you really have a tent you need help setting up? You came camping by yourself to come here to see me?"

She pulled off his sunglasses and gazed into the depths of his soft, dark eyes, seeing past the purple bruising to the kindness of his soul. "Yes," she whispered.

Garrett's eyes glistened. He blinked rapidly a few times, then smiled.

She opened her mouth to explain herself, but before she could say a word, he pulled her close until she was pressed against him from head to toe. He held her tight and buried his face in her hair.

Roberta opened her mouth to speak but gave up before she said a word. Any talking would have been drowned out by the thunderous applause around them.

Epilogue

Are you finished yet? How long have we been in this stupid duck blind, anyhow?"

Roberta slapped her thigh in frustration. "It's not a duck blind, it's a raccoon blind. If there were any raccoons out there, they're gone now!"

"Robbie." In his cramped sitting position, Garrett rested his elbows on his knees and bowed his head to drag his hands over his face. "You're in credit and collections. You work in the accounting department. If the real photographer got sick, they should have found someone else to do this if they were running on a deadline, not you."

"Who? Mr. Mulderberry? I don't think his wheelchair would have made it up the hill, do you?"

"Robbie. . ."

"Oh! I know! Kathy! She's not due to have the baby for another week and a half. There's plenty of time left to do a photo shoot, right?"

"Robbie. . ."

Roberta waved the camera in the air, accidentally hitting him in the cheek with the strap. He barely noticed. "I suppose Joanie could have done it if she came back from the Bahamas a few days early from her honeymoon. She probably wouldn't mind."

He held his palms in the air toward her to silence her. "I give up! I know it's a small staff. I know you'll take some wonderful raccoon pictures for the magazine. This just isn't exactly my idea of what we'd be doing this weekend."

Roberta sighed and sagged. Neither had she pictured them huddled together under a musty canvas covering deep in the woods, trying to take pictures of a family of raccoons who allegedly were taking the ceramic statues out of a wealthy gardener's landscaping display and carrying them into the middle of the forest. She figured it was a stupid idea, trying to get pictures of them back at their den hoarding their treasure. However, the owners of the magazine she'd been working for during the past year and a half thought it would be a great story, but only if backed up by photographs.

"This is your fault they stuck me with this," she griped. "Who else on staff is married to a wildlife biologist?"

Before she realized what he was doing, Garrett removed the camera from her hands and pulled her close. He nuzzled her cheek and gave her a gentle kiss. "Yeah, you are married to a wildlife biologist, and don't you forget it." He kissed

123

her gently on the mouth. "Happy anniversary, Darling. We'll go out somewhere special tomorrow."

Roberta smiled. She loved it when he called her "darling" because it reminded her of when they first met, and her thoughts that one day the woman Garrett called "darling" would be a lucky woman. She was, indeed, a lucky woman.

After nearly making the biggest mistake of her life, God had directed their meeting, their courtship, and now here she was, married to her Mr. Ranger.

Using just her fingertips, she touched his chin, then ran her hand slowly down his throat to rest in the center of his chest. Feeling the increase in his heartbeat following the path of her fingers, she smiled in feminine satisfaction. Instead of kissing him, she drew small circles on his breastbone, maintaining a short distance between them, enjoying his reaction.

⚜

Garrett smiled at Robbie, sitting before him in her favorite camping clothes; her khaki slacks with one patched knee, her gray sweatshirt dotted with holes from stray campfire cinders, and the most disgusting pair of hiking boots he had ever seen. To top it off, she wore one of his Parks and Recreation hats, and as usual, it was crooked. The other rangers always laughed when they saw her wearing it.

He covered Robbie's hand with his own, pressing it against his chest, against his heart, where she belonged. He'd prayed for his perfect soul mate, and God delivered her.

"I love you, Mr. Ranger," she whispered.

With his free hand, he tipped her chin up, then leaned forward to kiss her. "And I love you too, Mrs. Ranger."

At Arm's Length

Chapter 1

"Miss McNeil, could I see you in my office right away, please?" The intercom speaker echoed with a loud click as the company's president hung up.

Molly cringed. Rumor had it that big changes would soon be happening, and that usually meant downsizing. Since she'd never before been called into the owner's office, she suddenly worried that she was the first to go.

Her fears doubled when suddenly Janice appeared to relieve her when she hadn't been the one to ask for someone else to answer the phones.

With trembling hands, Molly dug her notepad and pen out of the desk and walked to Mr. Quinlan's office. She thought this would probably be a good time to pray, but beyond begging God to allow her to keep her job, her mind went blank.

"Come in. Sit down."

She tried her best to smile, but it fell flat. Molly sat in the chair in front of his large desk, grateful for the chance to take her weight off her wobbly knees. Mentally, she started calculating how long she could survive on her meager savings before she found another job.

Mr. Quinlan folded his hands on the polished metal desktop. Absently, she compared the shiny surface to his bald head. He flipped through a file. Her personnel file. Molly started to feel sick.

"You started in the mailroom, moved to file clerk, spent some time as...," he flipped the page, "...junior clerk in payables. You've been the receptionist for a few years now." He closed the folder and sat back in his chair, resting his hands on his protruding belly.

Her experience at Quinlan Enterprises wouldn't make an impressive resume, but perhaps the business courses she'd completed at night school would impress a future potential employer. She had hoped to be able to work her way up, but it now looked like the only place she was going was out the front door.

"Uh, yes...," she mumbled, forcing the words out.

He checked his wristwatch. "Janice will take over your current projects effective immediately. Have you removed your personal effects from the desk?"

Now she really felt sick. "No..."

He leaned forward, clasping his hands and resting them on top of her now closed personnel file. He opened his mouth to speak but was interrupted by a knock on the office door as it opened. A young man in an expensive suit hustled in and shut the door behind him.

"Sorry I'm late. You wouldn't believe the traffic." He glanced her way briefly, then turned to face Mr. Quinlan.

Molly forced herself to breathe. Mr. Quinlan acknowledged him with a nod. The young man, whoever he was, turned to smile a greeting at her, showing the cutest set of dimples and adorable crinkles at the corners of his eyes. His tall frame filled out the tailored suit to perfection, showing off broad shoulders and trim hips, a build that shouldn't have been confined in a suit.

Molly stared at him, transfixed by his eyes. A dark steel blue, the cool color oddly radiated a warmth that instantly led her to trust him. They contrasted perfectly with his black hair, which was meticulously cut and combed back, heightening his soft but still very masculine features.

As he lowered himself into the chair beside her, smiling the entire time, their gazes locked. Now that he was so close, she detected a spicy, deliciously male fragrance. Molly didn't usually like cologne on men, but this time, if she hadn't been already sitting and if this had taken place a hundred years sooner, she wondered if she might have fallen to the ground in a swoon. She told herself she was being ridiculous.

She hoped she wouldn't be asked to speak, because she didn't know if she could.

Mr. Quinlan nodded. "Molly McNeil, this is my nephew, Kenneth Quinlan."

The junior Mr. Quinlan shuffled to turn his body toward her as she remained seated and extended his hand, no doubt expecting her to respond.

She couldn't understand why she was being introduced to the owner's nephew when she was on her way out.

For five years she'd worked at Quinlan Enterprises. Molly knew every nook and cranny, every storage space, and she'd learned the location of almost every file in the building during her stint as filing clerk and office gofer. Later, when she took the receptionist position, she had made it a priority to know all the staff's job descriptions. That way she could transfer calls to the correct person the first time, as well as know enough to ask the right questions to take intelligent messages. It was something she took pride in, and that knowledge should have made her more valuable, not the first person to be fired. It only hurt worse to know she was being replaced by a junior employee.

She responded by giving Kenneth Quinlan the limpest handshake of her life.

"Pleased to meet you, Miss McNeil. Or may I call you Molly? Whichever you prefer, of course."

"M. . .M. . .Molly." She blinked at him, then continued to stare at him like he was from outer space.

❧

As he held onto her hand, Ken studied Molly McNeil. This was one woman who would not go unnoticed. Her flaming red hair would set her apart in any crowd. It was a shade he'd never seen before, a shocking orange-red in a wild array of curls he could only compare to Little Orphan Annie, in an adult sort o.

In contrast to her vivid hair, her clothing was businesslike and conse...e, a nice neutral shade that set the color of her hair even more apart. He didn't know much about women's hair, but as unique as the color was, he doubted it came from a bottle. As with every redhead he'd ever met, she, too, had green eyes and a smattering of freckles across her pert little nose. She was cute and fresh-looking, her expression unguarded and transparent as she stared at him in open astonishment.

"Please call me Ken. After all, we're going to be seeing a lot of each other."

As Ken slowly released her hand, her face paled, making him worry that something was terribly wrong. Since his plane was late, he'd phoned from the airport. Uncle Walter had said it wasn't a problem—he would be introduced to the person who would be showing him around when he finally arrived. However, she didn't seem very enthusiastic.

"We are?" she stammered, then glanced back and forth between himself and Uncle Walter with big round eyes.

Uncle Walter knotted his eyebrows. "Didn't Theresa speak to you this morning, Molly?"

"Uh, no. . ."

"Theresa was supposed to tell you that we've selected you to be Kenneth's assistant until he gets settled."

"Me? His assistant? That's what you called me in here for?" She sat completely still for a few seconds, then burst out into a very strange, humorless laugh.

Personally, Ken thought himself a nice guy, and the job of showing him around shouldn't have been so unnerving to cause anyone to react so strangely. He struggled not to give away any indications of his bruised ego.

Uncle Walter stood. "Well, Kenneth, I know you said you'd be happy with the back desk in the accounting department, but I wanted to let you know Nancy volunteered to give you her office."

Ken stood in response. He hated being called Kenneth, although it was a step up from being called Kenny, a name he'd suffered with through childhood. He'd only managed to shake being called Kenny when he turned twenty-five. He hoped it didn't take another twenty-five years to be referred to as just plain Ken, because if so, he had another twenty-three years to go.

"I told you, I don't want to be in the way, and I don't want to disrupt the status quo. The back desk will be fine." He turned to Molly. "Before we start, I do have a few things to take care of, and I have a number of boxes in Theresa's car."

His uncle tipped his head slightly, turning again to Molly. "Since you're going to be working closely with Kenneth, you'll have the empty desk beside his, as soon as we move the things we have stored in it. Perhaps you could find a home for those old files and move your personal effects while Kenneth gets settled."

Ken extended his hand to Molly again. This time, she grasped his hand firmly, making him not want to let go. Her hand was small and soft, and this time, all the color had returned to her face as she returned his handshake. "I'm looking forward to working with you, Molly. See you in about half an hour."

With that, he turned and headed for the parking lot.

~⚜~

Molly watched him go until he disappeared through the opening to the lobby. She tried to let it sink in that she'd been assigned to be the boss's nephew's assistant. She couldn't imagine what she might be able to show him that he wouldn't already know. Ken Quinlan had been running the Winnipeg production plant for the past two years, so he was more than familiar with the company and the way things ran. Even though she couldn't remember ever having seen him before, she didn't think she knew anything he didn't.

She also wondered what he was doing here, at the Vancouver office. Unless she was wrong, it appeared his move was permanent. So far she hadn't seen an announcement that they'd hired a new manger for his old position, but that didn't mean there hadn't been one. She wondered how to find out what was going on, and how it could possibly involve her.

Mr. Quinlan's voice broke her mental ramblings. "I'll speak to Theresa about not informing you of our decision. My apologies."

Molly struggled to contain her blush as Mr. Quinlan shook her hand. She'd never been good at accepting apologies, so she forced herself to smile, then cleared her throat. "I guess I should work on clearing out that desk."

She took her leave and headed for her temporary desk, dreading what she would find. Whenever anyone had old files or archives too difficult or inconvenient to put away, they stashed them inside the drawers in the spare desk where no one could see, so she doubted Mr. Quinlan knew what he was asking. It was only when the filing department had time that those old files were eventually returned to their rightful place in the storage areas or in the attic. It would take far longer than half an hour to clear even a portion of what had collected over time.

During her many trips back and forth to the back of the storage room, she overheard whisperings of gossip from a few of the other single women that they thought the only reason she got the job was because Ken liked her.

The thought that someone of Ken Quinlan's background of money and privilege would be interested in her on a personal level was preposterous. She was only a lowly office clerk. He was part of the owner's family. Besides, she'd never met him in person before today, she'd only spoken to him on the phone, no more than anyone else in the office.

Molly therefore concluded that they were angry because they wanted the job she'd been given.

The allotted half hour passed too quickly. She was nowhere near ready when Ken signaled his readiness to start. She left everything scattered in haphazard piles and abandoned the mess to be sorted later. First, Molly formally introduced him to everyone individually, allowing a few minutes to chat at each stop. Before she knew it, it was lunchtime.

Standing at the two disorganized desks in the rear corner of the office, Molly bent to reach for her purse, when a light touch on her arm made her breath catch.

"May I take you out for lunch? I regret that we didn't have time to talk before being thrown together. I'd welcome the opportunity to get away from the rest of the staff and listen to your ideas, and I'll let you know my goals. I'd prefer we talk in private. Or do you have other plans?"

Actually, she did have other plans, but she wanted to get off on the right foot with the boss's nephew, especially now that he was her immediate supervisor. "I just have a few errands, I can always do them after work."

He smiled, and her heartbeat quickened. Molly tried to smile back without looking like a simpering fool and wondered how long it would take to get used to him.

Rather than drive, since he'd been sitting for hours on the plane, they walked a few doors down to a small Italian restaurant that specialized in quick lunches for their business-oriented clientele. They were soon seated at a small corner table.

Molly folded her hands in front of her, expecting to hear him outline her expected duties. Instead, he asked her general questions about procedures and morale and if there was anything in her opinion that was a concern. In no way did he sound condescending or patronizing, only honestly concerned. Immediately her apprehension about working for him dropped. She was just starting to explain how they arranged the vacation schedule when their food came.

Molly stared down at her plate. Even though she hadn't been a Christian long, the pastor's sermon on remembering Jesus every time you ate and drank had hit home. It had been a sermon meant for communion, but she'd taken it very much to heart for every day. The trouble was, she hadn't been in a public restaurant since she made her decision, except for once after church with the church crowd. She didn't know what to do, especially with a stranger.

❧

Ken glanced down at his plate, then back up at Molly. He hated moments like this. He'd never been shy about pausing for a word of thanks before eating in a public restaurant, but he was usually with people he knew. He didn't want to look overbearing, and even worse, he didn't want to embarrass Molly, or himself, for that matter. He deliberately kept prayers before a meal short, but when he lunched with a client or associate who wasn't a believer, he only closed his eyes for a second or two in order to be as discreet as possible before he carried on with the business at hand. He didn't like to do that, but unfortunately, today was one of those times.

Across the table from him, Molly seemed to be studying her plate. As far as he could see, everything looked fine. The meal was what she ordered, something she claimed was her favorite house special. Since she wasn't paying any attention to him, he was ready to discreetly close his eyes for a brief, private prayer, when

Molly closed her eyes, bowed her head, and clasped her hands on the tabletop in front of her.

He blinked at the realization of what she was doing. He'd seen more subtle ways for someone in doubt of their surroundings to pause for a word of grace, but with that hair, he doubted anything this woman did could be subtle.

"Molly?"

Her eyes opened and her cheeks reddened.

"Would you mind if I said grace?"

The change from her open mouth and red face to her beaming smile almost made him feel lightheaded.

"I'd love that!"

A few people briefly turned their heads at her sudden exclamation. Quickly, Ken composed himself, bowed his head, closed his eyes, and folded his hands in his lap under the table. "Dear Lord, thank You for the food You've given us, and the day before us. Thank You for Your kindness and mercy, and for Your blessings in the days to come. Amen."

He picked up his fork, prepared to start eating, but noticed Molly staring at him.

"Yes?"

She turned her head from side to side, checking to see if they were being watched or if anyone around them was listening. "You're a Christian!" she said in a loud whisper.

"Yes."

"For how long?"

Ken narrowed one eye. This was not a question he'd been asked before. Everyone he knew didn't have to ask. "Since I was seven years old."

Her eyes opened wide with wonder. She grasped the edge of the table with both hands and leaned forward. "Wow. . . ," she murmured.

The brilliant green of her eyes drew him like a magnet. He felt like an idiot, staring at each other across the table while their food cooled, but he couldn't look away.

It was almost like another person was asking, but Ken heard his own voice. "How about you?"

She sat back in her chair and smiled. "A week ago last Wednesday!"

He'd never spoken to a new believer before, at least not that he knew of. He didn't know what to say, so he said nothing.

"Where do you go to church?"

"I just arrived in Vancouver this morning, so nowhere, yet."

"Have you ever been to Vancouver before?"

"A couple of times."

"It hardly ever snows in the winter here. Some years it doesn't snow at all. I hear Winnipeg gets tons of snow. I couldn't imagine what it would be like. It really doesn't rain in Vancouver as much as people say it does, and there's so much to see and do. Have you ever been to Science World? It's not just for kids, they have. . ." Her voice trailed off and her smile dropped. "Sorry, I think you'd asked me about vacation scheduling."

Ken tried not to shake his head. So much had been said since then, he couldn't remember what he asked.

He listened politely as a more subdued Molly explained about day-to-day happenings in the office. Before he knew it, they were finished lunch and back at the office.

For most of the afternoon, he spent his time in the accounting department studying their larger clients' transaction histories. At the same time, out of the corner of his eye, he watched Molly diligently piling and sorting old and dated files, then placing them in boxes once they were in order.

At the end of the day, everyone filed out except for Molly. Nancy, the accounting department supervisor, offered to stay, but Ken sent her home as well. Even Uncle Walter left, leaving himself and Molly the only ones remaining in the building.

Ken walked to the desk as she dropped the last file into a box. "You can go home, Molly. I don't want you to stay on my account."

She shook her head. "No, it took me all day to get these sorted, I don't want to stop now. Everything is put away that goes in the main storage room. All I've got left is what goes in the attic. It should only take me an hour, and then I won't have it hanging over my head. This way we can get a fresh start tomorrow. I don't mind."

"Then I'll help you. Together we can do it in half the time."

❧

Molly fumbled with the box in her hands and let it drop with a thump on the desktop.

Since it was Friday, her original plans were to play volleyball with the young adult group at church in the evening. However, because she'd used her lunch break to talk to Ken, she now had to make a choice—to do her errands after supper or go play volleyball, because she didn't have time to do both. But, if Ken helped her, then there was a chance she could still play.

She raised her eyes. All she could do was stare at him as he stood before her, waiting for her to say something. Ken Quinlan wasn't here to do filing. Obviously he was being set up for a supervisory or management position. No doubt his presence had something to do with the rumors everyone was passing around. Even though she didn't know the long-range plans, word was this move was permanent.

She cleared her throat and turned toward Ken. "You're going to put stuff away in the dark, dusty storage room?"

He shrugged his shoulders and gave her a grin that made her breath catch. "Why not? Unless you don't want my help."

"You know this isn't just carrying boxes to the attic and leaving them on the floor. I have to take out every single file, pull out whichever box they belong in, one at a time, and put them all away so someone can find them again, if needed."

"I know how archived files are stored, Molly. We're required to keep files for seven years. They have to go somewhere."

Molly looked at his suit, which probably cost as much as her entire wardrobe. "If you have asthma or dust allergies, you'll never survive up there. Do you have any idea how dirty it is in the attic? You'll ruin your suit."

"There's only one way to solve that." As he spoke, Ken slipped off his suit jacket and slung it over the back of his chair. Next, he loosened and pulled off his hand-painted silk tie and laid it over the jacket.

He rolled up his sleeves and picked up one of the larger boxes. "Lead the way."

Chapter 2

Molly opened her mouth, then snapped it shut. If Ken wanted to put files away in the filthy attic, she couldn't argue. After all, he was now the boss.

Molly snuck a peek at him as he lifted the largest box and settled it securely in his muscular arms. Even minus the suit jacket and tie, he was still every inch a professional. A five-o'clock shadow darkened his jaw, and dark circles outlined his eyes, making her wonder how long he'd been awake, especially considering his early morning flight and the time-zone change. Despite signs of fatigue, he continued on.

She was aware of his every footstep behind her as they walked through the office and up the back stairs to the storage room.

Molly groped around the corner for the switch and flicked it on, cringing at the layer of dust beneath her fingertips. The single bulb barely lit the room, which was probably a blessing in disguise, because the dim light didn't allow a complete picture of the thick dust and grime. The few occasions she'd spent any amount of time here, Molly had brought a change of clothing and a kerchief to cover her hair. This area was cleaned once a year whether it needed it or not, and she suspected it was more than a little overdue this year.

Molly pushed the stool with her foot rather than touch it, leaving a circle on the floor where the dust wasn't quite as high. When she stepped up, she looked down to see a trail of her own footsteps and wondered what the dirt would do to Ken's imported patent leather shoes.

Rather than contemplate the filth, she told herself that the sooner she started, the sooner she would be home. She turned and stood on her tiptoes atop the stool to reach the "N" box from five years ago.

"I can do that, Molly."

"It's okay," she mumbled between her teeth as she pulled out the dust-covered box. She knew her functional dress would launder better than his silk shirt and the expensive slacks for his tailor-made suit. "I think it will work better if I find the boxes, since I know where most of them are. I'll hand them to you, then you put the file away and hand the box back to me."

She took his silence for agreement and handed him the first dust-covered box. He opened it, inserted the file, returned it, and Molly slid it back. They continued in silence, slowly working their way down the shelving unit, until they were at the corner next to the stair opening.

Molly slid the stool to the corner, located the next box she needed, and pulled, but it was stuck. She pulled harder, but still it didn't budge.

"Let me try that. I'm taller than you, I can maneuver it easier."

"No," she mumbled between her teeth as she pulled harder, "I think I've got it. It's just—" The aged cardboard ripped. With the release of tension, Molly's whole body jerked backward. The piece of torn cardboard in her hand did nothing to help regain her balance as she flailed her arms. The stool shot out from beneath her feet. Molly toppled backward.

"Molly!" Ken shouted behind her.

His hands touched her back as she tumbled down. They grunted in unison as she thumped against him then crashed into the doorframe together. A sharp bump at the small of her back propelled her slightly forward before she crumpled to the ground at the same time as a sickening crash echoed on the stairs behind her.

Molly tried to scramble to her feet, but her skirt caught on the metal shelving unit. When she tried to push herself up, her shoe slid in the layer of dust, and the pull of the skirt held her in place. She yanked her skirt, not caring about the sound of ripping fabric, and clambered toward the stairs, where Ken lay, arms and legs splayed.

Molly's heart pounded as she wondered if she should try to move him or feel for a pulse.

Before she reached him he moved one arm. He started to push himself up, then groaned and sank down again. She scrambled down three steps, plopped her bottom down on the stair, and helped pull him up by the shoulders until he was in a sitting position, leaning against the metal stair railing. His teeth were tightly clenched and his eyes squeezed shut. All the color drained from his face.

"Ken! Ken! Say something! Are you all right!?"

He clutched his arm tightly and slowly his eyes opened. His words came out slow and strained. "I don't know."

❧

"You did WHAT!?"

Molly lowered her head and buried her face in her hands. The bright and cheerful music from the worship team at the front of the sanctuary did little to lift her sagging spirits. "I said, I nearly killed my boss's favorite relative."

Robbie's hand rested gently on Molly's shoulder while Garrett snickered behind her. She heard a muffled "oomph," and Garrett was silent.

"Come on, Molly," Robbie said in a sympathetic whisper. "What really happened?"

Molly shook her head without removing her hands from her face. "I'm serious. He was helping me put some old files away, and I knocked him down the stairs, and he broke his arm, and it's all my fault. And he was such a nice guy."

"Molly, he's not dead, and I'm sure he still is a nice guy. Bones heal."

"I know he'll heal, but tomorrow morning they're going to fire me. I should wear my pajamas to work, because they're just going to send me right back home again."

Garrett's deep voice sounded from behind Robbie, but Molly couldn't look at him as he spoke. "They won't fire you, it was an accident. Accidents happen, Robbie should know. Right, Robbie?"

"Never mind," Robbie mumbled. Garrett grunted again and stayed silent. Robbie's voice brightened. "The service is about to begin, but we'll pray for you. And him too. What's his name?"

Molly finally looked up at her friends at the exact second the volume of the music lowered. The overhead lights dimmed, and the screen with the music words lit up. The worship leader's voice boomed a welcome to the congregation over the PA system.

"His name is Ken."

❧

Ken squirmed in his seat, barely paying attention. The organist played a somber hymn at a low volume while the minister read a few highlights from the bulletin. His arm still hurt, but at least his wrist wasn't throbbing quite as badly as it was yesterday. He'd awakened yesterday in a daze, waiting for the effects of the bad dream to pass. Instead, reality set in. The pain didn't stop. He really had broken his arm.

Every movement on the hard wooden pew irritated the massive bruise on his back, and the support strap of the sling dug into his neck. Again, he shifted to sit straight to compensate for the unnatural lean to support the weight of the cast.

He peeked to follow from Aunt Ellen's hymnal as they started singing. He certainly wasn't going to make any attempt to hold anything until the swelling in his fingers subsided, which they told him would be about a week. The doctor at the emergency department told him he had been lucky to get away with "only" a broken arm, a slight fracture in his wrist, a few sprained fingers, and a lot of bruising. His shoulder hadn't been dislocated, it was "only" a pulled ligament. He really didn't feel so lucky. He hurt all over.

He still couldn't believe what had happened. This morning wasn't much better than the morning before. The only thing that made all the pain and inconvenience worthwhile was that he'd been able to prevent Molly from falling down the stairs and breaking her neck.

Molly.

Miss Molly McNeil was really something. Uncle Walter had said he had the perfect employee to show him general procedures from the ground up. Of course, he hadn't taken that to literally mean from the bottom of a stairwell. He smiled to himself, then quickly lowered his head. He winced at the kink in his neck and stared at the hymnal before anyone noticed his mind was elsewhere.

He liked Molly. He liked her outspoken spirit, her dedicated work ethic, and the way she carried herself. She was also a believer. Despite her junior position in the corporate structure, she made great efforts to do her best, to know her job, and to pay attention to what went on around her. It made her a valuable asset to the company, at least in his eyes. First impressions were important in the professional world, and every time he'd phoned through from the Winnipeg office he'd thought highly of the way the receptionist handled his calls. Now he'd finally met her in person.

He even liked her fiery red hair. Not that she was his type, but if she wasn't an employee, he might have tried to get to know her better. After Molly had dropped him off at his aunt and uncle's home Friday night following his visit to the hospital, and when Aunt Ellen finished fussing with his injuries, he'd asked about her. Uncle Walter didn't know Molly was a Christian, and therefore had no idea what church she attended, but Ken could plainly see she didn't attend this one. He could have picked her hair out of any crowd from a mile away.

The congregation stood, the movement causing him to focus his thoughts on where they should have been in the first place. However, when the worship time was finished and the congregation bowed their heads, Ken's prayers drifted to Molly McNeil. He asked God to hold her up, because he knew she felt terrible about what had happened.

Despite what he'd already discovered to be a quick tongue, she possessed a kind heart. She'd been very upset while they were at the hospital. A number of times throughout the examination and steps to set the break and fit the cast he thought she was going to cry. He'd tried to assure her it wasn't her fault, but he knew he hadn't convinced her.

He could hardly wait until work tomorrow, when he would see her again. It would be easier to talk to her a few days after the incident occurred and emotions weren't running so rampant.

⁂

Molly deliberately drove extra slow on her way to work. She had only been joking when she told Robbie she would wear her pajamas to work, but she hadn't been joking about the likelihood of getting fired.

When she drove Ken to Mr. Quinlan's home after the hospital, the scene she witnessed showed her that Mr. and Mrs. Quinlan loved Ken like the son they never had. Not much had been said except for fussing over poor Ken, although they'd assured her they knew it was only an accident. But, after the shock wore off of seeing him with his dirty and battered clothes and the cast on his arm she wondered if Mr. Quinlan would have second thoughts.

She buried her face in her hands as she waited for a red light. A million things could have happened. He could have broken his neck and ended up in a wheelchair. Or he could have been killed. For the millionth time, she praised God that compared to the possibilities, he was relatively fine.

Still, it was all her fault. She was responsible. She wanted to make it up to him, but first she had to face him.

A car horn behind her jolted her to attention, and she took off with a screech of rubber.

As she passed a florist, she wondered if maybe she should stop and buy flowers. Men bought flowers for women all the time to express what words could not. However, some things were beyond an apology.

Reluctantly, Molly pulled into her parking space. She dragged her feet all the way in past the front door of the gaping office tower. A couple of the sales staff stood talking in the lobby as she opened the door. Conversation instantly stopped as soon as they noticed her, and they blatantly stared at her.

Molly kept walking.

She continued through the foyer and into the open area of the main office. As soon as people saw her, a collective hush grew.

Molly wished she could melt into the cracks in the floor. She kept her sights focused straight ahead as she walked to her new desk.

"Molly? Could I see you for a minute in private, please?"

Molly cringed. Ken stood in the doorway of Mr. Quinlan's office. He wore a suit, but the left sleeve hung empty. At waist height, his still reddened and puffy fingers stuck out from the white cast beneath the jacket. He smiled, but the effect was completely negated by the dark circles under his eyes.

As she approached, Mr. Quinlan rose and left his office

People started whispering. Molly forced herself to breathe.

She followed Ken inside, and he closed the door. Instead of sitting in Mr. Quinlan's chair, he sat in the same chair he'd sat in on Friday and nodded for her to sit as well.

"Hi, Molly."

"Hi," she choked out. "How are you?" Molly bit her lip at the inaneness of her question.

"I'm okay. It still hurts, of course, but I'll heal. I wanted to assure you that neither myself nor Uncle Walter hold you in any way responsible. It was an accident."

Molly felt her throat tighten. "But it was my fault, and I'm so sorry. I don't know what to say or do, but I've been thinking of you all weekend. I remember when I fell. You pushed me away so I wouldn't tumble down the stairs. That made you fall down instead of me, and look what happened. I don't know how I can ever thank you, or how I can make this up to you."

She gulped, barely able to fight back tears, although she didn't know why it mattered. At this point she had nothing left of her dignity anyway.

∞

Ken forced himself to smile. Molly's recollection of that split second was accurate. He wouldn't have mentioned it, but since she did, she forced him to deal with it. "I don't want your thanks, but I'll tell you what I do want. It seems I'm going to need more help than I originally planned. Instead of just a week, I'd like you to be my personal assistant until I'm out of the cast."

Her face paled. "Me? After what I did to you?"

"It's not your fault, Molly. Really. And yes, you."

Her eyes trailed down to his throbbing fingers, tightly encased in the plaster cast, then back up to his face. He held himself stiffly, avoiding attempting to analyze why it was so important she agreed.

"Of course I'll help. It's the least I can do. If you can trust me."

"If I didn't trust you, I wouldn't have asked."

Her voice trembled. "Thank you."

Ken stood, very pleased with the way things were turning out. "This afternoon I'll have you type up a few letters for me. Normally I would just type them myself on the computer, but I'm obviously not going to be typing for awhile."

Molly stood in front of him. "Yes, well. . ." She looked down at his arm again. The jacket had slipped back on his shoulder, exposing more of the cast, which, due to the nature of the break, encompassed his wrist and extended past his elbow, partway up his upper arm. "At least it's your left arm."

He didn't want to tell her, but he knew it would come up sooner or later. "I'm left handed."

She stared at his swollen and aching fingers, then covered her face with her hands. "Oh, no. . ."

Chapter 3

As she slowly lifted her head, their gazes locked. She blinked rapidly a few times, her lower lip quivered, her eyes became glassy, then watery, and one lone tear slid down her cheek. "I'm so sorry. . . ."

Ken couldn't stop himself. He knew he shouldn't touch her, especially if there was the slightest chance any of the staff could see through the mini-blinds of his uncle's office. But he did it anyway. He lifted his right hand, gently rested his fingertips on her cheek, then brushed the tear away with the pad of his thumb. Another tear soon followed.

Ken felt like he'd just been sucker-punched in the gut. A woman's tears had never affected him like this before, but this time he had no doubt of Molly's sincerity.

"Don't worry, Molly. I'll heal. We can make the best of it."

Molly nodded, stiffened her back, and clasped her hands in front of her. All she wanted was to go to her new desk and begin her new duties, but she had to gain control of herself first. She wanted to trust Ken when he said neither he nor his uncle held her responsible for the accident. But responsibility aside, she was most thankful Ken wasn't seriously hurt.

Briefly, Ken outlined his schedule for the day and gave Molly her instructions. As soon as he was done and she left to begin her new duties, Mr. Quinlan joined Ken inside the office and shut the door.

As she walked to her newly assigned desk, she could feel everyone's eyes on her. Her first impulse was to stand up and yell out that it was an accident and for everyone to mind their own business. However, these people were not only her workmates, some of them were her friends. Also, being a Christian, she wanted to show everyone Christ's love and that she was grateful for the forgiveness offered her, which meant she shouldn't snap at them for their understandable curiosity.

While she doubted Mr. Quinlan had made an announcement about the circumstances concerning poor Ken's broken arm, she knew that in every organization there was always someone who discovered details which should have been considered private. She couldn't figure out who in this case might have found out she'd been the cause, but she could tell everyone knew.

As she worked, Molly purposely kept her head down. Since she made such a point of ignoring everyone around her, they eventually filtered their attention away and carried on with their own business.

Unfortunately, coffee break came too soon. Molly accompanied the usual group of ladies into the lunchroom. The second she sat at the table, she was surrounded.

"How did you do it?"

"What were you really doing up there in the storage room?"

"How mad was he?"

"How come Mr. Quinlan didn't fire you?"

"What's he like?"

Molly plunked her mug down so abruptly that coffee sloshed out.

She buried her face in her hands. "It was an accident," she muttered. She'd already embarrassed herself by crying in front of Ken, but the latest onslaught of questions was again driving her to the verge of tears. She didn't want to cry in front of her workmates too. The situation was bad enough already.

"Come on, you guys, leave her alone. Can't you tell she's upset? How would you feel if you broke the boss's arm?"

Molly peeked through her fingers to see Janice shooing everyone away.

Janice. Whom Molly had resented for awhile yesterday when she thought Janice had stolen her job, even though it wouldn't have been Janice's fault. The force of the guilt was almost overwhelming. She knew there had to be a Bible verse for that somewhere, but she couldn't think of one. Tonight she would ask Robbie, but for now, she wanted to be a good Christian example for Janice. The pastor's sermon yesterday had focused on that exact theme, but she hadn't understood the importance of being a good Christian example. Molly could see she was going to learn a lot on Sunday mornings.

For lack of something more dignified to do with her hands, Molly grasped her coffee mug and blinked away the sting of pending tears. "Thank you, Janice."

Janice simply shrugged her shoulders.

Molly opened her mouth, wanting to share her faith, but she couldn't think of an opening that wouldn't sound forced, and therefore destroy her credibility. Pastor Harry had said the greatest tool in sharing one's faith was friendship. Only then could one earn the right to be heard. So, instead, they chatted amicably until it was time to return to work, with Molly only inserting a few comments about attending church into the conversation.

Before she left the lunchroom, Molly poured herself another coffee, then paused. She knew Ken was a coffee drinker but suspected he didn't want to pour a hot beverage with the wrong hand. She also doubted he would ask a co-worker to do it for him because he didn't know anyone that well. Therefore, Molly selected a spare mug from the cupboard and fixed him a cup exactly the way she remembered from their lunch together and headed in his direction.

She found Ken busy at his computer, pecking at the keyboard with one finger while muttering under his breath. His suit jacket lay draped sloppily across the back of his chair, giving more prominence to the white sling and the reason for his frustration.

When she placed his mug on his desk, he stopped typing and looked up at her. Molly smiled weakly. "I thought maybe you could use this."

Ken's bleak expression caused her hand to tremble as she slowly lowered her own mug to an empty spot on the desk.

"Thanks. I'm glad you're here. This is much harder than I thought it would be."

"I guess you're probably having a hard time typing. Sometimes I try and use one hand to type while I'm eating a sandwich, and it doesn't work very well." She covered her mouth with her hands. "Oops! We're not supposed to eat at the computers. Crumbs and stuff, you know. You won't tell Mr. Quin. . .uh. . .your uncle, will you?"

He grinned, but the smile didn't reach his eyes. "As long as you don't tell when I do it."

Molly smiled back. She had the feeling she was going to like working with him.

Ken leaned back in his chair and ran his fingers through his hair. "Typing is bad enough, but the mouse is driving me nuts."

"The mouse?" Molly picked up his mouse, unlatched the bottom cover, removed the mouseball, and inspected the rollers for dirt. "There's nothing wrong with this mouse."

He sighed again. "It's so awkward with my right hand."

"Working a mouse is easy. How hard could it be, even with the other hand?"

"Have you ever tried to work a mouse with your left hand?"

"Well, no. . ."

Ken shoved the keyboard to the side, picked up the mousepad, and placed it on the left side of the keyboard, stood, and stepped aside. "Be my guest."

Molly tried not to let her mouth hang open. Gone was the softness in his face she'd witnessed a few minutes ago, replaced by tight lines on his brow and the hardening of his lips. He stretched out his free arm with an abrupt movement, signaling her to sit in his chair.

Molly reassembled the mouse and placed it on the mousepad. She sat quickly, before anyone in the office could notice their contest. As requested, she laid her left hand over the offending mouse and began to guide it through the program he had open.

"This isn't hard."

"Open the Brentwood file."

Carefully, Molly aimed the mouse, ran it down the list, and then clicked. Nothing happened. "Oops, I used the wrong button. They seem to be reversed for the wrong hand." Just as the words left her mouth, she squeezed her eyes shut. "I didn't mean the wrong hand. I meant the left hand."

Her comment was met with silence.

She slid the mouse to the list again, but the arrow went in the wrong direction.

"Oops."

Working very slowly, she guided the mouse to the correct entry and tried to stop it from wiggling when she used her ring finger instead of her index finger to click with the left mouse button.

Finally it worked.

"Now open their financial file."

She didn't know if she wanted to go through it again. "I think you've proved your point. I'm sorry, Ken. I really haven't thought about how right handed the world is. The keyboard even has the calculator part on the right side. I'll bet back home you have one of those ones that splits, and you can move it to the left, don't you?"

"Yes, I do. I've ordered a new one, but it hasn't come yet. Not that there's a rush now. I won't be able to use it for eight weeks."

Molly cringed. At that moment she made up her mind to attempt some basic tasks using her left hand, just so she'd remember how difficult this was going to be for him. She didn't know much about stuff designed for lefties, but she did know specialty scissors and baseball mitts were twice the price of the regular ones. Of course that didn't matter for now. He couldn't use his left hand if he wanted to.

"Would you mind entering this information and then checking the spread-sheet for me?"

Molly nodded. She normally didn't like someone looking over her shoulder when she worked, but in this case, she had to grin and bear it. If the situation were reversed, she didn't know if she would have been so gracious.

From the first moment she met Ken, she couldn't help but like him. He was soft-spoken, yet that didn't take away from his obvious authority. She'd never met anyone like him and wondered if he was like this because of his Christian upbringing.

She knew only two people who were raised in a Christian home, her friend Gwen and Gwen's brother Garrett, whom she'd been seeing much more often lately since Garrett married her best friend, Robbie. She'd never thought about how kind to others they both were as adults, because she grew up with them. For them, that behavior was normal. Likewise, it seemed normal for Ken. If this was typically the way a person who was raised in a Christian home behaved, she wanted to know more.

She switched the mouse back to the right side to finish Ken's task, then returned to her own desk.

She had just started her own work when Ken's voice beside her made her jump.

"Are you busy for lunch?"

Molly's fingers froze midsentence. Work and conversation around them stopped.

The library book she was supposed to return on Friday was still in her car, and the outfit she had at the drycleaners and her photographs were still waiting to be picked up. The list of supplies she needed from the stationery store was still tucked inside her purse, and now she was late paying her phone bill. But it wasn't Ken's fault she'd spent all weekend fretting about what happened instead of doing what she was supposed to.

Molly lowered her hands from the keyboard to the desktop and turned toward Ken. She didn't know what he wanted to talk about, but it apparently was something he didn't want to discuss with the rest of the office watching—and they were definitely watching.

Her errands would have to wait until evening. "I guess not," she mumbled

He smiled, and she immediately knew she'd done the right thing. "Great. Where should we go?"

With Molly sitting in the chair as Ken stood beside her, his poor swollen fingers were directly at eye level, reminding her that everything he did, including eating, had to be accomplished with one hand. Unless she was also expected to cut up his food, their choices were limited. She doubted he would be able to eat a sloppy burger with one hand, and there was a great Chinese place around the corner, but she didn't think he'd be able to manage chopsticks with the wrong hand. She could barely manage them with her right one.

"Why don't we go to the same place as last time? They have great ravioli."

"Sure. Let's go now and beat the rush."

Beating the rush was never an option before, but being the boss's relative gave one privileges that lowly office staff like her could only dream of. Molly hit save and stood. "I guess we should probably drive this time. I'll go bring the car out front for you."

"No, I'd like to drive this time. I obviously didn't get out to buy a car on the weekend, but Uncle Walter offered to loan me his car any time I need it. Let's go now."

Without a word, and feeling the stares of everyone in the office as they left together, Molly followed Ken to the underground parking. She shouldn't have been surprised that he had Mr. Quinlan's keys in his pocket.

Slowly, he backed the large car out of the narrow stall. Molly didn't like big cars, which was why she owned a small economy import. She wondered what kind of car Ken had, which then made her wonder if he had sold it, because he had just mentioned that he was going to buy a car when he had more time. That made her wonder how long he intended to stay in Vancouver. Rumor had it that this was a permanent move. Ken buying a car versus renting one would prove the rumor true.

The electric window on her side of the car rolled down. "Molly? Is something wrong? You can get in now."

"Oops," she muttered as she scrambled into the car and fastened her seatbelt.

"You'll have to give me directions. I remember how we got there when we walked, but I obviously can't take the car through the short cuts."

Molly pointed to the right. "Two blocks that way, then one block left. You said you were going to buy a car. Wouldn't it have been better to have your car shipped, or have someone drive it out for you?"

He shook his head. "Someone I knew wanted to buy my car, so I thought I would just do that." He grinned. "I'm anticipating not having to plug my car and still have it start."

Molly stared at him while they waited for the red light. "Plug it in? I didn't know they made electric cars for everyday use."

He shook his head and turned into the parking lot. "No, it's not an electric car, but it is winterized for the harsh prairie winter climate. It's got a block heater and an interior warmer, so I can get in a nice warm car after it's been sitting outside all day and it's twenty below outside."

"I can't imagine that," she mumbled. Still, the bottom line was that he had intended to buy a car over the weekend. Molly suspected the reason he hadn't was because of his inability to sign the registration papers or the other legal forms for transferring his driver's license.

"I was also going to look around for a house once I got here too, but we decided to put my stuff in storage for a little while. Uncle Walter and Aunt Ellen insisted I stay with them until I'm out of the cast."

Molly cringed. Something else that was her fault.

Once they were seated and their orders had been taken, Ken's expression turned serious. "I'm afraid we're going to have to discuss business. I was tied up all morning, and I have a big meeting first thing this afternoon, so this is all the free time I had. I hope you don't mind."

She was quickly coming to understand how Ken was moving rapidly up the corporate ladder. Even temporarily handicapped, he still carried himself in a style that left no question as to his authority, despite his age. His manners were impeccable, his words gentle but firm. He left no question of who was in charge.

"Tell me about Trevor Chapman. So far all I've learned is from his corporate file, the status of their account, their needs, but nothing about what the man is like to do business with, his preferences and concerns. As receptionist, you spoke frequently to all our clients, big and small, including Mr. Chapman."

Now she was starting to realize why she had been chosen to assist him. Not that she had been involved in sales, but she did have a lot of contact with all their business associates, even if it wasn't for the specialized dealings of day to day operations.

As best she could, she told him about Trevor Chapman, how everyone always jumped through hoops for him, that he expected everything immediately if not sooner, and was rather impatient if things didn't happen the way he wanted. She also knew Trevor Chapman was allergic to his granddaughter's new Pekinese puppy, whom the little girl had thoughtfully named Missykins.

Ken stared blankly at Molly. He didn't know much about Trevor Chapman, but he did know the man traveled only in very small and elite circles. "You know him personally?"

Molly laughed and waved one hand in front of her mouth as she finished her bite. "Of course not. I chat with people when they're on hold and I don't have another call coming in."

Ken studied Molly. Chatting was one thing, but he failed to see how a business client's granddaughter's puppy and his medical history could possibly enter a conversation.

"You know, someone really ought to change that music over the phone line when people are put on hold. It's really bad."

Ken had never paid attention to the music. He tended to ignore it and worked on something else while he waited.

She didn't wait for his response before she started talking again. "I have a friend who's got a great collection of Christian CDs. It sure would be nice if we could put one of those on instead of that elevator music. But I guess we can't do that, can we?"

He raised one eyebrow but said nothing. Molly's face reddened, which Ken thought quite amusing.

"Oops. It was only a suggestion. Forget it. It probably wouldn't work."

He'd never even remotely considered putting Christian music over the company telephone system. He made a mental note to discuss the idea with his uncle.

"Since you've been a Christian since you were a little kid, I'll bet you've got a great CD collection too, don't you?"

He was beginning to wonder when he was going to get a chance to speak. "Most of my CDs are packed in a box in storage. But you're welcome to go through the few I brought. They're in a box at my uncle Walter's house."

"I still have a box I haven't unpacked, and I've been in my apartment for three years."

Ken shook his head. He thought they were going to talk about Trevor Chapman's company, but he'd obviously been wrong, although he wasn't quite sure what they had talked about.

Soon they were back in the car and on their way. He turned south and checked the dashboard clock. They had plenty of time.

"Ken? Where are you going?"

Fortunately, Ken had a good memory for numbers. He'd memorized the address before they left for lunch. "I already told you. We have a meeting with Trevor Chapman and his associates."

Molly's face paled. "We?"

Chapter 4

Molly remained silent, staring out the window for the rest of the drive to the highrise office tower in the middle of Vancouver's downtown core, where the meeting would be held.

Ken had been to Vancouver before, and like the last time, he was in complete awe of the height and majesty of the unique buildings. However, he was not here to be a tourist. He had things to do and people to meet.

While he circled around the underground parking facility searching for a parking spot, Molly's grumbling about small cars and big cities gave him cause to rethink his choice when it came time to buy his own car. He finally found a spot on the opposite side of the lot from the elevator. He pocketed the keys, wiggled one arm into the sleeve of his suit jacket, draped the other side as best he could over his left shoulder, and they started walking through the lot.

"You never told me I'd be going to a big meeting today. Look at what I'm wearing!"

As they walked, Ken analyzed what she deemed inappropriate. She wore a black blouse accompanied by a loose green skirt, along with shoes the exact same shade as the skirt. Compared to her vivid hair, her outfit was subtle and controlled, and he liked it. He didn't know if Molly had done it on purpose, but the skirt and shoes were the exact color of her eyes. Wide, gorgeous eyes. Laughing eyes, eyes that hid nothing, a gateway to her soul. Eyes a man could get lost in, perhaps for a lifetime.

Ken cleared his throat, lifted his free hand to his tie, wiggled it, then let his hand drop. "You look nice."

He opened the door to the area containing the stairwell and elevator, and Molly pushed the button for the elevator. The light indicated the elevator was on the way down.

"I don't do shorthand or anything like that. I don't know why you need me to come with you."

His experienced secretary back in the Winnipeg office hadn't done shorthand either. He was almost positive that such a skill was a lost art. "I know you don't. I just need someone to take notes for me."

Molly opened her mouth, but no words came out. Instead, her gaze dropped to his fingers sticking out from the confines of the cast. All the sparkle left her eyes. He had tried his best to be gentle with his words, but facts were facts. He couldn't write.

"This is a really important meeting, isn't it?"

He nodded and felt the knot of his tie again. Not only was it their largest client, Trevor Chapman was a powerful influence in the business community, and his recommendation would go far to obtain new clients or shake up current ones. This was also Ken's first time representing Quinlan Enterprises in his new capacity, even though it hadn't become official yet. Uncle Walter had decided they would wait until he was out of the cast before making the official announcement, and Ken agreed heartily with that decision.

The chime sounded, indicating the elevator had arrived. After a few people exited, Ken waited for Molly to precede him. Instead, she waited for him to go first.

Automatically, he began to move his left arm to gesture to Molly to go first, but the weight of the cast and twinge in his shoulder caused him to wince. He suspected he would find it difficult to use his right hand instead of his left to make gestures that were previously automatic. He could also foresee that when this whole thing was over, he would be doing a lot less talking with his hands.

Molly finally started to step forward, but since they took so long to move, the door started to close. Before he thought to use his right arm, Molly beat him to it, gave the door a push, and held it open for him.

Ken stiffened. He was still old-fashioned enough to hold a door open for a lady. It felt wrong for a lady to hold the elevator open for him.

Once inside, she released the door and let it close. He carefully aimed one finger at the button for the top floor and pushed. He didn't get it dead center, but he did hit the correct button. As a leftie, he generally found he was more adept at using his right hand for such things than righties were at using their left. He found it both amusing and annoying to discover, one incident at a time, what he was good at and when he struggled. Fortunately left-handed people were more adept at using their right hand than right-handed people were at using their left. He suspected that tendency would be the only thing to save him in the eight weeks to come.

After the elevator started to rise, Molly turned to him. "Your tie is crooked. I didn't want to say anything in front of anyone."

Ken smiled. He couldn't tell if it was straight without using both hands and admired Molly's discretion. He started to raise his free hand to do the best he could to fix it under the circumstances but stopped when Molly spoke.

"Let me do it for you. It looked like it bugged you earlier. You'll never get it straight by yourself with only one. . . Uh, I mean, without a mirror."

Molly stepped exactly in front of him and raised her hands. Ken drew in a deep breath, then forced himself to relax when she touched him. This morning Aunt Ellen had helped him with his tie, but it didn't feel like this. Molly's gentle touch seemed personal, even though he knew that wasn't her intent. He looked down, willing her to make eye contact, but instead, all her concentration remained fixed on his tie. She diligently gave it a gentle tug, wiggled it with both hands, then gave it a pat. He tried to blame the odd sensation in his chest to the motion of the elevator.

"There you go." She stepped back as a ringing telephone broke the silence. "You'd better answer your cell phone."

"I don't have my cell phone with me. I still have to obtain a local number and get it connected."

They both turned to stare at the closed compartment containing the emergency telephone. A second ring confirmed their suspicions.

Ken scrinched his eyebrows. "I've never heard one of those things ring before. How about that?"

Molly nodded. "Me neither. What do you think we should do?"

"Do? Nothing."

Molly glanced from side to side, then pulled the small door open. "I have to answer it. What if it's an emergency?"

"That's impossible. That phone is meant to be used for people who might be trapped in the elevator to call out, not for anyone to call in."

"Well, maybe there's something wrong at the top, and someone has to tell us something."

"I don't think so. I think—"

"Hello?"

Ken cringed. She'd actually answered it.

She laughed. "No, you've got the wrong number. There's no one here by that name."

He sighed, waiting for her to hang up, but instead she shook her head and touched her finger to the body of the phone.

"You've got the wrong number. I mean yes, that's the number you dialed, but you won't believe this. The number you called is inside an elevator."

Molly laughed and nodded. "Yes, I'm very serious."

The elevator continued to rise. Ken looked up to the number display above the door. They were halfway to the top floor. "Say good-bye and hang up, Molly," he said quietly.

She shook her head at him while she continued to listen to the caller. Fortunately the elevator was still moving upward. Chatting with a client on the office phone was one thing, but he couldn't believe she'd answered the phone in a moving elevator.

"Yeah, this is the main elevator in the Stevens Building downtown. You know, the big brown building with the row of blue windows all the way up the side. The one beside the big trees where they had that newscast show in the spring, where they had that segment on the baby birds that hatched in the middle of busy downtown. Remember, they ran a contest to name the baby birds."

Ken was beginning to see how Molly had learned about their best client's personal life and medical history. "Molly. Please. Hang up," he ground out between his teeth.

"No, I never did hear who won the contest. Only it wasn't me."

The elevator slowed. "Molly. . .hang up that phone. . ."

"Really? I think those are cute names. You should have won."

The door opened. A woman and two men stepped forward, but they skidded to a halt just short of the entrance to the elevator.

Molly laughed. "You're kidding. That's really funny!"

The three people nervously glanced between each other, backed up a step, and the elevator door closed without anyone getting in. The elevator resumed its journey upward.

Ken glared at Molly without saying a word.

"Oops. I think I'd better go. I'm almost at my floor. Bye." She fumbled the phone as she hung up and slammed the small door closed. "Uh, it was a wrong number."

Before he could gather his thoughts, the elevator once again slowed. The doors opened to the top floor. "I can't believe you did that."

"Don't tell me you can ignore a ringing phone!"

"If it's not my phone, yes, I can."

Molly harumphed and stomped out. "Well, I can't. Which way are we going?" She stopped short, coming to a halt so quickly Ken nearly bumped into her from behind.

Between the off-center weight of the cast and the inability to move his left arm, he couldn't regain his balance, forcing him to steady himself against the wall. He hoped no one had seen him swaying like a drunk. As he regained his balance and raised his head, Molly was staring at him.

"Ken? Are you all right? Do you want me to take you back to the office so you can lie down or something?"

Ken felt his ears heat up. "I'm fine. We're going to 2510. According to the sign, it's to the right."

⁂

They were welcomed into Trevor Chapman's large office, where they were seated in a couple of the large chairs arranged in a half circle in front of his desk. The door opened, and three more people entered.

It was the three people who hadn't entered the elevator.

Molly cringed, then did her best to smile when they were introduced.

She'd embarrassed Ken. She hadn't meant to, but as usual, she hadn't thought before she acted, and again she was sorry. Molly made up her mind to sit and be completely quiet and to not speak unless spoken to.

With that thought firmly in place, the meeting progressed well. Ken gave her a small notepad he'd had in his suit pocket, and she soon had pages and pages of notes. At the conclusion of the meeting, the other people left first. As she and Ken stood, Mr. Chapman shuffled a few objects on his desk, one of them a picture of a darling little girl holding a puppy.

Mr. Chapman beamed when Ken picked up the framed photograph to admire it. "That's my granddaughter and her new puppy."

Molly peeked over Ken's shoulder. "Oh! So that's Missykins! What a darling little dog." Sheepishly, Molly raised her eyes. "Your granddaughter is cute too."

Mr. Chapman smiled like a typical proud grandpa.

"You know, I'd bet you'd like the dog better if you could get close to her without breaking out into a rash," Molly offered. "I once knew someone who was seriously allergic to dogs and cats, and he bought some over-the-counter stuff that really helped. I could phone and ask him what it was."

"It was a nonprescription remedy?"

Molly nodded. "Yes, it was. It will really help if she bathes the dog before you get near it and keeps it well brushed. Did you know more people are allergic to cats than to dogs? It's not the hair that's the allergen—it's the dander."

Out of the corner of her eye, she saw Ken squeeze his eyes shut then make a very halfhearted smile. She tried to keep smiling. Judging from his reaction, she'd embarrassed him again.

"Thank you, Miss McNeil. I'd appreciate that."

Molly pointedly checked her wristwatch. "I guess we'd better go. It was nice finally meeting you after speaking to you so often."

He simply nodded, they exchanged handshakes, and Molly and Ken left.

The second they were seated inside the car, Molly could no longer hold back. "I'm so sorry, Ken. I didn't mean to embarrass you. But you should hear him talk about his granddaughter. I know he would love to share her joy in the puppy, but he just can't get near it without feeling the effects for days. And he—"

"It's okay, Molly. You don't have to explain."

"But. . ." At the touch of his warm hand on top of her fingers, Molly let her voice trail off.

"Don't worry about it. Everything went just fine." He started the car.

Ken retraced their route back to the office. She noticed he got a little mixed up with some of the one-way streets, but she decided not to say anything, until he got really lost. Therefore, Molly spent the trip gazing out the window, studying the tall buildings, and commenting on some of the landmarks they passed, negating the need for a real conversation.

❦

Ken tried not to appear too relieved when he finally made it to the Granville Bridge. He could tell a few times she'd nearly corrected him when he turned down what he later found to be the wrong street. The restraint surprised him. In the short time since they met, he'd discovered that Molly didn't mince words. The first thing she thought was what came out of her mouth, which should have been a detriment. Oddly, he found the trait rather appealing, even though at times he feared what she might say next. She was as bold as her hair, and as difficult to blend into what should have been a dignified setting. Even when her comments and observations had no connection with the current conversation, she still managed to charm everyone around her. Himself included.

Ken smiled. She wasn't his type in the slightest. Bold, brassy, and once she got started, she talked a mile a minute. He preferred to stay in the background until he analyzed all components of a situation.

But he liked her anyway. He liked her too much. He'd felt a stab of something he didn't want to think about when she mentioned the male friend with the animal allergies. It gave him great satisfaction when she left the impression she no longer associated with the man. He didn't want to think of why it was important.

Chapter 5

Molly gave the dry cleaner's plastic wrapper one hefty shove into the garbage container and let the lid slam shut as she ran to catch the ringing phone.

"Hi, Molly. It's Ken. I was wondering if you were busy."

She glanced at the time. Resigned to the fact that it might be days before she could do her errands at lunchtime, she had done everything right after work, and because of that, in addition to the need to do some serious housecleaning, she hadn't eaten dinner yet.

The only reason she could think of why Ken would call her at home would be because he couldn't read the notes she made at the meeting, although she'd tried extra hard to make them legible. She didn't want to think that she'd be putting in endless hours of unpaid overtime during her allotted time as his assistant, but the guilt that his predicament was her fault nagged her. She didn't mind spending some extra time with him, but she was starving.

"Yes, actually. I was a little busy. . . ." She let her voice trail off.

"Oh."

Molly's heart fluttered. He sounded disappointed. "Why do you ask?"

"I was hoping you hadn't eaten yet and could join me for dinner."

Molly glanced at the freezer, where her frozen meal was still stored. She hadn't even turned the oven on yet. She ran one hand down her faded T-shirt and looked down to her ratty jeans with a hole in one knee. "I haven't had dinner yet either, but I'm not dressed for going out. So, sorry, not this time. But you're welcome to come over later."

"How about if we order in? All you have to do is give me your address and the directions. Just remember to talk very slowly."

Molly cringed. She couldn't imagine trying to write with the wrong hand, but when she heard him typing as she gave him directions, she smiled. When she was done with the instructions, she heard him hit the print button.

As soon as she hung up, her first impulse was to change into something more presentable, but she didn't have time. Instead of changing her clothes, she ran her brush quickly through her hair, then did a mad scramble to tidy up her apartment, which included folding her futon back into the couch, stuffing some of the clutter into her armoire, and kicking the rest under the couch.

She had just placed the last dirty glass into the dishwasher when the buzzer sounded. Ken arrived at her door with a large bag in his hand, but no briefcase.

He was still wearing his suit, minus the tie. Inwardly, she cringed, wishing she had taken the few minutes to change, at least into jeans that didn't have a hole in the knee.

"You brought Chinese food? I was expecting we were going to order pizza. How are you going to eat that?"

He smiled, showing tiny crinkles at the corners of his eyes, making Molly almost forget about how hungry she was. Now that he was here, she was relieved he'd shown up with their dinner in his hand, rather than having to wait even longer for something to be delivered.

"You don't have to eat Chinese food with chopsticks, Molly. You're allowed to use a fork. Honest."

She tried to fight it, but Molly couldn't stop a blush from creeping into her cheeks. "Come in," she mumbled as she backed up, allowing him access.

"Nice apartment. Which way is the kitchen?"

She backed up one more step. Her home was a small bachelor suite consisting of one big room—the status of which depended on whether she had her futon opened into a bed or folded into a couch—plus a kitchen and a bathroom. "Over here." Molly pointed to her right. She could only imagine what Ken thought of her apartment in comparison to Mr. Quinlan's house, which she had seen when she drove Ken home from the hospital. Her entire apartment could fit into the Quinlans' living room.

She'd already set the table, so after a short prayer of thanks, they quickly dug into the food.

"Have you lived in Vancouver all your life? Tell me some of the interesting things to see and do here. You've already mentioned Science World."

Molly smiled. Tourists.

"They built it for Expo '86, but now the SkyTrain is part of the local transit system, as is the SeaBus. I haven't used either one a lot except for showing visitors around town, but it's quite an experience, especially if you've never been on a monorail before."

"I've seen it going down the track on Terminal Avenue."

"I often take out-of-town friends and relatives to either Science World or the Lonsdale Quay, which is a massive marketplace, or sometimes to the IMax Theater and Gastown on the weekend. It's a lot of fun. You can park at the Park-N-Ride, then get a one-day transit pass."

"That sounds like a nice idea. I'd like that. Is it best to go in the morning or afternoon?"

"In the morning, definitely."

"Great. Should I pick you up, or do you want to pick me up?"

Molly opened her mouth, about to tell him all about how they'd expanded the system since it had originally been constructed, but the words caught in her throat. She hadn't been meant to issue him a personal invitation, but if he'd taken it that way, she didn't want to hurt his feelings. "Are you sure you want to go to a market and go riding around town?" she asked, but what she really wanted to ask, and didn't, was if he really wanted to see her on the weekend after being with her all week long.

"That sounds like a good introduction to living here." He smiled again, and she wondered if he knew she couldn't say no to him when he kept looking at her like that.

"Don't your aunt and uncle want to show you around?"

His smile never faded, and she could have sworn his eyes twinkled. "I'd rather go with you."

Molly forced herself to smile back. "Uh. . .okay. . . ." She stood and fumbled with the dirty dishes and piled them into the sink. "I guess we should go over those notes now."

Ken's smile dropped, and he blinked. "Notes?"

"You know, the notes from the meeting this afternoon."

"The notes were very comprehensive. Did you miss something? I didn't think you'd want to see them again. I left them at the office. We could go over them tomorrow if you want."

Molly stared openly at him. If he hadn't come to work, she didn't know why he came. They hadn't talked any business so far, and it didn't appear they were going to.

"Besides your aunt and uncle, you don't know anybody in Vancouver, do you?"

"A few people. Why?"

Molly continued to stare at Ken as she tried to figure out what was going through his mind.

"Would you mind if we moved to the couch? After sitting up in stiff office chairs all day with the weight of this cast, my back is killing me."

Rather than sit in silence, Molly turned on the television. Ken parked himself on one end of the futon, and she sat at the other. After an extended silence, the only sound in the room being some pathetic attempt at a new sitcom, Ken turned to face her.

"If you're tired, maybe I should leave."

Molly checked her watch. It was still early. "I'm not tired." She rubbed her fingers under her eyes, hoping she didn't have dark circles. "Why do you think I'm tired?"

His answering grin quickened Molly's pulse. "You've been so quiet. I was beginning to wonder if something was wrong."

Nothing was wrong. She was still trying to figure out what he was doing there, but she couldn't simply ask him. In the back of her mind, she thought the answer might be that he simply wanted to be with her. The idea both flattered and terrified her.

She stared at him as he stared back at her. "There is something I wanted to ask you."

A smile lit his face. "Ask away."

Her Bible sat where she'd left it on the coffee table, stuffed full of every scrap of paper she could find. She leaned forward and flipped through her many markers and opened her Bible wide open. "Right here, there's a couple of verses that I don't understand, and I'll bet you could explain them to me."

Ken's smile dropped. He cleared his throat, and his hand rose to where his tie would have been, had he been wearing one. His fingers splayed, patting the vacant spot, and his hand fell. "I'd be happy to help, if I can."

Slowly, Molly worked her way through all her markings and notes, stopping only briefly to bring in a snack of cookies and milk. Ken managed to answer all her questions in a manner she understood. By the time they worked through everything, Molly appeared to be reeling with information overload.

Ken watched Molly as she closed her Bible and returned it to the coffee table beside the pile of scrap papers she'd used instead of bookmarks. While not the reason he'd come, their time had been. . .productive. But at least he'd accomplished one step in the right direction. She'd committed herself to spending a day with him. He'd taken the chance and overstepped his boundaries by fishing for an invitation, something he'd never done before. Molly had been properly polite, even though she'd been less than enthusiastic, and agreed to accompany him, for which he was tremendously relieved.

"I didn't mean to stay so late. It's nearly midnight, and we both have to get up for work in the morning."

She accompanied him to the door, where they stood staring at each other.

"Thanks for the invitation."

Her curious frown changed into a sly smile, the change making Ken correct his posture and want to stand closer to her. "I think you invited yourself."

He smiled back. He'd never met someone who so openly spoke the first thing that ran through their mind. "That's true. But you graciously took me up on it. Thank you."

Her face reddened. "Well, thank you for bringing supper. I was starving, and that was really good. Sure beat the frozen dinner I was going to have."

The last thing Ken wanted to do was stand at the door throwing thank you's back and forth like a couple of spastic parrots. What he wanted to do was. . . kiss her.

His gaze dropped to her mouth, and then he hastily returned his attention to her eyes. He liked Molly. She was different than anyone he'd ever met. She was honest and refreshing and a new believer. Unfortunately, she was also an employee. With her penchant for speaking her immediate thoughts, he could only imagine what would come out of her mouth if he did what he wanted to do or gave her any indication of what he was thinking.

He opened the door. "See you tomorrow. Good night, Molly."

Ken raised his hand, about to pound his fist on the desk, then lowered it to his lap before anyone noticed. The novelty of having to do everything with the wrong hand was quickly wearing off and, unfortunately, so was the empathy people gave him, and likewise, offers of assistance.

At first he'd refused to allow his aunt to help him get dressed, but by the time he'd finally managed to at least cover all the essentials, she'd still had to do up his shirt buttons. Uncle Walter had to tie all his ties so he could simply slip them over his head. He didn't care about not looking completely professional, and he preferred not to wear a belt with his suit than have anyone help him with that.

He'd cut himself shaving with the wrong hand, so he resigned himself to borrowing his uncle's electric shaver, even though it didn't give as close a shave as a razor. He was sure he'd missed a few spots, but he was running so late he'd let it go. Not only did he not want to be late himself, but because he had to depend on Uncle Walter for a ride, he nearly made his uncle late too. Again, Aunt Ellen had offered her car, but he didn't want to leave her stuck at home all day just because he couldn't make it out the door on time.

Briefly, Ken considered growing a beard and wearing sweatpants and a T-shirt to work. This evening he would have to go shopping, because he owned only two shirts with sleeves wide enough to fit over the cast.

The doctor had predicted that in a week he would probably regain partial use of his fingers. Their mobility would be severely hampered by the piece of cast separating his thumb, but at least he'd be able to do simple things like gel his hair himself. He felt like a little kid when Aunt Ellen gelled his hair for him. After she'd finished, it then occurred to him he could have squeezed some gel straight onto his brush with the one hand he could still use and done it that way.

He sat and stared blankly at his computer screen. The screen saver came on.

"Ken? Do you need some help?"

He turned his head and looked up. Molly stood beside him, her brows knotted as she studied him.

It wasn't her fault he couldn't aim the disk into the narrow slot on his computer properly the first time, or that he couldn't hold a pen yet. "No, thank you. This is something I have to do myself."

She shrugged her shoulders. "Suit yourself. I'm going for coffee break. Want me to bring something back for you?"

Ken stared at the pile of papers that littered his desk. He'd been struggling all day and worked through lunch to meet a deadline. He wasn't quite done, and he was tired and frustrated. Despite the satisfaction it would have given him to swipe the growing stacks of paperwork into the garbage can, he neatly pushed them to the side and stood. "I think I'll go with you."

They'd almost made it to the lunchroom, when Ken thought he'd better make a detour into the washroom. The over-consumption of coffee was catching up with him, and with his limited mobility, he didn't want to embarrass himself. He swallowed his pride and asked Molly to pour his coffee for him and told her he would join her in a few minutes.

When he finally arrived at the lunchroom, Molly was sitting at a table and talking with Janice, the woman who had been temporarily assigned Molly's job as receptionist. In the two days since the switch, while Janice was doing an adequate job, he'd already heard comments that both staff and clients had missed Molly's bubbly voice on the phone.

A full cup of coffee sat waiting for him on the table at Molly's elbow. As he approached, he couldn't help but overhear their conversation.

"Really? I've never been to church in my life. I wouldn't know what to do."

Molly smiled, causing Ken to smile as well as he continued to listen, even though he hadn't intended to eavesdrop.

"I know what you mean. I've only been twice, but it's great. Already I've learned so much."

Upon his arrival, conversation stopped.

Janice stood. "I think it's time for me to get back to work. I'll talk to you later, Molly."

Ken nodded as Janice left, then sat in the chair she vacated.

Guilt roared through him. Molly had been a Christian for less than two weeks, and she was already witnessing to an unbeliever. He couldn't remember the last time he shared his faith outside a church setting. He tended to do his Christian service in activities amongst those already saved, or at least among those with whom most of the battle had been won and they had already ventured within the church doors.

"I was beginning to wonder if you changed your mind and went back to work."

His face flamed. The convenience of wearing sweatpants to the office was becoming less of a distant possibility. Rather than reply, he sipped the coffee.

All he could think of was Molly's efforts to speak of Christianity to Janice. If this was the typical way a new Christian behaved, with this refreshing enthusiasm and vigor, he wanted to watch her.

He'd been once to his uncle's church and knew the main core of the congregation was made up of older and well-grounded Christians. Since Molly still had lots of questions, if he could bring her to a weekly Bible study, it could serve two purposes. Molly would receive instant answers to her questions in a learned and experienced atmosphere, and secondly, some of the enthusiasm of her new faith would rub off on him.

Ken smiled into his cup, hoping Molly hadn't noticed. There was also a third reason. He simply wanted to be with Molly outside of the office.

For lack of something to do with the one hand he could move, Ken wrapped his fingers around his cup and smiled up at Molly. "I have a question for you. Will you accompany me to Bible study tomorrow night?"

Chapter 6

Molly scrambled to tidy up the kitchen after her rushed supper, pending Ken's arrival. Of all the things she thought he might say during coffee break, inviting her to attend a Bible study meeting with him would never have occurred to her. She nearly dropped her plate on the way to the dishwasher as she remembered his reaction when she asked him why he had asked. His face had flushed and his ears had turned red. Again, she'd spoken before she thought of what she was saying, and by doing so, she'd embarrassed both of them. She grinned as she tucked her glass in the rack. Ken was kind of cute when he blushed, although he never did answer her question.

Her smile dropped as she continued to wonder why Ken would invite her to his church's midweek Bible study. She suspected that it was because he didn't know anyone yet, yet she didn't see him as the type to be shy at a first meeting. He certainly wasn't shy with her.

When the buzzer sounded, Molly was ready. Just as the last time she saw him outside of work, tonight she wore jeans, only this time they were hemmed and didn't have any holes. Instead of a T-shirt with a cartoon character in vivid color on the front, she had chosen a sedate long-sleeved blouse. She'd even fastened her hair back with a clip for some semblance of dignity and control. Tonight she would be quiet and sedate. This time she wouldn't do anything to embarrass Ken, especially in front of the people who would be his Christian family at his new church.

She stood at the door and opened it as soon as she heard the swoosh of the elevator doors. At the sight of Ken approaching, Molly nearly fainted. Instead of the prim and proper custom-tailored suits she'd become accustomed to seeing him wear, he now wore a nylon jogging outfit with a jacket made of the same fabric as the pants, and a matching T-shirt. The only thing that didn't quite match was that instead of sneakers, he wore leather shoes.

"I'm ready," she stammered.

"I've got some good news and some bad news."

Her heart began to pound. Her first thought was that he'd had an accident with his uncle's car. She couldn't think of any good news. "Tell me the bad news first."

"The people who host the Bible study came down with the flu, so it's canceled for tonight."

"Oh." She wondered why he hadn't phoned to say so. She'd also been invited to another Bible study by her friend Robbie. If Ken had phoned, she could have taken him there. Now it was too late, because it had already started.

"But the good news is that the evening is now open, so you and I can do anything we want. We can have a Bible study with just the two of us. Or if you'd rather go out, we can catch a show or something."

A door down the hall opened and one of her neighbors stepped out, fiddled with the lock, then very slowly headed for the elevator. Molly didn't feel like having her nosy neighbor listen in on their plans for the evening.

"Come in, and we'll decide on something."

He entered her apartment very quickly and pushed the door closed behind him, making Molly suspect his preference was for an invitation. Thankfully she'd folded up her futon, just in case he came in for coffee after their Bible study was over.

"I have a few more markers in my Bible for some stuff I was going to ask tonight. I guess I can ask you instead. I'll make a pot of coffee."

He shook his head. "If you want coffee, that's fine, but none for me. I'm trying to cut down."

"Then I'll make tea instead. I'll be right back. Have a seat."

When she returned, he had already opened her Bible to the first marker, but instead of sitting on the end of the futon like last time, he parked himself in the middle. He patted the spot beside him. "Shall we pray before we start?"

Molly nodded and slowly lowered herself beside him.

"Have you ever been to an organized Bible study?"

Molly shook her head. Ken nodded and smiled. Adorable crinkles appeared in the corners of his eyes. The warmth of his smile did strange things to her stomach.

"What usually happens is everyone sits around and chats, and when things are ready to start, the leader will ask if there are any prayer requests or praise items."

Molly stared blankly at him. She had no idea what he was talking about.

"Sorry. Let me rephrase that. Generally, everyone is asked if they have anything to tell the group. Something they would like the group to pray for, either for themselves or a special friend or family. Or, if there is something that was prayed about at a previous meeting and came to pass or just something happened where God blessed them, they might want to tell the group about it. If something concerns them, whether it be personal, or a world issue, like war or a natural disaster, or something they feel strongly about that they would like the group to pray about. Or even someone they know who is having difficulty and they feel led to pray about it."

"Oh."

"Often one person in the group will write those things down, but not always. It depends on the group."

"You're kidding. Like a journal?"

He nodded. "Exactly. It's called a prayer journal. Some people keep them for their own personal prayers too."

"Wow. I don't think I could be organized enough to do that."

"Not everyone does that. I don't."

In a way, she found that difficult to believe.

"And then we pray. Sometimes the group will take turns, sometimes the leader will briefly summarize everything that was mentioned. Again, it depends on the group."

"But that sounds so. . .organized."

"Organization is not a bad thing, Molly."

She recalled the socks and odd shoes hidden under the futon. "I guess."

The first thing she thought of was to pray for Ken and his broken arm, both for a quick healing and also for a minimum of discomfort and awkwardness while he mended. Instead, she mentioned a few family issues and then stopped.

Ken was easy to talk to, but she had to remember that he wasn't her friend, he was her supervisor. Therefore, she wasn't sure how much she should tell him or how ingrained in her life she should let him become.

She still wasn't sure what his official capacity was going to be at Quinlan Enterprises. During management meetings he contributed along with the other supervisors, and he certainly did his share of the workload and more, which was evidenced by plenty of overtime. While he was doing actual work, she could never forget that Ken Quinlan was part of the corporate family.

Talk was that he was going to be the branch manager, because he was the production manager in the plant, but no one could see that there was anything wrong with the current manager. Craig was doing a good job and ran things efficiently; his relationships with both the staff and clients were without complaint. It didn't seem the style of Quinlan Enterprises to fire someone who was doing a good job and then give the job to a relative. The trouble was, no one knew what was going on, and in the face of the unknown, rumors abounded.

Throwing caution to the wind, Molly shared a few other personal concerns. Her boss or not, she trusted him.

Scariest of all, she actually liked the man. She could empathize with everything he shared with her. Except for his wishes to settle in, both in business and personal relationships, most of what he said for prayer requests and praise items didn't center around himself but around others.

"Want to pray now?" he asked.

All she could do was nod. Something was happening here, and she wasn't sure what to do, or how she should feel about it.

Molly folded her hands in her lap and closed her eyes, but they shot open at the touch of Ken's larger hand on top of both of hers. His eyes were closed, and at the same time as he gave her hands a gentle squeeze, he smiled slightly and sighed. His expression was relaxed and open, like he was preparing himself to talk to an old friend.

Quickly, Molly closed her eyes again. Even though they were sharing a prayer time, she felt like she'd just invaded a private moment, studying him when he didn't know she was watching.

"Dear Lord, thank You for this time together. . . ."

She listened as he prayed for all the things they'd talked about. She'd never thought about praying out loud. When she had accepted Jesus into her heart only two short weeks ago, Robbie had done all the praying, and all she'd done was nod because she was so choked up she couldn't speak. This time, as she listened to Ken and agreed with everything he said, she did the same, nodding at times to signal her thoughts even though no one could see her except God, which was okay.

"Amen."

Molly nodded. "Amen," she added quietly.

For a few moments, neither of them spoke. They simply sat staring, half smiling, into each other's eyes. He had nice eyes. She'd noticed his eyes the first time they met. She hadn't seen many people with such blue eyes with black hair. It set him apart. Ken Quinlan was a good-looking man.

Molly yanked her hands away. He was also her boss.

He took her withdrawal in stride. One scrap of paper at a time, they paged through her Bible and removed all her markers and read her notes, and he explained everything in an easy to understand manner.

The evening passed quickly, as it had the last time he'd visited. As soon as he noticed the late time, Ken apologized and headed to the door.

Molly clasped her hands in front of her. This night was truly special in ways that she couldn't begin to list. Not that she did a lot of talking, but praying out loud with Ken gave her prayers a special emphasis and created a bond with Ken like she'd never experienced with anyone. "Thank you for doing this with me. I'll never forget this night. Is there anything I can do to show you how much I appreciate this?"

Ken smiled, and he grasped her hands. "Yes, there is. Something unexpected came up for Saturday, so I can't do the tourist thing with you. But I'd love it if you came to church with me on Sunday."

Molly gulped. She had gone to church with Gwen, Robbie, and Garrett last week, and she'd promised to go again with them the coming weekend. However, since Ken was apparently hesitant about going to his new church alone, she felt obligated to go with him. She supposed her friends wouldn't mind. They would simply be pleased that she was going.

Molly allowed Ken to lead her from his church's foyer toward the sanctuary, where they stood in the entranceway while she got her bearings.

The grand, old, stone building sported a majestic vaulted ceiling that took her breath away. Stained glass windows and carved images of Jesus in the stations of the cross adorned the walls, adding a touch of history to the grandeur. Rows and rows of wooden pews filled the large room. In the corner, an elderly lady played a massive pipe organ, the old style very much in keeping with the rest of the surroundings.

The somber organ music echoed softly, and the murmur of low voices could be heard as people shuffled into their seats. Molly thought she'd seen something like this on the history channel, depicting some of the classic old churches in Europe. The Old World majesty and beauty of Ken's uncle's church was unlike any building she'd ever seen before, much less been inside. She could feel God's presence in this magnificent place.

All the people she saw milling about radiated money. Most were older, many old enough to be her parents. This morning she'd chosen a rather dressy outfit because she knew Ken would be wearing a suit. Every man in the congregation wore a traditional suit and tie, and every woman was dressed in the same style. She had made the right choice. She wasn't overdressed at all.

Ken gently touched the small of her back as they ventured into the sanctuary, and spoke softly. "I don't know anyone here yet. I was introduced to some of the people last week, but I really wasn't in any frame of mind to be sociable."

Molly forced herself to smile and nodded. So far the worst injury she'd ever sustained was a sprained ankle from her first and last attempt at skiing when Gwen dragged her up to Whistler Mountain for a weekend last winter. She couldn't imagine actually breaking a bone.

In addition to the broken arm, she could only imagine how bumped and bruised he had been from the fall down the stairs. She wondered, if it were her, whether she would have even gone to church so soon.

Mr. Quinlan and his wife walked in, waved to them, and sat down about halfway up the aisle.

"There's Uncle Walter and Aunt Ellen. Don't worry. I know it's awkward for you. They don't expect us to sit with them. Let's sit over there."

Molly gulped. She didn't know how she was supposed to function in the same social setting as her boss. She gritted her teeth and told herself that she wasn't here to socialize. She was here only to worship God, and so were they.

Molly nodded and followed Ken to an open spot very close to the back row. She slid in first, which ensured that she sat at Ken's right side. When they were as comfortable as possible on the hard wooden seats, she continued to study the sanctuary.

"Impressive, isn't it?"

It was past impressive, it was breathtaking. She continued to stare at the polished wooden ceiling and the massive, dangling crystal light fixtures.

While she was still staring at the chandeliers, the lights dimmed and the volume of the organ lowered. The minister stepped forward and greeted the congregation, which Molly guessed to be about 350 people, with the seating capacity about three-quarters filled. After a short prayer, everyone reached forward to pull their hymnals from wooden pockets in the backs of the pews in front. The people turned to the correct page, the volume of the organ increased, and the congregation began to sing. A few people sang in harmony, and it sounded wonderful.

Molly didn't know any of the hymns, and she didn't know how to read music, so she did her best to follow Ken, who sang beautifully. The majesty of the building and the Old World sounds of the timeless music filled Molly with a sense of awe and reverence for God's glory as they continued with a few more selections.

When they were done, the room echoed with the sounds of everyone closing the hymnals at the same time and muffled thuds of their being tucked back into the slots. Molly expected a small disturbance as the children were dismissed, as happened last week when she went to Robbie's church, but the minister started right into his sermon.

Molly tried to look around discreetly then leaned to whisper into Ken's ear. "Where are the kids?"

He leaned to whisper back. "There aren't many here. Most of the congregation is the same age as my aunt and uncle, but the kids go downstairs to children's church before the service begins."

"Oh."

The room was completely silent except for the odd shuffle as the minister began his sermon. Molly listened intently. He spoke on faith and how faith was proved by action.

"When the waters became rough, the disciples feared the boat would sink in the storm. They saw Jesus, and Jesus was walking on the water. And they believed. But, who was the one man who had enough faith to step out onto the choppy seas?"

Molly grabbed Ken's arm. "I know the answer to that one!" she whispered to him. She didn't know if she was supposed to raise her arm, and since this wasn't a classroom, she didn't. "Peter!" she called out loudly enough for the pastor to hear all the way at the front of the large room.

The people in front of her flinched at the sound of her voice. Ken's arm stiffened beneath her touch. The minister stopped talking, and about half the congregation turned to stare.

Molly felt her face flame as the silence dragged.

The minister cleared his throat. "Uh, that's correct. It was indeed Peter."

At his confirmation of the correct answer, a few more people turned to stare. The minister waited for everyone's attention to return to the podium before he continued speaking.

Molly clasped her hands tightly in her lap and listened in silence. If he didn't want anyone to answer questions, why did he ask? The man continued with his sermon, delivering a good solid message, and the congregation sat still, soaking in every word, except for one man who started to doze until his wife poked him.

They sang one more hymn at the conclusion of the service, and everyone quietly filed out of the sanctuary into the foyer, where small groups of people stood, engaged in different conversations.

"You must be Walter's nephew. Sorry I didn't get a chance to talk to you last week. Welcome." The pastor turned to Molly. "I'm Pastor Gregory. Welcome to St. Augustine's."

"Hi. I'm Molly McNeil. I'm with Ken." Molly adjusted her purse strap on her shoulder and shuffled her Bible back and forth between her hands while she waited for him to say something about the way she'd shouted out in the middle of the service.

Pastor Gregory simply smiled. "I'm pleased to meet you, Molly. Would you and Ken like to join my wife and me, Ken's aunt and uncle, along with a few other people at our home for lunch?"

Thankfully, Ken didn't answer. He looked at her, and Molly took that to mean that he was leaving the decision up to her.

"No, not this time, but thanks for asking." She didn't want to lie and say she was busy and hoped he wouldn't insist, because she really had no reason to turn down the invitation except for debilitating fear.

He smiled. "Another time, then. If you'll excuse me. . ." He glanced back and forth between herself and Ken, then left to join another group of people.

Ken's hand touched the small of her back. "Come on, let's get out of here."

She didn't need a second invitation. They were out the door without another word.

"Where would you like to go for lunch?" he asked as he fished the car keys out of his pocket.

Molly didn't know much about church life, but she did know that her friends who went to church regularly commonly went out for lunch following the service, whether it was to a restaurant or to someone's house. She did want to go out for lunch, but she felt a little overwhelmed by the whole experience. "I don't know. Where do you want to go?"

His ears reddened. "I'm actually not all that familiar with the restaurants around here. I was hoping you could pick something. . . ," he glanced down at his cast, ". . . appropriate."

Guilt washed through her. Just as when they went out to lunch from work, their choice of menus was severely limited to things that could be eaten with one hand, and things that didn't need to be cut.

"I don't know this area of town, so I don't know what the restaurants around here serve. How about if you come to my place, and I'll make us something?"

His face brightened. "Sure. I'd like that."

Molly chose grilled cheese sandwiches and fries. Not only was it very much finger food, it was also one of the few things she had enough of on hand to feed two people.

After a short prayer of thanks, Molly poured a blob of ketchup onto her plate, then pushed the bottle across the table.

Ken nibbled one fry without the addition of condiments. "What did you think?"

"I'm not sure. I've only been to church twice before, and this was really different."

"Every church is somewhat different. Most churches tend to be a combination of the personality of the pastor and a reflection of the lifestyle of the congregation."

"I guess that makes sense. I didn't know Mr. Quin. . .uh, your uncle, was a Christian. That's really neat."

"Most of my family are Christians."

"You're so lucky. Most of my family think I'm kinda nuts."

His eyes twinkled, and one corner of his mouth turned upwards, fighting an all-out grin. "Kinda? Can I reserve judgment?"

Molly let her mouth drop open. She'd never heard Ken make a flippant reply before, and didn't know what to think.

She lowered her head and dipped a fry into the blob of ketchup on her plate, then twirled it into a design. "No comment."

He didn't reply but continued to grin across the table.

"So what was your church like back home?"

"Very similar."

"Tell me all about it. Where you come from, your family, how you grew up? What do you do for fun?"

"Fun?"

"When you're not working, what do you do?"

He smiled. "I like to cycle."

"Cycle?" Molly couldn't imagine anything more boring. Even though she wasn't into attempting physically challenging sports, she had tried skiing. Last summer she had made a few camping trips with her friends. "You mean, like, on a bicycle?"

"That's usually what cycling is, Molly. Riding a bicycle."

She tried to imagine him on a bicycle. From what she'd seen so far, she doubted it was an ordinary bike like hers. Rather than her usual fare of cutoffs and a T-shirt, his clothing probably matched the bike.

"I'll bet you wear those special shorts with the padded seat, don't you?"

His ears turned red. "Of course."

"I hear the area around Winnipeg is really flat. You're going to be in for a big surprise when you try to cycle here in Vancouver, where it's really hilly."

He smiled. "Oh, I'm used to the hills. My last trip, I went to Idaho."

Molly choked on her milk. "You took your bike to Idaho?"

"Yes. That's where we decided to go this past summer."

"We?"

"A group of college friends. Before I left, we talked about meeting halfway on the Trans Canada Highway next summer, then heading south, probably from

Calgary. You don't happen to cycle, do you?"

She'd never made it out of the metropolis of Greater Vancouver and the surrounding suburbs, never mind hundreds of miles. She couldn't imagine it. "Where do you sleep?"

"We camp along the way."

Molly could see she'd greatly underestimated him. The first time they'd met she thought he looked quite physically fit, and now she knew why.

He told her about a few of his long cycling trips and some of the things that happened along the way, both funny and frightening, earning him a great measure of respect in her eyes. The contrast between "Ken the Professional" and "Ken the Adventurer" astonished her and combined into a fascinating package. She would never underestimate him again.

Time disappeared quickly, and they only realized it was suppertime when Molly's stomach grumbled. Rather than stop in the middle of sharing their stories, they ordered pizza as they continued talking. Before she knew it, it was nearly midnight.

Molly escorted Ken to the door. Even though he still appeared comfortable after being in his suit all day, Molly was sagging. Her skirt hung limp, her blouse was hopelessly wrinkled, and her hair had fallen out of the clip long ago. She couldn't remember the last time she'd sat and talked for so long with one person. Maybe she never had, but she had thoroughly enjoyed every minute.

She opened the door and stood in the doorway.

"Thanks for today, Ken. I know that sounded lame, but I don't know what else to say. I had a really nice time. I really enjoyed going to your church too."

He smiled. "That's great. Next Sunday we can go to your church."

"Uh, I guess so."

He stepped closer; his eyes darkened and his expression softened. He lifted his hand, gently brushing the backs of his fingers to her cheek, then rested two fingers under her chin.

Molly's heart started to pound, both fearing and anticipating what was going to happen next.

His voice came out low and gravelly. "Good night, Molly." He tipped her chin up and tilted his head. As his head lowered, his eyes drifted shut.

Molly couldn't stop herself. As much as she knew it was a bad idea, she wanted him to kiss her.

And he did. His kiss was soft and gentle and chaste, and much too short.

Briefly, when they separated, he held her chin between his thumb and forefinger, then released her as he backed up a step.

He turned, and without saying another word, he walked away.

Chapter 7

K enneth? Is that you?"

"Yes, Aunt Ellen, it's me. Sorry to wake you."

They'd left the lights on, and he had been as quiet as possible when he came in, leaving him to suspect that his aunt was waiting up for him.

"It's okay. I wasn't sleeping." Ken's eyebrows raised at the sight of his aunt, already walking down the stairway, bundled in her housecoat and wearing her big fuzzy slippers. "You're certainly out late. I was beginning to worry."

"Sorry. We lost track of the time." Ken tried to keep a straight face. He'd never lost track of time like he had today. As well, he usually didn't talk about himself so much, but Molly, full of innocent questions, kept pumping him for more. He didn't know who had been more embarrassed when Molly's stomach grumbled the need for supper: her, because of the surprise, or him, because he should have kept track of the time and been more courteous.

After they'd eaten, they hadn't felt the march of time until he had had to fight back a yawn.

"I saw you at church with the receptionist. It was nice to see you bring her to church, especially after what happened."

Now Ken really had to struggle not to smile. He could feel Aunt Ellen's unasked hints for more information hanging above his head. He simply nodded.

"She looked so ill at ease. You two left so quickly. One minute you were there, the next minute you were gone."

"That was only the third church service she's been to in her life. She's a new believer, and it's all quite new to her."

Aunt Ellen raised one eyebrow. He could almost imagine a neon question mark hovering above her head. "I was worried that you'd had an accident or something."

He couldn't help it. Ken laughed. "Why don't you just ask me if I spent the day with Molly and what we did?"

She had the grace to blush, but said nothing.

Ken grinned, then winked at his aunt. "We had a nice day together, and that's all I'm telling. Good night, Aunt Ellen."

He climbed the stairs and went to bed, but he didn't fall asleep. All he could do was stare at the ceiling. Over and over, he went over his day with Molly. Normally she dressed casually for work, but he imagined she'd worn her best outfit to church. She may have looked prim and proper first thing in the morning, but by the time the day was over, she'd been charmingly crinkled and her hair delightfully mussed. She'd enchanted him even more, the messier she became.

But, his aunt's words had been a poignant reminder. Molly was the receptionist, an employee. So far, it hadn't been important, but today, things had changed. He knew it hadn't been wise, but he'd kissed her, and she hadn't exactly pushed him away.

He couldn't help but like her. He'd only meant to disciple and help her on the way to becoming well-grounded in her faith, but they'd become distracted and talked about so many things he couldn't begin to recall them all. He'd had a wonderful time, and it seemed only natural to kiss her. Then when she responded, it was all he could do to back away.

Ken shifted positions, trying to get used to the weight of the cast resting on his stomach. He'd been having trouble sleeping and suspected that tonight would be worse, but for different reasons.

He closed his eyes, but it didn't help. Still he could see visions of Molly.

At church, the second she'd seen his aunt and uncle, she'd changed from being in awe over the magnificent surroundings to an awkwardness he couldn't immediately define. At first he'd thought it was because of the employer/employee issue, but when she said she didn't know his uncle was a Christian, he was absolutely floored.

Alone in the quiet darkness, it gave him time to reflect on why this bothered him so much.

All his life, he'd been raised that it was God's will to spread the gospel and that a Christian was to let his light shine before men. Uncle Walter was not shining if Molly couldn't tell that the man who was her boss for five years was a Christian. He knew Molly thought Uncle Walter was an honest man, honorable, and fair in his dealings, but plenty of non-Christians were good men. If there was nothing to set his uncle apart as a Christian, then he wasn't doing what God wanted.

In a lot of ways, he was very much like his uncle, which made him take a good hard look at his own Christian walk. Ken didn't like what he saw.

By witnessing to Janice, who was clearly an unbeliever, Molly had already once reminded him that he didn't go out of his way to talk to people about Jesus. Those Ken talked to were either already believers, usually in a Bible study setting, or, if not, they were close to making a decision from someone else's evangelistic outreach and the prodding and discipling had not been instituted by him.

Would people he saw every day be able to set him apart as a Christian? Would they recognize his faith by his words and actions? If he honestly had to think about it, the answer was probably not.

Molly, on the other hand, while she didn't deliberately show off that she was a Christian, made no effort to hide it. From the first day he met her, when she awkwardly but obviously started to pause to say grace before their first meal together, he could tell beyond a shadow of a doubt where her heart was, and that was with Jesus.

Ken wanted the same. He didn't want to be simply a nice guy. He wanted not only for the world to know he was a Christian, but he wanted to be able to share his faith. There was no better place to do so than to walk side by side with a new believer. As a new believer, he planned to be there for Molly when she had questions and to challenge her when she needed it. And likewise, she would no doubt be a challenge to him.

He smiled to himself, lying on his back in the dark, empty room. The decision brought a spark of joy to his heart. That was what he was going to do.

His uncle's church was a fine old congregation. From what he'd seen, most were well settled in their faith and continuing to grow in their own way, but he could tell Molly wasn't comfortable there.

He closed his eyes and smiled again. God was guiding his steps already, before he'd even consciously made his decision. Next week he was going to be in a church setting with people more his age. If Molly's enthusiasm and expectations for the normal order of a church service were any indication, he was going to the perfect place.

Next week their plans had already been confirmed. He was going to Molly's church.

Molly pulled into her assigned parking spot, but before she got out of her car, she rubbed her sleepy eyes then checked to make sure she hadn't smeared her makeup.

She was dog-tired, and it was Ken's fault.

He'd left in plenty of time for her to catch a good night's sleep, but she'd spent half the night staring up at the ceiling.

Up 'til now, she had to admit that she had been fooling herself. He'd made his intentions perfectly clear by kissing her, and she'd been stupid enough to kiss him back. Whatever was happening, it wasn't going to work, and she had to stop it before it went any further. The man wasn't exactly her boss, but at some point, he might be. So far no one knew what the long-range plans were, but Ken wasn't there to be regular office staff. When plans were announced, they were going to be big.

Above all, she couldn't forget what happened to her best friend. Robbie had started dating her boss's son, who had claimed to be a Christian then gradually started missing services until they'd barely attended anymore. After they got engaged, Mike started an affair. Molly was positive it hadn't been the first and told Robbie exactly that. In the end, when Robbie found out, instead of begging for forgiveness and trying to make it up to her, Mike had Robbie fired. Robbie lost her fiancé and the job she'd held for five years within the space of an hour. Not that Mike had been a loss, but Robbie's job was. She'd since found another job, but she'd struggled at the time.

Molly had now just passed her fifth anniversary with Quinlan Enterprises, and she had no intention of letting the same thing happen to her. Not that Ken could possibly fake being a Christian, but Robbie's experience only emphasized the fact that it was not a good idea for anyone to date their boss. Not only that, Ken came from a background of money and privilege. He grew up rich, his family could afford to give him a university education, and he didn't appear to be doing without anything he wanted. Molly, on the other hand, had grown up in a rather seedy neighborhood, something she hoped he would never find out. She couldn't allow anything to develop between them, no matter how nice he was or how much she liked him. It was too dangerous, both personally and professionally.

As she entered the building, a strange emotion gripped her when she walked past the reception area and past her desk. Correction, her old desk. As much as she desired a promotion, she missed her duties as receptionist. She liked meeting people and talking on the phone. It gave her a great deal of satisfaction to know that as soon as Ken's arm healed, he would no longer be needing her as his assistant and she could return to her regular duties.

She hustled into the lunchroom to get her first cup of coffee for the day, but instead of hanging around to chat, she immediately went to her desk.

Ken and Mr. Quinlan arrived a few minutes later. Mr. Quinlan merely nodded at her on his way past, as he did every morning when he walked by her at her usual station in the reception area. Ken, on the other hand, smiled and slowed his pace, just to make sure she acknowledged him with a returning smile.

Instead of going to his desk beside her, Ken continued on to talk to the office manager and shut the door. Molly worked by herself for nearly an hour until Ken returned.

"Molly, can you please come into the boardroom with me?"

Molly cringed. Her first thought was that she was in trouble over something she might have done wrong. After all, the things she had been given were far from the usual duties given to a receptionist. She'd taken a few business courses at night school, but she didn't have any actual practical experience. She was just getting that now—the hard way.

She remembered on Friday she had struggled for hours with a task that should have taken only fifteen minutes. She didn't want to receive a reprimand for poor work. If she were returned to her regular job now, it would be an obvious demotion, something she didn't want to happen. Her next thought was even more frightening. After he'd kissed her last night, once they were in the boardroom and the door was closed, would he kiss her again? Part of her was terrified he would, yet part of her wanted exactly that.

Molly mentally kicked herself. The man was her boss. Last night when he left, they were both too tired to think clearly, and the entire incident had been a mistake. It wouldn't happen again.

She followed him into the boardroom in silence. When he closed the door behind them, her heartbeat quickened.

"I thought we'd best do this in private."

Molly's knees started trembling. Her feet remained glued to the floor as she watched Ken walk to the computer and pull out the chair in front of it. He then dragged another chair beside the one he'd already moved and sat in that one.

When she didn't move, he turned to look at her, eyebrows raised. "I need this done right away, and I can't take the chance that it will be overheard while I dictate it. We don't have much time."

"Dictate?"

"Unfortunately, this is the unpleasant part of management. I have a meeting in ten minutes, but first I need to do up a disciplinary letter to one of the production supervisors. I don't have time to type this with one hand. I know you have other work to do, but you type faster than I do."

She struggled to hide the relief that the letter wasn't directed at herself, because after her performance Friday, she probably deserved it. She tried to be accurate as Ken stood behind her and read the text on the monitor as she typed. In only a few minutes, the letter was done, and printed. Ken picked up the pen with his right hand, held it over the paper, and froze. He switched hands, lowered himself into the chair, then lifted his Bible casted arm to align the pen to the paper. Again, he hesitated.

Once again, he put the pen in his right hand, and this time he touched the pen to the paper; however, he still didn't sign his name.

"I can't do this," he mumbled.

"Then do your best to initial it."

Ken gritted his teeth and slowly and sloppily forged out his initials.

"Do you want me to find a signature of yours on file, and get a stamp made up? That would save you having to sign things."

"I'm afraid that's not legal. The doctor told me that it would take a couple of weeks, and my fingers would be more mobile. He said I'd be able to write awkwardly, but enough to get by. Until then, this will have to do." Ken checked his watch. "I don't need you to take notes at this meeting, I just have to give some instruction to the production staff, then discuss this letter with Frank. But I need you to be ready at two-thirty, because I have to go over the quarterly totals with the western regional manager."

Molly nodded as Ken dashed out the door, leaving her alone in the large and empty boardroom. She pushed the chairs back into position, tidied up the computer, and returned to her desk.

Ken's behavior had been nothing less than professional, exactly what she thought she wanted.

She didn't know why she felt slighted.

❧

Molly raced in the door after the Bible study at Robbie's house just in time to catch the phone before the answering machine clicked on. Strangely, it was no surprise to hear Ken's voice.

"Good, you're home. How did it go?"

Molly smiled as she shuffled out of her jacket. "Great! Too bad you couldn't come. Everything went just like you said it would, with the way some people prayed with prayer requests and praise items, and someone really did write everything down in a prayer journal, and we talked about all sorts of things, and I got to meet some more people from my new church, and we had cake and coffee afterwards, and well, it was great."

She paused to breathe, kicking herself for running off at the mouth after Ken's simple question.

After a short pause where neither of them spoke, Ken's voice came out low and husky. "Did you miss me?"

"Yes, I. . ." She cut herself off. She had missed him. Of course a lot of her prayer concerns had to do with him, and since the Bible study was at her best friend's house, it was easy to share. Molly cleared her throat. "Yes, it was too bad you had to work late. Robbie's husband also became a Christian at a young age. You would have enjoyed talking to him."

She could hear the smile in his voice. "Maybe next time."

For once, she didn't comment.

"Another reason I'm calling is that Uncle Walter is going out of town tomorrow. I have to take his place at a Chamber of Commerce function tomorrow night. I was wondering if you'd like to come with me. I'll need help keeping track of who's who since I've never met any of these people before, except for Trevor Chapman."

She didn't know whether to be relieved that he was calling about business or not. She also didn't want to know why it would matter. "Sure, I can go. I guess I can take some kind of notes."

He laughed. "It's true that it's a business function, but I don't want anyone to think you're my secretary, Molly. What I need is for everyone to think you're my date."

Chapter 8

Molly lifted one arm to carefully snip the price tag off her new dress, stood on her tiptoes, and tried to get the best view she could using the bathroom mirror. She'd never attended a Chamber dinner before. She'd never attended any kind of business function. Receptionists didn't exactly get engraved invitations to those kind of events. Therefore, she had no idea what to do, what to say, and especially no idea what to wear. Ken had given her a few guidelines. With his suggestions in mind, Molly had run off to buy a new dress on her way home from work.

The lady at the store had helped a lot. When Molly told her what she needed the dress for, the woman squealed some comment about her red hair and ran off to get what she called the perfect selection. The woman was right, the dress was perfect. . .except for the price.

Molly had never before bought such a dress as an impulse purchase. Buying a new dress was an all-day excursion, requiring at least six trips into the changing room to make up her mind. However, today she didn't have the luxury of time.

She picked the price tag out of the sink where it had fallen, and shuddered. If she had impulses like this too often, it would bankrupt her. She hoped she would have occasion to wear it again before it went out of style.

The buzzer for the entrance sounded, signaling Ken's arrival.

Molly checked her watch. He was early, and that was bad, because she wasn't ready. She ran to push the button for the door, then ran into the bathroom, hoping she could apply her face before he made his way up the elevator. She had meant to put her hair up, even though she knew the unruly mass would never stay that way. Instead, all she had time to do was hastily apply her lipstick and brush on some eye shadow and a couple flicks of mascara before she heard the bell of the elevator in the hall.

※

Ken raised his hand to knock on Molly's apartment door, but before his fist made contact, the door opened wide. Molly appeared in the doorway. "Is this okay?" she asked as she twirled around.

She stopped suddenly and faced him dead on, her arms slightly spread, not giving him time to cover his initial reaction.

Ken tried not to let his mouth hang open. He thought she'd looked nice and presentable on Sunday, but today, she looked. . .different. The cream-colored dress she wore was perfect for the occasion, a combination of silky fabric with a bit of lace to make it extremely feminine yet still suitable for a business function. At the same time, the dress presented an undertone of what he could only call sass. A little voice in the back of his mind reminded him that she had purchased this dashing little number just for him, for tonight. While it showed nothing indecent, she looked ravishing. She was every man's dream come true—a gorgeous and classy woman, wanting to look her best just for him, yet still maintaining her innocence. For the evening, she was his.

All he could do was stare. This was Molly.

"You don't like it," she mumbled and looked down to the floor.

"Oh, but I do!" he exclaimed. Ken cleared his throat and lowered both the pitch and volume of his voice, trying to recapture a bit of dignity. "You look. . ." Words failed him. He wanted to show her how much he liked it. He wanted to touch her, to hold her, to run his hands down the smooth fabric. He wanted to kiss her, and not to stop like he had on Sunday. He wanted to kiss her well and good.

He tried not to blush. He'd told himself he was going to stick to business or church-related activities, yet he couldn't stop himself from asking her to be his date for tonight.

Ken cleared his throat and smiled politely. "You look nice."

Her unsure little smile made him stand straighter.

"I just have to go comb my hair and I'll be ready to go. Please come in."

Rather than be snoopy, when Molly disappeared into the bathroom Ken closed the apartment door behind him, but remained in the foyer. A pretty pair of shoes the same color as her dress sat on a small rubber mat. They were sleek and snazzy, and had killer heels.

"Okay, let's go." She leaned her hand against the wall and slipped a foot into one of the ridiculous shoes.

"You're not really going to wear those, are you?"

She wiggled her foot until it was all the way in, then bent over and picked up the other shoe. She leaned back against the wall for balance, then slid the shoe on her other foot. "I'm not even going to answer that."

"How are you going to walk?"

As she straightened, a taller than usual Molly stood in front of him. She snorted in a manner Ken thought quite unfeminine, greatly contrasting with the intriguing combination of the dress and high shoes along with a matching purse he hadn't seen before. In direct defiance of his question, she stalked past him, stood outside the door, and jingled her keys in the air.

Ken couldn't help himself. He laughed. He was still laughing as he walked into the hallway and waited for her to lock up. "Sorry," he said, knowing that by laughing he was showing her he really wasn't, "but far be it from me to understand women's shoes."

"You're just jealous because your shoes are boring."

He'd never considered shoes to have a personality. They kept his feet warm and dry. He thought the smartest thing to do would be to not reply.

"Do you know for sure where we're going?"

Ken nodded. "Uncle Walter said it's close to the Stevens Building."

"Yes, but do you know exactly where it is?"

"I have the address."

Molly snorted again. This time Ken didn't laugh.

"I thought so. I'll give you directions."

The Chamber of Commerce dinner was a surprisingly pleasant affair.

Molly dutifully stood beside Ken whenever he spoke to someone else he hadn't met before and tried not to laugh every time he not-so-discreetly glanced down to her shoes. Her feet were killing her, but she would die before she told him so.

All of the married business owners and executives had their spouses with them, and the few single men present had brought dates. Molly could tell the difference. The wives held their own in conversations, the girlfriends tended to cling. Molly refused to cling and did her best to contribute what she could to the conversations, telling herself that it was just as easy talking to these prominent business owners and managers in person as it was over the phone.

She knew who many of these people were, having spoken to them before. However, she didn't let anyone know how she knew their names, because she didn't want anyone to know she was only the receptionist.

All evening, Molly tried her best not to run off at the mouth or get distracted. She was here to help Ken schmooze with those who were to be his peers. Amongst all these important people, all dressed in their fine clothes, it was easy to remember to act dignified and, mostly, to be quiet.

Ken often asked if she knew who some of the people were, and for the most part, Molly could recognize them by their voices once a conversation began.

After allowing a respectable amount of making the rounds, the emcee requested that everyone please be seated for dinner. Cards at the place settings indicated they were to sit at the same table as Trevor Chapman and his wife, and a couple that Molly had never spoken to before.

She wanted to sit down and rest her aching feet, but Ken's touch stopped her. "I just wanted to give you a word of advice, Molly," he whispered in her ear. "They won't be saying grace here, and I generally find it more comfortable to just quietly close my eyes in private for a quick word of thanks, with my hands folded in my lap under the table. It would be different if it were just the two of us, but this is quite a crowd, and it's a business function. I've found out the hard way that if you're too obvious, it makes people ill at ease, and a chance to speak about it later is lost."

His words immediately recalled the first time they'd dined together and neither knew the other was a Christian. While she wondered if anyone here was as well, she took his words to heart. For herself, she didn't care. The people at the office acted a little strange at first, but they quickly got used to her praying over her lunch bag. Only one person had made a snide comment, but she'd told him what she thought of his rude remark, although afterward she was sorry she'd snapped at him. She couldn't afford to do that here, but like Ken, she also wouldn't ignore God just because she was out in public.

The meal was served, and conversation flowed at their table.

Heather Chapman tapped Molly on the shoulder, as they sat side by side. "Molly, I just had to tell you this. I thought you'd like to know that Trevor bought that allergy product you suggested, and we asked for Missykins to be freshly bathed before we arrived. The symptoms have been reduced to a minimum. It means so much to our granddaughter to have her grampa play with her little dog. I wish I could find a way to thank you."

"Maybe Trevor could sign a one-year contr—" A nudge at her ankle cut off her words.

Ken quelled her with one glance, then turned to the Chapmans. "That's so good to hear. I had a dog when I was a boy. I have nothing but fond memories of all the family playing with him."

Molly clamped her lips shut. She was only teasing, but obviously Ken didn't understand the joke.

Heather Chapman pulled out a small pocket-sized photo album entitled Gramma's Brag Book and proceeded to show off a score of photographs of their granddaughter, a few of which featured Missykins.

Molly couldn't help but smile. One day she would learn the little girl's name.

Immediately following the dinner, the mayor stepped up to the microphone. Between the dull monotone of his voice, the aftereffects of the delicious meal, and the relief to be off her aching feet, Molly struggled to keep her eyes open. Her eyes had almost drifted shut when a gentle touch on her hand startled her to complete wakefulness. Ken's fingers slowly intertwined with hers and remained linked.

Instead of staring at their joined hands, she looked up to his face. He smiled warmly.

"I agree," he whispered. "It can't be much longer. You can do it."

Heat rose in her face. She'd been caught almost dozing off. Abruptly, she turned to stare intently at the podium, knowing that as long as she could feel Ken's gentle grip, she would remain fully alert.

The mayor's words droned on into oblivion while Molly tried to figure out first why Ken was holding her hand and, second, what she should do about it.

The first and most common reason for holding hands was mutual affection. She couldn't deny that she liked him. The memory of his short but very poignant kiss still lingered in the forefront of her memory, which only emphasized that she had allowed things to go too far. She couldn't let a relationship develop. Ken was her supervisor. Even if he wasn't, they were working side by side, together most of the day. If it didn't work out, spending all day at work with him would be unbearable. She couldn't allow it to continue.

But if she pulled her hand away she would embarrass him. Everyone was supposed to think she was there as his date. But as her date, perhaps his peers expected him to hold her hand. Many of the other couples present were holding hands, she suspected for the same reason.

The thought lifted a weight off her shoulders. This was a business function, not a date. At the end of the evening, they would be back to business-only.

But for the moment, Molly decided to enjoy the comfort of her hand within his, without guilt. Tomorrow life would be back to normal, again.

Ken smiled to himself. The mayor continued to drone on and on, but Ken's plan was working. Not only was Molly staying fully awake throughout what was surely the most boring speech Ken had ever heard in his life, but the feel of her hand in his kept him awake too. A few discreet glances around the room confirmed his suspicions that more people were affected than just them. Unfortunately, the mayor was the only one not to notice his effect on the crowd.

Ken glanced down for a moment at Molly's small hand clasped in his. While he felt bad that the main event of the evening had turned so boring, he appreciated the excuse to hold her hand. Yet, he couldn't forget that Molly was an employee. He had told himself before they arrived that he had no business crossing the line, yet he was doing it again.

Instead of paying attention to the mayor's droning speech, Ken thought about Molly. For now, he might manage to fool himself that he was holding hands purely to keep them both awake. However, at the end of the evening, their relationship had to go back to purely business and church-related functions. As much as he regretted his decision, it couldn't be any other way.

At the close of the speech, it was almost painful when they had to separate their hands and applaud.

Coffee and wine flowed as the crowd mingled once again, signaling his cue to leave. They said their good-byes and were soon back in his uncle's car. The entire drive, Molly chattered incessantly. Ken listened politely, nodding on cue, hoping she couldn't see him trying to fight a grin. He was actually getting used to the way she chattered continuously. Still, he liked the musical quality of her voice. As he looked for an empty space in the visitor parking at Molly's apartment complex, he smiled at yet another amusing anecdote.

Even though she knew Ken was only being a gentleman, Molly smiled politely and allowed him to escort her all the way to her apartment. Too late, she realized she had let herself get carried away with her motormouth, but she couldn't help it. She was past nervous, she was scared to death.

She couldn't help it, she liked him. A lot. Too much. The man was her boss. But it wouldn't work. It couldn't. If she encouraged him, one wrong moment could mean disaster, both for her personal life and her career.

If she were smart, she would have told him she could see herself inside, yet when he turned off the engine and exited the car, she didn't say a word.

Once at her apartment door, she could barely keep herself from shaking as she dug the keys out of her purse and inserted the key in the lock. The second she stepped inside, she toed off her shoes, vowing never to wear them again. She turned to thank Ken for the evening and send him on his way, but he followed her inside and closed the door.

Molly blinked. "Would you like a cup of coffee or some tea, maybe?"

"No, I just wanted to thank you for accompanying me in a more private setting than the community hallway."

Molly gulped. The only reason a man would want a private setting would be for a good-night kiss. Which was exactly what she knew couldn't happen.

Her mind raced while she thought of something to say, while she forced herself to breath.

Ken spoke before she could think of the right words.

"I want to tell you how much I've come to value you in the short time we've known each other. You're a tremendous asset to the company in the way you greet people when they come inside for the first time, in addition to the way you handle everyone on the phone."

She knotted her brows. Company? Asset?

"You've also been a tremendous help to me both at the office and now tonight. I wanted to say thank you properly."

A million thoughts zinged through her head as she tried to figure out what he meant by "properly." As different as the evening was from a typical date, she had enjoyed herself, except for the mayor's boring speech, but the meal was lovely. The dessert was absolutely heavenly. If his idea of a proper thank-you was to offer to pay for the dress, she just might scream.

Her heart pounded as he stepped closer, but instead of bending to kiss her, he reached out his unencumbered hand and grasped one of her hands. Butterflies fluttered in her stomach as he ran his thumb up and down her wrist.

"I appreciate everything you're doing for me. I look forward to working with you as my assistant. I believe tonight will be the only time we'll need to see each other outside of the office for a business function, so I won't be interrupting your social calendar again."

At his smile, her heart constricted. She didn't have a social calendar. If he was saying what she thought he was saying, then he didn't want to see her again except for at work. While it was exactly what she had convinced herself she wanted to hear, it hurt to hear him say it.

"Of course, that doesn't include this Wednesday night's Bible study. I look forward to that very much. I enjoy answering your questions and hope I can be of continuing help to you as you continue to grow in your Christian walk. It will be nice to attend a study with people my age." He smiled, showing off the little crinkles at the corners of his gorgeous blue eyes, making her heart beat faster. "You've got to admit, the average age of my uncle's congregation is at least a decade and a half beyond me."

Molly gulped. She didn't want to see whatever was happening between them end and go back to being business-only, yet she knew it was for the best. By him still offering to attend Bible Study meetings with her, she truly was getting the best of both worlds. Ken was a great boss, and a wonderful Christian example. He had a wealth of knowledge accumulated since childhood, and she wanted to learn all he had to teach her.

Yet she didn't want the best. She wanted Ken, and that was wrong.

He leaned down. Molly closed her eyes to feel the softness of his lips on hers, but it didn't happen. He brushed a soft kiss against her cheek, then stood upright once more.

"If there's ever anything I can do for you, you be sure and let me know."

All she could do was stare up at him.

"I'll see you Sunday morning. Thanks for inviting me."

Molly's heart pounded. She seemed to recall that he had invited himself, but her mind was reeling too fast to contradict him.

He gave her hand one last gentle squeeze and released her. "Good night, Molly."

The door closed behind him. Ken's muffled footsteps faded down the hall and disappeared.

Ken frowned as he left the elevator and headed back to the car. He had clearly outlined his position, and Molly had readily agreed. He hadn't wanted to separate business from pleasure, but he had no other alternative. To do otherwise wouldn't be proper.

From now on, the only personal interaction they would have would be for the purposes of evangelistic outreach, which was helping a new believer become grounded.

It wasn't exactly what he wanted, but there was no other way. Outside of work, he would only see Molly for Bible studies and church services.

But there was one good thing that had come out of the situation. He'd never looked forward so much to Sunday.

Chapter 9

Ken pushed the button for Molly's apartment, then headed for the elevator when she buzzed the lock open. She was waiting for him when he arrived at her door.

"You're wearing a tie."

"Yes, I. . ." Ken raised his hand and out of habit wiggled the knot. Today Molly was wearing a casual outfit that he'd seen her wear to work.

"You've got to take it off."

"We're going to church, Molly. I haven't gone to church without a tie since I was a boy. As it is, I should be wearing the jacket."

Before he could protest, Molly reached forward and tugged the tie into a wide circle around his neck. He didn't want to fight her, especially when she seemed so determined, so he let her remove it. Unfortunately, before he realized how far she'd pulled it, she'd pulled it all the way open instead of simply slipping it over his head.

Ken stiffened and mentally counted to ten. He was getting tired of asking Uncle Walter to tie all his ties for him. He'd only just come to the point where he had enough strength without pain in the fingers of his left hand to squeeze a bit of his hair gel into his right so he could fix his hair by himself. If nothing else, he was experiencing lessons in humility like never before.

Ken cringed as she threw the tie inside, hoping it had at least landed on the table. "Let's go," she said and physically turned him around and pushed him out the door before he could make an attempt to retrieve it.

They pulled into a parking lot bustling with cars and people. A few young boys who were playing catch in an empty portion of the lot stopped when a woman called to them from somewhere Ken couldn't identify. He was surprised the woman would allow the children to play outside before church, taking the chance they would mess their clothes. As the boys approached, he noted they wore jeans and sneakers.

On their way past, one of the boys dropped his softball. Instinctively, Ken picked it up. Once it was in his hand, he realized he wasn't in a position to throw it with any degree of accuracy.

"You're not thinking of throwing that, are you?" Molly asked, confirming that she also doubted him.

"You don't think I can throw this without hitting a car, do you?"

Molly's cheeks turned an adorable shade of pink. "You don't really want me to answer that, do you?"

He tossed it in the air a couple times as they continued walking toward the building. Ken caught it just fine, but he always caught with his right hand. It was his throwing hand that was out of commission.

He decided that dignity came before pride. He handed the ball to Molly. "Here. You throw it. If you can."

Instead of throwing it, she motioned to the boys, who came running once they saw their ball was in the hands of a woman who had no intention of throwing it back to them from the parking lot.

"That's what I like about you, Molly. I never have to guess what you're thinking."

Her brows knotted. He wanted to assure her that he hadn't meant his comment to be an insult, but before he could speak, they arrived at the main entrance. A pleasant older couple handed them a bulletin, and they entered the building.

Once they were out of earshot, Ken nudged Molly and leaned toward her. "See. He's wearing a suit and tie."

Molly snorted. "I've only been here a couple of times, but I can tell you that besides the pastor, this man is the only one wearing a tie. The pastor won't even be wearing a suit."

Ken could barely believe his eyes, or his ears. The lobby was filled with people, almost every one of them chatting or laughing. The children weren't standing with their parents, but instead, they gathered in swarms in various groups throughout the room.

Just as Molly had promised, not a single man he could see wore a suit or a tie. Many people wore jeans, both men and women. He'd never seen anything like it. Music echoed from what he assumed was the sanctuary, only it wasn't an organ, it sounded like a whole band, and he thought he recognized the song from one of his CDs.

As they continued to walk toward the sanctuary, he saw a young couple about their age standing in the middle of a small group of people. The woman held a young baby in her arms, and the man was showing pictures to everyone surrounding him. Everyone around them chorused oohs and aahs as he proudly displayed them.

Like a typical woman, Molly gazed at the group with stars in her eyes. Ken thought Molly would make a wonderful mother and wondered if he would be a good father someday. He'd come from a happy home, his parents were still happily married, and they had been good role models. In the back of his mind, he wondered what kind of wife Molly would be for whatever man could keep up with her.

Before he could ask if Molly wanted to join them, a deep voice behind him called Molly's name.

Ken turned to see a tall man standing directly behind him. A short, little blond woman gave Molly a big hug.

"This is Robbie, my best friend, and this is her husband, Garrett." Molly beamed ear to ear. "I introduced them to each other. Garrett's a forest ranger."

Ken blinked, unable to figure out what one had to do with the other.

Garrett glanced down at Ken's cast, then back up again. He shrugged, then extended his right hand to greet him. "You must be Ken. We've heard so much about you. We've been praying for you." Garrett leaned forward and lowered his voice so only Ken could hear his next comment. "I think you're going to need it."

Ken didn't think he wanted to know the details. "Thank you," he said, averting his gaze to Molly, who wouldn't make eye contact.

"Never mind them. Let's go sit down." Molly pulled him into the sanctuary. Instead of pews, the seating consisted of rows of padded stacking chairs. Except for a single cross at the front, the room was void of any decoration. The starkness of the room indicated it was used more as a multipurpose room than a specific sanctuary.

As in the lobby, people milled everywhere, and the room was filled with the buzz of voices. The only difference was that in the quasi-sanctuary the voices were slightly softer. A group of teens hovered in the back, laughing and cajoling each other before they shuffled to their seats, not with their parents, but with other teens, the sole occupants of the back three rows of that side of the room.

On a slightly elevated stage, just as he had suspected, was a whole band. There was a drummer, an older gentleman who was wearing a suit jacket with jeans and no tie playing a bass guitar, and a younger man wearing faded jeans who was playing a bright red electric guitar. In profile, a very pregnant woman played the glossy black grand piano. Ken couldn't believe his eyes at the odd combination.

Not long after they sat, more people filed in to take their seats. Ken found the place a little overwhelming, but at the same time, it had a certain appeal, despite the lack of order.

The lights dimmed, the room quieted, and a man in a matching shirt and slacks, with a tie and no suit jacket, stepped to the podium. As he welcomed everyone present, a screen lowered from the ceiling, which signaled the congregation to stand. Everyone sang a rousing chorus Ken recognized from a CD he had in his car, complete with hands clapping to the rhythm. Ken couldn't believe his eyes, or his ears.

At the close of the song, the man, who was evidently the pastor, encouraged everyone to greet those around them. After the clamor died down, he read a few highlights from the bulletin, then called one of the teenagers from the back corner to the microphone.

The youth shuffled his feet as he nervously looked around at the congregation, then down to the floor. He tapped the microphone with one finger, blew into it, then backed up a step.

"Uh, yeah," he stammered, as he finally raised his eyes. "I wanted to tell you all about how we're doing for our raising money thing for the youth group going to Bible Quest this year. Uh, like, we're still a few hundred bucks short 'cause we need to rent a bus. Like, lots of the kids in the youth group don't come to church, you know, and their parents aren't gonna be paying anything. So we're going to have like a banquet or something next weekend after church. It's going to be lunch. Tickets are five bucks and come see me or Ryan and I'll sell you some. Someone will phone you during the week to tell you what to bring, because it's a potluck. That's all I was gonna say."

The boy shuffled back to his seat, where a couple of his friends patted him on the back for a job well-done.

Ken remembered his days of attending youth group. Most of his memories of his youth were happy, except for being called Kenny. But what stuck in his mind was the youth's comment that many of the group wanting to attend a youth-oriented Christian function came from non-Christian homes. He wanted to do everything he could to see that no one who wanted to attend would be left out.

The pastor called the ushers to the front for the offering and led the congregation in a short prayer.

He couldn't provide transportation himself, but he could help pay for the bus. His biggest problem would be his inability to write. He leaned to whisper to Molly. "Can you pull the offering envelope out of your bulletin?"

Her raised eyebrows registered her surprise, but she scrambled to pull it out, then studied it as if she'd never seen an offering envelope before.

"Quickly, Molly. Just write youth group on it and leave the rest blank."

She dug a pen out of her purse, scribbled in the middle of the envelope, then froze, the pen hovering above the total line. "How much?"

Since he still couldn't write out a check or legibly sign a credit card receipt, he had to pay for everything he purchased in cash. Therefore, he had a sizable amount of money in his wallet. He hoped it was enough to pay for the bus. "I don't know exactly how much I've got on me. I don't have time to count it. Leave it blank."

Molly handed him the envelope as the basket drew closer. Ken emptied all the bills from his wallet into the envelope, licked it, and tossed it into the basket in the nick of time.

A different man stepped forward to lead everyone to worship in song. It included one hymn, played with bass guitar and drums in a way Ken had never heard and couldn't quite decide if he liked. The rest of the worship songs were contemporary choruses, none lacking in commitment or sincerity, just not what he was accustomed to in church. Yet, he found the simple words and easy-to-follow melodies moved his heart in a way he hadn't expected. Halfway through the worship time, the children were called to the front for a short prayer before they were dismissed to their classrooms, when they ran out of the room hooting and screaming. A few parents laughed and groaned in frustration from their own children's antics, and the worship time continued.

When the pastor returned to the podium for the sermon, everyone settled in with their Bibles and followed the sermon notes on the back of the bulletin. Ken peeked over Molly's shoulder, as he wasn't sure of his ability to hold his Bible steady and turn pages with one hand. He expected that in one more week, he would, but not yet.

Every once in awhile, the pastor paused to ask a question. To Ken's surprise, many people called out the answer. When a key point was made, people freely called out a resounding "Amen," and once someone from the back row called out a friendly heckling joke in response to one of the pastor's questions, at which the congregation laughed.

Ken had never been to a service like this in his life.

Right on time, the pastor drew his sermon to a close, and everyone bowed their heads in prayer. At the pastor's "Amen," the worship team, who had returned to the stage, began to play, and the words for "Jesus Loves Me" appeared on the screen.

Ken smiled. He hadn't sung "Jesus Loves Me" for years, in fact, probably not since he was ten years old. He sang wholeheartedly with the rest of the congregation. After the third verse, the accompaniment cut out and the congregation repeated the first verse without instruments, creating a unique resonance in the large room.

The sincerity and beauty of the unaccompanied voices filled his heart like he'd never experienced. An attitude of sincere worship flowed through the building, touching his soul.

Ken closed his eyes as he sang, letting the simple words really sink in. Jesus loved everyone in that room, and Jesus loved him too. Even though he'd known it for years, something moved deep inside his heart.

When the song ended, a silence filled the room. In a soft and gentle voice, the pastor asked that if anyone wanted to ask Jesus into their hearts they should step forward, and everyone else was invited to have coffee and visit.

A few people rose and stepped forward, and many others began gathering their belongings to join their friends for coffee.

Ken turned to Molly to ask if she wanted to stay, but his voice caught. Molly's eyes were still closed, and tears streamed down her cheeks. All he could do was stare.

Her eyes drifted open, she brushed her sleeve across her eyes rather indelicately, smearing black smudges across her cheeks. She sniffled, then smiled at him, her eyes wide and still glassy with tears. She'd never looked more beautiful.

Her voice cracked as she spoke. "Jesus loves me, Ken."

Ken couldn't breathe. At that moment, he knew that not only did Jesus love Molly, but Ken loved her too.

Chapter 10

Naturally Molly didn't have a tissue in her purse, so she quickly introduced Ken to some of the people who had attended the Bible study at Robbie's house and dashed off to the ladies' room to blow her nose and do a temporary repair to her face.

When she returned, Ken was still with her friends. He joined very little in the various conversations going on around the circle of people, and every time a child screamed, he flinched. His eyes darted back and forth through the crowd continuously, but he didn't seem to be looking at anything in particular.

She rejoined the group as one of the youths approached, asking who was going to buy tickets for their fundraiser lunch the following Sunday. Garrett reached for his wallet, as did Ken, but as soon as his hand touched his pocket, his hand froze.

Molly knew he'd suddenly remembered he didn't have any money left on him, but she didn't think he wanted to tell everyone he'd already given it all to the youth group. Instead, she put her hand on his arm. "No, Ken, this is my church, so it's my treat," she said loudly enough for everyone in the group to hear. She pulled out enough money for two tickets, then realized that by buying him a ticket, she was again inviting him to attend church with her next week.

After she tucked the tickets into her wallet, she glanced over her shoulder. "Want a cookie? It looks like if we don't get one now, the kids will get them all."

His eyes widened as he turned to face the refreshment table. A little boy busily helped himself to three cookies and a few sugar cubes and then ran off to join his friends.

"Uh, no, thank you. I think I'll pass."

Garrett stepped closer to Ken. "I hear this might be a little different than what you're used to."

Again, Ken's eyes darted from side to side, this time focusing on a few people sharing some outrageously funny joke. Everyone in the small group roared with laughter, then the men smacked each other firmly on the backs while one of them reenacted a golf swing.

Ken's hand went up to where the knot of his tie should have been, his fingers grasped thin air, and he quickly dropped his hand to his side. "I have to admit I'm used to a more conservative setting."

Molly laid one hand on his arm. "Would you like a coffee? I'll pour it for you."

He shook his head. "No, thank you."

She couldn't blame him. She couldn't imagine what it must be like to be limited to using only one hand, and the wrong one at that.

"If you don't mind, I need one. I'll be right back."

Before he could protest, she hurried away. Since there were only a couple of people at the coffee urn, she wouldn't have a long wait.

From a distance, she saw Garrett and Ken talking in her absence. At something Garrett said, Ken nodded, and both men broke out into wide grins. Molly stared at the two of them. Ken was such a handsome man.

As they continued talking, Garrett broke out into a full laugh, making Molly wonder what it was that Ken said, and hoped it wasn't about her, even though she suspected it might be.

She hurried to pour herself only half a cup of coffee and didn't bother to take a cookie. Instead, she returned to Ken's side. "Are you guys talking about me?"

Ken's ears turned red.

Garrett gave her a cocky grin that spoke for itself. "Would we do that?"

"Never answer a question with a question," Molly mumbled.

Neither of them said anything to give her a hint, and she wasn't sure she wanted to know.

Garrett cleared his throat. "Are you two coming for lunch? Everyone's going to the same place as usual."

All she could do was glance at Ken, who was being unusually quiet. Without meaning to, she looked down at his fingers sticking out of the cast. Only having been to what she knew was the local lunch hangout pancake restaurant twice, she wasn't quite sure of the menu and didn't know if they served anything a person wouldn't have to cut. While Ken would never give any indication of being ill at ease, she didn't want to put him on the spot. Above all, she didn't want to embarrass him amongst strangers. As it was, he'd taken his chances at the Chamber dinner. He was lucky the menu was stir-fried steak with rice, but afterwards she remembered his comments that he was prepared to go through the drive-thru hamburger joint on the way home if he couldn't eat the dinner.

She couldn't do that to him.

"Ken and I have other plans. Maybe another time, okay?"

Robbie looked at her funny, but she wasn't about to explain herself. Not that she wanted to give her friend the impression that anything was going on between her and Ken, but she didn't have time to explain.

Ken's eyebrows raised momentarily, and he turned back to Garrett and extended his hand. Garrett grasped it and they exchanged a handshake. "It was a pleasure meeting you, Garrett, and your charming wife. I'm sure we'll see each other again soon."

Garrett nodded. "Yeah. Bible study at our house, Wednesday night. I hope you don't have to work late every Wednesday."

"No, something unusual came up last week. I'll be there. Thanks."

Molly could barely contain her excitement. Not only would Ken be a great addition to the group, but since he didn't know anyone in town, she hoped he and Garrett could get to know each other better. After learning of Ken's long bicycle trips, she was sure they would have a lot to share about various adventures in the great outdoors.

They took their leave quietly, but once in the car, Ken turned to her without starting it. "So what are these other plans we're supposed to have?"

She felt her face flush, so she winked to try to bluff away her nervousness. "The plan is to go somewhere where you don't go hungry."

"Yeah. After all, I'm a growing boy."

Molly's mouth gaped open, unable to figure out his uncharacteristic comment. "Something like that."

He inserted the key and turned it, starting the engine. "You show me where you want to go. I just have to make a short stop first."

It didn't take a lot of guessing when he made a stop at the bank machine. She was going to offer to treat him, but if he was going to all this trouble to get some money, she suspected he was determined to pay. Rather than bruise his ego, she said nothing. Besides, it gave her some extra time to decide on a small family restaurant she knew well.

❧

Once they were seated, Ken saw that Molly's choice of restaurants was, once again, a good one. They didn't have to wait long, and the food was excellent. After a pleasant meal and enjoyable conversation over their lunch, Molly rested her elbows on the table and cradled her coffee cup in her hands. "Well? What did you think?"

He blinked and stared at her. "The food's good here."

"Not that. I meant this morning."

Briefly he looked into his coffee cup, glanced around the restaurant, then back at her. "I like your friends."

"You'll meet most of them again on Wednesday. I heard Garrett invite you to their house for their Bible study meeting."

She smiled bright and wide and Ken smiled back. He still didn't know what to make of the service, but he didn't want to think about that. He couldn't take his eyes off Molly. Her eyes sparkled as all her attention focused on him. If she kept looking at him like that, he didn't know how he could carry on an intelligent conversation. "Garrett seems nice, and he's quite fond of you."

"Yes, I've known both him and his sister, Gwen, for years. I'll have to introduce you to Gwen, you'd like her too. We went to high school together. Gwen and Garrett are twins, and they've been Christians ever since I've known them. In fact, they both made their decision to follow Christ when they were kids, just like you. And Gwen is single."

"That's nice." While it was great that her friends were established Christians, Ken didn't especially want to meet another woman. It unexpectedly bothered him that Molly was so anxious to introduce him to her single friend. He'd met the woman of his dreams. Now all he had to do was convince Molly that he was the man of her dreams.

She smiled at him, for no reason in particular, which did strange things to his insides. He never wanted it to stop. If this was what it was like to be in love, he liked it.

"I know you probably have a lot of stuff to go through on the quarterly reports, but it would be a real shame for you to have to miss Bible study two weeks in a row. Actually more, because when you were going to take me to your uncle's church's study, it was canceled. You must be catching up to some degree. You don't think you'll have to work overtime again, do you?"

"No, that was a special project."

"That's good. I'll bet you haven't had a chance to go out and do much besides work since you got here. Have you gone out to see the sights and get familiar with the city or meet anyone?"

"No, not really."

"That's too bad. It's really a beautiful place to live. With the mountains to the north and the flatness of the Fraser River valley, I think Vancouver is one of the most beautiful places on Earth. But of course I can say that, I've lived here all my life and haven't had the chance to see much else except for pictures in magazines and stuff."

"I generally travel only as far as I can go on my bike. Of course, that's often a round trip of eight hundred miles and takes us about a month."

Molly laughed and scrunched her nose, which was even more adorable than her usual shining smile. Ken wished he had a camera to keep the moment with him until the end of time. As it was, he thought he could sit and listen to her musical voice forever.

"That's still more than me. I haven't done any traveling. The farthest I've been from here is Kamloops. But it's a beautiful drive. Not that I was driving. It was when I was a teenager and my parents were driving. I suppose you have to travel light when everything you need has to be on your bike or in your backpack. Did you at least take a camera?"

Ken wondered why Molly was so talkative. While she did tend to talk a lot whenever they went out together, she'd never chattered so incessantly before. In a way it was both comforting and frightening that he was able to follow her conversation, even though he couldn't remember for the life of him where the discussion had started. "Yes, I take my camera. When I finish a roll of film, I mail it home so it's all waiting for me when I get back. We keep the load as light as possible."

Molly poured herself another cup of coffee from the decanter on their table. "I love to take pictures. I once got an honorable mention in a photo contest." She grinned and took another sip, holding the cup to her lips as she waited for him to respond.

Ken frowned. Maybe she'd had too much coffee and that was what was making her so hyper. He wished he could find out what time it was. Since they'd arrived he'd lost track of how much coffee she'd consumed, but it had been a lot, and they hadn't been there that long. In addition to what she'd had at church, he didn't think it was a good idea for her to drink any more if it was going to affect her like this.

He tried to be discreet, but he couldn't read the time on Molly's watch and he didn't want to ask. On the way home from work on Monday, he was going to buy himself a wristwatch with an expansion bracelet so he could get it on and off without needing assistance with the clasp like a three year old. He glanced around the restaurant, but there wasn't a clock on any of the walls. By the time he looked at Molly again, she was staring at him, probably waiting for him to respond to her last statement, which he had to struggle to remember.

"I'd like to see that picture. Did you save it?"

Her head bobbed up and down so rapidly her hair bounced. Ken decided he was definitely going to cut her off the coffee.

"Yes!" Molly exclaimed. "It's the one hanging above my futon. That sunset picture. I took it at Stanley Park."

"Ah. Stanley Park. It's mentioned in much of the tourist literature."

Her hand shot across the table so fast it startled him. She clasped her fingers around his wrist and broke out into another wide smile. "You mean you haven't been to Stanley Park yet?"

"Uh, no."

"Would you like to go? There's lots of great stuff to see and do there. There's totem poles and lots of fields, trails, the zoo, the aquarium. . . It's even got a couple of beaches. I never swim in the ocean—it's too cold for me, but lots of people do."

It was perfect. Not only could he get her away from the restaurant's bottomless coffee pot, but it was a way to spend the rest of the day with Molly. "That sounds interesting. Let's go."

❧

Molly smiled, trying not to show her relief to have something to do besides talk. She'd talked so much she could feel an annoying rasp in her throat, and because of that, she'd drunk far too much coffee. She hadn't meant to talk Ken's ear off, but ever since they'd left church he'd been looking at her funny, and she didn't know what to make of it. Every time conversation lagged, a strange half smile appeared on his face, but he didn't say anything—he just stared at her. In the intimate setting of the restaurant, she couldn't stop herself from jumping in to fill the voids in the conversation. At least if they went sightseeing in a crowd, they could just watch the attractions without needing to fill every moment of silence.

Within the confined quarters of the car, she couldn't stop herself from telling him about all the local tourist hot spots. By the time they parked the car, she was tired of listening to herself, and she suspected Ken was too. As expected, he hadn't said much, but then she hadn't exactly given him much opportunity.

Rather than give him a choice, Molly led him to the animals rather than the aquarium complex. Molly wanted to go to the petting zoo, even though it was designed for children. The last time she'd come to the petting zoo she'd taken a friend's child, just so she could go into the pens with the animals and not look foolish. Today she didn't care.

Once inside the enclosure, she headed straight for the feed dispenser and popped in a few quarters to get a handful of the animal chow. She didn't think Ken would feed the baby sheep and llamas even if he did have two hands, but she had no such hesitation. She enjoyed petting the baby animals. She could hardly wait until she could afford a house of her own so she could get a dog. Until then, the petting zoo would have to do.

"Uh, Molly. . . We're the only adults in here without children."

"Don't worry. They won't notice. Besides, they make money from people buying food for them. Think of it as a fundraiser."

At his lack of response, Molly bent down to offer some food to one of the smaller goats who seemed to be left out when the larger and more aggressive animals got ahead of it. Her next favorite was the tall llama. After that, she stuck her hand into the pen for the small Vietnamese potbellied pig, a little black fellow whose imaginative name the sign showed as Porky. At first little Porky was hesitant, but once he got up enough nerve, he enjoyed the food she offered.

"Ken, come here. Pat him. He really likes it. Have you ever touched a potbellied pig before? His hair is really strange. It's bristly, but not unpleasant."

"I can't say I've ever patted a pig. I think I'll pass."

She scratched the little fellow behind the ear. Porky closed his eyes and leaned into her hand.

"I'll bet your name isn't really Porky," she whispered to the little pig. "I'll bet it's something very suave, like Black Bart or something, isn't it?"

"Molly? Are you talking to that pig?"

"Don't worry. He's not answering."

Molly turned to look at Ken over her shoulder to add further to her comment, but before she could say what she intended, the large llama appeared behind Ken. No doubt hoping for some food, it lowered its head and nudged Ken in the back. Unfortunately, he hadn't been expecting it. The llama pushed him forward, causing Ken to stumble. His right arm flew up as he attempted to regain his balance, but with the other arm in the cast, he couldn't right himself quickly. He grabbed hold of the wooden siding for the pen and managed to stay upright, but barely.

Molly stood as quickly as she could. Since the llama had once done that same thing to her, she would have expected it, but she suspected Ken had never been inside a petting zoo in his life. Some of the animals did tend to get aggressive, and she knew from experience that he would be head-butted again. The last thing she wanted was to embarrass him.

"Come on, I've said hello to all my favorites. Let's go somewhere else. How about the aquarium?"

Before he had a chance to reply, Molly grabbed his hand and pulled him out.

Chapter 11

Clicking computer keys, clattering calculators, the whirring of the photocopier, and the electronic tones of ringing phones surrounded Ken. Ignoring everything and remaining seated, he used his foot to push his chair away from his desk and arched to stretch his back. He was on the verge of completing another project, and it felt good.

He couldn't type properly or write yet, but at least he could finally operate the mouse half decently. Most importantly, he could now hold a pen firmly enough to sign his name if he angled the cast properly and leaned crooked. With this newly acquired skill, his next step would be to sign the lease papers on a new car.

Ken closed his eyes and drew in a deep breath. He lifted his left arm then rested the cast on top of his head to support the weight while he arched his back again and flexed his aching shoulder. It was the only way to ease the stiffness out, which was driving him nuts after keeping it immobile for so long. Fortunately, from his position at the rear of the office, no one could see him, if anyone had any mind to pay attention to what he was doing. He didn't know how he was going to stand much more of this, but he didn't have any choice. On top of everything else, just as his doctor had predicted, it was starting to get itchy in there.

Out of the corner of his eye, he sneaked a peek at Molly, who was working very hard to convert the labor costs on another project proposal. All thoughts of work fled his mind.

Sitting in his chair, leaning back with his arm still resting on top of his head, he watched Molly. He'd seen so many different facets of her personality yesterday, and it had only served to strengthen how he felt about her.

The woman who had grabbed him by the hand and forcefully pulled him out of the petting zoo had burst into tears over the simple but meaningful words of a children's song. The woman who had charmed his company's most important client had talked to a pig. He didn't want to compare her one-sided conversation with the little animal to his own rather one-sided conversation with her at lunch. Then, for a complete turnaround, instead of a diet of nonstop chatter, during their journey through the aquarium they'd shared a very comfortable silence as they walked slowly through the complex.

Since it had been busy, at one point he had held on to her hand so they wouldn't become separated in the crowd. When the crowd thinned, he hadn't let go, and Molly hadn't pulled away. They'd spent much of their visit walking around the exotic fish and aquatic displays hand in hand, and he'd thoroughly enjoyed himself. The aquarium had been interesting, but being with Molly in the dark complex lit only by the backlight from the aquariums made it enchanting.

The only thing that would have made a great day perfect would have been if he could have kissed her when he left.

He was completely and totally in love with Molly. Now if only he could figure out what to do about it.

He'd never seen an employee out of the working environment before, much less dated one. The situation called for extreme caution, because he didn't want to place Molly in an awkward position in front of his uncle or the rest of the staff. Still, he had every intention of pursuing this as a serious relationship. He'd already kissed her and she'd responded, so he didn't fear that whatever it was they shared wasn't mutual, at least to some degree.

Suddenly, Molly turned her head and looked at him, catching him staring at her. He should have felt stupid leaning back in his chair with his arm on top of his head, but he didn't. Her beautiful emerald green eyes opened wide, her mouth gaped slightly. She stared up at his arm, then quickly reverted her gaze back to his eyes. For lack of a better idea, he smiled at her and said nothing.

She lowered her voice so no one else in the area could hear. "Ken? Is everything all right?"

His smile widened. "Just fine. It's almost lunchtime. Want to beat the rush?"

In the silence of her apartment, Molly slowly spooned a serving of beef stew out of the slow-cooker and onto her plate, then stood and stared at it.

Something strange was happening, and she didn't know what to do. This afternoon she had looked over at Ken to ask him a question, but Molly couldn't believe what she was seeing. The question she was going to ask disappeared in a puff of smoke. Ken had shed his suit jacket and was lounging back in his chair doing absolutely nothing. His tie was loosened around his neck, the sling hung empty, and his arm was raised straight up with the cast lying on the top of his head. And then, when he saw her looking at him, all he did was wiggle his fingers and grin like an idiot.

She hadn't expected Ken to take her out for lunch again—after all, they'd had no urgent business to discuss and no important clients to visit. They'd left ahead of the rest of the staff, but once inside the car, she took advantage of the only private moment they were going to have. Ken was careful with his appearance and hated to look unkempt, even to the extent of his tie being crooked. For however long he'd been sitting in that ridiculous position with his arm on top of his head, he'd flattened his hair in the middle. In addition to looking silly with crooked hair, she couldn't look at him with a straight face because the flat spot reminded her of how it got that way. Not only that, if he went out in public like that, he would have been embarrassed.

Therefore, she'd attempted to fix it. That had been a mistake.

She'd never forget the silky feel of his thick hair as she ran her fingers through it in her efforts to fluff it back up again. While she knew men used hair gel to keep it in that particular style, it was never something she'd used herself. She'd been surprised at the stiffness of it on top, and she couldn't help but investigate the texture of it and experiment with a couple of the hardened strands.

At some point he had closed his eyes, and while she was busy trying to figure out the texture and shaping of his hair, another sappy grin had drifted onto his face. When her fingers stilled, his eyes opened halfway. The usual steel blue had darkened to a blue-gray, and his attention fixed on her mouth. If they hadn't heard the voices of a couple of women leaving the building, she wondered if he would have kissed her.

Molly stared at her supper, which was now starting to cool, and she hadn't taken a single bite. She wasn't hungry, but she knew she should eat. Just as she reached for the cutlery drawer, the buzzer for the door sounded.

"Hi, Molly. It's me, Ken. Are you busy?"

Molly stared at her untouched supper. Not that she was hungry. "No, I'm not busy. What are you doing here?"

"I forgot my tie yesterday and was wondering if I could come up and get it."

Sure enough, his tie was still draped over the kitchen chair where she'd tossed it Sunday morning. "Come on up," she said as she pushed the button to open the main entrance.

Since she hadn't touched her supper, she scraped the stew back into the pot, stirred it, and put the lid back on. By the time she rinsed the plate and tucked it into the dishwasher, Ken was knocking on the door.

"Hi." He stood grinning in the entranceway. "I hope you don't mind. I was just in the neighbor. . . Wow, what's that delicious smell? I hope I'm not interrupting your dinner."

Molly shrugged her shoulders. "I haven't eaten yet."

He craned his neck to look into the kitchen, which fortunately was tidy. "Me neither."

That was a hint if she'd ever heard one. "You're welcome to stay. There's plenty." She'd planned to divide it up into a number of servings and freeze it. While she tended not to be very organized, when it came to suppers, she could do that much. Besides, it saved her from having to cook some other day.

"That would be great. I'm starving. I owe you big time."

"Don't tell me you were at work all this time?"

He shook his head. "No. I was held up with the insurance agent. I got a new car today. Want to go for a test drive?"

"You bought a car? In one day?"

"I knew what I wanted, and I didn't exactly buy it. It's leased. That way I get to claim it on my income tax." He closed the door behind him and walked into the kitchen. "Can I help with anything?"

"No, there's nothing to do." She pulled out a couple of plates and cutlery, poured two glasses of milk, and sat down. In the same space of time, Ken picked up his wayward tie, awkwardly folded it as best he could, and tucked it into his shirt pocket. He shucked off his suit jacket but didn't remove the tie he was already wearing. After a short prayer, they began to eat.

"This is delicious. You're a good cook."

Molly felt herself blush. "I dumped a bunch of stuff into the crockpot this morning and turned it on. That doesn't take a lot of effort or imagination. I didn't even have to get up much earlier than usual."

"Did you get the recipe out of a cookbook, or did you just make it up?"

"Make this up? Me? Are you kidding? It was in the book that came with the slow-cooker. I followed the instructions." Molly couldn't believe she was discussing cooking techniques with him. As she shared her limited knowledge of cooking skills, then listened to some cute stories of his misadventures of cooking for one, she had to smile. Perhaps she had the wrong impression, and all Ken had in mind was mere friendship. He hadn't wanted to kiss her after all. Probably her lipstick was smudged, and he didn't know what to say.

She didn't want to be disappointed, but it was best in the long run. Whatever his final position in the company ended up being, it would still be an executive capacity; after all, he was a Quinlan. She'd never be able to relate to his friends or his lifestyle. Most likely, despite her dreams of promotion, all she would ever be was the receptionist, a job she enjoyed but wished paid better.

"Thank you for a lovely dinner. Now how about if I take you out for a drive? You can show me some noteworthy points of interest to us tourist types, and I'll treat you to coffee and dessert."

It was a deal she couldn't refuse.

He didn't say anything about the car, but without a doubt, it was priced well beyond her own means, leased or not. Since they'd already been through Stanley Park, she directed him to the outlying areas.

"You'd mentioned something about the SkyTrain and a marketplace a few weeks ago. I don't have any plans for Saturday. Can I take you up on it this weekend?"

She hadn't remembered specifically saying she volunteered to play tour guide, but she couldn't say no without looking churlish. Besides, now that she knew his intentions, she could relax in his company, knowing friendship was all he sought. "Sure. Wear comfortable shoes. We'll be doing a lot of walking."

"Comfortable shoes? Is there any other kind?"

Molly gritted her teeth. She had a closet full of shoes to match every outfit she owned, and then some. There weren't many in the pile she'd select to walk for hours at the crowded marketplace.

Instead of describing the points of interest out the window, Molly turned to face Ken as he drove. He obviously didn't have a clue about women's shoes, which was evidenced by his reaction to the spikes she'd worn to the Chamber dinner. As many suits as he appeared to own, their primary hues were all in very basic, functional, and boring colors. "Just how many pairs of shoes do you own?" she asked, crossing her arms and narrowing her eyes.

His brows knotted as he turned the corner. "Four. If you count my boots and my sneakers. How many pairs of shoes does a person need?"

She could see it in her mind's eye. Basic black, basic brown, white sneakers, and felt-lined boots for a person living in a snowbound winter climate. Exactly four. He didn't even have to think about it. "You're such a...a...," she paused and waved one hand in the air, "a man!"

He blinked. "Is that bad?"

"Typical male," she grumbled.

"Excuse me."

Molly cringed at his sarcastic response. She did mean to tease him, but she hadn't meant to insult him. She opened her mouth to apologize, but as he turned his head, his little grin caused her heart to skip a beat and start up in double-time.

"You're teasing me!" she huffed and stared out the window again.

"Me?" He had the nerve to laugh. "Never."

"That does it. We've seen enough of the landscape. You owe me dessert. And it had better be something chocolate."

❦

"Thank you all for coming. I'll see you all again this time next month."

Molly closed her notebook and stood as the board of directors did the same. She'd never been to an executive meeting, and she could sum it all up in one word. Dull. Although nothing could have been worse than the mayor's speech at the Chamber of Commerce dinner.

She'd tried her best to take good notes, but out of the corner of her eye, she'd seen that Ken had also taken some notes of his own. To anyone who was watching, it wouldn't have looked strange to see Ken writing with his right hand, but Molly knew better.

Once they had returned to their desks, Molly wheeled her chair beside him and immediately explained what she had written down, just in case he couldn't understand her writing or had questions.

"I saw you writing too. What kind of notes were you taking?"

"Nothing," he mumbled. "Did you write down Malcom's question? I can't remember now exactly what he said, but I do know that whatever it was, I thought he had a good point and I wanted to take it up with Uncle Walter later."

Molly paged through her notes, then pointed to the correct spot. "Right here."

He nodded as he read, and while his attention was on her notes, Molly sneaked a peek at his. It was a single page, which he had pushed to the far side of his desk. But she could see it anyway.

There were only a few words on the paper, and they were printed in a large and almost illegible scrawl.

"That's great. I wasn't sure if you caught that. And what about. . ." His voice trailed off as he looked up and saw where she was looking. His mouth snapped shut. He grabbed the paper, crumpled it up with one hand, and aimed for the garbage can.

Molly grabbed it out of his hand before he threw it. "No, wait, let me see that. It wasn't too bad." Before he could protest, she smoothed it out in front of her.

"I couldn't believe it. I couldn't write with the wrong hand—it was all I could do to print—and as it was, I struggled to do just a few words. It took so much of my concentration for each individual letter that I lost track of the meeting. It was like I was back in kindergarten."

Molly giggled. "I'll bet you were a cute kid in kindergarten."

He tried to snatch the paper, but Molly slapped her hand on top of it.

"I was funny-looking and everyone laughed at me because I was the only one wearing glasses."

"Glasses?"

"Yes, glasses. I wore glasses from a very early age."

"You wore glasses as young as kindergarten?" Molly leaned closer to study his eyes. His gorgeous deep blue eyes. "I've never seen you in glasses. I don't see that you're wearing contacts."

"I had that new laser surgery about a year ago." He grinned wide. "No more glasses. What a difference, huh?"

She didn't know what to say. She had never seen him in glasses, so she couldn't tell. But he was mighty good-looking without them. He was probably just as handsome with glasses; in fact, they would probably add a touch of dignity, since he was an executive. Not liking where her thoughts were headed, Molly returned her concentration to the paper in front of her.

"I think my notes are fairly comprehensive."

"You've done a good job, as usual, and we're nearly done. How would you like to join me for dinner? I'm on my own tonight and have no intention of cooking."

"Sorry. I've got something all defrosted. I'm cooking supper at home."

"Oh."

He looked so dejected, she couldn't help but feel guilty, although she didn't know why. Molly sighed. "Would you like to come over for supper?"

His sullen expression changed instantly into a hopeful smile. "That sounds great. We should be finished soon. I'll follow you home."

Molly tried not to groan.

Chapter 12

Ken followed Molly very carefully. Not only did she take a few shortcuts only the locals would have known about, but her driving was rather erratic. He'd already noticed that the population of the area in general tended to drive too fast and follow too close, to say nothing of aggressive tendencies, but it surprised him to see that Molly was no different.

He sighed and reminded himself not to be judgmental and that most likely after a few years of living here his own driving habits would change to match the general population.

Molly's poor driving habits aside, Ken felt a strange satisfaction to know that even though they were in separate vehicles, they were headed for the same destination. Molly's home. He smiled to himself as he dreamed about the possibility of one day being in the same car, driving home together after a long day at the office.

His original plan to buy a house shortly after his arrival had changed. At first, the delay was only due to the cast as there was no way he was going to be unpacking with one arm. Now, however, he had no desire to buy a house because he would have been buying it alone. When the cast was off and he could move out of Uncle Walter and Aunt Ellen's house, he had decided to rent something instead. He wondered what it would be like to buy a home with Molly at his side, permanently.

Molly waited for him as he found a spot in the visitor parking, and she complained about the traffic the entire trip up to her apartment. He didn't think he needed to add anything. She said it all, and then some.

The apartment was considerably less tidy than the last time he'd visited. He had a suspicion, which was further evidenced after observing the condition of her desk day after day, that what he saw of her home today was closer to its usual state than what he'd previously witnessed. He thought that Molly would probably appreciate a housekeeper more than most people.

"Is there something I can help you with, since you didn't expect to be cooking for two?"

She shook her head as she washed her hands in the kitchen sink, then wiped them on the dishtowel. "No, you probably wouldn't be that much help anyway." Her hands froze. "I mean, with only one hand what could you do?" Her face flushed red. "I mean, no, I don't want any help."

Ken bit his lip. Once Molly opened her mouth, he always knew exactly what was on her mind. Yet as tactless as she seemed, Ken could appreciate it. Since she

200

treated him with nothing but open honesty, he could simply relax and be himself. He hoped she was equally as relaxed in his company.

Rather than go into the living room to sit on the couch by himself, he pulled out one of the kitchen chairs and sat down so they could talk while she prepared supper. He watched as she bustled about the kitchen. For one of the rare times since they had met, she was silent, probably because she was following the instructions on the box. Her back was toward him as she worked.

It felt rather domestic, and he liked it. His preference would have been to help her, and when he was out of the cast, he hoped to do that someday. His thoughts drifted to the picture of both of them tidying up the kitchen after supper, of washing and drying dishes together, as a couple. The next addition to the domestic picture in his mind was the addition of children and a dog or two.

Ken rested one elbow on the table and leaned his chin into his palm as he slouched forward, still watching Molly. She held the lid above the saucepan, whose contents were now simmering, while she stirred.

"Have you ever thought about getting married?" he asked.

The metal lid crashed down, landing askew on the saucepan and tottering a few seconds until Molly straightened it. She turned to face him. "Married?" She shrugged her shoulders. "I guess so. When the right man comes along."

"Tell me about your Mr. Right."

Molly turned the heat down and stared at him like he was from outer space. "You want to hear about my Mr. Right? The man of my dreams I haven't met yet?"

According to him, she'd met the man of her dreams, all right. She just didn't realize it yet. He merely had to convince her of it. "Yes. Tell me about the qualities you want to find in your life's mate."

Molly crossed her arms over her chest, tilted her head, scrunched one eye, and stuck the tip of her tongue out the corner of her mouth. She looked up to the ceiling for a few seconds, then turned to him. "First, he'd have to be a Christian."

Ken smiled. So far so good. "And then?"

Molly's eyes glazed over, her expression became dreamy, and she turned to study a blank spot on the wall. "No matter what, he's got to love me the same way I love him. Like, totally nuts about each other. Not love at first sight, I don't believe in that. Like best friends, but with a major spark. You know. Romantic stuff. We'd both be in love totally and completely, faithfully, till death do us part, and all that rot."

Ken smiled. He couldn't have said it better himself, although he would have worded it differently.

Molly sighed. "A good job would help. But it wouldn't really matter, as long as he's ambitious and motivated. I expect to continue working. I wouldn't even care if I made more money and became the major income provider. I took some business courses at night school, and I plan to work my way up." She stopped staring at the wall and made eye contact. Her dreamy smile made Ken's chest tighten.

After Ken's cast came off, Uncle Walter was going to make the announcement that Ken was to be named as vice president of Quinlan Enterprises. That would begin the five-year transition leading to Uncle Walter's retirement, and then Ken would take over as company president. Of course Uncle Walter would still be honorary chairman because he owned the company, but Ken was going to effectively run the entire corporation. That was why he went to college, and he'd excelled at all the courses he needed. When he started working for Quinlan Enterprises, he'd started at the bottom and worked his way up, not simply taking over because of his name. He'd worked, and he'd worked hard because he had to prove his worth—that he wasn't being given preferential treatment because he was family. The respect he received from the employees was well deserved. He'd earned it the hard way.

Now everything was coming to fruition. Over the next five years, he was going to put both his experience at the working level and all his administrative knowledge into practical application. It was what he'd wanted to do from the time he graduated from high school. He wondered if that qualified as "a good job."

He smiled. "And then what?"

Molly tilted her head and rested one finger on her cheek as she thought for a few seconds. "I wouldn't care what he looked like. I mean, it would be nice if he was good-looking, but what's in the heart is so much more important. I hate it when you meet someone who is so good-looking they're stuck on themselves."

While Ken knew he wasn't the most handsome man to grace the face of the earth, he tried to take care of himself. He was careful with his appearance, doing the best he could with what God gave him.

"And he should be able to hold his own in a conversation and stand up for himself." Molly's cheeks reddened and her voice lowered. "I sometimes tend to dominate a conversation."

"No!" Ken exclaimed, trying to feign shock. "Really?"

She stuck her tongue out at him and turned away. For once, she didn't comment. Ken laughed.

"What about kids?" he asked, ignoring her silence. Besides, he knew it wouldn't last. "Do you want to have kids?"

Molly nodded. "Of course. A nice house in the suburbs, 2.4 children, the white picket fence. I want it all!" She raised both hands in the air and twirled in a circle, the picture of glee, then turned back at him, smiling ear to ear. She lowered her hands and shrugged her shoulders. "I guess that's about it. What about you? Do you want to get married someday?"

Ken smiled. Not only did he want to get married, he wanted to get married soon, and he knew exactly to whom. "Yes, I do."

That same dreamy expression appeared on Molly's face. She dropped herself into the chair opposite the table from him, rested her elbows on the table, and cupped her chin in her palms. "Tell me about your Miss Right."

He looked straight at Molly. "She'd have to be a Christian."

"Yeah. I figured that. And?"

"Like you, I'd marry for love, nothing else. And if the perfect person didn't come along, I'd stay single."

Molly didn't say anything, so he took advantage of it and continued.

"My position at Quinlan Enterprises is obviously stable, so it's not important to me if the woman I marry works or not. If she wants to work, fine. If not, I'd like her to be involved in some kind of ministry function. Or maybe church secretary if that's what she wanted, and that could be a volunteer position, because we'd be able to afford it."

"You seem to have things pretty mapped out."

He smiled. "No, not really. Those were just a few ideas. I'd also want to be part of a team in some form of ministry. We're talking future dreams here, not necessarily reality, right?"

She shrugged. "I guess so. What else? What would she be like?"

He knew that without hesitation. She'd have untamable red hair and smoky green eyes, be bold and lively, and never lack for cheerful conversation. She would have a smile that lit up a room. "Looks aren't important. What's important is what's underneath. Intelligence, ambition. Waiting for her Mr. Right, which would be me."

Molly scrunched her eyebrows and cocked her head to one side. "Waiting?"

Ken cleared his throat. "Uh, you know. Not promiscuous."

"I would think that most women aren't promiscuous. It's just that you see so much news about those that are, but really, it's not the norm."

"I know that. But I don't know how many women are waiting for marriage nowadays."

"Waiting for marriage?" Her voice trailed off. He could see the exact second she put two and two together. "Oh!" She snorted rather indelicately and laid both palms on the tabletop. "You know that really bugs me. Men expect that of a woman, but when the shoe is on the other foot, it's different."

Ken stiffened and leaned back in his chair. "Not always."

Molly snorted again.

Ken rested his free hand on top of the cast, the closest he could come to crossing his arms while his mobility was so restricted. What he expected was not unreasonable, nor was it impossible. He was ready to let the subject pass when Molly's mouth dropped open, she leaned toward him, and stared deeply into his eyes. At her scrutiny, his face heated up.

"Well, maybe not always, but. . ." She leaned closer, never wavering from a stern eye contact. Her eyes widened and her brows raised. "You've never. . ."

Now his ears burned too. It was a subject he felt strongly about, but he had never discussed it with another living soul, especially a woman.

"You're saving yourself for marriage! That's so sweet!"

What he really wanted to do was cover his face with his hands, but since he had the use of only one arm, he bent his head forward, pinched the bridge of his nose, and shook his head. He was twenty-seven years old, graduated near the top of his class in college, and was about to become vice president of a major corporation. He had always been an active member of his church and took God's word about love and marriage and chastity very seriously. For all his commitment to doing his best to follow God's direction about avoiding temptation, the last thing he would have been expected to be called was sweet.

When he looked up, she was still staring at him. Molly placed one hand on his shoulder. "You know, just because a woman hasn't been a Christian all her life doesn't mean she would give herself away. There are lots of women out there who are waiting, you know."

He didn't know if she was speaking in general terms or if she was speaking of herself. He was afraid to ask.

Molly backed up a bit. "What about kids? Do you want kids?"

Ken cleared his throat. "Yes, I want kids. I'm an only child, and even though we had a large extended church family, I always wanted brothers and sisters. Or even a cousin would have been nice. When I get married, I want kids. I never thought about how many. Just more than one."

"I have one brother. But when I was a kid, I wished I had a dog instead."

He allowed himself to relax, since the conversation was drifting into more comfortable territory. "I had a dog when I was a boy. I'd like a dog too. But I wouldn't allow my daughter to call it Missykins."

Molly giggled. "Me neither!"

Ken smiled. "Well, I guess that makes us a perfect match, don't you think?"

She laughed out loud, which made Ken doubt she took him seriously, even though he'd never been more serious in his life. Obviously the light touch wasn't going to work.

The timer for the stove dinged. Molly spooned some kind of ground beef and pasta mixture onto two plates. "Another famous gourmet meal. Just read the instructions on the box."

It took Ken a few seconds to realize that she was comparing it to the recipe for the stew they'd had yesterday.

After a few words of thanks, they began to eat. Ken had never eaten anything like this in his life, but it wasn't bad, considering.

"You could do this, you know, even with one hand."

"Naw," he mumbled. "I'd prefer you to do it for me."

Molly choked on her mouthful.

Ken rapidly shook his head. "I didn't mean I want you to cook for me. I meant that I enjoy your company and that includes mealtime. I'd cook for you if I could. In fact, when I'm out of the cast, I'd love to cook a meal for you." If that's what it took, he'd do anything.

She mumbled something he couldn't hear, and he didn't dare ask her to repeat herself.

Fortunately he managed to steer the conversation after that to less personal territory. After dinner, he would have liked to help her do the dishes but didn't want to take the chance of dropping anything. Rather than allow him to watch her clean up the kitchen, Molly shooed him into the living room. He heard everything getting piled into the sink, and before he knew it, she joined him on the futon.

With a flick of the remote, she turned on the television, and they enjoyed a few programs, interspersed with much conversation. The domesticity of it all appealed to him, and he wanted more.

Now to figure out how he was going to achieve that.

Chapter 13

Molly studied the spreadsheet on her computer, then wrote down a few notes so she could remember how she'd figured out her latest entry. She knotted her eyebrows as she studied the endless statistical data, absently winding the pencil through her hair as she read. She was so lost in thought that when the phone at her elbow rang, she jumped. The pencil tangled in her hair, and when she pulled it out, it caught in her earring. A ping clicked in her ear as the earring unfastened and flew into the air. The pieces bounced off the edge of the desk, fell to the floor, and rolled under her desk.

"Molly speaking. May I help you?" she mumbled into the phone as she tried to see where her earring had gone. "Hmmm," she mumbled as she tipped her head to the side, trying to look under her desk at the same time as she listened to Janice's questions. "It's in the second drawer in the folder marked 'Correspondence.' Yeah. You're welcome. Bye."

The second she hung up, she pushed her chair back, bent at the waist, and continued to check farther underneath the desk. She found the main piece of the earring easily, but the small back fastener was nowhere to be seen. A small glint caught her eye, so she dropped to her hands and knees and crawled under her desk to retrieve the missing piece. It ended up being only a broken shard of something she couldn't identify, but since she was already on the floor, she remained under the desk to try to locate it. Not only were they her favorite earrings, they were a gift from Gwen.

Voices drifted from above the desk as footsteps approached. "Surprise, surprise. They're both gone again."

"And it isn't even lunchtime."

"Why do some women have all the luck? What's she got that I ain't got?"

"Ken Quinlan, that's what."

"How in the world did she do it?"

"Take a guess, Francine."

The first woman made a disgusted sound and made a rather rude comment. The voices faded as the women walked away.

Cautiously, Molly backed up, slowly raising her head inch by inch to scan the area to see if anyone noticed her. Everyone in the vicinity sat with their noses glued to their work, so she rose as nonchalantly as she could and sat back in her chair.

Did people really think something was going on between her and Ken?

His chair was empty, but she heard his voice coming from Mr. Quinlan's office.

She hadn't tried to hide the fact that he'd taken her out for lunch on a number of occasions, but she was mortified to hear that the rumor mill had reared its ugly head to make more of things than really happened.

The last thing she wanted was to damage Ken's reputation, or her own. In the future, she would make sure they were not gone at the same time so people with overactive imaginations could no longer weave their tall tales. Naturally she liked Ken. But to think she had any claims on him was ludicrous.

The first time she'd had the mistaken impression that his interest might be other than friendship was the weekend he'd kissed her. As pleasant as it was, afterward he'd obviously thought twice about it, because the next day at work, he'd distinctly told her their relationship would be strictly business except for Bible or church-related stuff. If he had considered anything other than friendship, it had taken only one day to change his mind.

For a few minutes on Monday she'd wondered what was going on in his head when she caught him watching her with that sappy grin on his face. But when he appeared at her doorstep to get his tie, he had only sightseeing on his mind and that was fine with her.

Yesterday, after spilling his guts about his dreams for finding the ideal woman, she knew that what he felt for her was strictly a platonic friendship, otherwise he wouldn't have said such personal things.

When Ken returned to his desk with an armful of papers, Molly took the opportunity to dig out some files she needed from the back room. For the rest of the day, she made sure when she needed something, even if it was only a piece of paper, she fetched it when Ken was busy at his desk, so people could see she wasn't with him. Also, when Ken was gone, she made sure that she spent as much time as she could in plain view of as many people as she could, right at her own desk.

All day long, Ken had the feeling something was wrong. Many times he'd caught Molly sneaking little glances at him, watching him but never saying anything. He would get completely immersed in his work, and then the next time he would look up, she would be gone. If he left to do something, when he got back, there she was, as if she'd been there all along. If he didn't know better, he would have thought she was avoiding him.

The thought terrified him.

The worst part was that he didn't know what he'd done wrong. Sure, he'd laughed at her obsession with shoes, but that was days ago, and besides, he didn't think that was something worth getting the cold shoulder over. He wanted to ascertain what was wrong. She'd been fine for most of the morning, but at some point, something changed.

He had to find out what it was.

By the time the work day came to an end, he was a nervous wreck. Sure enough, Molly appeared back at the desk just long enough to tidy up her mess.

He saw her open the drawer for her purse, ready to leave. Without him. He couldn't let the sun go down on her anger. Or whatever it was that was bothering her.

"Molly? Could I see you for a minute please? In private?"

Her hand froze, she yanked her purse out of the drawer, slammed it shut, and hugged the purse to her body like a shield. "Now?" Her eyes darted around the room, as if she was searching for someone or something.

Which only confirmed that something was terribly wrong.

"I'm kind of in a rush. Can't you just tell me here?"

His heart clenched. "No. Can you come into Uncle Walter's office?"

Again, she looked skittishly around the room. He felt sick. If he'd done anything to hurt or frighten her, he'd never forgive himself.

He stood tall and walked into his uncle's office, and Molly eventually followed. At a distance. He motioned to the two chairs and closed the door. She remained standing, her posture rigid.

"Molly, please, tell me what's wrong."

"Wrong? Nothing's wrong."

Rather than contradict her, he tried to act calm and wait her out. His stomach clenched when she avoided looking directly at him.

"Okay, I'll tell you what's wrong. Have you picked up on any of the rumors yet?"

"No, I haven't." Relief washed through him. If all that happened was that word was starting to circulate about him being named vice president or taking over Uncle Walter's presidency in five years, then he'd worried for nothing. Even though they didn't want anyone to know until the official announcement was made, he knew that in large organizations sometimes information leaked out. He no longer cared, as long as nothing was wrong between himself and Molly. He wished he could understand why the news had affected her so much that she was now avoiding him, but at least it was something he could deal with. "So?"

"So we shouldn't be going out for lunch so often."

He failed to see why not. Most high-ranking executives with controlling interest had personal secretaries or assistants, and they often lunched together.

"And it's getting worse, you know."

"Worse?"

"Do you want to know what I heard this afternoon?"

"You heard something?"

"I heard a couple of the guys laughing about more than just business going on in the boardroom. And they weren't the only ones talking."

Ken frowned. The employee's personal affairs were their own business, but if employees were using company time for personal liaisons, he would have to follow it up with disciplinary action.

"And now we're in here with the door closed."

"What's that got to do with anything?"

"You don't get it, do you?" She waved one arm in the air, in the other she continued to hug her purse next to her body. "People are spreading rumors that we're having an affair!"

"An affair? That's ridiculous."

Molly sighed loudly. "Tell me about it."

He stepped closer to Molly. The anger in her eyes made them sparkle and it made her cheeks flush. She radiated energy. Her anger spoke righteousness, and he loved her for it. "An affair implies something tawdry and short-lived. Nothing could be further from the truth."

Molly nodded. "You're telling me."

"You're far too valuable for a tawdry affair. You deserve to be courted properly."

"Yeah, and I think—" She gulped, and her eyes widened. "I beg your pardon?"

"Tonight's Bible study. May I take you out for dinner before we go? Oh, didn't you say you were in a rush to go somewhere?"

Her eyes widened even more and her mouth gaped as she stared at him in open astonishment. "Uh. Yeah. Right. I was. Bye."

Before he had a chance to say another word, she turned and ran.

❦

Molly had barely changed into her jeans when the buzzer for the door sounded. She knew who it was. It was Ken, and he was expecting her to go out to dinner with him.

It was probably rude of her to turn and run out on him at the office when he had been expecting a reply about dinner, but his remark had thrown her so off guard, she hadn't known what to do.

She tried to figure out what he meant by courting her properly. They were friends. He was her boss. He probably had millions of women after him, women more in his social and economic circles. Or at least he would, once he got settled. If he was lonely, then he needed to meet more people. Quickly.

Knocking sounded on the door. She opened it and nearly fainted. Gone was the suit and tie. Ken stood before her in jeans, a casual shirt, and a light jacket.

He grinned and handed her a flower. A single long-stemmed red rose.

He bowed his head slightly. "Hi."

She nearly choked and had to struggle to speak. "Hi, yourself. What is that for?" She tried to convince herself he had merely run into someone selling flowers and had bought it out of an act of charity. It didn't mean anything personal.

"It's for you."

Very delicately, she took the flower from him, scrounged through the cupboards for the only bud vase she owned, and placed it in the middle of the kitchen table. Before she left the room, she inhaled its sweet fragrance. No man had ever given her flowers before, and therefore, she knew she would always treasure this moment. She dreamed of the day a man would give her a flower as more than a kindhearted gesture. One day it would be for romance. But until then, she could dream. She wished Ken was more her type, but he wasn't.

Everything about Molly shouted casual, but Ken was seriously suit and tie, although he looked fabulous in jeans. Almost everything Molly did was spontaneous. Ken had his whole life planned out. He was well on his way to being rich. She. . .wasn't.

Molly cleared her throat. "I've got the perfect place in mind for dinner. Really casual. It's always crowded and loud because lots of people take their kids, but the food's great."

Ken smiled, and Molly forgot what else she was going to say. One day, when he did start courting someone, that would be one very lucky woman. And she knew the perfect person.

❧

"Ken, I'd like you to meet my friend Gwen."

"Pleased to meet you, Gwen."

"Pleased to meet you too, Ken."

Molly stifled a giggle. Ken and Gwen. The combination sounded so silly, but there was nothing silly about the way they looked together as they chatted in the noisy living room. Gwen was taller than Molly, thinner, and with the understated grace of a model. She couldn't help but picture Ken in his usual suit with his usual dignified demeanor, well mannered and gracious, as always. They suited each other.

Just like Ken, Gwen also tended to be quiet and reserved when in a crowd. Gwen had class. Gwen also had hair that behaved and didn't look like she stuck her finger in a light socket every time the weather got a little damp, which in Vancouver was almost always.

Molly laid a hand on Ken's free arm, then hastily pulled it away when she realized she was touching him. "I've known Gwen for years, and Gwen was one of the people who helped me find Jesus."

He smiled and nodded at Gwen. "I've heard quite a bit about you."

Gwen laughed softly. "I've heard a lot about you too. We'll have to talk."

Molly watched the two of them smiling at each other. Her own smile began to drop, but she forced it back.

Robbie's voice drifted from the kitchen. "Gwen? Who are you talking to?"

Robbie and Garrett rounded the corner arm in arm. Molly caught them exchanging a glance that made her long for the day someone would look at her like that, and that someday she could be as in love as her friends.

"Oh, Ken, Molly. We didn't hear you come in."

Before she could say anything, the doorbell rang and more people entered. Everyone stood and chatted for a few minutes, then took their seats. Molly quickly sat in Garrett's big armchair, which left Ken to sit beside Gwen.

They shared a number of prayer requests, which included praying for Ken and his broken arm. Molly cringed as a few of the people kept looking back and forth between herself and Ken. Before she'd come to know Ken so well, she'd been very distraught as she told the group that she'd been the one responsible for his injury. She had barely managed to not break down and cry in front of them when she asked for prayer for the situation. Now, here he was, in person. She didn't know what to make of the way everyone kept looking at them.

Ken seemed not to notice the sideways glances. She forced herself to smile when Ken thanked everyone for their prayers, and they moved on to the topic of their study.

Every once in awhile, she sneaked a peek at Ken and Gwen, sitting side by side. They were comfortable together. When the study was over, they remained seated, engrossed in conversation while others socialized around them.

Molly squirmed in her chair. It was exactly what she wanted, but seeing them together, she wondered why she didn't feel very happy.

Chapter 14

Molly told Ken he could just drop her off, but he insisted on escorting her all the way up to her door. Once there, she couldn't very well turn him away, so she invited him in and put the kettle on to boil for tea, since it wasn't that late.

She nearly dropped the teapot when she turned around and saw him standing in the doorway to the kitchen instead of where she left him, sitting on the futon.

"I thought I'd see if I could do anything to help."

"With one hand? I don't think—" Molly slapped her hands over her big mouth. She'd done it again.

"Don't worry, Molly. You don't have to watch what you say around me. I'm a big boy, and I'm fully aware of my limitations. But praise God they're only temporary." He raised the cast slightly and grinned. "Besides, I can still reach the top shelf with my other hand. You can't."

"Very funny."

"It's true."

Molly scowled. "I don't need anything on the top shelf." When Gwen came over, it was Gwen who reached the stuff on the top shelf. Molly busied herself finding the box of tea bags and searched through the cupboards for a bag of cookies that she knew she had somewhere.

"I like your friends. Thank you for inviting me. I guess I'll see them all again on Sunday."

"Yeah." Last week Gwen hadn't been there, but she would be there next Sunday.

He didn't say anything but continued to stand in the doorway, watching.

"I thought you and Garrett would spend all your time talking about camping and the great outdoors."

"I really didn't have a lot of time to talk to him. The evening went so fast."

Molly poured the boiled water into the teapot. "I know," she mumbled, concentrating intently on her aim. "You spent all your time talking to Gwen."

"What did you say?"

She turned the cookie bag upside down and dumped some cookies onto the plate. "Nothing," she muttered under her breath while she shoved the bag back into the cupboard.

"I don't remember you telling me that Garrett and Gwen are twins. That's fascinating. I understand they have a very unique relationship."

She took a spoon and fished the tea bag out of the pot and splatted it in the sink, perhaps throwing it a little too hard. "Yeah."

"Did you know that when they were young, they did a number of magazine ads and even a commercial? It's too bad they didn't have VCRs back then. Gwen said she would have liked to have saved a copy to show her children someday."

Molly slammed the lid onto the teapot. "You spent enough time talking to her. I'm surprised she didn't tell you her life's story."

Instead of turning and walking into the living room, Ken stepped forward. Before she had a chance to start pouring their tea, he rested his fingers on her cheek, drawing her complete attention to his eyes. His beautiful dark blue eyes. Eyes that saw down into her soul. Only inches separated them.

"Mostly, we talked about you."

Her heart started pounding, and she couldn't control it. She wanted to move. She couldn't. "Me?"

His thumb brushed under her chin. Butterflies fluttered in Molly's stomach. She reminded herself to breathe. Ken's voice came out in a deep whisper. "You know what I want to do, don't you?"

He tilted her chin up. The butterflies engaged in battle. She tried to keep her eyes open. She really did. But they drifted closed of their own accord as their lips touched. And she was lost.

❧

Ken kissed Molly, and in so doing, the last remaining reservations of why he shouldn't be doing this were gone. He kissed her gently at first and then with all the love in his heart. He wanted to wrap his arms around her and envelop her completely as he kissed her, but the best he could do was run the fingers of his right hand through her soft, silky hair. With his left arm fixed in a forty-five degree angle, he could only touch his fingertips to the side of her waist.

When she raised her arms and wrapped them around his neck, he thought his heart would burst. He was kissing the woman he loved, and she was kissing him back.

It took great restraint to stop. Instead of releasing her completely, he held her until he could let go without feeling like a piece of him was missing.

"I think we should go into the living room," Molly said at the same time as she picked up both mugs, now filled with lukewarm tea.

Ken picked up the plate of cookies and followed her. He set the plate on the coffee table and sat on the left side of the futon. While Molly placed the cups on the table and picked up the remote for the television, Ken patted the seat beside him. "Please sit beside me."

Her eyes widened, but she didn't comment. When she actually did sit beside him, his breath released in a rush, and it was only then he realized he'd been holding it. Without hesitation, he slipped his arm around her until she leaned into him, and he held her in a loose embrace.

The program droned on. It was supposed to be a sitcom, but Ken wasn't paying attention. Molly was warm and comfortable as she leaned against him, settled in for the duration of the show, which he hoped was an hour long. It was very rare for her to be silent for so long, and he hoped it was because she was enjoying the closeness as much as he was.

After about ten minutes, as he knew would happen, Molly was the first to break the silence. She turned and forced direct eye contact while his arm remained around her shoulders. "I thought you just wanted to be friends."

"I do. There's more than one type of friend, you know."

No answer came, and Ken smiled to himself at her lack of response as she settled back in. He could almost hear the gears whirring around in her head. The type of friend he wanted Molly to be was the happily ever after kind. The kind a man wanted as his best friend and helpmate during the day and his lover at night. That one in a million woman, chosen for him by God, to be together for the rest of their lives, the mother of his children. He wanted to marry Molly. But just as he had promised, before he asked for her hand in marriage, he fully intended to court her properly.

By the close of the program, she still hadn't said anything, so Ken thought it was a good time to make a graceful exit. Despite how he wanted to kiss her, he left her at the door with a chaste kiss on the cheek. Now all he had to do was figure out what to do next.

❧

Ken heard her before he saw her. Or rather, he heard a strange hush and a few people calling out her name in greeting as she walked into the office. He knew she was very sensitive to potential gossip concerning his attentions toward her in the office, so Ken tried his best to concentrate on his work and not look up until Molly slid into her chair at the desk beside him.

"Good morning, Molly. And how—" He lifted his head and blinked a few times, but the sight before him didn't change. "What have you done to your hair!?"

A different Molly faced him. The red was gone. Instead of the vivid and lively color he'd come to know and love, it was some kind of lifeless, dull, dark brown. The bounce was also gone. It lay flat and tame and sluggish and in an orderly style. It didn't suit her at all.

He stood and walked the two steps to her desk so he could speak without the entire office listening in. He did his best to ignore those around who were pretending they weren't watching or straining to hear their every word.

"It's a henna." She shook her head to show it off, and it still didn't bounce. "Do you like it?"

He hated it.

She ran the fingers of both hands through it, and it fell heavily when she let it go. He started to lift his free hand to also run his fingers through it to examine the loss, almost needing to feel it as proof that she'd really done it. At the last second, he clenched his fingers and dropped his hand to his side, remembering they were in plain view of anyone who cared to look. And they were looking.

It finally hit him. Molly was right. He had to be very careful about what he said and did around her. His obvious shock and the way he'd approached her without thinking just proved to the entire office staff that she meant more to him than simply a mere employee. If anyone else had done something so drastic with their hair, it might have garnered a raised eyebrow, but nothing more.

When he first met Molly he'd been amazed by the striking color of her hair. The more he saw her, the more it continually fascinated him how she could never get it under control. It enchanted him, just as the woman beneath the wild hair.

"Is it permanent?"

"No, after a few washings it comes out. I think. But it's supposed to be really good for your hair. I'm not sure about the color. What do you think?"

He didn't know very much about women, but there were certain things he knew a man had to be careful about when expressing his opinions. He suspected this was one of them. "I think, uh, that it might be a little," he struggled to find the right word, "dark."

"I did it last night. I might have used a little too much or left it on too long or something. I'm not sure I did it right, and I don't think I got it all out. It was really late."

He wondered why in the world she would have stayed up late to play with her hair, which was perfectly fine the way it was. Not that it was late when he left, but when he arrived home at his uncle's house he'd gone straight to bed. He had fallen asleep right away and dreamed of little children with bright red hair.

"There was nothing wrong with your hair."

She ran her fingers through it again. "It never behaves and when it gets damp it gets so wild and frizzy. Don't you ever want to change your hair just for the sake of something different?"

He patted the top of his head. He'd worn it in the same style for years. It looked fine and was easy to care for with regular trips to the salon. "No."

She shrugged her shoulders. "Well, I think I might regret this, but at least I can say I tried it. I'll probably wash it out as soon as I get home from work tonight."

Ken decided that tonight he would leave her alone. He understood the standard brush-off joke when a woman didn't want to date someone, she would use the excuse that she had to wash her hair. In this instance, it was legitimate, and in this case, he would encourage it.

"I have plans for Friday night, but don't forget that you promised to take me sightseeing on Saturday."

"Of course. I haven't forgotten."

Rather than give the office more to speculate on, Ken returned his attention to the project on his desk.

He could hardly wait for Saturday.

❧

As soon as Ken pulled up, Molly ran to the car and hopped in. During their excursion to the zoo and aquarium at Stanley Park, they somehow ended up holding hands. At the time she didn't attach too much significance to it since every tank was surrounded by a close crowd and they didn't want to get separated. However, after the way he'd kissed her, claiming some kind of friendship she never dreamed would involve kissing, she wanted to make sure that this time there would be no opportunity for more of the same.

Today she was going to take him to the marketplace. Unlike the aquarium, today they would be in bright daylight where everything was busy and offered no privacy.

"I'm going to introduce you to the SkyTrain today. We're going to leave your car at the Park-N-Ride. Go that way." She pointed in the right direction.

"Your hair looks nice."

It didn't look any different than normal. She ran her fingers through it, then fluffed it up. "Thanks. I had to wash it a number of times over the past few days, but I got most of the henna out. It's almost back to my natural shade. I guess I'll never do that again. Maybe I'll get it cut instead."

"No!"

Ken's sudden exclamation made Molly jump. She turned to him, and not only did his cheeks turn red, his ears flushed too. She couldn't remember knowing a man who blushed before, yet again she'd caught Ken doing it. She found the trait rather endearing.

His voice lowered and he cleared his throat. "Of course, it's your decision, but I like your hair the way it is." He turned into the parking lot and found a space.

They walked to the station, bought their tickets out of the machine, and climbed the stairs to the platform to wait for the next SkyTrain.

"I've never been on a monorail before. This should be interesting."

"Thousands of people take it every day. It's part of the regular transit system, no different than a bus, except it's above the ground. Plus there's no traffic."

The next train approached the station, slowed, and when it came to a stop, the doors whooshed open. Molly led Ken into the nearest car.

"Isn't anyone going to check our tickets?"

"No. It's an honor system. They have random checks. Someone might come check and see if we have our tickets somewhere along the ride."

They sat down. Electronic chimes sounded to signal the doors closing, and the train started moving.

"How fast does this thing go?"

"I'm not sure. I think up to forty miles an hour. It actually goes pretty fast.

I must admit I was nervous at first with a fully automated system."

"Fully automated?"

"Yes. There's no driver."

Ken's face paled, and Molly wondered if he would bolt, except the car was already in motion. "What do you mean, no driver?"

Molly rested her hand on his shoulder. "Don't worry. It's run by a computer, but they do have people at the main control center. It's always monitored."

"You're serious. There really isn't a driver?" He glanced forward. They were in the center car, and they couldn't see the first car, but Molly knew all the cars were identical, because none required staffing.

She smiled, imagining his reaction to her next statement. "Don't worry. If anything happens, the system simply shuts down."

He looked out the window to the ground, about twelve feet below as they whizzed along. "Then what? Does everyone have to jump?"

"No, everyone just waits until it moves again. There's a radio in every car in case of emergency, see?" She pointed to the unit, clearly marked to be used only in time of emergencies. "Problems don't happen as often as they used to."

"Why doesn't that instill me with confidence?"

Molly couldn't help herself. She laughed. "Relax, I'm teasing you. The technology works really well. Stops between stations are extremely rare. Enjoy the ride."

He mumbled something under his breath about his perfectly reliable car sitting idle in the parking lot, but Molly couldn't fully understand what he was saying. She decided not to comment further and leaned back in the seat.

As the monorail continued on its path through the city, Molly filled him in about the districts and municipalities they passed through, the points of interest, and then a bit of history as the train went underground at the downtown core of Vancouver. In due time, they arrived at the end of the line where all passengers exited. Most walked to the SeaBus terminal.

Molly didn't take the SkyTrain or the SeaBus often, but had done it enough to know the routine. Having been born and raised in the Vancouver area, she could tell by watching which people were boarding the SeaBus for the first time, observing their first shaky steps as they walked from the solid land onto the floating portion of Vancouver's public transit system as it bobbed slightly in the water. Ken was no different.

Once aboard, she led Ken to the front seats against the window. Molly bit her bottom lip as Ken tried not to look too enthralled with the uniqueness of the next part of their journey. She suspected that if he were younger, his face would have been pressed to the glass, just as the young boys beside them. They passed Stanley Park and the floating fueling stations for boats on the river, past a massive ocean container vessel, then pulled into the docking station in North Vancouver. Most of the crowd traveled from the SeaBus to the market.

"Here we are. The Lonsdale Quay."

He tilted his head back to take in the sprawling three-story complex. "It's huge."

The first section she led him to was the food court, where she stopped to buy her favorite snack. "Try this. It's great." She held the morsel up to his face.

He craned his neck backward. "What is it?"

"I'm not sure what's in it. Mostly seafood mushed up and wrapped in some kind of Oriental-type white stuff."

"No, thanks. I think I'll pass."

Molly popped it into her mouth and savored it, bite by bite. "Coward."

"Yes, but I'm a live coward."

She licked her fingers, then pinched her thumb and index finger together and gave them a loud smacking kiss as she moved her hand away from her mouth. "You don't know what you're missing."

"That's fine with me."

Molly snorted and led him to the next concession.

"You're not buying something else strange to eat, are you?"

"Yup."

After that, Molly led him around the market, which varied from artisans displaying and constructing their wares, curio and souvenir shops, produce, and entrepreneurs selling everything imaginable.

She was about to lead him outside so they could sit on the bench beside the Burrard Inlet and rest their feet for a few minutes before they went to the next level when his hand closed around hers and pulled gently.

"Wait. I want to go in here."

"But that's a toy store."

"I know. Something caught my eye."

As far as Molly could remember, Ken was an only child and didn't have any cousins, so she knew he didn't have any nieces or nephews back home. She didn't know who he might want to buy a toy for, but since they'd looked at nearly everything at the marketplace, she allowed him to lead her into the toy store.

He went straight for a rack of stuffed toys, where he dropped her hand and picked out a small fuzzy bear.

He held it up and smiled. "Perfect."

Without another word, he proceeded to pay for it, and they left the store.

Molly led him outside to the bench, flopped down, stretched out her feet while wiggling her toes inside her sneakers, arched her back, then turned to Ken. While she was curious about the bear, she did manage to hold herself back from asking, because it was probably none of her business.

He fumbled with the bag enough to grasp the bottom with the fingers that were sticking out of the cast, reached inside with his free hand, and pulled out the bear. "This is for you." He laid it in her hands, and then to her surprise, he raised his hand and ran his fingers through the bottom strands of her hair. "It's the same color as your beautiful hair. Without the henna."

Molly stared at the cute little bear. In its own little way, it seemed to be smiling at her, almost laughing, if a toy could do such a thing. She tried not to think about the odd color of her hair except when she was buying clothes, and at that time, she usually considered it a curse. When she met new people, the first thing they generally commented on was her flaming, wild hair. To see the same color on a toy was indeed a shock to her system. It looked better on the bear than it did on her.

"I don't know what to say. Thank you."

She lifted her head, but instead of what she expected, his fingers drifted to her chin and he leaned his face close to hers. "You're welcome," he whispered against her lips, then brushed the lightest of kisses to her mouth.

Against her better judgment, she was disappointed when he didn't kiss her again. Instead of sitting back in the chair immediately, he only moved a few inches away, smiled, and maintained eye contact, making her hope he was going to kiss her again despite the public setting. When a noise sounded behind them, Ken leaned back fully on the bench but sustained eye contact. Most important, his contented little smile highlighted the adorable crinkles at the corners of those eyes she was beginning to know and love.

Despite the unusual location, Molly considered what he'd done quite romantic. Acting outside his conservative nature, he surprised her and she was delighted, even though she shouldn't have been.

"Let's get back inside. We made it about halfway through, we still have lots to see."

He never lost his smile. This time, when Molly stood, Ken reached out for her hand, as if she needed help up, then didn't let go. After the little flutter her heart made when he kissed her, she didn't want to protest, so they continued on to investigate the shops hand in hand.

As they passed a boutique displaying a few souvenir T-shirts in the window, Molly stopped. "Wait. This is what every tourist to Vancouver has to have. I'll bet you don't have anything that says 'Vancouver' on it, do you?"

"But I'm not a tourist. I live here now."

"That's beside the point."

Not giving him any opportunity to protest, she pulled his hand and led him into the store, where she saw someone holding one of the shirts up to a light, which was part of the display inside the store. After being exposed to the light, the black and white sketch outline drawing came alive with colors.

Molly shook his hand, just in case he wasn't watching. "Wow, look at that! The shirt changes in the light. Did you see it?"

"That's fascinating. I wonder how it's done?"

Molly yanked one off of the rack and held it up to his chest. "Perfect. Don't move."

Before he had a chance to open his mouth, she rushed off to pay for the T-shirt.

Within a few minutes, Molly returned to Ken and held out the bag toward him. "This is for you. It makes you a proper tourist."

"But I already told you, I'm not—"

She held one finger in the air to silence him. "Consider it an initiation. Everyone has to have a shirt that says 'Vancouver' on it. I've got one too."

"Thank you, Molly. I don't know what to say."

"Then don't say anything. Come on. We still have lots of stuff to see."

When he reached for the bag, Molly stuffed it into her purse instead. This way, he would have his only available hand free to hold her hand. She didn't want to think of why she wanted it so badly. Monday, when they were back to work, it would be business as usual, but for now, she planned to enjoy herself, which mostly included a good case of the warm fuzzies from being with Ken.

They wandered past all the small shops, but every once in awhile, she made sure she led him back to someplace she could buy a snack.

"Don't you ever quit eating?"

Molly finished the last prawn in the bag from her latest purchase and threw the tail in the garbage bin. "This isn't really eating. It's snacking. All the calories I consumed today are canceled by the diet cola."

"I'm not even going to comment."

She also chose not to mention that Ken had consumed a fair amount of food himself, especially considering how much he complained. Even if he protested today, one day she would get him to eat seafood. "I just want to get one more thing, and I think we'd better head home."

He nodded. "It's probably not a good idea to wander around here after dark, is it?"

"I don't know, but I'd think not. We're a long way from home."

He checked his watch. "Fine by me. Let's head back."

Molly redirected him to the place that sold the little seafood rolls and asked for two, determined this time to at least get him to taste it. To her horror, she discovered that after paying for the T-shirt, she didn't have enough money left in her wallet.

She lowered her voice to a whisper. "Ken, can you do me a favor? Can I borrow some money?"

"I'd be more than happy to buy it for you, Molly."

She shook her head. "No. I want to buy one for you. You've really got to try this. I'll pay you back. I promise."

One side of his mouth quirked up. "Let me get this straight. You're borrowing money so you can buy me something I have no intention of trying."

Her face flamed. "Something like that."

His laughter rang out, a cheery sound that made Molly's heart beat faster, which was something else she became determined to control. "A deal I can't refuse." Once he paid for the two rolls, the clerk presented them to Molly, and she turned to give one to him.

Molly delved into hers immediately, savoring every bite. Ken stared at his in such a way that she wondered if he had the use of both hands if he would be picking it apart like a little kid before deciding if he was actually going to risk taking a bite.

She nudged him with her elbow, since both her hands were busy. "Taste it. It's really good."

He took the smallest bite known to man, then rolled it around in his mouth before swallowing it almost painfully. "Sorry, but I really don't like seafood." Sheepishly, he handed it back to her.

Molly sighed. "I'm not shy. I love these things." Gustily, she ate Ken's roll, then licked her fingers. "Okay, let's go home."

"I guess we've both eaten so many snacks that stopping for supper is a foolish idea."

Molly nodded and tried to hold back a burp.

Chapter 15

Molly slid into the seat of the SkyTrain car, and Ken slid in beside her. "There are far less people going home than on the way here, aren't there?"

"Yes," Molly said. "This is normal for a Saturday. Remember, for most people, this is suppertime."

"We've been sitting here for a long time. Why aren't we moving?"

"The SkyTrain turns around here. See, behind us." Molly pointed to the opening where the switch for the track was, just beyond the wall. "This is where the trip begins eastbound, so the train will just sit here for a few minutes until it's time to go. It's a schedule thing." Molly turned her head, but Ken was looking around the car. He tilted his head back as he read the ads displayed in a neat row along the curved edge of the ceiling of the car.

"Look at that. There's an ad for a 3-D movie. I remember when I was a kid, some cereal box had a 3-D picture on it, and they enclosed the glasses to go with it. I was fascinated by it. I was about nine years old and attempted to draw some 3-D pictures. My mother saved a few, even after all these years. It's harder than you'd think it would be, you know. I can't imagine a whole movie in 3-D."

"You mean you've never been to a 3-D movie before? Are you serious?"

He nodded, then shook his head. "Never."

Molly started to push him out of the seat, forcing him to stand. "You don't know what you're missing. Let's go."

"But we haven't even gone one stop."

"I know. It's right here. Let's go." Molly continued to nudge him until they were both out of the car. "I haven't seen this one yet, and I hear it's really good. It's all taken underwater."

The chimes sounded, the doors swooshed closed, and the SkyTrain moved away, leaving them standing alone on the platform.

"I can't believe this. We left the train. We just got on it. We didn't even go one stop."

"You're going to enjoy this. I know it. This way."

She nearly dragged him out of the station, up the escalator, and toward the convention center. They walked slowly up the stairs and down the long side of the convention center until they arrived at the entrance to the IMax Theater.

From a distance, Molly squinted to read the board above the ticket booth which showed the features and times. She shook his elbow when she found what she wanted. "We're in luck. The one I want to see starts in half an hour. We can buy our tickets now and enjoy the scenery for awhile. It's really pretty from up here, isn't it?"

"Where are we?"

"This is the Burrard Inlet. We just crossed it on the SeaBus. Over there, see? That way is Stanley Park."

"I knew that. I meant this place."

The wind ruffled his hair as he turned to look down the inlet. She imagined he could have been a pirate, facing into the wind off the bow of his ship, ready to experience yet another adventure. The only thing that marred the image of a brave adventurer was that one sleeve of his jacket hung empty, and she could see the cast and sling peeking through the opening. Molly wondered what pirates did in days of old when they broke an arm.

"It's called Canada Place. It was built for Expo '86, but now it's a convention center. The IMax Theater is part of the complex."

He leaned over the railing, three stories above the water, inhaled deeply, and closed his eyes as another ocean breeze ruffled his hair. "There's nothing like this where I come from."

"I think we should go buy the tickets now. We don't want to miss out on getting great seats." She started to reach for her purse, but Ken's hand on her arm stopped her.

"Please, it's my treat. Don't embarrass me by insisting."

Molly snapped her mouth shut. As if she needed more reminders. The difference this time was that here she could put the tickets on her credit card, especially now that she knew exactly how much, or rather how little, she had in her wallet.

Instead of waiting inside for the show to start, they returned to the railing to enjoy the view and the fresh sea breeze. Fighting the chill of the wind, Molly wished she had worn a warmer jacket but wasn't willing to give up the delight of the moment. She struggled to control a shiver. After a very poorly suppressed shudder, she crossed her arms and hunched her shoulders.

Ken stepped closer, and she thought he was about to suggest they go inside since he couldn't do up his jacket because of the cast. To her surprise, he slipped his arm around her shoulders and pulled her close. She fit neatly into the opening of his unbuttoned jacket, with the hardness of his cast pushing gently against the side of her waist. She looked up and opened her mouth to protest, but no sound came out as he grinned down at her.

"You looked cold. One thing I've learned so far is that you West Coast people don't know how to dress for cool weather. I'd bet you don't own a pair of proper winter boots, do you?"

All Molly could do was shake her head. She no longer felt the cold. It was true, the size of him sheltered her from the wind, but the heat generated came from within.

"See? And you're keeping me warm now, too, since I couldn't do my jacket up."

She knew they were supposed to be checking out the scenery, but she continued to look up at him.

His voice lowered in pitch, and he nuzzled his face into her hair. "We're good together, Molly."

Molly's heart hammered in her chest. He was right. They were good together, and not just to keep warm. He kept her disorganized habits in place, and she loosened him up. He quieted her down, and she brought his gentle nature to life. They laughed at the same things, and the same issues upset them both. She liked being with him. She simply liked him. A lot. More than liked. She loved him.

At the realization, Molly's head spun. Before she could think about it, she felt Ken nuzzling his face into her hair. Then he kissed her temple.

Her heart skipped a beat, then started up in double-time. She couldn't deny it. She did love him. If she turned her head just a little and lifted her chin, she could allow him to kiss her properly. If that happened, without moving too much, she could turn and slip her arms under his jacket and hug him and kiss him right back.

The cool wind on the other side of her head ruffled her hair.

Molly stiffened. She couldn't entertain the thought of kissing Ken now. They were outside a major public attraction, in front of a bunch of people, all strangers.

She squeezed her eyes shut. It didn't matter where they were. Ken was her boss. She couldn't love him.

Molly stepped back. Immediately she missed his warmth. "We should go in now," she stammered.

Once inside, Molly headed straight for the concession.

"Surely you're not going to tell me after all the food you've consumed today, you're hungry."

Her stomach churned. Maybe if she ate some junk food, it would calm her down. She selected the cheapest candy in the display and carefully counted the exact change to the clerk, leaving exactly two cents in her wallet. "I can't watch a movie without a snack. It's not right. It's a rule."

He didn't say a word, but she could imagine what he was thinking. Candy in hand, Molly directed him toward the entrance to the theater room, where two ushers were distributing the special 3-D glasses to patrons as they entered.

Ken groaned softly. "Don't tell me everyone is going to be wearing those horrible green and red glasses."

He almost stopped walking, but Molly pushed him from behind, determined to focus all her attention on the upcoming movie instead of Ken and what he was doing to her system. "You really haven't been to one of these before, have you? They're not red and green. They look just like regular sunglasses. The movie is in beautiful bright vivid color. It looks just like a regular movie when you put the glasses on, only better, because you could swear that some of the stuff is almost in your lap. It's a real experience."

Ken mumbled something under his breath that Molly couldn't hear, so she ignored him.

The short line inched forward, taking them along with it. They received their 3-D glasses and found their seats.

Ken wiggled the arms of the glasses and held them up to the light. She tried not to laugh at his incredulous expression as he examined them. "These are cardboard. And they're green. Both sides are the same. Are you sure about this? Is this some kind of joke?"

"Trust me. It's different when you're wearing them. Just be patient, okay?"

Before the lights dimmed, Molly struggled to open the bag of licorice, concentrating intently on the little perforated line that was supposed to make it easy. The plastic stretched but refused to tear, making her think that if she couldn't find a pair of scissors in her purse, she should ask for her money back, especially since she'd spent the money she was supposed to have used for her fare home on the candy. She froze for a second as it dawned on her that now she was going to have to borrow more money from Ken to get home. She tugged at the plastic wrapper again, on the verge of desperation when Ken spoke.

"I still don't notice anything any different. Everything's just darker."

Molly gave the plastic another pull, only succeeding in stretching it worse. "They're polarized or something. I don't know how they work. All I know is that they do."

She lowered her head, raised the bag, and opened her mouth, ready to rip it open with her teeth.

"I told myself when I got my laser surgery that I would never wear glasses again, not even sunglasses. Look what you've done to me."

With her mouth wide open and teeth bared mere inches from the bag, Molly paused from her mission and raised her eyes to study him. Ken sat beside her, already wearing the large cardboard 3-D glasses. He scanned the surrounding area, alternately looking through the glasses, then picking them up so the arms remained sitting on his ears, holding the lenses above the level of his eyebrows as he studied the area without looking through them.

"What are you doing?" she whispered between her teeth.

He let the glasses fall back to rest on his nose and turned to her, grinning like a little boy. He scrunched up his nose, making the glasses rise on his cheeks temporarily and drop once more.

Molly's heart skipped a beat. The man was still good-looking wearing oversized cardboard glasses.

They slid down his nose, and he pushed them back into place with his index finger. "So much for my dignified image. Have you ever seen a vice president with cardboard glasses?"

"Vice president?" Molly glanced around the theater, which was rapidly filling up. She wasn't aware Quinlan Enterprises had a vice president. She scanned the crowd around them once more. "There's no one from work here. The only one I know here is. . ." Her voice trailed off. "You. . . ," she whispered.

She stared at him. His 3-D glasses were crooked, and he was still grinning. "What?" he asked.

Suddenly things she'd heard started falling into place. She'd known the production manager's position was safe from being replaced, as was everyone in the office. The only person who would be leaving within a few months was Mr. Rutcliffe, who was about to retire. Everyone knew Ken wasn't going to take that position because Mr. Rutcliffe's assistant was being trained for the job and was doing well, and Ken had nothing to do with either one of them. It all suddenly made sense.

It was Ken. Ken was going to be the vice president. That was the big shake-up rumor said would be happening. Rumor also had it that the senior Mr. Quinlan would be retiring in a few years. When a president left, it was natural that a vice president stepped up to take his place. Even though he was only twenty-seven years old, Ken was being set up to be the future president of Quinlan Enterprises.

She had fallen in love not only with her immediate supervisor but also with the man who was soon going to run a national corporation. When that happened, she, and all the rest of the staff, would be calling Ken "Mr. Quinlan." Molly felt sick.

"Say something. At least tell me how ridiculous I look. But don't sit there with your mouth open."

Molly snapped her mouth shut. All she could do was stare at Ken, who still wore a devastatingly attractive grin beneath the oversized cardboard glasses.

The lights dimmed.

The entire theater stilled and all was quiet. Except her heart. It was pounding so hard surely the erratic thumping echoed through the whole place.

A deep voice boomed through the speaker system; spotlights illuminated the speakers and screens and the cameras in the rear of the large room in sequence as the narrator gave the audience a tour of the workings of the IMax Theater, saving Molly from having to comment.

"This is fascinating," Ken whispered in her ear. "I can't believe all this technology for a movie."

"Yeah," Molly mumbled over the bag, now firmly clenched in her teeth while she tugged at it increasingly harder. All the electronic wizardry in the world wasn't helping her get the sugar she needed so desperately. At the moment she didn't care if she pulled out a tooth—she needed that candy. She was almost ready to scream when it finally gave way, except she was pulling so hard the wrapper tore completely in two. Red licorice nibs flew into the air, landing on everyone around her.

"Mommy! Mommy! It's raining candy!"

People around her stared, and the mother hushed the child while the demonstration continued.

Molly shrank down into her chair, hunched as low as she could. She could hear Ken's muffled laughter beside her as he picked a handful out of his lap. He leaned toward her, then deposited a small handful into her open palm. "Here. It's not exactly manna from heaven, but I managed to recover a few."

She mumbled a thank you and prepared herself to watch the show with her diminished supply of candy as the opening credits and film's title expanded in huge, full 3-D across the screen.

"Wow. This really works. Look at the letters. They seem to pop right off the screen. These green glasses are really something."

Since everyone around her started to become engrossed in the effects in front of them, Molly straightened, determined to enjoy the show, except her mind went blank.

As the movie unfolded, many people reached out as if they could actually touch the images they saw. Everyone in the theater flinched when one of the fishes in the presentation jumped out of the water and the 3-D effects made it appear it was going to land in the viewer's lap. The entire audience laughed, right on cue, and the movie continued.

About halfway through the feature, Molly felt the light brush of fingertips on her left shoulder. She turned her head to see Ken's arm drift behind her neck, then settle in around her other shoulder.

She turned her head to respond, although nothing she could put into words would come out.

He leaned his head to whisper in her ear. "We're not in the back row, but it is a movie theater. You didn't expect me not to put my arm around you, did you?"

No words came. A million jumbled thoughts rolled through her head. She couldn't concentrate on the movie, despite the spectacular 3-D effects.

She considered her options. She could handle being friends with him, except it appeared he no longer had merely "friendship" in mind. Between all the hand-holding and the times he'd draped his arm around her, she'd never had any friend touch her so much. She'd certainly never had any of her friends kiss her.

His words of "courting her properly" echoed through her head. She tried to imagine what it would be like to date him.

While going shopping to the market and movies and volleyball night at church were her style, she doubted those activities would suit the future president of a large and growing corporation. The closest she'd been to attending a high-class affair, not counting the Chamber of Commerce dinner, was when she'd gone with friends to see *Joseph and the Technicolor Dreamcoat* at an upscale live theater presentation at the Queen Elizabeth Theater. The price of the tickets had been horrendous, and while she'd enjoyed the live acting, she'd felt terribly out of place during intermission. A few ladies were wearing gowns that had likely cost more than her entire wardrobe. Aside from attending theater productions she couldn't afford, she had no idea what the rich and famous did for fun, or if they had fun at all.

If she did start dating Ken, she didn't know how she would be able to face the people she'd worked with for the past five years. Some of them had come to be her friends. Some of those same people would soon begin to hate her for anything they would perceive as favoritism from the boss, especially when plans for Ken's position were announced. She couldn't blame anyone who did, because if the situation were reversed, she would probably feel the same.

There had already been rumors concerning her time spent alone with Ken, so already her reputation was becoming questionable. She couldn't allow her good reputation, or Ken's, to become sullied.

They belonged in separate worlds. Everything about him shouted class and position, education, dignity, and grandeur. Molly liked her casual, laid-back lifestyle. She liked her one-room apartment because it was less area to keep clean.

She tried to think what would happen if she threw caution to the wind and dated him anyway. That would mean working with him while dating him, and she knew that wasn't a good idea. After Robbie's relationship with her boss's son ended in disaster, Robbie had been promptly fired. She didn't think Mr. Quinlan would fire her when she and Ken broke up, but she couldn't be positive. Even if he didn't, she couldn't see working side by side with Ken every day if a relationship ended badly, especially if he was to be the future president. She'd have to quit before she was fired.

She'd almost worked herself into a sweat when Ken's fingers moved on her shoulder, reminding her that she sat snuggled into his arm. She wondered if his periodic movements were involuntary, or if he was doing it on purpose to remind her that his arm was around her, apparently to stay.

In front of her in panoramic glory, fishes swam, birds flew, and underwater plants swayed. It all went by in a blur. Ken gave her shoulder another gentle squeeze, a tender and very personal touch reminding her once again that he considered this a date. When they left this morning, she had thought their day together would be a friendly outing showing a tourist around town, yet now they were snuggled together in the dark. To anyone watching, they were a couple, regardless of what was going through her head.

All she knew was that it wouldn't work. They were too far apart in everything in life, both personally and professionally. That she'd already fallen in love with him didn't matter. They were too wrong for each other.

"Molly?" Ken's voice whispered in her ear. "Look at me for a second."

He drew his arm away, but instead of sitting back in his chair and letting his arm drop into his lap, his fingers brushed her chin, tipping it up slightly. "The movie is almost over. May I kiss you while it's still dark?"

It was nice of him to ask, except he didn't give her an opportunity to answer.

Without removing the cardboard glasses, he tilted his head and kissed her, slowly and gently, and with such a tender sweetness Molly resented the slow brightening of the house lights which caused them to separate.

He backed up slowly, released her chin, and removed his 3-D glasses. His open and unguarded expression made Molly want to kiss him again, but she didn't dare.

His voice seemed deeper than usual, with a delightful low and husky quality she'd never heard from him before. "This movie was a wonderful idea. Thank you for suggesting it."

Molly couldn't move. She became aware that Ken had reached up and was slowly pulling the 3-D glasses off her face. He let them fall into his lap, then brushed her cheek with the backs of his fingers.

Here he was, her Mr. Right. But how could her Mr. Right be so Mr. Wrong?

The people beside her stood, ready to leave, forcing Molly to pay attention to what was going on around her. They stood and prepared to exit the theater. Ken carried both pairs of glasses and dropped them into the bin as they left. The second they walked outside into the cool night air, his hand grasped hers, and they followed the crowd to the SkyTrain station.

They barely said a word the entire journey home, and Molly didn't force it. She didn't want to spoil the moment. In one short day, everything had changed. Yesterday they were simply friends. She still hadn't figured out what they were today. She only knew everytyhing was different, and it was wrong. As much as she enjoyed his romantic attentions, she needed his friendship back.

As before, he escorted her up the elevator, through her apartment building, and waited quietly beside her while she unlocked her door. He stepped inside, confirmed there had been no intruders in their absence, and Molly accompanied him back to the door.

Before she met Ken she'd never been at a loss for words, but now words evaded her. She didn't know how to tell the man she loved that it wasn't going to work, that they could only be friends and nothing more.

She didn't know if it was good or bad that they would still be together all day at work, but at work, it was business. No tender touches and, especially, no kissing. The thought nearly broke her heart, but not nearly as much as not being able to see him again. Perhaps functioning at the office side by side she would see enough of him to enjoy his company, yet abide by the rules of office etiquette to keep a safe distance.

Ken stepped closer, and Molly gulped. She was already backed against the wall in the small entranceway and had nowhere to go, short of sliding against the wall and retreating in fear.

Mere inches separated them. She didn't know what she expected him to say, but he surprised her when he didn't say anything. Without a word or preamble, he kissed her exactly the same way he had kissed her in the theater, only this time they didn't have to worry about the house lights coming on, or crowds of people around them.

She didn't want the beauty of his kiss to stop. Molly knew this would be the last time she kissed him and the last time she could see him away from the office. It was too dangerous to her heart. Throwing caution aside, she slid her arms under his jacket and kissed him back with all the love in her heart.

When he finally backed up, Molly needed to catch her breath, and it appeared Ken had the same problem.

He still didn't say anything.

Molly hoped by the time they saw each other next at work, they wouldn't be so tongue-tied.

He brushed a light kiss to her cheek. "Good night, Molly. I'll be here at the usual time tomorrow." He turned and left, shutting the door behind him.

Molly blinked at the closed door. Tomorrow was Sunday.

She hunched her shoulders and buried her face in her hands.

Tomorrow was Sunday, and he was coming to church with her, and there was nothing she could do about it.

Chapter 16

Molly didn't know how she did it, but she made it through Sunday relatively unscathed. She groaned and sank against the door after Ken left, trying to will her heart to stop pounding.

He'd picked her up right on time, dressed in his casual best for church, proudly announcing the lack of a tie. After church she'd almost forgotten about the youth group's fundraising luncheon, but Ken hadn't. Most of the congregation retreated into the foyer to talk while the teens set up the banquet tables and laid out the food. Everyone else had been requested to bring a contribution for the potluck lunch except her.

Gwen suggested that word of her cooking skills had leaked out, and that was why she hadn't been asked. Ken joined all her friends in teasing her about it, although in the end Ken was the only one who defended her culinary talents. He especially enjoyed talking with Garrett. The whole time they were together in front of her church friends, Ken faithfully held onto her hand. She couldn't pull away in front of everyone without worrying about hurting his feelings, so she managed to convince herself to enjoy his company for one more short day.

Except the day wasn't very short.

Somehow, after the banquet, they'd ended up back at Robbie and Garrett's house. Again, Ken got distracted talking to Gwen; the difference this time was that Molly had participated in the conversation, having no choice because Ken wouldn't let go of her hand.

They ordered pizza for supper and attended the evening service, followed by dessert and coffee at a nearby coffee house. They were together from practically sunrise to well after sunset.

He was finally gone, but not before he'd kissed her with such intensity it rocked her to her soul.

She had a wonderful day with him.

She couldn't let it continue.

Molly went to bed but spent most of the night staring up at the ceiling.

❦

Ken smiled as he waited for his computer to boot up. The love of his life was due to walk in the door in seven minutes, and he could hardly wait.

Things were going perfectly. He'd spent another day at her side, most of it with her soft, tender hand enclosed in his. They'd enjoyed their time together, and when the day ended with a heart-stopping kiss, he knew future happiness was

231

within his grasp. In only a few weeks the cast would be off, and he would be able to hold her properly. Life was good.

He knew he was beaming from ear to ear when she sat down at her desk, right beside his, but he couldn't help it. It wouldn't be much longer and he would ask for Molly's hand in marriage, and then the world would know they were together.

"Good morning, Molly."

She sat with her head bowed, shuffling a stack of paper. "Good morning," she mumbled, not lifting her head.

Ken turned away and returned to his work. If Molly was still going to be sensitive about the rest of the staff's reaction to them as a couple, he would respect her wishes, although her less than enthusiastic greeting stung.

She didn't speak much to him all morning.

She didn't want to go out for lunch.

She was away from her desk a good part of the afternoon.

She was taking things a little too far.

By the end of the day, Ken was ready to scream. She was ready to leave. Without him.

"Molly? Would you like to go out for dinner?"

"Dinner? Tonight?"

"Do you have other plans?"

She stiffened and glanced from side to side, and her posture relaxed when she saw they were alone in their corner of the office. "No, I don't have other plans. That would probably be a good idea. I think we should talk."

Ken narrowed one eye. Talking was exactly what he had in mind. However, judging from Molly's reaction, he didn't think they were going to be talking about the same thing.

"Leave your car here. We'll pick it up later."

"Later? But. . ." She shrugged her shoulders. "Okay, I guess so."

During the drive to the restaurant, a sinking feeling settled in the pit of his stomach. All through the meal, every time the conversation gave indications of drifting to serious topics, he quickly steered the discussion to more pleasant subject matter. As well, every time conversation lagged, he made sure to introduce a new topic, keeping things as animated as he could. He'd never talked so much in his life.

Molly appeared to be enjoying their evening together, but he didn't want to give her a chance not to. He ended the evening much sooner than he would have preferred in order to quit while he was ahead.

He mentally kicked himself for pushing her to leave her car at the office, because this would give no opportunity for privacy in which to kiss her good night properly. He respected Molly too much to kiss her in the middle of the company parking lot.

To his relief, after much protest, he convinced her to allow him to follow her home so he could ensure her safety. When they arrived at her building, after escorting her up the elevator, he quickly checked her apartment for intruders, then left with only a quick peck to her cheek before she had a chance to say anything.

Ken started his car, then smacked the steering wheel with his fist. This was the first and last time he intended to play silly games. Tomorrow things would be different.

Molly pulled into her parking space and fought back a yawn as she turned off the engine. After yet another sleepless night, she still couldn't figure out what had happened. For all her intentions, she never got a chance to tell Ken that she couldn't see him again outside of work. He'd been funny, witty, charming, and everything she'd ever dreamed of in the perfect male. Except he was her boss and out of her league. He'd been the perfect gentleman, and she'd fallen even more in love with him, if that were possible.

She craned her neck to check her makeup for signs of smears in the rearview mirror, then entered the office building. Around her, conversations hushed as she headed for her desk. She heard a few badly muffled shushes and a short giggle. It gave her a bad feeling, solidifying even more the reasons she shouldn't be in any type of relationship with Ken. She'd worked too hard and too long to let everything come crashing down around her.

The first place she checked on her way to her desk was Ken's area, but fortunately he wasn't there, he was in his uncle's office. She tried not to appear too relieved, because she could feel people watching her as she approached, even though some were pretending to concentrate too intently on their work for first thing in the morning.

Then she saw it. A crystal bud vase containing a single rose sat on her desk. It didn't take a lot of guessing to know who it was from, even though there was no card. Molly plunked herself into her chair and stared at the flower.

Ken's voice drifted from his uncle's office. "Good. You're here. I need you to type up a quick confidential memo for me."

The second she walked into Mr. Quinlan's office, Mr. Quinlan left, shutting the door behind him, leaving her alone with Ken. She didn't have to turn around to know that half the office was straining to see through the open miniblinds to check out what was going on.

She cleared her throat and stiffened her posture. "Before we get started, I want to talk to you about the flower."

"Ah, yes." He smiled, making Molly's foolish heart flutter. "It was a difficult decision between that rose and another blossom I couldn't identify but smelled quite pleasant. I thought the rose suited you better. I hope you like roses."

"Oh, of course I like roses, they're my favorite flower, especially that two-tone kind you picked. I think that variety is called. . . Hold on. Quit distracting me."

Molly stepped closer, then, remembering the curious stares of the rest of the staff backed up again. "You shouldn't have done that."

"Why not? Men send flowers to women at work all the time. There's no rule that says because we work together I can't send you flowers. While on company property we have certain decorum to adhere to, and I have no intention of crossing that line during working hours. As much as I hate to say it, if you received flowers at the office from another man, you'd accept them and enjoy them all day wouldn't you?"

"Well, of course I would." Not that any man had ever sent her flowers at work, but she assumed she would enjoy them.

"Then don't you think that it's logical to do the same when it's from me?"

She considered it very different when the man who had sent the flower was seated at the desk next to her and was one day going to take over the company. "No. We can't be doing this while we're working here, together. You could send me flowers and we could date and stuff if I was working somewhere else, but I haven't quit yet, so you can't do this."

He grinned. "I'm the boss, or at least one day I'm going to be. I can do anything I want. If that includes sending flowers to the beautiful woman who sits next to me, then I will. So enjoy the rose." His grin widened. "As long as you think of me when you look at it."

Molly opened her mouth to protest but realized it was no use. His self-satisfied smile told Molly she had already lost this battle. Except she had a beautiful rose on her desk to enjoy, from the man she'd fallen in love with.

"Have I just been bamboozled?"

He grinned again. "That depends on your perspective." Ken checked his watch. "I have a meeting in half an hour. We'd better get that memo done."

He was gone for most of the day, which made Molly wonder if that were the reason he'd sent the flower, although she had the impression he really hadn't planned on being gone so long. Whenever she thought no one was looking, she reached out to touch the soft, silky petals and inhale the heady fragrance, then pushed the vase back to the corner of her desk.

It was beautiful and so romantic, and it did make her think of him.

Again, she didn't get the chance to tell him they shouldn't see each other, because he'd told her that while at work, they would stick to strictly business.

She didn't want to think about what would happen after work.

She didn't get a choice. Ken finally arrived back at the office at nearly quitting time, obligating her to stay overtime to type his notes from the meeting as he dictated them.

He didn't want to take the chance of forgetting anything overnight since he had nothing written down. By the time they finished, they were the last ones remaining in the building except for the janitorial staff.

"I owe you for staying so late. May I buy you dinner?"

"You bought me dinner yesterday."

"Then this time you can buy me dinner."

Molly opened her mouth, but nothing came out.

"Just kidding, Molly. I'm going to put it on my expense account. Let's go."

She studied him as he stood in front of her. After typing his notes, she knew it had been a critical and laborious meeting. Dark circles shadowed his eyes, alluding to a poor night's sleep in addition to a stress-filled day. Yet, he would still take her to a fine restaurant, be a perfect date, and she knew she would enjoy herself thoroughly, even if he almost fell asleep in his plate.

"Maybe this isn't such a good idea. You look so tired. Maybe we should both just go home."

Ken shook his head. "We both have to eat, and I'm sure not cooking."

The words were out before Molly had a chance to think about what she was saying. "Then why don't you come over to my place, and I'll cook something simple for the two of us."

"I can't ask you to do that, as much as I appreciate it. You've cooked for me so often I feel guilty. But I am tired. Why don't we pick up some burgers and take them to Uncle Walter and Aunt Ellen's place? We can put our feet up and relax. They'll be in the den watching television, so they won't intrude."

Going to his home, or at least his temporary home, was the perfect opportunity. Molly could say what she had to say when the time was right, and then leave. "That's a great idea. Let's go."

As soon as they walked in the door, Molly was again reminded of why she shouldn't be with Ken. As Ken reached for the closet door, Molly studied the fine house, set in the exclusive British Properties of West Vancouver where many movie stars and millionaires lived. The first time she'd been to Walter Quinlan's home she hadn't seen much, because that was the day she'd broken Ken's arm.

At the front entranceway, the marble floor of the foyer met with a rich burgundy carpet for a room that was big enough to be a living room, except its only purpose was to be an opening to go to the "real" rooms in the huge house. A grand winding staircase led to five bedrooms upstairs. To the side of the sweeping staircase was the opening to a vast living room filled with furnishings and trinkets so expensive she dared not breathe on them, never mind touch them. To the other side was the kitchen and a massive dining room, and then down the hall was a den and a family room, all of which had to be kept clean. The main bathroom, with the glass shower enclosure, the Jacuzzi bathtub, and double sinks, was bigger than the kitchen of her apartment.

She couldn't associate the word "relax" with being in this home, yet Ken was perfectly comfortable here.

Ken opened the closet. "Let me take your coat." Molly's heart clenched. She'd watched him at the office. He could lift his coat with one hand to hang it on a coathook, but it took two hands to use a hanger. She could see the effort required to hold and steady her coat with the fingers sticking out of the cast while he maneuvered the hanger to fit into the sleeves with his right hand.

"Let me do that," she mumbled, and took the coat back.

He didn't argue. Instead, he waited, then led her into the kitchen, carrying the bag of food. His aunt made a brief appearance, then left them alone, which Molly greatly appreciated. After pausing for a prayer of thanks, they began to eat.

Molly didn't feel comfortable in the kitchen either. She supposed the room was supposed to look domestic, with copper pots and antique utensils hanging as decorations, but it only emphasized the differences between them.

Molly didn't belong in the same social circles as someone who thought a place like this was normal. Her whole apartment could fit into the living room of this house, with room to spare.

"This isn't right. Your first time as my guest, and we're sitting in the kitchen. I should have set the dining room table and lit some candles."

Molly couldn't imagine eating fast-food hamburgers on the white lace table-cloth atop the dark wooden table, using fine china.

Her vision blurred as she projected what it would feel like to sit with Ken in his aunt and uncle's elegant dining room. The lights would be dimmed, and rather than the standard cliché of sitting across the table lengthwise from each other, they would be sitting side by side.

The candlelight would reflect in Ken's dark blue eyes, making them shimmer as he gazed lovingly into her eyes. He would smile, and she would smile back, just like in an old movie. He would be wearing a tux with a pristine white shirt and she would be wearing a flowing white gown, and then he would tell her that he loved her as much as she loved him. Violin music would sing its haunting strains in the background, and lovebirds would twitter in the air.

The muffled thwack of the fridge door, followed by a soft clunk, jolted Molly out of her dreamland.

"Sorry, I forgot you like ketchup with your fries. Here you go."

Molly blinked, hard, as she came back to reality with a thud. They were sitting in the kitchen, the ketchup bottle on the table in front of her.

"Uh, thanks." She opened the lid and squeezed a blob of ketchup onto the corner of the plate. She'd never eaten fast-food fries on a plate in her life.

Ken plucked off the top bun of his burger and picked out the pickles, popped them in his mouth, then reassembled his burger.

She could relate to the way he ate a hamburger.

Molly shook her head. She didn't want Ken in her idealistic romantic fantasies, and she didn't want to like the way he ate. She wanted to find something about him that she didn't like, something she could focus on to make ending things easy. She couldn't think of a single thing, except that maybe his nose was a little too big.

Molly swirled a few fries in the blob of ketchup. "You shouldn't have given me that flower at work, you know."

"We already went over this. Besides, you spend more time at work than at home, so I gave it to you where you would see it the most."

She narrowed one eye. "That's not what I meant. I meant you shouldn't have given it to me in the first place."

"Sure I should have. I wanted to give you a little something special."

She didn't want anything special from Ken, little or big. He was too easy to fall in love with—she didn't need help or encouragement. Now it was too late, and it couldn't continue.

"I don't know what you're trying to do, but this isn't going to work."

"I disagree."

Molly shook her head. "You're so focused. You've got your whole life planned! You have solid goals that you've been working on for years. You're so organized, and I'm. . ." She glanced around the massive pristine home he felt so comfortable in and compared it to her one-room apartment. Unless she was expecting visitors, her floor was littered with books and magazines, a few stray socks, and other odds and ends. She tried to set the futon back into a couch when she wasn't running late but often forgot to put her pillow away. She usually dusted and vacuumed once a week but frequently forgot. She did her grocery shopping the day after she ran out of food. ". . .I'm not."

"I know that. It makes you more interesting."

"Look at you!" She waved one hand in the air. A blob of ketchup from the fry she was holding splatted onto her plate. Before more dribbled, she shoved it into her mouth. "You're the most comfortable in those custom-tailored suits, perfectly pressed, with perfectly matched ties. My favorite clothes are a five-year-old T-shirt and jeans with a hole in the knee."

Ken smiled halfheartedly. "Opposites attract?"

"And another thing." She waved both hands in the air, now that both were free. "How can I face the people I've worked with for five years? You're going to run the company. Probably own it one day! You know how people talk. I've already heard some wild rumors about our hot relationship."

The halfhearted grin turned to a full smile. "Hot relationship?"

Molly crossed her arms and glared at him.

He patted his tie, cleared his throat, and controlled the smile. "You don't have to worry about what people will say. When we get married, you won't have to work at all, unless you want to. You wouldn't necessarily have to work for Quinlan Enterprises either."

"What!?"

"If you felt awkward, I wouldn't mind if you quit and went elsewhere to work. I'd understand."

"Married!?"

He shook his head, then rose to his feet. "I'm sorry—I'm doing this all wrong."

Very slowly, he turned her swivel chair so she now sat facing him. With his hand resting lightly on the wall for balance he sank to one knee, and once aptly positioned, he reached out to grasp her left hand with his right. "I love you, Molly McNeil. Will you marry me?"

All Molly could do was stare at him. He couldn't love her.

It had been easy to fall in love with him, and she imagined that many women before her had fallen for his kind and gentle ways. She couldn't imagine how he could possibly have fallen in love with her. She didn't have a gentle bone in her body.

"This can't be happening. There's a logical explanation for this. Everything in your life is all mixed up, and you're just a little confused. It's a psychological reaction. The shock of breaking your arm, being uprooted and thrown into staying with your aunt and uncle, the move to a completely different city halfway across the country, the new job, and enormous responsibilities. Soon you'll settle into a new routine and be able to think more clearly. It's all been too overwhelming for you."

He shook his head and squeezed her hand gently. "No, Molly. I'm thinking very clearly—more clearly than in my entire life. I love you, and I want you to marry me."

Molly yanked her hand away. "No! It isn't right." She jumped to her feet, sending the chair skidding back behind her. "I can't. You don't."

Ken rested his hand on the wall for support and rose to his feet. "I do, Molly."

His choice of words nearly made her heart stop beating. His "I do" echoed through her head. Wedding words. The ultimate vow of love and devotion.

"You can't. This is all wrong. I wouldn't be seeing you if I hadn't broken your arm. This whole mess is my fault. We can't see each other anymore."

Before she burst into tears in front of him, Molly grabbed her purse off the floor and dashed out of the room. She ran through the entrance hallway, slamming the front door behind her.

She ran all the way to the car and took off without taking the time to fasten her seatbelt. Before she turned the corner, she glanced in the rearview mirror. The door of the mansion opened, and Ken appeared in the doorway as she drove away.

His shocked expression burned into her heart. But he would see she was right, and he'd get over it.

It was herself she wasn't sure of.

Chapter 17

Feeling more bleary-eyed than she ever had in her life, Molly pushed open the office door.

If this was what it was like to be in love, she wanted no part of it.

Through all the hours of staring up at the ceiling in the dark, she had come to a decision. She was wrong. At first she thought it would be better to work with Ken and keep their relationship strictly business rather than never see him again. Now she knew different. She couldn't work with him. She couldn't see him every day and ignore the pain of wanting what she couldn't have, or worse, pretending everything was okay, when her life would never be okay again. As soon as he settled in and made some friends in his own social circle, he would find a woman more suited to him. Molly knew she couldn't bear the pain of watching that happen.

She had to leave the job she loved to keep her sanity. Except, since she couldn't afford to be without an income, she would request to be relieved of her duties as Ken's assistant and return to her position as receptionist, which was the farthest away she could be, yet remain in the same building. For as long as she could bear it, she had no alternative but to suffer through each day until she found employment elsewhere.

When she walked into the main office on her way to her desk, Ken's chair was conspicuously vacant. Fortunately, no one watched her as she approached her desk, and all appeared normal.

But it wasn't normal. Life would never be normal again.

She hung up her coat and headed for her desk, then froze momentarily as Mr. Quinlan's office door opened. Ken walked out, but instead of turning toward his desk, he continued walking. He did not approach her, but Molly was close enough to notice the dark circles under his eyes and his bleak expression as he walked into Nancy's vacant office and closed the door.

"Molly, may I see you in my office, please?"

Molly flinched at the sound of Mr. Quinlan's voice. This was the perfect opportunity to make her request, yet she wanted to run and hide.

Molly stiffened her posture and walked past her desk to Mr. Quinlan's office.

"Please close the door."

As she lowered herself into the chair, memories roared through her mind of the day she was called into Mr. Quinlan's office and assigned to be Ken's assistant. How suave and sophisticated, yet friendly and gentle he was when they first met. How she'd immediately liked him, how well they worked together. How deeply and honestly he lived his faith and the excellent example he'd been. Most of all, how quickly she'd fallen completely and totally in love with him. The picture of how he lowered himself to one knee as he professed his love and proposed marriage flashed through her mind. She didn't think she could possibly love anyone more than she loved Ken, but soon he would see that she wasn't right for him.

Mr. Quinlan sat at his desk, her personnel file in his hand. "Effective immediately, you will be returning to your position of receptionist. You've done an admirable job, and your efficiency will be noted for future reference. Next time an opening comes up, you will be given first consideration."

Molly's stomach clenched. The possibility of a promotion was now in sight. At one time, it was exactly what she wanted, but now that the moment was upon her, she felt no sense of triumph or accomplishment. Two minutes ago all she wanted was to get her old job back. Now she had it, and the victory was hollow.

Mr. Quinlan continued. "If you're wondering the reason, Kenneth has requested a transfer back to the Winnipeg office. He'll be leaving tomorrow."

Molly gulped. "Tomorrow?"

Mr. Quinlan nodded. "Yes. He's booking his flight now."

Molly's breath caught. She immediately thought of when Robbie was engaged to Mike. When the relationship fell apart, Mike had Robbie fired. But rather than having her fired, Ken had made her job more secure.

Typical of Ken, he did nothing in half measures. After making sure she would be okay, he was making the breakup as final as could be. He was leaving.

Her mind reeled. Ken had moved from the place of his birth halfway across the country to be here. He'd left his friends, his family, and his home church, everything he knew, to become the future president of Quinlan Enterprises. He'd been preparing himself for this job all his life.

Molly turned her head to stare through the slats of the mini-blinds at the closed door of Nancy's office, knowing Ken was sitting on the other side.

She began to think through their relationship. Ken didn't act on impulse. He prepared for everything in his life, through research and planning, until he had the greatest chance of success. He thought everything out to its last possible conclusion. She knew he felt confident about taking over Quinlan Enterprises. He wasn't leaving because he didn't want the job. He was giving it up because of her.

But in the same way he had worked and planned toward his future career, Ken wouldn't act on impulse in his personal life either. Yesterday Molly had been positive that no relationship between them could work. Yet Ken had asked her to marry him.

She knew that Ken took the commitment of marriage seriously. Just as he put all of himself into striving toward his future career, he also had been saving himself personally for the one woman who would be his wife. If he didn't love her enough to know that marriage between them would work, Ken Quinlan would never have asked. It wasn't in his nature to take chances.

He really did love her, and he had no doubts concerning their future together. Molly continued to stare across the room at the closed door.

First she had broken his arm, and now she'd broken his heart.

She had to trust that he knew something she didn't.

Molly stood so fast she nearly knocked the chair over behind her. "Excuse me," she said to her boss, who had been watching her the whole time she had been lost in thought. "I have to talk to Ken."

Ken stiffened his back and sucked in a deep breath. He wanted to make his separation from the head office of Quinlan Enterprises as quick and painless as possible.

He couldn't believe how his world had come crashing down around his feet in such a short time.

Molly's words echoed through his head.

"I wouldn't be seeing you if I hadn't broken your arm."

He thought she loved him too, but obviously she didn't. Even if she didn't love him now, he'd thought she at least liked him, and that one day she possibly could love him the same way he loved her. He would have accepted her rejection of his marriage proposal if he could continue to try to establish a relationship. But he'd completely misread her. She'd only been seeing him out of guilt and pity. The knowledge stabbed him where he would never recover.

He couldn't in good conscience terminate her employment because of his own poor judgment in overestimating their relationship. Nor could he handle being in her presence every day without the pain of defeat and loss of even her friendship. In order to do the admirable and right thing, he had no alternative but to return to his old position. Either he could continue on as production manager at the Winnipeg plant for the rest of his life, or he could seek a management position with another company. Neither choice was what he wanted, but he felt drawn to return to what was familiar, at least for now, until he could regain his bearings.

Of course his uncle had been disappointed at his decision, but he'd understood. Ken knew he was leaving with his uncle's blessings, as well as wishes that time would heal things to the point where he could return. But Ken knew that could never happen. As long as Molly was in Vancouver, he couldn't be.

The airline section of the phone book sat open in front of him. Ken had just begun to dial when the door burst open. He flinched when Molly slammed the door shut behind her with a bang.

Molly marched to the front of the desk and thumped the phone book shut. He started to open his mouth, but before he could protest, she grabbed the phone out of his hand and whacked the button down with her finger, knowing full well that due to his lack of mobility because of the cast, he couldn't stop her.

She stood before him, breathing heavily, the phone in her hand.

"Can I help you with something, Molly?"

"I can't allow you to do this. You can't abandon your career." She dropped the receiver into the phone cradle and crossed her arms. Her chest rose and fell quickly with her angered breathing. Her mane of unruly hair surrounded her face in a halo of color, the red a testimony to her rising temper.

"I've simply had a change of plans."

He didn't know what he expected Molly to do, but as usual, he wasn't even close. Before he realized what she was doing, she stomped around the desk, stood beside his chair, and stared down at him, her clenched fists planted on her hips. She was vibrant and beautiful and he loved her from the depths of his soul.

"I can't let you pack up and leave. Your family is counting on you. You've worked up to this your whole life. You can't leave because of me."

Ken opened his mouth to speak, but Molly raised one finger in the air, silencing him, which was fine. He was too afraid to hope for what he knew he couldn't have.

"You know things have to be different before we could possibly have any kind of relationship, don't you?"

Ken's heart pounded. His mind reeled and his heart pounded in his chest with the hope she meant what he thought she meant. If she did mean it, he didn't want to wait.

He turned his chair to face her, then stood, inwardly loathing the cast that held his left arm immobile. If there ever was a moment he needed to hold Molly properly, it was now. Since he couldn't wrap his casted arm around her, he rested his fingers to the side of her waist and cupped her chin with his other hand. He swallowed hard, forcing the words out.

"Did I hear you say 'relationship'? Does this mean you've changed your mind?"

Molly raised her hands, and Ken closed his eyes for a brief second at the gentle touch of her fingers on his cheeks. She raised herself on her toes and brought herself closer. His heart soared in the hope that she was going to kiss him. He knew a major portion of the office staff could see them through the office window, but he didn't care. If Molly was touching him in plain view of anyone in the area, it could mean only one thing, that his prayers for the love of the perfect woman were coming true.

"I love you too, and I'm so sorry about the way I acted. I can't live without you, and if you think we can make it work, despite everything, then I trust you."

Ken's heart pounded so hard he almost felt lightheaded. He remained with his feet firmly planted on the ground and cleared his throat. He stared into Molly's beautiful green eyes, begging God with all his heart and soul that this time he would receive the answer he wanted. "Then will you marry me, Molly? Let me warn you, I don't want a long engagement."

She raised herself even closer. "Me neither," she whispered against his lips.

Ken closed his eyes. If she meant what he thought she did, then she had just accepted his proposal. Soon Molly would be his wife, and they would be happy together for the rest of their lives.

He waited, wanting from the depths of his soul for Molly to kiss him, but she didn't. "I guess you know what this means, then?" She spoke against his lips.

Ken couldn't think. His brain refused to function. "What?" he barely managed to ask.

Her soft lips pressed against his, and just before she gave him the best kiss of his life, she mumbled, "It means I quit."

On the
Road Again

Prologue

I hear you're going to become an auntie."

Gwen Lamont nodded. "Yes. When I teased Garrett and Robbie and said it would probably be twins, Robbie went all pale and I thought she was going to faint."

Uncle Chad snickered and sipped his coffee.

The chair next to her scraped the floor and Garrett sat down beside her.

Gwen plunked her elbows on the table and rested her chin in her palms. "Hey, Bro'. Is Robbie feeling better?"

"Yes, no thanks to you. She's lying down."

Gwen lost her smile. "I was just teasing, I didn't mean to scare her." When her brother just shrugged his shoulders, Gwen turned to her uncle. "So, Uncle Chad. What's wrong? I can tell something's bothering you."

A loud sigh told her she was right. "Jeff has to take the summer off for a hernia operation, but I'm under contract to run doubles. I asked the boss, but he said the company can't be without the team for that long. I'm going to have to find another partner, but good drivers are hard to find."

"Oh, come on, Uncle Chad. I'm sure lots of people can drive a truck. How hard could it be?"

Garrett made a strange sound under his breath but didn't comment.

Uncle Chad slammed his fist into the table. "It's much harder to drive a truck than people think."

"Oh, come on now. The hardest part would be having to sit next to you for days on end."

"I didn't think you, of all people, would be like this, Gwen."

She couldn't hold back her laugh. "Why? I speak the truth."

She felt a poke in her arm. She turned to her brother. "What?"

"If it's so easy, prove it. You have all summer off."

"Pardon me?"

He crossed his arms over his chest and leaned back. "I dare ya."

"You've got to be kidding."

Garrett jerked his head toward their uncle. "If you think driving a semi is so easy, you can be the temporary driver."

"It's called a tractor-trailer, not a semi," Uncle Chad muttered under his breath. "Amateurs."

Both men stared at her, and she glared back at Garrett.

Over the years they had constantly challenged each other, much to the dismay of all who knew them. Seldom did either of them back down, but this time Garrett had gone too far. While it was true that, as a teacher, Gwen had all summer off and didn't have plans except for a few outings with her friends, the last thing she would ever have thought of doing would be spending all her time with Uncle Chad.

On the other hand, as a truck driver, her uncle Chad visited lots of interesting places all over North America, even though he seldom stayed long anywhere. Sometimes it was just a day before he picked up his next load and kept going. Often he and his driving partner had remarkable tales to tell of the fascinating places they visited. As a child, she had been amazed at the stories her uncle told. He was also part of a network of Christian drivers who traveled together when their paths crossed.

Garrett was right. Once her classes for the school year were over, she had no plans for the summer. Now that her two best friends were married, one of them to her brother, she was starting to feel left out.

They continued to stare at her, and Garrett raised one eyebrow. "Forget it, Uncle Chad. She knows she can't do it."

She crossed her arms over her chest and glared back. "I don't imagine it's much different than pulling the camper or boat, except it's bigger and heavier, and it's farther than the campsite."

Uncle Chad grunted.

"Coward," Garrett taunted.

Gwen glanced toward the calendar on the wall. She had two months and then school would be over, leaving her nothing to do but stare at her four walls.

Garrett turned to Uncle Chad. "It's not a job for a woman, anyway."

Gwen rose and stomped to the drawer and pulled out the phone book.

"What are you doing?"

"I'm going to register for classes and learn how to drive a truck. By the last day of school, I'll have my Class-One license, and my name better be painted on the door of that rig."

Garrett laughed.

Uncle Chad groaned.

Gwen dialed. She could hardly wait 'til the first day of summer.

Chapter 1

The blast of the air horn sounded just as Gwen stuffed the last pair of socks into her duffel bag.

"I can't believe you're really doing this."

Molly approached Gwen's bedroom, one hand waving in the air as she walked. Molly's husband, Ken, stood silently in the hall, keeping a respectable distance.

Gwen yanked the zipper shut. "I've got nothing better to do all summer, and Uncle Chad needs the help."

Molly planted her fists on her hips. "But you just barely got home from school and you're already leaving. We were planning a party to see you off. You're going to be gone before everyone's here."

Gwen hitched the strap over her shoulder, then grabbed her camera. "Sorry. The load's gotta go."

Molly snorted. "You sound like a truck driver."

"I am a truck driver. Starting right now."

She walked past Molly, smiled a greeting at Ken, then walked through the living room. Garrett sat on the couch with their mother, eating the goodies that had been laid out for the party. He waved, then popped another meatball into his mouth, but she caught the wink and the approving gleam in his eye before she left the room.

A few of her friends and her aunt Chelsea surrounded the truck, which was parked in front of the house. Uncle Chad bowed from his position beside the passenger door and pointed to the scripted handwriting next to the door handle.

"You did it!" Gwen gasped. "That's my name on your truck!"

Aunt Chelsea poked her husband in the ribs. "Don't get too excited, Gwen, Dear. It's not permanent. It will only last until the next rain, I'm afraid. So, enjoy it while you can."

Uncle Chad cleared his throat and checked his watch. "Let's get going, Gwen. We've got lots of miles to make by dawn Monday."

Gwen looked up at the mountains to the north, and then to the flatness of the Fraser Valley to the south. High school was out, and the Vancouver summer had begun. All the spring flowers and fruit blossoms were gone, but her mother's cherry tree was full of cherries, even though they were still green. All the other trees and bushes were lush with deep green foliage. Her mother's rose bush with its fragrant blossoms was in full bloom, and the wisteria growing up the trellis was starting to open its lavender buds. The strawberries were ready to be picked and eaten, and her mother had given her a tub to snack on as they drove.

Gwen knew she would miss everyone, but she told herself she would only be gone a week. She'd be back for a few days and catch up on all she missed before the next load sent her away from home.

She opened the door and was in the process of hoisting herself up into the cab when Robbie's voice sounded behind her. "I can't believe you're doing this, Gwen."

Gwen laughed. "I think I'm hearing an echo. Molly just said the same thing."

"Doesn't that tell you something?"

She pushed her duffel bag and camera behind her into the bunk, closed the door, fastened her seatbelt, and leaned her head out the open window. "Yes. It tells me I've been too predictable all my life. See you in a week."

With another blast of the air horn, they were on their way to the terminal to pick up their first load.

❧

Lionel Bradshaw waited for the dispatcher's signal to begin fueling, glad to be outside. All the other drivers were hanging around in the dispatch office instead of the lunchroom, and the place was getting crowded. Word had it that Chad was due into the yard shortly with his temporary driver—his niece who had the summer off from school. They all could hardly wait to see the kid and have a good laugh. Frankly, Lionel pitied the poor girl, who probably had no idea what was being said about her. He couldn't help but be annoyed at Chad. He should have seen this coming and found someone else.

Sometimes drivers brought along wives or girlfriends who had their Class-One, claiming they actually drove when their own allotment of driving time was up. But those women didn't really drive. They were a ruse so the driver could make more miles without getting caught on an infraction. Everyone knew what was really going on. Short of someone falling asleep at the wheel, there was no way to catch them. Lionel praised the Lord that such an accident hadn't happened to anyone there yet, but everyone knew, one day it would.

He could understand if, in desperation, Chad had asked a nephew to help drive, regardless of a young age, but a girl. . .

Of course she had to be old enough to drive to get her Class-One license. Still, Lionel thought Chad had more sense. Most of all, he had always looked up to Chad, as a Christian brother, to do the right and honest thing.

He'd just finished checking the oil when Chad's unit pulled up behind him at the pump. First Chad hopped out of the driver's side. Then the passenger door opened.

It wasn't a girl who hopped out at all, but a gorgeous, dark-haired woman about ten years older than the student he'd been expecting—a woman who would rival many men for height. Even though she wore sneakers, she walked smoothly and evenly, with the grace of a model.

"Lionel, this is my niece, Gwen. She's going to drive with me for the summer until Jeff comes back."

She stood in front of him and extended her hand. "Pleased to meet you, Lionel."

Despite her height, she had delicate hands. Woman's hands. Lionel quickly checked his palm for grease, then wiped it on his jeans, just in case. "Yeah," he muttered as he returned her handshake. "Same."

She stood almost eye-to-eye with him, not more than an inch shorter than he was, not breaking eye contact. Her boldness was one thing in her favor, but he knew she couldn't possibly be prepared for what awaited her inside the dispatch office. Even Lionel couldn't stand the off-color remarks and had left.

Lionel finished fueling and pulled his truck forward to allow Chad to drive up to the pump. Rather than going back to the dispatch office, he remained outside to check her out without everyone else watching.

"Uncle Chad? The man in the window waved so you can get your gas now."

"It's not 'gas,' it's diesel. And we call it fuel."

"Oops."

Lionel frowned. She would never survive.

While Chad filled his tank, Lionel and Chad talked about the upcoming routine maintenance on their units. He couldn't help but notice Gwen soaking in every word, even though she added nothing to the conversation.

When they were done, they walked into the dispatch office together to get their running orders. The room fell into silence, and Burt, the dispatcher, raised his eyes from the calculator. "Lionel, your load'll be ready soon. You've got a set of dry joints for Casper." He turned to Chad. "So this is your new driver. I'm Burt. You have a high cube van for Bismarck. The rear's dragging and the yard shunt is hooking the switch, so you've gotta slide the bogeys." He stared straight at Gwen, waiting for a response.

Her face went blank and, without moving her head, she quickly glanced at Chad, who nodded ever so slightly.

She smiled at Burt. "No problem," she said.

A number of muffled snickers echoed in the room. Lionel didn't laugh. In a way, he felt sorry for her. Burt had deliberately tried to intimidate her. When he'd first started driving, it had taken him awhile to understand the lingo. As a new driver he had been allowed a lot of leeway, but he could see they wouldn't cut any slack for Chad's niece. Simply because she was a woman, she would face a certain amount of ridicule with their own company drivers, but he wondered if she had any idea what she was in for once she got out on the road, where it was survival of the fittest.

Now that the show was over, rather than file into the lunchroom with everyone else, he joined Chad and Gwen as they went outside and prepared to leave.

Gwen glanced back and forth between the two men. "I have no idea what he just said. They didn't talk like that in driving school."

"Burt's just trying to confuse you with the lingo. Don't worry about it."

"Lingo? That was another language."

"He just meant that John's busy hooking up Dave's load and we have to adjust the axle weights ourselves if we want to get going sooner." Chad turned to him. "Lionel, you want to help slide the bogeys?"

"Sure."

Chad headed for his truck while Lionel led Gwen to a trailer in the rear of the complex.

"Why do I have a feeling the bogeys we're talking about have nothing to do with Humphrey Bogart?"

He couldn't help but smile. He was glad she wasn't going to let Burt bother her. He said nothing.

"I'm really a teacher, you know. But if I'm going to do this for the summer, I want to do it right."

"We're going to adjust the axle weights by sliding the trailer wheels."

They waited while Chad backed up his rig to hook up to the trailer.

"Now that he's under, we have to crank up the dolly legs."

He was about to grab the dolly handle, but Gwen beat him to it and began cranking. "I'll do it. It's not much different from our camper."

He had to give her credit. It wasn't easy, but unlike any other woman he had seen, she was actually working instead of watching.

Once the landing supports were fastened up under the trailer, he led Gwen to the rear and pointed to the track. "The back axle slides along the frame rails. You set the back brakes, pull the pins, and, in this case, Chad will pull the trailer forward while the bogeys," he patted the back tire, "stay in place, which puts the wheels closer to the back of the trailer to shift the weight distribution. Each hole shifts the weight about three hundred pounds. Then we put the pins back in, release the brakes, and send it over the scale. Hopefully we got it right and won't have to do it again."

She ducked her head underneath and looked at the frame rails. "So that's sliding the bogeys."

Lionel nodded. Chad stuck his head out the window. Lionel pulled out the pins, waved his hand in a forward motion, and held four fingers in the air with the other hand. "Ahead four holes!" he yelled.

"This is called a long box," Gwen said.

He nodded.

"It's fifty-three feet long."

He nodded again.

"It's got a reefer, but we won't know until we get the paperwork if we have to keep it running, right?"

Lionel shook his head. They were such elementary comments, but it meant she was trying to understand. "This is also an insulated trailer, but this one is equipped with what we call a heater, only meant to keep a load from freezing in the winter. Since it's summer you don't have to worry about stuff freezing."

"Oh."

The trailer groaned, heaved, then finally slid smoothly ahead four holes. Chad hopped out of the truck. Lionel replaced the pins, locked them, and Chad checked everything. "Gwen, you take the set over the scale, and I'll go get the paperwork."

"Okay."

There was no need for him to stay there, so Lionel accompanied Chad to the office while Gwen climbed into the cab.

They hadn't gone far when the engine roared, a big puff of black smoke poured out, the truck lurched, then went silent. The engine chugged to a start again, and this time it moved forward toward the scale, slowly, if not quite smoothly.

"Are you sure you're doing the right thing with someone right out of driving school? Have you heard what the guys have been saying about you getting your niece to drive?"

"I don't care what the guys are saying, as long as they don't say it where Gwen can hear. She may be inexperienced, but Gwen is my niece and she's capable of whatever she puts her mind to. We all made our mistakes when we started."

While Chad went into the office, Lionel waited outside, watching Gwen scale the load more slowly than anyone he had ever seen. He clenched his jaw. Yes, he'd made mistakes, but he had the support of all the other drivers. All Gwen would have was Chad.

Chad stepped outside and waved, the trip envelope in his hand. "Hey, Lionel. You're ready to go now too. Coming with me?"

He watched her pull the load onto the street and park it. She didn't know the difference between gas and diesel, but the woman had at least managed to scale the load without running into the shed. "Yeah. I think I will."

❧

Once they were out of the city, Gwen picked up the handset for the CB radio and reached down to turn it on while Uncle Chad drove. "What's our handle?"

"CJ. For Chad and Jeff. But you can think of your own. Lionel's handle is Lion King."

"I wasn't thinking of calling him in particular. But I guess he's better than no one."

Uncle Chad laughed. "I'm sure Lionel would be pleased to hear that."

Gwen giggled, grateful for the chance to relieve some stress. She'd anticipated a few snide remarks, but she hadn't expected to be laughed at. No one knew she'd heard, but she'd picked up on a few of the things being said about her behind her back, especially after she stalled the truck on the way to the scale. She knew she would have to work extra hard to earn any degree of respect in this predominantly male profession. Still, she thought the drivers where Uncle Chad worked would have behaved better, if for no other reason than company loyalty to one of their own.

Apparently not.

At least Lionel had helped her, although he wasn't exactly enthusiastic.

"Lionel is a Christian, you know."

"It must be nice to have someone you can relate to on the road. Some of the drivers are pretty rough around the edges, aren't they?"

"Yes, they are. And Lionel's single too. He's your age, and not bad-looking, I mean, as far as young men go."

Gwen squeezed her eyes shut. She couldn't deny anything her uncle said about Lionel, especially the good-looking part. He wore his dark blond hair in a lazy, barely-combed-back style, looking like it would fall into his eyes at any moment, yet it never did. His hairstyle served to bring attention to the dark green of his eyes, which were particularly mesmerizing. His eyes added to the mystique of his lovely smile, a feature he didn't appear to display very often. His nose had a small bump, indicating it had been broken at one time. The combination gave him an almost standoffish appearance, which probably suited the solitary life of a trucker.

"Don't start on me, Uncle Chad. I know Garrett and Robbie and now Molly and Ken are happily married, but I'm perfectly satisfied with my life the way it is. I'm not on the lookout for a husband. If God places Mr. Right in my path, fine. If not, that's fine too."

"He's a good Christian man. Well grounded in his faith, and he lives a Godly life."

Gwen sighed and bent to check out the buttons and dials on the main unit of the CB radio. "He's a truck driver."

"I've been a truck driver all my life. It's an honest living, and there's nothing wrong with that."

She rested the handset in her lap. "For you, no. But I couldn't live like that. You're away so often for such long stretches. Then, when Aunt Chelsea is used to you being gone all the time, all of a sudden you're home again, sometimes without leaving the house for days. You're either totally absent or underfoot. That would drive me nuts. I don't know how you two do it."

"You're right, Gwen. It's not an easy lifestyle."

"I know how hard it was for Jenny and Sarah. So many times you weren't there for their school concerts or their youth group functions. I know you tried your best to be around for the really important stuff, but I know many times they were disappointed when you couldn't be there."

Sadness filled her uncle's eyes. "I know," he said quietly. "Being a truck driver is all I've ever done, and I'll do it until I retire. Your aunt Chelsea is a remarkable woman. The divorce rate is very high among truck drivers. God has held us together throughout the course of our marriage. But, thanks to laptop computers and E-mail, staying in touch with family and friends has been easier over the last few years. Most of the truck stops have E-mail access these days. Also, with cell phones, if either of us gets lonely or an emergency happens, instead of having to track us down wherever we are in the continent and leave a message we won't get for hours or even days, now we're just a phone call away. It's better than it used to be."

"I'm sorry, Uncle Chad. I need more of a regular lifestyle than that. I could never marry a truck driver."

"You don't have to marry Lionel to be nice to him."

"I was nice to him. I just don't want to start anything. Okay?"

"Okay. Now go ahead and call him. I know you're dying to play with that CB."

She grinned as she turned on the main switch. The radio crackled for a couple of seconds while she adjusted the channel. "I don't know what to call myself. Mind if I just use your handle?"

"Oh, sure."

"CJ calling Lion King. You got your ears on, good buddy? Do you copy? Over."

"Lion King. Over."

"Uh, Gwen," Uncle Chad said softly before she could think of something worthwhile to say to Lionel. "Truck drivers don't really talk like that on the CB. Especially if it's just the two of us on at the moment. Just talk normal."

Gwen gritted her teeth. Something else she had done wrong. "Oops." She pressed the button to talk to Lionel. "I just wanted to test the CB. How far is the range on this thing? Over."

"About five miles. Over."

"Really? That's not a lot. I don't know what to say. Is it true that you talk back and forth on this thing for hours and hours while you're driving?"

She waited, but there was only silence.

"Gwen," Uncle Chad mumbled, "you're supposed to say 'over.' "

"Oops." She pushed the button again. "Over."

She heard him laughing over the radio. "It took me awhile to get used to that, but now it's second nature."

Gwen exchanged smiles with Uncle Chad but remained silent since he hadn't said "over."

Lionel's voice again came over the radio. "And yes, truckers really do talk on these things for hours. It helps fight the boredom through some of the long stretches. Sometimes, when we've been driving too long in the middle of the night, the chatter helps keep us awake. You can ask Chad about that some time. Over."

She continued to chat with Lionel, every once in awhile giving the handset to her uncle. When all topics were exhausted, they turned the radio off.

"The laptop is behind me under the bunk. How would you like to type up an E-mail to your aunt Chelsea, or maybe Garrett? We're going to stop in about half an hour and have dinner, and the truck stop has E-mail access?"

"Really? You mean I can type while we're driving?"

"If the battery is low, I've got a converter to plug it into the cigarette lighter."

"I had no idea driving a truck was so much fun!"

Uncle Chad smiled thinly but didn't comment.

She started to type but had difficulty concentrating. Her mind kept drifting back to Lionel. Chatting with him back and forth on the CB was just like talking on the phone with an old friend she hadn't seen for years. Although, she suspected she would be saying the word "over" in her dreams tonight. She couldn't remember much of what they said, but he had a wonderful sense of humor. At the same time, she sensed a closely guarded heart, which was no surprise. The lifestyle of a truck driver was very much the life of a loner, and he was a trucker by choice.

Being a teacher, Gwen was usually in the middle of a crowd of people, either in her high school classroom all day long or in adult church activities on evenings and weekends. She loved being busy. Even though she couldn't relate to someone who chose to stay solitary most of the time, she could respect his choice. Uncle Chad had been a trucker all his life, and he fit into both ends of the social spectrum. When he was in town, he was active in his church and with his family.

By the time they arrived at the truck stop, she had managed to compose two E-mail messages. She sent them off and they joined Lionel in the restaurant. Gwen had never been so hungry in her life, although she couldn't figure out why, since they'd been sitting most of the time. She chalked it up to the excitement of her first truck driving job and, after they paused for a word of thanks over their supper, she ate gustily.

"I've never seen a woman eat like you."

Gwen paused mid-chew to see Lionel watching her. She gulped down her mouthful and dabbed her mouth with her napkin. "I'm really lucky, I've never had to watch my weight. Guess it's because I'm so tall and have a high metabolism."

Uncle Chad nodded. "This is nothing. You should see her twin brother."

Lionel's eyebrows raised.

"Uncle Chad!"

"Never mind. We don't have time to sit and drink coffee. We've got to make Bismarck by Monday morning. Because this is your first trip, we'll be making more stops than usual. Make a quick visit into the washroom. This is the last time we're stopping for a long time."

Gwen tossed the money for her portion of the meal on the table and stood. She had been warned. This was the life of a trucker, and she had committed herself to it for the summer. "I'll be right back."

Uncle Chad was waiting for her in the truck.

"You've got to pay close attention to the way you shift in the mountains," he said. "We'll be arriving in St. Regis at about three A.M. I'll explain as we go."

"You mean we're driving through the mountains at night? We're not stopping somewhere to sleep?"

"In tourist season we want to avoid driving in the mountains during the daytime."

"You didn't tell me that before."

"I didn't? I'm sure I did. People tend to drive crazy around trucks. Even if we're driving faster, they still feel they have to pass us. Campers are especially bad, because often people aren't used to pulling the weight, and they don't leave themselves enough time to pass. I've been in countless close calls. The best solution is to drive as much as possible at night during tourist season."

There were so many things he'd told her in the past about the business of truck driving, but Gwen was positive this hadn't been one of them. If so, she might have changed her mind.

"Is Lionel going to be with us too?"

"Yup."

"Are you two going to yap on the CB?"

"Nope. Need both hands. There's a lot of shifting. You watch and learn. Didn't they take you through the mountains in driving school?"

"They did. We went up to Squamish, and I learned how to use the Jake brake, but that's nothing like going through these mountains."

"Nope. Got a few tricky corners, and in the daytime, lots of traffic."

Gwen cringed. She sat in silence as he drove, listening to her uncle explain why he shifted and changed speeds when he did. Every once in awhile she glanced behind them in the rearview mirror to see Lionel's rig following behind.

"We're making good time. But I'm almost out of hours. We're going to stop in St. Regis and sleep."

Gwen looked behind her at the bunks. She had been inside Uncle Chad's truck before, but it was another matter to live in it for two months with only the occasional stop at home. She wondered who got the top bunk and what she would do about the bathroom in the morning.

"For your first trip, Lionel and I will sleep in the trucks, and you can stay in motels. You need a good night's sleep, because you're driving in the morning."

Chapter 2

The waitress refilled their coffee mugs and dropped a handful of cream packets onto the table. Lionel added two of them to his coffee and talked to Gwen as he stirred. "You ready for this?"

She nodded and sipped her coffee without saying a word, which somehow didn't surprise him. After they parked their rigs at the truck stop following her first trip through the mountains at night, he noted that, although she was tired, she wasn't rattled. The three of them had enjoyed a pleasant chat as he and Chad walked her to the motel. He had teased her about getting a good night's sleep before her first long driving day. Instead of being nervous, she told him how much she anticipated driving the next morning.

Now it was the next morning and they were almost ready to go.

She took another sip of her coffee, leaving the cup at her lips as she spoke. "So now we get fu-el," she enunciated slowly, glancing back and forth between himself and Chad with a teasing twinkle in her eyes. "Just exactly how much fuel does a truck hold?"

Chad had just taken a large bite of his cinnamon bun, so Lionel answered. "Two hundred and twenty gallons. We get fu-el," he drawled out, "once a day."

"See. I'm learning. By the end of the summer everyone will think I'm a seasoned driver."

Lionel chose to reserve judgment. Just because she knew the difference between gas and diesel, that didn't make her an experienced driver, or even a good one. So far, the only actual driving he'd seen was when she pulled over the scale, and she'd stalled the engine. Today he planned to see for himself what she was like on the road.

"Uncle Chad said that we wouldn't usually stop so often, but for my first trip they've allowed us extra time, the same as a single driver. I feel bad to be slowing things down."

Lionel smiled and continued to talk as Chad ate in silence. "They always make allowances for a first trip. Just one word of advice. Keep careful records in your logbook. Government regulations are very strict. When you're trying to make miles, every quarter hour counts. Don't forget to count fueling or when you have to take a. . .uh, stop to visit the ladies' room or pick up a snack as driving time. If you take a quarter hour off driving time, log it as such. The minutes add up. When you're out of driving hours, that's it. You have to stop. A lot of companies do random checks to compare your tach card with your log entry, not only to make sure you weren't speeding, but to compare when you were stopped with what your log-book says."

"Thanks for the advice." She stopped to grin, and all Lionel could do was stare. He didn't have much experience with women, especially considering the lifestyle of a long-haul trucker, but Gwen was not what he expected. Gwen wore simple and comfortably worn clothes. Her dark shoulder-length hair was combed neatly, but she hadn't fussed with it. Nor did she wear any makeup. If she had tried to flirt or act provocative, it would have had an opposite effect. Her relaxed nature impressed him more than anything.

He didn't meet many of the drivers' wives. They tended to stay in the trucks, hiding from the surly drivers. Sometimes, though, some of the drivers brought girlfriends who openly tried to impress their men. Often they tried to impress any man in sight, and they dressed accordingly. Of course, the truck stop "lizards" always caked on their makeup and they all wore provocative clothing to lure the men. The entire package sickened him.

He had spent many hours praying for those women, unable to understand why anyone would want to live a life so full of sin. Both before and after he made his career choice as a truck driver, he'd seen this tragedy repeated often. He hadn't been raised in a Christian home, but he had been taught right from wrong. Since becoming a Christian in his early twenties, his heart had always gone out to women who would throw themselves away like that.

Gwen didn't act like she cared if she impressed anyone. She obviously didn't care if she impressed him, in particular, even though by now Lionel was certain Chad had told Gwen he was single. That fact didn't seem to make a difference, and he was relieved.

On their walk back, after seeing Gwen to her motel room last night, Chad had made a point of telling him Gwen was single too. Lionel had replied that, quite honestly, he had no interest in a relationship, including and especially one with Chad's niece.

❧

Chad checked his watch. "We should have been moving half an hour ago. Let's get going."

They made a quick check of the pins, trailer seals, brakes, and the air lines and were soon ready to go. Gwen hoisted herself up into the driver's seat, and Chad climbed slowly into the passenger side, stretched, and settled in, as if he didn't have a care in the world. It wasn't the way Lionel would have felt if a beginner were driving his truck.

Slowly the truck inched to the highway entrance. At least this time she didn't stall the engine.

The truck entered the highway, jerking and speeding up a little more each time she shifted until finally reaching the posted highway speed limit. Soon he was driving behind them, which was where he wanted to be in case they had trouble.

He didn't hear from them on the CB all morning, although he didn't think it was because she was too scared to operate the radio while driving. Instead, he suspected Chad was explaining things as they were going.

The first time he heard from them was lunchtime, and that was only long enough to learn they were pulling off at the next rest area for a sandwich. Lionel always anticipated the first lunch stop on a new trip if he was traveling with Chad. Chad's wife stocked his fridge with all sorts of yummy treats, and Chad always shared. Eating at too many greasy-spoon restaurants over the years had given him an appreciation for a nice cold sandwich and fresh fruit, especially if it was from the fruit trees in Chad's back yard.

When he pulled in, Gwen and Chad already had a few bags containing their lunch piled on one of the picnic tables.

"Aunt Chelsea sure makes a great lunch. Now I remember where I learned to pack the fridge in the camper in a way that makes use of every single square inch of space. Who wants a strawberry?"

He noticed she didn't wait for a reply before placing a sandwich and a small handful of strawberries on each of three plates. She left the rest in the tub in the center of the table.

Lionel stared down at their lunches. "Paper plates? We're eating on paper plates?"

"Oops, I forgot the napkins."

"Napkins?"

When Gwen ran back to the truck, Chad turned and whispered to him, "The wife included them this time, for Gwen."

Gwen hustled back and handed out napkins, along with pieces of cake, each on a fresh paper plate, a plastic fork tucked neatly on the side. "This is just like camping, except I wash dishes instead of using disposable stuff. It's more environmentally friendly."

Lionel picked up one of the utensils in question. "Plastic forks too?" He shook his head. "Gwen, we travel as light as possible, and that doesn't include tableware. We eat fast, so the sandwich doesn't get put down, and the same with the cake. Then we just go."

"If you eat too fast, you'll get indigestion."

"I've never had indigestion, and I've been doing this for ten years."

"Then you're just lucky."

"Luck's got nothing to do with it. I'm perfectly capable of eating sensibly, and I do, most of the time."

"Do you know the four basic food groups?"

He crossed his arms over his chest. "Bread, dairy, meat, and fruit and vegetables. Do you brush your teeth after every meal?"

She stuck up her chin at him, scrunched up her nose, and bared her teeth at him.

Lionel barely suppressed his laugh. She could give it right back to him, and he liked that. "Okay. But do you floss?" he asked. "And do you—"

Chad raised one hand, cutting him off before he could finish his sentence. "Stop bickering and let's eat."

After a short prayer of thanks, they ate.

Most of the women he knew picked and nibbled at their food, but when Gwen ate, she ate every bit as fast as he did, and she ate just as much. Yesterday, when they stopped for supper, he couldn't help but notice how much she'd eaten. Now he was wondering if this wasn't unusual for her.

Their hands bumped as they both reached for the last strawberry.

He grinned. "Who gets the last one?"

The second he hesitated, she grabbed it and popped it into her mouth. "Me. If you snooze, you lose. I put everything out, so you clean up. I'm making a trip to the little girls' room."

Before he could protest, she was gone.

Chad snickered beside him. "Did I tell you that her brother usually doesn't have a chance?"

Lionel looked down at the empty tub. "Thanks for the warning."

Again Lionel followed them down the highway, but this time they chatted on the CB. For awhile they discussed an interesting topic her pastor had brought up at the last church service. He was surprised and pleased when she offered to leave a tape of that particular sermon in his mail slot at the home terminal when she got back. Spending most weekends on the road, he couldn't attend church services as often as he would have liked. Whenever he could, he tried to be at one of the truck stops which scheduled informal, non-denominational services.

They drove straight through to Billings, arriving at the rest area on the edge of town as the sun was setting. Chad had made coffee before they arrived for a last quick break together, because from here they would be going separate ways.

Gwen hopped out of the driver's side, reached her arms to the sky, and twisted her back. She froze and blushed when she caught Lionel watching. "I guess I'm not used to sitting for so long."

He smiled. "You get used to it. The seats are constructed with good back support, and some have special custom adjustments. Still, it helps to get out and walk around whenever you can to try and stay in shape."

She pressed her fists into the small of her back and arched. "I can see that. A walk sounds like a good idea. Who wants to go?"

Chad shook his head as he settled in with his coffee. "Not me. I like being fat and out of shape."

Lionel looked around the nearly deserted park. He didn't think it was a good idea for a woman to be walking alone in a place like this at nightfall, but he suspected she would go anyway. "I could probably use a stretch. I'll go with you."

They helped themselves to the coffee and began their walk with mugs in hand.

"How was your first day driving?"

"Good. My last couple of shifts I never missed a gear. But truck driving is a lot different than what I expected."

Lionel figured as much. Most of the girlfriends and wives who came along only wanted to see the countryside. Since she was a teacher with the summer off, he suspected Gwen was expecting to experience a cross-continental summer vacation and get paid for it as a bonus. "Most women find that," he said.

"I knew a lot of people drove like idiots around the trucks, but I had no idea it was this bad. They have no concept of just how big or how heavy that truck is, and because of that, how long it takes to stop. We can't make split-second maneuvers. They just think we can simply turn the wheel and zip out of the way for them when they do something stupid."

Her response caught him off guard. He had been expecting her to say something about not being able to stop and check out the scenery. "Summer is the worst season for bad drivers."

"Uncle Chad said the same thing. Some guy, with his wife beside him and a car full of kids in the back seat, just whipped in front of me and cut me off when it took him longer to pass than he thought. Then he got mad when I was too close to his bumper until I could slow down. You should have seen him, I could tell he was swearing at me. Then the kids poked their heads in the back window and stuck their insolent little tongues out at me."

He sipped his coffee. "Unfortunately, that kind of thing happens all the time."

She turned to him and smiled. Even in the twilight, she had a lovely smile. His heartbeat picked up speed and his throat tightened.

"Yeah. Uncle Chad calls them four-wheelers. That's so funny."

He cleared his throat. "Yeah. Real funny."

He listened to her expound on her driving experiences of the day, but rather than hearing what she said, he paid more attention to how she said it. Instead of carrying on like a kid with a new toy, albeit a rather big toy, she was making comments he could relate to as a fellow driver. Her thoughts and impressions were the same as his own on his first few trips.

Chad's voice echoed from the distance. "Come on, you two! Time to get moving!"

Gwen giggled. It was a lovely, happy sound. "Sorry. I didn't mean to yak your ear off."

They hustled back to the trucks, and he noted this time Chad was driving. They entered the highway, and at the intersection he replied to the blast of their air horn with a short blast from his, and turned right while Chad and Gwen continued.

He wanted to turn on the CB but didn't since in only a few minutes they would be out of range. The silence disturbed him more than it ever had before.

For the first time in ten years, Lionel felt lonely.

He turned on the radio louder than usual and headed for Casper.

❦

Gwen ran her finger down the map. "We're almost there. Lionel said he'd be at Salt Lake City about ten, so we're right on time."

Uncle Chad applied the Jake brake to slow the engine. "Yes, but it was strange of Lionel to send an E-mail. I can't remember the last time I got one from him."

"Really? I thought you would be in contact with him a lot."

"No. Remember, we didn't become truck drivers because of our typing skills."

Gwen couldn't hold back her laughter. The last few days were an education like she had never imagined. After they'd delivered their first load, even though she knew they wouldn't be dispatched straight back to home, she'd expected to at least head in that direction. Instead, they'd been sent to some place in Iowa, and then to Denver. Finally they were heading in the right direction, even if they wouldn't be back to Vancouver and her nice soft bed for another three or four days. More than her bed, what she most looked forward to was her bathtub, and after that her mother's strawberries.

The truck stops had functional showers where the drivers could see to their personal needs and then move on, without necessarily sleeping. She compared it to a library, where a person would borrow a book, relax for a short while, and then leave. Renting a shower seemed strange. However, since the drivers basically lived in their trucks, there was definitely a need for such amenities.

While most of the truckers she met were generally friendly, many had trouble with the idea of a woman being part of a driving team. She also found a great many of them lacking in social skills. Her uncle tried to take their stopovers in the Christian-oriented truck stops when they could, but when traveling in a straight line to make time, they often didn't have any choice when they stopped.

For this trip, when they stopped for the night, she slept in the motels or rented a room at the truck stop and Uncle Chad slept in the truck. Next trip, they would be taking turns, one sleeping while the other drove, like a real doubles team.

"He beat us. There's his truck."

Gwen raised her head. Although the highway was dark, the parking lot of the truck stop was well lit. The outside temperature was still more than comfortably warm. Instead of waiting for them inside the coffee shop, Lionel was sitting on his running board, his legs stretched out, his head leaning back against the part of the cab that stuck out where the sleeper began. She wondered if he was sleeping, because she'd been learning, the hard way, to rest in strange places and positions whenever time permitted.

"Gwen, Honey, I'm not feeling great. I think I need a little sleep. You go in with Lionel and I'll grab some Zs in here."

"Are you okay? You're not coming down with something, are you?"

He shook his head. "Probably not. Your aunt Chelsea packed me a new bottle of vitamin C, so I'll take a few and lie down. Now go stretch your legs."

She didn't want to leave him alone but had to trust that he'd been doing this all his life and knew what he was doing. She hopped out of the truck and approached Lionel, who opened his eyes and stood when she neared his truck.

"Hi," she said.

Lionel stood and brushed some dirt off his jeans. "Hi, yourself. How's the driving today?"

They started walking toward the building. "Really good. It's so amazing, the number of miles we've done in such a short time."

He held the door to the coffee shop open for her and they walked to a small table in the center of the restaurant. The waitress poured their coffees, described the specials of the day, and left them with menus.

Gwen studied the menu. It hadn't been that long since she had eaten supper, but she was already hungry. While she decided whether she should have a muffin or go all out and have a hamburger and fries, she tried to ignore the loud group of men at the next table. Normally, she wouldn't have paid attention, and she hadn't meant to eavesdrop, but a few of the men were being so obnoxious she couldn't help but overhear. When one of them commented on his wife at home and, in the next sentence, mentioned his girlfriend in another town, Gwen's blood went cold.

"I know. It bugs me too."

She looked up at Lionel. His mouth was drawn into a tight line, and he was holding his menu far tighter than necessary.

"Uncle Chad and I spent a lot of time talking about stuff like that. I know it's not an easy lifestyle, but they've both remained faithful for over thirty years."

"Most men are. It's guys like that joker at the next table who make me sick."

Gwen glanced up at Lionel. She saw more than righteous anger in his eyes. She saw pain. Infidelity, the breaking of the ultimate trust in another human being, always angered Gwen. Fortunately, she had never been involved in a relationship where she had been personally hurt by unfaithfulness, although the first time she'd met Robbie, who later married her brother, that was exactly what had happened to Robbie. From Lionel's bleak expression, she wondered if he had also experienced the same thing. She wished she knew him well enough to talk about it.

"Hey, buddy!" A man with a tattoo of a snake on his forearm rested his elbow on the table next to them and leaned closer to their table. "Wanna introduce me to the little lady?"

Gwen stiffened.

Lionel didn't move as he muttered out of the corner of his mouth, "Get lost."

"Maybe she's not a lady."

His grip on the menu tightened even more. "She's more of a lady than you've ever met."

The man leaned back in his chair and tilted his head to comment to the rest of his friends at the table. "Hey, guys. He doesn't want to share."

Gwen couldn't believe what she was hearing. The worst part was that they were talking about her. She didn't know what to do, so she remained silent.

Lionel slapped his menu on the table. "She's a driver, not someone who would get involved with slime like you."

The man called out a crude comment and the rest of the men with him laughed uproariously. Lionel's face hardened even more and he started to open his mouth, but Gwen feared what might come out and, worse, that once he said something, a fight would start. She quickly laid her hand on Lionel's wrist and gave it a gentle squeeze. "Ignore them," she whispered between her teeth. "Let's just go."

His eyes narrowed and his lips tightened.

"I mean it. I wasn't hungry anyway. Let's go."

He slapped enough money on the table to cover the cost of the two cups of coffee and they both stood.

A wolf whistle pierced her ears. The man made a very crude comment about her figure as she walked away.

Lionel's pace hesitated in front of her, but Gwen stopped dead in her tracks. Anything Lionel said at this point would instigate a fight, but as a woman she could get away with telling the man she didn't appreciate his comments. She whirled around, stomped to their table, and smacked her palm down onto the checkered surface.

"Say that to my face. But before you do, know that I am a Christian. I live my life the way God wants me to, and I'm happy. Because of God's love and what His Son, Jesus Christ, did for me, I know where I'm going when my days on earth are over. Do you? Think about it. Do you have the strength to do anything other than show off to these guys from the safety of a crowd? Let me tell you something, tough guy," she sneered and leaned closer to his face. "When you're not shooting off your big mouth in front of these other tough guys, think of your wife, who you've cast aside like garbage. Do you think she'll stand beside you and support you when you're old and weak? Will these guys be with you then? Will anyone? I know Jesus is with me, every minute of every day. He's always there. I'll be praying for you."

Gwen stood, still fuming, her breath coming out in shallow bursts, her fists clenched tightly at her sides. Gradually she became aware that every person at every table was staring at her. Complete silence filled the room. Even the waitress stood stock still in the corner, the coffeepot in her hand.

Lionel grabbed Gwen by the hand. "We're leaving."

Without protest, she let him lead her outside to his truck. He unlocked the door, they both hopped inside, and he locked it again. "I'd offer you a coffee, but I don't think you need the caffeine." Without asking first, he reached into the fridge and handed her a juice box. "I know the place is a mess. It'll only take a minute to straighten up, though."

He kicked aside some clutter from the floor, flicked a switch to release the bunk bed, raised it, and secured it to the back wall. Next he lifted up a fold-down table and clicked it into place. The music from a popular Christian CD began to play.

"Sit down. Take a deep breath. Relax."

Gwen sank into the chair, thunked her elbows on the table, and buried her face in her hands. "I don't know what came over me."

Lionel poked the straw into the juice box and pushed it across the table toward her. "He was a pig."

She shook her head. "That's still no excuse for my behavior. That wasn't kind or loving, and that wasn't going to open his heart to Jesus."

"I don't know if kindness would be effective in a situation like that. Your delivery certainly caught the attention of everyone in the place."

Gwen raised her head.

"Seriously. I don't think anything could make him change right now. But one day your words will come back to him, and one day they might make a difference."

"Really?"

He nodded. "Oh, yes. You certainly made an impression. And not only with the jerks at that one table."

Gwen buried her head in her hands again. She hadn't wanted to make an impression, but she couldn't deny that she had. She would never be able to show her face in that particular place again. Still, she was driving for only two months. This was Lionel's life, and after making such a scene in his company, she had just made it impossible for him to go back.

"It's difficult to be a witness for Christ on the road, but it can happen. I'm an example of that. Don't be too hard on yourself. God uses all kinds of situations for His glory, even if we don't know it at the time."

Her ears perked up. Gwen had been raised in a Christian home and had made her decision to follow Christ when she was young. She loved to hear stories and the testimonies of people who turned their lives over to Christ when they were adults. One of the best moments of her own life was when her friend Molly became a Christian after many years of witnessing and praying for her. She had personal proof that prayer worked.

Even though she didn't know the man's name, and even though he had insulted her terribly, Gwen knew, right then, that she had to pray for him.

Lionel looked at her from across the small table. One corner of his mouth tilted up. He reached across the table and covered both her hands with his larger ones. "Let's pray for him."

She didn't know how he knew what she was thinking, but she couldn't have agreed more. They joined hands over the table and prayed for the man, for God's mercy and kindness to touch him, for the man to open his heart to salvation in

Christ Jesus, and that he could become a witness to the unsaved once he turned his life around. They also prayed for the man's wife, for God to hold her up, that she could forgive her husband and their marriage could be saved.

"Amen," they said in unison.

Gwen lifted her head and opened her eyes slowly. She wasn't sure, but she thought Lionel's eyes were a little too shiny.

He blinked and turned away, causing her to wonder if the dim lights and shadows were playing tricks on her.

Lionel checked his wristwatch. "It's getting close to midnight. Chad will want to drive a few more hours before you two stop for the night, and I've got to make some miles too. Maybe I'll catch you on the flip-flop."

Gwen stood but didn't leave the cab. She wasn't sure what had happened, but something special had passed between them. Although she prayed with other people all the time, this was different.

She watched him as he prepared to make a pot of coffee. Lionel was a nice Christian man. Still, even though she could see so many good things about him, she knew she could never get involved with him. All her life she had seen the heartache and disappointments her cousins and her aunt Chelsea endured when Uncle Chad wasn't around.

Gwen knew her own personality and needs well enough to know she needed more solidity and more togetherness than that from the man who would be her husband.

Knowing the lifestyle up close, Gwen had vowed she would never get involved with a truck driver. When the summer was over and her time as a trucker was over, she would never see Lionel again. The thought saddened her, but that was life.

Yet, for now, for the summer, they could be special friends.

Gwen opened the cab door and hopped to the ground. "I'll go wake up Uncle Chad. See you next time our paths cross."

Chapter 3

Burt handed Gwen the envelope containing the running orders. "No appointment on this one. You've got to get it there as fast as you can without breaking any laws. It's a specialty piece of machinery for a plant breakdown in Evansville, Indiana. Every day they're shut down costs them ten grand, and four hundred people are out of work until you get there."

Gwen cringed. She knew the doubles teams got all the priority and rush loads, but she never thought of a situation like this.

"If you get there in the middle of the night, it doesn't matter. Call that number on the envelope when you're an hour out of town. By the time you pull into the lot, they'll have a crew standing by, ready and waiting."

Uncle Chad nodded. "I'll drive first through the mountains, then you take over when I'm out of hours."

Gwen nodded.

They drove to the manufacturer's plant to pick up the load. When it was ready, they hooked up, made sure it was blocked properly, checked the trailer, and within half an hour they were on the highway.

"This is it, Gwen. Our first real doubles trip, and it's a dandy."

"Yes." It was a tremendous responsibility, unlike any she had ever faced. Every day she accepted the accountability of her students, the mentoring and guiding of young lives, but that was on an ongoing basis. She had never before been forced into such an urgently critical situation. Now, from a different perspective, she saw Uncle Chad's job in a whole new light. Being a truck driver was more important than driving widgets from A to B. At times, people's livelihoods depended on them. Their driving skills might very possibly be the determining factor in the failure or success of a business. If that business was the predominant industry in a small town, the fate of an entire community might rest in their hands.

This time Gwen didn't feel like chatting on the CB as the miles went by. Even though they were days away from their destination, the urgency of the need for speed was always on her mind. Unlike her first trip, when she thought they were traveling so fast, this time, considering the urgency of their load, they seemed to be moving in slow motion.

They reached the start of their journey through the mountains and leaving the West Coast as darkness fell. The ups and downs and the curved roads only seemed to taunt her, reminding her this would be the slowest portion of the trip.

As they continued, she watched Uncle Chad downshift, preparing to make the most difficult ascent in this section of the mountains. At least the worst part of the trip was nearly over.

"Uncle Chad? What's that noise?"

They were both silent as a ticking sound suddenly increased in volume.

"I don't like the sound of that," he muttered.

A loud bang and the grinding of metal on metal jolted the entire unit. The truck rocked and lurched as the engine seized. Gwen grabbed the door handle with one hand and braced herself against the dashboard for support while her uncle fought with the wheel, forcing the truck to the side of the road. They came to a very sudden, complete stop.

Gwen's heart pounded as she forced herself to breathe. "This is bad, isn't it?"

"I don't even have to look, I know what's happened. The truck's thrown a rod. It's very bad."

"Can you fix it?"

Through the glow of the dashboard lights, she could see a very humorless smile on his face. "Fix it? No. I have to call a tow truck. The repairs are a major job, and very expensive. The truck will be down at least a week."

She stared into the rearview mirror at the trailer they were pulling. "But we've got to get that machinery to Evansville as soon as possible."

He reached between the seats and pulled out his cell phone. "They'll have to dispatch another truck to come and get it. We're not going anywhere."

❈

Lionel pulled into the terminal compound and backed his load against the fence.

The trip had been a long one, and he was tired. He'd left Portland later than usual, so he'd parked his truck for a few hours at Seattle instead of driving through their rush hour. It was now nearly midnight, but he was almost home. When he finally got back to his North Vancouver apartment, Lionel planned to sit outside on the balcony and watch the lights of downtown Vancouver from across the Burrard Inlet to wind down. From a distance, he always enjoyed watching the hustle and bustle of the Vancouver nightlife. Then he would crawl into his nice soft bed for a good long sleep, since he wasn't going to be dispatched out.

"Here's the paperwork, Burt. See you tomorrow."

"Whoa! Lionel! Not so fast."

He waited while Burt finished a phone call and hung up.

"Sorry about this, Buddy. I don't have any drivers in town with any hours left. I've got to send you out."

"Out? I've only got three hours left before I have to book off. Send me in the morning."

Burt shook his head. "No can do. Chad's broken down in Snoqualmie Pass with that hot load for Evansville. It will take you three hours to bobtail there. Then you can sleep. You're taking the doubles load. We can't delay eight hours. Get going."

Lionel fueled his truck and left as soon as he could. In nearly ten years he'd never done a doubles run, and he wasn't looking forward to it now. He didn't want to think of driving a very rush load almost all the way to the East Coast. He had just come into town after being away for over a week. He only wanted to eat something and go to sleep. The only good part of this trip would be that, since Chad had been dispatched from home tonight, he would have a fridge full of good food, which now he would share.

Thinking of Chad's fridge made him think of Chad's wife. At times, Lionel was almost jealous of Chad and the closeness of his family, how they managed to overcome the trials of long absences. He used to think about coming home to a wife and kids anxious for his return, but he knew that was a fantasy. His parents hadn't been able to keep their marriage together, no matter how much or how little time they spent together. Experience had shown him that, when put to the test, the one woman he would have called "special" turned out to be no different than his mother. Chad had indeed been blessed to have a woman like Chelsea as his life's partner.

Briefly Lionel wondered what life would be like with a special woman to welcome him home with open arms after a long absence. The first woman who came to his mind was Chad's niece. He knew Gwen was single because Chad had told him so. As well, Gwen had chosen to drive around the continent all summer, which proved Gwen truly didn't have anyone she called special to stay home for. He didn't know why a woman like Gwen was still single at thirty years of age. He was thirty-one and single, and he planned to stay that way.

Lionel shook his head to break away from his mental meanderings. Gwen was a teacher—a people person. She was in her element in a crowd, both with children and adults. Everyone liked her. He had seen that firsthand. Every time she came into contact with people, they warmed up to her. For someone to whom people gravitated, the temptation was too great. Absence did not make the heart grow fonder. He'd learned that the hard way.

He slowed his speed as he approached the glow of headlights near the summit of Snoqualmie. A tow truck was already hooked up to Chad's Kenworth. Lionel parked behind the rig and stood to the side. He watched as the truck was pulled out from under the trailer. Shaking slightly, the trailer settled onto the landing legs and, when it was on solid ground, the tow truck pulled Chad's truck clear.

Chad appeared at his side. "Threw a rod," he mumbled, shaking his head.

Lionel also shook his head. "Bad stuff. Down time?"

"Figure a week and a half. Maybe two."

"Taking it home?"

"Yeah. Most of the repairs should still be covered under warranty."

"Expensive towing bill."

"Figure so."

Lionel said a short prayer of thanks for Chad that, since this was a major job, the truck had broken down fairly close to home.

He turned to climb back into his own truck and get ready to hook up to the trailer but stopped dead in his tracks when he saw Chad climb into the passenger side of the tow truck. Chad waved as they started moving.

Lionel abruptly pushed his truck door shut, ran to the tow truck, and banged on Chad's door once with his open palm. The tow truck stopped. Chad rolled down the window.

"Where are you going?" he shouted over the noise of the engine. "I was told this load had to go doubles to Indiana and it was hot."

Chad nodded to the side of the road.

Lionel turned his head in the direction of Chad's nod.

"I've got to go with my truck," Chad said. "You're driving with Gwen."

Lionel's breath caught as he saw Gwen standing stiffly at the side of the road beside the trailer. Her duffel bag was slung over her shoulder. A number of grocery bags and a few other items lay at her feet. Her shoulders were hunched, her arms were crossed over her chest.

This was not the same Gwen who had pitched in on her first trip to help slide the bogeys, or held her own when Burt tried to make her look foolish in front of the other drivers. She hadn't shown any sign of weakness then. The size and weight of driving a tractor-trailer unit hadn't intimidated her either. When she lost her temper at the truck stop a few days ago, her righteous indignation had instantly earned the respect of many truckers, and his too.

Gwen now looked terrified. And all she had to do was get into his Freightliner.

"I can't drive with your niece."

"You don't have a choice. She's the other half of the doubles team, and this half has to stay with the downed truck."

"I can't."

Chad sighed. "I don't like it either, but Gwen doesn't know anything about mechanics. I can't leave her in charge of such an investment. Jeff just got out of the hospital, so I can't expect him to look after this. Face it, the company doesn't see her as a woman. They only see a licensed driver and a load that's got to move."

"It's not that she's a woman," Lionel stammered, "it's that she's. . .uh. . .I mean. . ." He couldn't finish the sentence. Even though she was a beginner, she was a qualified driver. He also knew she was no shrinking violet if trouble came up. So far they got along well enough when they were together, both in the serious stuff as well as the good-natured teasing. They had shared a very special moment when they'd prayed together.

What he didn't want to think about was their being together, all day and all night, without a break for over a week. Most important, it was neither right nor proper, even if they were on the road and on the job, to travel with a woman, day and night.

His gut twisted. Being with her all day didn't bother him half so much as being with her all night.

"There's no option here, Lionel. I have to go with my truck, and Gwen is going with you. The load's already been delayed three hours. You've got to get moving."

Moving. He thought of what it would be like. Technically, in any twenty-four-hour period, on a critical load like this, both of them would drive ten hours apiece. Interspersed in those twenty hours they'd have a number of breaks totaling four hours to fuel, eat, and see to personal needs. Basically, the truck didn't stop. There would never be a time they would be resting or sleeping at the same time. This was work.

He stiffened his back and squeezed his eyes shut. *Dear Lord, please give me strength. I can do all things through Him who strengthens me,* he prayed. It could be done, and it would be done

Lionel walked to Gwen. "I'm out of hours. I'll hook up, and then you're driving."

☙

Gwen knew she would be driving through the mountains at night at some point, but she never imagined this.

She had barely managed to get familiar with Uncle Chad's truck, and now she had to get to know this one. Most of all, she had to get used to Lionel.

He hadn't said anything, but Gwen knew Lionel wasn't comfortable with the situation. For that matter, neither was she. With Lionel in the passenger seat, she'd never felt so scrutinized in her life, including the time she took her driver's test for her Class-One license. The multiple shifts required for mountain driving were bad enough, but the job was made much worse with Lionel watching her every move. She wished the breakdown could have happened on the prairies. Then again, if it had happened any farther from home, she wouldn't have been driving with Lionel, but a stranger.

Rather than feeling sorry for herself, Gwen chose to thank God that she was teamed with someone she knew, at least a little. Most of all, even though Lionel was a man, he was a Christian, and since Lionel knew her uncle, he would have to answer to her uncle Chad for any potential misdemeanor.

The situation could have been worse. Much worse.

She tensed with another shift. Lionel cringed, anticipating that she would grind the gears. She had done much better with Uncle Chad because Uncle Chad hadn't been worrying about his precious truck, at least not that she'd seen.

"This is your first time driving through the mountains at night, isn't it?"

Gwen stiffened. It was her first time driving a truck through the mountains, period, day or night. "Yes."

"You're doing good. I mean, for a beginner. You handled that last uphill curve really well."

"Thanks."

"Was it you or Chad driving 'til Snoqualmie? I'm asking because I want to know how many hours you've got left."

"I can do ten hours."

Even though the only light inside the cab was from the dash lights, she could see him sag into the seat. "Great. I've just come back from a long trip, and I was right at the end of ten hours by the time I reached Snoqualmie. I've got to have a sleep. Are you okay with that?"

"Sure."

"Wake me if you need anything. I won't be far away."

She couldn't tell if he was being sarcastic or trying to be funny. As nerve-wracking as it was to be driving alone, having him sleep instead of watching every mistake she made was infinitely better. She would rather die than wake him. "Sure."

"Stop whenever you need to have a stretch or a snack. I probably won't wake up."

"Okay."

"If you want, I can make a pot of coffee for you before I bed down. Got any questions?"

"No questions."

Silence hung in the air. Gwen downshifted as they slowed for another hill.

"Are you always this talkative? Are you concentrating that much on your driving, or is it me?"

Gwen released a rush of air. She hadn't meant to let him know she was so tense. "I think it's a little of both."

"I guess we should talk."

What she really wanted was some silence so she could think. A million thoughts had churned through her mind while she waited the three hours for him to arrive. Now that they were actually on the way to Indiana, everything she thought she'd worked out in her mind dissolved into mush. "I suppose."

"If we're going to be living together, we should lay down some guidelines."

Gwen gripped the steering wheel so tightly her knuckles turned white. "We're not living together!"

He had the nerve to laugh. "I knew that would get you. Seriously, though, we should talk now. I don't want you to sit and stew for hours while I toss and turn trying to get some sleep. Let's get it over with so we can both relax."

She was glad for the distraction of driving. "That's a good idea."

Once more silence hung in the air. He ran his palm over his face, then pushed his hair back over his forehead. "Honestly, Gwen, I had no idea this was going to happen. The thought never occurred to me that I wouldn't be driving with Chad. I'm sorry."

His blunt honesty impressed her. "If you had known, would it have made a difference? Would you have refused the load?"

"No. I couldn't have refused, because that's ground for dismissal unless it's justifiable as a safety violation. I just wish I would have been better prepared."

"I know what you mean. I thought about it for three hours, and I'm still not prepared."

Lionel chuckled softly. "What I was thinking about more than anything else for the last three hours was Chad's fridge full of food." When she didn't join in laughing at his little joke, he cleared his throat and the humor left his voice. "Anyway, since we're stuck with each other, we should come to a few decisions and make a few agreements, although I don't know where to begin."

Gwen winced at his word "stuck." It stung, even though she'd been thinking the same thing not long ago.

Before she allowed herself to wallow in self-pity, she recalled the routine she had developed with her uncle, and then, imagining Lionel's reaction, she couldn't stop a grin. "Who gets the bathroom first in the morning?"

"Bathroom? But. . ." His voice trailed off. "Very funny."

Thankfully, the darkness hid the blush she knew flooded her cheeks. "Seriously, I've never had to think about stuff like that in quite this way, and I probably never will again. My first trip was different. We actually stopped to sleep. Uncle Chad stayed in the truck and I got a room. This isn't going to be like that, is it?"

"No. The truck won't stop except for fuel and for us to eat and stuff."

Gwen knew it might be difficult to get used to at first, but Uncle Chad was family. She could have handled that. Living out of the truck with Lionel, she didn't know. "We'll have to take things as they come, a few hours at a time, I guess."

Lionel nodded. "Yes."

"I guess you should sleep then. Is this curtain the same as the one in Uncle Chad's truck? I looked at it but never got to test it."

"They are the same, and they're very soundproof. Looks like I get to test it first. Good night, Gwen."

"Good night, Lionel."

He turned and crawled into the bunk behind the seats. The rasp of the Velcro signified the closing of the heavy Naugahyde curtain, which was double thick and insulated, covering the back area from floor to ceiling, making it as effective as a solid wall between them. Then she heard nothing except for the sounds of the engine and the hum of the tires on the pavement.

This was it. For the first time, she was truly driving alone. There was no one in the passenger seat to coach her, no one to help her when she didn't know what to do. She had known from the time she made her decision to do this for the summer that this time would come, but now that it had, everything was different.

She was on her own, in more ways than one. While technically she could ask Lionel anything, she couldn't allow him to think she was stupid beyond her inexperience.

Gwen forced herself to concentrate on her driving. In the daylight, on the flat lands, she would think about Lionel and this whole situation.

Chapter 4

Gwen's stomach grumbled about the time the sun began to rise. Technically, it was breakfast time. But she had been driving all night. She was starving.

All night long she hadn't heard anything from Lionel. She'd managed to convince herself he'd be awake by the time she was ready to stop. She didn't want to embarrass either one of them, in case he slept like her brother, Garrett, with his mouth open and snoring. Unfortunately, he was still sleeping, and she didn't want to find out the hard way.

The night's darkness and quiet provided the perfect opportunity for some serious thinking. As she drove down the nearly deserted highway, she tried to imagine what it would be like to be with Lionel for however long it took to deliver this load and make their way back home.

Thinking of her brother solved her problem. Gwen had always had a special relationship with Garrett, beyond that of normal siblings, because of their special bond as twins. They had been almost inseparable all their lives. She'd missed him terribly when he moved away from home to live on-site as a park ranger and then, later, when he married Robbie. She chose to handle spending time in close quarters with Lionel the same way she did with Garrett—only this time, instead of being a brother by birth, she could relate to Lionel as a brother in Christ.

Uncle Chad spoke highly of Lionel. In fact, there were times he hadn't let up and she told him she didn't want to hear any more praises of Lionel. Gwen was tired of the attempts at matchmaking, not only from Uncle Chad, but from all her friends and family. The matchmaking intensified when she was the last one left unmarried and became even worse when she turned thirty.

Even though she didn't know Lionel well, he seemed nice enough. Still, she wasn't interested in a relationship, especially with a truck driver. The circumstance she now found herself in, and the fact that she didn't like it, proved how much she thrived on her regular school hours. She needed a more predictable and stable environment than the uncertain agenda of driving a truck. Molly and Robbie had been right. She shouldn't be doing this, but it was too late to turn back. She was obligated to Uncle Chad by her promise and bound to the company by a contract. When the summer was over, she would have learned a valuable lesson, namely, never to do anything on impulse again.

A sign ahead indicated a place to stop, so she did. The process of slowing down and parking didn't awaken Lionel, therefore she rationalized he must have been exhausted. She left him to sleep and went into the restaurant without him.

"Table for one?"

Gwen cringed. "Yes." She'd never gone into a restaurant alone before.

When the waitress left her with a coffee and a menu, it felt odd not to be chatting with someone. The awkwardness was worse after she gave the waitress her order. She would rather have prepared her own meal, in a rush or not, instead of sitting all alone in a room full of people, all of whom had someone to talk with, except for her. However, Lionel was sleeping beside the fridge, preventing her access, so she had no other choice if she wanted to eat. Next time she would make a sandwich before he went to sleep.

Instead of letting the time drag until her meal arrived, Gwen pulled a book out of her purse and read until the waitress returned. She continued to read as she ate, trying to ignore the stares of people as they passed on the way to their own tables. As much as she enjoyed the book, she vowed never to eat alone in a restaurant again. She paid the bill without lingering and hurried back to the truck.

She finally heard the rasp of the Velcro curtain opening as she started the engine. Lionel poked his head through the opening. He winced and blinked with the morning light, then stepped into the center of the cab wearing a well-used T-shirt and wrinkled jeans. This time the lock of hair that forever threatened to fall into his face really had.

"Good morning," she said. "Have a good sleep?"

He grunted something she didn't understand and left the truck carrying a small duffel bag. She couldn't tell if he was annoyed with her for some reason she couldn't fathom, or if he simply wasn't a morning person. Gwen killed the engine, pulled her book out of her purse again, and settled into the passenger seat so she wouldn't have to think about it.

She re-read the same page three times before she slapped the book shut in frustration. With the curtain open, she couldn't shake the overwhelming sensation that she didn't belong here. Not only was she invading Lionel's personal space, his belongings and blanket and pillow strewn atop the bunk behind her emphasized that this truck was his home, and she was trespassing.

At the sound of the door opening, she opened the book as if she had been reading the entire time he was gone. Lionel hopped up into the cab freshly shaven, wearing new clothes, his hair combed and slightly damp, and unlike on his departure, he was smiling.

He nodded at her as she remained sitting. "Sorry, but you're in my chair. You have to keep driving. I haven't booked off for eight hours yet." He held up a small paper bag. "I gather you've already eaten, so I bought myself a muffin for breakfast. I fully intend to eat it now while it's still warm. Want me to make coffee, and we can get moving?"

"Sure."

All traces of his earlier mood were gone, making her think that, perhaps, she had imagined it. Since he wasn't talking, she shuffled into the driver's seat and tried, once more, to read until the coffee was made and it was okay to start driving. Despite the lack of conversation, he still distracted her, and she still didn't finish the page.

Gwen studied him out of the corner of her eye as she pretended to read. She couldn't detect any signs of discomfort or nervousness. Unlike her, he seemed relaxed and perfectly content making coffee for the two of them before they carried on with their day. While the coffee dripped, he tidied up. He organized his personal effects, raised and secured the bunk, and stowed a few things in the overhead storage bins.

The atmosphere felt entirely too domestic, and she didn't like it.

He squatted to open the small fridge. "You take your coffee with milk and one sugar, right?"

"Uh, yes, I do," she mumbled, refusing to be pleased that he remembered.

He poured two cups of coffee into travel mugs and tucked them into slots in the dash. "Ready. Away we go."

Gwen tucked the book into her purse, pushed her purse behind her and under the bunk, buckled her seatbelt, and turned the key. He said nothing as she inched to the highway entrance, and he remained silent as she went through the process of shifting and accelerating until she was up to highway speed.

Once they were traveling smoothly, he lifted his coffee out of the holder and sipped it slowly. "I wasn't sure how well I'd sleep in a moving truck, but I was out like a light. I briefly remember a bit of a disturbance, which must have been when you pulled into the truck stop, but I must have gone right back to sleep."

Gwen checked her watch. "You didn't get that much sleep. It's only been six hours."

"That's as much, if not more, than most truckers get in one stretch on the road. It's more like a series of long naps than bedding down for the night."

Now she was convinced she wasn't cut out for this life. She hadn't discussed the nitty-gritty of sleeping schedules with Uncle Chad, but she needed a good night's sleep, every night, on an ongoing basis.

"Are you getting tired, Gwen? It's probably been a long day for you. If you want to stop, we can."

"I'm okay. Besides, it's only another couple of hours and we can trade spots."

She remained silent while Lionel bit into his muffin.

The silence didn't last long. "So, is driving a truck all you thought it would be?"

She laughed a very humorless laugh. "It's nothing like what I thought it would be."

Lionel nodded. "It's kind of a skewed home-away-from-home kind of thing. I spend more time in my truck than I do in my apartment."

"You probably don't have a single live plant, do you?"

"Yes, I do. I have a cactus. It's not doing too good, though."

Gwen didn't comment.

He took another bite of his muffin, closing his eyes while he savored it. "This is sure different than trying to grab a bite while I'm driving. I could get used to this."

"Don't count on it," Gwen mumbled.

"Did you say something?"

Gwen shook her head. "Nothing worth repeating."

Silence hung in the air while he held the mug close to his face, inhaled the heady scent of the coffee, and then drew a long sip. As he spoke, his deep voice made a strange echo inside the metal cup. "I've never done team driving before. I've often wondered what it would be like, day after day with the same person. I would think they would have to be very unique friends."

"I guess. Or relatives."

He tucked the mug back into the holder. "That doesn't count. I know Chad is your uncle, but that was only a temporary arrangement. I'm thinking about Chad and Jeff. They've been a driving team for, must be, twenty years. They spend more time with each other than they do with their wives."

"That's true." She'd thought about that very thing over and over and still didn't have an answer as to how or why it worked. The inside of the truck seemed a lot like her family's camper. Every bit of space was well planned, every square inch used. But it wasn't very big when two people spent days, or even weeks, at a time in it without a chance to get away from each other.

He popped the last of the muffin into his mouth. "I've been asked to run doubles a few times, but I like things just the way they are. I'll always run single."

From what she'd seen, Gwen didn't doubt that. Lionel very much fit the image of a loner. She worried that, because of this fact, there would be an uncomfortable silence between them. However, that had not been the case so far. To the other extreme, for a supposed loner, he talked an awful lot. "I've noticed that your truck is different inside than Uncle Chad's."

Gwen listened while he explained the differences in design. Apparently Uncle Chad's truck was one of the few makes that came from the factory with the standard option of bunk beds, which gave Uncle Chad and Jeff more space to call their own in a very limited environment. Needing only one bed, Lionel had chosen the option of a fold-down table.

If a person didn't get claustrophobic, Gwen could see how a person could live like this, because the cab wasn't too much different from a motor home interior, except smaller and without cooking facilities. The only bad part: there was no bathroom.

Lionel checked his watch. "That's an eight-hour break for me. Minus the stop back there, that's about seven hours of driving time for you, which is plenty for a beginner. Want to trade places, as soon as we find a place to pull off?"

Just the thought of taking a break made Gwen sag. It hurt her pride for him to suggest she needed preferential treatment as a beginner, but truthfully she was tired of driving. "Yes, I'd like that."

She drove in silence while Lionel told her more about the different options and what life was like living out of a truck, until they reached the next rest area.

Rather than switching places and continuing, they hopped outside for some fresh air. Lionel jerked one thumb over his shoulder in the direction of the picnic area. "Let's have a short walk, and then away we go."

Gwen eyed the ladies' room. "In a minute."

❧

Lionel flipped on the cruise control once they reached highway speed. He hadn't expected to sleep well, but to his surprise, he had. Unlike every other rush trip, where he had to grab a quick bite on the run, or eat while he drove, he'd enjoyed his breakfast at a leisurely pace. More than that, he'd enjoyed having someone to talk with in a private, quiet, and smoke-free setting.

He'd suggested to Gwen that, rather than crawling straight into the bunk, she ride for awhile and wind down. Even though she was exhausted from her first long stint of driving alone, she took his advice and was now sitting beside him staring out the side window in silence.

"I see you brought a sleeping bag and your own pillow."

She nodded but didn't turn her head. "Yes. I was supposed to get the top bunk, and I didn't want to use Jeff's personal stuff."

He'd noticed exactly what she brought, since he had helped carry everything from the side of the road into his cab. Besides the sleeping bag and pillow, she had exactly one duffel bag, her purse, and a camera. He didn't know a woman could travel without half a dozen suitcases. He'd carried more bags of food from Chad's fridge than Gwen's personal effects.

"I guess by now Chad is back home and everyone knows what happened. Do you want to e-mail your family and tell them everything is okay?" At least he hoped everything was okay. She'd been so quiet he didn't know what she was thinking, and he didn't know why it mattered to him what she thought. Gwen was just another driver, and this was just another job, and very soon it would all be over. Life would be back to normal and he would be alone in his truck once again.

She turned her head. "That's a great idea! I'd forgotten you could do that."

"The laptop is in the lower compartment, on the same side as the fridge."

He didn't want to interrupt, nor did he want to intrude. She focused all her attention on the computer while she typed, then turned it off.

"I'm going to sleep now. Is it okay if I tuck this under the seat? I'll sleep better knowing you won't have to crawl under the bunk to pull it back out again."

Lionel sighed. "I guess this is one of those things that we knew would come up when we talked yesterday." He waited for her to respond, but she didn't. "We're probably going to have some awkward moments since we're going to be in close quarters for a long time. I want to be sure we respect each other's privacy and personal space. If you ever want some time alone when we're moving, just go to the back and close the curtain, and don't worry about hurting my feelings or anything like that. I don't want to invade your privacy, and that includes going underneath the bunk if you're on top of it, sleeping or not. I trust you'd have the same courtesy for me. If that curtain is closed, it stays closed unless there's an emergency."

He glanced quickly at her, then returned his attention to the road.

"That sounds good. I think I'm going to go to sleep now. The bunk is easy to take down, isn't it?"

"Yes, it works on a hydraulic mechanism. Just undo the clips. They're easy to figure out. See how it's done?"

"Yes, I can figure it out. Thanks."

The bunk thumped slightly as it settled into place. The curtain slid closed, and the rasp of the Velcro announced the finality of the separation.

He had wanted to say good night or something but couldn't figure out exactly what to say. Now he'd missed his chance.

Lionel reached for the CD player, but his hand froze before he touched the play button. The heavy curtain was an excellent sound barrier, but he didn't know how effective it would be against the music. Often he heard music through the walls of his apartment when he was trying to sleep. Since he kept such an irregular schedule, he didn't have the right to ask his neighbors to turn their music down, especially during the day when most people were at work. They probably weren't even aware when he was home, since he was there so seldom. He suspected that, despite the claims of the salesman as to the soundproofing quality of the curtain, it still wasn't as good a sound barrier as a wall. He tried to recall if he'd heard music in the background when Gwen was driving and he was sleeping. He hadn't heard a thing, but he didn't know if that was because she had had it on so quiet or if he'd slept that heavily. Somehow he doubted she'd put the music on at all.

He made a mental note to test exactly at what volume they could have the music playing when driving so as not to disturb whoever was sleeping at the time. He felt guilty now knowing that Gwen had driven most of the night in the boring silence.

Since Lionel had agreed to not touch the curtain once it had been closed, he left the music off, leaving him with only his thoughts for company.

On any trip, he did a lot of thinking while he drove, sometimes about important things, sometimes not. This time he could think only of Gwen. He wasn't sure he liked that.

For the past few years he hadn't thought much about women. After his experience with Sharon, he knew he would never get married, and because of his unpredictable schedule, he seldom dated. Except for the few times he wanted a little female companionship, there was no point.

Now he had no choice but to spend days and days with a woman he'd just barely met. Nothing would have adequately prepared him for this. The only consolation was that Gwen couldn't have foreseen this happening either and was equally caught off guard.

All was silent from behind, making him wonder if she was sleeping well. He didn't know if he would be able to hear the slight creaking of the bunk when she moved, but since he heard nothing, he assumed she was sleeping soundly.

Lionel frowned and focused his attention on the road. The only thing that should concern him was that she be well rested in order to drive safely.

He thought back to their previous conversations. In that short space of time, he'd seen many sides of Chad's niece. She had an easy sense of humor, yet there was nothing funny about the way she confronted those morons who had all but accused her of being a truck stop lizard. She had demonstrated a confidence and strength of character he didn't see often in a man or woman. She had shared her faith in the strangest way he'd ever seen, but he had a feeling that, one day, her words would come back to at least one person in that room, and the firmness of her conviction could make a difference.

Even though she had only taken up driving a truck on a dare, she showed no lack of respect for the profession. Instead, she treated him as an equal, despite the differences in education level between her years of university to obtain her teaching degree and his minimal pass in high school. He had judged her unfairly, assuming that because she was a woman, she couldn't do the job.

He was wrong. The woman had moxie. She wasn't a bad driver either. She was also adapting well to life on the road.

He continued to drive in quiet, checking his watch more often than he ever had before, wondering how long she needed to sleep. Finally, after six hours and forty-seven minutes of driving alone, the rasp of the Velcro sounded behind him.

"Hi," he said, knowing he was smiling much more than he should have been. "Sleep well?" A sign ahead indicated a rest stop coming up, so he began to slow down.

She smiled back as she slid into the seat and buckled her seatbelt. He forced his attention to the road.

"Yes, I did. I must have been more tired than I thought. I didn't hear a thing. That bunk is much softer than I figured it would be. I was out like a light. It sure feels strange to be waking up at this time. I feel like eating breakfast, but it's nearly supper time."

"Most truck stops have bacon and eggs on the menu 'round the clock."

She scrunched up her nose, which on a woman should have been cute, but when Gwen did it, she only looked miffed at his suggestion. "That's too greasy. I like something more healthy for breakfast."

"Don't start that again."

Gwen laughed but didn't comment.

Lionel pulled into the stop without being asked. Her little smile as she ran out of the truck for the amenities building did something funny in his stomach, but he passed it off as not having eaten for awhile. When she returned, he was already digging into the fridge.

"Let's eat now," he said. "I think I'm hungry too."

Lionel made coffee while Gwen carried the bag of sandwiches to the picnic table. When she didn't comment on the lack of tableware he considered teasing her about it, but when they stopped to pray, he no longer felt like fooling around.

They ate in silence, and Lionel didn't miss the conversation. He felt comfortable with Gwen, more comfortable than he'd felt with anyone in many, many years. They didn't need to fill the silence with meaningless words.

They both chose the same moment to stand, clean up the mess, and return to the truck. Lionel drove only as far as the next truck stop, where they fueled. When they were done, they went inside the restaurant for a cup of coffee. The sun was setting, and from here they would be driving most of the night without stopping, except to switch drivers.

Lionel sat back, cradling the cup in his palms as Gwen pulled a scrap of paper out of her pocket then plopped her purse on the table. She pulled out a calculator, a ruler, a pencil, and her driving logbook, then started writing. She checked back and forth from the paper to the logbook, drawing little dots and making notes in the logbook. She then used the ruler to draw perfectly straight lines joining the dots.

He finally couldn't stand it. "What are you doing?"

She didn't look up as she pressed one finger on the page and dutifully added up all her figures. "I'm doing my logbook."

"With a ruler and a calculator?"

She still didn't look up. "I strive for accuracy," she mumbled as she wrote down the total, then began to add the next column.

He peeked over at the volumes of notes she'd made, then shook his head. "You don't need to write all that stuff down. They don't need to know exactly how much time it took to fuel, how long it took you to eat, what you dreamed about, or anything else I'd rather not discuss. All you need to have in there are your driving hours, the hours you've worked but weren't driving, off-duty hours, and time sleeping. Four things. That's all they need to know."

"I want to do this. Like a journal."

He opened his mouth to protest but snapped it shut again. Teachers probably did stuff like that all the time, so it was probably second nature for her. Out on the road she would soon see such detail was unnecessary.

She pulled a separate piece of paper out of the back of her logbook, also scribbled with notes. "So up until now, you've driven eight hours and fifteen minutes, and I've driven nine and a half in this twenty-four-hour period."

"You've figured out my driving time in your logbook?"

"This is pretty calculated, you know. It's not as easy as driving a total of twenty hours, leaving a window of four hours that the truck doesn't move. It's different when you have to figure that once each of us has driven ten hours, we have to rest for eight in between. We can't have an overlap where there won't be an eight-hour break between the last time someone drove with the other having enough driving hours to fill the break. If that happens, the truck can't move."

She added a few more numbers to the paper. "So if you drive one and three-quarter hours tonight, that ends your legal allotment for the day. I have half an hour left, but that will bring us to midnight, where I can start on the next twenty-four-hour period, so I can keep driving. I've had my eight-hour break, and you haven't."

Lionel shook his head and stared at her. He hadn't ever gone into such detail. He'd never needed to.

She frowned and started to draw a table on the same page. "I figure I can draw up a schedule so we can actually get twenty hours of driving between the two of us in each twenty-four-hour period, including the eight-hour breaks between, fueling the truck once a day like you said, and eating and personal time, and do it quite comfortably."

"You're drafting up a schedule?"

She slid the paper across the table and pointed to a chart with that day's date and the times written down until that moment. "We can stay here in the restaurant for another half hour." She snapped the book shut, laid her pencil down, and smiled ear to ear. "So that means we can relax and have dessert. I'm having a piece of that peach pie in the front case. With ice cream."

Lionel didn't comment. He'd never relaxed on schedule before. He ordered a chocolate donut.

Chapter 5

Gwen settled into the passenger seat and clicked on her seatbelt. Lionel hadn't seemed too impressed with her attempts at making a schedule. But it was the only way she knew to accomplish the maximum allowable driving time while they had such a critical load. She would have thought that since a trucker had to live by a schedule, he'd be used to such things. Apparently not.

He didn't speak until they'd reached highway speed, and then his voice startled her. "I've been thinking."

Gwen cringed. She should have felt this coming. They hadn't even spent one day together and already it wasn't going to work. She stiffened her back and turned to look at him as he drove. She could see his profile in the lights of the dash. Out of nowhere the thought struck her what a handsome man he was. Not only that, but he'd been helpful and considerate. Every nice thing Uncle Chad had said about him was right. She quickly erased those thoughts from her mind as she cleared her throat. "Yes?"

"When I drive at night I usually have the music or the radio on, or even in the daytime when there's no one to talk to. It helps fight the boredom of the long stretches. The curtain is supposed to be really soundproof. We should test it with the music and see if we can have it on without disturbing each other."

Gwen blinked. "Uh. . .sure. . ." She glanced behind her at the bunk. Since they had known Lionel would be the next one to have a sleep, they had tucked her sleeping bag underneath, and his blankets and pillow were piled in the corner of the bunk, ready for him. She didn't want to go there.

Gwen mentally kicked herself. If she was scared of getting in the same area as a pile of blankets, she had to have a screw loose. Without another word, she climbed into the bunk, flicked on the small light, closed the curtain, and listened.

His muffled voice drifted through the curtain. "Can you hear that?"

The constant hum of the motor was louder than the music, because she couldn't hear a thing. "No!" she called back.

She waited a few seconds and he called out again. "How about now?"

This time she could actually hear it. It was still soft enough that it wouldn't keep her awake. "You can make it louder. It's still okay."

This time she could almost make out the words, and that would disturb her. However, she didn't want to be unrealistic. If this arrangement was going to work, she couldn't infringe too much on his routine, and that included the volume at which he played his music.

Gwen glanced at the pile of blankets in the corner of the bunk.

She tended to sleep completely bundled up and liked to have the corner of her blanket or, in this case, sleeping bag tucked under her chin and over her ears, no matter what time of year. Because of that, she'd always had difficulty sleeping in the summer heat. Despite the summer heat, she couldn't sleep with her ears uncovered. She didn't know why she did it, but she couldn't remember ever sleeping any other way. A completely unexpected bonus of her temporary summer job was that the truck was air-conditioned, so she found sleeping comfortable. She'd slept better last night in the truck than she had in the past month at home.

The only way to know if the music would disturb her would be to lie down as if she were about to really sleep.

Very slowly she unfolded Lionel's blanket. She wasn't going to wrap herself in his personal blanket, but she did lie down and pull just the corner of it over under her chin and over her cheek and ear, as if she were going to go to sleep.

She could still hear the music, but it would never prevent her from falling asleep. Gwen closed her eyes and snuggled her face into the fuzzy fabric and tried to imagine that she was really ready to fall asleep. It wasn't difficult. The blanket was thick and soft, not what she figured a man's blanket would be. Besides the soothing feel of the blanket against her face, it held a faint, spicy, male fragrance.

Gwen smiled. She liked this fragrance, and it was familiar to her, even though she couldn't remember from where. At first she considered that she might have dated a man who wore the same thing. She inhaled it again, then sat up with a start as she realized what it was. She'd smelled this scent from her brother's sleeping bag when she'd borrowed it. Garrett was a very basic kind of guy, not into cologne or other trappings. What she was smelling wasn't cologne, it was deodorant.

She pushed the blanket away and hurriedly folded it up as she called through the curtain. "That's fine. If I was lying down to sleep, that wouldn't bother me at all."

Once everything was neatly back in the corner, she parted the curtain and slid back into the passenger seat, grateful that, in the dark, he couldn't see the blush she knew was on her cheeks.

"I had that on volume level eleven. Are you sure that wouldn't bother you?"

Heat spread into her cheeks even more as she nodded quickly. "Positive."

"As long as you're sure."

Gwen turned her head, studying whatever was out the window, even though it was pitch black and she couldn't see a thing. "I'm sure."

They continued to chat about nothing in particular until Lionel's allowable driving time was up. He pulled into the next rest area, but instead of just switching drivers, they decided to go for a walk and stretch their legs.

The rest area was deserted. The moon was almost full, so even with no artificial lighting except for the lights shining from the window of the amenities building, the picnic area was not in total blackout.

Gwen tapped Lionel on the arm. "Want to jog around?"

His little grin made crinkles appear in the corners of his eyes. "Do better than that. Race ya." He took off laughing and without saying, "Go."

Years of competing with Garrett had conditioned Gwen to shift into high gear instantly. Lionel hadn't gone far before she bolted after him.

She caught up quickly, but when she did, he quickened his pace, which forced her to speed up too. She caught up to him again, but he ran faster still. Gwen ran for all she was worth, and by the time they neared the end of the circular path around the area, she was ahead of him.

She raised her hands in the air as they crossed the imaginary finish line where they began, beside the truck. "I won! I beat you!" she gasped.

Lionel stood still and bent at the waist, resting his hands on his knees for a few seconds before he straightened. "Whew!" he panted. "I'm more out of shape than I thought."

Gwen shook her head while she also struggled to catch her breath. "Me too. I'm not used to this anymore."

Without any further discussion, they walked around the path once again as their breathing and heart rates slowed to normal. Then they hopped back into the truck, this time with Gwen in the driver's seat.

After driving awhile, Gwen couldn't hold back a giggle. "I suppose I should tell you that I jog around the field before school twice a week with my students to keep in shape. Our jog often turns into a race. I don't always win."

His answering smile quickened her heartbeat, even though their race was long over. "I suppose I should tell you that I sit all day."

"You didn't do too bad for someone so old and out of shape."

His hands went to his stomach, which, from what Gwen had previously seen, was not the least bit out of shape. "I'm not that bad. I do make an effort to get some exercise. And I'm not that old, I'm only thirty-one!"

"I'm thirty, and I beat you."

"Let's see if you can beat me on the last day of summer, after you've been driving for two months. I think that's enough time to lose that edge. And you will lose it."

Gwen opened her mouth to issue a challenge but snapped it shut before she spoke. A situation exactly like this had gotten her into this mess in the first place. Only, for something that was such a mess, she really was enjoying herself.

Lionel turned the radio on and they rode without conversation, until he yawned. "I think not getting enough sleep is catching up with me. I'm tired. If you don't mind, I'm going to crawl into the back."

She shook her head. "Not at all. Good night."

When the curtain closed behind her, Gwen turned the music down to a level slightly lower than what Lionel had said when they tested it earlier. After a few songs, she hadn't heard from him asking her to turn it down, so she assumed he was able to fall asleep without difficulty.

This time she was more relaxed driving alone in the night, although driving through the flatlands of Colorado instead of through the mountains at night might have had something to do with it. She enjoyed the music and was pleased to see that many of the CDs in his collection were also her favorites.

At sunrise Gwen pulled into a truck stop, but this time Lionel poked his head out before she left the truck. "Sleep well?" she asked.

He mumbled something that might have been a yes, and Gwen tried to stifle her smile.

"What's so funny?" he grumbled as he sat on the edge of the bunk to tie the laces on his sneakers.

"Are you always crabby in the morning?"

"I'm not crabby. The light's too bright."

They walked together into the building but parted ways as soon as they entered. As soon as Gwen sat at the table, she made a note of the time in her logbook, then pulled out the novel she'd half-read and ordered a coffee while she waited for Lionel.

She read a whole chapter by the time he joined her, and again all traces of his earlier mood were gone. His hair was combed and slightly damp, he'd shaved, and he wore new clothes.

"Later today when we stop and fuel, I've got to do laundry. This is the last of my clean stuff. Remember, I didn't make it home after my last trip. They dispatched me straight out."

She hadn't thought about doing laundry. After her first trip with Uncle Chad, they'd had a couple of days at home. Even though she didn't do much other than laundry and make a number of phone calls the first day, she didn't think about the possibility that she might have to do laundry away from home.

Another good thing about being single and living at home was that she didn't have to worry about coming home to an empty fridge. When she got back, her mother had made a feast for dinner and then invited not only Garrett and Robbie but also Molly and Ken. As expected, Molly nattered on and on about what a dumb idea it was for her to be driving all summer. Gwen had passed off the remarks, but now, when it was too late to do anything about it, she could acknowledge that, even though she'd had a nice enough time with Lionel, Molly was right. She was crazy for doing this.

Lionel ordered bacon and eggs, which was fine for him because it was breakfast and it was, after all, six in the morning. However, Gwen had been driving for seven hours, and she was famished.

The waitress didn't bat an eyelash, but Lionel nearly choked on his coffee when Gwen ordered a hamburger and fries with all the trimmings. She waited for him to comment, but this time he didn't take the bait.

This time they didn't linger. As soon as they were finished eating, they climbed back into the truck, ready to roll. They needed to save their non-driving time for later so Lionel could do his laundry.

Gwen liked the early morning best of all. It was nearing the end of Lionel's eight-hour break, and even though the meal helped refresh her, she was more than ready to switch drivers. She needed to relax.

As she continued to drive, an eagle soared overhead. The sunrise had been beautiful, but now that it was daylight, she wanted to take in the beauty of the fields and meadows on either side of the highway and take some pictures. During her short time as a trucker, she'd already seen many different kinds of birds and animals, including a fox or something at the side of the road a few miles back. From time to time, cute little gophers scampered across the highway.

"It sure is pretty in the morning," she sighed. "Everything is so fresh, the heat of the day hasn't made the birds and animals seek shelter yet."

Lionel raised one finger in the air and leaned back in his seat. "There are animals out at night too. You just don't see them."

"Yes, I have. Last night I saw a couple of deer at the side of the road. Their eyes caught the headlights and they froze when the light was on them, just like the textbooks say they do."

"I didn't mean the deer. In some parts you'll see moose too, by the way. I was talking about other critters. Snakes and lizards and things that go bump in the night."

She turned her head, gave him a big, fake, toothy smile, then turned back to the road. "Don't try to frighten me by talking about bats and bugs and stuff. They don't scare me, so don't waste your time. My brother is a forest ranger, and you wouldn't believe the animals and creepy crawlies he's been so kind to show me over the years."

He grinned back. "I had to try. So unseemly creatures don't scare you. Big, loud-mouthed truckers don't scare you. Tell me, what does scare you?"

Gwen shrugged her shoulders. "I don't know. Lots of things." One thing that was scaring her right now was Lionel, even though there was nothing big or loud-mouthed about him, nor did he have scales or smell bad. He made her feel comfortable, which in itself wasn't a bad thing, but he made her feel too comfortable. There were times they didn't need words, they knew what the other was thinking and acted accordingly. The only person she'd ever experienced that connection with was her brother, but that wasn't the same. They were twins, and over the years she'd learned that the bond she shared with Garrett was unique.

She didn't know anything about Lionel beyond what Uncle Chad had told her and what she'd learned herself in the past couple of weeks. And now, traveling across the continent with a man she barely knew, she should have been frightened, or at least nervous. Instead, beyond the few awkward moments she knew would happen, she trusted him completely. She shouldn't have. She felt comfortable around him. And that made her nervous.

"What scares me is one of the kids in my Sunday school class. I teach grades eight and nine from Monday to Friday, but on Sundays I got the grade fives this year. There's one boy in the class who I think spends his spare time dreaming up something bizarre to do when he gets to church. Last month he came with his hamster in his pocket. I put it in a box so I could teach the class without the distraction, but the critter chewed its way out. The worst part was, after we caught it and put it in a hamster-proof container, he asked me not to tell his parents about what he'd done so he wouldn't get in trouble."

"What did you do?"

"I know his parents fairly well, and it was something they should have known, but I couldn't tell because there's a trust involved in being his Sunday school teacher. I have to be an example to him, which means not betraying a confidence."

"That's a tough one."

"But I got him back." Gwen laughed, in spite of herself. "I made him write a note of thanks to everyone who helped catch his hamster. Then the parents of the children who received the notes phoned his mother to say how nice Jeremy was for doing that." She laughed again. "But I didn't say a word to anyone about the escapist hamster. He still doesn't know how his parents found out."

He pretended to shudder. "Remind me never to hold you to a promise." Gwen knew he was smiling, but even knowing that, she turned to acknowledge his unstated approval.

"So tell me, what else has he done to you that he scares you so much?"

She opened her mouth to continue when another little gopher ran onto the road ahead of them. But instead of running all the way across, he stopped in the middle of the highway, directly on the center line. He sat up on his cute little behind and looked straight at the truck bearing down on him.

At the speed at which the truck was moving, she knew the turbulence as she passed would knock him off his little bottom and send him rolling on the pavement, which would probably hurt him. Gwen turned the wheel slightly and aimed the truck to hug the shoulder line so she could pass him as far away as possible. Suddenly, the gopher decided to run. Instead of going back the way it had come, it ran to her side, directly in front of the truck.

"No!" she called out. "Not that way, little fella!"

Gwen felt a bump.

Lionel muttered something nasty under his breath.

Gwen's stomach rolled. She tightened her grip on the wheel, and her eyes started to burn.

"I hate when that happens," Lionel mumbled. "You'd think they would. . ." His voice trailed off.

She knew he was looking at her. She refused to turn her head. The burn in her eyes worsened, and her hands started to feel shaky.

"Gwen?"

She swallowed hard. "I used to feed them at the zoo when I was a kid." Her chin quivered. She clenched her teeth but she couldn't stop it.

He mumbled something else she couldn't hear. "Pull over," he said, more loudly.

She quickly swiped at her nose with the back of her hand, then grabbed the wheel again, holding it much tighter than she needed to. She choked the words out, trying to keep her voice steady. "We can't stop here."

"Yes, we can. That's what the shoulder is for. Pull over."

She needed to be tough. She wanted to show him she could act like a professional. People ran over gophers all the time on the flatlands. She had to show him she could be strong, even though she'd just murdered one of God's innocent woodland creatures with twenty tons of mobile machinery. The poor little thing hadn't had a chance.

Gwen's vision blurred, and she couldn't blink it away. One tear trickled down her cheek.

Gwen pulled over.

The second they were at a stop, before Lionel had a chance to undo his seatbelt, she dashed straight for the bunk. "I'm really sleepy. I don't think I need to wind down. Good night."

And she whipped the curtain shut.

Chapter 6

Lionel stared at the closed curtain, his mouth wide open, the words he was going to say forgotton. His hand still rested on the seatbelt clip. He hadn't had enough time to press the button and release it.

She'd moved faster than the truck ever had, and the closed status of the curtain was as effective as a fortress wall.

He'd run over many gophers in his career as a driver, and he still found it upsetting. Most of the other drivers joked about it, trying to out-macho each other, but he knew he wasn't the only one who felt bad when it happened. He wanted to tell her that, but she'd run off before he could say a word. Now she was sequestered behind the curtain, which he'd promised never to touch.

Not that he knew what to do with a crying woman, but he wanted to do something. One thing he did know. He didn't want to sit and stare at the curtain while she cried. He couldn't hear her, but he knew what she was doing. He'd never felt so helpless in his life.

Lionel slid into the driver's seat and turned the radio on. As soon as he reached the speed limit, he flipped on the cruise control.

He had nothing to do but drive and listen to the music.

Things had gone so well until this point, although nothing had gone like he expected. He could understand that she was upset about running over the gopher, but it bothered him that she'd shut him out and not allowed him the opportunity to help her deal with it.

He'd counted on, and even looked forward to, the next few hours, wanting to enjoy the morning, talking to her as he drove, before she crawled into the bunk for a sleep. Instead, he was alone in the driver's seat again, and she was in the back crying.

As the miles rolled by, he tried to think of something he could say when she got up. Besides the standard rhetoric that it happened to every driver at some point, the best he could come up with was to tell her there was nothing anyone could do to avoid them. She probably wouldn't derive much comfort from being told that in the eyes of the company or an owner operator who had his life's savings tied up in his truck, risking an accident wasn't worth a little gopher. Nor did he think she'd get much consolation if he told her to be grateful it wasn't something bigger, like a moose, that she'd hit.

He remembered a few years back when one of his friends hit a moose outside of Thunder Bay. Thankfully the driver hadn't been badly hurt, but the truck had sustained heavy damage and the trailer had gone over into the ditch on impact. The weight of the load had busted out the roof of the trailer. It had taken an entire crew three days of picking through the muddy, stagnant water to recover everything. Then it took a year and a half for the head office to settle all the damage and loss claims. Very few people realized that much of the cost of an accident wasn't covered by insurance, which made the company not look favorably on accidents caused by wildlife.

By noon she still hadn't appeared. Lionel tried to convince himself that it wasn't a major deal because she'd been in the bunk only four hours and she was due for a sleep anyway. When his stomach grumbled, he stopped at a truck stop, pulling into an area of the parking lot he thought would be the quietest. Leaving the motor running so the roar of it wouldn't disturb her when he started it again, he dashed into the building, bought a sandwich and a coffee, and ran back. Since the curtain remained closed, he ate his lunch alone as he drove.

By mid-afternoon Lionel thought he must have checked his watch a couple of hundred times. He was beginning to wonder if she would ever come out, when the rasp of the Velcro sounded.

He purposely kept his focus straight ahead. "Good morning, Stranger. Sleep well?" he asked, then kicked himself. By being too cheerful he didn't want her to think that he knew she'd been doing anything other than sleeping.

"Yes, thank you." She slid into the passenger seat.

No words passed between them as he drove. He pulled into the first rest area and hopped out of the truck to catch a breath of fresh air when she went into the amenities building.

He waited as she tossed her purse up into the truck. "Want to go for a walk before we get moving again?"

She nodded but didn't comment so he started walking, expecting her to follow, which she did.

This time the silence bothered him. He had so many things to say but didn't know how to start. The things he felt he should say jumbled with what he wanted to say but couldn't, until he couldn't tell one from the other. Lionel decided to keep quiet.

"Uncle Chad told me it would probably take awhile to get used to sleeping in a moving truck. He said some drivers never sleep well, that he and Jeff sleep and drive in five-hour shifts. But I haven't had any trouble sleeping."

"Me neither."

"I'm really sorry, it's after three o'clock, and I didn't let you get into the fridge. You must be starving."

Lionel grinned. "I stopped and grabbed a quick sandwich at a truck stop. I couldn't believe it when you slept through. After all, there was food involved."

She shot him a dirty look, but he kept his gaze fixed forward and bit his bottom lip to stop himself from smiling. She continued when he pretended not to notice her scathing glare. "That's not all that surprising. I was really tired because I didn't get enough sleep the day before. Or the night before. Or whatever you call it when you sleep these strange hours."

He shrugged his shoulders. "I've never really thought about it. It's something you just get used to."

"Or not."

"I suppose. Are you hungry? If you want to make a quick snack, that's fine, but I really have to do some laundry, so we have to allow for a long stop at the next truck stop. That will have to be our real supper break, while we're waiting for the washing machine and stuff."

"I just woke up. I don't want supper."

He laughed, letting himself relax, grateful that everything appeared to be all right, after all. "Right. You're the one who had a hamburger and fries for breakfast."

"That wasn't breakfast. That was supper at six in the morning. Now it's time for breakfast at," she checked her wristwatch, "three forty-seven in the afternoon."

This particular rest area was much smaller than the one they'd stopped at the day before, so they found themselves finishing their walk around the picnic area in a very short time. They were about to leave the grassed area and return to the parking lot when they heard a child squeal with delight.

"Mommy! Mommy! He took it!"

"Don't move, Sweetie. Mommy wants to take your picture."

They watched a woman crouch down to take a picture of a little girl feeding bread to a black squirrel beside one of the tables.

Lionel's gut clenched at the sound of Gwen's sudden intake of breath. He remembered her comment that, as a child, she'd enjoyed feeding the gophers at the zoo. He had a bad feeling she was thinking of a gopher that wouldn't ever get fed again.

He grabbed her hand. "Let's go. We don't want to get behind schedule. You know all about schedules."

She stiffened but allowed him to lead her to the truck.

He fished in his pocket for the keys. "You want to drive or ride?"

Her voice, when she answered, wavered slightly. "Either way, whatever you want."

He stuffed the keys back into his pocket and grasped both her hands. "Gwen, I know you're upset about it. It's okay to be upset. Even us guys feel bad when we hit an animal. Even little ones like gophers."

Being at virtually the same height, she seemed closer than she really was. If she were shorter, it would have given him some distance as she stared at him with those big round eyes—eyes that started to well up with tears. She blinked a few times and the moisture cleared.

He dropped her hands and slid his palms up to her shoulders, which probably wasn't very smart, because it only drew her closer. The softness of her hair as it brushed his fingers made him want to run them through the dark locks. Her hair was an unusual color, a brown so dark it was almost black, and even though she hadn't had a shower in two days, it still looked fresh. It shone in the afternoon sunshine with a natural luster he thought would have looked good in a shampoo commercial. He knew he shouldn't be touching her hair, or any part of her, but he couldn't move away.

"You probably think I'm such a ninny. I know it was just a gopher. It's not like it was someone's dog or anything."

He wound his fingers in her hair, amazed at the silky feel of it. "You're not a ninny."

He spread his fingers and watched as her hair slipped between them. He then returned his attention to her beautiful chocolate brown eyes. As soon as they made eye contact, she bit her bottom lip, her eyes grew moist, welled up, and overflowed.

"Aw, nuts. . . ," he mumbled. He pulled her forward, and when she didn't resist, he surrounded her with a hug. Her chin rested exactly on top of his shoulder as they stood. She sniffled again, right beside his ear, sending a feeling of dread through him that she was going to start sobbing her guts out, right in the parking lot.

Now he really didn't know what to do.

Very gently he rubbed small circles on her back, doing his best to soothe her. She didn't cry but, instead, let go a ragged sigh. The tension in her shoulders relaxed beneath his touch, so he didn't stop. Lionel closed his eyes. A few strands of her hair tickled his nose. Instead of turning his head away, he pressed his cheek into her hair.

He knew what he wanted to do. He wanted to kiss her. Very slowly he began to turn his head until his whole face was buried in her hair. All he had to do was touch her chin with his fingertips to turn her head just a little and he would be in just the right position.

At the realization of what he was about to do, his eyes bolted open. He backed up about an inch, creating some distance between them. As soon as he pulled away, Gwen also stiffened and backed up, completing the separation.

She swiped her eyes with the back of her hand and sniffled. "Thanks, I feel better now. We've got to get going, we've got miles to make."

❧

Gwen started to slow the truck as they approached the exit for the truck stop, noting the time on the dashboard clock. "I've driven for nine hours today, you've driven for seven. We've already used two hours of non-driving time, but we can still get in ten hours each for this twenty-four-hour period if we hurry. Tell me all that we need to do, in case I've forgotten something."

Lionel checked his watch. "We have to fuel and do our trip fuel sheets, then update our personal fuel log as well as our trip logbooks. While we're stopped and we still have daylight we should clean the clearance lights and windows and check the tires. Plus you want to have a shower, and I have to do my laundry. We were going to have supper too. We'll never do it."

Gwen tilted up one corner of her mouth while she downshifted, organizing the details and guesstimating how long each step would take. Lionel opened his mouth while she was still thinking, so she quickly shook her head to silence him in order to take a few more seconds to calculate her plan. She turned her head for a second to catch his attention. "We can do it if we organize ourselves efficiently."

"Oh, yeah. Right," he grunted, and crossed his arms.

Gwen slowed their speed to a crawl and rolled up to the pump. "We can do this." She applied the hand brake, but before she released the seatbelt, she grabbed a pen and a napkin from the slot and calculated how long each duty would take as she wrote the details of her plan. "You begin fueling, I'll start the laundry and reserve the shower. While I'm doing that, you clean the windows." She stuck her tongue out of the corner of her mouth as she figured out how long the washer would run and tried to recall how long the fueling and maintenance took them yesterday. "When everything is in the washer, I'll come back and do the clearance lights and tires. Then I'll go have my shower. You'll be finished with the fueling and the windows by the time I'm done, and by then the washer should be finished. We can throw everything in the dryer and then go have supper. We can do the paperwork while we eat. By the time we're finished the clothes should be dry, then we can move out."

He didn't speak, so she handed him the napkin as proof that she was right.

"Come on, Lionel, we don't have much time."

"I don't believe this." He looked down at her notes on the crumpled napkin. "I'm traveling with the Schedule Queen."

Gwen reached across the space between the seats and poked him in the arm. "Trust me. This will work."

He handed the napkin back. He spoke so softly she could barely make out what he said. "You missed calculating how many seconds it would take for me to brush my teeth."

She glared at him and crossed her arms. "Did you say something?"

"Nothing worth repeating," he grumbled as he unclipped his seatbelt then reached for the door handle.

Gwen loudly cleared her throat, making him freeze in place. She purposely didn't say anything but narrowed her eyes and gave him her best dirty look, one she'd perfected on her brother.

He raised his palms in the air toward her and sighed. "Okay, I give up. We'll do it your way."

Gwen immediately stepped into the back and pulled out her bag of dirty laundry. "Where's your stuff?"

He opened the door and started to leave, but stopped at her question, leaving one leg sticking out as he answered. "The rags are in the bin underneath where your clothes are, like they usually are."

"No, not that. I meant your clothes. The stuff you need washed."

"Oh, that's in a bag in the bin on the bottom left. It's. . ." His voice trailed off. The door closed, but instead of being outside to start fueling the truck, he appeared beside her in the cab. "I'll do the laundry."

Gwen stiffened and tightened her grip on her own laundry bag. She didn't want a man going through her personal things. "It's okay, I can do it. You go fuel the truck."

He shook his head and pulled a bag out of the bin he'd told her to check, but didn't give it to her. "You fuel the truck. I'll do the laundry."

They stood, neither one moving, staring at each other, neither giving up his or her bag of laundry.

Gwen bowed her head and pinched the bridge of her nose. "We don't have time for this. It's okay, Lionel. Really." She reached for the bag, but when she grasped it and started to pull, he didn't let go. Gwen squeezed her eyes closed. "Lionel, I assure you, you don't own anything I haven't seen before."

His cheeks reddened, but he still didn't let go.

She pulled a little harder. "I have a twin brother. I've washed a man's underw. . .uh. . .personal items before. It's not a big deal. Come on, we don't have time for this." It wasn't that she was anxious to do his laundry, but there was no way she was going to let him wash her underwear.

"As long as you promise to dump the load in the machine without looking."

"I promise. Now let go."

Reluctantly, he released his grip. While he was acting mildly complacent, Gwen hopped out of the truck and ran to the front counter to make the necessary arrangements.

On her travels with Uncle Chad, when they'd stopped at night she got a motel room, so she'd always had the comfort of her own bathroom, shower included. Then, in the morning when she was done with the room, she tidied up the truck while Uncle Chad had his shower. This was going to be her first experience with renting a truck stop shower.

She told herself that the facilities would be similar to those available at the various campsites she'd been to over the years. After she put her name down, she went into the truck stop's Laundromat, pulled a few pairs of jeans out of Lionel's bag, and stuffed them into the machine with her own jeans. Then she dumped everything else into another machine without looking, along with the few things of her own that needed washing, just as she'd promised.

She hustled back to the truck and quickly wiped off the clearance lights, walked around the unit to check the tires, then stood behind Lionel as he stood on the running boards, busily cleaning the windows.

"I'm going to have my shower now. Catch you in about twenty minutes." She retrieved her small overnight bag and some clean clothes out of the larger duffel bag and jogged to the shower area.

It wasn't exactly relaxing, but the shower left her feeling clean again, which she supposed was the point. She stuffed her toiletries back into her bag as she contemplated her last duty, that of transferring their clothes from the washer to the dryer. Then she would be meeting Lionel in the restaurant for supper.

Life on the road was vastly different from anything she'd ever experienced. Any other time she'd gone to a restaurant for dinner with a man she'd worn a skirt, a nice blouse, and, even though she usually didn't wear a lot of makeup, she always put some on when she went out on a date. She hadn't brought a single tube of lipstick with her for her truck-driving stint, and she certainly hadn't brought a curling iron.

Gwen peeked over her shoulder before she left the room and caught a glimpse of herself in the mirror. She paused, studying her image to see what everyone else saw.

Her hair was still damp and hung loosely to her shoulders. She wore no makeup, and her fine-dining attire was a T-shirt with the faded logo of a Christian summer camp where she'd counseled a few years ago. Her jeans were so well-worn the right knee almost had a hole. Her battered sneakers had seen better days, but they were the most comfortable she owned. She looked like a slob. A clean slob, but a slob just the same.

Not that she had to dress up for Harry's Truck Stop Cafe.

She imagined this would be what married life was like—not having to care what she wore, coordinating dinner with a man in between work, laundry, cleaning, maintenance, and other chores. She ran her fingers through her hair to fluff it and let it fall. No matter what she did, in her present state, nothing would improve.

While she was taking the classes for her Class-One license, a few friends had not-so-graciously pointed out that spending the summer trucking around the continent in her old clothes wasn't going to do anything for her single status. She was so tired of the well-meaning yet annoying attempts at matchmaking that she could hardly wait to get away. However, now that she was here in a hole-in-the-wall truck stop in the middle of the continent, she knew this wasn't what she had in mind.

So far her experiences on the road hadn't been bad, although she felt very sorry for Uncle Chad with his truck breaking down. She thanked God she hadn't been driving when it happened, because she knew, without a shadow of a doubt, it wasn't her fault. However, she had been driving when that poor little gopher met its demise, and that was her fault. Except for killing the gopher, she was enjoying her summer so far.

Gwen slung her overnight bag over her shoulder and headed for the Laundromat. She transferred everything from the washers to the dryers and nearly bumped into Lionel in the doorway. "Great timing," she said. "You done?"

"Yes, are you?"

She nodded. It was suppertime, and not a minute too soon.

The second the waitress took their orders, Lionel spread a pile of papers and notebooks over the table. "This was a good idea. I think we really can do all this stuff in two hours and get in our full driving time. I'll do the fuel log and fuel trip sheets." He pushed both drivers' logbooks toward her. "Here. You can kill two birds with one stone, since you're so good at it." His hands froze, his eyes widened, and his face paled as he met her eyes. "I didn't mean that the way it sounded. I meant that you're good at making notes on my times in your logbook, so you can do both logbooks. Not that you're good at killing things. I meant doing two things at once. Like when—"

Gwen bit her bottom lip, reached over the piles of paper, and laid her hand over his, interrupting him before he dug himself in deeper. She really did appreciate his attempts to make her feel better. Lionel was really a sweet man, if one liked the loner type. "It's okay. I know what you meant. Let's get this paperwork cleared before the food comes."

Chapter 7

Lionel didn't bother to try to hide his smile. "Good morning. Or afternoon. Or whatever. Did you sleep well?"

She yawned as she flopped into the seat and clipped on her seatbelt. "Yeah, I did."

Without needing to be asked, he prepared to stop at the first rest area or truck stop they came to, just as she'd done for him as soon as he woke up. It had been only a few days since they'd been driving together, but in those few days he suspected they had seen more of each other and done more talking than most married couples did in a month.

While he hadn't thought they would argue, he had traveled alone for so many years that he had expected her constant companionship to get on his nerves. At the very least, he'd expected to do a lot of reading in the bunk to get away from her while she was driving, but he'd been in the bunk only to actually sleep.

Again, she'd driven all night while he slept, and then he'd driven until midafternoon while she slept. He tried not to feel guilty about Gwen driving the graveyard shift hours, but because Chad's breakdown happened when he was out of hours, it hadn't left them any leeway. Now they'd fallen into a pattern. While the hours she was driving were easiest for a beginner, with the least amount of traffic on the road, he knew it wasn't fun to drive all night alone in the dark. He had also worried about how the change in her sleeping patterns would affect her, being up all night and sleeping in the early day, but she had adapted well.

Just like yesterday, he'd started getting antsy about noon, anticipating when she would wake up.

He checked the time. It was nearly three o'clock. "We'll be at Evansville before midnight. We've been making great time, and you've been doing real good. Are you sure you aren't going to be making a career change in September?"

"Not a chance. They need me at the high school, and the kids at church would miss me. I'd miss them too. Besides, my sister-in-law is going to have a baby and I want to watch her grow big and round. I also have to laugh at Garrett every time he makes a fool of himself getting ready to become a father and going through the pregnancy with her. I can hardly wait for him to go to prenatal classes and watch all those ghastly films. It's my sisterly duty to remind him what he's in for."

"I'm sure he'll appreciate your efforts."

She smiled and stared off into nowhere in particular, making Lionel wish she would smile like that when she thought of him.

"He will, strange as it sounds. By the way, can I use your laptop? I have to send him an E-mail and see how they're doing. Robbie was going to have an ultrasound, and I think she's had it by now. I just want to make sure everything is okay."

"You know you can. You don't have to ask."

She turned her head and gave him a big smile.

He smiled back, his heartbeat quickened, and his chest swelled, knowing that this time her smile was for him.

Lionel cleared his throat and forced his attention back on the road. There was only one explanation for his sappy reaction to her simple gratitude. He was losing his mind.

He pulled into a rest area and waited inside the truck when she ran off to the amenities building, watching her every step until the door closed behind her. He couldn't believe that someone who ate so much could be so thin.

After this short stint was over and she was back with Chad, they would see each other only a few times when they crossed paths on the road or ended up back home at the Vancouver terminal at the same time, which wouldn't be often. After the summer was over, he would never see her again because she was going back to her teaching job, and he would continue with his life on the road.

He would be ten times a fool if he thought they could begin dating once life returned to normal. He'd been down that road before, and life had taught him well that it would never work. He had done his best to spend as much time as possible with Sharon when he wasn't away on the road. He had really thought they could be happy, because the time they spent together had been good, yet they weren't miserable when they were apart. The happiest day of his life had been the day she said she'd marry him. Up until that point, his relationship with Sharon had been everything his parents' relationship hadn't been.

Even though his father wasn't a trucker, his father traveled a lot for business. Looking back as an adult, he could see the deterioration of his parents' marriage, and he had vowed not to make the same mistakes.

When he was a kid he'd been witness to their many fights. He couldn't count the times as a child he'd hidden under his bed, praying to a God he really didn't know or understand to make the yelling stop. The screaming usually started the day before his father began his preparations to leave for yet another business trip. Even worse than the screaming matches, he'd had to endure his mother's constant complaints until his father returned, a mother telling her child what a jerk his father was and how his father didn't care about them.

He remembered when it stopped. It was when his mother found someone else.

The divorce was quick, but the custody arrangements had been painful. As he grew up, he'd avoided going home, because from Monday to Friday he had to listen to his mother correct everything he did so he wouldn't turn out like his father. Every weekend he'd had to listen to his father tell him what a selfish and ungrateful woman his mother was. Living with his mother on the weekdays and his father on the weekends, he'd had a difficult time making and keeping friends. He couldn't see his school friends on the weekends, because custody arrangements said that he lived at his father's house on the weekends, and his father insisted on his staying there all weekend. Then he couldn't see the few kids he'd met in his father's neighborhood during the week, because his mother wouldn't take him to his father's house on "her" time.

He would never do that to a child. Even before he became a Christian, Lionel promised himself that his marriage would be forever, and that no matter what troubles happened, he would do everything he could to make it work.

When he met Sharon, what attracted him the most was her independence. When they were apart she anticipated his return, but she had other things in her life to occupy her thoughts and her time. Both their lifestyles suited his being a trucker. They could function apart, and when they were together again, they were happy as well. As far as he could see, and according to what she told him, every time he left she missed him, but wouldn't pine for him, and eagerly awaited his return. A few weeks before what would have been their wedding date, he thought he'd surprise her when he'd been rerouted and come home early. The surprise had been on him. When he knocked on her door, she was with someone else.

He jumped at the sound of the truck door opening. Gwen hopped in and headed straight for the back. She rolled up her sleeping bag and raised and secured the bunk. She tucked her personal effects, including her overnight bag, into the bin they'd said would be hers, and pulled out his laptop computer. "I'm ready to go."

Lionel watched as she took her place in the passenger seat and fastened her seatbelt. The woman was efficient and organized beyond belief. She was a good driver, yet she recognized her limitations as a beginner and was anxious to learn. When they stopped she did her share of the maintenance, even checking the oil. Still, doing what had until recently been considered a man's domain, she was every inch a woman. Even without makeup and in her wrinkled old clothes, Gwen Lamont was beautiful, inside and out. She had a heart of gold and a soul that radiated the love of Christ. One day some man would be lucky to have her.

Lionel found himself jealous of a man who so far didn't exist. He was realistic enough to see that he could have no future with her. He couldn't enter into a relationship that could never have a happy ending.

As he geared up the truck, she booted up the computer. While she waited for it, she gazed out the window and sighed. "It looks like this good weather is going to be over soon. When I was outside I could see big ugly gray clouds in the distance, and they're getting closer. I guess in this part of the country in the heat of the summer that means a thunderstorm is coming, doesn't it?"

"You never know. The clouds could disappear as quickly as they appear. Or we could miss it entirely. Actually, a little rain would be a nice break in this heat."

"Yes, it sure has been hot, way hotter here in Kansas than at home. Have I told you yet how grateful I am that your truck is air-conditioned?"

He grinned and quirked one eyebrow. "No. Tell me."

"I don't think I've ever slept so well in the heat of the summer. The air conditioning is perfect when I. . ." Her voice trailed off. She lowered her head and began furiously typing her messages. "Never mind."

Lionel flipped on the cruise control when he reached cruising speed. Their pattern had been that he would drive for a couple of hours, then they would stop and fuel and eat. He would have an early supper, she would completely ignore his comments and have what she called a late breakfast, despite the time of day. Then she would drive for a few hours before he crawled into the bunk for a sleep. The pattern was comfortable, and it hadn't taken long to get used to.

As they continued eastward, the clouds in the distance billowed and expanded with a speed he'd never seen. In the blink of an eye, the sky became dark.

Gwen stopped typing and reached over to turn off the air conditioning. "This is so strange. I don't like it, it's kind of scary. Does this happen often?"

A gust of wind rocked the truck.

"No, this doesn't happen often." He studied the clouds. Everything had happened too fast, and he didn't like it either. He also didn't like the sickly yellow-green color behind the gray of the clouds.

Another gust of wind hit the truck. "This isn't good, Gwen. Turn on the weather station."

Without question and without finishing what she was doing, she closed the laptop, laid it at her feet, and pushed the designated button on the radio that automatically zeroed in on the local weather station, no matter where in the continent they were.

A blast of hail pelted the truck at the exact second the announcer's voice came on the radio. Gwen turned up the radio in order to hear, and the steady drone and bang of the hail nearly drowned out the voice.

". . .no funnel clouds have touched the ground so far, but Doppler radar indicates a severe line of thunderstorms accompanied by hail and heavy winds. Persons in the southwestern portion of the state should seek immediate shelter as it continues to travel northeast. I repeat, we have a tornado warning in the southwestern portion of the state. . . ."

Lionel set the windshield wipers onto high. "We're in serious trouble like this in the middle of nowhere. Grab the map and see if there's an overpass nearby. We're sitting ducks out here."

A flash of lightning lit the sky, immediately followed by the crash of thunder directly above them. The hail instantly became so thick he couldn't see past the hood, pummeling the truck in fierce torrents, the ensuing onslaught battering the roof and hood in a deafening roar.

The truck started to slide. "Hang on!" he yelled over the din of the hail pounding them as he fought with the wheel. He struggled with all his strength to regain control. "And pray like you've never prayed before!"

He geared down and steered against the force of the wind and the hail as it pushed the truck. Until he could bring the unit to a full stop, they would continue to slide. Only when the truck was at a stop would they be safe, if he could do so before they toppled over in the ditch.

"I know you can do it," Gwen whimpered beside him, and then she started to pray.

He heard her, and he wanted to pray too, but he had to pour all his energy and concentration into working against the wind, guessing where he was going, and trying to stop. If he touched the brake, the wheels would lock up, the truck would jackknife, and they would go over in the ditch.

He had no idea if there was anyone else on the road. It was the major interstate highway, and there would be other traffic besides them in the middle of the day, but he couldn't see where he was going or what he was doing. In the ten years he'd been driving, he'd never hit a snowstorm that blinded him as much as this summer hail. He wouldn't know if another car was on the road until he rode over it or hit it.

He frantically continued to gear down, fighting with himself not to touch the brake. After an eternity, when he was almost at a stop, he couldn't stand it anymore and stomped on the brake. The truck slid a few feet, shuddered, and settled with a jerk. Immediately he killed the motor and yanked on the parking brake.

Lionel turned to Gwen. Her face was pale, her eyes wide. "Don't move!" he called over the clanging of the hail. "Stay in the seat, and don't take off the seatbelt!"

The falling hail outside the window surrounded them completely in a pasty gray void, but even in the dim, filtered light, he could see the fear in her. He'd never been so scared in his life either, but he knew that the safest thing to do was to remain seated, with the seatbelt on.

"How do we know where the funnel is?" she yelled across the space between the seats.

"We don't."

She squeezed her eyes shut and pressed her folded hands to her heart, but she didn't touch her seatbelt.

Lionel closed his eyes and prayed. For their safety. For the safety of those around them, if there was anyone around them. And mostly for Gwen, that no matter what happened, to him or the truck, she would be safe.

As suddenly as throwing a switch, all was quiet, except for the pounding of his heart.

Slowly Lionel opened his eyes. Within seconds the sky brightened and sunlight appeared. The wind stopped.

He looked outside.

The truck sat at an angle on the highway, blocking two lanes, the right rear tire of the trailer hovering over the edge of the ditch. Three inches of hailstones covered the ground. Mixed with the layers of hail, branches and tree limbs were strewn everywhere.

He checked around them for other vehicles. No one was in the ditch as far as he could see, but three cars were scattered as haphazardly across the highway as he was. All were upright.

"Looks like we caught only the outer edge. We're safe."

They both unfastened their seatbelts at the same time and stood. His legs felt like they were made of rubber, but he couldn't stay in the seat a moment longer.

He met Gwen halfway between the seats. Lionel needed to touch her. To press her body close to his and hold her tight. To feel her heartbeat and, by experiencing the movement of her breathing against him, have the proof he needed to confirm that they were still alive. But he didn't have that right.

His hands shook as he cupped her face.

Her eyes widened at his touch. Her voice was raspy and wavered as she spoke. "No flying cows out there?"

His own voice shook as he spoke, and he couldn't control it. "No, no flying cows."

He thought his heart had started to slow its pace, but when he felt the light touch of her fingers on his chest, pressing over his heart, he lost it.

Without a word or a thought of the consequences of his actions, he tipped her head and brought his mouth down on hers and kissed her for all he was worth. Her arms wrapped around his back, and all thoughts of why he shouldn't be doing this were forgotten. He kissed her with everything he had, from the bottom of his soul. For the desperation with which he kissed her, she kissed him back in equal measure. Maybe he had died and gone to heaven.

The muffled thud of a car door closing reminded Lionel that he was very much still on earth.

Very slowly he pulled back an inch, but only an inch and no more. If she pulled away from him, he thought his heart would surely tear in two. When she removed her hands from his back, he trailed his fingertips down her cheeks, keeping contact with her chin, needing to touch her, even in this small way. Instead of backing up, she rested her hands on his shoulders and, fortunately, remained silent, giving him the time he needed to think.

Lionel cupped her chin. Not moving, simply staring into her eyes, at that moment his heart said he loved her, but his head said it wasn't possible. His common sense said they were nothing alike, but his soul said she complemented him where he was weak, and he would support her when she needed someone to hold her up as well.

He bent his head and brushed a short kiss to her lips, then released her.

Her face flushed and she backed up. "We'd better go outside and make sure everything's okay." In the space of two seconds, he was looking at the closed door, and he was alone inside his truck.

Gwen walked through the puddles of water and melting hailstones. She stopped beside the back trailer tires, drew in a deep breath, pressed her palms against the trailer, and leaned her forehead against it as well. The cold of the metal wall soothed the heat from her face but did nothing to still her pounding heart or strengthen her wobbly knees.

He'd kissed her. And she'd kissed him back.

No one had ever kissed her like that before. It had been scarier than the tornado. She hadn't seen the tornado, but she had more than felt its effects. Conversely, she had seen Lionel but didn't yet know the effects of what had happened between them. One thing she did know, Lionel Bradshaw was more dangerous than any tornado could ever be.

It was panic. Pure and simple.

Not that she would have kissed just anybody, tornado or not. She didn't understand the instant friendship that had developed between them, but she was sure it had something to do with being with him almost nonstop, day and night. What she felt with Lionel confused her. This was different from anything she'd ever experienced, different from any relationship with any of her other friends, people she'd known for years. The immediate bond had thrown her, and panic made her respond.

There was no other explanation. She couldn't get involved with a trucker. She had a life and a routine to get back to, a life and a routine she knew and liked and was comfortable with.

After kissing her like that, Lionel left her feeling far from comfortable, and she didn't like it.

Very soon she had to go sit in the truck with him, not being apart from him unless one of them was sleeping, and pretend everything was okay.

Fortunately, they were near their destination, and soon they would be on their way home. By the time they were back to familiar territory, Uncle Chad's truck would be fixed, and life would be back to normal, or as normal as it could be, considering she'd never done anything like this before.

The thud of the truck's door sounded. She peeked under the trailer to see Lionel hop off the running board and approach one of the three cars nearby. People had exited the other two, but no one had come out of the little red one.

A surge of dread coursed through her. Her first thought was that it might be an older person—perhaps someone had a heart attack. She had never been more frightened in her life, and the sheer weight of the truck had made it ten times safer than a car. She couldn't imagine what it would have been like for the other people.

She ran around the rear of the trailer, straight for the car.

Lionel opened the door before she arrived. She heaved a sigh of relief and skidded to a halt when instead of a person slumped over the wheel, inside was a woman clinging to two very frightened, screaming children.

Although she'd had some first aid training in her studies to become a teacher, she was much more comfortable handling crying children than sick or injured adults.

Before she could take charge, Lionel coaxed the woman, a little boy, and a preschool-aged girl outside. The boy wouldn't let go of his mother's leg, but the little girl practically jumped into Lionel's arms, threw her arms around his neck, and sobbed freely while he stroked her hair.

A man from one of the other cars approached. "Radio says it's petered out. Nothing touched down, a few homes and buildings damaged, nothing completely destroyed, some minor injuries, no deaths."

"Praise the Lord," Lionel murmured into the little girl's hair.

The moisture had cooled the air somewhat, but the summer sun and blue skies were back. If it weren't for the branches scattered on the ground, or the cars and truck helter-skelter on the highway, Gwen would never have been able to tell anything out of the ordinary had happened.

When the little girl was returned to her mother, Gwen and Lionel began their check of the air lines and tires before they resumed their journey. Not a word was spoken as they walked around the truck and trailer, falling into the same pattern they had every time they stopped, needing no elaboration.

Without asking, Gwen hopped through the driver's door and started the engine. "It's over," she said as she engaged the clutch and threw the stick shift into first gear. "We made it."

Lionel grinned, a cute little boyish grin that quickened her heart, even though it shouldn't have.

"It's not over yet," he said. "After all that excitement, I have to visit the little boys' room."

Gwen groaned. Life on the road was a challenge in more ways than one.

Chapter 8

After she finished fueling the truck, Gwen parked it and walked into the restaurant.

When they first pulled into the truck stop she had gently suggested that Lionel shower after all the tense moments. Instead of being embarrassed, he'd burst out laughing, made a rather bad joke, and told her she'd have to fuel the truck and wash the windows herself. He had still been laughing when he walked into the truck stop office with his overnight bag slung over his shoulder, while all she could do was sit in the truck with her mouth hanging open.

She couldn't believe the things that passed as conversation between them. She didn't speak to her brother about the things she'd discussed with Lionel, yet she very much enjoyed the time she spent with him. There was only one explanation. She was losing her mind.

By the time she joined him in the truck stop's coffee shop, there were two cups of coffee on the table and Lionel was reading the menu.

"Finally. I thought I would starve to death by the time you got here."

Gwen refused to get into an argument about why women took longer to get dressed and ready than men. That was one of many topics she didn't want to talk about with him but somehow always fell into. She slid into the chair and picked up the coffee cup, which he'd fixed just the way she liked it.

She took a slow draw on the coffee, savoring it, hardly able to believe that, after all that had happened in the few hours since she woke, it was only her first coffee of the day. Across the table, Lionel had nearly guzzled his entire cup. "You shouldn't be drinking coffee after all this," she mumbled over the cup. "You should be drinking something to calm yourself, like a nice soothing blend of herbal tea."

He closed both hands around his throat, crossed his eyes, and made a gagging sound. A family seated at the next table turned to stare.

"Stop it," she ground out between her teeth. "You're embarrassing me."

"Herbal tea? What else do you think I should do, take up knitting? Or I know. Needlepoint!"

Gwen sighed in exasperation. "I know a few men who knit. It was only a suggestion."

He stopped the theatrics, leaned forward to rest his elbows on the table, and finished the last of what was in the cup. "I was only fooling around, Gwen. You should know that by now."

The waitress returned with refills and took their orders, sparing Gwen the need to comment. As had been their pattern, Lionel ordered supper fare and Gwen ordered a nice brunch, since for her it was the first meal of the day.

When the waitress left, Gwen watched Lionel take a long, slow sip of his second cup. The laughter had left his eyes, the moment had passed. They were on a mission, and it was time again to get on with the job.

In contrast to his silly actions, when faced with a crisis his behavior was quite sober. He'd recovered quickly when thrust into the position of driving with her to take the critical load of machinery across the continent, especially considering the unusual circumstances in which they'd found themselves. His treatment of her while traveling together was beyond reproach.

His performance in the face of the tornado was exceptional. If she had been driving, she was positive the truck would right now be lying on its side. Her stomach clenched at the memory of the rear tire partly overhanging into the ditch. A few more inches and the trailer would have gone down, then the truck, and them along with it. The way he'd comforted the hysterical child had almost brought her to tears.

Lionel was a nice man, and she thanked God she had been teamed up with him. Things could have been a lot worse. They both agreed that no matter where in the country they were on Sunday morning, they would attend church together. If they weren't near a big city with a church that had parking facilities to accommodate the truck and trailer, then they would hopefully find a small truckers' chapel on the road wherever they were. Failing that, they had agreed to simply stop and have their own worship time, just the two of them, at the side of the highway, if necessary.

The clink of Lionel returning the cup to the saucer broke her out of her musings. "Actually, there is something I've got to talk to you about."

Gwen cringed. They'd talked about so much in the time they'd spent together. Some personal, some not. About family and preferences. Lifestyles. Their faith and beliefs. Considering the amount of time they'd been together, there wasn't much silence in the truck. They'd used the CB radio only a few times because they'd talked about so many interesting and important things, they didn't need the meaningless chatter with strangers.

Tonight they would be at their destination, and their critical trip would be at an end. She didn't like the serious tone of his voice, because it gave her a feeling he was going to tell her something she didn't want to hear.

"Why don't you ever use the cruise control? At first I could see why, what with you being a new driver and all, but really, it's great once you get used to it. I know it feels funny not using your feet when you drive, but it saves a lot on fuel. We would save money if you used the cruise control."

Cruise control? All she had been able to think about for the past few hours was the way he'd kissed her and how good she felt in his arms, and what the next few days of driving together would be like. She couldn't believe he was thinking about gas mileage.

Gwen shook her head. "You've got cruise control on your truck? You're kidding, right?"

"You didn't know? I use it all the time. Certainly you've seen me engage it. Or Chad, when he uses his."

"Uncle Chad never showed me cruise control. I didn't know you could even get cruise control put on a truck."

"It was an option when I bought the unit, and it was a good decision."

"I've never noticed you turning it on. Or maybe I did and didn't realize what you were doing. I didn't know you'd be concerned about fuel economy in a big thing like that."

"Especially in a big thing," he emphasized the words, "like that. Driving a truck is a business, and it's important to minimize expenses. We go through 220 gallons of diesel fuel a day. It's an expense that adds up quickly."

"I think someone should invent a solar-powered diesel engine."

He shook his head at her inane statement. "Do you know what you just said?"

"You know what I meant."

He squeezed his eyes shut for a second. "Unfortunately, I think I do."

She wanted to ask what he meant, but the waitress delivered their meals. After a prayer of thanks, Lionel checked his watch. "We'd better eat and get going quickly. Even though we've had some down time, if we hurry we can still make it before midnight."

⁓⁂⁓

As instructed, Lionel used his cell phone to call the factory when they were an hour away.

Unlike the rest of their trip, much of this portion was made in silence. Gwen hadn't said much since they left the truck stop, so neither had he. To fill the void of silence, he'd turned on the radio. The news reported minor structural damage to some homes and businesses, and as the man from one of the cars during their brief encounter with the tornado had said, there were only a few minor injuries, and that was it.

Apparently life was back to normal.

Except Lionel didn't know what normal was anymore.

He felt a certain satisfaction knowing they had done a good job as a team to deliver their payload as quickly and efficiently as possible, but that also meant their journey was over. He didn't want to think about what came next.

When they reached the city limits, he pulled out the paper with the directions he'd been given on the phone and directed Gwen through the outskirts of the city to the industrial area.

While they waited for a traffic light that was only a few blocks away from their destination, Gwen turned to him. "Are you sure you're not going to be embarrassed about this?"

Lionel blinked. "Embarrassed? What for? We've made great time."

She turned her head forward. "That you're a passenger and that a woman is driving."

The light turned green, so she started moving the truck forward.

He grinned. "Not as embarrassed as you're going to be."

"Me? I don't care about being seen driving a truck. That's what I planned to do all summer."

He raised his arms and linked his fingers behind his head as he leaned back in the seat. "I know. But in four minutes you're going to have to back the trailer into the loading bay."

"Uh. . .back up?"

"You know. Driving backwards. Going in reverse to maneuver the trailer through a teeny little tunnel-like path to the warehouse door so they can unload their machinery, while at an angle, judging from the age of this complex. The only way to see what you're doing is by looking in the mirror. In the dark. Plus you have to match the trailer door to the warehouse door within inches. Don't forget, you've got to get it straight."

"Oh dear. I'm not very good at backing up. When I first started this, I thought it would be just like backing the tent-trailer into the campsite, but on a larger scale. It turned out to be not as easy as I thought."

"Most beginning drivers practice backing up a load at the truck stops where there's lots of room. I did when I first got my license."

"I haven't had that kind of time. I haven't practiced at all except for the minimum needed to pass my test."

"I also spent a little time doing a temporary stint doing yard shunt work, so I'm better at backing up than most long-haul drivers. I'm open to bribery. I'll back it in for you. For the right price."

When no answer was forthcoming, Lionel wondered if he should duck to avoid flying objects.

Fortunately for him, she slowed and stopped in front of a gate, where a security guard used a radio to announce their arrival, then pointed them in the direction of the shipping/receiving area.

Just like many industrial areas in the older sections of various cities, this was exactly what he'd expected. When the neighborhood was designed, the distance between the buildings and property lines and fences had considered only the five-ton trucks and smaller trailers. In the olden days, most shipping areas had been designed for a maximum trailer length of forty-five feet, which was the longest standard trailer length at the time. Then in the early 1990s the standard had changed to forty-eight-foot trailers, and not long after that, the new standard size had become fifty-three feet, which was what they were pulling. In a tight area like this, those eight feet made a big difference, especially for a beginner.

He opened his mouth to volunteer to switch places and back it in for her, but she spoke first.

"Okay, I give. What's the right price for you to back it in? Quick, before they notice."

He opened his mouth to say the first thing that popped into his mind, but stopped himself in time. He had almost said he would back the trailer in for a kiss. "I'll think of something later. Let's trade places."

Because of her height, he didn't have to adjust the seat, and they switched drivers in seconds flat. A man appeared at the driver's door, and Lionel rolled down the window to talk to him. He calculated the distance to where the man was pointing, shifted into reverse, jackknifed the unit as he backed up to get around the corner, and backed in. They both hopped out, and he cranked down the landing legs while Gwen locked the trailer brakes and unhooked the air lines. When they got the signatures for delivering the load in good order and all was settled, he and Gwen hopped back into the truck and exited the compound. Again, Gwen was driving.

"We did it." He could hear the pride in her voice. It wasn't her first trip, because she'd already been out once with Chad, but this was her first doubles run, and it had been a dandy. It was his first-ever doubles run as well, one he would never forget.

"We make a good team. I think we must have done it in record time."

"What now?"

Lionel flattened the map in his lap and pulled his flashlight out of the glove box. "We go to the terminal at Evansville and report in, turn in the paperwork, and book off until the next load."

Just the thought of booking off for a sleep made him yawn. "Sorry," he said, making no effort to cover his mouth. She'd probably seen him do far worse already, and he simply didn't have the energy left to be polite. He'd been driving for twelve days without any time off, and the last few weren't exactly at a normal pace. He'd been getting less sleep than usual, and the pattern they'd fallen into had him going down for the night around midnight. It was nearly one in the morning. "I figure it will take about an hour to get to the terminal building from where we are." He yawned again.

"Why don't you have a nap? I've got a good memory. I'm a teacher, remember. Read me the directions, and I'm sure I can find my own way there."

Lionel started to fight another yawn, but gave up; after all, there was no point. "I think I'll do that," he said through his yawn. "Don't be afraid to open the curtain on me. I'll just kick off my sneakers and lie down just like this for a short nap. Wake me up when we get there. See you in an hour."

At her nod, he went to the back, pulled down the bunk, crawled in, and pulled the lightest blanket over his shoulders. He couldn't remember his pillow being so soft or the motion of the truck being so soothing.

He knew he was falling asleep with a smile on his face. They delivered their load in good time, Gwen was driving, and all was fine.

"Lionel? Lionel? Wake up."

Slowly he opened one eye, then the other one. Gwen's face above him slowly came into focus. "Are we there already?"

She smiled, and he smiled back. She was smiling at him. He closed his eyes again to help him remember this moment.

She grabbed his shoulder and started shaking him. "Wake up!"

His eyes sprang open, but he grabbed his pillow and rolled his face into it to filter out the light. "Five minutes. . . ," he mumbled and closed his eyes again.

In the back of his mind, something wasn't connecting. Something was wrong, different than it should have been.

He sat up with a jolt and blinked repeatedly. It was daylight.

"Why did you let me sleep so long?" The entire truck shook at the same time as a thud sounded. "What's going on?" Instead of hearing trucks, he heard the grinding of what he thought might be conveyors and the clanking of machinery. "Where are we?"

"I think we should talk."

Since the curtain was wide open, he looked forward out the front window of the cab. Not only was it daylight, but they weren't at the truck terminal anymore.

Gwen's cheeks darkened. "We're going back to Kansas."

"Kansas? What are you talking about?"

"It kind of happened like this. You were sleeping so soundly I didn't have the heart to wake you, so I took the paperwork into the terminal myself. I asked about how I was getting home, now that this big rush is over. I thought maybe I could fly home, but they said they have another rush load, and their own drivers are already dispatched out, so he gave it to us. It's a short hop back to Kansas for a doubles team. I thought about what you said about getting fired if you refused a load. I didn't want to take the chance that they could fire you because of me, so I accepted it. That's where we are now, we're at a roofing place. We're taking a load of shingles to repair a church roof. The owner of the business is donating them. Seems the pastor there is an old friend. He wants them delivered as soon as possible. I left you to sleep and we're at the shingle place now. I didn't even do too bad a job of backing it up myself. They directed me to a big wide open loading area, so it didn't matter that it was a little crooked. I thought I'd wake you up and tell you what was happening before the noise and shaking woke you up."

"Let me get this straight. You accepted a load, drove there, and they're loading the trailer right now."

"Yes. You won't believe what happened. While you were sleeping, for the first time I got to be part of a real convoy."

All he could do was blink and stare at her.

"It was so much fun! I always wondered how trucks could go in such tight formation like that. Uncle Chad and I traveled with other trucks, but this was the first time I've been with more than three at a time. But now I was part of a real convoy! And I was driving all by myself! I think there were ten trucks all together in the line. We chatted on the CB and everything."

"But—"

"Now I know how they do it. Courtesy, and signaling. I closed in on the truck ahead of me, signaled left, and then pulled out into the passing lane and sped up. There wouldn't have been room for the length of the truck in between any in line when I wanted to get back, but all I had to do was signal right, and the truck I wanted to get in front of just flashed his brights to let me know he's going to fall back, and he was ever-so-nice and let me in."

"When—"

"And I made sure to double click on my turn signal to say thanks because Uncle Chad said to always do that. I'm never going to feel the same when I get back home and I'm driving my car."

"I—"

"Some people are such selfish morons behind the wheel of a car. It would be so nice if everyone could drive like those truckers. I don't know why people have to be so aggressive and nasty and risk their lives to get ahead by fifteen seconds. But anyway, here we are, almost ready to go with our next priority load. Were you going to say something?"

Lionel buried his face in his palms. "I was going to book off for a day before I accepted another trip. I've been driving for twelve days, and I need a break."

"I know, but I didn't know what to do. I'm sorry."

He shook his head. "What time is it?"

"It's a little after seven in the morning. We're not far from the terminal, don't worry. If there's something I forgot, we can go back on our way to Kansas."

He raised his head and checked his watch. "I went to sleep at one. What have you been doing for six hours?"

"Don't forget, it took an hour to get to the terminal after you fell asleep. I checked for E-mail, and I got a message from Garrett and Robbie. They said my mom's cherries are all ready, and they're all eating more than usual without me there. Garrett reminded me that I missed the strawberries. They're all gone now too."

"Never mind the fruit from the back yard. What have you been doing all this time?"

"It took me an hour to get here from the terminal."

"That's two. What about the other four hours?"

"I went into the lunchroom."

"By yourself?"

"I wasn't alone. There were all the other drivers going in and out. Lots of them sat for awhile and talked to me. The graveyard shift foreman sat with me for awhile, and we talked too. Some of the warehousemen came in every once in awhile to talk to me, but I don't think they were supposed to do that. Everyone was really nice. Although, I didn't get any time to read my book. I don't think it's ever taken me this long to finish a book in my life."

Lionel flopped down on his back and stared at the ceiling. First she'd participated in a convoy, and now she'd gone into a building full of truck drivers and night shift warehousemen, a gorgeous woman all by herself. Of course she hadn't had a minute alone.

"They bought me coffee and everything. Some of them even offered to share their lunches, since I couldn't get to the fridge because you were sleeping. They were all so nice."

"I'll bet they were."

"Since you're awake, you might as well come with me. There are a few men here who invited me to come into the lunchroom while I wait for them to finish loading the shingles. They're really nice too. I told them my driving partner was sleeping in the truck. They suggested I leave you alone, but I thought it best to wake you up."

Lionel slapped his hands over his eyes and groaned. "You did the right thing. Let's go join them for coffee."

They made good time on the road, although driving alongside the tourists in the daytime slowed them down to some degree. They finally reached their destination mid-afternoon. Gwen promised Lionel they would book off for a day, no matter what, so they could both catch up on some much-needed sleep. She could feel the effects of three short nights' sleep in a row herself. Knowing how tired he was after being away from home for so long made her almost feel guilty about accepting the load, but she had had to make a decision. She would have felt guiltier if he'd lost his job because of her.

Gwen read the directions to Lionel as he drove through the small town. They headed into an older district in the town's core, where the homes were smaller and—one thing Gwen would never have noticed before she started driving a truck—the roads were narrower.

"It should be just after the next left."

They approached a rectangular old church building. Dark green bushes dotted with red flowers stood on either side of the front doors. They appeared to be in better condition than the building. The white slatboard walls were peeling in sections, and the short steeple was peeling more than the rest of the building. It didn't have a cross on it, but the sides were open, indicating a bell inside. Gwen wondered if they actually rang the old bell on Sunday morning and what it would sound like. Orange tarps covered sections of the roof, and the parking lot was empty except for one small car and a huge blue disposal bin.

Lionel drove carefully into the parking lot, going slowly over the old cracked surface.

"What's your church like at home?" he asked.

Gwen looked at the tattered building. "It's nothing like this. The church I go to at home is huge. The building is only about fifteen years old and very modern, inside and out. I've always appreciated a classic old building, although this one is more classic than most."

They walked inside and found their way to the pastor's office. A man close to retirement age sat behind a very cluttered desk, talking on the phone. The room wasn't much bigger than the desk. He motioned them to a couple of chairs and they squeezed into the limited space while he ended his call.

"Welcome! I'm John Funk, the pastor of this humble place. What can I do for you?"

Lionel stood and returned the pastor's handshake. "We've got a load of shingles for you, Pastor Funk. They're from a friend of yours in Indiana."

John Funk pumped Lionel's hand faster. "Praise the Lord! The roof wasn't in very good shape as it was, but the wind and hail finished it off. Those shingles are an answer to prayer. Please, call me John."

Lionel nodded. "Pleased to meet you, Pastor John. I'm Lionel, and this is Gwen."

Gwen shook the man's hand in turn.

Pastor John checked his watch. "You're here much earlier than I ever hoped you would be, and I appreciate it. You must be hungry. Would the two of you like to be my guests for dinner?"

Gwen shook her head. "No, that's okay. I know my pastor at home is always having people over for dinner, and I don't know how his wife does it on short notice. But thanks for the offer."

Pastor John smiled warmly. "Your pastor at home? So you're a believer? Praise the Lord. About that dinner, I happen to know it's leftover turkey dinner, and there's lots."

Gwen opened her mouth to decline, but before she spoke, she turned to Lionel. At the mention of turkey dinner, his whole face lit up. She imagined he didn't get many home-cooked meals and, of those he did, probably very few were full turkey dinners, first day or leftovers.

She knew his answer without asking.

"Thank you, that would be lovely. We'd be delighted to join you for dinner. But only if it's no trouble for you or your wife."

"I'll phone and check, but I know what the answer will be. I've been married to the same woman for thirty-seven years, and I'd like to think I know her reactions. Just don't tell her she's predictable."

The phone call yielded exactly the results he'd expected. While Pastor John locked up the church, Lionel locked up the truck. Within minutes they stopped in front of a small white slatboard house. Rather than fences, evergreen hedges separated the yards, the twisted old shrubbery denoting the age of the well-established and well-kept older neighborhood.

A gray-haired woman dressed in jeans and a bright green T-shirt waited in the doorway. "Welcome, Lionel and Gwen. I'm Freda. You don't know how much it means to have those shingles here so soon. John can get started on some of it tonight. Hopefully it will be done in a few days and we'll be ready for the next rain."

"A few days?" Gwen asked. "Why do you think it's going to take that long? It's not that big a building. You don't mean you're going to do it all by yourself?"

He shrugged his shoulders. "It's a small congregation. Today is Friday, so everyone is at work. They have their own messes to clean up and repairs to make on Saturday. I won't ask anyone to work on the church roof on Sunday. I doubt most of them are aware of the extent of the damage to the old roof. But it will get done."

Gwen looked at Lionel, and Lionel looked at her. They both raised their eyebrows and nodded at the same time.

Lionel turned back to Pastor John. "We've got a day here before we have to take another load out. If you've got a couple of extra hammers, we can help with the roof, and it will be done before Sunday morning."

"I can't ask you to do that. You're not even a member of our congregation."

Lionel glanced at Gwen and smiled. Her heart swelled with pride for him as he spoke.

"We're all members of God's congregation, no matter where in the world we live. If you've got hammers, you've got help."

Gwen nodded. She didn't want to be a burden, and she certainly didn't want to sit and do nothing while Lionel worked during the short amount of time they had off. "I'm not too bad with a hammer either," she said.

The Funks joined hands. "I don't know what to say...," Pastor John drawled.

Lionel grinned from ear to ear and patted his stomach. "Just say it's supper time!"

Gwen elbowed him in the ribs. "That was delicate," she muttered under her breath so only Lionel could hear.

He laughed and followed the Funks into the house.

After a prayer of thanks for the food, the gift of the shingles, and the unexpected help to install them, they enjoyed the wonderful meal Freda set before them. Not that the truck stop food had been bad, but it hadn't taken long for Gwen to become tired of greasy fare, which made her consider the leftovers an extra special treat. Lionel ate with utter abandon, devouring everything on his plate as if it were a king's meal placed before a starving man.

She nudged his ankle under the table. She had meant just to get his attention, but at the contact he froze, fork in midair, and stared at her. "Yes?" he asked.

"Nothing," Gwen mumbled.

He obviously didn't get the hint, because when Freda passed him more food, he gratefully accepted it.

Freda offered more to Gwen, but she shook her head. "This has been wonderful, but I've eaten so much. Thank you, I couldn't eat another bite."

"But I have homemade cherry pie for dessert."

Gwen really was full, but she couldn't refuse the kind woman. "Just a small piece would be lovely. Thank you."

Lionel's eyes lit up. "Homemade pie?"

Gwen couldn't stand it anymore. When Pastor John rose to clear the table and Freda went to the counter to cut the pie, Gwen turned and whispered to Lionel. "I can't believe you. You look like you haven't seen food for a week. Aren't you embarrassed?"

"Me? You should talk. You're the one with the hollow leg. I eat like this once and you think it's a big deal, but you're the one who orders a second helping of fries at six in the morning."

She was about to comment on the unique seasoning of the fries in question, when Freda returned and placed two plates of pie, topped with ice cream, in front of them. "So, where are you folks from?"

"We're from Vancouver, Canada."

"You're a long way from home."

"Yes, we are."

"I hear it rains a lot there."

Gwen smiled. "It rains a lot, but it's not as much as people think it does. I really don't mind the rain."

Lionel harumphed beside her as he dug into the delicious homemade pie. "I hate the rain."

Gwen took a nibble of her pie. "You were the one praying for rain just before we ran into the hail."

"I never did."

"You did so. You said that you wanted a little rain to break the heat."

One eyebrow quirked. "I might have said that, but I certainly never prayed for it. You like rain so much, you probably prayed for it. You just won't admit it."

The sparkle in his eye gave his thoughts away. Even though she knew he was teasing and goading her to put her foot in her mouth, she was having too much fun to stop. Gwen opened her mouth to tell him that the reason they were caught in the storm was his fault, when she heard the older couple chuckling. She snapped her mouth shut and lowered her head to pick at the piece of pie in front of her.

Freda smiled and snickered. "Don't mind us. As pastor and wife, we've seen a lot of marriages over the course of the years. More couples would benefit from this kind of friendly banter. How long have you two been married?"

Gwen felt her face heat up. She glanced at Lionel out of the corner of her eye, noting that he was also blushing.

Gwen delicately dabbed her mouth with her napkin. "We're not married."

Freda's cheeks reddened as well. "I just assumed. . . You're traveling together. . ."

Lionel laid his cutlery down on his plate. "Gwen started driving with her

317

uncle, but an emergency breakdown teamed us together on short notice. Since we're driving team, the company sent us on another priority trip, which was your shingles. We actually just met at the beginning of the summer."

Freda's hands rose to her cheeks. "Oh!"

"Yes. I must say it was a surprise to both of us, but God was gracious to team us together as Christians. To tell the truth, this is the first time since we've been traveling together that we have some time off and don't have to drive all night. I was wondering if you could recommend a motel nearby."

Both of them stared at Lionel as he spoke. Gwen chose to keep silent. She knew what they were thinking.

Lionel's ears flamed. "The motel room is for Gwen. I'll be sleeping in the truck."

Freda turned to Gwen. "Nonsense. You don't have to get a motel. Please, be our guest in our home for the night. There's just the two of us here, we have a spare bedroom. You're more than welcome." She stopped to smile, making Gwen think of how much of an art it was for the woman to recover her composure so quickly. "You'd be welcome even if you weren't helping fix the roof of the church."

Gwen noticed she didn't offer for Lionel to also be a guest in their home, nor had Freda suggested that she take her to the motel after all and that Lionel stay in their guest room so he wouldn't have to sleep in the truck.

She tried to think of a way to politely decline in favor of the motel, when Pastor John spoke.

"If you sleep here instead of across town at the motel, we'll get an earlier start on the roof."

Gwen smiled. "That would be lovely. Thank you. Now let me help with the dishes."

Chapter 9

Lionel sat outside the church and waited for everyone to arrive. The sun was up and he was refreshed and ready.

He couldn't believe it when Pastor John had left him with the key to the church so he could have washroom facilities when he needed them. The old building didn't have a kitchen or a shower, but it had the basics, and that was all he needed. In his travels as a trucker, it was more than he had most trips.

What astounded him the most was the trust involved in giving him the key. They had just met the night before, and nothing would have stopped him from loading up anything of value from inside the church and leaving in the middle of the night. Of course, they had Gwen at their home, and he wasn't going anywhere without her.

He'd phoned the nearest terminal to book off the day, and they had told him he would have had the weekend off anyway, since there wasn't a load out, which was fine with Lionel.

It gave him extra time with Gwen, which was exactly what he wanted since they would now be on their way home and their time together would soon be over. Not that being up on the roof and banging away at shingles was exactly quality time, but it was as close as he would get. It was quieter and more private in the truck when they were driving, but that was work, and with work came limitations and boundaries.

He looked up at the roof. Whatever he said and did today with Gwen would be on display to not only a minister but the entire neighborhood. He looked up at the clear blue sky. God was always watching, day or night, in public or in the privacy of his home and his truck. Rather than being intimidating, the knowledge gave him great comfort. Today he didn't have to think about calculating maximum driving hours or crossing any personal lines while in the confines of his truck. He could concentrate everything he had on Gwen, and he prayed that God would bless their short time together away from business.

Pastor John's small car pulled into the parking lot, and Pastor John, Freda, and Gwen climbed out.

"Good morning, Son. Did you sleep well?"

"Yes, Sir, I did."

He had slept well. After dinner they'd cleaned up and talked and prayed together before Pastor John dropped him off for the night. On the short drive back to the church, Lionel thought Pastor John was on the verge of asking him about his relationship with Gwen, but at the last minute held back, which was a good thing. Lionel didn't know the answer.

After their experience with the edge of the tornado, he'd thought briefly that he could have been in love with her, but recognized that the panic of the situation had intensified his emotions. Of course he liked her, and he liked her a lot, but it couldn't be love, not after such a short amount of time. However, whatever was happening between them had hit him hard and fast. When they parted ways, Gwen would be taking a piece of him with her. He vowed that, today, he would do all he could to discover more about this fast friendship and make the most of it, although what he felt for her at this point extended beyond anything he'd ever felt in his heart for any friend, male or female.

"I haven't re-shingled a roof in years, but I remember how it's done and all the steps. I want to tell you again how much I appreciate this. Freda won't be coming up on the roof, she'll be inside the church doing some paperwork, and she's brought drinks and meals. We brought something for breakfast for you, since we all ate at home."

Lionel wiped his hands on his pants and accepted an English muffin with bacon and eggs inside. "This is great. Thanks." He gobbled it down while Gwen and Pastor John set the ladder against the eaves.

Gwen returned with something in her hand. He expected her to hand him a napkin, but instead it was a small white bottle. "Put this on. It's sunscreen."

"Sunscreen? What do I need this for?"

"For your right arm, but do both."

"I beg your pardon?"

She grabbed both his wrists and pulled his arms forward and together. Her touch caught him so off guard that he nearly dropped the bottle.

"See? Look at the difference. Your left arm is nice and tanned, and your right arm is white."

"So? That happens all the time. It's from driving with my arm out the window."

"Exactly my point. Don't you think you'll look stupid with one normal arm and one beet red arm if you don't put on lots of sunscreen?"

He wanted to protest, but for such a minor point, despite how silly, he didn't want to look stupid in front of Gwen. It shouldn't have mattered, but it did.

Lionel splashed on the sunscreen and rubbed it into his arms and face. "This stuff stinks. I'm only doing this for you, you know."

She harumphed and turned her back to him, but he caught her rolling her eyes. "Spare me. Such a sacrifice. How will I ever live with myself?"

"You can make it up to me later."

She made a sound almost like a snort, which surprised him. He didn't know what to say, so he said nothing.

Once everyone was sufficiently coated with sunscreen, Freda held the ladder and they climbed up to the roof. The first chore was to pull off the old shingles and tarpaper and toss everything into the disposal bins below. He'd discovered one bin on each side of the building. He imagined they would overflow them both by the time they were done.

The old shingles were brittle and often cracked. He cleared one section, then moved to start in another place when a hunk of shingles and tarpaper flew over the peak toward him. It fell apart mid-flight, with a large section falling near his feet and sliding down the roof and into the bin. A smaller section of broken shingle sailed over his head, and another small section hit his back.

"Hey!" he called out. "Watch it!"

A scuffle sounded, and Gwen appeared from the other side of the peak. "Oh, Lionel! I'm so sorry! Are you okay?"

He forced himself to grimace. "No, I'm mortally wounded." He slapped both palms over his heart. "I need first aid. Artificial respiration would help."

Another small piece of shingle hit him in the stomach. "In your dreams," she muttered, and disappeared over the peak once more.

He couldn't help but smile as he bent to pull off another section. It would have been nice, but what he pictured in his mind was more personal than artificial respiration. It hadn't been long since they'd met, but he caught himself calculating the days until they were back at the home terminal. At first he hadn't wanted to drive with her, and now he wasn't ready for their time together to be over.

It had bothered him more than he cared to admit when she had said she was considering flying home. He didn't know she'd been uncomfortable with him, even though the situation they found themselves in, especially as Christians, was admittedly difficult.

Lionel froze, then stared at the torn tarpaper in his hand without really seeing it. He had just realized he wanted more than a driving partnership with Gwen. He wanted a real relationship, both business and personal, something that would last. Today was probably going to be the only day he could use to build their relationship into something deeper. Once they were driving again, he couldn't say or do anything that would make her feel compromised or ill at ease when they couldn't get away from each other in the close confines of the truck.

When summer was over she would go back to her life as a teacher. Lionel wanted to be able to call her up when he was in town and spend as much time with her as she would allow. When they were apart, he would have his computer. He could always practice to improve his typing and send her E-mail messages, although he didn't want merely a long-distance relationship. He needed the real thing.

"Coffee time!" Freda called out from below.

Lionel wiped the damp hair off his forehead. He rested his hands on his hips as he surveyed what they'd done so far. Only one section remained to strip, then they would begin stapling on the tarpaper. After that, they'd have to get the bundles of shingles lifted up onto the roof and start nailing them down. He had no idea how long such an area would take.

Gwen climbed up over the peak and stood beside him. "It didn't look so large from the ground, did it?"

"No. I'm glad we started at sunrise."

"Yes, it's already starting to get hot."

The stubborn lock of hair fell into his face again, and he swiped it away. "I don't think it ever cools down in this part of the country."

"That's what I've heard too."

He steadied the ladder at the top while she climbed down, and they joined Pastor John and Freda in the shade. When Gwen went inside to wash up, he added the milk and sugar to her coffee, then sat on the grass and stretched out his legs, waiting for her to return.

The pastor and his wife discussed some church business between themselves, which was fine with Lionel, because he didn't feel like talking anyway. He lay down on his back on the cool grass, linked his fingers behind his head, and looked up at the clear blue sky, waiting for Gwen's return.

While he waited, he anticipated her pretty smile as she took that first sip of the coffee he'd poured for her, just the way she liked it. She truly appreciated the little things he did for her, which made him want to do more.

He quickly nixed the idea of doing her laundry. She'd made it more than clear she didn't want him looking at her stuff. Of course, he didn't exactly like the idea of her handling his underwear either, even if it was to save time. He tried to think of something else.

Another thing she seemed to appreciate was when he played her favorite music in the boring moments on the road. Not that there were many boring moments. They seemed to fill almost every minute with conversation of some sort. Even when they weren't laughing about something stupid one of them had done, their serious moments were equally as pleasant. They'd been open and honest with each other, talking about things he'd never spoken to anyone about, even his best friend. Yet, for everything they discussed, no matter how personal, they both had been able to tell before they'd reached the point of prying into an area best left alone. Every time they'd prayed together had been special too.

Not moving from his stretched out position on the ground, Lionel closed his eyes and smiled at his own thoughts. He'd caught himself plotting to impress a woman, something he'd never done, not even with Sharon, the woman he'd asked to marry him. At the time he hadn't seen it. He could now, in hindsight, see where Sharon had worked to impress him without his knowing it, and it had worked. She'd done all the right things to feed his ego, and after living with the dysfunctional relationship between his parents, he hadn't seen it coming. He'd been too starved for her attention to realize she'd been stringing him along. Instead of missing him when he was out driving, his absence had been convenient for her.

Gwen was different from anyone he'd ever known. She'd done nothing to impress him. Instead of feeding his ego to make him putty in her hands, as Sharon had done so well, Gwen pointed out his flaws and liked him anyway. She laughed with him, understood his weaknesses, and accepted him exactly as he was. Likewise, she took it in stride when he teased her. Even when they were working, they had fun together.

"Lionel? Are you sleeping?"

If he was, he would have been dreaming about her. He opened one eye. "Just relaxing."

"I see you poured my coffee. Thank you." He watched as she took a long, slow sip, cradling the mug in her hands and smiling, just like he knew she would.

He opened the other eye. "So, do I get a tip?"

Her eyes sparkled, her mouth opened, and he anticipated a smart comeback, but instead she glanced at the Funks, who were not necessarily paying attention but would clearly hear anything she said.

"Put it on my tab," she said, winked, and took a second sip.

As soon as they were finished drinking their coffee, the three of them returned to the roof and tore off the last of the old shingles. Soon they had the new tarpaper laid out and stapled down, and next came the job of moving the new bundles of shingles from the truck to the roof.

Using a winch and a few lengths of rope attached to the steeple, Pastor John rigged up a way to raise the bundles of shingles to the roof. They worked quickly as the dwindling coolness of the morning gave way to the full heat of a summer day. Gwen pushed the bundles out of the trailer, Pastor John worked the winch, and Lionel insisted on being the one to distribute the bundles on the surface of the roof. As he carried each new bundle farther and placed it where it would be needed, he could feel the effects of the unaccustomed physical labor. Every bundle seemed to become heavier than the bundle before it. By the time he heaved the last one into place on the far side of the roof, he was dripping with sweat. He ached all over. He couldn't see people doing this for a living. He much preferred sitting in his air-conditioned truck.

With every kink in his back and twinge in his arms, he reminded himself that this was work for the Lord.

He sat on the peak to rest, not having the energy to climb down the ladder for a glass of water. Gratefully he accepted one that Gwen brought up to him. He drank most of it, then, when no one was looking, he dumped the last bit of it over his head and wiped the soothing cool water down his face and over the back of his neck.

The work of nailing down the shingles wasn't as bad as carrying them, but the heat of the noonday sun made it more difficult to endure and finally forced them to stop.

Freda filled four glasses from a pitcher, then picked up two glasses, kept one, and gave one to Pastor John. Gwen also picked up two glasses and handed one to Lionel, standing very close as he took it from her hand.

She leaned toward his ear. "Don't pour this one over your head, okay?" she whispered. "It's lemonade, and this time it would be sticky."

He opened his mouth to protest, but he couldn't think of a thing to say.

Gwen pushed her damp hair off her face and smiled at him. Temporarily, he felt better. "Actually, it was a good idea, and I did the same thing after you did. Only no one saw me."

"I'm not used to this heat. It's really wiping me out."

"The heat doesn't help, but you're the one who insisted on carrying all the shingles yourself. Are you crazy?"

"I couldn't let an older man carry those heavy bundles up there in the heat. I'm in the prime of life, you know." He made a fist and pressed it into the center of his chest. As he spoke, he could feel the wetness from his shirt seep between his fingers. The gel in his hair had given up its hold long ago and his damp hair hung in his face. He didn't care enough to push it back.

In order to protect his knees when he knelt on the shingles, he'd worn jeans instead of shorts. The denim was also wet with sweat and stuck to his legs. His feet ached, made worse because granules from the shingles had worked their way inside his sneakers. He didn't want to take his sneakers off, fearing that once they came off he'd never get them back on. He hit himself in the chest a few times and grunted like an ape. And why not? he thought, because by now he probably smelled like an ape.

One corner of Gwen's mouth tilted up as she scanned him from head to toe. "Prime of life, huh? You look it."

Lionel looked at Gwen. Even damp from the heat and showing the signs of heavy work, she still looked good.

"Come on," he said, tilting his head toward the Funks. "Let's eat."

While Freda opened the cooler, he went inside the church to wash up and splash some cold water on his face.

He longed for the air conditioning in his truck but settled for the quasi cool of the shade in the churchyard. While they ate, Pastor John shared many funny stories of his experiences over the years. Lionel looked forward to hearing his sermon Sunday morning. Being able to attend a service inside a real church was a rare treat for him, since he spent most weekends on the road.

Too soon they were back at work, nailing down the shingles. He didn't know why he thought he would be able to talk to Gwen while they were working, because she was spending all of her time on one side of the roof helping Pastor John, and he was working alone on the other side of the building.

"Supper time!" Freda called from below.

Lionel dropped the hammer without a second's hesitation. He was the first to wash up and be ready.

In the middle of their prayers before the meal, Freda's cell phone rang. She excused herself to answer it, and when she returned, her face was pale. Pastor John excused himself while the two of them talked in private, then returned.

"A crisis has come up. One of our youth is in the hospital from what appears to be a gang-related incident, although he appears to have been an innocent bystander, not directly involved. I'm going to join the family in the hospital, and that means I'm not going to be able to do any more work on the roof today. I don't expect to be back before nightfall."

Gwen gasped and raised her hands to her mouth. "You mean there are gangs here? In a small town like this?"

"There are gangs everywhere, unfortunately. Although he was in the city when this happened. I hate to stop now, but this is critical."

Lionel checked his watch. "We've still got lots of time. Leave us here and you go see to that family."

Freda glanced between them, shuffling her feet.

Lionel smiled at her, knowing what she was thinking. "Don't worry about us, Freda. If you feel you should go, then go. We'll be fine."

The Funks glanced quickly between each other. Freda reached into her pocket and picked a key off her key ring. "You've already got the church key. Here's our house key. Help yourself to anything in our home, with our gratitude. We appreciate all you've done for us. I don't know when we'll be back." She grasped his hand, then Gwen's. "Thank you."

"You're welcome," Lionel and Gwen mumbled in unison.

Without further ado, the Funks hurried to the car and drove off.

Lionel rested one fist on his hip as he swiped a damp lock of hair off his forehead and gazed upward to the half-finished roof. "Do you think we stand much chance of getting it finished before nightfall? How much is done on the other side?"

"More than on this side, but there's still lots to do."

He sent Gwen up the ladder while he steadied it, then climbed up himself and got back to work.

Earlier he had worked alone in silence, but he'd heard Gwen and Pastor John talking as they worked. Even if he couldn't hear the words they'd been speaking, he'd heard the sound of happy conversation. Now all he heard was the hammering and the resulting echo in the distance. It wasn't nearly as comforting.

By the time they reached the peak, Lionel estimated under an hour until the sun would set. They worked quickly, with Gwen curving the shingles over the peak and holding them in place as Lionel hammered them down as fast as he could. Now that they were finally close enough to talk, he didn't. It would have taken too much energy to speak and hammer at the same time. Stubbornness alone kept him going, boosted by the challenge to beat the sun before it disappeared.

"We did it!" Gwen half-cheered and half-groaned as he hammered in the last nail.

Lionel laid the hammer down. He'd never worked so hard in his life. He was so thirsty his throat felt like sandpaper, and his sweat-soaked T-shirt stuck to his chest in a most uncomfortable way. All he had the energy to do was groan as he let himself sink down, half-lying and half-sitting on the roof. He leaned his back against the slope of the roof, resting his elbows behind him on the peak, and bent his knees to use his heels to brace himself from sliding down.

"The sun will be down in a few minutes."

"Yeah," he mumbled. He wanted to pull the wet T-shirt away from his skin, but he didn't want to do something so disgusting in front of Gwen. Besides, he didn't think he could move.

To his shock, she sat down beside him. He wanted to shift away, but he was too tired. If he had to get up, he wouldn't sit down again, he would go all the way and get off the roof. Fortunately, he was downwind. They sat in silence and watched the sky turn colors as the sun set.

"Isn't the sky beautiful?" Gwen asked with a wistful sigh. "Is it really true that if the sky is all pink and purple, it will be good weather the next day?"

"Sometimes, but I'm always moving, so I don't stay with the local weather system for long."

"It's finally cooling down a little."

He didn't think so. He figured the temperature still hadn't dipped below ninety, and even though he was covered in sweat, he was still too warm. He wasn't used to the heat, and he didn't like it. That's why he had air conditioning in his truck. He could barely stand himself—he didn't know how Gwen could sit so close to him. He also wondered why women didn't sweat like men.

Gwen sighed again. "Old towns like this have always fascinated me. I wonder if some of the buildings nearby are heritage buildings?"

"I dunno," he muttered, trying to shuffle over with the least amount of effort.

She pointed north. "I think that area with that lit-up cement square in the middle and the flag is the town core. I'll bet the dark building is made of brick, and it's the police station. That one with the flag in front would be city hall. What do you think?"

All he could think of was the need for a cold drink and a clean shirt. "Probably."

"You know those old black and white movies, where at the end the people sit on the flat rooftop of some old apartment block, looking out over the city? We're kind of doing the same thing. Isn't that fascinating?"

He thought that women were supposed to find that kind of thing romantic, not fascinating, but romance was the last thing he felt. He was sweaty, tired, thirsty, and he didn't feel like talking. What he wanted was a long shower, then a bed. "I guess. I don't watch old movies."

Gwen stretched. "We should get down before it's totally pitch-black. I guess the only way we're going to get back to the Funks' house is in the truck. I hope their neighbors don't mind."

At this point, Lionel didn't care who minded. With every movement, his muscles protested as he slowly made his way down the ladder and then steadied it while Gwen climbed down.

As they approached the truck, which he had parked on the farthest corner of the small parking lot after they had all the shingles out, he nearly groaned aloud. He knew they'd be using the truck to get back to the house, but what he hadn't considered was that it was still hooked to the trailer, and he couldn't take the set through the residential neighborhood.

"Oh, dear," Gwen mumbled. "We've got to unhook before we can go."

If it wasn't so far, he would have considered walking. He really didn't want to go through all the work of unhooking, but he didn't have a choice. He stood in one spot, staring at the truck and trailer, trying to motivate himself to move.

He felt Gwen's light touch on his forearm. He gritted his teeth, forcing himself not to cringe away from her touch, but he really didn't want her touching him when he was like this.

"Lionel? Is something wrong?"

He shook his head to get himself moving. "I'm just thinking about unhooking so we can get going." He arched and twisted his sore back and began to unlatch the handle for the dolly legs.

Gwen didn't move. "I know how you feel. I'm so tired. I don't know if I can lift my arms."

It gave him little satisfaction to know he wasn't the only one feeling the aftereffects of the physical labor from sunrise to sunset, literally. He gritted his teeth and cranked down the dolly legs, and Gwen unhooked the air lines and set the back trailer brakes.

Once they arrived at the house, Gwen let him shower first, and he was soon back in the truck. It was all he could do to drive back to the church parking lot. He couldn't remember ever being so tired. The second his head hit the pillow, he was out like a light.

Chapter 10

Gwen yawned as they drove into the church parking lot. She had no idea pastors got up so early on Sunday. She vividly remembered watching the sunset not all that long ago, and now, barely after sunrise, she was back at the church again.

Pastor John tried the front door of the church, but it was locked solid. A knock received no reply, and a check inside the windows showed that all inside was dark. Gwen walked across the parking lot to Lionel's truck, which was also dark and quiet inside.

She rapped lightly on the door. "Lionel? It's me. Are you sleeping?"

Nothing happened.

She knocked a little louder. "Lionel? Can you hear me?"

Still nothing moved. She stepped up onto the running board and peeked in the window. The curtain was drawn across the bunk area, and all was still.

Gwen knocked louder. "Lionel! Wake up! We need the church key!"

Finally the curtain moved. Gwen hopped down and waited beside the door until it opened.

Lionel leaned over the seat, one hand resting on the steering wheel, the other straight and supporting his weight as he leaned on the seat. His hair hung in his face, his eyes barely squinted open, and she'd never seen a more sour expression. "What time is it?" he mumbled.

"It's 6:42 A.M."

"What are you doing here?"

"Pastor John wants to get ready for the Sunday service, and he needs the key for the church."

He grumbled something under his breath and backed up very slowly. As he bent to retrieve the keys from the compartment in the dash, he flinched and pressed his left fist into the small of his back as he slowly straightened.

"Lionel? Are you okay?"

"I'm fine. Here's the keys." Instead of bending over and handing them to her, he tossed them from where he stood.

Gwen felt a little stiff herself after all that hard work yesterday. Knowing Lionel did most of the heavy lifting, it didn't take a rocket scientist to know what was wrong. She also knew where he stowed his clothing and overnight bag for his first trip out of the truck when waking up, and he'd have to bend and stretch to get at it.

"Do you want some help?"

"No. Just let me wake up a bit."

"Okay. See you in a few minutes." Not that she thought he'd be any better once he switched his brain into gear.

She pushed the door closed to save him the agony of reaching for it. Before she took her first step, she heard him groan from inside the cab. She hurt inside knowing he was suffering, but she wouldn't invade his privacy to get his overnight bag for him.

Pastor John opened the door, punched in the alarm code, and continued inside. Gwen stood inside the doorway, watching the truck and waiting.

The passenger door opened and Lionel emerged, very slowly. He held himself poker-straight as he walked, without his usual speed or bounce, first trip of the morning or otherwise.

She held the door open for him as he entered. She noticed he was wearing the same clothes as when he left Pastor John's house the evening before, and he was very wrinkled.

"Are you sure you're okay?"

He didn't speak. But if looks could kill, she would have been six feet under.

She stayed in the foyer, not wanting to make it too obvious she was waiting for him. When he finally made his appearance, she followed him back outside. "Freda stayed home, and I'm supposed to drive you back because she's making you breakfast. It should be ready any minute. Are you ready to go?"

He opened his mouth like he was going to protest, and then his face sagged and his eyes closed while he spoke. "That would be great. I can't believe how stiff I am. I've got muscles that hurt where I didn't know I had muscles. This is so embarrassing."

They walked together to the car. "Don't be embarrassed. That was hard work, and for a lot of years you've had a job where you sit all day."

He winced as he used the roof of the car to support himself as he lowered his aching body into the car. "Rub it in, why don't you?"

She grinned. "Today you can pamper yourself. Freda's making you a wonderful bacon and egg breakfast, just the way you like it, and then we can relax and enjoy the service. After the services, she's invited us back as their guests for lunch. I thought it would be nice to go for an afternoon walk, which isn't a bad idea, because then you won't seize up completely. Then, after supper, we can go to the evening service. When was the last time you've been to church twice in one day?"

"Never."

"See? Today will be a real treat for you."

"Right."

"They're so grateful for the roof, it's almost embarrassing. They've invited us to stay with them tonight too, but I don't want to impose on their hospitality."

"Me neither. But our only other choice is to have you hole up in a motel because we won't have a load out until Monday evening, and then only after we take the empty trailer back to the terminal in Topeka."

Gwen parked the car in front of the house. "Oh, and one more thing. About the service. I didn't bring anything to wear except jeans and casual tops. What about you?"

"Same."

She frowned. "I hope we don't stick out too badly. I have no idea what everyone will be wearing, although the building itself is less than formal."

"I've never thought about what to wear. I've only ever worn jeans to church."

She stared at him. "Really?"

"Well, I've got this pair of khaki pants, but they're not much different than jeans, they're just a different color. But I didn't bring them, they're still at home."

Gwen remembered the family routine of going to church on Sunday as she grew up. As a girl, her mother made her wear pretty dresses to church, which annoyed her because she wasn't allowed to run outside and play with the boys when the service was over. As a teen she'd gone through a rebellious stage where she'd worn only jeans and T-shirts to the service, but it hadn't taken long to grow out of that. Looking back, she realized her parents had it easy if that was the worst thing she'd done in her growing up years. Now, as an adult, she usually wore the same comfortable but suitably nice outfits she wore to school.

She thanked God for her Christian parents and her loving family, including her extended family, her uncle Chad and aunt Chelsea and her cousins.

"You told me you became a Christian as an adult. Does that mean your family never went to church when you were growing up? Not ever?"

His face hardened. "The only time my parents went near a church was for a wedding or a funeral."

She didn't think his brusque tone was exactly sarcasm, but if he didn't want to talk about it, she wouldn't press it.

They knocked on the door, and Freda enthusiastically welcomed them back. While they ate, Gwen joked about it being a rare treat to have two breakfasts in one day. Then she excused herself to dress for the service.

The three of them arrived back at the church as the worship team was beginning to practice the songs for the morning.

"We're sorry for making you so late in getting back," Lionel said as he held the door open for Gwen and Freda.

Freda smiled. "I always get here at this time. I usually drive John early and go back home so he can pray in private before the service and make sure everything is okay in the building. The worship team gets here about eight o'clock, and I come back about eight-thirty to set up the table at the door and hand out bulletins until the ushers get here. I'll introduce you to the few people who also come early, and then leave you alone."

Gwen smiled at Lionel. If she wasn't mistaken, he looked nervous. She grew up going to church, but she suspected he felt out of place at an organized service where he didn't know anyone. A piece of her heart went out to him. She touched his hand, slipped her fingers between his, and held on. "Come on. Let's go get introduced, and then we'll visit with people until the service."

⁂

Lionel smiled as Freda introduced them to one of the church's elder couples. The couple welcomed them and asked what he thought were the usual questions when greeting a newcomer, but he only half paid attention.

Gwen was holding his hand. He suspected she could sense his nervousness and was trying to make him feel better, but whatever the reason, Lionel determined to make the most of it. For today, the people here would perceive them not as a driving team, but as a couple, and that was exactly the way he intended to behave.

He closed his hand around Gwen's and gave her fingers a little squeeze. In response, she turned toward him and smiled. A smile meant just for him. He listened politely as she chatted with the growing group of people who surrounded them.

Word seemed to spread that they were from out of town, because soon they were joined by another couple who started asking questions about Vancouver as a vacation spot. Lionel gave them a list of the usual tourist traps around town, then confessed that he hadn't been to most of them because even though they were right in his back yard, he spent most of his time traveling around North America, living out of his truck. Still, he thought Vancouver was one of the most beautiful places on Earth, and told them so.

He listened to Gwen tell tales of her favorite vacation activity, which was camping in the Provincial parks around British Columbia. He recalled her telling him that her brother was a forest ranger, so he supposed her love for the great outdoors was something that ran in the family. He thought that for someone who seemed to thrive in a crowd, camping seemed a rather solitary activity.

More people entered, and many approached to chat. Lionel liked the friendly atmosphere prevalent throughout the whole place.

When the worship time started, he was pleased to know a couple of the songs, and Gwen knew most of them, although none were in a style they were used to. He was used to a single guitar or taped music, and Gwen was used to a very polished and practiced worship team. This group of people was somewhere in the middle. What they lacked in skill they more than made up for in eagerness and unpolished natural talent.

Unfortunately, he had to let go of Gwen's hand, because the congregation clapped to a couple of songs, something he wasn't used to, but Gwen joined in with enthusiasm. Gwen also raised her hands with a number of people in the congregation and prayed openly, while Lionel kept his hands at his sides or joined in front of himself and remained quiet. Knowing her passion for Jesus in her life outside

331

church, her behavior inside wasn't surprising. He liked it.

As soon as they sat for the pastor's sermon, Gwen pulled out of her purse the smallest full-version Bible he'd ever seen. As soon as they were finished with the Scripture reading, he again sought her hand. Her reaction indicated she hadn't expected it, but she didn't pull away.

He thoroughly enjoyed the pastor's sermon, and the service ended with a solemn and meaningful hymn.

"You said we were invited to Pastor John and Freda's for lunch after the service?"

Gwen nodded. "Yes. I think they're going to invite someone else, and we also have to wait until everyone is gone so he can lock up the building."

Lionel looked around the room. He'd always gone alone to church services, whether it was at home or on the road. This time, sitting beside Gwen, the room filled with people of all ages, was different than anything he'd ever done. It felt good. It felt right.

When they stood to talk with another couple who asked about their travels, he didn't drop her hand. Since life on the road was new to Gwen, he let her answer all the questions. Driving had become mundane for him years ago.

She was open and honest with everyone she spoke to, whether it was a child or an adult, and she spoke as an equal to all. He could see why she loved being a teacher. Everyone paid rapt attention to her, as did he. They never had a moment alone until the church doors were locked, and even then they talked in the parking lot with more people before they finally managed to get away.

All through lunch and the rest of the day, he participated little in the many conversations going on around him. He usually didn't feel comfortable in a crowd, but being with Gwen was different. Whether it was a small private group or the entire church congregation, he had Gwen at his side, and things that used to bother him were no longer important. Any time he was hesitant about saying anything or felt the push of too many people around him, she seemed to sense his hesitation and jumped into whatever topic was current until he could regain his bearings.

They were two halves of a whole.

If he was unsure before, he was sure now. He was deeply and fully in love with Gwen Lamont, his temporary driving partner.

Chapter 11

"Good-bye! Thanks again for everything!"

Gwen waved at Pastor John and Freda as they drove out of the church parking lot, beginning the trip back to Topeka and, ultimately, home.

She turned to Lionel. "They were such a nice couple. I'll have to write to them when I get home."

Lionel patted his pocket. "Yes, and I can't believe all the food they gave us. I got their E-mail address. I can't remember the last time I actually wrote a letter to someone. I don't like typing, but I like writing even less. Guess it's a guy thing."

"Or a lazy thing. Or maybe you're just too cheap to buy a stamp."

"You wound me."

Gwen didn't answer. She doubted anything she said could wound him, although she was starting to feel a wound opening in her own heart.

They were on their way home. Lionel had a program in his computer designed for truckers which calculated that in only thirty-two hours, they would be home. She wasn't sure she was ready to get home. The last week had been one unlike anything she'd ever experienced.

For all they'd been through and all they'd done, the week had gone fast, yet in other ways, it seemed like forever.

"I figure we'll be in Topeka in a couple of hours, and then we're going home, and you'll be back with Chad."

His words hurt her. They shouldn't have, but they did.

After a heavy silence, Lionel was the first to start talking. Gwen could only listen. Thankfully, he avoided any topics to do with home, and she didn't say anything to change that. Instead, she tried to convince herself that thirty-two hours of driving was really a long time, and when those hours had passed, she would be grateful to be separated.

"Here we are. This terminal is a lot bigger than the one in Evansville, isn't it?"

"Yes."

She followed him inside, dragging her feet every step of the way.

The dispatcher was a huge, balding man with an enormous potbelly and a cigarette hanging out of his mouth, which Gwen thought was no longer allowed in most workplaces.

"Your load's been delayed," he mumbled around the cigarette. "Won't be ready 'til late, likely after ten at night."

Gwen turned to Lionel. "It's barely past noon. What are we going to do?"

He shrugged his shoulders. "Nothing we can do. We've got to find some way to kill time."

Gwen checked her watch, but it hadn't changed. "What are we going to do for over ten hours?"

He shrugged his shoulders again. "Usually I either nap or sit around and read. Sometimes I take in a show. Do some grocery shopping. Laundry. Stuff like that."

All those things made sense, but she couldn't see killing ten hours that way. "We don't need to go grocery shopping for days."

His little grin quickened her heart. "I should have guessed you'd think of food first."

Rather than respond in front of the dispatcher, she walked outside, and Lionel followed close behind, snickering all the way. "I have an idea. Women usually like shopping, and we both like eating. Let's combine the two activities. Since both of us only brought jeans and T-shirts, we can go buy ourselves some nice clothes and go somewhere nice for supper, since this is the last of our leisure time. From here, it's straight home. Let's make it a special night together."

Gwen's heart skipped a beat. She'd been thinking so much about this being near the end of their time together, it was almost obsessive. To hear that he also had been contemplating the same thing was strange. She wished she knew how he felt about the matter but was too afraid to ask. She swallowed hard. "I'd like that."

She waited while he went back inside to ask the dispatcher for directions. They ended up at a nearby mall where they could park the truck without its being in anyone's way. After enjoying the Funks' hospitality and Freda's good cooking, thinking of the greasy truck stop food over the next couple of days heightened Gwen's anticipation for a fine restaurant meal tonight.

"I've never been shopping for clothes with a woman before. I hope you don't take forever to decide on something and then try on everything in the store three times."

Gwen laughed. "Don't worry. I'm not especially fond of shopping for clothes, so I make my choices quickly. I think part of that comes from shopping with my brother. I can help you pick something nice too."

"Great. A woman picking my clothes. Isn't this every man's worst nightmare?"

"Depends on your perspective, I guess. Garrett appreciated me picking his clothes. I think part of the reason he likes his job so much is because they provide a uniform, so there's nothing for him to buy except his boots."

It didn't take long to pick a nice shirt and matching slacks for Lionel. She couldn't put her finger on why, but the whole procedure of picking clothes for him was different from picking clothes for her brother. She decided it was because Lionel actually fit the normal, off-the-rack clothes.

For herself, Gwen selected a functional mix-and-match skirt and top that wouldn't crease too badly when she stuffed the outfit into the bottom of her duffel bag. Lionel waited behind her as a clerk opened the fitting room.

"Going to model it for me?"

"Model it?" she stammered. "Why?"

"Isn't this the time a man is supposed to tell a woman how beautiful she looks when she buys something new?"

She didn't want him to tell her anything of the sort. She didn't want to get too familiar with him as a man. As it was, she had enjoyed holding clothes up to each other and the resulting playful banter far too much. "No, I'm not going to model it. Go sit down somewhere."

After she paid for her purchase, Lionel insisted on carrying both bags. "That wasn't too painful," he said, holding the bags up as if they were some kind of conquest. "We still have lots of time left before supper."

"We're not done. We have to buy shoes."

"Shoes?"

"I only brought my old beat-up sneakers. Did you bring anything else to wear on your feet?"

"Yes. I always have a pair of black rubber boots in the truck."

She didn't want to give him the dignity of a response. "Let's go in here, they have a sale."

It took them longer to select shoes than the clothing, but finally they managed to choose something relatively inexpensive yet comfortable.

Again, Lionel insisted on carrying all the bags. "I didn't realize buying clothes would be such a major undertaking. After all this, I keep thinking I'm supposed to buy you jewelry or something."

"I don't wear jewelry. I only wear a watch and earrings. You're safe."

Without warning, his hand wrapped around hers and he stopped dead in his tracks, forcing Gwen to stop as well. She turned to him to see if something was wrong when he stepped closer, leaving only a few inches between them. His voice dropped to a low, gravelly rumble. "Maybe I don't want to be safe."

Her heart pounded. Such strange things had happened to her heart in the past few hours, she wondered if she should see a doctor.

He pointed to a bench a few feet away. "Wait here."

Lionel strode into a jewelry store before she had a chance to protest.

Rather than stand in front of the store with her mouth hanging open, she demurely sat on the bench, looking anywhere other than the jewelry store. He returned in a few minutes, empty-handed. "Let's go back to the truck to change."

Gwen nodded, grateful he hadn't bought anything, and they walked back to the truck. "How are we going to do this?"

"Flip a coin to see who goes first?"

Gwen won the flip, so she told Lionel to change first because she didn't want to wait outside alone all dressed up.

Lionel took only a few minutes, but those few minutes transformed him. Compared to the usual T-shirt and jeans, he was a different man in cotton shirt and pleated slacks. She tried to imagine what he would look like with the finishing touch of adding a tie, but he didn't need one. He'd changed from attractively rugged to dashingly handsome. Apparently clothes did make the man. He'd even touched up the gel in his hair.

He ran his hand along his jaw. "I wish I could have shaved, and I need a haircut. But this is as good as it gets away from home. Your turn."

Gwen hopped inside and pulled the curtain closed. She'd only remembered at the last minute to buy pantyhose and a slip, and considered it quite unfair that women had to dress in so many layers. She drew the line at buying a new purse when she already had another good purse at home. To make it worse, she hadn't brought any makeup, nor had she brought a curling iron. Even if she would have had the time to use the curling iron or apply the makeup, she refused to buy anything more for one dinner date, especially when this really wasn't a date. It was only Lionel. Her temporary driving partner. They were only doing something different than the usual routine for dinner. Nothing more.

Getting dressed in the back of the truck was nothing like any other time she'd prepared herself to go out to dinner with a man. The only mirror inside the truck was the rearview mirror, so she didn't get a full look at herself when she was ready. But she didn't need to look. Without makeup and not being able to touch up her hair, she felt plain.

When she emerged from the truck, Lionel held out one hand to help her down.

His smile made her foolish heart flutter. "You look lovely, Gwen."

She didn't think so, but didn't want to be impolite and contradict him. Instead, she concentrated on how good Lionel looked. She grinned. "You don't look too bad yourself."

He reached into his pocket. "There's only one thing missing."

"You're not missing anything. You look great."

"Not me. You." He reached into his pants pocket and gave her a small box.

She stared at the small blue velvet box. It was from the jewelry store. "I can't accept this."

He stepped closer and twined the fingers of one hand in her hair. His emerald green eyes bored into her, and his familiar touch seared her to her soul. She had to remind herself that it was only Lionel. "My poor heart will break in two if you turn me down."

She thought he was laying it on a bit thick, but opened the box anyway.

It was a pair of gold earrings, made of a gemstone the same color as the blue of her skirt. She suspected they were sapphires, surrounded by ribbons of gold dangling down. They were gorgeous, and they looked expensive.

"Thank you," she choked out. No man had ever given her a gift like this before. She'd never had a serious enough relationship with a man where such a gift would have been appropriate. "I don't know what to say."

His fingers brushed her cheek. "You've already said thank you. That's enough." And then his lips brushed hers.

She tried not to enjoy it, but before she had a chance to think about it, he backed up, and it was over. "Going to put them on?"

Rather than climb back up into the truck with him standing behind her, Gwen stepped up on her tiptoes and used the side mirrors on the truck to change earrings. The simple task had never been more difficult because she couldn't stop her hands from shaking. Finally, after a number of failed attempts, Lionel removed the earrings from her trembling fingers and slid them in for her.

Very gently he brushed the earrings with his knuckles, then rested his fingers under her chin. All she could do was stare into his gorgeous green eyes. If he tried again to kiss her, he wouldn't have to bend down at all. With the shoes on instead of her sneakers, they were exactly the same height.

Her eyes drifted shut, but instead of the kiss she expected, his thumb caressed her lips, then he stepped away.

"They look good on you. Now let's eat. All that shopping made me hungry."

She didn't resist when he grasped her hand and they began walking. "It's a block north and two blocks east. We drove by it on the way to the mall. Looks like a nice place."

"I guess," she mumbled.

The restaurant turned out to be a cozy little place. The lights were turned down, slow, relaxing strains of music drifted through the air, and the room was quiet with the absence of children.

The hostess showed them to a small booth table in the corner, where Lionel slid in beside her. She was about to tell him to move and sit across the table from her, but he gave her an adorable impish grin that made her brain freeze. All thoughts of protest fled her mind.

She grabbed the menu and studied it intently. Instead of looking at his own menu, he slid one arm behind her back, snuggled up beside her, then pointed to one of the items listed on her menu. "That's what the dispatcher recommended. He also said the chocolate cheesecake here is excellent, so save room for dessert."

Gwen couldn't concentrate. She could feel his breath on her neck. Not that she didn't expect him to breathe, but it was distracting having him so close. If she turned her head, they'd bump noses.

She snapped the menu closed. "That's what I'll have, then." She didn't know what it was, but she wasn't going to open the menu again.

Without warning, he covered her hand on top of the closed menu.

"I enjoyed going shopping together. It would be nice to do it again some day."

"I don't really like shopping," she mumbled. "What we did today was buy exactly what we went for, then leave. That's the way I always shop."

"I know. I shop that way too. That's why I like shopping with you."

Gwen shuffled away a couple of inches on the seat and turned to face him, needing to crane her neck back so she could focus on his face, he was so close. All he did was give her a goofy grin. Gwen wondered if maybe he needed glasses or something.

While the waitress took their orders, she slid a respectable distance away.

He opened his mouth to start talking, but Gwen was too nervous about what he would say, so she quickly said the first thing that popped into her mind before he had a chance to speak first. "When I checked my E-mail today, Garrett told me Robbie's ultrasound showed something really interesting. He sounds really excited, so it must be something good, but he didn't say what they found out. He also said that she's feeling better. She's just past her first trimester, and he was worried about her being so sick all the time."

Suddenly, Gwen snapped her mouth shut. She couldn't believe she'd just started to discuss her friend's morning sickness with Lionel. She'd found him easy to talk to, and they'd shared some very personal things, but this time she knew she'd finally gone too far. Lionel couldn't possibly want to hear about how sick Robbie had been.

He leaned back and crossed his arms over his chest, and that dopey grin came back. "Have you ever wondered what it would be like to be as in love as your brother and your friend?"

Gwen sighed and stared into the yellow candle in the center of the table. "What they have is really special. It's funny how they met. We were all camping together when they fell in love. It hit him right smack between the eyes. I'd never believed in love at first sight until it hit my brother. Everyone saw the signs but him and Robbie. It was almost laughable. He was falling all over himself, behaving like a lovelorn puppy, anything to be close to her, and she couldn't see it. He couldn't even tell he was acting like an idiot around her."

Lionel shifted closer, the dopey grin unchanged. "Really?"

"Yes, and they're so different. He lives for the great outdoors, and she'd never done anything outside the city limits. Like night and day, those two. Yet they're perfect for each other."

He flipped a lock of her hair and rested his finger under her chin, leaving her no choice but to meet his gaze. "Does that make you think of anyone else?"

"Yeah. . .kinda. . ." Gwen stared into his eyes. Lionel was such a handsome man. He was intelligent, but probably very few people realized his potential because he didn't spend long enough in one place for anyone to really know him. She wondered if he knew his neighbors. Uncle Chad's neighbors really didn't know him because he wasn't around in the evenings or on weekends. Being a fellow trucker, Lionel's lifestyle would be the same. She already knew he'd been to what he called his home church only a handful of times because he was out on the road almost every weekend.

At first she had him pegged as the strong, silent type. In a crowd he was thoughtful and serious, but the more she got to know him, the more friendly he became, and he really was a lot of fun once he let his guard down and was away from a crowd. He had a quick wit and an easy laugh, and she had never enjoyed being in anyone's company so much.

Gwen wrapped her hands around her coffee cup and picked it up. "Yes. My friend Molly and her husband, Ken, are like that too."

Dinner turned out to be a barbecue steak dish, which Gwen thoroughly enjoyed. Tonight Lionel didn't tease her about the volume she ate. In fact, he didn't tease her about anything. She would never have pegged Lionel for the sensitive male type, but tonight he was different, and she couldn't figure him out.

They lingered a sufficient amount of time after dessert and then left the restaurant.

It was already dark outside, and although the air was still hot, it wasn't uncomfortable. They turned in the direction of the mall, and Gwen held out her hand, expecting him to take it because they'd walked hand in hand on the way to the restaurant.

He picked up her hand, but instead of letting their joined hands dangle between them, he lifted her hand to his mouth. Her knees turned to rubber when he kissed it, let go, and slipped his arm around her waist.

She barely realized they had started to walk. She slipped her arm around his waist for lack of someplace better to put it.

"What are you doing?"

"I'm trying to be romantic. Is it that hard to tell? If it is, then I must be doing something wrong."

Gwen tried not to choke. He wasn't doing anything wrong. But this was Lionel. The man she argued with every day about whose turn it was to crawl under the trailer and check the slack adjusters. She didn't want to be romantic. Yet they were walking down the street arm in arm.

Since they were exactly the same height with her shoes on, every step was in perfect unison, as accurate as marching, except their pace was leisurely and slow. His arm around her waist felt comforting and secure, and right.

They stood outside the truck door while Lionel fished in his pocket for the keys. "I guess this is it. Our date is over."

Date? Gwen swallowed hard. Without question, tonight something had changed between them. She just wasn't sure what. They hadn't merely gone out to share a meal. They had breakfast, lunch, and supper together every day, but nothing about tonight had been the same as any other day. He'd been sweet and kind and attentive to her every need. He'd also been serious in everything he'd said and done.

She thought of the way he'd kissed her hand. He wasn't trying to comfort her over something she was upset about, nor had panic and mayhem driven them into each other's arms.

There wasn't any other way to describe it. This had really been a date.

He inserted the key into the lock but didn't turn it.

"I want you to know that I will never take advantage of you and never put any pressure on you when we're in the truck. Just like that curtain is the separator for personal privacy, once we get inside the door of that truck, that's the line. We can't do anything that could jeopardize our working relationship in any way, not when we have to stay side by side for days without being able to get away from each other. I like you a lot, Gwen, and the only way I'm going to be able to handle this is to make the rules very specific. I don't know about you, but I can't mix business with pleasure."

Gwen nodded. "No, we can't do that." This wasn't a nine-to-five job. What little space they could call home was mobile. They'd seen each other at their worst, and they had no normal routine. There were no boundaries, no rules, no guidelines.

He stepped close to her. "So this is the end of our evening out, where a man takes a woman home. Here we are, our traveling home." His hands cupped her face. "So this is where I kiss you good night."

As Gwen's eyes drifted shut, Lionel kissed her with such an aching sweetness she didn't want it to end. She wrapped her arms around him and kissed him back, not caring that they were standing in the dark mall parking lot. He was tender and gentle yet held her so firmly that the bond between them was almost a tangible thing. When she thought he was pulling away, he instead tilted his head and kissed her again.

By the time he stopped kissing her, her knees felt wobbly. All she could do was watch as his eyes drifted open slowly. Very gently he touched her cheek, and then his hand fell to his side, completing the separation.

"Wow," he murmured.

She didn't know what had happened, but she couldn't have expressed it better. Her world would never be the same again. "Yeah," she mumbled back. "Wow."

One corner of his mouth tilted up in a lazy half smile. "Will you still respect me in the morning?"

Gwen blinked. By morning they would be on their way home. In fact, within an hour they were supposed to be on their way home. She shook her head to bring herself back to reality. "Not if we're so late picking up our load that we get fired. You wait out here, I'm going to get changed first."

She yanked the door open and hopped up. Lionel closed it softly behind her once she was inside.

Gwen's hands shook as she pulled her duffel bag out of the bin. Every other time she'd kissed a date good-bye, that was it, it would be days before she saw him again. When a man looked like he was starting to get serious, she always had sufficient time to evaluate the relationship before she saw him again. This time she didn't have that option. Lionel was waiting outside. She wouldn't have that separation for thirty-two hours.

The importance of being so specific about drawing the line between work and their personal lives finally sank into her addled brain. When they were inside the truck and working, there was no room for romance, and that's exactly what was happening. Strange as the situation was, she'd never had such a romantic evening in her life as what she'd just experienced with Lionel, and no man's kiss had ever affected her like this.

Gwen had never changed her clothes so fast in her life. If she couldn't have the time to recover from the rapid change in whatever it was that composed their relationship, and if she couldn't change the setting of being confined inside the truck with him, then the change in clothes was the best she could do to emphasize the separation between a date and work.

She pulled out her grubbiest jeans and oldest T-shirt and slipped her feet into her beat-up old sneakers. As a finishing touch, she messed up her hair.

The transformation was complete.

She was back at work.

Chapter 12

What do you mean, there's been a change in our running orders?"

The dispatcher tossed the trip envelope through the window onto the counter. "I said the customer got a rush order and put the load for Vancouver off 'til another day. Now they've got a priority load for Phoenix. They need it picked up as soon as they're finished with it. A doubles team can get it to Phoenix in thirteen hours. That's you."

Lionel ran his hand down his face. It had taken awhile, but he'd finally managed to focus his thoughts on something else after he'd kissed Gwen and gotten his mind back to where it should have been in the first place. Driving.

He'd planned to treat Gwen special and show her how much she meant to him on their last bit of personal time together, but now things had changed. Once they delivered the load in Phoenix, they'd probably have another layover, and he didn't know if he could handle the pressure. He'd crossed the line, and he could never go back. He'd almost told Gwen how much he loved her, but had stopped himself before he blurted it out.

If they drove straight through to home, he wouldn't have to worry about crossing the line again. More than that, if he could keep things professional in the confines of the truck, he wouldn't have to risk hearing that she didn't feel the same way about him. If she didn't, their time together would be unbearable. He couldn't handle that. If she was going to tell him she didn't like him at least a little, he didn't want to hear it until they parted ways, possibly for the last time.

His gut clenched. He didn't want to plan what it would be like saying good-bye for the last time. He needed more time, but not like this.

"So, what's it gonna be?"

Lionel shook his head to clear his mind. He turned to Gwen. "Have you got a Green Card?"

If she didn't, it was his only chance of refusing the load and getting another load through to Vancouver, and home. Without a Green Card, crossing the border to take their first load to Evansville, they would have to be dispatched straight back home without doing jobs with an American origin and destination. Legally, they got away with delivering the shingles only because it was a mission of mercy after the tornado.

She stiffened. "Of course I've got a Green Card. Uncle Chad made sure of that so we wouldn't get caught in a spot."

So much for that.

By the time they arrived at the client's warehouse, the last pallet was being loaded onto the trailer. They hooked up and were ready to roll before midnight.

"I guess this is what being a doubles team is all about," Gwen said. "The rush loads and unusual stuff."

Lionel was used to rush loads. Every driver got a few rush loads. It was just that the doubles teams got the rush loads that went farther. For him the unusual part was driving with someone else, and then falling in love with the other driver.

He turned to Gwen. "Who sleeps first? You've been driving all night until now, so maybe you'd like a change of pace. If you want to go have a sleep, go ahead."

"That's really nice of you. I think I will. It was hard switching back to regular living hours at the Funks' house, and it's caught up with me. Good night, Lionel."

"Good night, Gwen."

At the sound of the curtain sealing shut, he allowed himself to relax. He'd almost said, "Good night, Darling."

He had it bad. The night was going to be long. . .and lonely.

❧

The sun had been up for hours before Lionel heard the rasp of the Velcro behind him. He smiled and quickly glanced behind him. "Good morning, Stranger."

She mumbled something he didn't quite understand.

"Have a good sleep?"

She mumbled something else under her breath.

"What's wrong? Are we not a morning person today?"

This time he thought he understood what she mumbled, and it sounded amazingly similar to "Shut up." Lionel pretended to gasp in shock and caught the dirty look she shot him as she sank into the seat.

Part of him told him not to push his luck, but part of him couldn't leave it alone. "I think you're going to need extra sugar in your coffee this morning. Or is this the kind of morning grumpies that can only be fixed with a double order of fries?"

"It's breakfast time," she grumbled to the window.

"Ah, yes. Time for whole wheat cereal with two percent milk and a glass of orange juice."

This time she didn't answer, and Lionel stayed silent. He wondered what she was really like in the morning, under normal circumstances. So far this was the only day she hadn't been cheerful when she woke up, although he had to remind himself that for two days she'd slept at the Funks' house while he'd slept in the church parking lot.

It struck him that he knew what she liked for breakfast. He wondered how many husbands knew what their wives liked for breakfast.

He stopped at the first place they came to, which happened to be a truck stop. While Gwen freshened up, Lionel headed into the restaurant.

Gwen sank quietly into the chair across the table from Lionel. "I'm sorry. I didn't mean to be so crabby. I'm not usually like that in the morning."

"No problem."

Yes, there was a problem, but she didn't want to tell him what it was, because he was the problem. For the first time since she'd been out on the road she had not slept well, and it was all his fault.

After their date she had changed clothes in the truck, but he had waited and changed from his nice new clothes to his old jeans and typical T-shirt when they got back to the terminal. The change had hit her in a completely unexpected way. She'd taken one look at him when they got back into the truck, and the first thought that had run through her mind was that the scruffy Lionel was the familiar Lionel, the man she knew, the man she loved.

She was in love with a truck driver.

She noticed he had ordered coffee for her, but he was drinking juice. It felt good to know that at least some of her good habits were rubbing off on him.

He pushed a menu across the table. "This is a switch. For you it's really breakfast time at seven in the morning, but I feel like a bedtime snack. I'm really tired after driving all night. Soon as we eat and get moving, I'm going to crawl into the bunk for a sleep. I hope you don't mind."

"Of course I don't mind." She needed the time to think, but rather than being glad to be rid of him, she felt comforted knowing he was close by, behind the curtain, because she would be thinking about him.

Once the summer was over she wouldn't see him often, if at all. His job as a trucker kept him away from home, and her job as a teacher kept her restricted to staying in town. The only free time she had was on the weekends, and a trucker's busiest times away from home were from Friday to Monday.

It had taken half the night, but she had come to a few conclusions. The first was that for the short time they had left, she wanted to be near him and to spend as much time as she could with him. The professional boundaries, which he had stated were in effect while they were driving together, were perfect and clear. Despite the constant close proximity, there was no temptation, because both of them knew not to cross the line. Personal interaction beyond conversation while driving was unacceptable inside the truck. Inside the truck they were partners only. Anything else would mean disaster, both professionally and personally.

As the meal progressed, she could see he was fading fast, which wasn't surprising. He was long overdue for a sleep, and she felt guilty for sleeping so long. She could see why trucks traveled in convoys and chattered on the CBs. It was necessary to keep each other awake and alert.

He crawled straight into the bunk, and she was sure he was asleep by the time she reached highway speed. The countdown to home had begun, and this stopover in Phoenix gave her extra time to think. This delay was in her favor, and she thanked God for it.

"I did a good job backing it in, don't you think?" Gwen couldn't help but be proud of herself. It was only her second time backing a load in, and it was straight.

He grinned and winked. "It's okay."

It was better than okay. She'd done a marvelous job. Of course, the lighting helped. The modern facilities were well lit, the compound was paved, and she had lots of room to back in straight.

Gwen yawned, making no effort to hide it. "What now?"

Lionel walked into the customers' building and returned in a few minutes. "I just called dispatch. They don't have a load out for us right away, so we're to call in in the morning."

"It is morning. One in the morning."

"Nice try. I saw a motel on the way in with lots of room to park the truck. We'll unhook and go there."

She let Lionel drive while she sagged into the seat. The short time it took to back up into the shipping bay had been more stressful than the entire trip.

Lionel reserved the room while Gwen dug her personal effects out of the bins. Lionel stuck his head through the door. "You've got room twenty-four." He picked up her duffel bag and opened the room for her.

"Wait!" she called. "Can I borrow your computer? I want to check my E-mail. Garrett might have answered me back."

He dumped her stuff on the bed and peeked into the bathroom while she booted up the computer.

"This is great." His voice echoed as he spoke into the bathroom. "Don't turn in the key in the morning, I want to have a real shower. I'll wait for you to be finished with my computer. I've got some stuff to catch up on while you sleep."

Gwen phoned the clerk for an outside line and set the modem to dial while Lionel opened all the drawers in the small desk.

"Hey! A Gideon Bible! Cool!" He turned, grinned, and started flipping through it. "I check for these every time I need to rent a room."

Gwen mumbled her approval while a long E-mail came through. "You'd better read this. It's from Uncle Chad."

He read the message over her shoulder.

Hi, Gwen,

Hope you're having a great time on the road with Lionel. Like I said before, he's a good Christian and a righteous man and I know he'll treat you right.

Lionel puffed out his chest. "See? A good reference from your uncle. I see the beginning of a beautiful relationship."

Gwen smacked him in the arm. "Quit fooling around. This is important. Keep reading."

> *The truck is fixed, right on time, and until you return, they have me running singles. As an unofficial favor, the dispatchers have put me on low priority runs in order to give me more time at home, including weekends.*
>
> *I know I can't ask you to stay away forever, but if things are working out with you and Lionel, it would give me a very special time with the family if you could stay out on the road awhile longer. At the time I am writing this, you are somewhere between Topeka and Phoenix. The longer you are gone, the more time I have with my family. This is a rare opportunity for us, but I don't want to put you in an uncomfortable position with Lionel. This is being done as a favor only and cannot go on indefinitely. But they will pass the word amongst the dispatchers not to send you and Lionel home to Vancouver for a little while longer if you agree. Whatever you decide, I will understand.*
>
> *Love always,*
> *Uncle Chad*

"Wow," Lionel muttered. "What are you going to do?"

Gwen looked up at him as he stood beside her. "I don't know. What do you think?"

The silence dragged. Lionel turned to stare at the bed in the middle of the motel room and rammed his hands into his pockets. "We should pray and talk about it in the morning."

Gwen's heart nearly stopped. They'd prayed together many times, and every time they had, they had sat together and joined hands. But that was never in the middle of a motel room.

He picked up his laptop. "I'll see you in the morning. Good night." In the blink of an eye, he was gone.

Gwen closed the door and watched him through the crack of the curtain as he hopped up inside the truck. The light went on in the bunk area as he set up the table to get ready to do his paperwork on the computer.

She had assumed he meant they should pray together, but he'd obviously meant in private. She wanted to pray with him. It would have been right to pray together, but not proper to do so sitting on the bed in a motel.

Gwen changed into her pajamas and crawled into bed, preparing herself to talk to God about the decision she had to make.

Of course, Uncle Chad wanted to take advantage of this limited opportunity to spend more time at home. Whenever he booked off, he didn't get paid, and under his contract he couldn't book time off unless it was for specified vacation time or something critical.

Over the years she had seen many times where her aunt had nearly broken down, she'd missed her husband so much. As an adult, Gwen could understand the anguish of separation of a husband and wife, different from the way her cousins missed their father.

She wanted him to spend more time with Aunt Chelsea and her cousins. But at what cost to her?

Gwen stared blankly at the closed curtains, knowing that on the other side was Lionel in his truck.

If she decided to go straight home, she would be denying Uncle Chad something she knew had been difficult for him to ask. Would she be selfish to refuse?

If she decided to continue driving with Lionel, she didn't know what would happen. She enjoyed being with him, both when they were driving and when they weren't. Except for his being a loner and a truck driver, she couldn't help but love him. But that only made things worse.

She was an adult and a Christian, but that didn't mean she was immune to temptation. She would be setting herself up for torture if she continued driving with him and had to maintain an emotional distance. She didn't know if she could handle the situation if she said yes, but she didn't know if she could live with herself if she said no.

Gwen closed her eyes and prayed like she'd never prayed before.

Lionel stared up at the ceiling of the truck. He'd given up on his paperwork. He'd been lying in the dark for hours, but he still couldn't sleep.

They'd just been given the perfect excuse not to go home, to spend days, even weeks, exclusively with each other.

Not that doing Chad a favor wasn't a good thing, but he wanted her to do it because she wanted to be with him, not just for Chad's sake. However, the impropriety of the situation they found themselves had just become even more of a stumbling block. Until now, traveling together had been beyond their control, something thrust upon them when there was nothing either of them could do about it. Now it had become a choice.

They needed to pray about this together, but he wasn't going to hold hands and sit on a bed in a motel room to do so. He loved Gwen with all his heart and soul. He wanted to spend the rest of his life with her, to make her his wife and the mother of his children. God said to flee from temptation, and even though it meant not praying together, he'd flown. He needed to outline the hands-off rules in the truck for a reason, and those rules applied tenfold in a motel room.

Lionel rolled onto his stomach and buried his face in the pillow. He knew what he wanted, but he didn't know what Gwen wanted.

Above all, he didn't know if she could trust him.

But then, he didn't know if he could trust himself.

The matter was out of his hands. It was Gwen's decision for now, but ultimately it was God's direction that would determine what would happen tomorrow and in the days and weeks to follow. He knew what he wanted but didn't know what was best, or right. Rather than pray for his own selfish desires, he rolled over, once again on his back, pressed his hands over his heart, squeezed his eyes shut, and spoke out loud, "Father God, Thy will be done!"

Peace filled his soul. The future was out of his hands, and in God's, where it belonged.

Lionel rolled over and managed to drift off to sleep until his ringing cell phone jolted him out of his dreams.

After listening to the dispatcher, he threw on his clothes, hurried outside, and knocked on Gwen's door. He shouldn't have been surprised to see her already dressed and ready to go. After all, it was daylight.

"The dispatcher just called. We've got to go now. Give me a few minutes to shower."

She waited for him in the truck, and when he was done, they drove the three blocks to the terminal in silence. He usually teased her to see if she'd slept well. This time he wasn't in the mood to joke around. Not a word was said when they walked together into the dispatch office.

The day shift dispatcher held two envelopes in his hands. "You've got a choice between two loads. A through load for Vancouver, or a consolidation, then a couple of drop shipments ending up in Buffalo. Both are ready now. What'll it be?"

Lionel clenched his teeth so hard his jaw hurt. The dispatcher stared at him, expecting it to be Lionel to make the decision. Lionel kept silent and looked at Gwen. His heart was pounding and his palms were sweating. He forced himself to breathe. Gwen turned to him. All he could do was nod once.

The dispatcher turned to Gwen.

Gwen stiffened her back, sucked in a deep breath, and turned to face the dispatcher.

The seconds ticked on like hours.

Lionel thought he might throw up.

Chapter 13

Gwen swallowed past the frog in her throat. "Buffalo," she said.

The dispatcher handed her the envelope from his right hand, but her hands were shaking too much to open it, so she turned and held it out to Lionel.

His face was pale, his eyes were wide open, and he didn't move, not even to raise his hand to take the envelope from her as she held it in front of him.

His voice came out in a hoarse croak. "Buffalo? Are you serious?"

"Yes." She still could barely believe her own answer. She would be lying if she said she was doing it as a favor to Uncle Chad. The favor was merely a good excuse. She was going to Buffalo because she wanted to spend more time with Lionel.

Last night she'd prayed for God to tell her to go home. No such answer came.

The boundaries and codes of conduct were stated before their feelings for each other became an issue. He made her feel safe, and she trusted him. It had stung for only a minute when he bolted out of the motel room. More than anything, she saw the actions of a man who didn't cross any lines best left alone.

God's rules and boundaries gave freedom instead of restrictions. If she followed the guidelines of God's Word for her life, she had the complete freedom, providing she made wise and moral choices, to follow the desires of her heart. As soon as they returned home, whatever was between them would be over. God had provided a way to make it last a little longer, and for that she was grateful.

She felt the envelope pulling out of her fingers. Lionel cupped her elbow and ushered her outside. "I think we have to talk. In private."

They walked outside but didn't go to the truck. It seemed like neither of them wanted it to be that private.

"You're sure about this?"

All she could do was nod.

The color returned to his face, and he smiled. "Then let's see what we've got." He opened the flap and pulled out a stack of papers, mumbling as he read the top sheet. "We leave here and go to El Paso and pick up a part load, then we start a series of drop shipments. All the bills of lading are here. Directions too." He paged through them one at a time, still muttering under his breath. "San Antonio, Oklahoma City, Birmingham, then the final drop in Buffalo." He slapped the heel of his palm to his forehead, still holding the wad of papers, and squeezed his eyes shut. "This is the most screwball series of drop shipments I've ever seen! These are all short hops in between. We'll be spending all our time in layovers!"

"Should we go back and take the Vancouver load?"

His face paled instantly. "No!" A blush spread over his cheeks, and his ears turned red. He cleared his throat, and his voice lowered in volume. "I mean, this is just fine. It's just the kind of thing you would love as a beginning driver. This is what's known as a paid tourist run. We can take our time, and you can probably even get some good pictures. Providing we're somewhere it's worth taking pictures."

Gwen beamed. "Great! I was beginning to wonder if I would get a chance to use my camera."

Lionel's voice changed to a melodic intonation. "Then we shuffle off to Buff-a-lo." He grinned and stuffed all the papers back into the envelope.

"If you start singing, I'm going back and taking the Vancouver load."

He laughed and darted toward the truck before she could snatch the envelope out of his hand. "Catch me if you can!" he called out as he ran.

Gwen smiled and walked to the truck. She had done the right thing.

❦

"I think you're wrong. I don't understand why you say this is going to be a wacky trip." She'd entered the dates and the destinations in the computer three times, and every time the answers were the same.

"It's because that program doesn't allow for the most important variable."

"I thought you said this program was the best."

"It doesn't account for fickle clients."

"Oh."

Gwen figured out that if all went well, since today was Thursday, they could be at the final destination Saturday, which she figured wasn't bad at all. Lionel had just laughed and reminded her that the customers didn't keep the same hours they did.

So far all had gone well. They'd arrived in El Paso at six in the evening on Wednesday. It had taken an hour for the customer to finish loading. They'd eaten another wonderful truck stop meal and left at eight. It was now Thursday just after sunrise. They were going to pull into San Antonio, the first point where they'd have to unload something, and then they would keep going.

"Let's go to the customer's warehouse first. We can eat and shower after we unload, which should take us to lunch time."

"Sure." Gwen packed up the computer. She was becoming accustomed to using Lionel's laptop while they were moving. Using her big desktop computer at the school would never be the same.

"Who gets to back it in?"

Gwen patted her seatbelt. "I'm a passenger. You do it."

Everything went smoothly, and soon they were at the truck stop outside of town. After they finished fueling and showered, Gwen took the laptop into the truck stop and downloaded their E-mail, then took the laptop into the restaurant.

Lionel sipped his coffee while she opened the Inbox.

"You're like a kid with a new toy with that thing," he grumbled. "Will you give it a rest?"

"I told you, I'm expecting something from my brother. There's nothing for me, but you got something from your friend Randy. The subject title is 'Happy Birthday.' Is it your birthday?"

He took another long sip. "Whatever."

"It is! Why didn't you tell me? How old are you?"

"It's not a big deal. I'm thirty-two."

"Well, happy thirty-second birthday. I could have at least gotten you a card."

"I don't want a card. It's just clutter in the truck."

"Then I can get you a piece of cake. Give me the dessert menu."

"If you have even the remotest idea of ordering a piece of cake with a candle on it, I'm leaving."

"If you think I'd do that to you, then you don't know me very well."

"Sorry," he mumbled. "Someone did that to me once, and I never want to go through that again for the rest of my life."

Gwen watched him stare into the bottom of his coffee cup. On a number of occasions she'd been the instigator to set up singing waiters, sparklers for candles on a cake, and the whole package for a birthday in a restaurant. However, she would never consider doing that to Lionel. Whoever did that must not have known him very well. "I can't imagine who would do that to you."

"It was my ex-fiancée," he mumbled.

Gwen couldn't stifle a gasp.

"Yes, I was engaged once. A few weeks before what was supposed to be our wedding day, I came home early and found her with someone else."

"Oh. . .Lionel. . .I'm so sorry. . ."

He swished around the dribbles in the bottom of the cup, not looking up. "Don't be sorry. It hurt at the time, but shortly after that I met Jesus. We wouldn't have been right for each other, I can see that now."

Gwen thought of the few relationships she'd had with men, none of which had ever come close to being serious. "Still, it must have been awful."

"I lived." He checked his watch. "I don't feel like sitting around here. Let's go."

Not a word was said as they walked to the truck, but she didn't like him being so sullen. It wasn't like him. She didn't want to make a big deal of it, if Lionel didn't want a fuss. Still, everyone deserved something special on their birthday. She knew they would be driving straight through to Oklahoma City, so she didn't have time to buy him a small gift or even a card, which she would have done, despite his calling such things clutter.

While he inserted the key in the lock, Gwen laid the laptop on the running board and stepped between Lionel and the truck.

"What are you doing?" he asked.

She cupped his chin in her hands. "Happy birthday, Lionel."

Then she kissed him. Not just a little brush-on-the-lips kiss, but a real, big, loud, smacking kiss. She even made a popping sound when she pulled away.

"Hey!"

She snatched up the laptop, pulled the keys out of the lock, opened the door, and hopped in before he had a chance to regain his bearings. "I thought you said we should go. I'm driving."

By the time they pulled into Oklahoma City it was ten at night. The client's warehouse was closed up, but a night watchman opened the gate and told them to back the trailer in and leave it until morning.

Since they had all the time in the world, Gwen backed it in, doing it slowly and trying it a number of times just for the practice. Together they cranked down the dolly legs and set the trailer brakes.

Gwen peeked under the trailer and called out to Lionel. "If you knew this would happen where we'd be stuck here like this in the middle of the night, we should have stopped in Dallas."

"What for?"

"I've never been to Dallas."

Lionel shook his head. "We're in a truck and pulling a fifty-three-foot trailer. We can't exactly go touring around the city and visiting all the local hot spots."

"I could at least have taken some pictures."

"You got a picture of the skyline."

Gwen rested her hands on her hips. "That was from out the window, and we were moving at the time."

"Well, here we are in Oklahoma City, and we're not going anywhere. Take all the pictures you want."

"It's midnight!"

"There's lots of stars to take pictures of. Look. There's the Big Dipper." He pointed up. "There's Polaris, which the Big Dipper points to. It's the tail of Ursa Minor, which is supposed to be a bear, but most people call it the Little Dipper."

"That's fascinating. How did you know that?"

"I spend a lot of time in the middle of nowhere in the middle of the night, so I've had time to study the sky. It's really quite remarkable."

Gwen looked up. Not a cloud disturbed the crystal-clear images of the night. The beauty of God's creation shining above had always awed her, but it had never touched her like right now. "It doesn't have the same feel from the industrial estate as it does from a deserted rest area off the highway, does it?"

"Nope."

If it wasn't for the concrete and buildings around them, the setting would have been rather romantic. The quiet night, the beauty of the stars above, and, most of all, the kind and handsome man beside her. The night watchman had gone back to his post at the gate, leaving them alone. It was the perfect time and place for Lionel to kiss her, and not a silly, smacking kiss like she'd given him on his birthday, but a real, sizzling, melt-your-socks-off type of kiss.

"It's late. We've got to get up early in the morning and get going, so I'll drop you off at a motel. I'll drive."

❧

Lionel couldn't believe he was doing this. He'd consented to wait inside the truck while Gwen ran into a large wholesale mega-store for a few groceries. He again checked his watch and questioned her definition of the word quick. He'd managed to get some reading done, but he'd been too distracted to really concentrate. He wanted to be with her, and the waiting was killing him.

Once they arrived back home, he didn't know how he was ever going to run singles again. At first he'd worried that being with someone would drive him nuts, but instead he was going nuts without her. She'd been gone less than an hour.

"I'm back. Let's go."

She tossed a small bag into the fridge, and then hoisted a large box behind the seat. A bag around it prevented him from seeing the markings.

"What in the world is that?"

"It's a surprise. I thought you were in a rush to get moving."

He studied the box. For the size of it, apparently it wasn't heavy.

"Mind your own business! Now get going."

He almost made a teasing comment about a nagging wife but stopped himself in time. He wondered what it would be like to be married to Gwen. If he'd been anxious for her return when she was only at the store, he could only imagine what it would be like during the long separations when she was tied to the school and he was out on the road.

They picked up the trailer, turned the music on loud, and then headed to Birmingham.

Conversation was light and playful until mid-afternoon, when Gwen was suddenly silent. After a couple of minutes she spoke again. "I've been thinking."

Lionel cringed. "Is something wrong?"

"If we just drove like normal, we'd arrive Saturday at three-thirty in the morning, and no one is going to be there. I was thinking that we should kill some time out here. Relax, take it easy, and enjoy ourselves away from the city. We really don't have to be there until eight-thirty in the morning, so let's do that."

He had a feeling there was more to her suggestion than met the eye. "What have you got in mind?"

"I want you to stop at the next rest area."

That was easy. Too easy. But he did anyway.

Once in the parking area, he killed the engine and reached for the door handle.

"No! You wait in the truck."

"Gwen. . .you're making me nervous."

"I have a surprise for you."

Now she really was making him nervous.

She pulled the box outside, but before she closed the truck door, she shot him a quelling look.

Lionel laughed. The woman could definitely hold her own, and he loved it. If they did pursue their relationship after their driving together was over, he knew Gwen possessed the strength to endure the separations. However, he wasn't sure he did.

"You can come out now!"

Gwen stood beside the picnic table, the large white bag covering something large in the center.

"Tah-dah!" She whipped off the bag.

"It's a portable barbecue."

She grinned from ear to ear. "Yes!"

"Okay. . ."

"I'm going to barbecue supper today. We've got lots of time."

Visions of baked potatoes and medium-rare T-bone steak danced through his mind. He loved barbecued corn on the cob, steamed to perfection after being wrapped tightly in tinfoil. Or mushrooms would be even better.

"I bought those special foot-long wieners, and whole wheat hot dog buns. And carrots. I even got a can of beans. I didn't know if you had a can opener, so I bought one, just in case. I love cold beans."

"Uh. . .sounds delicious."

Her grin widened. "This is my favorite camping meal. When I first started talking about driving a truck with Uncle Chad, I compared it to camping. Now that I've been doing it, I can see some things are the same, but not really."

"That makes sense."

"Never mind. Here, you scrape the carrots."

The domesticness of what they were doing hit him in the gut like a sucker punch. Gwen chattered away about camping and the school and her family, but all he could think about was what it would be like if they had a family of their own. About what it would be like to spend quality time together. Kids playing at their feet, and then settling in for some private time together when all was quiet for the night.

The healthy whole wheat buns seemed to contrast the questionable food value of the wieners, but he was surprised to find how much he enjoyed the simple meal. He also admired Gwen's ingenuity at the small disposable propane cartridge she'd purchased rather than the large cylinder on most propane barbecues.

"You've been awful quiet. What's on your mind?"

Marriage. Kids. A house in the country. A dog. Little league games. "Nothing in particular."

When all was tidied up and the small barbecue packed up inside the truck, they lay on their backs on the grass to enjoy the sunset until the stars began to wink their way out in the evening sky. When they started to feel the chill from lying on the grass, they walked back to the truck and headed to Alabama.

Gwen checked her watch. "What's taking them so long? I thought this was supposed to be a priority shipment."

"This is another thing that the computer program doesn't take into account. Overtime. The people who got called in are on overtime since it's Saturday. One of them told me that if they work for four hours they get paid for the day, at time-and-a-half. So if I count on my fingers correctly, we will be out of here at precisely one in the afternoon."

"That's not right."

"That's the way it goes."

Gwen sighed. She knew that as a teacher she was sheltered from such things, but she knew the course of human nature. To be delayed by what she felt was a worker cheating an employer, even if it wasn't her employer, annoyed her. "We don't have any choice, do we?"

"Nope."

By the time they were done, Gwen was more than ready to go. She almost laughed at herself. When she'd first started driving with Lionel, his compulsion to always keep the load moving annoyed her, and now she was no different.

This time Lionel had a nap in the afternoon, and she slept earlier in the evening than usual as they traveled. Both of them were wide awake in the middle of the night, so rather than getting a motel, they kept going. They caught the sunrise just over the New York state line. Since she was driving, Lionel took a picture out the window with her camera.

"I'm going to miss being in church on Sunday," Gwen sighed. "I can't remember the last time I missed a service, I mean, not counting since I started driving with Uncle Chad."

"We don't necessarily have to miss. Lots of the truck stops have small chapels for truckers passing through."

"Really?"

"Really. I just happen to have a directory of where they are." He pulled a little book out of the glove box. "We're in luck. We're not far away from one right now."

"Really?"

He grinned. "Really."

Gwen pulled into the parking lot of the truck stop as directed, and they walked around the back to a long, narrow building that looked suspiciously like a converted trailer. The only windows were in the back doors, and it was so small there was room only for one row of pews down the side, with a small altar at the front. Gwen thought it rather cozy, and not too different from the Funks' little church, except this one was a very miniature makeshift version. She noted Bibles in the pews, as well as tracts everywhere, including on a small table in the back.

At the front, a fiftyish man dressed in a western style shirt and jeans, who was probably the minister, was talking and laughing with another man whom Gwen pegged as another trucker.

"It's so early. What time do things usually start?"

"Usually at seven-thirty. This is all volunteer time for the minister. Services are short. After they're over, no one hangs around because most of the ministers have their own congregations to go to for regular Sunday services. Besides, we're all wayfaring strangers who have schedules to keep for early Monday and have to keep moving."

"That makes sense, I guess."

A few more men entered while they spoke. Right at seven-thirty the minister stood at the front and welcomed everyone.

Gwen leaned to whisper in Lionel's ear. "There are only eight people here, including us, and I'm the only woman."

He leaned back to whisper his reply. "I hope you didn't expect any different. The most I've ever seen on Sunday morning is a dozen, and I do this a lot."

She straightened and waited as the minister slipped a tape into the machine and hit the button.

If Lionel was used to such small gatherings, it would explain why he was so stiff at the Funks' church, which she considered small compared to the large congregation that attended her church back home.

The sound of a few good old-time gospel songs filled the air, and the small gathering of people sang heartily. Gwen enjoyed hearing the low male voices, as back home the prominent voices she heard were female. It set a different mood to the worship time.

The minister preached an enthusiastic sermon on the miracles of Jesus, and although it was short, it was refreshing after a busy and long week on the road.

". . .and go with God's good wishes!"

Everyone stood. Three of the men immediately went outside and drove away, two of the other drivers stood outside and talked, and the same man who was there when they first arrived began talking to the minister again.

Gwen followed Lionel outside and stood next to the small building where the sun was bright and the summer breeze ruffled her hair. "It's been a long time since I've heard such a good evangelical message."

"Yes. I gave my heart to Jesus at a service very similar to this."

Without saying so, Gwen had a feeling it wasn't long after his ex-fiancée had broken his heart. She couldn't imagine what it would be like to go through such heartache.

"Whenever I'm close to Fargo, I always stop in at that little chapel, or else the church run by the pastor who performs the services. He's an ex-trucker turned minister, and he knows what it's like to live like this."

"That's really nice." Gwen smiled and rested her hand on Lionel's arm. "It was a lovely service."

"I don't know if any of those truckers or the minister would appreciate you calling it lovely."

"You know what I meant. So, now what?"

"We shuffle off to Buffalo, get a room for you when we get there, unload at seven A.M., and go to the terminal to see what kind of outbound load they've got for us. Then we're on the road again."

Chapter 14

Lionel stared at the gray building looming before him. After all these years, it was so familiar, even though it had been a month since he'd last seen it. At this moment he hated it. They were home. It was over.

He couldn't think of anything worthwhile to say, so he said nothing. They walked to the dispatch office in silence together. For the last time.

Burt took their trip sheets and logbooks. "Long time, no see, Lionel. If it isn't the other half of our doubles team. Now that you're back, Jeff is ready to drive again, so it looks like you came home just to be replaced." Burt laughed at his own comment.

Lionel didn't find Burt the least bit amusing. He noticed Gwen didn't have anything to say either. Lionel emptied out his over-stuffed mail slot, and they turned and walked out.

He drove Gwen home and helped carry her personal belongings inside. Over the past month she'd accumulated much more than the one duffel bag, sleeping bag, and pillow he'd carried into his truck when he picked her up at the side of the road at Snoqualmie.

She told him to keep the barbecue, to consider it a belated birthday gift. He'd never received such a special gift in his life.

They stood in the open doorway.

Gwen studied the ground and shuffled her feet. "It feels strange to be home."

"I know what you mean. It's the same with me. After being gone a long time, it's familiar, but it's not."

Silence hung in the air.

Gwen shuffled her feet again. "Strange as it sounds, the first thing I'm going to do is have a long, hot bath. With bubble bath."

He smiled. "Same. Just with no bubbles."

More silence hung between them.

Lionel grasped her hands and cleared his throat. "Can we continue seeing each other? I'd like to call you when I'm in town and take you out and stuff."

"Yes, I'd like that."

"So I guess this is it."

Her sad little smile ripped him in two. If he had to say good-bye to the woman he loved, he was going to do it right. He threw his arms around her and kissed her with everything he had in him until the sound of someone walking by caused them to separate.

He stared into her beautiful brown eyes. Eyes that were starting to well up with tears.

He couldn't watch her cry. Not like this.

"See you sometime," he croaked out.

Before she could reply, he walked to the truck as quickly as his dignity would allow and drove home.

In an attempt to settle himself, he proceeded through what had always been his normal routine after getting back from a long trip, except that he'd never been gone for so long before. He listened to the messages on his answering machine, wiped a thick layer of dust from the television, and got his laundry started. He didn't want to open the fridge. Even his cactus was dead.

He'd dropped Gwen off only a few hours ago, but already he felt the gaping void in his life.

He needed her in so many ways. She was attractive in all the ways a man found a woman attractive, but most of all, seeing each other at their best and their worst, in addition to falling in love with her, she'd become his best friend.

They had no future together. She was bound to her job as a teacher, working days and off weekends, and he was limited to the hours of his trips, leaving evenings and away all weekend.

He stared out into the night from his apartment's balcony.

Across the inlet, the lights of downtown Vancouver glowed. He could see the pointy sail-shapes on the roof of the Canada Place convention center, lit brightly from below. High in the city, the Harbour Centre towered high above most of the other buildings, showing off the odd shape of the revolving restaurant on top, topped by the spire to make it even taller in the Vancouver skyline. The many office towers only showed about half their lights on, being a weeknight and already past midnight. To the right of downtown, Stanley Park was pitch black, but from the park, headlights of moving cars streaked over the Lion's Gate Bridge in little white lines, which was the way he'd come home, into North Vancouver. From directly below him, honking horns and the roar of the odd car echoed upward from Marine Drive, even up to the twenty-fifth floor.

Lionel had always found peace in watching the city from a distance, keeping himself separate and untouched by the commotion of life below. Tonight it only made him feel lonely.

He slid the patio door closed behind him. In the quiet of his small kitchen, he began the last untouched chore—digging through what had accumulated in the company mail slot in his absence. He found the usual forms questioning his handwriting on a few log entries, fuel bills, and a warranty reminder. At the bottom of the pile, he found a tape.

Lionel picked it up. A Post-It note attached identified it as being from Gwen, put there when she'd just begun her second trip out, the day of Chad's breakdown in Snoqualmie. On her first trip she'd promised him a tape of the sermon they'd talked about over the CB radio. Since she hadn't expected to see him, she'd tucked it in his mail slot for when he got back.

The label identified the topic as "Friendship—God's Way."

He slipped the tape into his cassette player but couldn't press the button to listen to it. Lionel knew it was going to describe someone he'd just left, someone he wanted to share his life with, but by the nature of their lifestyles they would seldom cross paths, until they drifted apart forever.

He didn't listen to the tape. He crawled into bed and stared at the ceiling all night.

⋙≫

Gwen stared at the pile of books for the courses she'd be teaching in the coming school year.

Very gently she touched her earrings. The earrings Lionel had given her in Topeka. She hadn't taken them off since she'd been home.

She studied her class list for the coming year. As their teacher, she had always thought she would make an impact on all the young lives she touched. But now, looking at the names, even knowing that some might, one day, remember her fondly in years to come, in almost all cases she was just another ship that passed in the night. Once they left her classroom, she would never see them again.

Gwen fingered the earrings again. She hadn't seen Lionel for nearly two weeks, the longest two weeks of her life. She'd received many E-mails, loaded with typing errors and apologies for them. Many he signed with his CB handle, The Lion King. They were all bittersweet. She didn't want to read his words, she wanted to hear his voice. In person.

She'd made the biggest mistake of her life when she agreed to keep driving with him. While she'd enjoyed their time together, the love between them had blossomed in a way neither of them could have foreseen. Yet they never talked about it. They were both too aware that it couldn't last. When he'd kissed her good-bye at the door two weeks ago, it was more than saying good-bye to the man she loved. She was also saying good-bye to her best friend. Ripping off her right arm couldn't have hurt much more.

Gwen reached for the phone. She wasn't doing herself any good by dwelling on it. Instead of getting herself even more depressed, Gwen needed to talk to someone, and the person who could best make her laugh was her friend Molly.

At the same second she touched the phone, the doorbell rang.

She opened it to see Lionel standing in the doorway, holding a single red rose. "I've missed you."

Gwen's throat clogged. She could barely choke the words out. "I've missed you too."

She didn't ask if he wanted to come in. She didn't need to. Gwen put the rose in a glass of water, and they sat together on the couch.

Lionel grasped both her hands. "There's something I have to tell you. I'm going to sell the truck."

Gwen's stomach knotted. Driving a truck was all he'd ever done. It was his life, and he loved it. If he'd just discovered a fatal medical condition that was forcing him to quit, she didn't know what she would do. She struggled to speak past the tightness in her throat. "Why?"

"These last two weeks have been the worst of my life. I can't do this anymore. Not without you."

She couldn't think of a thing to say. She opened her mouth to tell him that she had been miserable without him too, but he touched his index finger to her lips. "Please let me finish. I've thought a lot about this, and it's not a decision I've made lightly."

Gwen nodded and he lowered his finger.

"I can't leave you for days and weeks at a time. These last two weeks have been. . .well, not good. I can't live like that indefinitely."

She opened her mouth to tell him she would never be unfaithful, but he spoke before she could say a word. "You promised you'd let me finish. I know what you're thinking, and you're wrong. You're nothing like Sharon. I know you won't find someone else while I'm gone. I don't want to stop driving because I don't trust you. It's because I miss you too much, and driving just hasn't been satisfying anymore without you."

"I don't know what to say."

His grip on her hands tightened. "I love you, Gwen. Until I find a buyer, I'll still have to drive, but whenever I'm in town, I want to spend all the time we can together. I'll do whatever I can to make this work. If that means quitting driving, then that's what I'm going to do."

Gwen gulped. "Make this work?"

He shook his head. "I'm doing this all wrong. What I really came here to do was to ask if you'd marry me. If it's too sudden, then we'll date and stuff until you're as sure as I am that this is God's will for us, to love each other forever, to have and to hold, for better, for worse, for richer, for poorer. The whole package. I love you, Gwen. Will you marry me?"

Gwen's vision blurred. "I love you too. And yes, I'll marry you. Under one condition. Don't sell the truck."

His kiss was immediate and welcome. When his mouth released hers, he held her firmly in his arms, and she never wanted him to let go.

"I don't care about the truck," he mumbled into her hair.

"Well, I do," she said. "I loved living on the road. But I don't think it's something I could do forever. Like when it's time to have children. About a year driving together sounds good, though."

He murmured her name and buried his face farther in her hair, but otherwise didn't speak.

"I'll take a leave of absence from teaching and drive with you. Uncle Chad says Burt is going to retire in about a year, and he heard Burt mention your name as a possibility for his replacement. Do you think you'd like that?"

He cupped her face in his hands. "Yes, I would. I'd love to drive with you again. But, before you step foot in that truck again, you need more than your Class-One license. You need a marriage license. And then we'll run doubles again."

Gwen grinned. "Really?"

Lionel nodded. "Really."

"Does that mean I get my name painted on the door? You've got 'The Lion King' painted on the driver's door."

"After we get married, that will make you 'The Lion Queen.' How's that?"

"Then that makes the truck 'The Lions' Den.' And then we'll be. . ."

Lionel grinned. ". . .On the road again."

My Name Is Mike

Chapter 1

God grant me the serenity
to accept the things I cannot change,
courage to change the things I can,
and the wisdom to know the difference.

M y name is Mike, and I'm an alcoholic."

"Hi, Mike," murmured the roomful of people.

Mike Flannigan cleared his throat and scanned the crowd. There were about fifty people in the room.

"This is my first AA meeting, and I'm not really an alcoholic. I'm only doing this because I don't have a choice."

Most people in the crowd smiled wryly.

Mike cleared his throat again, not having received the sympathy he thought he should have. "I was forced to be here by my probation officer."

Mike stopped speaking and scowled at Bruce, expecting Bruce to lose his insipid grin. Instead, Bruce turned around to the crowd with a wide smile and waved. A number of the people in the crowd smiled and waved back, more nodded in understanding. Mike couldn't believe it.

He'd seen from the previous two people who stood at the front that nothing was sacred here. Both of them, a man and a woman, had said some very personal things—private types of things that he wouldn't say to his best friend. Yet they'd poured out their hearts to this roomful of people. While it was obvious many knew each other, he could tell many were also strangers or, at best, only casual acquaintances. He vowed he would never expose himself like that, and he certainly hadn't expected the group to welcome Bruce.

"I'm only here because I got caught drinking and driving. I made a mistake, that was all."

Mike hustled back to his chair. The crowd applauded gently, just as they had for the previous speakers. An older man rose and walked to the podium.

"My name is Claude, and I'm an alcoholic."

"Hi, Claude," the crowd responded.

"I'm not going to give you my usual drunk-a-log tonight. Besides, most of you have heard it before."

The crowd laughed.

"I'm going to tell you about my first meeting. I see we have a few first-timers

365

here tonight, and it got me thinking. Maybe because I'm coming up to my seven-year cake."

Everyone applauded.

Mike leaned to whisper to Bruce. "What's a seven-year cake?"

Bruce leaned toward Mike and whispered back. "It's the anniversary of seven years without a drink. They bring a cake to the meeting, and everyone has a piece. It's a small celebration."

Seven years without a drink. Mike couldn't remember the last time he'd been seven days without a drink. Maybe he did drink a little too much, but it was nothing he couldn't handle. He just lost it for one night, and he got caught. That was the only reason he was here.

Claude continued. "I didn't think I had a drinking problem. I was on the brink of losing my job. I stopped getting invitations from my family because I ruined every family gathering. The only friends I had left were drinking buddies, and their friendship depended on when my money ran out. Still, I couldn't go a day without a drink. Then my wife left me because of what my drinking was doing to her and the kids. That's what brought me to my first meeting. I had nowhere to go but up because the next step was straight to hell. Hitting bottom is a different place for each of us, but we all have one. For some it's a job. For some it's money. For some it's personal. The thing that made me stop and take a look at myself was when Michelle left. That was the day I knew I had to change. It was hard, but nothing would have been harder than life in an empty apartment with only a bottle for company."

Claude paused, and the crowd remained silent, respecting Claude as he fought with his memories. "You first-timers, think of today, your first meeting. Life gets better from here. Join a twelve-step group. Get in touch with your Higher Power. Go to meetings often, every day if you have to, and mark today on your calendar. Today is the first day of the rest of your life."

The crowd burst into rounds of applause as Claude returned to his chair.

Mike clapped weakly. Claude seemed like a happy guy. He wondered if Claude had gotten back together with his wife.

Mike listened politely to what the remaining speakers had to say. When the hour was up, he aimed himself for the door. He didn't care if Bruce was behind him or not. He would wait for Bruce in the parking lot. He almost made it out when Claude stopped him.

"So when was your last drink, Mike?"

Mike stiffened. "Yesterday." And he was going to have another one the second he got back home.

"Before you take that next drink, think of what you heard today. I look forward to seeing you again soon." He stuffed a piece of paper in Mike's shirt pocket and turned around to talk to someone else.

Fortunately, Bruce was right behind him, and they headed straight for Bruce's car.

Mike stared out the car window the entire trip home without saying a word. He wondered how Claude knew what he was thinking. He didn't have a wife to lose, and since he would one day take over his father's company, his job was set for life. However, what Claude said about his friends held a note of familiarity. Mike tried to think of a single friend who had stood beside him when he'd been arrested. Not one had made any effort to help him. In fact, some of them had laughed.

Only because of Claude's implied suggestion, he would not drink tonight.

He flicked on the television and parked himself on the couch, but he couldn't sit still. Especially today, Mike felt the absence of a glass in his hand as he sat alone. Rather than dwell on it, he stomped to the bedroom to change and go to bed early since there was nothing decent on television. When he began to unbutton his shirt, a crumple sounded in his pocket. Inside was the piece of paper Claude had given him. Instead of the AA rhetoric he had expected, it was a simple handwritten note.

"Therefore, if anyone is in Christ, he is a new creation; the old has gone, the new has come!" 2 Cor. 5:17

Mike stared at the note. The words "he is a new creation" were heavily underlined.

He stared at the paper in his hand. He didn't need to become new. The old Mike was just fine. What he needed was to get some sleep. He threw the paper on the floor and crawled into bed.

❧

Patricia Norbert picked up the ringing phone. "Hello?"

"May I please speak to Bruce?" a shaky baritone voice asked.

"I'm sorry, he's not home. Is there a message?"

"Do you know what time he's going to be back?"

Patricia checked her watch. The caller's tone made her suspect it was one of her brother's probation cases. Bruce's supervisor was constantly telling him not to give out his home number. If it was an emergency, they were supposed to contact the answering service and the message would be forwarded. Again, it appeared Bruce thought differently.

"Not until late. Is there something you need?"

The voice laughed hesitantly. "I need to ask him for an address."

Patricia frowned. Just like their father, Bruce never discussed personal details of his case histories. However, in this case, Bruce had left a note on the fridge for her because he was hoping for a certain call.

"May I ask who's calling?"

"It's Mike. Mike Flannigan."

Patricia rested her finger on the note. "Can you wait for a minute, Mike? Bruce asked me to let him know if you called."

Patricia pulled her cell phone out of her purse, walked into the living room where Mike wouldn't hear what she said, and dialed Bruce's cell number.

"Bruce? It's Patty. Mike called, just like you said, and he wants to talk to you."

"He probably feels the need for another AA meeting. I had a feeling he might, and that's good. But I can't get out of here for another hour, and the meeting starts before then. The address is on the fridge. I guess he'll have to take a cab because he lost his license. I wanted to take him just to make sure he went, but I can't. Oops. I gotta go."

Patricia didn't know much about Alcoholics Anonymous except for what Bruce had told her. Evidently, the group's history started in 1935 as a Bible study but had been watered down in its spiritual content to include more people who needed help. Although she failed to understand how anyone could let alcohol strip a person's common sense and dignity, she respected any organization that helped people get their lives back together. She also knew that many people found Christ through the AA program.

If Bruce considered Mike worth breaking the rules for, that was all Patricia needed to know. She walked back into the kitchen and pulled the note off the fridge.

She checked the time and picked up the phone. "Mike? Bruce left the address and time right here, but the meeting starts in half an hour. If you have to wait for a cab, you'll be late for the meeting. Bruce thought it was important for you to go, so I can take you. I've got your address. I'll be there in ten minutes." Patricia hung up before Mike could reply. She locked up Bruce's house and was on her way.

As Patricia pulled up to the address on Bruce's note, it was all she could do not to stare at the front of Mike's house. Due to Mike's being one of her brother's cases, she certainly hadn't expected this.

The main story's brick front contrasted elegantly with the white vinyl siding used on the second story. The deep red Spanish villa-style shingles and shutters finished off the stateliness of a beautiful executive home. Tall trees graced the professionally landscaped property, and the driveway, rather than being plain cement, was cobblestone.

Whoever Mike was, Mike had more money than she'd ever have if he could afford to live in the Kerrisdale area of Vancouver and have a house like this.

Patricia knocked. A man answered the door. He was tall, and she guessed him to be in his mid-thirties. He wore his dark brown hair in a short, stylish cut which emphasized his chiseled features. His clothes fit him so perfectly she suspected they were tailor-made. While he wasn't movie star handsome, he was better than average. Patricia wondered if he was ill because he was pale, and his hands were slightly shaky.

She straightened and patted her purse strap on her shoulder. "I'm looking for Mike Flannigan."

His face paled even more. "Are you Bruce's wife?"

"No, I'm his sister, Patty. Are you Mike? I'm here to take you to the meeting."

He nodded and glanced at his wristwatch. "I guess we should go then."

She backed up a step while he grabbed a waist-length leather jacket from eside the door and locked up.

Conversation in the car was stilted, which Patricia could understand because f the awkward situation. When the usual pleasantries were done, she drove to the ddress on Bruce's note in silence.

They arrived at a stately church building not far off Cambie Street. Bruce's nstructions said that the room they were looking for was in the basement, but hey wouldn't have needed further instructions. The noise would have led them to he right room. The cloud of cigarette smoke was another dead giveaway. They rrived with only minutes to spare, so they hurried in.

Once inside, they were welcomed openly. When Patricia greeted newcomers t church, she always asked a few simple questions, such as where they were from nd if someone else had invited them. However, no questions were asked here, not ven their names, which Patricia thought quite odd, but probably suited the Anonymous part of the name Alcoholics Anonymous.

They were shown to the coffee table at the back and told to help themselves uickly before the meeting started. Patricia didn't take any coffee because it was vening, but Mike poured a large cup for himself, and they quickly found two eats together near the back.

A man stepped up to the podium and welcomed everyone present. With ittle preamble, he introduced another man, by first name only, as the first peaker. Mike sat stiff as a board beside her, cradling the Styrofoam cup with oth hands in his lap.

Patricia had some experience with a few of the members of her church fam-ly coming from alcoholic backgrounds, but nothing would have prepared her for he things the speakers said at this meeting.

The first speaker told of how when he was drinking, his wife hid or dumped ll the liquor in the house. She timed him from when he left work to make sure he didn't stop at the bar, yet by the time he arrived home, he'd had plenty to drink, and no one could figure out how he got it. The man now laughed at himself, dis-gusted by how pathetic he was. He had devised a way to store his liquor in the windshield wiper container under the hood of his car and drank on the way home through a tube he'd run to the driver's seat. Now that he'd been sober for a num-ber of years, he could laugh at himself, but he shared with the group that he wished he could be as creative on the job and with his family as he had been when he was desperately finding ways to get enough to drink every day.

A woman told of how she thought drinking with the right crowd would fur-ther her career. She blamed management favoritism for passing her up for every promotion until one day she took a hard look at herself from a hospital bed. In what was supposed to be a dignified moment, she had been so drunk she tripped in her high-heeled shoes and broke her leg. Confined to the hospital for a couple of days, and without access to alcohol, she had time and a clear head to think about the direction her life was going. She discovered that she no longer associated with those who should have been her peers. The right crowd gradually stopped hanging around with her because her personality changed when she drank, until the only people who would put up with her were those she never would have associated with five years ago.

Patricia fought back tears at the testimony of a man who told how his wife finally left him because of his drinking. She had begun the process of a court battle to limit his visitation rights to his children, but for the time, he still had his two teenaged children every second weekend. One day, his daughter, knowing her father was drunk again, decided to walk home alone late at night rather than call him for a ride home, and was brutally attacked. The day he took her home from the hospital was the last day he'd had a drink.

Patricia couldn't understand how people could let their lives be so controlled by drink, but at the same time, she couldn't deny that it happened.

She was pleasantly surprised to hear the meeting end with everyone repeating the Lord's prayer.

At the closing amen, she turned to Mike. She didn't know what it was he had done to have Bruce assigned to him as his probation officer, nor did she know how bad his drinking problem was, only that Bruce thought it was important for Mike to attend this session. As she opened her mouth to speak, her words stuck in her throat. Mike's face was expressionless, hard and closed. He stood quickly, crushing the empty cup as he rose.

"I've got to get out of here," he mumbled.

They had almost made it to the door when an older man stopped them.

"Mike! Good to see you again." The man pumped Mike's hand and patted Mike on the shoulder with his other hand.

Mike didn't respond. His face tightened, and his whole body stiffened.

The man turned to Patricia. "I'm Claude, and I met Mike yesterday at a meeting last night. It's good to see him here." He released the handshake, but one hand remained firm on Mike's shoulder. Patricia could see that Mike was raised to use good manners, because even though it was obvious Mike was not comfortable, he allowed himself to remain captive to Claude's firm hand still on his shoulder.

"I went to a meeting every day for many months when I first joined AA. I knew myself well enough not to risk going home to an empty apartment, because it would only remind me of what I didn't want to face. I knew until I could get a handle on my new life that if I spent night after night alone, I would end up drinking again. Are you two, uh, together?"

Patricia didn't want to embarrass Mike because she didn't know any details of his life, or his case, so she didn't want to tell the man the only thing she knew about Mike was his name and address. "Yes, we're together," she mumbled.

Claude nodded. "It's so noisy here. How about if we go out for coffee, to talk away from the crowd? Mostly, the smoke here bothers me. You don't smoke, do you?"

Patricia shook her head, and she was relieved to see that Mike did the same.

"Good. Let's go to the donut place down the street. I'll see you there." He turned and left before either of them had a chance to decline.

"What do you want to do?" Patricia asked Mike, checking her watch instead of looking at his face. "I've got plenty of time."

"I don't care," he mumbled. "You're driving."

She wondered if Mike was always this surly but chose to give him the benefit of the doubt.

They pulled into the parking lot of the donut shop at the same time as Claude. The girl behind the counter appeared to know Claude well, so Patricia assumed Claude was a regular customer. They were soon seated in a corner booth.

"Well, Mike, I'm not going to ask if you're enjoying your first meetings, because I sure didn't when I first started." Claude paused to chuckle, then poured some sugar into his coffee.

Mike didn't see anything funny. He'd never been so uncomfortable in his life. The only reason he was there was as a condition of his probation. While it was true he probably did drink a little too much, he didn't have a problem. He certainly wasn't an alcoholic—he never drank before lunchtime, and he was no skid-row wino. He had a nice home and a good job, and he never drank cheap booze just to get drunk. He only drank the best. After all, he could afford it. The only reason he felt shaky and on edge was because he was probably coming down with the flu.

"It looks like you've never been to a meeting before, have you, Patty?"

She smiled weakly. "No. Is it that obvious?"

Claude nodded and smiled. "Oh, yes."

Mike looked at Bruce's sister. She wasn't hard on the eyes. She was just what he considered the right height for a woman, about five and a half feet, and she was kinda cute. He figured she was about thirty. Her light brown hair was slightly wavy and hung loose, accenting her wide eyes and pouty little mouth. What he liked best was her blue eyes, large and expressive, taking in everything around them in wide-eyed fascination. She was different from the other women he knew. Patty Norbert's expressive eyes hid nothing. He could tell she had been frightened by the more aggressive people in the meeting room, and most of all, she obviously felt out of place. It was as if she had the words "I don't belong here" stamped across her forehead.

Most of the women he'd seen at the meetings had a hard-bitten edge to them, which he could understand. It seemed a good number of the people there had been through a major trauma or had some kind of hard-luck story, which was why they were there. Patty had been even more uncomfortable than he was, and it bothered him that she had been put in that situation because of him.

Mike lowered his head and stared into his cup. At any other time, he could have appreciated getting to know a woman, but tonight all he could think of was the things he'd heard.

"What brings you to AA, Mike? Last night you said you got caught drinking and driving."

Mike looked up at Claude and Patty, both of whom were studying him. He could have easily snowed Claude, but since his connection to Patty was through her brother, his probation officer, she would know there was more to the story.

He looked straight into Patty's eyes, her beautiful blue eyes—innocent eyes. He didn't know why she had come with him, but he didn't want her there. If Bruce couldn't accompany him to any of the mandatory twice-weekly AA meetings, he would rather go alone.

"It's a condition of my probation. I'm going to use it as part of a plea bargain when my court case comes up."

He noticed she blinked and stiffened. That was good.

"I had a little bit too much to drink one night, and had an accident. I didn't want to take a Breathalyzer test, so I took off, but they caught me. It's just a first offense. My lawyer told me that I'll probably get off with a slap on the wrist or a very short sentence if I behave and go to AA meetings like a good boy."

Her eyes widened even more, and a light gasp escaped. "You drove away? What if the people in the other car were hurt?"

Mike stared down into his cup. It hadn't bothered him at the time. All he'd thought about in his drunken state was his own skin. But now that it was over, the guilt was starting to get to him. "It was only one guy in the car," he muttered, not looking up. "He wasn't hurt too badly. I found out he only had a broken arm or something." His lawyer had told him the man couldn't work for a few months because of that broken arm, but Mike figured it wasn't so bad. It would be a little vacation, paid for by the man's insurance, and he'd be getting a new car out of the deal.

Patty said nothing, which was fine with Mike.

Claude didn't even blink. "So you've been charged with DWI and leaving the scene. What did your friends say?"

He stared up at Claude. "Nothing. It's not their problem. It's mine."

"Nice friends you've got."

Mike didn't want to think of his friends and how much they'd let him down. None of them would lend him the money to make bail, and they were all too drunk to come and pick him up from the police station. He'd had to call his dad, who wasn't pleased to have his thirty-three-year-old son call in the middle of the night, getting him out of bed to go down to the police station to pay his bail.

Tonight, when he needed someone to talk to after all he'd been through, most of his friends chose, instead, to go to the club like any other night. The rest of them had gone to Trevor's house where they could get drunker quicker and partake of substances they couldn't be seen using in the bar. He wasn't in the mood for that, especially not so soon after someone had been hurt because of him. For awhile he had been tempted, but a comment he'd heard at the first meeting stuck in his mind—that drinking had become the most important thing in the speaker's life. Mike had been reaching for a drink at the time that he recalled the comment.

It made him think, maybe he did have a bit of a drinking problem. That was why he'd called Bruce to take him to another meeting. The conditions of his probation stated a minimum of two meetings a week. Bruce had encouraged him to do more. Last night Claude had said he'd been to a meeting every day when he first started going.

He gulped down the last of the coffee, then thunked the cup on the table. "I can handle this on my own."

As soon as the words left his mouth, he knew he'd made a mistake. A change came over Patty. The shock in her face softened, her eyes widened, and her mouth opened slightly in the saddest expression he'd ever seen. She felt sorry for him, and that was the last thing he wanted. He didn't need anyone to feel sorry for him. He had gotten into this mess himself, and he was going to get himself out.

Thankfully, he didn't have to say anything. Claude also lowered his cup to the table and checked his watch. "This has been good, but I've got to get up early for work tomorrow. What about you two?"

Patty checked her watch as well. "Yes, I work as the secretary for our church, and sometimes my hours are flexible but not this week. I've got to be in early tomorrow morning."

Mike stood. "I've got to be at work in the morning too." He wasn't going to tell them he worked for his father's company, and he showed up for work at whatever time he got himself together in the morning. He was the office manager, and it was no one's business what time he got there.

They left together, and Mike followed Patty to her car. On the way home, they passed a large church, which she pointed out was where she worked. He'd known a few people who went to church over the years, but he'd never met someone who actually worked for one.

This time, they actually talked during the drive home. He found Patty pleasant and easy to talk to. He'd meant to shock her with the reason her brother was his probation officer, but now that she knew, she wasn't judgmental, nor did she turn her nose up at him. She just talked to him like everything was normal.

Mike needed normal. All his friends were laughing at him for being stupid and getting caught. His family, especially his father, was furious, and even though Mike hated to admit it, rightfully so. At work, he knew everyone was whispering behind his back. He didn't like to admit it, but it hurt.

Too soon, they were parked in front of his house. He politely thanked Patty and went inside. She'd been nice to give him a ride when he needed it and, after all the awkwardness was over, she'd been quite pleasant to talk to. Most of all, she hadn't snubbed him or talked down to him like he was a low-life, being one of her brother's cases. He appreciated that right now more than she would ever know.

Since Mike would never see her again, he wouldn't have the opportunity to thank her properly. Therefore, Mike decided to send her flowers in the morning. He didn't know where she lived, but he did know where she worked.

Chapter 2

Patricia sat on the secluded park bench, enjoying the warm sunshine. She smiled as the little brown squirrel snatched the piece of bread from her fingers. It ran a safe distance away and held the morsel between its tiny paws. While it ate, it kept a watchful eye on everything around, trusting nothing, not even her.

Just like Mike.

Patricia sighed. She couldn't get him out of her mind.

She turned her head briefly to glance at the church. She always enjoyed taking her lunch break outside at the park next to the church, but today she needed the escape more than ever.

He'd sent her flowers.

She'd often received flowers for special services and banquets and set them out, but no one had ever delivered flowers specially for her.

The only thing on the note was the word "Thanks," and his name. She wasn't sure if it was a simple thank you for the ride, or for something more.

He'd said almost nothing to her until Claude took them out to the donut shop and asked Mike for details as to why he went to the meetings. She knew Mike's answer was meant to intimidate her and make her back off. She'd been in ministry long enough and counseled enough people to know what he was trying to do.

What had surprised her was the way he'd responded to her in the car during the drive home. She'd only meant to be friendly, recognizing that he felt abandoned by his friends and family. She'd kept the conversation light and carefree, and he'd responded. After he began to relax, she'd asked him a few questions and listened to his opinion, to show him that he had value as a human being. Once he let his guard down, he'd been very pleasant to talk to. She'd actually enjoyed their conversation.

Apparently, when he wanted to, Mike could be quite charming. If it hadn't been for the fact that she knew he had a severe drinking problem, and that he'd tried to run from the law in an effort to save his own skin, and that drinking and driving appeared to be a habit of his, and that he had tried to manipulate her, she might have fallen for it. She also had no doubt that he was used to getting his own way.

As interesting as she found Mike, she knew it wasn't smart to get involved in any of Bruce's cases, especially this one. Just like she wouldn't get involved when

her father was counseling someone, unless she was specifically asked, she was n[o]
going to get further involved with Mike, especially since Mike wasn't a Christia[n]
She couldn't miss his disapproval when she told him she worked for the churc[h]
Still, something about him fascinated her, although it was probably because h[er]
heart always went out to those in need, and she could see he needed a friend, bad[ly]

The little squirrel finished his bread and approached cautiously for mor[e]
Patricia moved very slowly so as not to scare him. When he took it, she remaine[d]
bent over, waiting until he was far enough away not to be frightened when s[he]
moved to sit up.

Suddenly, the squirrel darted away. She sighed and flopped back on the benc[h]
She'd thought the little squirrel was becoming more used to her because, unless [it]
rained, over the past few weeks she had fed it almost every day.

"Hi, Patty. Mind if I join you?"

Patricia screeched, and all the bread flew out of her hands. At the same tim[e]
as she turned her head to place the semi-familiar baritone voice, Mike steppe[d]
into her line of vision. He was wearing sunglasses, pleated dress slacks, and th[e]
same leather jacket he'd worn last night, over a pale blue dress shirt. His chee[ks]
were slightly pink from being outside in the breeze, and his hair was pleasant[ly]
mussed. The combination gave him a roguish appeal.

She pressed one hand to her pounding heart. "Mike! You scared me. Wh[at]
are you doing here?"

He smiled as he scanned the ground, noting the scattered pieces of bread. "[I]
needed to go for a walk, and before I knew it, I was here. May I sit down?"

She knew his home was a fair distance away, not what she would call [a]
leisurely walking distance. She wondered how he got there. "Of course you ca[n]
have a seat." She shuffled over to give him room. She knew Mike also had a jo[b,]
yet they were miles from downtown or any industrial estates. She knew he wasn['t]
driving, and again wondered how he got there.

"This is a nice little spot. I went inside the church, but the pastor told me yo[u]
were on your lunch break, and that I'd find you here." He sat beside her, leane[d]
back, rested one elbow on the back of the bench, crossed one ankle over the oppo[o]
site knee, and smiled.

She stared into his face. Even with the sunglasses hiding his eyes, he wa[s]
quite a handsome man. Different from last night, today he oozed confidence an[d]
poise, and he was even more attractive when he smiled.

"I was just feeding the squirrel," she said, looking past the bread on th[e]
ground, and into the trees. The squirrel was gone, and she doubted it would b[e]
back today. She checked her watch. "It's almost time for me to get back to work[."]

At her words, which she had meant only as a hint that she couldn't stay out[-]
side much longer, Mike's expression changed. His smile dropped, he sat straigh[t,]
then slumped. Resting his elbows on his knees, he picked off the sunglasses an[d]
buried his face in his palms. "I'm not going back to work. My dad fired me today[."]

"Oh. . . Mike. . . I'm so sorry."

He shook his head, not removing his hands from his face, his sunglasses dangling from his fingers. "I shouldn't have come here, but I needed someone to talk to."

Her heart went out to him. If he had come to her, a virtual stranger, then she would stay with him on the park bench and let him talk. If she was late getting back to work, she knew her father would understand. She knew Bruce would also understand her involvement, since it was Mike who had sought her out, not the other way around. She could always do the church bulletin tonight, or come in Saturday to finish it, although she hated leaving things until the last minute. However, people were more important than the bulletin. She waited in silence to let Mike continue when he was ready.

"I don't understand. Dad has always stuck up for me and helped me out before. He paid my bail and made arrangements to have my car released from the impound yard. Now, since I can't drive it, he also arranged to have it fixed. Everything was fine, just like usual. But today, when I told him I went to another AA meeting, and without my probation officer this time, he changed. He told me what a disappointment I was, and that my services were no longer required. He told me to clean out my desk and get out."

He paused to draw in a ragged breath. "You know the first thing I wanted to do? My first thought was how bad I wanted to go home and have a drink. I was desperate for the quickest way to get home. Then I caught myself. My first meeting, one of the speakers said he knew he had a problem when he admitted that the most important thing in his life was getting that next drink. That's all I could think of. The quickest way to go home and drink myself into oblivion. So I came here instead."

Patricia sat still, watching Mike, and thinking. If she understood correctly, his father's company was apparently quite large and successful, judging from the way he was dressed and the exterior of his expensive home. From what Mike had said yesterday, this was the first time he'd been arrested, but from his comment about his relationship with his father, it sounded like this was not the first time he'd been in trouble.

In her experience with counseling, she'd seen many times when a parent or spouse, by excusing wrong behavior, covering it up, and even making excuses for it, unwittingly encouraged it to continue. She suspected Mike's father was such a person.

However, she couldn't understand why Mike's admission that he had started going to AA meetings would cause the support to stop. In what seemed an ongoing pattern, Mike finally admitted to having a problem and was actively doing something about it, even though it had initially been forced on him as a condition of his probation.

Patricia thought it was a tremendous step forward for Mike to want to talk about going to the meetings, now that he admitted he needed help. Help he apparently wasn't going to get from his friends or family.

"Do you believe in God, Mike?"

He sat up and looked back at her, squinting in the sunlight. "Yeah, I believe in God," he mumbled. "I've even been to church a number of times with, uh, well, someone I used to know."

"Going to church isn't the same as believing in God."

"I said I believed."

"But in what? Look at all of this." She swept one hand through the air, encompassing the serene park with the stately church building behind them, the magnificent trees in front of them, and the beauty of the brilliant blue sky above. "Acknowledging that a supreme God created all of this, as well as you and me, and knowing it up here," she tapped her index finger to her head, "isn't the same as knowing this same God loves you, no matter what you've done. You've got to know it in here." She pressed her palms to her heart. "God loves you enough to have sent His Son, Jesus, to take the punishment for your sins, and the slate can be wiped clean. That's what you've got to believe. God can help you overcome this, if you let Him."

Mike blew out a breath of air tersely between light lips. "What is this? *Touched by an Angel?* Should I call you Monica? Are you going to start glowing?" He put his sunglasses back on and scowled.

Patricia sucked in a deep breath and let it out slowly. She refused to let his sarcasm affect her. He was hurting, so he was striking out at her in a misguided attempt to deal with what was happening to him.

"You blew it, Mike, and you blew it real bad. Now you've got to do something about it."

"Well. That was certainly what I came all this way to hear."

Patricia crossed her arms over her chest. "You know that it's time to take a good look at yourself and do something before you ruin your whole life."

"Thanks for the encouragement."

"I'm telling you this as a friend, Mike."

"My friends would feel sorry for me, not rub my face in it."

"I'm not rubbing your face in it. If I saw one of my friends starting to get involved in something wrong or harmful, I would say something. I trust that if I started to do something bad, I know many people would say nothing, but my real friends would tell me I was doing something wrong, even though I might hate them for it. They would try to steer me in the right direction, no matter what the cost, and I'd do the same for them. That's true friendship."

"Is this your way of saying you want to be friends?" His face brightened. Mike straightened his shoulders and shuffled closer on the bench. He removed his sunglasses and smiled so that one corner of his mouth tipped up a little more than the other side. Patricia's breath caught. His utterly masculine appeal and the teasing winkle in his eye would have most women melting at his feet.

Patricia wasn't falling for it. The stakes were too high. Mike needed someone to push him in the right direction and to keep him out of trouble while he reevaluated his life and allowed himself to be touched by God's love.

She cleared her throat. "Yes, I think we can be friends."

He reached forward and picked up a lock of her hair, rubbing it between his fingers. "Or is there something more? I think I see the beginning of a beautiful relationship."

Patricia slapped his hand away and crossed her arms. She wasn't playing some kind of foolish dating game, she didn't play hard-to-get, and she certainly wasn't into his macho routine. "Forget it. I meant as a platonic friendship, and you know it. One false move and it's over. *Capiche?*"

"*Capiche.*" He grinned, which made her doubt his sincerity, but she had to take him at his word, such as it was. "How would you like to cement our friendship by going out for dinner with me? Just to talk. Then maybe we can go out somewhere afterwards. It's Friday night. I never sit home alone on Friday night. You wouldn't want to be the one to cause me to fall into temptation and start drinking, would you?"

Patricia narrowed her eyes. "I'll join you for dinner, but don't read anything into it. If we go out anywhere else, it's going to be to another AA meeting."

His smile dropped to a frown. "You're kidding, right?"

"Wrong. If you want to go out for dinner, fine, but only if you go to another meeting after." A meeting where she knew they would see Claude. Claude had slipped her his phone number in the parking lot of the donut shop when Mike wasn't looking. After she'd mentioned at the coffee shop last night that she worked for the church, Claude whispered to her that he was a Christian, too, and that he wanted to help Mike. Between Bruce and Claude, Mike would be in good hands. Tonight, however, it was up to her to take Mike to the AA meeting, because she knew Bruce had a committee meeting.

He smiled again. "Okay, you win."

Patricia stood, being very obvious about checking her watch. "One more thing. I'm way behind since I'm so late getting back from lunch. If you really want me to join you for dinner, you've got to do my filing." She smiled as sweetly and convincingly as she could.

He leaned back on the bench, crossed his ankles, and linked his fingers behind his head. At his broad smile, a dimple appeared in his left cheek. "You're kidding, right?"

"Wrong. If I'm going to get out on time, I need help. Besides, unless you call a cab, you don't have a way of getting home. You're stuck here until I take you home, so you might as well do something constructive."

"The pastor won't mind?"

"He won't mind at all." Above all, she couldn't let Mike go home, at least not yet. Her father would understand that Mike needed something to do to keep his mind off his troubles until he got a handle on things. "You can start by doing some photocopying, then sort and file clippings and notes for future sermon topics, and then you can file the week's receipts."

He shrugged his shoulders and thankfully followed her inside without protest.

※

Mike dutifully did what he was told, but he watched Patty constantly out of the corner of his eye.

The woman was sharp. Usually he had women eating out of his hand by now, but not Patty. He knew this time he wasn't exactly a prime catch, considering the reason they'd met in the first place. She made it more than plain he wasn't going to win her heart by playing for sympathy. Not that he wanted her to feel sorry for him. That was the last thing he wanted.

The first time he met her, he thought she was shy and reserved, but when he met her on her own turf, she stood her ground and called it like she saw it. More than anything, she made him think.

He tucked the last receipt into the folder and closed the filing cabinet drawer, then stood back to watch her work. The woman was organized and efficient but at the same time, warm and friendly when she answered the phone. Likewise, she radiated sensitivity when someone wandered in to ask a question or arrived for an appointment with one of the pastors or the church counselor.

He could see that everyone liked her. He liked her too. However, the fact that she was his probation officer's sister complicated the issue.

He'd always thought someone who worked in a church would be more subservient, but he was wrong on that one. She could take it and dish it right back. The way she showed up on his doorstep to take him to the AA meeting without being asked should have given him the first indication of what he was up against. He'd always thought he picked up on people quickly, but he could now admit that when he'd met her for the first time, his brain had been too foggy to process everything clearly. She'd only been quiet and demure because she'd been out of her element.

Mike watched Patty, busily typing up the church's Sunday bulletin. She was just as focused at work as she had been at the AA meeting. While at work, all her concentration focused on the papers in front of her. She occasionally glanced up at the computer screen as she typed. Not once did she look at him, as much as he wanted her to.

Mike leaned back, resting his elbows on the top of the filing cabinet. "I'm all done. Got any more urgent and critical tasks for me? Pencils to sharpen? Paper clips to sort?"

She stopped typing and straightened the stack of papers in front of her. "Everything I've given you needed to be done. All jobs, however insignificant they appear, are important."

Mike snorted. "Spare me. I don't give the kids fresh out of school the menial junk you've dumped on me."

She folded her hands and rested them on the base of her keyboard. "Have you always had such a bad attitude?"

"I don't have a bad attitude. You're just bossy."

"I'm not bossy. I'm an efficient adjudicator."

"You're bossy, and you're enjoying it too."

"I didn't give you anything I wasn't prepared to do myself. But now all I've got left is the bulletin, which you can't do." She tilted her mouth and closed one eye, no doubt thinking of some other meaningless task to keep him occupied. Part of him was amused at her attempts to keep him busy, but something deep inside appreciated what she was trying to do, as much as he hated to admit it.

He actually found it funny that it was so easy to figure out what she was trying to do. The woman was transparent. Every emotion and every thought was written on her face. He would bet she never played Poker, because if she did, she would be lousy at it.

"I really don't have any other work you can do, so I'm going to give you something else." She opened her drawer and pulled out a Bible.

Mike cringed.

She flipped it open about three-quarters of the way through and handed it to him. "I want you to start reading. This is the book of Matthew, the start of the New Testament. Start at verse eighteen. Do you have a Bible at home?"

"I said I'd been to church before. I didn't say I was a Bible scholar."

"You don't have to be a Bible scholar to read it. Besides, Bruce told me that the AA program is based on biblical principles, so, therefore, you should know something about the Bible. And that can only happen by reading it."

"I don't believe this," he grumbled.

At her answering scowl, he broke out into a wide grin and held the Bible to his heart. "But for you, I'd do anything."

Patty rolled her eyes. "Give it a rest. This, you don't do for me. You do it for yourself. Now sit down and start reading. I have work to do."

Chapter 3

This wasn't what I meant when I suggested dinner."

Patricia fluttered her eyelashes and smiled sweetly. "But I love this place." She tried not to laugh at his answering scowl. She knew he wanted to go someplace that would have been suitable for a date, so she picked the place that was the furthest extreme from date-worthy she could think of. Sir Henry's Fish and Chip Palace fit the bill perfectly. "I can't remember the last time I had fish and chips." Sir Henry's was less a restaurant and more a combination of take-out and a glorified lunch counter. Most importantly, they didn't serve alcohol.

"There are only four tables and a counter. They don't even have menus. This place is a hole in the wall."

"I like to think of it as cozy."

He grumbled something she couldn't quite make out, which was probably for the best.

"Quit complaining, and let's order. We don't have much time."

They looked up at the menu board, told Henry what they wanted, and sat at a table after Mike insisted on paying, which she knew he would. It was another reason she'd picked Sir Henry's. The food was cheap.

"When Henry calls our number, we're supposed to go pick it up, but he'll probably bring it to our table."

Mike harumphed. "Call our number? We're the only ones in here!"

"Shhhh! Not so loud! Their main business is take-out, but we don't have time to sit in the lineup at the drive-thru today. You must admit the place has character."

Faded red-and-white-checkered curtains hung cafe-style on tarnished brass rods with huge ornate ends, making her think they were the same ones Henry had up in 1973 when he opened the place. The marred tabletops were stained, but always clean, likewise the old wooden chairs, most of which sported different fabrics of different generations on the padded seats. What the place lacked in furniture, it made up for in photographs. Every space on the wall held a framed photograph either depicting the restaurant over the years, such as a faded blown-up shot of Henry's opening day, or some part of Jolly Ol' England, which had been snapped by Henry himself or sent to him by a relative still living there.

Mike rolled his eyes. "Yeah. Right. Character."

Since the place was small, they heard the sizzle of the deep fryer. She didn't normally eat such greasy fare, but she made the exception for Sir Henry's, since the food was so good. "You're really going to enjoy this. I promise."

His scowl turned into a smile. "You know, for some reason, I believe you. I don't know why, but I do."

Patricia chose to accept his comment as a compliment, whether or not that was how it was meant. She smiled, rested her elbows on the table, and said nothing.

Mike studied a photograph of Big Ben, then folded his hands on the table and turned to her. "Before we go any further, I want to apologize. I'm not usually such miserable company. I don't know what's come over me. I can only use the excuse that I'm still trying to sort out what's happened, and I haven't been myself lately. I don't know why I'm talking to you like this. You seem to bring it out in me."

"Honesty is always the best policy."

He shook his head. "Not if I'm trying to impress you."

"You're not supposed to be trying to impress me. You're supposed to be working your way through this and straightening out your life. I can only imagine how difficult this has been for you." She also suspected it was going to get harder before it got better, as that was usually the case when someone started working through such a long-term problem, especially when there was an addiction or compulsive behavior involved. "Besides, your charm is lost on me. I want you to work on whatever it takes to clean yourself up and move forward with your life. All I want to be is friends."

When their dinner was ready, Henry couldn't leave the long line-up of cars at the drive-thru window, so Mike picked up their order at the counter when Henry called out their number. Mike both grumbled and joked at the same time about their still being the only ones inside as he placed the tray on the table, which Patricia thought quite endearing. In a way she couldn't quite figure out, he had a charm about him that naturally made people gravitate toward him. Fortunately, she was immune.

She bowed her head and folded her hands on the table, and Mike followed her lead, waiting as she prepared herself to pray.

"Thank You, Father God, for this day of new beginnings and for Your wisdom as You guide us through the path You've laid out before us. Thank You, also, for this food and for new friends to share it with. Amen."

"Amen," Mike mumbled.

He didn't complain about her praying in a public restaurant, which would have probably been more public if they weren't the only people there besides the owner. Still, Patricia chose to interpret his acquiescence to her prayers as encouraging.

Mike took his first bite cautiously, paused, then smiled. "As much as I hate to admit it, this is pretty good."

Patricia smiled back and agreed. Throughout dinner, Mike playfully complained about everything around them, but she noticed he ate every morsel in front of him.

When she was done, she dropped her napkin on top of what she couldn't finish. "I'm stuffed. We'd better go."

Mike checked his watch. "Yes. I don't want to walk in at the last minute again."

On the drive to the meeting, Mike compared what he saw as every short-coming of Sir Henry's with the finer points of the restaurant he had wanted to take her to. He also made it plain that dinner tonight would have been a date, which was exactly what Patricia wanted to avoid.

Even though she didn't know him very well, she easily figured out that Mike used his natural charm to his advantage. It wasn't hard to see that he knew women in general were attracted to him. She also had no doubt he'd used the same technique to get himself out of trouble. Often.

It made Patricia very much aware of the sheltered life she'd led. Sometimes she appreciated it, sometimes she didn't. In times like this, she did. She knew that men like Mike left trails of heartache in their wake, and she had been spared from the experience so far. At thirty, she had dated before but never had what she would call a serious relationship. She had carefully dated only well-grounded Christian men—never bad-boy types like Mike.

The downside of her love life was that, even though it was unintentional, most men had been intimidated by her father, many having future dreams of ministry themselves. While naturally she could share in their excitement, she often felt used, or set on a pedestal as her father's daughter, neither of which she wanted out of the man who would one day be her husband.

This meeting was also in a church building. Just as they turned into the parking lot, Mike spoke up.

"You know, I really don't know anything about you, other than you work at your church. I guess you also attend there, and stuff."

Patricia smiled. "All my life, except when I went to Bible college."

"Bible college, huh? I guess that shouldn't surprise me. Do you live close to the church too?"

"Yes, I do. But not close enough to walk. If you're wondering why I had my car."

"No, not at all. Just wondering, that's all. The first time I talked to you, you were at Bruce's house."

She couldn't imagine why where she lived would concern him. "I was just borrowing his computer that night because I don't have a scanner. I'm not there often. Come on, we should go in."

"How exactly did you know about this meeting? Did you talk to Bruce? Is he putting a note in my file that I'm here?"

"No, I haven't spoken to Bruce. If you want to tell him, fine, I can vouch for you. Claude told me about this last night in the donut shop parking lot."

Mike's step faltered. "Claude? Do you know him? Does he go to your church or something?"

Patricia shook her head as Mike caught up, and they entered the building together. "Nope. Never met him before last night. I thought you knew him."

It was Mike's turn to shake his head. "I only met him at my first meeting. He slipped me a note with a Bible verse on it. I guess there must be quite a few Christians in the program."

"That's what Bruce says."

Sure enough, they hadn't been in the meeting room long when Claude appeared. Without being prompted, he sat beside Mike, and the meeting began.

As happened at the previous meeting, Patricia listened to everyone share their stories. A couple of people went quite in-depth with personal testimonies, but most of them only grazed the surface of their own stories while they shared words of wisdom with the group. One man in particular had the entire crowd in stitches. His delivery was hilarious, but his real message wasn't funny at all. Despite what had happened in his life, this man named Gerry had a wonderful attitude, and she wondered if Mike would be able to look back on his life some day and be able to laugh like that at the stupid things he'd done.

At the close of the meeting, they remained seated.

Claude slid his chair so it was turned toward both of them. "In a few weeks, it's going to be my seven-year cake, and this is my home group. I would be honored if both of you would be here to share it with me. I'd also like you to meet my wife, Michelle. She's going to be here for the occasion. The only times she comes to meetings is when it's an anniversary cake for me."

Before she had time to think about it, Mike pumped Claude's hand. "We'd love to come, and we're honored to be asked. Right, Patty?"

Patricia hadn't realized people would automatically consider them a couple, yet that was exactly what happened. She wondered how she could let Claude know they weren't as together as they appeared. "Uh. . .of course. . .we'd be delighted."

Claude beamed. "Great! I'll look forward to seeing you there."

Mike didn't smile. "Today I'd swear that some of the thoughts and feelings of some of the people who got up to speak were taken right out of my own head. I've got to ask, if you don't mind telling me, once you went to your first meeting, did you go back and drink for awhile?"

"No, I didn't. Since I went to my first meeting, I haven't touched a drop of liquor."

"Not a single drink? Never? How did you do it?"

"The first thing I did was get rid of all the booze. All of it. Even when Michelle and I got back together, nothing was saved. Not even for when company came over. No liquor in the house, not even for holidays, or any day, after that. Even the bottle of wine Michelle kept for cooking. Everything I had from the liquor cabinet, and especially my secret stash. It all had to go. I knew I had to avoid temptation. Have you done that yet, Mike?"

Mike was silent too long, which gave away his answer. Also, Patricia recalled when he showed up at the church, Mike had commented that it was either that or go home and start drinking, which doubly confirmed her suspicions. He did have liquor still in the house. Patricia poked him in the ribs with her index finger. "He's going to do that tonight, aren't you, Mike?"

"I. . .but. . ."

"Aren't you, Mike?" she asked again.

Mike cleared his throat and stiffened in his chair. "Yes. Of course."

Having received the answer she needed, she turned back to Claude. "What else helped you as you straightened yourself out?" She wanted to ask him exactly when he turned his life over to Christ, but didn't want to further intimidate Mike, who was being uncharacteristically quiet and pensive.

"After I got rid of all the booze, I joined a twelve-step group."

"What's that?"

"It's a twelve-week study on the twelve steps of AA. Every week the group discusses one step, and we all work at applying it to our lives."

Patricia nodded. "Bruce told me a little about that. He said they are all based on Biblical principles."

"Yes. I have quite a few Scripture references in my notes. I've already volunteered to lead the next program. I highly recommend that you do it, Mike. Actually, a few other new members are also interested. So if you want to do it, we can get a group started next week. But you can only do this if you're serious about turning your life around. It will only work for you when you're prepared to really apply yourself. Are you ready?"

Patricia turned to look at Mike. He sat silent in his chair, and his eyes flitted around the room, taking in the people who had shared their testimonies. His gaze stopped on one man in particular, whom it was obvious had been drinking before he arrived.

After awhile Mike cleared his throat. "Yes. I'm ready."

Claude stood, so Patricia stood also, and then Mike.

"Great," Claude said. "Give me your phone number, and I'll start arranging a time and meeting place, and I'll get back to you. If you'll excuse me, I have to go. I have a date with my wife tonight."

Claude grinned and left.

❦

Mike sat in silence the entire drive home, staring out the window.

There had been a man, drunk, at the meeting. He'd never seen anything more pathetic in his life. Going drunk to an AA meeting was like. . .swearing in church or something. It wasn't right.

When he was on his way home after getting fired, he felt like someone was telling him to go see Patty. It was so clear it was almost audible. He'd listened because he knew if he didn't, he was going to start drinking the minute he arrived home. It wouldn't have been long after that, considering the state of mind he was in, he would soon have been too drunk to even stand. Then, knowing his luck lately, Patty would have shown up and dragged him to a meeting, and he wouldn't have fought her.

He would have been just like that drunk at an AA meeting. Pathetic. A loser.

When his father told him that his services were no longer required, the only thing on his mind was going home and drinking himself into oblivion. It had been the first and foremost thing on his mind, until he convinced himself to go see Patty.

He tried to figure out when getting the next drink had become the most important thing in his life.

He couldn't.

He really was an alcoholic.

They stopped in front of his house, so he pushed the car door open and turned around. "Thanks for the ride, Patty, I. . . Where are you going?"

She exited the car and closed the door behind her, so Mike did the same.

"We're going to dump all the booze in your house."

"We?"

"Yup."

Mike didn't move from beside the car, but Patty walked to his front door and waited.

He couldn't remember ever meeting someone so pushy. Only this time, they were on his turf, not hers. He was supposed to be the one giving the orders.

She crossed her arms and tapped her foot. "Are you coming or not?"

He shrugged his shoulders and started walking. He felt numb from his new revelation and probably needed someone to point him in the right direction for a little while, and Patty seemed just the right person to do it. Not wanting to look like he was giving in too easily, he squared his shoulders and forced himself to grin. "Do I have a choice?"

She shook her head. "Nope."

He unlocked the door and punched in the code for his alarm, then hung her jacket in the closet. "Welcome to my humble home."

She scanned the entranceway, noting the marble tile, ran her hand over the carved wood on the door. She then tilted her head to look up the spiral staircase leading to the loft. "Nice place."

"Thanks." The house was clean and tidy, but that was only because the house-keeper had been there today. Since he no longer had a job, it looked like he would have to clean up his own mess for awhile.

"We might as well get right to it. Where do you keep everything?"

He led her downstairs to the rec room. First her eyes widened at the sight of his home-theater television, then she turned her attention to the recessed bar, taking in the colored lights reflecting in the mirrors behind, and then the tooled wood of the bar unit itself, which was the focal point of the room. He'd built the bar with his friends and had spared no expense, including the mahogany top and custom-built leather stools.

Without saying a word, Patty gathered all the bottles on display and started pouring everything down the sink. She didn't miss a beat, pouring all the contents of every bottle without first reading the labels, nor did she check how much was actually in the bottles before she started pouring. One bottle's seal hadn't even been broken. Without hesitation, she cracked the seal and dumped it too.

Mike tried not cringe when she picked up his bottle of the most expensive whiskey money could buy and poured the golden liquid down the sink with the rest. Next she opened the bottom shelves and dumped out everything else she could find.

The strong smell of sweet liquor permeated the air. Strangely, it turned his stomach.

He stared at his bottles lined up on the bar top. He counted an even dozen empty bottles. His mind went blank. It was all gone, every last drop. A woman he barely knew had just poured hundreds of his dollars down the drain.

She ran the water to complete the process. "Where's the rest?"

He spoke before he realized what he was saying. "In the linen closet."

"And the linen closet is. . .?"

Mike shook his head. He couldn't believe he'd told her, but he recognized that it was for his own good. He walked upstairs in a daze, straight to the linen closet where he reached behind the pile of towels and pulled out his secret last bottle.

Fortunately, she didn't question why he kept a bottle hidden when he lived alone. He wasn't sure he knew the answer.

Without a word, she marched into the kitchen and dumped it down the sink. "I'll take the empty bottles home and put them in my recycling bin for pickup, so you won't have to handle them again. What can I put them in?"

Woodenly, he found a few empty grocery bags and followed her as she returned downstairs to the rec room. He watched as she put the bottles, one by one, into the bags.

The sound of clinking glass cruelly nagged at him as she picked everything up, reminding him what had just happened.

It was gone. Everything was gone.

He couldn't keep the sarcastic edge out of his voice, and he didn't care. "You enjoyed that, didn't you?"

She sighed. "No, I really didn't. It was such a waste. But Claude was right. It's for the best."

Mike bowed his head and pinched the bridge of his nose with his thumb and index finger. "I'm sorry. I didn't mean that. I know you're only trying to do what's best. I appreciate it, even if you can't tell."

The glass in the bags she was holding clinked again as Patty moved. "I think it's time for me to go."

Something in his chest tightened, gripping his heart like a vise. It was too early for him to be home alone. Nothing was on television. He didn't have anything to do. Just the thought of her leaving sent a stab of dread through him.

He rammed his hands into his pockets, but he couldn't keep still. He shuffled his feet, then stared at the empty shelves behind the bar.

This was it. He really had no choice. He was completely cut off. He had nothing unless he walked or called a cab to go to the closest bar for a case of beer, since by now all the liquor stores were closed. He could call one of his friends to bring him something if any of them were home and not already at the club. But he didn't want to drink. He couldn't. He didn't want to see his friends, because by now they would all have consumed their share of alcohol. He would be the only one not drinking.

"Please. Stay."

"Stay? But. . ."

He opened his mouth to speak, but nothing came out. He didn't have any right to further inconvenience her. For the past three evenings, he'd kept her from her normal routine and her own friends, friends who were no doubt upright and respectable, friends who would never walk on the wrong side of the law, friends who probably didn't drink anything stronger than tea and liked it that way.

He wondered what her friends were like. He knew that she'd been raised going to church, then after graduating from high school, she'd attended Bible college, and right after that, she'd gone to work for her church. He suspected that everyone she knew, both friends and family, were Christians like her.

Mike had only ever known one person who was a Christian. Robbie was different from anyone he'd ever met—so different that for awhile he thought he'd been in love. He'd even asked her to marry him. Because she went to church, and he did believe in God, he'd attended church with her. But organized religion wasn't for him, and he quit going after a few months. He'd convinced Robbie to stop going, and hoped to keep it that way, but every once in awhile, she asked him to go back, which he didn't want to do.

In the end, his interest strayed to someone he thought more his type, someone who had no interest in anything to do with God or church. That hadn't worked out either. Since then he'd dated a lot, but as soon as a woman looked like she was getting too serious, he ended it.

Of course, frequently women only went after him for his money, but he expected that. It went with the territory, and he treated them accordingly. Whenever he broke up with a woman, there were never hard feelings, and life went on. It was all for fun, usually on both sides. For the last few years, all his relationships had been shallow, and he hadn't been drawn to any woman in particular.

Until Patty. She was special. He liked her. She was tough and confident, but at the same time, sweet and innocent. She lived what she believed—standing up for what was right according to her God, no matter what. She had convictions. Strength. But at the same time, she was every inch a woman, tender and delicate. For the first time in a long time, he felt drawn to her by something he couldn't name, but it wasn't right. The woman was pure and wholesome, raised in a sheltered environment, and she chose to keep living that way.

He was none of the above. He'd been a wild and spoiled teenager, and he hadn't settled down much as an adult. He did what he wanted, when he wanted, the way he wanted. He lived to excess. But now, everything he'd done had caught up with him in one way or another. He'd broken the law and finally been caught. Because of his carelessness and disregard for the law or safety, someone had been hurt. Up until recently, he hadn't cared about anybody but himself.

Worst of all, there was no way to hide the severity of what he'd become from Patty, because she was his probation officer's sister. What she didn't already know, he had a feeling she would soon find out.

Then she'd hate him, and he'd deserve it.

Patty checked her watch. "All right," she said. "I'll stay, but not too long. I have a ladies' breakfast in the morning."

Chapter 4

Patricia wasn't sure if she was doing the smartest thing by staying, but she didn't know what else to do. She couldn't tell what was going on in his head, but something was happening in there, and she didn't think it was a good idea to leave him alone.

Mike smiled weakly. "Can I get you something to drink? I might have some tea or something here somewhere. I've got lots of mix, er, soft drinks in the fridge."

"Thanks for asking, but I'll pass."

She followed him upstairs into the living room where he flipped on the television, a newer, large-screen model, and sat in the center of a giant, well-stuffed couch. The room was well decorated in tones of blues. Everything was color coordinated, including a framed painting of a horse in a ranch scene hanging above a black gas fireplace, accented with polished brass. It was definitely masculine, yet comfortable.

Patricia sat in the armchair across from him. "You have a lovely home." She couldn't understand, though, why anyone living alone would need two televisions.

"Thank you." He laughed quietly. "I have to tell you, I seldom use the living room. When my friends come over, we usually head straight downstairs into the rec room, after everyone raids the kitchen."

She didn't know whether she should feel honored for the special treatment or bad for him, since it was also possible the only reason they were in the living room was that he felt too awkward about going down to the rec room after watching her dispose of his liquor. Over the years, she'd known a few people who had quit smoking, and a part of the addiction was the breaking of bad habits and lifestyle patterns. She imagined that quitting drinking had many similarities.

"So after you have your breakfast with the ladies tomorrow morning, what are you going to do?"

"I'm going out shopping with a friend. What are you doing tomorrow?"

"I have no idea, but I guess I'll think of something. Maybe I'll head to the shop and see how they're coming on my car."

As the hour passed, they watched a sitcom on television in comfortable silence. At the end of the show, Mike politely thanked her for staying. She gathered up the bags of empty bottles and went home.

⁂

Patricia settled into the passenger seat of Colleen's car, pushed her back into the chair, stretched her aching legs, wiggled her toes, and groaned. "I can't remember the last time I've done so much walking. My feet are killing me!"

"But it was worth it! Look at all the great stuff we bought."

"You mean the great stuff you bought. I only bought a new soap dispenser for the church."

"But it's a great soap dispenser." Colleen started the car. "I think your purse is ringing."

A muffled ring sounded. "It's probably Mom wanting to know if I'll be around for lunch after church tomorrow."

As quickly as she could, she dug under Colleen's parcels for her purse and pulled out her cellular phone. "Hello?"

"Hi, Patty. It's me. Mike. Did I catch you at a bad time?"

Patricia gasped and put her hand over the phone. "It's not my mom," she whispered to Colleen. "Excuse me. This might be private."

Colleen turned off the ignition, and Patricia stepped out of the car and closed the door. "Hi, Mike. Is something wrong?"

"No, nothing's wrong. I was just wondering if you could do me a favor. I hate to ask, but none of my friends are available. My car is ready, and they don't want to leave it here outside over the weekend. I, uh, was wondering if you could come here and drive it home for me. I'll pay for a cab for you to get here. It's at Arnie's Auto Repair, just off Main Street."

Patricia checked her watch then glanced over at Colleen. "Actually, my friend was just about to drive me home. She can drop me off there instead."

"Thanks, I appreciate it. See you whenever you get here. I owe you."

Patricia turned off the phone and got back into Colleen's car. "Change of plans. I need you to drive me somewhere. I have to do a favor for a friend."

"A male or female friend?"

"None of your business."

"Ah. That kind of friend."

Patricia stared out the window. Colleen could think what she wanted. Maybe it would be safer for Mike if people thought she was dating him. She would suffer with the well-meaning but erroneous impressions of her love life, which was always a curiosity item around the church circles, but it would lessen the questions. Most of all, she wouldn't betray the confidence of Mike's personal life and the real reason they were together.

Come to think of it, she'd only meant to take him to one meeting. Since the day she met him, she'd seen him every day.

"Going to give me more details? What's he like? Where did you meet him? Does he go to our church? Do I know him?"

Patricia put on her best smile. "Shut up and turn left at the next intersection."

Colleen smiled right back. "I can take a hint."

The entire way to Arnie's, Patricia gritted her teeth, listening to Colleen humming "Here Comes the Bride."

Mike tossed his keys into the air and once again stuffed them into his pocket while he waited alone, outside, beside his car.

His car was fixed, and it was killing him not to drive it. It was the stupidest thing. If he needed a ride, he could simply have called a cab, or, if he really wanted to start thinking of saving money while he was unemployed, he could take the bus.

It wasn't so simple when he needed someone else to drive his car. For a brief few seconds, he'd considered driving it home himself without a license. After all, he'd been cold sober for four days, and he was certainly a good driver. Unless he got a ticket or, heaven forbid, got in an accident, no one would ever know.

Except Patty. As soon as she knew his car was home, she would ask about it, and he knew he couldn't lie to her. He didn't want to disappoint her, and suddenly it mattered more than ever that he obeyed the restrictions of the charges against him. He got himself into this mess, and it was nothing he didn't deserve. He was going to get out of it the right way, with dignity.

Once again, he needed Patty. The only friend he'd been able to get in touch with was Wayne. However, he could tell that Wayne had been drinking. Therefore, he didn't want Wayne to drive his car.

How quickly things changed.

A red compact pulled into the lot. Patty exited and waved, but instead of the car immediately leaving, the woman who was driving hesitated and gave him an obvious going over. Any other time, he would have smiled, waved, and winked, openly flirting with any woman who paid him attention.

This time, he didn't feel like it. He smiled only at Patty as she started walking toward him, and the little red car drove away.

"Hi," he said as she approached. He couldn't keep his feet still. He left the side of his car, walked to her, then took the bag she was carrying from her hand. He smiled brightly and walked side by side with her back toward his car. "I really appreciate this. To show you how much, I want to take you out for dinner."

She shook her head. "Don't be silly. This is nothing."

They stopped beside his car. Before he realized what he was doing, he lifted his free hand and gently ran his fingertips along her soft cheek, slowly brushing away a stray lock of her beautiful brown hair. He didn't drop his hand, touching her chin as he spoke. "It isn't nothing to me, and I know what you're thinking. Yes, I can afford to take you out to dinner. I'm not quite derelict yet. I can easily get another job. I may have charges pending against me, but that doesn't make me unemployable. You deserve a special thank you."

She didn't fight his touch but stared up at him. It was the first time she'd stood so close to him, allowing him to assess her in a different way.

Their height difference was just about perfect. He didn't look down to see what kind of shoes she wore, but at the moment he was about five or six inches taller than Patty. To his way of thinking, that was just right for kissing. He knew she was about thirty, but with her sheltered lifestyle in mind, he wondered if she'd ever been kissed properly. He hoped not, because he wanted to be the one to do it.

She shivered slightly in the cool spring breeze then backed up one step, forcing him to drop his hand. "This is your car?"

He quirked up one side of his mouth in a lopsided smile. "Yeah." Patty had such beautiful eyes. He'd noticed the blue of her eyes when they had dinner together, but he hadn't been close enough to fully appreciate them. He'd never seen eyes such a pure blue without the aid of colored contacts, but she wasn't wearing any. That beautiful sky blue was natural, and especially striking with her brown hair. He'd only ever seen the lighter blue eyes with blonds.

"You never told you had a fancy car. It looks really expensive. I'll bet it's brand-new too."

"Yeah, it's a limited edition, and it is fairly new." Unlike the other times they'd been together, today she wore a touch of eye shadow but no lipstick, although he suspected it had simply worn off. He found it strange that she'd worn makeup to go out with other women for breakfast but she didn't wear it for him. He'd always thought it was the other way around, at least it had been for most of the women he'd known.

He watched as she stared at his car in wide-eyed fascination then ran her hand cautiously over the hood of the low-slung sports coupe. "You trust me to drive this?"

He trusted her with more than just his car—he trusted her with his life. "Of course I trust you, or I wouldn't have asked. I also trust that you won't argue with me, and you'll drive it to where I say I want to go."

"I've been shopping all day. I really don't feel like going anyplace fancy. Besides, I'm not dressed for it."

"Then where we're going will be perfect." He opened the driver's door and bowed with a flourish. Her mouth opened then snapped shut, and she begrudgingly got in.

After he gave her directions and they were on their way, he selected a CD, turned it to a low volume, and settled back in the seat. He'd thought he would feel awkward being a passenger in his own car. Normally, he didn't like being a passenger in anyone's car. The first time Patty picked him up, he felt strange, but the second time, he'd been relaxed. Now, in his own car, he didn't mind her driving at all.

"How did you get my cell number?"

"I phoned your place, but when I got the answering machine, I called the church, in case you were there. I ended up speaking to the pastor. He wasn't going to give me your number, but when I gave him my name, he must have remembered what a good job I did sorting those paper clips, because he gave it to me without hesitation after that."

Her lips tightened, but she didn't say anything. Now more than before, he considered it a mark in his favor to have obtained her cell number so easily.

She pulled into the parking lot. Mike couldn't help but smile when she parked in a spot far away from the rest of the other cars. He always did the same thing to preserve the pristine paint on his car's doors for as long as he could.

She handed him the keys, and he pushed the button for the alarm.

"I can see why you alarm your house, but your car?"

"It's better to be safe than sorry."

He guided her up the steps and escorted her inside his favorite bistro where a table was waiting despite the lineup.

"You made a reservation?"

He shrugged his shoulders and patted the cell phone hanging on his belt. "They know me here."

Unlike the last time they had dinner together, Mike didn't complain about a single thing, even in jest. This time he didn't have the pressure of going to an AA meeting hanging over his head. Also, he wanted to make it up to Patty for being so difficult the last time they were together, because he usually wasn't so hard to get along with, nor did he usually complain so much. His behavior embarrassed him, and he wanted to make it right.

When the waiter asked what they wanted to drink before he took their order for their meals, his usual drink order nearly slipped out of his mouth before he thought about it, it had become so ingrained in his routine. Patty ordered coffee, and before he had a chance to speak, asked him in front of the waiter if he wanted a coffee as well, sparing him the awkward moment.

The warm coffee didn't feel right, so he pushed it aside and concentrated on entertaining Patty. Today she was there as his date, and he treated her as such.

When their meals came, he hesitated when Patty stopped to pray before they ate. This time was different than when they were at Sir Henry's, because the restaurant was crowded. However, either because of the crowd, or out of consideration for him, she made her prayer quick and to the point, and it was over so fast he barely noticed.

He had to admire her. It was important to her to say grace before each meal, even in public, and she was sticking to that. She had not backed down even though she knew he really didn't want to pray. Despite the possibility of his protests, she had done what she considered the right thing, which was to thank God for the meal, not caring that people might stare at them in a public place.

As the evening progressed, it wasn't difficult to make Patty smile. It was important to him that she enjoy herself, and it was easy to get her to do so. Her face was an open book. In the same way he could tell when she was annoyed with him or nervous in an unfamiliar situation, he could also see that she was enjoying herself now, and he was encouraged. He very carefully steered the conversation away from his troubles and anything that might be considered business or to do with church, and simply had a good time.

Mike was extremely pleased when she didn't argue with him about the bill, which was the smallest he could remember, because there was no alcohol consumed with the meal.

He left his credit card on the tray with the bill and turned to Patty while the waiter completed the transaction. "You're certainly a cheap date. We're going to have to do this more often."

Instead of an answer, Patty held her palm to her mouth and yawned, and then her face turned red. "I'm so sorry! I'm really tired after running around all day, and all this good food is putting me to sleep. I have to get up early for church in the morning. We should be going."

Her response didn't do wonders for his ego, but Mike chose to conclude that since she hadn't given him a negative response, they would indeed do this again.

When she pulled his car into the driveway, instead of turning it off, she started searching under the seat and behind the visor.

"What are you doing?" he asked.

"I'm looking for your garage door opener. I assume you're going to want to keep your car in the garage rather than the driveway for the next few months."

He hadn't really thought about it. "Actually, the battery was dead, so it's in the house. I'm sure the limits of not driving don't include moving the car from the driveway into the garage. After all, it's on my own property. Don't worry about it."

They both exited the car, and Mike waited for Patty to come around to his side.

"Can I use your phone book?" she asked.

"Sure. What for?"

"I have to call a cab so I can go home."

Mike stopped in his tracks, and Patty also stopped walking.

"No. Don't do that." He glanced at his car then back to Patty. "Take my car."

"Take your car? But. . ." Her voice trailed off. "I can't do that."

"Why not? I'm obviously not going to be using it."

"You trust me with your car?"

"You're a good driver. Take it."

"I can't."

"I already said you can. You've got to get home."

She looked back and forth between him and the car. "How do you know I won't abuse it, or drive carelessly, or sell it and take off with the money or something?"

Mike laughed. "Just by saying those things, you've proved that you wouldn't."

"But you barely know me."

His mouth opened, but no words came out. It was true—he didn't know her all that well in some ways, but in others, he knew her better than she thought. Dozens of Patty's finer qualities ran through his head as he considered what he could tell her that he already knew about her.

She was kind, yet firm. She'd gone out of her way to be helpful, but at the same time knew where to draw the line. He thought she had a great sense of humor, although at times she bordered on sarcasm, but her sharp wit only proved her intelligence. Her sense of right and wrong was as solid as black and white. He even admired her for her unwavering Christianity, which, by itself, said a lot about her. She was a good leader, although she tended to be bossy, but by being so, she also displayed confidence and a great strength of character, which she would need. After all, he knew how headstrong he could be, and that was what she was up against.

He liked her, and he liked her a lot. He couldn't think of a single thing to say that wouldn't sound sappy, so he stuck with "I trust you."

Instead of the fast comeback he expected, she stood before him with her mouth hanging open. Her confusion only magnified her sweetness.

He wanted to kiss her.

"Well, I guess I should go home. Good night, Mike." She jingled his keys in her hand.

Before she turned around, Mike glanced at his car, then back to Patty. "This is so backwards. I'm supposed to be the one to say good night and drive away."

She shrugged her shoulders. "Life seldom goes the way we think it will."

Mike stepped closer. "Thanks for picking up my car. More than that, I really enjoyed being with you tonight." He'd enjoyed himself more than he had in a long time. They'd discussed nothing important, only relaxed in each other's company, enjoying the moment exactly as it was—simply spending time together. He wondered if this was what it was like to really fall in love.

Patty smiled, sending a warmth through his heart. "Yes, it was nice."

He was hoping for a better summary than nice, but Mike decided to take what he could get. "May I kiss you good night?"

"Sure."

Before he could move closer to embrace her and kiss her properly, she turned her head all the way to the side, tilted up her chin, and tapped her index finger to her cheek.

Mike smiled. If she wanted to play games, that was fine with him. He was good at playing games.

Instead of a quick peck on the cheek, he nuzzled his face into her hair, inhaled the apple fragrance of her shampoo, and smiled as he nibbled and kissed her ear. Very slowly and gently, he rested his hands on her shoulders and moved his mouth to her cheek, brushing gentle kisses closer and slower as he worked his way to her mouth. Gently, he brushed the underside of her chin with one finger, then two, until he was ready to turn her face toward his and kiss her fully.

Just as he was about to claim her mouth, she stepped back, breaking contact except for one hand remaining on her shoulder, preventing him from doing what he wanted.

"Watch it. I know karate. I took a women's self-defense course. Of course, I could always call my brother on his cell phone and tell him to come and beat you up."

Mike let his hand drop from her shoulder. "Beat me up? But. . ." He couldn't imagine anyone asking such a thing of a probation officer, whose job held very rigid restrictions against violence and using unnecessary force. Unless she was speaking of Bruce in the capacity of a big brother, protecting his little sister from unwanted advances. "Not funny," he muttered.

"I didn't mean it to be funny. Good night, Mike."

Mike watched the taillights of his car disappear in the distance. Patty Norbert won this round, but he'd win the next.

Chapter 5

Patricia sighed as she hung up the phone. In the back of her mind, she had hoped that Mike would have shown up at church yesterday, but he hadn't. She didn't want to miss him, but she did.

She buried her face in her hands. She'd almost melted in his arms the last time they'd been together. She thought she was being so smart, offering only her cheek when she knew he wanted more, but he had quickly turned that situation to his favor. She'd given him an inch, and he'd taken a mile. The trouble was, his actions had heightened all her senses. For the moment, she really had wanted him to kiss her.

She wished she knew what had been going through Mike's head. It seemed her inexperience with men was inversely proportional to his experience with women.

Michael Flannigan, Jr., was dangerous.

If it was anyone else, she would simply refuse to see him again, and that would be the end of it. But she couldn't. She had his car.

She had underestimated him.

It would never happen again.

The phone rang again, bringing her attention back to where it should have been in the first place, away from Mike and back to her job, which was the administration of serving God's people.

After successfully dealing with a parent who insisted that her child was too developed for the toddler class, and kept insisting the three year old be moved into the grade one class, Patricia needed a break.

Today was a day that demanded an early lunch break. Nothing would soothe her nerves more than the friendly little squirrel at the park bench, who hopefully had missed her handouts all weekend.

Patricia gathered a few slices of bread along with her sandwich and went outside.

Sure enough, the little brown squirrel appeared not long after she sat down. Just like every day, she leaned over, holding a small piece of bread gently in her fingers, encouraging the little creature to take it from her hand. When he finally approached and took it, Patricia slowly sat back on the bench, picked another morsel of bread out of the bag, and waited for it to finish the treat, all ready to give it the next one.

"Hi, Patty. Mind if I join you?"

Patricia screeched, and the bread flew out of her fingers. The squirrel fled.

"Oops. Did I startle you? Sorry."

Patricia pressed her palm to her pounding heart. "Mike! What are you doing here?"

He shuffled beside her on the bench. "I was just in the neighborhood and thought I'd stop by. It wasn't like I had anything better to do."

She wasn't sure if she was supposed to feel complimented, so she said nothing.

"Cute little chipmunk. I guess I scared it away."

"It's a squirrel. Chipmunks have a stripe down their backs, and their tails are short. A squirrel has a long bushy tail, and they come in all colors."

"I knew that." He grinned. "I was just teasing you. Can I feed him with you?"

"I'm not sure he'll come back, but if he does, you're welcome to try. He's still really shy about taking the bread out of my hand, but we're working on it."

They both sat back on the bench, talking quietly about nothing in particular while they waited for the squirrel to return. After awhile, it didn't, so Mike leaned back, crossed his ankles, clasped his hands together over his stomach, and generally made himself comfortable. The breeze ruffled his hair, and he closed his eyes and sighed contentedly. Just looking at him made her think how much he must have needed this stress break. It was the same reason she enjoyed taking her lunch outside with the squirrel.

"How did you get here?" she asked.

He didn't open his eyes. "I rode my bike. For two reasons. First, I cashed in my membership at the gym to save money, then I thought I'd get some exercise. And I missed you." He opened one eye and smiled. Patricia's breath caught. "I guess that's really three reasons, and they weren't in the right order."

She didn't want him to miss her.

"I see my car in the parking lot. I'm glad you're using it."

"Uh. . .yes. . ." She felt her cheeks heat up. It was a rare treat to drive such a car, because she would never be able to afford such a machine, even if she ever had an inclination to own a car like that. She also wanted to drive it when no one she knew would see her with it, so she figured that taking it to work and back on Monday would get it out of her system.

"Claude called me this morning. He said that special group is starting tonight, and we'll be meeting at his house. I called Bruce, and he's going to come with me to the first few meetings. So I won't be able to see you tonight."

Patricia wondered why he was telling her this, because even if she had plans for the evening, they wouldn't have been with Mike. But still, part of her wanted to know what he was doing, strictly because she was concerned for him as one of Bruce's cases, of course.

He checked his watch. "I think your lunch break is over, it's time for you to get back inside. I'll phone you or something."

To Patricia's shock, he simply stood and walked away. As she gathered up her lunch containers, out of the corner of her eye, she watched him mount a mountain bike that had been set near the side wall and ride off.

Patricia sighed as she sat down at her desk and pulled out the notes her father had made from the budget meeting. It was going to be a long day.

~~~

Patricia leaned forward on the park bench, her hand outstretched. Just as the day before, the little brown squirrel approached slowly. She loved it when it took the bread from her fingers, and now she would have to handle the little creature with patience, until the day it wouldn't run too far away to eat the treats she gave it. One day she hoped she would be able to take a picture of it from close range while it was eating.

When it was mere inches away, it froze.

"Hi, Patty. Mind if I join you?"

Patty screeched, the bread once again flew from her fingers, and the squirrel darted away.

She leaned her elbows on her knees and buried her face in her hands. "Hi, Mike."

"Are you trying to feed that chipmunk again? Do you feed that thing every day?"

"It's a squirrel, and yes, I do feed it every day. I've been working very hard to get it to take the bread from my fingers."

"Oops. Sorry."

She straightened and took a sip of her juice as he slid beside her on the bench. "How did the meeting go yesterday?"

His whole body stiffened. "I don't know how to describe it. At first, it was a kind of a get-to-know-you thing. By the end we're supposed to be pouring our guts out to each other, so we can't be total strangers. Claude opened with a prayer, which was okay, I guess, and then we went over AA's first step, which is 'We admitted we were powerless over alcohol and that our lives had become unmanageable.' It was so strange. We could all relate to each other, and we all could admit that. But it was different to actually say it out loud. Know what I mean?"

Patricia nodded. "Confession is good for the soul. There is tremendous value in verbalizing your feelings to solidify your position in a difficult situation."

He blinked and stared at her. "Okay. . . ."

Her cheeks burned. She hadn't meant to turn into counselor mode. That was Bruce and Claude's responsibility. "Sorry. I sometimes get carried away. There's an old saying that confession is good for the soul."

"What was really different was praying about it. Thinking about it is one thing. Telling someone else is another. But to close my eyes and talk to God about it, well, it's something I've never done before."

She laid one hand on his forearm as she spoke. "You can talk to God about anything, Mike. The best part is, He's always there to listen."

"I guess. Hey! Look. Your chipmunk is back."

Very slowly, Patricia bent at the waist and held out the piece of bread. The little squirrel took the morsel and scampered a safe distance away. They sat in silence watching it eat. When the critter was done, instead of approaching for more, it scampered off into the bush.

"So, what are you doing tonight?"

"This is Tuesday. Every Tuesday I go to a Bible study meeting. Want to come?" She forced herself to smile, but inside, her heart pounded, and she nearly broke out into a cold sweat. She wanted him to come. She would have preferred to talk to him about God one-on-one, but she also knew that he would benefit from a group situation with other believers. Mike believed in God, but at the time, he had been more than a little sarcastic as she told him about God's love for His children. She didn't know how much he participated in the prayer, but he did say he talked to God, which was encouraging.

"I don't think so. I'm not really into that kind of thing."

She tried to hide her disappointment but knew she wasn't doing a very good job when he leaned forward and grasped her hands within his. "Is it important to you that I go?"

Patricia didn't know what to say. It was important. She wanted him to have a right relationship with God, but she didn't want him to begin his journey of discovery because of her. He had to do it for himself. "No, not really."

Silence hung in the air for a short time. She was about to ask about arranging to return his car when he started talking about nothing in particular, just yakking. Patricia enjoyed talking to him so much that she didn't realize the passage of time until Mike checked his watch, announced that it was time for her to get back to work, and left.

He walked away before she realized she had missed the chance to ask him about the car. She wondered if he did it on purpose.

❧

Patricia hit Save and tidied her stack of papers before she went into the kitchen to get her lunch as well as a couple of pieces of bread that she stored there for the little squirrel.

As she sat on the bench to eat, she thought about last night's Bible study meeting, part of her regretting she hadn't been more direct with Mike and specifically requested that he come, and part of her being glad he hadn't been there.

They had covered the story of Jonah, focusing on how much Jonah would have suffered in the belly of the fish. Although it was often hard work to follow God's will, it would have been easier on Jonah if he'd just done what he had been told to do in the first place. Their discussion naturally followed to a more personal level, and a number of the people present shared recent experiences where they felt led to do something out of the ordinary for God and told about how they'd handled it.

She hadn't shared about Mike because she didn't want to risk breaking confidentiality, but the lesson further solidified in her own mind what she was called to do, which was to guide Mike through this trying time and help him build a relationship with Jesus as his Savior.

A movement on a nearby tree caught her eye. Quickly, she returned the uneaten part of her sandwich to the container, ripped off a small piece of bread from her special stash for the squirrel, slowly leaned over, and held it out. The little brown squirrel approached cautiously, then in the blink of an eye snatched the bread from her fingers and ran into the bush.

"Hi, Mike," she called over her shoulder without looking as the squirrel retreated out of sight.

The grass rustled behind her. "How did you know I was coming? I scared your chipmunk again, didn't I?"

"It's a squirrel."

He grinned as he shuffled in beside her. This time he carried a small backpack. He withdrew a sandwich, grinned, and placed it on the bench. "It's not exactly going out for dinner together, but I brought dessert." He removed a couple of store-bought pieces of cake, also nicely wrapped, and put them down with the growing lunch pile.

"Uh. . .thank you."

He unwrapped his sandwich and took a bite, so Patricia also took a bite of hers.

"There is a reason for this, you know."

"There is?" Patricia couldn't remember anything special about the day.

"It's the anniversary of our first meeting. Kind of like the celebration of our first date."

She nearly choked on her sandwich. "First date? We haven't had a first date."

"That's not my fault. So are we on for tonight?"

All she could do was stare at him. After she got home from the Bible study meeting, she'd spent many hours in prayer, agonizing over what to do and thinking how she could show Mike how much God loved him. She had to make him see God as more than simply the Supreme Creator, but also his heavenly Father, who sent His Son, Jesus, to take the punishment for his sins.

As a ministry, she could make no allowances for dating, even if he was her type, which he wasn't. Most importantly, she couldn't risk becoming emotionally involved, because it would jeopardize her mission.

Patricia cleared her throat. "No."

He shrugged his shoulders, but didn't lose the grin. "Oh, well. I had to try. Bruce is taking me to another meeting tonight anyway. I'm not sure I'll see you tomorrow. I've got an interview for a job, and I don't know what time I'll be finished."

"Mike! That's great!"

Before she realized what she was doing, she looked down to see that she had wrapped her fingers around his.

She jerked her hands away, then folded them in her lap. "I have to get back inside soon. We should finish up."

He had the nerve to wink as he bit into his sandwich.

※

Mike sat on the bus, staring out the window. He wanted to hit something.

Hard.

The interview had gone smoothly, until he told them he would need a day or two off in a couple of months when his court case came up. He knew he would probably get off, or if he did get anything, it probably would be only a fine and a suspended license for awhile. At the worst, he might have to spend a few weekends in jail. His father had hired one of the best lawyers in town to defend him. That, plus showing the judge that he was being such a good boy by attending AA meetings without protest, according to the terms laid out for him, plus that it was a first offense, all would act in his favor.

He didn't get the job. Because he was honest about his pending court case, they suddenly became uninterested. If he had said nothing and just taken a couple of days off sick when his court date came up, no one would have known.

They didn't hire him because of that.

And for that, he'd missed having lunch with Patty.

Already he missed her. He hadn't been without her for a day, and he missed her.

He stomped all the way from the bus stop into the house, his big empty house. He threw his jacket on the couch, stood in one spot, closed his eyes, and yelled out in frustration. It hadn't been exactly the job he would have chosen, but anything was better than sitting home alone in an empty house all day, every day.

Mike checked the time and laid his hand on the phone. He wanted to see Patty. If he couldn't see her, he had to talk to her.

He didn't dial. Instead, he thought about what was happening. He had never been so compelled to spend time with a woman. With the odd exception, by now, most women would have been eating out of his hand, and he would be enjoying himself immensely.

But Patty wasn't. He wasn't even sure she wanted to spend time with him at all.

Every time they were together, she seemed to enjoy herself, and she certainly seemed comfortable enough with him. Still, he could tell something was bugging her. It bothered him that she was his probation officer's sister, and it was probably a breech of confidence or crossing into forbidden territory to be seeing her, which meant it wasn't a good idea to get too attached to her.

He couldn't help it. She'd done nothing to encourage him, in fact, just the opposite. She'd refused to go out on a date with him, and she wouldn't let him kiss her properly. She never called him; he had always been the one to either call her or simply just show up when she couldn't get away.

Mike released the phone. He wasn't going to call her, and he wasn't going to show up on her doorstep.

For the first time in his life, he didn't know what to do.

Mike looked at the Bible she'd lent him, still lying on the kitchen counter where he'd left it since she'd given it to him a week ago. He had no idea on what page to start reading, so he didn't touch it.

Since he couldn't think of anything else to do, Mike walked into the living room and sat on the couch. He started to reach for the remote but didn't pick it up. He didn't want to watch television. He had to think.

Any other day, he would be pouring himself a drink and nursing it while he thought about what was bothering him, until whatever it was faded in importance or his brain became so dulled he forgot what he was so worried about in the first place. This time he couldn't, because Patty had poured everything down the drain, which had been a good thing. If there had been anything left in the house, he would have been into it by now.

All he could do was stare at the blank television.

He wanted to phone Patty, to pursue a relationship with her, but he couldn't. She wasn't his type. She was a decent and caring person, putting her time and needs aside to do what was best for others. She deserved better than him. She deserved a man who would treat her right. Looking back on his past relationships, he'd never treated a woman right, and he'd been too self-centered to care.

She was also his probation officer's sister. Not only was he positive he was crossing some kind of line he wasn't supposed to, he wondered what Bruce would do when he found out that one of his alcoholic law-breaking cases had the hots for his sister.

Mike buried his face in his hands. To even think of Patty in such a way was insulting to her. What he felt for her was far beyond physical attraction. But whatever it was, it wasn't right. She was smart enough to know it and to try to keep him at a distance. It was because she was so nice that she wasn't doing a very good job of keeping him away.

On the other hand, Mike couldn't let it drop. She was too good to let go. He just didn't know what to do about it.

Therefore, he did the only thing he could. He folded his hands in his lap, closed his eyes, and for the first time in his life, he prayed to a God whom, up until recently, he had ignored, and hoped that God would listen anyway.

Chapter 6

H i, Patty. Busy tonight?"
Silence hung over the line. Mike held his breath.
"Uh. . .no. . . ."

He forced himself to exhale. He hadn't seen her or talked to her in two days, and he was going crazy. "I was wondering, if you weren't busy, if we could go out for dinner, someplace quiet where we could talk and without the caveat of attending another AA meeting afterwards."

"Uh. . ." Her voice trailed off, and silence again hung over the line.

Mike waited. He wasn't going to beg. It wasn't his style.

"I don't know if that's such a good idea."

He flushed his style down the toilet. He needed results more than he needed to salvage his pride, which was already in tatters anyway. "Please? We'll have a nice time. I know we will, and I'll behave."

"Uh. . .well. . .I guess so."

He pulled one fist down in the air while making a closed-teeth triumphant smile and thinking "Yessss!" in his head. "That's wonderful," he said calmly. "The only catch here is that since you've got my car, you've got to pick me up. But I'll pay for the gas."

"Don't be silly. And about your car, I think it's time I gave it back."

"We can talk about it tonight. How's that?"

"I guess so."

"Great. Can you pick me up at six?"

"Sure. But remember, I have church tomorrow morning, so this can't be a late night."

"No problem. See you later."

Mike smiled as he hung up the phone. It was going to be the best Saturday night of his life.

By the time she arrived, Mike was composed and ready. He shaved for the second time that day and gelled his hairstyle to perfection. He chose a casual black shirt and his black jeans, knowing how sharp he looked in the monochrome ensemble, which would be suitable attire no matter where they went. He grabbed his favorite leather jacket, clipped his cell phone to his belt, and locked up as soon as his car pulled into the driveway.

He picked a suitable restaurant once he saw how she was dressed. Today she wore a loose-fitting jean skirt and a pretty pink pullover top. It pleased him to see that this time she'd applied a little bit of makeup, but her hair still hung loose, just the way he liked it.

The same as every time he joined her for lunch at the park bench, their evening together was pleasant. Since he knew before he asked her out for dinner that she would pray before they ate, he was prepared when she did. After she'd said the expected thank you for the food and friends to share it with, he was very honest in his answering "amen," because he felt the same way.

When they were done, she drove him home, and he invited her in so he could ask a few questions.

First he made coffee, then sat beside her on the couch and opened the Bible she'd lent him to the page he had marked.

"I cannot tell a lie. I didn't start reading where you told me to."

She raised one finger in the air and opened her mouth, but he raised his hand to stop her before she got the wrong idea and became disappointed with him.

"I flipped through and read all the verses you had colored in yellow. I figured if you thought they were important enough to mark up your Bible for, then that was what I should be paying the most attention to."

"That's not necessarily true. When I do highlighting, it's when I'm reading and something has a special meaning to me at the time. Those things aren't going to hit you the same way, especially since this is your first time reading it through."

"What do you mean, reading it through?"

"Reading it cover to cover. Although I had told you to first read the New Testament. I've read the Bible through four times now, four different versions. I have a guidebook that says how much to read in both the Old and New Testaments each day, and it gives a small commentary on those verses. The idea is to read the entire Bible through in one year. It's dated. You start January first, kind of like a New Year's resolution kind of thing, and finish up the same year on December thirty-first. But the very first time I read it, I simply started at Genesis 1:1 and read some every day until I got to Revelation 22:21. I think it took me about five months."

Mike stared at the Bible in his hand, then flipped through the pages. He didn't know much about the Bible, but he did know that Genesis was the first book and Revelation was the last. Not only was it really thick, but he found out the hard way that it wasn't like reading a best-selling novel. Some of the verses he had to reread four times in order to fully comprehend the meaning of a single sentence, and even then, he knew without a doubt that he'd still missed stuff. He couldn't imagine reading the whole thing through, especially different versions in which he knew the wording was slightly different. "Wow. . . ," he mumbled.

"Did you have something you were going to ask me?"

"Oops. I lost my place. It was something about Moses and Jesus."

She laughed. "There are more references to Moses and Jesus in the Bible than I could count. I guess you'll have to reread it and then ask me when you find it again."

He stared at the closed Bible. He'd taken hours paging through it and reading the verses she'd highlighted. However, it had been both interesting and thought-provoking, and he supposed it wouldn't hurt to go through it again. "I guess I don't have much choice."

"It really would be a better idea for you to start where I said, the beginning of the book of Matthew, and read it through. That way, you'll be reading everything in context, and it will be easier to understand."

Mike shrugged his shoulders. "I guess you would know."

Patty checked her watch. "I have to go. Remember, I have church in the morning. You know you're invited if you want to come. It's not like you've never been there before." She smiled, and Mike's heart nearly went into overdrive.

"Yeah. I know," he choked out.

She stood. "Can I borrow your phone book? I have to call a cab."

Mike shook his head. "Forget the cab. Take the car. I'm not using it, and it's getting late. You'll wait a long time for a cab on Saturday night, and I'd feel better knowing you're in my car."

"I really shouldn't."

Mike stood as well and grasped her tiny hands in his. Her skin was so soft, and he didn't often have the chance to touch her. Very slowly and gently, he massaged the tender skin of her wrists with his thumbs, enthralled how such a simple action could move him so much. "You won't take my heart, so please take my car."

"I. . ." Her voice trailed off and the cutest blush colored her cheeks.

Mike smiled. "If you don't take the car and go now, I'm going to embarrass myself and start spouting poetry."

She yanked her hands out of his, walked quickly to the door, then nearly ran outside.

"Wait!" he called out, and ran to catch up to her, which he did as she opened the car door. He made sure to lower his voice so his neighbors couldn't overhear, in case anyone was outside. "I didn't get a good night kiss."

Before she had a chance to protest, he tilted her chin up and brushed a soft kiss quickly to her lips, then backed away.

She looked up at him, her eyes wide. His heart pounded, making him question why, because he really hadn't done anything all that exciting, although what passed between them was special in a way he couldn't name. It made him want to kiss her again, properly this time, but he didn't dare.

"Good night, Mike," she said in almost a whisper, then sank into the car and drove away.

Mike watched until she turned the corner, but he couldn't make his feet move.

He knew where he was going in the morning. Strangely, it wasn't entirely to be with Patty.

He couldn't remember the specifics of a single verse he'd read, but what he had read made him want to know more about the God who created him. Was it possible that God really did love him as much as the verses he'd read had said?

❧

Patricia stood beside her mother as they greeted the earliest of the congregation to arrive and handed each person a bulletin. While her mother chatted with a friend, Bruce and his wife entered.

Bruce pulled a computer disk out of his pocket. "I brought that clip-art you were asking me about."

"Thanks! I really appreciate it. Let me go put it on my desk."

He followed her into the office. "I took Mike Flannigan to another AA meeting during the week. He told me that he'd been to another meeting with you, as well, before that one."

"Yes, that's right," she mumbled as she tucked the disk into the right file folder.

"I left a message on your answering machine last night, just to be sure I copied the right file for you, but you never called me back."

Patricia faltered for just a split second. "Sorry, I didn't get home until late. I must have forgotten to check for messages."

"Oooh," Bruce drawled, then leaned back on the filing cabinet. "Hot date?"

"Not really. I just went out to dinner with Mike."

Bruce froze. "Mike who?"

"Which Mike were we just talking about? Mike Flannigan."

"You went out on a date with him?"

"It wasn't a date. It was just dinner."

"Patty, going out to dinner with a man on a Saturday night is a date."

She muttered a denial under her breath but doubted he heard.

"Okay, I can see you don't want to talk about it. That's fine." He turned his head to gaze out the window and study the parking lot. "I was surprised to see you here this morning. I didn't see your car in the lot."

"I didn't bring my car."

"Is there something wrong with that hunk of junk again? Do you need a ride home?"

Patricia closed the desk drawer and walked toward the door, en route to the foyer. "I haven't made an appointment with the mechanic yet, but for now it's still driveable. Thanks for the offer, but I don't need a ride home. I brought Mike's car." At the beginning of the week, she didn't want anyone to see her driving it, but as time went on, she enjoyed it so much in comparison to her own car that she found herself not wanting to give it up. Besides, the use of it now had become very convenient, since her car needed a trip to the repair shop that she wanted to put off paying for.

Bruce quickly caught up with her, then stopped her about a foot out of the office doorway. "Mike's car? What are you doing with Mike's car?"

"I helped him pick it up after it was fixed, and the right moment hasn't come up to give it back."

"Right moment? How long have you had it?"

Patricia counted on her fingers. "Eight days."

Bruce sputtered and pulled her back into the office then shut the door behind them. "What's going on? Why has he given you his car? Do you know who he is?"

She blinked and stiffened her back. "He's just an ordinary guy who needs a little help to get his life on the right track."

"He's no ordinary guy. He has a history of drinking and I suspect some drug abuse even though this is the first time he's been officially charged. The fact is that he's in big trouble, and I don't think he's taking it seriously. He's rich and spoiled and manipulative, and he eats innocent women like you for breakfast."

She crossed her arms and stared at her brother. "I think you're getting carried away."

"He's bad news, Patty. Stay away from him. I mean it."

Patricia narrowed her eyes. She couldn't believe the way Bruce was behaving. "Aren't you being rather judgmental?"

"I'm his probation officer. It's my job to be judgmental. And I'm his probation officer for a reason. This isn't just a parking ticket. He deserves the charges he's been given."

"Maybe so, but whom I see is not your concern."

"It is when you're wrong. He's not the kind of man you should be seeing. Most of all, he's not a Christian."

"You don't know that."

"Yes, I do. I've seen him in action under pressure. You didn't see him the night he was arrested. I had to go down to the police station in the middle of the night when his rich daddy posted bail. He's not only a drunk, he's an arrogant drunk. Also, I'm not convinced that his performance at AA meetings isn't just an act because he thinks he can manipulate the justice system. He thinks if he shows the judge he's reformed, he can get a lighter sentence. I've seen it before with his type."

She couldn't deny that Mike had a bit of an attitude, but she refused to listen to Bruce insult him any longer. She really believed that Mike was trying. He'd started reading her Bible, even if it wasn't the way she'd told him to do it. It also shocked her to hear Bruce talk that way about anyone, especially Mike. She could understand how his experiences with people at his job would harden him to some degree, but she didn't want to think her brother could be so unforgiving and unwilling to give Mike a chance to redeem himself.

"I can't believe the way you're acting. Aren't you the one who pushed him into going to AA meetings so he could straighten out?"

Bruce dragged his palm over his face. "I'm sorry. I'm not usually like this. You're my sister. I don't want to see you get mixed up with the likes of Mike

Flannigan. I don't want him to take advantage of you or hurt you."

"So far, I'm the one taking advantage of him. Have you had a look at that car he's let me borrow without asking for a thing in return?"

"Don't think he won't. He'll ask for something in exchange when he knows you can't turn him down."

Mike's silly comment about taking his car versus his heart crashed to the front of her mind with a thud. She knew he was only teasing, but still, the remote possibility that he wasn't scared her. "I plan to give the car back as soon as I can, today if possible. But I don't want to hear you telling me who I can and cannot spend my time with. That's my business, not yours."

Bruce's face paled, and he backed up a step. "Sorry," he mumbled, and without further comment, he walked away.

Patricia felt sick. She'd just had a fight with her brother, whom she loved, over a man she barely knew.

What bothered her most of all was that Bruce was right. Mike wasn't her type. Mike was rich and spoiled, and he did have a bad attitude, and she could tell he was a ladies' man. Worst of all, she kind of liked him anyway, although she couldn't figure out why. If all that wasn't bad enough, even though she'd known all along that, according to all the rules, it wasn't a good idea for her to minister to him, God kept throwing Mike in her path.

Therefore, she would obey, and she would do what she could to guide Mike in a path to knowing Jesus Christ as his Savior, if that was what Mike chose to do.

She sucked in a deep breath, absently ran her hands down her sleeves to push out some imaginary creases, and returned to the foyer to chat with some friends who had just arrived.

⚜

Mike held himself straight and tall and walked into the church building. Even though it had been over three years ago, it wasn't like he'd never been to church before. He'd already been to this one a number of times, although it was during the week when it was quiet and business as usual, whatever that meant in a church. However, today it felt different with the buzz of people around him and music in the background.

It didn't take him long to find Patty. Her joyous laugh warmed him deep inside and drew him like a magnet.

He joined the small group she was with and stood beside her. He smiled, quickly nodded a greeting at everyone in the small circle, and moved closer to Patty when she noticed him. "Hi," he said, grinning ear-to-ear.

"Mike! What are you, uh, I mean, it's good to see you here."

He could feel the other women in the group staring at him, which happened often when he joined a conversation already in progress. This time he didn't care to smile back at the other ladies. The only person whose attention he wanted was Patty's.

She looked beautiful. She wore a lovely spring-type dress in a soft, flowing blue fabric and matching shoes. It was feminine and pretty, and it suited her.

"These are my friends, Colleen, Nancy, and Fran. And this is Mike."

He nodded at each as they were introduced. Nancy and Fran politely excused themselves and walked away together, peeking over their shoulders at him one more time before they turned the corner into the sanctuary.

Colleen stayed where she was. She glanced quickly at Patty then back to him. "So you're Mike, the guy with the car."

He would have preferred to be thought of with a more personal connection to Patty than the car, but at least it proved she had talked about him to her friends to some degree. He was glad she hadn't referred to him as the guy with the drinking problem. "Yeah. That's me. The guy with the car."

Patty shuffled her feet. "Maybe we should go sit down. If you'll excuse us, Colleen?"

Mike followed Patty into the sanctuary where she selected a couple of seats near the back.

"I'm so surprised to see you here." Her cheeks darkened. "I mean, not that I'm not happy you came, because I certainly am. I just didn't think you'd come."

"Life is full of surprises, isn't it?"

"How did you get here?"

"I was a good boy and decided to save some money. Instead of taking a cab, I took the bus. They sure don't run very often Sunday morning, so I had to get up really early. I guess I had better get used to it, huh?"

All she did was stare at him. Before she could say any more, the lights dimmed, the volume of the band increased, a man at the front welcomed everyone present, and the congregation began to sing.

Mike didn't know the song, but he followed the words on the overhead screen. This church wasn't much different from the other one he'd been to a few times several years ago.

Everyone sat while the worship leader mentioned a few newsworthy items, including a tidbit about a woman who just had a baby. They paused for a short prayer, everyone stood, and the music continued.

He'd never paid attention to the words when he'd attended services before, but this time he did. The message in the songs was simple and clear. One song in particular centered around grace, about God caring for every one of His children. Mike wanted to listen to the song again, but they moved on to the next one. He made a mental note to ask Patty after the service was over if that song in particular was available on CD.

When the songs were done, the pastor came to the front, welcomed everyone, and directed the congregation to open their Bibles and turn to the right verse.

He felt a nudge, so he leaned toward Patty.

She held her Bible open to the right place so he could read it with her. "Why didn't you bring that Bible I gave you?" she whispered.

"I've seen before how quickly everyone flips through their Bibles during a service. I'd never find the right place before everyone was finished reading it, so I thought I'd just sit back and listen."

The pastor read the verse and then began to expound on it, as well as a few others. The congregation and Patty faithfully flipped to the right verse as soon as he mentioned another reference.

The pastor's voice boomed over the speakers. "John 3:14–15 says, 'Just as Moses lifted up the snake in the desert, so the Son of Man must be lifted up, that everyone who believes in him may have eternal life.' "

Mike stiffened in his chair. That verse was the one that he'd meant to ask Patty about, but he lost his place. He thought snakes were bad things when mentioned in the Bible, yet as far as he could tell, Jesus had just been compared to a snake.

The pastor continued, explaining that what Moses had actually lifted up wasn't a real snake but one made of bronze, and the point was that those who looked up at it as instructed, believing that they would live, lived. Likewise, those who believed in Jesus as their Savior were saved from punishment for their sins because of their belief. The issue wasn't the snake at all, but having the faith to do what God said.

Mike sat with rapt attention, soaking in every word. It was as if the pastor's words of explanation and following practical application were meant just for him. A chill ran up his spine as he thought of watching Patty driving away last night, and how at the time he didn't know why he wanted to go to church today, only that he did.

Mike forced himself to breathe as he listened, not allowing himself to be distracted by anything going on around him. The pastor ended the sermon, everyone bowed their heads for another prayer, and the band at the front finished off the service with one last song.

The people around them rose and began to circulate and talk, but Mike remained seated. He wasn't in the mood to make small talk with strangers. A million thoughts cascaded through his mind.

"Well?" Patty asked beside him. "What did you think?"

Mike blinked and shook his head. "It was incredible. It was like he prepared that message just for me. That was the verse I wanted to ask you about and couldn't find. Aside from that, his sermon was easy to understand, the presentation was interesting. He didn't belabor the point too much, but still said all that was important to say. He made it so easy to understand. It sure didn't come together like that when I was reading it myself. I'm really glad I came. I learned a lot."

"Daddy is a very gifted speaker."

"He sure is. And he. . ." Mike's heart stopped, then pounded in his chest. "Daddy?"

"I wish I had the ability to deliver a message like that, but it's just not my gift."

His stomach tightened into a painful knot. "Daddy? The pastor is your father?"

"And every day he. . ." Her voice trailed off. "You mean you didn't know?"

He stared unseeingly at the empty podium. Most normal fathers didn't want him being in the same room with their daughters because he was such a bad influence, to say nothing of his reputation—especially in the past year. He could only imagine how much more so now that he was in trouble with the law.

Patty's father would never have been in trouble with the law, or with anything. Being a pastor, he'd probably never done a bad thing in his entire life.

He knew Patty had been raised in a pure and righteous home, but he had no idea it was that pure and righteous. He felt himself sink to a few levels below the common earthworm.

Mike thought he just might throw up. He was in love with the pastor's daughter.

Chapter 7

M ike? Are you okay?"

Patricia wanted to touch his forehead, but didn't because they were still in church. All the color had completely drained out of his face, and he was staring off into nothing.

He nodded, then shook his head. "Yeah, I'm fine. No. No, I'm not fine. I didn't know the pastor was your father. Why didn't you tell me?"

"I thought you knew."

She leaned back as Mike waved one hand in the air. "Of course I didn't know! How would I?"

"But you've spoken to Dad so many times. He even gave you my cell phone number, which he doesn't give out to just anybody."

He bowed his head and pinched the bridge of his nose, which Patricia didn't think was a good sign. "He calls you by your name, not by the title of Daughter."

"But what about Bruce?"

He still pinched the bridge of his nose, plus he shook his head. "That's a unique situation. We talk only about my personal life, not his—and especially not yours."

Patricia gritted her teeth, then stiffened in the chair. "Does it matter?" Most people knew she was the pastor's daughter before she met them for the first time. She didn't always like it, but she had become accustomed to living in her father's shadow. However, it was different when people got to know her first, especially out of church circles, and then found out she was a pastor's daughter. Then the reaction was often mixed. She saw it in people's eyes. Sometimes, the second they found out, suddenly she transformed from simply a nice girl to some deity of angelic perfection, especially after they found out she worked for the church. She was no angel, far from it.

Some of the color returned to Mike's face. "I don't know if it matters. I don't want it to matter." He glanced nervously around the room, then flinched when he saw her father. "Let's get out of here. I'll take you to lunch."

Quickly, she gathered her purse and Bible and followed him into the parking lot. Rather than go to the usual church-crowd lunch hangout, they ended up at a pizzeria.

All went well until the group at the table next to them ordered a pitcher of beer. She saw Mike staring at it and wondered what was going through his mind. She couldn't personally fathom why anyone would continually drink to excess, knowing the damage it caused, especially after long-term abuse, but she couldn't deny that it happened. After listening to the speakers at the few AA meetings she'd been to, she wondered if many of the people really could say exactly why they drank so much, because every single one of them openly admitted that drinking only made things worse.

She didn't like the way Mike was staring at the beer. He wasn't even looking at the people. All his attention was focused on the pitcher. For whatever reason people had for drinking so much, it didn't take a rocket scientist to figure out that stress made the desire to drink stronger. Judging from his reaction when he found out about her father and the way he scooted out of the church when they saw him, she knew Mike was stressed.

"Mike? Do you want to go somewhere else?"

He shook his head, his ears reddened, and he turned to face her. "I'm sorry. No. I'm fine." He reached for the menu sitting in the middle of the table. "Let's order."

Curiously, not a word was said about her father, or the service, or anything about church or the Bible. She was dying to ask Mike what he found so captivating about her father's sermon because she had noticed that Mike was glued to her father's every word, but a voice in her heart told her to wait and bring up the subject at another time, after Mike had dealt with what he considered a shock. Restraint had never been one of her strengths, and every time a silence lulled in their conversation, Patricia struggled to let Mike speak first.

He said very little when she dropped him off at his house, so little that she was afraid to bring up the subject of returning his car.

Patricia decided that she would wait until Monday to return it, and since Monday was usually a slow day, a good time would be during her lunch break, since she knew she would be seeing Mike.

❧

Patricia stood huddled in the church doorway, staring at the pouring rain. She didn't know how it happened, but instead of missing her little brown squirrel, she missed Mike.

She didn't want to miss Mike, but he had become such a regular part of her day, it felt odd that she was eating her sandwich without him.

A deep voice sounded behind her. "I guess he's not coming, is he?"

Patricia sighed. "No, Daddy, I wouldn't think so. He's only got his bike, and I've made such an issue about it being too expensive to take a cab, I know he won't do that just to sit and eat a sandwich beside me." Thunder rumbled in the distance. She sighed again. "He's definitely not coming."

"Bruce told me a little about him."

She tried not to cringe. She didn't know if that was good or bad, so she said nothing.

Her father stepped beside her but didn't look at her. Instead, he also stared into the rain as he spoke. "It sounds like he has a lot of things to work out in his life."

"Yes, he does. None of his friends are helping him. From what he says, not one has called or offered any support, and nobody has invited him to go do something that doesn't involve drinking or going to their familiar hang-outs. He must be so lonely, but on the surface, he's putting on a happy face. I know he's hurting deep down. He's just not letting it show."

"You be careful, Sweetheart. You don't have a lot of experience with people like him."

She turned toward her father. It was an echo of what Bruce had said. She wished she could pin the entire blame for her father's sentiments on Bruce, for tainting his opinion of Mike, but she couldn't. She was fully aware of her inexperience in these matters.

All her life, she rarely ventured out of church circles for both her social life and her job. She couldn't relate to Mike at all on many issues, and she knew he couldn't relate to her. Now that he knew the pastor was her father, the gap had widened even more. She realized that missing him now, the way she was, proved that being with him was more than a ministry. At some point it had become personal, and it shouldn't have.

"Daddy, am I doing the right thing?"

"I can't answer that. Have you prayed about it?"

"More than you can ever know."

"Then you're the one who can best answer that question."

She stared into the rain once more. "Bruce doesn't approve." She didn't want to ask for her father's approval, but she did want some kind of endorsement from him that she was doing the right thing.

"It's not up to me to approve or disapprove. This man is Bruce's client, and so Bruce sees this from a different perspective than you or I do. Bruce tends to see more failures in his line of work, and while I've seen a lot of heartache and tragedy in my time, I've also seen a lot of redemption in many people all else would have called hopeless. On the other hand, from a father's point of view, I don't want to see you hurt. But as a Christian, I want to see Mike turn his life over to the love and care of Jesus, no matter how he's lived his life up to this point."

That was also what Patricia wanted to see. However, it was more than just as a Christian sister.

She couldn't deny the truth of what Bruce had pointed out. She was fully aware of many of Mike's shortcomings from her own personal dealings with him. Romans 3:23 echoed through her head.

"For all have sinned and fall short of the glory of God."

In God's eyes, she was no different. For all her faith and good works, she was still a sinner, but she was justified by the blood of Jesus. More than anything, she wanted Mike to be justified too.

All her life, she had been spared from much of the heartache she saw around her. She had been raised in a wonderful home, full of love and support, surrounded by friends and family as well as the whole church, teaching her not only of God's love but also how to show God's love to others. She didn't know what kind of love or support network Mike had grown up with, but he needed someone to support him and push him in the right direction now. The second half of Luke 12:48 flashed through her mind.

"From everyone who has been given much, much will be demanded; and from the one who has been entrusted with much, much more will be asked."

She had indeed been given much, and it was now her turn to give much back.

Patricia turned to face her father.

She didn't say anything, but he nodded slowly, once.

"I'll be praying for both of you," he said.

Patricia returned to her desk. She also had a lot of praying to do. Tonight was Mike's special meeting with Claude's group, and they would be doing step two. She pulled the little AA pamphlet out of her drawer and read it.

(2) Came to believe that a Power greater than ourselves could restore us to sanity.

Quickly, she shoved it back into her drawer. She didn't know who was more insane, Mike or herself.

All day long, that one sentence echoed through her head. Even on the short drive home, she still couldn't get it out of her head or the ramifications of how it related to Mike.

Lunch had felt strange. Except for the few minutes she'd spent with her father, it was the first time in a week she'd been alone at lunchtime. Usually she ate her dinner alone, but today it felt strange being alone in the kitchen. In order to shake the sensation, she ate her dinner in front of the television—something she never did.

When something disturbed her, she always pulled out her Bible and paged through and read her highlighted verses until something jumped out at her, and then she read the surrounding section. She couldn't even do that, because she had given the Bible containing all her notes to Mike.

In less than two weeks, the man had invaded every portion of her life.

She had just decided to go to bed when the phone rang.

"Hi, Patty. Busy?"

"Hi, Mike. What's up?"

"I just got home from that meeting at Claude's house, and I really needed to do something normal, so I had to call you."

She wouldn't have called starting a phone conversation at ten at night normal. "Uh-huh," she mumbled, waiting for him to continue.

"It was a very strange meeting. For most of it we talked about all the stupid things we've all done over the years. You know, the insanity of it all. In the middle of the meeting, we all laughed about it, but really, it wasn't very funny when you think of it. We're all supposed to be responsible adults. It really made me think. At the end, we came to the part you probably want to hear about. We talked about how God could help us. I really believe that He can."

Her heart pounded. "That's great."

"I'm just not sure He would want to. I haven't exactly been a prime candidate."

"God loves you, Mike. Really. Why do you think He's put you among those people? He did it before any real harm was done."

She heard him suck in a deep intake of breath. "I guess."

Silence hung on the line.

"I guess I should let you go," Mike mumbled.

She couldn't completely stifle a yawn. "Yes, it's late. Are you going to come and visit me at lunch time tomorrow?"

His voice brightened. "Depends on the weather, but to be with you is worth the risk of catching pneumonia."

Patricia harumphed. "I don't think so. See you if the weather holds."

When she went to bed, she found herself praying for good weather, just because she wanted to see her little squirrel again.

In the morning her prayers were answered. It was a lovely day. The air was fresh and clean, the birds were singing, and the drops of water beaded and glistened off the pristine wax finish of Mike's car.

She hummed as she worked and then went outside for lunch early.

Mike joined her at precisely noon.

"No chipmunk today?"

"Yes, the squirrel was here. You scared it away again."

He emptied a sandwich, a couple of wrapped cookies, and a few pieces of bread out of his backpack. When all was laid out between them on the bench, he turned to her and grinned. "It'll probably come back. This time I'm ready."

She wasn't so sure the squirrel would return, but she didn't want to contradict him because she didn't know what he was trying to do, attract the squirrel or impress her by bribing the squirrel.

Since neither of them had started eating, Patricia paused for a prayer of thanks over their lunch, and they began to eat. Unlike most days, this time Mike was strangely silent. Patricia remained quiet, waiting for him to talk first, which he eventually did when he was almost finished with his sandwich.

"There's something I've got to tell you."

She nodded and waited.

"Yesterday, on the phone, when you said that so far, no real harm was done because of, well, you know."

Again, Patricia remained silent while Mike sorted out what he felt was so important to tell her. She had a feeling that a confession was coming, even though she had not asked for one.

"Well, that's not quite true. You already know that I left the scene of an accident, but that wasn't so bad. His insurance covered it and stuff. What I have to tell you is that I was engaged once. I didn't treat her very well. She ended up losing her job because of me."

Patricia tried not to show her shock. She didn't know what hit her harder, that someone had lost their job because of something he'd done or that Mike had once loved someone so much he had planned to marry her.

"I know she would have gotten another job quick enough. She was more than capable, and my dad gave her a good severance package—something he sure didn't give me. But now I know what it's like to get fired, and it's not a very good feeling. I'm not having as easy a time as I thought finding another job either. Last week I thought I had something, but as soon as I told my prospective employer I'd need some time off for my pending court case, they were suddenly no longer interested."

She stared blankly at him, trying to let it all sink in. Her brief experience with Mike had shown that he could pour on the charm when he wanted to, but deep down, he wasn't a bad guy. Knowing that once he had planned to marry someone contradicted her playboy image of him. The woman must have been very special to make him decide to settle down, and Patricia also wondered what had happened that caused them to split up.

"Do you still see her?" She was afraid to know the answer, but some sick part of her had to know.

"No. I haven't seen her since the breakup. It was rather unpleasant for both of us, and it was entirely my fault."

Patricia remained silent, afraid to ask, and not sure it was any of her business.

Mike turned his head, not looking at her as he spoke. "I was cheating on her. I was a jerk."

The bite of her sandwich became a lump of cardboard in her mouth. She swallowed it painfully and dropped the un-eaten remainder of the sandwich into the container.

Mike did the same. "It still bugs me, and it's been three years. It was the stupidest thing I've ever done in my life."

Patricia stared blankly at the trees.

He swiped what was left of his lunch into his backpack, except for one of the cookies, which he slid on the bench toward her. "I think I'd better go."

Without another word he slung his backpack over his shoulder, strode to his bike, and rode off.

Patricia watched the street long after he'd gone.

His words echoed in her head. He had said it was the stupidest thing he'd ever done. It shouldn't have mattered to her, because Mike was only supposed to be a ministry to her. God trusted her to guide Mike, to show him God's love, and God had orchestrated the timing to be when Mike needed it the most.

But it did matter. Her throat tightened, and her eyes burned. Mike was still in love with his ex-fiancée.

❧

Mike slammed the door behind him and kicked his sneakers off, not caring that he hit the wall with them, stomped into the living room, and flopped down on the couch.

He'd blown it. As soon as he told Patty he'd been engaged once, he'd seen a change come over her. But when he admitted he'd been cheating on Robbie—that was when he knew anything he'd ever hoped for was over.

But it was something she had to know. He knew there was no way she'd ever learn that from Bruce, because he hadn't told Bruce. They didn't talk about personal details of his past that weren't directly related to his drinking habits.

For now, Patty wasn't going to meet any of his friends, but that wasn't to say it would never happen. He didn't think it was likely that he would bump into Robbie on the street when he was with Patty, but the future possibility of either existed.

He didn't want her to find out that way. Therefore, he told her himself in what he hoped would be the least damaging way. He had expected her to be shocked, but he hadn't expected utter disdain.

Considering her upbringing, he could only imagine what she thought of him being unfaithful to the woman he was supposed to marry, which was the most important commitment a person would ever make.

He'd handled himself badly. He still didn't know why he had cheated on Robbie, because it had started so innocently. Suzie had started it, taunting and tempting him, and at first he'd simply flirted back, the same as he always did, but Suzie had kept at him. Before he realized what was happening, he was seeing Suzie on the side. If he'd been half a man, he would have broken up with Robbie then, telling her they weren't as suited as he originally thought, or he would have told Suzie to get lost, but he hadn't. The whole thing had fed his ego, and he'd made the most of it at the time, or so he thought.

Then Robbie had come in to work early and caught him with Suzie. The scene that followed had been so horrible he'd fallen into what he could now see as a pit of self-indulgence. For awhile, he'd been into such substance abuse that there were holes in his memory. There were days he couldn't remember where he was or what he'd done. Looking back, he almost couldn't believe he had been so stupid, that he actually could remember some of the things he'd done that were less than noble. He'd let everything spiral completely out of control. He'd lived his life going from one party to the next.

Except, he wasn't having a lot of fun. His life had no meaning. He had accomplished nothing. He now had the possibility of a jail sentence to look forward to, and it was his own fault. It wasn't just himself whom he had hurt. First, he'd hurt Robbie, both emotionally and financially, and now he'd physically hurt the man whose car he ran into. He'd run from the results both times.

Mike sat up on the couch and buried his face in his hands, speaking out loud. "God, if You're out there, and if You're listening to me, I'm sorry for the things I've done and the mess I've made. Please, I beg You to forgive me. And if You can, please help me make things right with Patty. I've blown it once. I don't want to blow it again. Lord God, she's so special. Show me how to treat her right."

He sat in silence, not moving. Today was Tuesday, and he knew that Tuesday nights Patty went to Bible study meetings.

He stood and walked into his bedroom, picking up Patty's Bible from the nightstand where he'd tossed it earlier. He'd asked God to help him, both to straighten himself out as well as to help him in building a relationship with Patty. If he was going to ask such things, then he thought it only fair to study God's word and to learn more about the God who supposedly loved him as much as Patty said.

Without putting the Bible down, he walked to the phone and dialed the church. Of course, Patty's cheerful voice answering made his pulse quicken.

"Hey, Patty. I've been thinking. You said you go to Bible study meetings on Tuesday nights. It's Tuesday, and I'd like to go. Am I invited?"

Chapter 8

Mike smiled a greeting as he shook hands with Gary and his wife, Melinda, the people who led the home Bible study meeting, and then made himself comfortable on the couch. As he hoped, Patty sat beside him.

Everyone present was looking at them. In people's minds, officially, they were together, and he liked it that way. To further enforce their assumption, he laid his hand over Patty's, patted it, then returned his hand to the Bible in his lap as he laughed at a joke someone made while they were waiting.

They were about to start when one more couple arrived, and everyone shuffled over to make room, which was fine with him because that meant Patty had to sit right up against him. When Mike looked up at the new arrivals, his heart skipped a beat.

It was Bruce and his wife. It hadn't occurred to Mike that Bruce would be here. He had assumed the crowd would be made up of Patty's friends. He didn't think about her brother.

Bruce smiled at everyone as he apologized for being late, but when Bruce looked at him, Mike could see a falter in the smile and a hesitation in Bruce's movements. No one else appeared to notice, but Mike was positive he hadn't imagined it.

Just as Patty had warned him, they opened with a shared prayer after Gary asked everyone present if they had any prayer requests. Mike had a few concerns, but he wasn't going to share them with this group of strangers, and he especially wasn't going to share them with Patty, because most of them were about her.

The lesson was informative and done in a casual presentation that Mike could relate to. Questions and comments were invited, and Mike remained silent while he listened. He was receiving enough information to process without asking for more.

Last night the group at Claude's meeting was completely different. They were all people much like himself; a couple of them believed in God; most of them didn't. One thing they all believed was that there was some greater power out there that could help them make a break from the addiction they all shared.

Tonight, many present, like Patty and Bruce, had been raised in homes where Christian values were taught and believing in God was never a question, God was always there. Like Patty, he didn't think any of them had ever had anything really bad happen to them, yet they depended on God anyway. A few people were present who made their decisions as adults, and even though it was hard to tell what had made them make the decision to become Christians, their belief and faith were strong.

Either way, everything that was read or commented on showed that God loved everyone, no matter what kind of people they were or what they were doing at that point in their lives. Mike found it fascinating, and he had to admire every one of them for standing up for what they believed.

When the study part of the meeting was finished, they all chatted as they helped themselves to coffee, tea, and some wonderful homemade cookies. Everyone talked to him except Bruce, which left him feeling strangely relieved.

On the way home, he wanted to go out for coffee or somewhere he could talk privately with Patty without her feeling intimidated, which she would have at his house. Even though it was his car, he wasn't driving and he couldn't protest when she took him straight home, making it very clear that she had no intention of coming in.

After his disclosure earlier today, he could see a difference in the way Patty treated him. It wasn't overtly noticeable, but she had erected a wall between them, and he had to find a way to break it down. It did encourage him that she had taken him with her tonight without complaint, which he hoped was a step in the right direction.

Once he was at home alone, Mike couldn't quell a feeling of agitation. Any other day, he would have poured himself a drink and parked himself in front of the television, but that wasn't an option. For a complete change of pace, in order to keep his mind busy, he turned the CD player on loud and played a few games on his computer. When he got bored, he did something he had never done before, which was to wash his kitchen floor since he no longer had a housekeeper to do it for him. He then vacuumed the entire house. After that, he dug through the fridge to see if there was anything worthwhile to eat.

Nothing soothed him.

Despite it being earlier than his usual bedtime, he decided to hit the sack early. As he reached for the light, he saw Patty's Bible lying where he'd left it, and instead of turning off the light, he picked up the Bible. This time, instead of paging through for the highlighted parts, Mike started at the beginning of the book of Genesis and read until his eyes would no longer focus. Then he drifted off to sleep.

He woke to the sound of birds twittering, which meant only one thing. It wasn't raining, and he would be joining Patty for lunch.

After a few unprofitable calls for jobs listed in the help wanted ads, Mike needed to do something to ease his frustration. A long bike ride was the perfect solution. He made and packed himself a lunch, including a couple of pieces of bread for the squirrel, and was on his way.

This time, as he leaned his bike against the church wall, instead of rushing across the grass to greet Patty, he stood in the shadows and watched her from a distance.

First she checked her watch, then emptied her lunch containers from the bag onto the bench, paused to pray, and took a bite of her sandwich. Then she tore a piece of bread off the extra piece she always brought and looked into the trees, waiting for the squirrel. Just looking at her calmed him and made him smile. She was kind and gentle, yet had a mind of her own and didn't hesitate or have second thoughts to do what she thought it would take to keep him in line. No woman had ever made him want to stay in line until he met Patty.

Mike sucked in a deep breath, hooked his thumbs into the straps of his backpack, and walked quickly across the grass. Just as he started on his path, the little brown squirrel began to approach Patty. It was too late to turn back, and even though he slowed his pace, the squirrel turned and fled.

"Hi, Mike," she called out without turning around.

Mike smiled. He wondered what she would do if one day it wasn't he who approached. The thought caused a knot to form in his stomach. He didn't want anyone else to approach her.

"I think I scared your chipmunk again," he said as he sat beside her on the bench.

She grumbled something he couldn't understand.

He tried to keep a straight face. "Pardon me? Sorry, I couldn't quite hear you."

"I said it's a squirrel. It has a long bushy tail. It's a solid color. It's a squirrel."

"Shh. Don't raise your voice so much. You'll scare it away."

"You've already done that," she mumbled under her breath.

Mike laughed and emptied his backpack. He held out a cookie toward her, waving it in the air. "I brought you a treat, but it's bound to be a disappointment after those wonderful cookies last night."

He held it in front of her, sweeping it in the air under her nose until she took it from his hand.

"You're welcome," he said, still grinning.

"Thank you," she grumbled.

He continued to tease her and tell jokes until she couldn't help but smile at him. The squirrel finally did return, and he sat completely still and silent while she fed it. Mike marveled at how a wild animal could be lured so close, even though he knew the answer. The same gentle spirit that drew the squirrel also drew him.

They stood at the same time when her lunch break was over. Mike slung his backpack over his shoulders and picked up her bag after she had deposited her empty containers into it.

With his heart in his throat, he grasped her hand and held onto it and, without saying a word, gave her a slight pull to start her walking back across the field and to the building. To his delight, she didn't pull her hand away as they walked together. He couldn't believe how wonderful it felt, something so simple as holding hands, compared to some of the things he'd done in the past with women he'd dated. Most of them, however, were far from pure, and their words and actions only showed what was in their hearts—they were as self-centered as he was. There had been times lately he'd come out of a relationship feeling used, and that wasn't the way it was supposed to be. A man and a woman were to cherish each other and treat the other with respect and dignity.

It was a bitter reminder that he didn't deserve a woman like Patty.

When they arrived back at the building, she stood with him until he mounted his bike. He wanted to kiss her so badly he was grateful for the distraction of holding the handlebars.

"Good-bye, Mike."

"Yeah. See you tomorrow."

She opened her mouth, but then closed it again. His gut clenched to think she could have been ready to tell him not to come back. He rode off before she had the chance to think about it. He planned to be back to share her lunch break, not only tomorrow, but every day.

⋘⋙

Mike touched up the gel in his hair and pulled his jacket out of the closet. Last night his friend Wayne had called to remind him that tonight was the annual car and truck show, and everyone had asked if he was coming this year. Of course, he was thrilled to be asked. He was very much looking forward to going.

He hadn't seen his friends and had barely talked to them since he'd been arrested. Seeing Patty nearly every day had helped him when he felt left out of their activities, but now that he'd made plans to spend the next day without her, he almost regretted it, because he knew he would miss her. He'd missed her terribly on Monday when it had rained, but he'd seen her for lunch every other day. On Friday afternoon, when he was about to call her to see if she would spend the evening with him, Bruce had called unexpectedly to take him to an AA meeting, which he couldn't refuse. What he had really wanted to do was to take Patty out. Today, now that Wayne was due to arrive any minute to pick him up, he wished that instead of Wayne, it was Patty who was coming to get him.

Mike shook his head. Even married men had to have a night or two out with the guys, and he wasn't even close to being married to Patty, no matter how much he wished he could be.

The thought nearly caused him to stumble. He did want to be married to Patty, but wasn't in a position to ask, even if he thought there was the slightest possibility she would say yes. Now that he'd told her what a jerk he'd been when he was engaged before, he doubted she would consider it. After all, who would ever want to set themselves up for heartbreak?

A horn honked in the driveway, so Mike set the house alarm, locked up, and jogged to Wayne's car. After they picked up their other three friends, they were on their way.

They laughed and had a great time, joking around all the way to the B.C. Place Stadium. The only thing Mike thought missing in the conversation was that for such old-time friends, they didn't talk about anything important. Even Wayne, who was supposed to be his best friend, didn't ask him how he'd been over the last few weeks, nor did he ask what AA meetings were like. Most of all, Mike wanted an opening to tell them that he'd done some thinking and to tell them that throughout all that had happened, he felt a deep inner peace. Somehow, he knew God was in charge of his life, and everything was going to be fine.

Soon they were mingling with the crowd, making the rounds touring all the new cars and trucks, and checking out most of the booths hawking automotive accessories of every imaginable description and possible use.

After stuffing themselves silly with corn dogs and French fries, Mike wanted to continue on and see everything else in the building, but before they got that far, they came to the beer garden.

His friends wanted to go in, because every year they made the beer garden the crowning glory of the whole auto show experience.

Mike froze. He didn't come here to drink. He came here to have a good time and look at the new cars and the latest toys that went with them. Sure, in previous years he had enjoyed the beer garden, but this year it wasn't on his agenda.

Apparently, none of his friends had considered that.

Travis gleefully announced the absence of a line and was the first one to enter, then Rick. Dave hesitated, but only for a minute.

When Mike didn't move, Dave stepped back and pulled him by the arm. "Come on, Mikey, old boy. If you're really on the wagon, you can have a soda."

Mike didn't want to sit in the beer garden and drink soft drinks while everyone else around him got drunk.

At his silence, Wayne nudged him. "This way, you can be the designated driver."

Mike stiffened. They had never had a designated driver before. Warning bells went off in his head. To his friends, his arrest may have served as a warning about getting caught drinking and driving, not about actually cutting back on their drinking habits. It dawned on him that the only reason he'd been asked to come with them was because they knew he was going to stay sober, and they wanted him to drive. "I can't be the designated driver. My license was suspended, remember?"

Travis patted him on the back. "Who cares? No one will catch you. Just drive the speed limit and stop for all the stop signs. Nothing will happen."

Mike backed up a step. While he knew that if he carefully obeyed every little rule of the road, the chances of getting stopped on a busy Saturday night were next to non-existent, but that wasn't the point. He had lost his license for a valid reason, and he fully intended to obey every restriction imposed upon him.

"No," he said bluntly.

Travis patted him on the back again, then nudged him to start walking into the beer garden. "Aw, come on, Buddy. You wouldn't want us to get caught or get in an accident because we were a little over the legal limit, would you?"

Mike stopped dead in his tracks and smacked Travis's arm away. He knew what they had in mind. It wasn't to be a little over the legal blood-alcohol limit. They planned to be a lot over the legal limit. "This is blackmail."

"It's not blackmail. We're your friends."

He turned to Wayne. "What would happen if I did get stopped, was arrested again, and your car was impounded? What would you do then?"

Wayne shrugged his shoulders. "That's not going to happen."

Mike clenched his teeth. No one thought it would happen to them, but sometimes it did. He never could have foreseen what had happened to him, but things like that happened all the time to people.

"No."

"Coward."

"I'm not driving. You guys are making a big mistake."

His friends, including his very best friend, Wayne, started quietly clucking like chickens.

"I don't need this. You guys are on your own." He turned and strode away into the crowd, ignoring their rude comments behind him as he walked. He didn't stop until he was outside.

Mike drew a deep breath of the cool night air into his lungs, but it didn't relieve the numb feeling inside. These were his friends. Every year they went to the auto show together, and every year they had a good time.

He leaned against the building, out of sight from other people going in and out of the door. That was all he ever did with his friends, have a good time. Thinking back, though, he couldn't really recall exactly what was so fun.

This year, in order to have their fun, his friends had planned this—to take advantage of him. What hurt the worst was their attempt at manipulation, trying to lay a guilt trip on him to get him to drive them home. By using his refusal to drink, the rest of them planned to get drunker than usual. They had seemed more chipper on the way there than usual, and now he knew why.

A couple of months ago, he would have been angry at being set up, but he wasn't angry. Yes, he was hurt, but more than anything, he felt sorry for them that they would go to such means to get drunk. They weren't going to have as good a time as they thought if they couldn't remember the next day what they'd done. Also, no matter how "good" a time they had, their alleged fun would not be worth the hangover. He'd been that route himself enough times to know. But then again, it never stopped him from over-indulging, nor was it likely to stop his friends today.

He was not going to give in and break the law or disobey the conditions of his probation so his friends could continue to drink. Any efforts to convince them to skip the beer garden and simply cruise the auto show, which was what they came for in the first place, would be fruitless. Their barbed comments behind his back on his way out foretold that nothing would be different upon his return.

Mike looked down the street. It had gotten dark hours ago, and even though he was in reasonably good shape and he was tall enough not to be considered an easy mark, this was not the best area of town to be out alone late at night, even for a physically fit grown man.

He unclipped his cell phone from his belt and began to dial Patty's number but stopped before he hit the last digit. He'd called her to bail him out when he had to pick up his car, but he wasn't going to inconvenience her again, especially so late on a Saturday night. Nor did he want to further humiliate himself by asking her to come all this way and rescue him after his so-called friends had abandoned him. Instead, he hit the clear button and returned the phone to his belt.

Mike checked his wallet only to discover that he didn't have enough money for a cab. He again looked down the street, ran his fingers through his hair, straightened his back, and headed for the nearest bus stop.

Being alone for so long waiting for the bus at night gave Mike time to think. After two transfers, and after regularly checking his wristwatch, he estimated the amount of time that his friends would be at the beer garden before they were asked to leave. From his seat in the back of the bus, he called directory assistance for the non-emergency number and dialed the police.

"Hello? I'd like to report a drunk driver."

After he completed the call, he closed his eyes and prayed, knowing that even though Wayne would probably hate him, he had done the right thing.

Chapter 9

Patricia spread her lunch out on the park bench but didn't open anything. Mike was late, but she was positive he was going to be there.

Once again, she checked the time. She hoped he was going to be there. He had phoned early Sunday morning and asked her to pick him up for church. Of course she couldn't turn him down. In the past month, she had seen amazing growth in Mike. She could see his perception changing, opening a little more every week to God's wisdom and leading. All day long on Sunday he'd been uncharacteristically quiet, and when he finally did speak, he had asked some very strange questions about friendship.

The best she could do on short notice was to show him the loyal friendship between David and Jonathan. When she asked why he was asking, he became evasive, which made her interpret his questions as a hint that he had decided to simply be friends and nothing more.

Being friends was also what Patricia knew was best, but against her better judgment, she wanted more than friendship with Mike. It wasn't going to happen, nor would it have been right in their given situation. All her counseling training and experience taught her that after a trauma or upheaval in a person's life, major decisions, especially matters of the heart, should be avoided until a significant amount of time had passed. Not only that, it was clear to Patricia that Mike still carried a torch for his ex-fiancée.

He'd also been very quiet when he joined her for lunch Monday. If he still hadn't snapped out of his doldrums today, she planned to ask him what was wrong.

This time she saw him coming before the squirrel showed up for his daily treat. Today she anticipated him telling her all about the special Monday evening meeting at Claude's house.

"Sorry I'm late. You should have started eating without me. This morning I was talking to Claude on the phone since he had the day off, and before I knew it, it was past time to leave." He shucked off his backpack and sat beside her. "The meeting last night was great." He began to remove his lunch from his backpack.

She opened her mouth to ask him about it, but he started before she could make a sound.

"The step of the night was 'Made a decision to turn our will and our lives over to the care of God as we understood Him.' And you know what? I did that, and I feel great."

He grinned ear-to-ear, and Patricia could see that he wasn't exaggerating. He looked great, unlike the quiet and somber person he'd been over the last two days. Today he was a different person.

"After the meeting was over and everyone left, I stayed and prayed with Claude, and it's like the weight of the world has been lifted from my shoulders." Instead of doing what she expected, which was to start eating his lunch, Mike enclosed both her hands in his. "God loves me, Patty. He cared for me even when I didn't care about Him. He's kept me safe, and He put you in my life. He put Claude in my life, and I don't believe that any of this is an accident. Most of all, Jesus has already taken the punishment for everything I've done. Just because He loves me."

Patricia stared at Mike. He radiated pure joy, and she thought her heart would burst with happiness for him. He had Jesus in his heart, and it showed. The only thing about being with him now that wasn't perfect was a tiny twinge of resentment that he hadn't made his decision with her, but she quickly pushed such thinking aside.

"Even if I do have to go to jail for a short time, I can handle that. I did wrong, and I still have to face the consequences of my actions. But from here on, I'm a new creation."

Jail. The word echoed in Patricia's mind, crashing into her heart. Spending time in jail was still a very real possibility for Mike. For today, he was living in a euphoric bubble, but as life returned to normal, daily routine would bring him back down to earth a little bit. She said a quick prayer in her head that Mike would never lose the enthusiasm she saw right now.

"I want to celebrate. I've never felt like this before."

She looked down at their joined hands, then back up to his face. She knew he still had more money than she did, despite his current unemployment status. However, he had shared with her that every time he thought he was close to getting a job, no one wanted to take the chance of hiring him before his court date, in case he had to go to jail. If that were the case, and if that trend continued, his money was going to run very low, very fast, especially if he did get a jail sentence.

The entrance of a new soul into God's Kingdom was the best reason for celebration there could ever be, both in heaven and on earth, no matter what unpleasantness lay in the future. For this, Patty wanted to celebrate with him, and for this, it would be her treat. "I think a celebration is a great idea." At her words, she felt an encouraging gentle squeeze on her hands.

She figured he would choose a convenient evening and name an expensive restaurant she probably couldn't afford, but she would treat him anyway. "What do you want to do?" she asked.

Slowly, he released her hands and gently cupped her face, cradling her chin between both palms. His voice dropped to a low rumble. "I want to kiss you."

Before she could protest or think of a good reason why he shouldn't, he leaned forward over the lunches spread between them on the park bench and kissed her. He kissed her slowly and fully and so sweetly it made her insides melt.

No one had ever kissed her like this. Her stomach fluttered, and her heart pounded. Then he broke the contact, let his hands drop, and it was over.

Patricia sat speechless. Gradually, a lazy and very self-satisfied smile came over his face, making him more handsome than any man had a right to be. "I've wanted to do that for a long time."

Patricia blinked herself back to reality and abruptly reached for her sandwich container. Not that she was hungry anymore, but she suddenly, desperately needed something to do.

A quick movement near the front of the bench caught her attention. She turned her head just in time to see the little brown squirrel run off into the trees.

She had forgotten about the squirrel, and this time it was her own movement that sent him scurrying away.

Mike made a strange choking sound and bit his bottom lip, like he was trying very hard not to laugh. "You scared Charlie Chipmunk."

She stared at him, not caring that her mouth was hanging open. She couldn't think of a single response. She couldn't even remind him that it was a squirrel.

"Don't you think we should pray and start eating? You have to get back to the office soon."

"Yes. Of course." Because he was a new child in Christ, she wanted to reach out and hold his hands while they prayed, but she was afraid to touch him. Since she already had her sandwich container in her hand, she opened it and laid it and the lid on the bench, then opened her juice container, as well as another containing some fruit cocktail, and spread everything out between them. The open containers, plus lids, effectively doubled the space between them.

"I think today you should pray," Patricia mumbled. She folded her hands in her lap and waited. She knew she was being immature, but she couldn't think properly.

"I'm not very good at this, but I know God knows what's in my heart." Mike cleared his throat and they both bowed their heads. "Dear Lord God. I thank You for this good lunch. And for Patty. Thank You for putting her into my life. Thanks for this special private place where we meet every day. Thank You most of all for Your love and for Your Son, Jesus. Amen."

"Amen," she said, then picked up her sandwich.

Mike also bit into his sandwich, and then talked around the food in his mouth. "I didn't have time to check it out, but did you know they're expanding the mall down the street?"

Patricia listened to him make cheerful conversation while they ate together, but for once she did very little talking. All she could think of was how Mike had kissed her. She tried to figure out why he would have done that, but the only thing she could think of was that he was so excited about his newfound discovery of

God's love for him that he acted impulsively, and since she was the nearest person, his enthusiasm spilled over onto her.

She wanted to talk to Bruce about what exactly was said at those meetings Mike attended, but lately Bruce had been very touchy whenever the subject of Mike came up. Since Sunday, she found herself avoiding Bruce, because she knew he would give her a rough time when he discovered she still had Mike's car.

If she couldn't get the information out of Bruce, she would have to go elsewhere. Even though she didn't know Claude except for the two times they'd met, Patricia decided to call him. She had no intention of prodding for confidential details of what Mike said at the meetings, because that was meant to stay within the boundaries of their meeting and was only for the ears of those who attended.

She needed to know that the things Claude was teaching Mike were spiritually sound. To do that, she needed an excuse to talk to him and broach the subject.

Because Mike had been a little late arriving, the lunch break seemed the shortest of her life, added to the fact that Mike was talking nonstop.

On the hour, she stacked her empty lunch containers in her bag at the same time as Mike tossed his empty containers into his backpack.

Mike stood and slung the backpack over his shoulders. "Oh, before I forget. Remember that this Thursday is Claude's seven-year cake, and you said we'd go to his special meeting."

Patricia couldn't hold back her smile. God knew the answer before she had formulated the question.

She very much looked forward to talking to Claude.

❧

"Patty! Mike! Good to see you two!"

Patricia smiled politely while Claude first pumped Mike's hand, then laid one hand on Mike's shoulder and patted him on the back with the other. She had always found it amusing the lengths men would go to not to hug each other, even when the situation warranted it. The bond between Mike and Claude was almost tangible, and her heart filled with joy for both of them.

Since Claude was busy talking to a great many people, Patricia did not protest when Mike led her to a chair, and they sat down to wait for the meeting to start.

This time, Patricia found the meeting slightly different. The few meetings she'd previously attended hadn't had a specific theme. Often the speakers didn't know what they were going to say until they got to the front; in fact, some of the speakers didn't know they were going to speak until they felt led to say something at that particular moment.

Today, many of the people present included Claude in their testimonies, either congratulating him for this, his anniversary of seven years without a drink, or saying what a help Claude had been to them in their individual quests for sobriety.

Claude came to the podium last. He briefly told of the happenings around his decision to begin attending AA meetings, and spoke of a man who had greatly helped him in the beginning. Her heart filled with joy for him when Claude elaborated on what AA circles called his "spiritual awakening." His experience was very much like what Mike had gone through; first there was a general belief in God as a Supreme Creator, but this grew to a more personal relationship as he realized the full scope of God's love in his life, despite the bad things that had happened. He gave all the credit for his accomplishments to Jesus, and at the end of his testimony, the crowd burst into rounds of applause. Brief glances to the sides showed Patricia that she was the only one with tears in her eyes. Quickly she wiped them away before anyone could notice.

When the meeting came to a close, Claude served everyone a piece of the largest Black Forest cake Patricia had ever seen. Since he was the center of attention today, she chose not to question him. Besides, many of her questions on where he stood spiritually were answered from listening to his testimony.

With a piece of cake in hand, she retreated with Mike to an empty spot in the room.

Mike stuffed the last of his cake into his mouth and swiped away a bit of icing from his chin. "Claude just asked me if I wanted to go to church with him on Sunday. I told him that I've been going with you, and then he said you were welcome to come too. You want to?"

Her first thought was to decline because she handed out bulletins with her mother, but she couldn't talk with cake in her mouth. Before she could form the words, another thought struck her. Last Sunday, when she had made the rounds amongst the congregation with Mike at her side, she had been very aware of Bruce nearby, and she got the impression that he hadn't been very pleased to see her with Mike. Nothing had been said, but his disapproval weighed heavily on her long after church was over. She didn't like confrontations, especially since she'd already told Bruce that she knew what she was doing by spending so much time with Mike. Even after that, Bruce's attitude apparently did not change. Not that she would skip church to get away from Bruce, but attending another church for one Sunday was a rare opportunity for her, and it gave her an excuse to avoid her brother.

Patricia nodded and swallowed. "Yes. I'd like that."

Mike smiled, making Patricia's foolish heart flutter. "Great. I'll get the address from him. As usual, you'll have to pick me up."

She knew she should have given him back his car long ago, but with her own car still needing that rather expensive repair, using Mike's car was too convenient. Besides, many of the miles she put on his car were from chauffeuring him around, so that made it acceptable for her to still have it.

She smiled back. "Name the time, and I'll be there."

❧

"Hi, Patty." Mike shucked off his backpack, dusted off the bench so he wouldn't have to send his good slacks to the dry cleaner, and sat.

Patty's eyes narrowed slightly as she checked out his clothes. She turned her head to look for his bike, which was exactly in the same spot as he parked it every day. "Why are you dressed like that?"

He sighed and ran one hand down the lapel of his suit jacket. Since it was his turn to bring lunch, he couldn't be late. He only had time to throw everything into his backpack before he rushed out the door. "I didn't have time to change. I went for a job interview this morning, and I got home five minutes after the time I should have left to come here."

"I wouldn't have minded you being late. Really. But you do look nice in the suit. How did it go?"

Mike sighed. "The same as last time. It looked really promising, but as soon as I told them about needing time off for court, they suddenly didn't think I was suitable."

"Don't worry, you'll get something soon."

"I don't know. I'm not so sure anymore." He sighed again. "Let's eat." He emptied all the containers from his backpack onto the bench between them, they paused for a prayer of thanks for the food, then dug in.

"If you were running late, I would have understood. All you had to do was phone, and I could have picked something up at the local drive-thru."

Mike grinned. "Honestly, I had everything made and wrapped before I had to leave for the interview. I just had to throw it all into my backpack and go."

The smile she gave him did funny things to his hungry stomach. "I didn't know you were so organized."

He held up a brown paper bag. "Hey. I even brought lunch for the chipmunk."

She rolled her eyes. "It's a squirrel. One day I'll bring an encyclopedia and show you the genus and species."

Mike laughed and bit into his sandwich. Today he appreciated the teasing because it distracted him from what was really on his mind. He had wanted to tell Patty that he'd gotten a job, because he really thought he had it. Now, after yet another failure, he was more than disappointed. He was downright discouraged. He usually didn't give up when he was going after something he wanted, but this time he didn't see any point in continuing to look for a job until after the court case was over and whatever sentence he received had been served.

He was about to point out that her little critter still hadn't shown up when he heard muffled footsteps on the path to the bench. They both looked up at the same time.

"It's Daddy." Patty checked her watch. "I wonder what he wants."

Mike's chest tightened. He often chatted briefly with Patty's father after Sunday services, but it was always only pleasant small talk, nothing personal, conversation suitable for discussion within the congregation. A few times, Mike had spoken to her father on the phone while waiting for Patty to answer, but that had been simply passing time, and there was never time or opportunity for a serious discussion. He'd been inside the church on a weekday only a couple of times because usually he joined Patty at the bench as soon as he arrived.

Now there was only the three of them, no one else anywhere nearby, no time constraints, and no distractions.

Patty leaned slightly closer. With her father approaching, he didn't want it to appear that he was too close to her, but he didn't want to look guilty by backing away too quickly. He forced himself to be still.

Patty's voice dropped to a whisper. "I'll bet Daddy will be impressed with the suit." She had the nerve to giggle.

Mike's stomach went to war with the sandwich. He'd never cared if he impressed a woman's father before. In fact, he hadn't met most of the fathers of the women he dated. Until now, he'd pointedly avoided them. Either that, or they had avoided him.

He reached up to pat where his tie should have been. He hadn't wanted it to dangle or blow around during his bike ride on the way there, so he had yanked it off as he was leaving. Now, when he wanted to make a good impression, he wished he'd kept it on. He also didn't feel completely dressed in a suit without a tie.

He tried to squelch the feeling of dread as he rose to his feet and nodded a stiff greeting. "Pastor Norbert."

Patty's father smiled warmly, but Mike's stomach wouldn't relax. "Hi, Mike, Patty. Sorry to disturb you, especially on this gorgeous day, but Cassandra Phillips is on the phone. She wants to talk to you about her daughter's Sunday school class. I told her you were on your break and couldn't come to the phone, but she started crying and said it was important she talk to you now. She said she's on her lunch break, too, and this is the only time she can call. I'm sorry about this. Would you mind?"

Patty sighed, stood, and turned to Mike. "I'm sorry, but I know what she wants to talk about. I shouldn't be long. Do you mind?"

He rammed his hands into his pockets. "No, not at all. I don't mind."

He supposed it was better coming sooner than later. With Patty gone, this would be the perfect opportunity for her father to talk to him about all the time he was spending with her. He suspected her father's sentiments about his character wouldn't be much different from Bruce's, and Mike couldn't blame him for that. He wouldn't be able to deny a word of why he shouldn't be in the vicinity of his sweet and precious daughter.

Mike struggled to prepare himself for the worst. He didn't want to take his hands out of his pockets, because he knew they were shaking. He didn't want to hear her father tell him to go away and not come back, because he didn't want to do that. Part of him told him to respect her father's wishes, but another part of him prepared to defend himself, even though he had no defense. If he didn't ever see Patty again, it would be like ripping out a piece of his soul. He couldn't do it.

Pastor Norbert checked his watch. "I wish I could stay out here and keep you company until Patty's done, but I have an appointment scheduled in two minutes. Maybe one day I'll have enough free time to join you and Patty out here for lunch. She tells me you make a great submarine sandwich."

Mike tried not to let his mouth hang open as Patty's father smiled, said a polite good-bye, and Patty and her father walked together toward the church. Mike heard them talking about the small child in question until they were out of earshot.

Mike sank to the bench. In the eyes of a righteous man like Patty's father, he was lowlife. Countless times he'd broken the law by drinking and driving, and the only thing that stopped him was being caught for the hit-and-run. Yet, even knowing that, Patty's father treated him as an equal, giving him a respect he didn't deserve.

He turned his head, meaning to watch them until they disappeared into the building, but a small movement caught his attention.

Patty's squirrel had arrived for its lunch. Mike studied it as it cautiously climbed up the side of the bench opposite to where he was sitting and then sat on the end, staring back.

Mike smiled. He was having a stare-down with a squirrel.

Very slowly, Mike lifted the paper bag containing the bread and reached inside. Inch by inch, the little squirrel tiptoed along the back of the park bench, until it was so close that Mike could reach out from where he was sitting and the little animal could take the food out of his hand.

He expected the squirrel to dart away with every small movement he made, but the squirrel remained still. He'd never moved so slowly in his life, but by using very slow movements, Mike managed to give the squirrel the pieces of bread, and it didn't run away.

The squirrel wasn't afraid of him. It was as if the little animal trusted him not to hurt it. In the same way, Patty's father had shown him in not so many words that he, too, trusted him.

Mike wondered what they knew that he didn't.

Deliberately, he kept his movements slow and steady, so as not to frighten Patty's squirrel. He held out another piece of bread, then kept perfectly still so the squirrel would again take it from his fingers.

Suddenly the squirrel darted away.

"Sorry I took so long."

Mike caught his breath, fumbled with the bag, and dropped it. The few remaining pieces of bread fell out onto the ground.

He looked up to see Patty standing behind the bench, both hands over her mouth, her shoulders shaking, and her eyes sparkling with glee. She'd never looked so beautiful.

"Don't say a word," he mumbled as he bent over to pick everything up.

"Me? Never."

"Yeah, right," he grumbled.

"I hope you don't mind, but after Daddy reminded me of your famous submarine sandwich creations, he got me started talking, and I think Daddy is going to join us for lunch sometime soon."

Mike smiled. Strangely, he didn't mind. In fact, he looked forward to it. "Not at all. Now finish your sandwich, because I'm not giving you your dessert until you finish your lunch."

❦

Patricia sighed as she started the next load of laundry, wishing she could be outside in the sunshine on a beautiful spring day instead of downstairs doing laundry. Since she had been busy every night that week, Saturday afternoon was the only time left to do her housework.

In the background, Patricia thought she heard a noise. She pushed in the knob on the washing machine to turn it off, tilted her head, and sure enough, she heard the doorbell again.

She ran upstairs and peeked through the blinds to see Mike at the door.

"What are you doing here?"

He grinned. "Hi. Got a bucket?"

"A bucket?"

He jerked his thumb over his shoulder toward the driveway. "My car is dirty. I came to wash it."

"You came all this way to wash your car?"

"Patty, the dirt will damage the finish." He shucked off his backpack and pulled out a sponge.

"I could have given you a sponge. You didn't have to bring one, you know."

"Yes, I did. This is a special sponge, manufactured in particular for use on cars. I bought this at the car show a couple of years ago."

She stared at the sponge. It didn't look different from any other sponge. She didn't want to ask how much he paid for it. "It's really not so dirty that you had to come all this way. I washed it last weekend."

Mike froze. "What did you use?"

Patricia cringed. "Dish soap. That's what I use on my own car."

He squeezed his eyes shut for a second, then smiled tightly. "That's fine, but from now on, please let me wash it myself, okay? Would you mind if I came by every Saturday afternoon to do it?" He removed two brightly colored bottles from his backpack. The labels boldly stated a guarantee to preserve and protect the finish on fine cars.

She nodded woodenly and left Mike outside while she ran into the house for her bucket. The last thing she had left to do was wash the floors, but she owned only one bucket, which Mike was now using. "Want me to help? I don't have anything else to do."

He removed the sponge she stored in the bottom of the bucket and left it at the side of the driveway. "Nope. But you can keep me company, if you want."

He carefully rinsed the bucket out three times with the hose, then turned to the house. "Can I have some warm water? It works best with the stuff I brought."

"You bought that stuff at the car show too, right?"

"Of course."

"I'm surprised you didn't buy a bucket at the car show."

He frowned, and his eyes narrowed. "Let's not get ridiculous."

She led him to the laundry sink where he filled the bucket with water exactly the right temperature, measured exactly two capfuls from each bottle into the water, and returned outside. He very diligently and tenderly scrubbed every square inch of the car, the whole time making sure not to touch it with his fingers until he had carefully washed away every speck properly, chatting very little as he worked.

When everything was cleaned to his satisfaction, he instructed her how to hose it down, two and three times in some places.

Patricia gritted her teeth. She didn't know how he trusted her to drive it when he didn't trust her to wash it.

After she hosed all the suds off, he double-checked it, then began to wipe it down with a special leather cloth.

"What are you doing? It's a warm day. The car will dry by itself."

He shook his head. "The water might spot. If you'll excuse me, I have to do this quickly."

Patricia couldn't stand it anymore. She would show him spots.

"Oh, Mi–ike. . . ," she drawled.

He glanced over his shoulder while he continued to wipe the car. "Yes?"

She opened the hose full blast for a few seconds, catching him squarely in the center of his back, then ran into the house, laughing every step of the way. He would forgive her if she made something special for dessert.

<hr />

Mike guided Patty by the elbow as they entered Claude's church. Since she was the pastor's daughter at her own church, Mike understood Patty having strong ties there. For today, though, he wanted to be here. Claude's church was very similar to Patty's, except for one big difference.

Bruce wouldn't be here.

Mike realized he was placing Bruce in an awkward spot, but he couldn't help it. As Mike's probation officer, Bruce's relationship with Mike was supposed to be strictly professional, and seeing Bruce at church encroached on Bruce's private life. He knew cops and other law-enforcement professionals couldn't mix their private lives with those over whom they had authority, and Mike could well understand that. After all that had happened, nothing lessened his respect for Bruce's authority, but if things continued the way he wanted, the situation could become very complicated.

Patty had driven him to a few of the required AA meetings, but he didn't want her to get involved, so he had now found other ways to get around. He knew some of the things said at the meetings would make her uncomfortable. Sometimes they made him uncomfortable, but they were things he needed to hear. He also had some thoughts of his own that he had shared at meetings that he didn't want Patty to hear.

The Monday meetings at Claude's house were closed to all except the specific people who had committed themselves to the intense twelve-step meeting. It was there that he could really let himself go, and he had.

Over the last three weeks, he'd shared some very ugly things about himself to the group, things he had never told anyone. Having to sort himself out in an honest and open manner among people who shared the same addiction forced him to take a hard look at himself, and he saw many things he didn't like.

He would work on those things. God had forgiven him for them, Jesus died to erase them, but he had still done them. A lot of what the meetings were forcing the participants to do was to deal with things from the past so they could move on. Of course he could see the wisdom of doing so, but that didn't make it any easier to do.

He jolted himself out of his thoughts when Patty touched his arm. "Look, there's Claude. Let's go talk to him."

Her touch made him want more. He would have liked to slip his arm around her waist, or failing that, hold her hand while they walked around as strangers in a new setting, but he didn't think that was appropriate in a church.

He wanted to show Patty how special she was and how much she meant to him.

Seeing her at lunch every day was satisfying to some degree, but it wasn't enough. He wanted to date Patty properly, which brought him back to seeing Bruce in a non-professional setting.

Bruce had seen him at his worst, and therefore, Bruce's opinion of him was understandably low. It was obvious to Mike that Bruce wasn't pleased about him spending so much time with his sister. However, Mike was determined to rise above Bruce's perception of him. He fully intended to treat Patty with the respect and dignity she deserved, and, with Jesus in his heart, Mike also intended to prove himself as a decent human being in Bruce's eyes. However, Mike didn't want to think about proving himself to Patty's father, the pastor. The very thought struck fear in his heart.

As they reached the circle of people, Claude introduced them to the small group, not as acquaintances through AA, but as friends. Mike liked that.

He said little, since Patty seemed to be doing a good job of holding up their end of the conversation. He also wanted to follow her lead if anything personal came up.

He only half listened to the conversation concerning the upcoming ladies' function, and his attention wandered to other happenings in the large foyer. Some people milled around a table containing books and pamphlets, and almost everyone else in the room stood around, chatting in small groups.

A family of a man and woman and two small children were greeted heartily when they joined the group standing next to Mike and Patty. Mike really wasn't listening, but when he heard the words "broken arm" and "car accident," he stiffened from head to toe.

The new man in the group had a cast on his right arm, and Mike didn't want to listen, but the words "drunk driver" echoed in his brain.

Mike felt sick. If the man attended this church, he probably lived nearby, and it wasn't far from here that he had his accident. His lawyer told him the lone occupant of the vehicle, a man, had only a broken arm, and it wasn't too bad.

He couldn't help it. He completely ignored Patty talking to Claude's wife about their baby-sitting ministry and listened to the group next to him. It appeared the whole family hadn't been to church for four weeks because his wife, who had been staying home with the young children, had had to go out and get a job while he wasn't working.

Four weeks. The time frame was too close for comfort.

Mike thought he might throw up.

He had to know.

Very gently, he tapped Patty on the shoulder and whispered in her ear that he had to have a quick word with the man in the group next to them. Sucking in a deep breath, Mike took two steps toward the group beside him.

Their conversation stopped.

The man with the cast on his arm blinked in surprise, then smiled. "You must be new here. Welcome to Faith Bible Fellowship. I'm Darryl. Sorry I can't shake your hand." Then he actually smiled.

Mike felt two inches tall.

"I'm Mike. Uh, Darryl, would you mind if I asked you something, uh, privately?"

Everyone in the group stared at him, but he couldn't find out what he wanted to know in front of them. It was hard enough facing only one person.

Darryl looked hesitant, but then nodded and smiled to his wife and stepped to the side with Mike, where they were still close by, but out of that circle of conversation.

Mike forced himself to look into Darryl's face and kept his voice low as he spoke. "I couldn't help but overhear part of your conversation—that you were in a car accident involving a drunk driver. If you wouldn't mind me asking, what night was it, where was it, and was it a hit-and-run?"

Darryl smiled. "I don't know what to say. It was on May seventh, on Main Street, in front of Hank's Outdoor Store. But it's okay. They caught the guy, so if you witnessed the accident, everything is all in motion. I'm just waiting for a court date to testify. It's nice of you to be concerned."

Mike's knees shook. He wished he could run away, but he couldn't.

He cleared his throat and rammed his hands into his pockets. He stared at the ground, because he couldn't look Darryl in the face as he spoke. "I'm afraid it's a little more complicated than that. You see, I was the drunk driver."

Chapter 10

Patricia glanced to the side briefly while she listened to Claude's wife. The woman was a joy to speak with, full of love for the Lord, but Patricia really didn't want to leave Mike alone. Being her father's daughter, she was a key figure in the church and was very used to making conversation with relative strangers, as everyone always felt they knew her and spoke freely to her. As much as some people felt they knew her, she often didn't know them. Sometimes she didn't even know their names. All her life, the one-sided familiarity had helped her develop the art of holding a good conversation versus meaningless chitchat with people she didn't know very well.

She thought it nice to see Mike meet up with someone he knew. From the little he'd said of his usual friends, it didn't sound like any of them ever went near a church, so this was a pleasant surprise.

Patricia turned to glance at Mike as he spoke to his friend one more time, and as she did, she lost all track of the conversation she was supposed to be paying attention to. All the color had drained from Mike's face. He was staring at the floor while the other man was staring at Mike. Neither of them was talking.

"Claude, do you know that man Mike is talking to?"

"No, not really. I think his name is Darren or something like that."

"Excuse me," she said, and quickly walked to Mike.

"Mike? Are you okay? You don't look well."

He cleared his throat. "I'll be okay. Uh, if you wouldn't mind, I have to speak to Darryl, alone."

Patricia blinked and backed up a step. "Oh." She glanced back and forth between the two men. Neither of them appeared pleased to see the other, but she would respect Mike's request and leave them alone. "I'll be with Claude and Michelle."

She watched Mike and Darryl while she listened to Claude and his wife. Instead of talking, Mike pulled a pen out of his pocket, they exchanged phone numbers and separated. Mike walked back toward her, so she quickly turned around, but first she watched Darryl as he rejoined his group. He said only a few words, and a woman in the group grasped Darryl's arm and stared wide-eyed at Mike's back.

Patricia stared up at Mike as he returned to her side.

"I don't want to talk about it," he muttered, then turned to Claude. "I think I need to go sit down. If you'll excuse us?" He nodded politely, and without another word, he led Patricia into the sanctuary where he chose seats in an empty section.

He sat in silence for a few minutes, staring straight ahead at nothing in particular as more people entered the large room. She was starting to worry in earnest when he finally spoke.

"That was the guy I hit."

A knot formed in the bottom of Patricia's stomach. Her first thought was that Claude had set Mike up for this meeting, but that wasn't fair to Claude. She knew Claude wouldn't do something like that without discussing it with Mike first. He also had said he didn't know the man, nor did Claude even get the man's name right.

She waited for Mike to continue, but he didn't. He continued to face the front in silence.

"Mike? If you want to leave, I'll understand."

He shook his head slightly but otherwise didn't move. "No. I need to be here." Very slowly, he turned to her and rested one hand on top of hers. "I'm sorry I'm not being very good company."

"It's okay. I understand."

The lights lowered, the congregation stood, and the first song began.

Midway through the worship time, Mike recovered his composure. He actually sang the last song, which they had sung at Patty's church one of the times he was there, making it the only song familiar to him. When the pastor began his message, Patricia found herself only half concentrating. Most of her thoughts centered on Mike.

She felt sorry for him. It was true that his actions had caused someone to be injured, and it was his fault, but knowing him personally versus thinking of him as the unknown bad guy altered her perspective in what should have been a black-and-white case of right and wrong.

The difference was that instead of passing it off, Mike was actively trying to change. She wanted to say something to let him know that he had her support, but sitting in church in a public setting while they were supposed to be listening to the pastor's sermon was neither the time nor the place. The only thing she could think of to show Mike she was on his side was to take his hand and hold it.

He flinched in surprise when she grasped his hand, but Patricia didn't let that bother her, knowing the last thing Mike would have been expecting would be for her to touch him. He turned to her and raised his eyebrows in a silent question, and Patricia gave his hand a gentle squeeze as an answer. Mike smiled and held on for the rest of the service.

After the closing prayer, as Patricia hunched over to gather her purse from under her chair, the man Mike had been speaking to appeared beside them. Mike stood abruptly while she remained seated.

Darryl nodded down in greeting at Patricia and then turned toward Mike. "When you first came to me, you really threw me for a loop, but I've had a little time to let it sink in. I think I'm ready to talk to you now."

Mike looked down at her. "Would you mind? I won't be long."

She didn't know what she was going to do in a strange place, but Mike needed the time. "Take as long as you need."

Mike and Darryl left the sanctuary and turned the corner, going down the hallway to speak as privately as possible, leaving Patricia alone. Fortunately, Claude and Michelle sought her out, and when she told Claude that Mike had gone to talk to someone, they said they would stay with her until Mike returned.

They introduced her to a few of their friends, and before long, Mike joined them. Darryl and his family were nowhere to be seen.

She doubted Mike would want to make social conversation, so they politely excused themselves and left.

"How would you like to come to my place for lunch instead of going to a restaurant? Or if you want, I can just take you home, if you'd rather be alone."

He buckled his seatbelt and turned to her. "It's going to be okay. Darryl and I had a good talk, but I have some serious thinking to do. In the meantime, lunch at your place sounds great."

It didn't take long, and they were soon at her house. "I hope you don't mind grilled cheese sandwiches. I know we have sandwiches every day, but I can't think of anything else to make that's fast, and I'm hungry."

"That sounds great. Can I help?"

"Sure. What do you want to do?"

He grinned. "Actually, I make grilled cheese sandwiches all the time, and I'm quite proficient at it. How about if you sit down, and I'll cook lunch?"

Patricia had never had a man make her lunch. It was an offer she couldn't refuse, so she sat.

Mike rolled up his sleeves. "Where's the frying pan?"

Patricia stood and pulled the frying pan out of the cupboard, laid it on the element, and sat back down.

Mike checked out the counter. "Where do you keep your bread?"

Patricia rose, walked across the kitchen to the breadbox, opened it, plunked the loaf in front of Mike, and sat back down.

"Where's the butter?"

She remained seated and pointed to the butter dish sitting on the counter, in what she thought was plain sight.

He removed the lid and looked inside the container. "Where's a knife?"

She pointed to the cutlery drawer.

"Got cheese?"

"I would think the fridge would be a good place to look."

He shrugged his shoulders. "Isn't it rude to rummage through someone else's fridge?"

Patricia got up again, opened the fridge, opened up the cheese compartment in the fridge door, handed it to him, and returned to the chair.

He cut a few slices of cheese and returned the remainder of the block to the wrapper.

"I just thought of something. What about—"

Patricia groaned and covered her face with her hands.

"French fries?"

She thought he should have guessed that frozen French fries were simply in the freezer. "Do you want me to make this lunch?"

He wiped his hands on his pants. "Naw. I'm almost done. But thanks for asking."

True to his word, soon the sandwiches were sizzling in the frying pan and a tray of fries was in the oven. After she pointed out the cupboard where the glasses and plates were stored, Mike poured the milk all by himself and served lunch. He hadn't asked if she had napkins, nor did she volunteer any, because that was the one thing she had run out of.

After lunch, rather than sit around, they went for a walk around the neighborhood, not talking about anything important, which was both relaxing and therapeutic.

For supper, Patricia laid everything out on the counter and did all the preparation, and Mike did the cooking.

Usually she attended the evening service, but today she didn't. Instead, they prayed together, asking for direction and guidance for Mike, and then she drove Mike home.

❦

"I missed you yesterday at church."

Patricia hit the Save key and nodded. "I went to a friend's church. I hope you didn't mind."

Her father snickered and patted her on the shoulder as he stood beside her, reading the screen she was working on. "Of course I don't mind. At times I worry that I'm tying you down too much. I like to see you get out with your friends."

Friends. She still wasn't sure what was happening between herself and Mike, but it wasn't just friends. All day Sunday, they hadn't talked about anything serious. She had given him plenty of opportunity to talk about meeting the man whom he had injured, but he hadn't. That was okay too. Experience had taught her that people needed time for something like this to sink in before they could deal with it. What he needed right then was a friend, and being with him when he needed her was part of her ministry to Mike.

The biggest problem was that she was getting too attached to him. She didn't know when it happened, but he had become more than a ministry, and that wasn't in her plan. She wasn't sure how he felt about her, or how he still felt about his ex-fiancée. He had kissed her, but that was at times when his emotions were running high and had gotten the best of him, and she really didn't know what was in his heart.

When everything should have been clearer, things were only getting cloudier.

Her father checked his watch. "I think your friend is going to arrive any minute. I gather he's the same friend you went to the other church with."

"Mmm. . . ," she mumbled as she typed. She didn't know what to say to her father about Mike. Bruce's disapproval was already hanging over her head, and she didn't want to hear the same from her father. Last night Colleen had phoned after the evening service, wondering where she was. After telling Colleen she had been with Mike all day, Colleen bombarded her with questions about a future with Mike that couldn't possibly happen.

Once Mike sorted himself out, he would move on to someone more in his social circle, someone who could keep up with his lifestylke, and she wouldn't see him again.

She didn't want to think about that.

"Hi, Patty. You weren't outside, so I thought I'd find you here. Since it was my turn to bring lunch, I didn't think you'd take off on me."

She hit Save one more time, and they walked outside to the park bench where Mike emptied sandwiches, juice, and some cookies out of his backpack.

They paused for a short word of prayer and ate in silence. The squirrel came, and Patricia fed it in silence.

When only a few minutes of her lunch break remained, Mike finally spoke.

"I know what I'm going to do about Darryl."

"And what is that?"

"I phoned him this morning, and we had a long talk. His medical plan while he's off doesn't pay as much as his salary, so his wife, who was staying home to look after their two young kids, had to go and get a job. Even though the insurance paid to fix his car, it's never as good as new, and they only have one car. Worst of all, he's lost some of the strength and mobility in his arm permanently, which is bad because he's an auto mechanic. His boss is going to give him a job in the parts department, but that doesn't pay as much, and it's not what he wants to do. But he doesn't have a choice."

She wanted to tell Mike it wasn't his fault, but that would have been a lie. It was his fault. He hadn't intended for this to happen, but that didn't alter the fact that it had.

"I read somewhere in the Bible, I forget where, that when a man takes something from someone else, he is to repay it all, plus a portion extra. I can't give him back the full strength of his arm, and he already told me he wouldn't take money, but I know what I'm going to do. I'm going to pay for him to take some kind of course while he's off work, so he can get a better job. It's not much, but it's the only thing I can think of."

"That's a wonderful idea. What did he say?"

"He said no, but I made him promise to talk it over with his wife. I don't see how they will be able to survive if they don't. I think he'll change his mind and accept in a couple of days. I also talked to Claude. He says that this kind of restitution is actually one of the steps that come later in the program. He said he knows how hard it is, but the only way to put all this behind me is to make peace with God, make peace with others, and then to make peace with myself."

Mike rested his elbows on his knees and clasped his hands, but he turned his head so he wasn't facing her as he continued. "Darryl said he forgave me, even before I told him that I would pay for a course. He said God forgave me too, but I don't know if I can forgive myself. What if I hadn't ever met Darryl outside of court? What kind of mess would his life be? It's still not going to be easy for him. The man is a Christian. How could God have let something like this happen to him? Worst of all, I did it."

Patricia felt a lump in her throat. "I don't know. Sometimes bad things happen to good people. Sometimes we know the reason, and sometimes we find out later. Most of the time, we'll only find those answers when we're with Jesus in God's Kingdom."

He turned, and the anguish in his face nearly brought tears to her eyes.

"I had better go," he mumbled. He swept the empty containers into his backpack and left before she could think of anything to say.

All afternoon Patricia worked with a heavy heart. Mike was overburdened with guilt, and he was obviously filled with remorse for what he had done. The man he'd hurt had forgiven him. God had forgiven him. Now if only he could forgive himself. She knew from experience that was often the hardest thing to do.

She pulled the AA pamphlet she had marked with the dates of the meetings at Claude's house out of her drawer. Tonight they would be working on step four "Made a searching and fearless moral inventory of ourselves." In the notes underneath it stated Haggai 1:7— "This is what the LORD Almighty says, 'Give careful thought to your ways.' "

That would be a tough one for Mike. He was already looking carefully at himself, and Patricia didn't think he liked what he saw.

Blankly, she stared through the office door and down the hall leading to her father's office. Her father already knew Mike was one of Bruce's clients, but she didn't know how much Bruce had told him. According to Bruce, Mike wasn't the type of man her father or the church would approve of. However, Bruce only knew the old Mike. The Mike whom Patricia knew was a new creation in God's sight, set apart and called by God to be one of His children.

For now, Mike needed the support of those around him more than she needed the approval of her father or her brother to continue to see Mike for what was no longer strictly ministry. Even more than that, he needed prayer.

She closed her eyes, remembering the way Mike had kissed her. Even though she knew it wasn't a good idea, she had kissed him back, and she would have kissed him longer if he hadn't been the one to move away first.

That was wrong. She couldn't allow him to distract himself from building his relationship with God. How she felt about him had to come second.

Patricia walked into her father's office. "Daddy, I need to pray about something with you."

~

Mike leaned his bike against the church wall and watched Patty trying to feed the squirrel.

It had taken a week, but Darryl had finally accepted his offer. For a few hours, he'd felt better about the way things were going, but then he'd gone to the step five meeting: "Admitted to God, to ourselves, and to another human being the exact nature of our wrongs."

He'd done a lot of wrongs. He hadn't thought much about it before, but when he lumped together all the wrong things he'd done, he was a pitiful excuse for a human being.

Patty raised her head and waved when she saw him. The squirrel took off.

Mike cleared his throat and strode across the grass, forcing himself to smile, although he felt far from cheerful. When he reached her, he sat beside her on the bench.

"See?" she said brightly. "I scared Sally Squirrel all by myself today."

His stomach churned. At least that was one rotten thing he hadn't personally done.

Today it was Patty's turn to bring lunch. Mike waited while she opened a small cooler on the ground beside her. She pulled out two submarine sandwiches, a container of potato salad, and a small cake, along with paper plates and plastic forks.

Mike blinked and stared at the cake. "Is it someone's birthday?"

"Nope. Do you like chocolate swirl?"

He looked down at the cake. "Uh, yes. Is it a holiday or something I've forgotten about?"

She shook her head. "No. I just wanted to give you something special."

A lump formed in his throat. He didn't deserve something special. He stared into the trees while he tried to think of something to say.

Her fingers touching his arm startled him. "I've been keeping track of what you're doing every Monday, and I know what you're thinking. God has forgiven you for everything you've done. All you have to do is lay everything at His feet. 'If we confess our sins, He is faithful and just and will forgive us our sins and cleanse us from all unrighteousness.' That's 1 John 1:9."

At the meeting last night, Claude had quoted that same verse to him and to everyone there. He tried to respond, but couldn't.

"God has forgiven you, Mike. Now all you have to do is forgive yourself." Before she finished speaking, she unwrapped the subs and gave him one. When she closed her eyes, Mike did the same. "Heavenly Father, I thank You for this food, for this day, for the abundance of Your love that You pour down on us every day, and for Your Son, Jesus, who died so that all our sins could be washed clean. Amen."

"Amen," he mumbled.

"Now let's talk about something fun. I want to go out tonight."

He blinked. "Uh-huh. . ."

"When was the last time you've been to the aquarium?"

"The aquarium? You want to go with me?"

He couldn't believe it. She actually laughed. "Of course I do. Who did you think I meant?"

He didn't want to think about that. Even though she'd never talked about another man, he knew there had to be someone out there who was right for her— someone who was more suited to her and more worthy than him. Patty was pure and innocent, and he. . .wasn't. He should have been staying away from her. That she was his probation officer's sister made it worse. He didn't want to think about her being the pastor's daughter. Every day he was with her, she brought more joy to his soul. The days he couldn't see her, it felt like a part of him was missing.

Now, for the first time, it was Patty who was asking him to spend time with her, instead of the other way around. It was an offer he couldn't refuse.

Mike cleared his throat. "I haven't been to the aquarium since I was a kid."

"Then you're in for a treat. I discover something different every time I go, even though it doesn't change much from year to year."

"I'll be looking forward to it. But isn't tonight Bible study night?"

"Yes, but Gary and Melinda's kids came down with chicken pox yesterday, so their house is under quarantine for awhile."

Mike shuddered at the thought. "What time do you want to go? Tell you what. Why don't you come over to my place and I'll cook dinner, and then we'll go."

She grinned, and Mike's heart flip-flopped in his chest. "Depends. Are you going to make grilled cheese sandwiches?"

He pressed one palm to his heart. "You wound me. I told you I'm an accomplished cook, and at my house I know where everything is."

"Well, praise the Lord for that! Name a time, and I'll be there."

He glanced at his wristwatch. He had enough food on hand so he wouldn't have to go shopping, but if Patty saw the way he kept his house, she'd never come back. "Six?"

"Six it is."

They shared the cake and he returned home, where he immediately began a flurry of housekeeping. The novelty of cleaning his house himself had worn off quickly, and as he worked, he grumbled to himself that the first thing he was going to do when he got a new job was to hire his housekeeper back.

After everything was picked up and the house was clean, he had a fast shower. When Patty arrived, he was ready.

Chapter 11

"Come on in. I hope you're hungry."

She smiled as she entered. "Yes, I am. Something smells good."

Mike patted himself on the back. They'd eaten together so often, he knew exactly what she liked. Patty was easy to please, so what he had prepared wasn't difficult. Many of the women he'd dated in the past would settle only for the most expensive, and the best, and certainly nothing home-cooked, especially by him. He had once interpreted it as sophistication. He now saw things differently.

What they had talked about last night at the meeting had to do not as much with the rotten things everyone had done but the motivations behind those things. For himself, it was self-centeredness that had driven him—not to succeed financially or have more than everyone else, because he already had more than he needed. Instead, after he sat down and really took a good hard look at himself, he saw everything he did was in some way related to feeding his ego and putting what he saw as his own needs, instead of the needs of others, first.

Starting today, he was going to put others first, beginning with Patty. He would work on the rest later.

Mike grinned. "Don't be too impressed. It's just a simple potato casserole recipe my housekeeper gave me because she felt sorry for me. I'm going to barbecue the steaks now that you're here. Want to come outside and talk to me, since everything else is done?"

He guided her through the house, smiling to himself at her reaction to his preparations. He had used the dining room table instead of the kitchen, and his setting included a tablecloth and cloth napkins as well as a small vase of flowers he'd snipped from one of the bushes in the yard. All in all, considering he'd never cooked dinner for a woman before, he thought it looked rather romantic, and he was quite proud of himself.

The only thing not perfect was that since it was summer, it was still light outside. For an added touch, he would have liked to have had it slightly dark and to have either candles lit or the crystal chandelier on low.

She followed him into the kitchen where he uncovered the steaks which were marinating on the counter and transferred them to a plate. He bit back a smile as she not very discreetly checked out the whole kitchen. He'd carefully cleaned up after himself, including washing the bowls he'd used in his preparations, so nothing was out of place. He'd scrubbed the counters and sink with some kind of cleaner his housekeeper had stashed under the sink and then gone on to sanitize the whole house with it. Just using it made his eyes water, but it was worth it. Everything was now spotless, and the house was the cleanest it had been for a month.

He led her outside where his built-in gas barbecue was heated up and ready.

Patty shuffled her feet, then sat in one of the padded deck chairs. "There must be something I can do."

The steaks sizzled as they touched the hot grill. "Nope. I've got everything under control."

She folded her hands in her lap and sat straight in the chair, her back stiff as a board.

"Relax, Patty. You're my guest."

"Sorry."

To be honest with himself, he was as nervous as she was, except he had something to concentrate on, which was cooking. Before, when he was nervous, he offset it by having a drink in his hand, but that was no longer an option.

If he had had anything left in the house, which, of course, he didn't because Patty had dumped it all down the sink, his first impulse would have been to offer her a glass of wine. This was an old habit he would have to break.

It had been five weeks and six days since he'd had a drink, and this was the first time that neither he nor his guest drank while he entertained. When he was a child, before he was allowed to drink, his parents always served alcohol when they entertained, which was the socially acceptable thing to do. He felt the absence, as much by the breaking of a lifetime of habits as the addiction itself.

"I've got coffee ready in the kitchen. If you want a cup, help yourself." He flipped the steaks over. "I don't mind if you rummage through my fridge. I'd like to make you a cappuccino, but I can't leave this."

"It's okay. I can watch the barbecue."

"No way. I said I was going to cook dinner, and by that I meant that I'm going to do it all. Tell you what. I'll make that cappuccino after supper." He already knew exactly what flavoring she liked in it. He'd bought a jar of it last week, waiting for the day he would have the opportunity to use it. He'd also bought a can of spray whipped cream for the occasion, just in case.

While he cooked the steaks, Mike told her a few jokes and some of his best and worst barbecue experiences over the years. She howled with laughter when he told her about the time his neighbor's dog dug a hole under the fence, then somehow managed to knock over the plate of cooked meat when he went into the house to bring out the rest of the food. He had come back into the yard with his friends, ready to eat, and discovered the dog had eaten the wieners and left the steaks on the ground, untouched.

Today he didn't want to eat outside. He transferred the steaks to a plate and ushered Patty to the dining room. First he pulled out the chair for her, seated her properly, poured the coffee, and then began to place the food on the table.

She ran her fingers over the cloth napkins, then sniffed at the flowers while he made a second trip back to the kitchen. Her eyes opened wide when he laid the potato casserole before her.

"Don't be so shocked. Not every single man lives on pizza and frozen dinners. It really was easy to make."

Next, he brought the dish of broccoli with cheese sauce out of the microwave.

"Don't tell me you made this yourself."

He grinned. "I'm good, but I'm not that good. The sauce is out of a bottle, but the broccoli is cooked to perfection."

Mike sat, tucked his napkin in his lap, and folded his hands on the table while she fiddled with her napkin.

He waited for awhile, then spoke. "Shall we pray before it gets cold?"

Her cheeks turned pink, which he thought quite endearing.

After they paused for a word of prayer, instead of digging in, she continued to stare at everything.

"Don't be shy. Do you want me to eat some first to prove to you that you're not going to die of food poisoning?"

Her cheeks darkened again. "Sorry. I'm just so caught off guard by all this. You really did make this all by yourself. I expected something different."

"Did you expect me to be like the single guys on television—to buy takeout and put it on my own dishes and pretend I did it myself?"

Patty stared at the ground and said nothing.

"I made dessert too."

"Boy. I don't know what to say. You went through so much trouble—just for me."

She didn't know the half of it. Preparing the food was nothing compared to cleaning up the house. It had been so bad, he would have died of embarrassment if she'd seen it. When his housekeeper came back, he would more fully appreciate all her hard work cleaning up after him.

He shrugged his shoulders. "It's not a big deal. Even if you hadn't come, I still had to eat. It was a nice change to be able to cook something special."

Her cheeks flushed, she lowered her chin, cautiously took a bite, paused, and then smiled. "This is really good. It would be perfect for a potluck at the church. Do you think I could have the recipe?"

Mike laughed. "No one has ever asked me for a recipe before, especially a woman. I guess so."

"No. Maybe I shouldn't. Next time there's a potluck, you can make this and bring it yourself."

Mike froze, his fork halfway to his mouth. "You're kidding, right?"

She smiled. "Wrong."

He'd never been to a potluck, and wasn't really sure what went on there.

All he knew was that it had something to do with eating.

When they were done, he brought out the dessert.

Patty giggled. "This is Jell-O."

"Yes. I boiled the water all by myself too."

She tilted her head to examine it further. "You were very artistic spraying on the whipped cream."

"I wish I had a cherry to put on top for a finishing touch, but my creativity only goes so far."

She glanced quickly at her watch. "I don't want to rush through this delectable treat, but if we're going to have time to walk through the aquarium without rushing, we're going to have to leave soon."

"Fine by me."

Soon they were in the car. Mike settled into the passenger seat and selected a CD while Patty drove. The novelty of Patty driving his car had worn off long ago, and he longed to be the one driving. Now the only time he got to sit behind the wheel was on Saturdays when he washed it while he cleaned the interior.

If he forced himself to think of something good, being without his car had a few side benefits. Despite the fact that he had cashed in his membership at the gym, he was in great shape from biking for miles every day. He was also getting to know the people in his neighborhood. He was on a first-name basis with the clerk at the grocery store, because he could carry only what fit in his backpack and had to shop every few days instead of once a week like he used to. Since he was unemployed, he had plenty of time to strike up friendly conversations with other people in line rather than fretting away the time, anxious to be out the door.

Patty's voice broke him out of his thoughts. "Remember, since this was my idea, I'm paying."

Mike sighed. "Patty, don't do this to me."

"If you don't let me pay, I'm going to turn around right now, and I'll drop you off at home."

Mike grumbled his reply.

"Good," she said. "Here we are."

❧

Patricia smiled sweetly as she tucked her wallet back into her purse and patted it. "There. That wasn't so bad, was it?"

He mumbled something she couldn't quite make out, but she decided not to question him.

Since it was a weeknight and only a couple of hours until closing, the complex was nearly deserted, which was fine with her. It was comfortably quiet, with the only noise the bubbling of the aquariums and the low murmur of conversations from a few small groups of people in various places in the section they entered. The backlit aquariums in the dark room gave it a strange ambiance of privacy in a public setting.

They walked around the room slowly, enjoying the colorful fishes and other aquatic species on display.

As they stood watching a small display of starfish that weren't really doing anything, she felt the warmth of Mike's hand enclose hers. He gave it a little squeeze, and then didn't let go.

"This is really relaxing. You had a good idea. Thank you for suggesting this."

She nodded. "I really like it here. It doesn't change much, but it's just as fascinating every time I come. When I get home, I always think about setting up my own fish tank, but it's not the same."

They moved to the next display, a tank containing some strange creatures that must have been some kind of fish, but just seemed to sit at the bottom of the tank like rocks with eyes. Mike lowered his head for a closer look, and Patricia held back a snicker at his boyish curiosity.

No matter how close he stood to a tank, and no matter whether he examined the tank's occupants or read the blurb about each species, he didn't let go of her hand.

By the time they checked out a few more displays, they were the only people left in that section of the room. Patricia thought it would be a good time to get him talking.

"You haven't told me about your meeting last night. You always tell me something about what you did, but this time you haven't."

She felt him stiffen.

"Yeah, well, it's kind of a scary thing, having to start making a serious list of all the things you've messed up in your life. After the meeting, I couldn't sleep, so I made my list last night. Claude warned us not to get obsessive about it—just list the major stuff. Well, my list isn't very pretty."

Part of her wanted to assure him that it couldn't be that bad, but truthfully, she didn't know it wasn't. She knew about his drinking and driving, and she wasn't stupid enough to think that the time he was arrested was the first time he did it. Bruce had also suspected that Mike had been under the influence of more than just alcohol at the time. It was a subject she didn't want to bring up. She also knew he'd fled the scene of an accident. The thing that bothered her most was that he had been unfaithful to the woman he had promised to marry.

He continued to stare into the tank. "Claude gave us a list of verses. I think he meant to encourage us, but I'm still not sure about all this. Last night I read them so many times I think I've got them memorized."

"Memorizing Bible verses is not a bad thing, Mike. I've got a number of verses memorized."

"The main verse of the night was 'Therefore confess your sins to each other and pray for each other so that you may be healed.' I forget the reference. It's in the New Testament somewhere."

Patty smiled. She knew it was in the book of James but couldn't remember the exact reference. "Confession is good for the soul. Really."

"We're supposed to talk about this 'exact nature of our wrongs' thing with another person, and Claude said it's a good idea to do it with a clergy person. You're kind of a clergy person. You work for a church, and you've been to Bible college. You already know some of my list of wrongs. Do you think that counts?"

She could hear the anguish in his voice. Some people were able to freely admit when they messed up and confess their failings. Others were not. In her years of counseling, she'd dealt with both types. Mike obviously fit in the latter category. "Sure. I think that counts. Remember: Your life is not for me to judge. Whatever you've done, good or bad, is only between you and God, but it does help to talk about it."

He cleared his throat, but his words came out in a low rumble anyway. "You already know about the charges against me. And you know what happened with Robbie. I've obviously had a falling out with Dad, and of course Mom is even more disappointed in me. No one at work is going to miss me, because I haven't been the best manager. The list goes on. I've even been rotten to my house-keeper—when she was my housekeeper."

He stopped talking and looked up at the description of the species in the near-est tank, but he wasn't really reading the words. Patricia waited for him to continue.

"Everything I've done, it all comes down to thinking of myself first and not caring about the rights or feelings of others, even my family. I did whatever felt good at the time, without regard for anyone else. It didn't matter if I knew I was going to hurt them." He turned and stared blankly into the next aquarium. "I don't know why you put up with me, but you're always there." He swallowed hard. "You know what's really humbling? God pulled me out of the pit I was in and placed me with so many people who could help me before any more damage was done. Bruce. Claude." He turned around and, not releasing her hand, reached up his other hand and ran his fingers down her cheek. "Most of all, you."

Patricia trembled at his touch. She had no idea that Claude's group would be doing something so deeply intense as this. Even in the strictest sessions, never had she pushed someone she was counseling to look at themselves so hard.

But then, she'd never counseled someone with such a powerful addiction, or who had made such a mess of his life. All she knew was that for those who applied themselves, with the help of God, the AA program worked.

Mike had displayed tremendous strength of character so far, especially since she understood the courage needed to honestly dig deep into oneself. He not only opened himself up to her and others, but he was moving past talking about it and was really doing something about it. Not many people could do that.

He prayed and read his Bible daily, trusting God completely for the guidance and instruction to be what God wanted him to be, and he was laying his life in God's hands, one day at a time.

"God loves you, Mike. With the sacrifice of Jesus, everything you've done is wiped clean."

He turned to her and smiled. "Yeah. I know. He really does, and it's great."

Patricia looked up at him, then closed her eyes and leaned her cheek into his palm.

Not only did God love Mike, Patricia knew that she loved him too.

❧

Patricia checked her watch. Again.

She had laid out the hose, Mike's special sponge, and the bottles of his favorite cleaners in the driveway. She'd also bought an extra bucket, which she had also left outside.

But Mike wasn't there.

For all Mike's failings, one thing she had learned about him was that he was punctual. He arrived faithfully at the same time every day for lunch, and since he started coming on Saturdays to wash his car, he also arrived at the same time every week.

For the first time, he was half an hour late, and Patricia didn't know what to do. She'd phoned his house and gotten the answering machine, and he didn't answer his cell phone.

She knew that he was on his bike. If he had an accident, except for his helmet, he was unprotected.

Once more, she went into the house to phone him. Just as the answering machine clicked on, she heard a strange clunking noise on her porch. Patricia dropped the phone and ran to the door.

Mike had arrived. She opened her mouth to tell him how scared she'd been that something had happened to him, knowing that in her next breath she would scold him for the exact same thing, but no words came out.

Something wasn't right. Instead of his jeans, he was wearing shorts. For some reason, he was wearing gloves with no fingers, he was breathing heavily, and he seemed taller than usual.

He panted as he spoke. "Sorry I'm late. It took me longer than I thought."

She first looked where he usually put his bike, but it wasn't there. Then she looked down at his feet. He was wearing inline skates.

She tipped her head back and looked up at him. He peeled the wrist guards off his hands, tossed them on the ground, then pulled the helmet off his head. A few locks of wet hair landed with a splat across his forehead. The rest of his hair hung in damp clumps, and a few drops of sweat dripped down his face. He swiped his arm across his forehead. "That was much harder than I thought it would be."

"You came all this way on those things?"

He let go a ragged sigh. "No. I had someone drop me off a few blocks from here, and I jumped through your neighbor's sprinkler just to look all sweaty. What do you think?"

"You don't have to be so sarcastic. It was an honest question."

He sank to sit on the bottom step, stretching his legs out and not making any effort to take the skates off his feet. "Sorry, I didn't mean to snap at you. I'm really hot and tired."

"I'll go get you some water."

She hadn't been gone long, but when she returned, instead of being on the bottom step where she left him, she found him stretched out, lying on the grass. He looked up at her from his position flat on his back. "Don't laugh. The grass is nice and cool."

"I'm not laughing. Just the opposite. I'm really quite amazed. It's quite a distance from here to your house. I wonder how many miles it is."

He lifted one foot in the air and began to undo the laces while still lying on his back. "I don't know. But it's too many miles to do this again. My ankles are killing me."

She looked to his car, parked in the middle of the driveway, ready to be washed, which was the reason he had come. "I bought another bucket, just for you to use for your car. I have to finish cleaning the house, so you do the car while I wash my floors, and then we can make supper."

"Sure." He pulled off the skates and thick wool socks and added them to the pile beside the porch. He then padded barefoot to the car, arched and stretched his back, bent to rub his ankles, and picked up the bucket.

Patricia left him alone so he could go to the basement and fill the bucket with exactly the right temperature water while she began to finish her housework.

He was still wiping the car by the time she was done, so Patricia headed into the kitchen to start making supper. She had expected him to walk in and offer to help, but when she had finished everything, including setting the table, and he still hadn't appeared, she headed outside to get him. She didn't make it past the living room.

Mike was lying on the couch, and he was snoring.

Out of curiosity, she picked up his cell phone that he had left on the coffee table. The battery was dead.

Very gently, she shook him. He opened one eye, then the other, and smiled lazily. "Huh?" he mumbled, "Did I fall asleep?"

"Yes. Now wake up. Supper is almost ready."

Slowly, he sat up, stretched, then rose and walked to the washroom, still barefoot, because the only footwear he had with him were his inline skates.

Patricia stared at the closed door. She'd spent the afternoon cleaning the house while Mike had washed the car. She had made supper while he made himself at home and had a nap.

It felt almost domestic, and she wasn't sure she liked it.

<hr/>

Mike sat in his study at his desk. A few weeks ago they had done step six. "Were entirely ready to have God remove all these defects of character." He'd found that step to be easy. After the time he'd spent with Patty at the aquarium talking about some of the things that made him tick, the good and the bad, he found it to be a real eye-opener to look at himself that way. Once he'd figured out the honest reasons why he had behaved so pathetically, he was more than ready to ask God to help him get rid of the garbage in his life.

Likewise, when the group had gone over step seven, "Humbly asked Him to remove our shortcomings." That wasn't difficult either. Not only was God the Creator of the universe, which included himself, God was also his heavenly Father, who wanted to help him. All Mike had to do was pray honestly and seriously about it, and he knew that God would help him work on removing those shortcomings.

However, what they were doing this week was getting harder. Step eight said, "Made a list of all persons we had harmed, and became willing to make amends to them all."

Mike held the pen in the air, but he wasn't quite ready to write any names yet. Making a list would be easy, but the caveat of the step was that for everyone he wrote down, he also had to be prepared to make amends to them.

He thought carefully of the people in his life whom he had harmed enough that he needed to make amends.

At first he was pleased with his completed list. It had only three names. For now, it was enough that he had made the list and was willing. He didn't want to think of next week when he would actually have to do it.

He folded the paper and tucked it into his Bible just as the doorbell rang.

It has been a long time since someone unexpectedly showed up at his door.

When he opened it, he made no effort to hide his smile.

Chapter 12

P atty! Not that it isn't great to see you, but what are you doing here?"

Patricia smiled. It was almost word for word what she'd said so often lately that she'd lost count.

"I was just on my way home, and since it's payday, I don't feel like cooking. Would you like to join me at Sir Henry's?"

Mike groaned out loud, but Patricia could tell he was only fooling around. They'd been to Sir Henry's a number of times, and every time, Mike had enjoyed himself. It was close, the food was cheap, and despite Sir Henry's unusual decor, they enjoyed the atmosphere of the place. Most of all, they appreciated the privacy, because most of the times they'd been there, they were the only patrons eating inside.

"Sure. Just let me lock up."

Again, they were the only people inside while the line-up at the drive-thru window was consistently five cars long. They waited patiently while Henry finished taking an order at the window.

"What do you think Henry would do if one day we came through the drive-thru instead of coming inside?"

"Shhh!" she whispered. "Don't talk like that. It might be too hard on poor Henry's heart."

Mike laughed, which Patricia thought a lovely sound. He didn't laugh often enough, and she wondered how she could get him to laugh more often. Of course, going through the AA program with all its soul-searching intensity, and the fact that his court date was looming closer, might have had something to do with it.

They gave Henry their orders and were about to choose a table when Patricia pointed to the display on the wall beside the cash register.

"Look. Henry has some new pictures."

Mike harumphed. "They're not new. He just moves them around on the wall so you think they're new."

"They're new."

Mike shook his head. "No, they're not. I've caught him switching."

"He was putting new ones up while he rearranged some old ones, that's all." Patricia pointed to what she thought was new since the last time they were there. It was a picture of all the pictures on the wall of the restaurant. "See? We would have remembered this one if we'd seen it before."

Mike's eyebrows raised. "He must be getting desperate."

"Either that, or he takes his camera everywhere."

While they waited, instead of sitting at a table, they walked around checking out all the pictures, something they'd never done before. They shared comments on many of them, especially the ones taken in various travel spots around the world.

Mike pointed to a photo of the Eiffel Tower. "What do you think of Paris as a honeymoon spot?"

Patricia opened her mouth, but no words came out. Up until recently, she'd never entertained the thought of a honeymoon, because she hadn't met a man she would have wanted to honeymoon with.

Mike smiled, and her heart went into overdrive. She wasn't supposed to be thinking of travel and honeymoon with Mike. She had started seeing him only as a ministry favor to Bruce, and somewhere along the way, something very wrong had happened to her plan.

Fortunately, Henry called their number. She deliberately chose the table farthest away from the pictures of Paris, she changed the subject, and they ate in peace.

Mike leaned his bike against the church wall and swiped some of the wetness out of his hair. The dismal gray of the rainy day suited his mood.

Today was the day he had to start step nine. "Made direct amends to such people wherever possible, except when to do so would injure them or others."

Since Patty wasn't sitting on the bench in the rain, he walked inside the building to join her at her desk.

She fumbled with the phone as she was hanging up with a call. "Mike! What a surprise! I didn't expect you today when it started raining."

He shrugged his shoulders. "I was halfway here when it started, so I figured I might as well come all the way. I was going to get wet anyway, no matter which direction I headed."

She smiled. "You're in luck. Since it wasn't raining when I was getting ready, I brought two sandwiches, and I just made fresh coffee."

For once, her cheeriness didn't affect him. "That's nice," he mumbled.

Her smile dropped. "What's wrong?"

He stared out the window at the rain, which was now coming down heavier. "I started to try making amends to the people I've hurt. I've already done what I can for Darryl. In the past few days, I've called my dad at least a half a dozen times and left messages for him to call me, and he hasn't. So I guess it's up to him now. The last one left is my ex-fiancée, but the number I have is out of service, and she's not listed in the phone book."

"Do you think she moved to another city? Or what if she got married and changed her name?"

"Don't know."

"I guess you don't know where she works?"

"Nope."

"What about a mutual friend?"

"Didn't have any."

"You mean you didn't know each other's friends?"

"Nope. Think about us. Except for the last little while, we wouldn't have had any mutual friends either. Your friends are all nice Christian people, and they hang around mostly with other nice Christian people. My friends are all party-hardy drunks like I was. There wouldn't be any mutual friends because you don't have a thing in common with a single one of them. I'm not sure I have anything in common with them anymore."

"I'm sure that's not true."

Mike turned to her. "It is true. Did you know that I recently phoned the cops on my best friend? The night of the car show, my friends spent most of the night in the beer garden, and I went home. I phoned the cops because Wayne was going to drive after drinking all night. After I called, the cops were waiting for Wayne in the parking lot. Since he hadn't actually got in the car yet, they told him to take a cab home and pick up the car the next day, which he did. He hasn't talked to me since. First it was just my dad, now there's another person who won't talk to me. I'm trying to make things right. I really am."

"Sometimes when we ask people for forgiveness, it doesn't happen, and there's not much you can do about it. Whether or not it was received on earth, it was received in heaven."

"Yeah. That's what Claude said too."

"Surely there's someone you can call to get her number."

He stared blankly into the rain again. "There is someone. Her best friend, Molly. I can't remember her last name, but I know where she works—if she still works there."

Patty's desk drawer squeaked open, and he heard a thump on the desktop. "There's one way to find out. Phone and ask."

Mike stared at the phone book. He could put it off, but the only person he would be hurting by not following through would be himself. He didn't know if Robbie could forgive him, but he wouldn't know if he didn't ask. In a way, if she refused to see him, it would make the whole thing easier.

He paged through and found the number for where Molly used to work and dialed. He noticed that Patty was shuffling papers, but her exaggerated motions indicated she was trying too hard to look busy.

"Good morning, Quinlan Enterprises," the receptionist chirped.

Mike cleared his throat. "May I speak to Molly?"

"Molly? Sorry, she quit before the wedding."

"Do you have any idea how I can contact her?"

"Oh. Is this personal? She's here. One moment."

The phone clicked, and some music came on the line. Strangely, instead of the usual horrible canned music that businesses typically used for people on hold, it was a Christian artist he recognized. He was beginning to enjoy the song when a male voice answered.

"Ken Quinlan."

"Sorry, I must have the wrong extension. I'm looking for Molly."

"Just a minute. She's right here." He heard the phone being shuffled. "Honey? It's for you. I don't know who it is."

Mike sucked in a deep breath.

Molly's voice came on the line. "Hello?"

"Hello, Molly. I don't know if you remember me. This is Mike Flannigan. I'm looking for Robbie, and I was wondering if you could give me her number."

Silence hung on the line, but it didn't last. "She's happily married! You leave her alone!" The phone shuffled again as it passed hands, but he could still hear Molly's voice. "Quick. Hang up."

The man didn't hang up, and Mike could hear him talking to Molly. "What are you doing? Who is it?"

"Remember I told you that before Robbie and Garrett got married, she was engaged to someone else, and the guy was a real creep? It's the creep."

Mike cringed, but it was nothing less than he deserved. Molly had never liked him from the first time they met.

Ken spoke again. "Still, what does he want?"

Whoever was holding the phone covered the mouthpiece with his hand. Mike waited while the two of them argued, and although he heard the differences between the male and female voices, he considered it a blessing in disguise that he couldn't hear what was actually being said.

Ken's voice came back on the line. "Molly doesn't want to talk to you, Mike, but maybe you can tell me why you want to talk to Robbie."

"I've been doing a lot of thinking lately, and I wanted to tell her I'm sorry and wish her the best."

Mike's heart pounded while more silence hung over the line.

Finally, Ken spoke. "For some reason, I trust you. Tell you what. I'll do better than her phone number. I'll give you the address so you can do it in person. Just so you know, Robbie and Garrett are now the proud parents of one-month-old twins."

His hand shook, but Mike wrote down the address and directions to get there. In the background, he could hear Molly nattering her disbelief that Ken, who was apparently her husband, was going along with him.

Mike hung up.

"Well? How did it go?" Patty asked.

"I need to ask you a favor. Instead of sitting here for lunch, can we go to the mall? I need your help picking out a couple of baby gifts."

⊰❈⊱

Mike knocked on the door. He didn't have to recheck the address that Molly's husband had given him. He recognized Robbie's car in the driveway.

The door opened. A very big man holding a small baby stood in the doorway. "Mike." He nodded. "Molly told us you called."

Mike extended his hand, then pulled it back because Robbie's husband needed both hands to hold the baby. Mike wasn't sure that Garrett wanted to shake hands anyway. After all, he could only guess what Robbie might have told her husband about him. He forced himself to smile. "You must be Garrett."

"Yes. We've met before."

Garrett stepped aside, allowing him to enter. Not too many men stood taller than Mike at six feet tall, but Garrett towered above him by a couple of inches. He had a husky build and a rugged complexion which hinted he worked outside. He appeared to be a man one would remember, but Mike didn't.

Thinking back during the time following the breakup with Robbie, he had fallen into a pit of heavy drug and alcohol abuse. Only recently could he admit to himself that he had suffered blackouts during that period of his life, and it bothered him. If that were the case, he didn't want to think of what he could have said or done, especially since Garrett wasn't exactly welcoming him with open arms.

The door closed behind him, and Mike suddenly felt very alone. Instead of just dropping him off, Patty had insisted on waiting for him in the car. He had found it comforting that even if she wasn't with him, she was watching. But now that the door was closed, the connection was broken, and he felt the loss.

"Robbie!" Garrett called. "You have a visitor."

Mike's stomach contorted as he laid the two gifts he'd brought on the coffee table and waited.

He had prayed about this moment more times than he could count, asking God to help him get proper closure to his relationship with Robbie, to give him strength and wisdom, and to help him be understanding of how much he'd hurt her if she didn't forgive him.

The more he thought about it, he also had prayed for Robbie, as he recognized this wasn't going to be easy for her either, but it was something they both probably needed to do.

Robbie appeared from around the corner, carrying another small baby. Robbie was exactly as he remembered her, except her hair was a little shorter.

He cleared his throat, but his words still came out gravelly. "Hi. Congratulations on the twins. I brought a little something for them."

Both Mike and Robbie glanced at the gifts he'd already set out on the coffee table.

Robbie cuddled the baby in her arms. "This is Tyler, and that's Sarah. Thank you."

Mike turned to see Garrett, still standing near the door, the baby in his arms, watching them.

Mike turned back to Robbie and cleared his throat again. "They're really cute.

And you look good too. How have you been?"

"Fine. And you?"

"Fine."

They stood staring at each other.

Mike rammed his hands into his pockets. "I know there's no way I can ever make it up to you, but after all this time, I want to say I'm sorry for the way I treated you. You didn't deserve that. I'm really sorry."

She didn't say anything for awhile. Her eyes widened, and he could tell her mind was racing. "That's what you came here for? To say you're sorry?"

"Yes."

Silence hung in the air.

Robbie's eyes glistened, but she blinked it away. "I don't know what to say. Every once in awhile, I've prayed for you."

His throat clogged. "I think it worked. I got myself into a couple of big messes, but God has really blessed me through it all, helping me as I try to pick up the pieces."

They stared at each other for awhile.

Robbie shuffled the baby. "I don't know where my manners are. Please, sit down. Would you like a cup of coffee?"

All the tension drained from him, and he gave her a shaky smile. "Don't make coffee for me. I'm hyper enough right now without adding caffeine."

Robbie smiled and sat on the couch, and Garrett sat beside her. Mike took the single armchair across from them.

At first glance, Mike thought that Robbie and Garrett were very different from each other, but at the same time, a good match. He was not only relieved that things were working out for her, but more than that, he was genuinely happy for her.

"I won't stay long. I know this is awkward for you, but it's something I needed to do, for a lot of reasons. Thanks for taking the time to see me like this."

"Actually, I never thought I would ever say this, but it's nice to see you again."

She actually smiled at him, and Mike knew that he had done the right thing. It released a bond he hadn't known had been weighing him down all this time.

"I know I handled myself badly, but we weren't right for each other. You two look so happy together, and now you've been blessed with two beautiful children."

Robbie nodded. "I think we both knew it at the time. It's amazing how God can make things work, even when we can't see it at the time."

"Yes."

"Are you married now, Mike?"

"No. There are a number of things I still have to work out before I can allow myself the privilege." He stood. "Speaking of that, I really should be going. I have a friend waiting for me outside in the car."

Garrett and Robbie stood as well. "Why don't you invite your friend in?"

While he felt infinitely better about Robbie and their past together, Mike didn't think it was a good idea to introduce the woman he loved to the woman he once said he would marry. "I really should be going. Maybe another time."

They walked him to the door where they both took note of Patty sitting in the car pretending to be reading a book. It was barely noticeable, but he saw Robbie and Garrett quickly exchange smiles.

"Tell you what," Robbie said. "We haven't decided on a date yet, but why don't you bring your friend to the baby dedication? That will also give us all a little more time for this to sink in. We'll let you know when it is."

Mike smiled. "That sounds like a good idea." He paused before he walked away. "Thank you again for seeing me, Robbie. You have no idea how much this has meant to me."

"Same."

Mike turned and walked to the car where Patty was waiting for him. He slid into the passenger seat, but she didn't drive away. Without using a bookmark, Patty tossed her book into the backseat, grasped the steering wheel with both hands, and turned toward him.

"Well? How did it go?"

He hadn't expected it to go so well, nor had he expected to feel so good after it was over. Robbie hadn't come right out and said she had forgiven him, but he could tell she had, long ago. She'd even been praying for him, and the knowledge touched him deeply.

He knew Patty also had been praying for him, and he felt both humbled and blessed because of it. And now, added to his relief from the burden of seeing Robbie, Patty's beautiful smile almost made him lightheaded. He wanted to tell her he loved her, but there were still too many unknowns looming in his future.

He smiled. "It went great. I'll tell you all about it when we get home."

❧

Mike walked into the garage and stood still, staring unseeing at his car. For the first time in a long time, his car was in his own garage.

He had settled with the insurance company for the costs of the accident, but in addition to that, it was time for the renewal of his annual premium, and his rates had skyrocketed. After more than two months without an income, for the first time in his life, money was getting tight, and he really was having to watch where the money was going.

Patty often cajoled him about needing to save money, and he could no longer dispute her reasoning for not renewing the insurance when he couldn't drive. Patty had a car of her own to drive; she really didn't need his, and it was an expense he could no longer afford. Patty had driven the car into his garage and parked it permanently. Last night the insurance had expired at midnight.

Her friend Colleen had come to pick her up immediately after supper, and shortly after that, Claude had picked him up to go to the step ten meeting.

"Continued to take personal inventory and when we were wrong promptly admitted it."

Mike fiddled with the knot of his tie and left the garage. As always, God's timing was perfect. Bruce was due any minute to pick him up. This morning was his court appearance, where he was going to promptly admit to the judge how wrong he'd been.

Chapter 13

Patricia entered the courtroom. Mike was already at his place in the front, sitting stoically beside a man whom she assumed was his lawyer. Bruce sat behind him in the front row. She quietly walked to the front and sat beside her brother.

"This is it, the big day," he whispered as she shuffled into the seat.

"Yes."

Patricia shuddered. She'd never been inside a courtroom before. Her only experience with court was court scenes on television. The real thing was far less dramatic. Everything was very formal. All the men at the front wore suits, including Mike. Even Bruce was wearing a suit, which was rare. She couldn't remember the last time she'd seen her brother in a suit, including church on Sundays.

Even from the back, Mike looked dashing in his suit. She had seen him in a suit only once before, on the day he'd shown up for lunch after what had been his last attempt to find a job before this court fiasco was behind him. At the time, she had laughed and teased him about trying to impress her father. She thought she was being very funny, but Mike hadn't laughed.

Unlike then, there was nothing funny now. This was the day they had been waiting for, the day that would be the catalyst to Mike's future.

He turned his head slightly, and she could see when he saw her out of the corner of his eye. He gave her a nervous smile, then turned his face forward and continued to sit stiffly with his hands folded on the table in front of him.

Mike's case was the first of the day. Still, the minutes dragged like hours.

"All rise!"

Everyone stood, the judge entered, and the court session began.

The way the clerk read the charges against Mike seemed so cold, and the sterile atmosphere in the courtroom made it worse. It was hard to believe that the Mike she knew and loved was the person who had behaved so callously only ten weeks ago. By the mighty hand of God in his life, he was a changed person. He had put his life in order and was moving forward again.

"And how does the defendant plead?" the judge asked.

Mike's lawyer stood. "My client pleads not guilty, your honor."

Mike jumped to his feet. "Wait, that's not what I said. I'm guilty!"

The lawyer turned to him. "Sit down, Mr. Flannigan," he whispered firmly. "I'm following your father's instructions."

Mike didn't sit. He turned to the judge. "I plead guilty, your honor."

The lawyer nudged him. "Stop it, Mike. You don't know what you're doing."

"I do know what I'm doing. I was wrong, it was my fault, and I'm guilty."

"But I can—"

The gavel sounded.

"Order!" the judge called with a firm voice. "Counsel, please approach the bench."

Patricia forced herself to breathe. She didn't want Mike to go to jail. She wished he could be let off. But he really was guilty and, in the eyes of the law, he deserved whatever the justice system handed down to him.

The entire courtroom was silent except for the lowered voices of the judge, the prosecuting attorney, and Mike's lawyer. She strained to hear what was being said, but only a low murmur of male voices was audible.

She watched Mike, alone at the front. The decision being made now would affect his whole future, yet he held himself bravely, sitting with his hands folded in front of him. Still, she could tell he was nervous, because as she looked to the side, she could see him tapping one foot. She'd never loved him more.

Both attorneys returned to their places.

The judge folded his hands in front of him and spoke to the courtroom. "Despite advice from his legal counsel, the defendant has pled guilty, and the record will remain as such. Prosecution has advised that the defendant has voluntarily made restitution to rectify the damage he has caused with the injured party, and this is admirable. However, this does not alter the fact that the defendant displayed a flagrant disregard for the law at the time of the infraction. Since this is a first offense, and knowing that the defendant has made restitution voluntarily, has been active in the AA program, and fully complied with the conditions and restrictions of his probation, I hereby sentence the defendant to prohibition from driving a motor vehicle for a period of one year, plus one hundred hours of community service."

He thunked the gavel on the stand and announced a thirty-minute recess before hearing the next case.

Everyone rose while the judge left the courtroom.

Patricia's heart pounded in her chest. God had indeed been merciful. He had spared Mike from a jail sentence.

Mike's lawyer thumped him on the back, and everyone turned to exit the courtroom.

As she also turned, she saw a gray-haired man who looked like an older version of Mike alone in the back of the courtroom. His eyes glimmered as he watched Mike leave the room, and as soon as Mike passed, he followed.

Patricia felt her eyes burn, but she blinked it back. His father had not had contact with him since he fired Mike, yet he had come to the trial. Mike hadn't known he was coming.

She turned to the front instead of filing out, leaving her the last person in the room. She hadn't known if praying for leniency was the right thing, so she'd prayed for God's will to be done and had then been ready to accept whatever sentence was handed down. She didn't know enough about how the system worked to know how Darryl told the prosecutor that Mike had tried to make things better for him, but he had, and she thanked God for the difference that fact had made in the judge's decision.

Bruce also must have submitted some kind of statement outlining Mike's progress under the terms and conditions of his bail and made comments and recommendations concerning Mike's progress and the projected outcome of his involvement with AA. He probably also reported his newfound faith in Jesus as his Savior, although she didn't know which would have more influence in the eyes of the legal system.

Now that it was over, she didn't know what would happen next. Of course Mike would be relieved and, now that there was no possibility of a jail sentence, she anticipated he would have no difficulty getting a new job. Soon, all would be back to normal.

She wondered if "normal" would include her.

Patricia sighed. It was time to get on with life, whether or not it included Mike. She turned, glanced once more over her shoulder at the judge's desk and the witness stand, and left the room. Her footsteps echoed sharply on the tile floor until she exited through the heavy door, which she shut firmly behind her.

Many people lingered in the hall, most of whom she didn't recognize from Mike's session, and who must have been waiting to go in for the next case. Though the hall was crowded, two people stood out. Mike and his father. They stood to the side of the doorway leading into the courtroom, staring at each other in silence.

Patricia couldn't intrude. She wanted to say something to Mike about the favorable outcome of the judge's decision, but this was not the time. This was his time to make peace with his father.

Very quietly, Patricia turned the other way, left the building, and went back to work.

Fortunately, her father didn't question how things went in court. She wasn't ready to talk about it. Since she wouldn't be visiting Mike in jail, she didn't know when she would be seeing him. Also, Mike would probably be getting another job right away, so he would no longer be joining her for lunch every day.

If he had made peace with his father, that meant he would get his old job back, and in that case, his old ties would be mended, and he would be back in the society circles he was accustomed to, which didn't include lowly, unsophisticated pastor's daughters.

Patricia buried herself in her work, trying to keep her mind occupied with anything but what the future held for her—with or without Mike.

When lunchtime came, she went outside, the same as she did every other day.

The squirrel joined her, but Mike didn't. Since he didn't come to scare it away, the squirrel ate every bit of bread she offered while Patricia left her sandwich untouched. Just in case Mike tried to call the church and she wasn't there, she left her cell phone beside her on the bench, not caring if the ring would scare the squirrel.

It didn't ring.

When she returned from her break, she looked for a message on her desk, but her desk was exactly as she left it.

All afternoon, the phone was silent, and Mike did not rush in with an apology for being late. The entire afternoon passed, but when the clock struck five, she had no idea what she'd done all day. All she knew was that Mike hadn't come, nor had he tried to contact her.

She walked to the parking lot where only two cars remained, hers and her father's.

She stared at her little white economy compact. She had enjoyed driving Mike's sports car even though it didn't suit her personality or the lifestyle of a pastor's daughter to be driving such an expensive automobile. Now, having her own car back, it further emphasized the differences between herself and Mike.

An empty ache settled in her stomach. He had his car back. He probably had his old job back as well and had reestablished the ties to his family and the lifestyle with which he was comfortable. His absence today, and his lack of a phone call, confirmed what she had feared would happen after his court appearance.

He didn't need her anymore. It was over.

⊰❧⊱

Mike stood at Patty's door, fiddled with the knot in his tie, rang the doorbell, and waited.

When finally the door opened, Patty blinked and stared at his suit, then quickly glanced to the side where he usually parked his bike. It wasn't there. Her stunned expression made him smile.

"May I come in?"

"Uh. . .yes. . .of course. . ." She stood to the side to allow him entry. "How did you get here?"

"Bruce dropped me off."

She checked her watch. "You were at the courthouse all day?"

Mike shook his head. His stomach knotted as he began to think that perhaps coming here like this wasn't such a great idea, especially when she found out what he'd done. "No. I had some errands to run, and Bruce drove me around. I asked him if he wouldn't mind dropping me off here. I hope you don't mind."

"Of course I don't mind."

"Actually, I was hoping that we could go out for dinner. Someplace quiet, where we could talk."

"Talk?" She backed up, which he thought rather strange and not like Patty.

"Yes. I wanted to thank you for all you've done for me. I want to take you out for dinner."

"Because it's over?"

He sighed, and all the tension left him. It had been a long and difficult ten weeks, and the wait was arduous, but it was finally over. The sentence was light and very much in his favor, if he handled himself properly.

"Yes," he said. "Because it's over."

He had tied up almost all the loose ends in his life. He'd done what he had promised and paid for Darryl's course. He'd had a long talk with his father and made things right there. He had arranged some of the hours of service for his sentence. He'd also made some very difficult decisions regarding the direction of his future.

There was only one thing he had to do now, and that was settle everything with Patty.

"I don't know. I'm really tired." She looked up at him. Her eyes glimmered, and she turned her head so she wasn't facing him.

For a second Mike thought maybe she was going to cry. Either that or she was overtired and was having some kind of female reaction related to the relief from the recent days of constant stress during the long process leading up to his court case. Now that it was finished, he, also, was exhausted—but excited at the same time. He could finally make some plans.

Patty looked up at him with bloodshot eyes. A pang of guilt shot through him. He didn't feel half as bad as she looked, and he felt bad that his predicament had taken such a toll on her. She didn't deserve to be saddled with his burdens. He hadn't slept well last night, but it hadn't occurred to him until now that perhaps Patty hadn't either. Still, no matter how tired he was, he couldn't let the day end without telling her what he had decided. He didn't want her to find out from Bruce tomorrow, so he had to tell her himself, today.

He stepped forward and took her hands in his. "Please? We can still be home early, in plenty of time for you to get a good night's sleep for work tomorrow."

She blinked fast a few times and faced him again. "Okay."

"We'll go somewhere simple, and cheap, just for you." He smiled, hoping his little attempt to cheer her up would help, but instead, she stiffened and pulled her hands out of his.

She picked up her purse from the floor and locked the door as they left. He suggested Sir Henry's Fish and Chip Palace, but instead of the reaction he hoped for, she simply nodded and turned in the right direction.

He tried to get a conversation started, but her response was less than enthusiastic. Now he worried more than ever that perhaps this wasn't the best timing.

The same as every other time they were at Sir Henry's, they were the only patrons inside, but the drive-thru lineup went on forever. Today, that suited him just fine. Henry was busy, so they had the place to themselves.

They placed their order, and Mike led her to a table. She didn't say a word, so Mike gathered his nerve and decided to simply start at the beginning.

"I talked to your father today."

"My father? When were you at the church? I was there all day and didn't see you."

"I didn't actually go there, I talked to him on the phone. You didn't answer the phone when I called, so I figured you must have been outside with your chipmunk."

She turned her head and stared out the window. "Yes, I managed to feed him the whole piece of bread for the first time in a long time."

His gut clenched. He was hoping she would say that she had missed him, but she didn't. Even a comeback that it really was a squirrel, not a chipmunk, would have been preferable to her bland response.

"Daddy never told me you called."

"Now don't be mad at him. I told him I wanted to tell you myself. Part of my community service is going to be spending a few sessions talking with the youth group and the youth groups from a few other churches about drugs and alcohol."

She turned and smiled at him, her first smile in a long time. He couldn't help but smile back.

"That's great, Mike. I'm sure they'll listen to you knowing how much you've been through."

"Yeah. Bruce thinks it's going to be a great ministry to the youth. He said they'd really listen to me, hearing it from someone who has experienced firsthand where it can lead."

"Yes, and you'll also have some stern warnings about drinking and driving."

He nodded. "You got that right."

"Especially when they see your car, they'll see the sacrifice it is to not be able to drive it."

"Yes, I'm sure they'll see it often too. Bob Johnson is going to have lots of fun with it."

"Bob Johnson? You mean Billy Johnson's dad? I don't understand."

"Yup. Bob Johnson. He bought it this afternoon. I sold it."

She covered her mouth with both hands and gasped. "You sold your car?!"

He shrugged his shoulders. "Yeah. Well, I can't drive for another ten months."

"But ten months isn't that long! Surely you could have waited for ten months!"

Mike turned his head and stared out the window. He knew how much she enjoyed driving the car, and he wished he could have let her continue, but he didn't have a choice. "I needed the money," he mumbled. "Bruce happened to mention how much Bob liked the car, being a collector's edition, and he made me an offer I couldn't refuse. I needed the money to pay the college."

"Oh, Mike, I didn't know! If you could have held on for just a little while longer, I'm sure you'll have no problem getting a job now that you know you won't be going to jail. I could have loaned you something if you were running that low."

Henry plunked the tray of food in front of them. "You two looked lost in conversation, and you didn't come when I called your number. Enjoy it before it gets cold." He turned and hurried back to the drive-thru window.

"I won't take a loan from you, Patty. I wouldn't be able to pay it back for at least a year, and I can't do that to you." He reached over the table and covered her hands with his. "Come on. Let's pray." He closed his eyes and bowed his head. "Dear Lord, thank You for Your blessings, for Your kindness, and Your mercy. Thank You especially for this day, the decision of my court case, and I pray for Your will to be done in whatever the future holds."

"Amen," she mumbled.

Mike took a huge bite of Sir Henry's special recipe. He had skipped lunch, and he was starving. Fish had never tasted so good.

"What about your father? I thought you talked to your father."

He swallowed and sipped his drink to wash it down to allow himself to speak. "I'm not borrowing the money from my father. For once, I have to be able to do something myself without my father behind me picking up the pieces."

"Didn't he give you your job back?"

"Not exactly. He did give me a job, but not the same one I had when I left. The job he gave me doesn't pay very well."

Her eyes widened, and the pity in them made him lose his appetite. The last thing he wanted was for Patty to feel sorry for him.

"This isn't coming out right." He covered his face with his palms, then rested his hands in his lap. "Patty, I wanted tonight to be special because I'm not going to be able to see you very much for a very long time."

Her eyes opened wide and she froze, with a lone French fry dangling from her fingers.

"You see, I'm going back to school."

"School?"

"Dad wants to retire in a few years, and I have no real management or business skills. I have to be able to take over the reins of the company and run it successfully. When I paid for Darryl's course, I also signed up for a business management course for myself. It starts in two weeks, and I should graduate next spring. I'll be going to school full-time and working part-time evenings and weekends, starting at the bottom instead of the top this time. I'm going to be working in the warehouse, driving the forklift and doing the stock. While I'm learning how to run a company in the daytime, I'll be seeing how it really works in a practical application at night."

"You're going to be a stock boy?"

He nodded. "I have to squeeze that in around my sentence of the community service, so that cuts into the time I can actually earn a salary, to say nothing of studying."

"Oh."

He wanted to reach over the table and hold her hands, but he could feel the grease from the fries on his fingers, so he didn't touch her. "So I'm not going to have much time to see you."

She gulped. "Oh," she muttered.

"I also talked about something else with your father."

She stared at him blankly.

Mike cleared his throat. "I asked if, as a pastor, he'd mind having a son-in-law with a criminal record."

"Son-in. . ." Her face paled.

Mike sucked in a deep breath. "Today closes the book of my past sins. You've helped me through it more than I can say. You've been such a prayer warrior for me. You've supported me when I was weak, and I want you to know how much that means to me. In a way, you've been my mentor, but I don't want you to be my mentor anymore. I want you to be my best friend, my help-mate, my partner."

He wiped his hands on his napkin, stood, then walked around the table. Once he was in front of her, he sank down on one knee, pulled the squashed French fry out of her fingers, and covered her hand with both of his. "I love you, Patty. I know this is asking a lot, but I'd like you to think about the possibility of getting married after I graduate. I know it's going to be hard, but knowing you're there for me at the end will make it all worthwhile."

Her eyes glistened, welled up, and tears streamed down her cheeks. "I love you too," she sniffled. "Of course I'll marry you."

Joy like he'd never experienced surged through him. Mike stood, pulled Patty to her feet, and wrapped his arms around her. He buried his face in her hair and inhaled the sweet fragrance of her apple-scented shampoo, doing his best to ignore the heavy smell of the deep fryer that always permeated Sir Henry's. He thought his heart would burst when she wrapped her arms around his back and squeezed.

The loud snort of Henry blowing his nose echoed behind him.

"That's so beautiful," Henry mumbled, and blew his nose again. "Can I take your picture? No one has ever proposed in my restaurant before."

Patty sniffled, they separated, and she looked up at him. Her beautiful smile almost made him lightheaded. "Do you mind?" she asked.

The woman he loved just said she would be his wife. He wouldn't have minded if Henry wanted to film a movie as long as he got a copy so he could look at it when the pressure of the next year threatened to overwhelm him.

He turned to Henry. "Only if you'll come to the wedding."

The flash of the camera was Henry's reply.

Epilogue

Patricia watched the tears form in her father's eyes. "I now pronounce you man and wife. You may kiss your bride."

Mike lifted her veil and kissed her, but instead of the short peck they'd discussed at the rehearsal, he embraced her and kissed her fully. She leaned into her new husband and kissed him back in equal measure, until she thought her knees would give out. The sound of her father clearing his throat brought them both to their senses.

Her father wiped his eyes, cleared his throat once more, and addressed their guests in the church, which was packed with standing room only.

"Before Mike and Patty walk down the aisle for the first time as Mr. and Mrs. Michael R. Flannigan, Jr., I want to read this Scripture that Mike requested. Psalm 103, verses 1–4.

"Praise the LORD, O my soul;
    all my inmost being, praise his holy name.
Praise the LORD, O my soul,
    and forget not all His benefits—
who forgives all your sins and heals all your diseases,
who redeems your life from the pit and crowns you
    with love and compassion."

Patricia smiled and squeezed Mike's hand. The next six months were going to be difficult; however, after two months of struggling to see each other between school, his job, and his community service requirements, they discovered that his suspended driver's license made it too difficult for them to see each other. So they just gave up and got married earlier than they had planned.

Autumn was a fine time for a wedding, and they didn't care that they couldn't take their honeymoon until after his graduation, although she did have a feeling that, when Monday came, he wouldn't exactly be in the mood for his first class.

He smiled back, squeezed her hand, and they began their walk down the aisle. Joy radiated from him, so unlike the first day she'd shown up on his doorstep.

He had changed and grown so much since they met, not only as a Christian, but also as a person.

After his court case, he had worked hard on the last two steps in the AA program, which were "Sought through prayer and meditation to improve our conscious contact with God as we understood Him, praying only for knowledge of His will for us and the power to carry that out," and, "Having had a spiritual awakening as a result of these steps, we tried to carry this message to alcoholics, and to practice these principles in all our affairs."

He hadn't come to know Jesus in the same way she had, but his love for Jesus was evident in every part of his life, both at school and on the job for his dad, and she loved him more every day because of it. He'd made new friends in the church, and he'd developed a wonderful ministry with the youth group, who loved him.

The church door opened to the parking lot, where four hundred people waited to shower them with rice. Instead of small bags, many members of the youth group held boxes.

A number of rice boxes began to shake, the sound increasing in volume. When she cringed, Mike leaned down to whisper in her ear. "Don't worry, I knew what they were going to do. I have a plan."

Patricia turned to her new husband. "You're kidding, right?"

Mike grinned. "Wrong."

They began their walk through the crowd of well-wishers, until they were at the section where the youth group was congregated. A split second before the torrent of rice poured upon them, Mike reached into his sleeve, whipped out a small umbrella, and opened it with a flick of his thumb. His free arm wrapped around her waist and pulled her close as the rice thundered onto the umbrella, slid down, and within a few seconds covered their feet.

Patricia raised herself to her tiptoes through the rice, wrapped her hands around his neck, and gave him a quick kiss, at which the crowd hooted.

"My hero," she whispered.

Mike grinned. "Yeah?"

She gazed into his smiling eyes, eyes that radiated with pure joy. God really had pulled Mike from the pit. After intense soul-searching, some hard work, and much prayer, everything in Mike's life was fitting into place. His future was set with his ministry, he was working toward high goals for his career, and within a couple of years, they would start a family. He'd met all the challenges and obstacles in his way first with prayer and then with courage and diligence.

Patricia grinned back. "Yes. You really are my hero."

And she wouldn't have it any other way.

A Letter to Our Readers

Dear Readers:

In order that we might better contribute to your reading enjoyment, we would appreciate your taking a few minutes to respond to the following questions. When completed, please return to the following: Fiction Editor, Barbour Publishing, Inc., P.O. Box 719, Uhrichsville, OH 44683.

1. Did you enjoy reading *Vancouver?*
   ❏ Very much—I would like to see more books like this.
   ❏ Moderately—I would have enjoyed it more if _____

   _____

   _____

2. What influenced your decision to purchase this book?
   (Check those that apply.)
   ❏ Cover   ❏ Back cover copy   ❏ Title   ❏ Price
   ❏ Friends   ❏ Publicity   ❏ Other

3. Which story was your favorite?
   ❏ *Gone Camping*   ❏ *On the Road Again*
   ❏ *At Arm's Length*   ❏ *My Name Is Mike*

4. Please check your age range:
   ❏ Under 18   ❏ 18–24   ❏ 25–34
   ❏ 35–45   ❏ 46–55   ❏ Over 55

5. How many hours per week do you read? _____

Name _____

Occupation _____

Address _____

City _____ State _____ Zip _____

E-mail _____

$\mathcal{H}$EARTSONG ❤ PRESENTS

Love Stories
Are Rated G!

That's for godly, gratifying, and of course, great! If you love a thrilling love story but don't appreciate the sordidness of some popular paperback romances, **Heartsong Presents** is for you. In fact, **Heartsong Presents** is the only inspirational romance book club featuring love stories where Christian faith is the primary ingredient in a marriage relationship.

Sign up today to receive your first set of four, never-before-published Christian romances. Send no money now; you will receive a bill with the first shipment. You may cancel at any time without obligation, and if you aren't completely satisfied with any selection, you may return the books for an immediate refund!

Imagine. . .four new romances every four weeks—two historical, two contemporary—with men and women like you who long to meet the one God has chosen as the love of their lives. . .all for the low price of $10.99 postpaid.

To join, simply complete the coupon below and mail to the address provided. **Heartsong Presents** romances are rated G for another reason: They'll arrive Godspeed!

YES! Sign me up for Hearts❤ng!

NEW MEMBERSHIPS WILL BE SHIPPED IMMEDIATELY!
Send no money now. We'll bill you only $10.99 postpaid with your first shipment of four books. Or for faster action, call toll free 1-800-847-8270.

NAME _____

ADDRESS _____

CITY _____ STATE _____ ZIP _____

MAIL TO: HEARTSONG PRESENTS, P.O. Box 721, Uhrichsville, Ohio 44683
or visit www.heartsongpresents.com